KARIBA

NYAMINYAMI'S KINGDOM

D1784212

ZIMBABWE

AFRICAN PUBLISHING GROUP
PO Box BW 350, Harare
ZIMBABWE

© David Martin, Pictures as credited, Maps and Published edition APG

Photographic credits. All David Martin except page 22, 32, 34, and 42, National Archives, 50, 54, and 80, Peter Ginn, 53, Viv Wilson, 56, Gregory Rasmussen, 60, Steve Edwards, and, 61, Joan Thomson

ISBN: 0-7974-1666-8

Design Paul Wade, Ink Spots, Harare

Printed by Cannon Press, Harare

CONTENTS

KARIBA

ZAMBIA

LAKE

K

N

Chete Is.

CHETE

Chete

Siabuwa

🏠 22

🏠 23

🏠 24

Binga

🏠 25

🏠 26

🏠 27

CHIZARIRA

NATIONAL   PARK

🏠 21

Sengwe

Sebungwe

CHIRISA

SAFARI   AF

Mlibizi

🏠 28

🏠 29

TO KAMATIVI

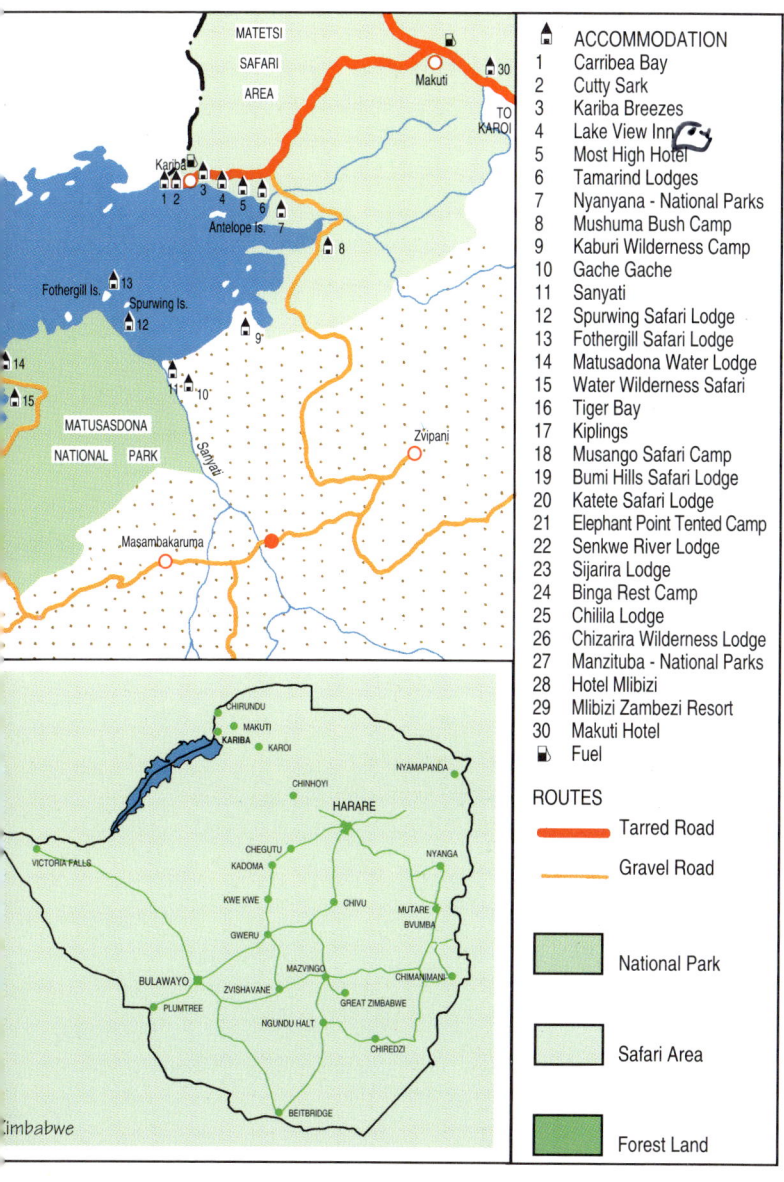

ACCOMMODATION

1 Carribea Bay
2 Cutty Sark
3 Kariba Breezes
4 Lake View Inn
5 Most High Hotel
6 Tamarind Lodges
7 Nyanyana - National Parks
8 Mushuma Bush Camp
9 Kaburi Wilderness Camp
10 Gache Gache
11 Sanyati
12 Spurwing Safari Lodge
13 Fothergill Safari Lodge
14 Matusadona Water Lodge
15 Water Wilderness Safari
16 Tiger Bay
17 Kiplings
18 Musango Safari Camp
19 Bumi Hills Safari Lodge
20 Katete Safari Lodge
21 Elephant Point Tented Camp
22 Senkwe River Lodge
23 Sijarira Lodge
24 Binga Rest Camp
25 Chilila Lodge
26 Chizarira Wilderness Lodge
27 Manzituba - National Parks
28 Hotel Mlibizi
29 Mlibizi Zambezi Resort
30 Makuti Hotel
⌕ Fuel

ROUTES

━━━ Tarred Road

─── Gravel Road

National Park

Safari Area

Forest Land

5

ACKNOWLEDGEMENTS

I am particularly grateful to Martyn Doggrell for lending me the luxurious Wild Goose motor cruiser to explore Lake Kariba. The Wild Goose, the unique Malindi Station Lodge in Hwange (co-owned with Dr Tom Raub), and Pyramids Estate near Inyati Mission in northern Matabeleland, belong to his father-in-law, architect Mike Clinton, and they combine three quite distinct safari destinations unrivalled in scope in Zimbabwe.

Kariba is wider than the English Channel separating Britain and France. And like that channel, the opposite shore hides a multitude of secrets through the frequent veil of haze.

On that far shore one meets some of Kariba's most accomplished residents. Cephas Mabalini, chairman of Luyando Gillnet Fishing Cooperative Society, and member Patrick Mutale. Andy Williamson at Bumi, Steve Edwards of Musango, Gary Douglas and "Spike" Williamson at Fothergill, and Graeme Lemon, who operates his own upmarket tented safari camps.

Once again I am extremely grateful to Godfrey Ncube, a lecturer at the University of Zimbabwe, who allowed me to use his outstanding M.Phil. paper which explores the hitherto neglected history of northwestern Zimbabwe. Kevin Walsh, also of UZ, checked the geology section, which was also read by Tim Broderick, an expert on Kariba's geology and palaeontology.

Two of Zimbabwe's leading experts in their fields, Dr Kit Hustler (ornithology), of Wild Horizon Safaris, and Meg Coates Palgrave (flora), who runs her own operation, produced the attached checklists. I am also indebted to Maurice Wood, Judy Boyd and Phyllis Johnson for their support and encouragement.

A special thank you must be saved for two regular British visitors, Ian and Patience Smith, who took the outstanding cover picture of a lion and crocodile disputing the remains of an impala.

Finally I am grateful to the owners of the Wild Goose and Zimbabwe Sun Hotels, whose generous support made the publication of this Guide possible.

David Martin
Kariba

INTRODUCTION

Like many schoolboys before and since, and prior to being exposed to a particularly wild Atlantic storm in a tiny fishing boat off the Cornish coast, I had visions of becoming a mariner.

The sea, and its supposed calling, was much romanticised at school by landlubber teachers. The Atlantic taught me a sharp, non-classroom lesson, dispelling any notions I had of such an occupation.

More recently I finished editing a book, Hobo, by David Lemon (African Publishing Group), who had single-handedly rowed from Kariba to Victoria Falls and back in a tiny cockleshell boat.

Kariba, I learned, is really an inland sea rather than a lake where the swell, certainly when viewed from a boat so small, can reach an intimidating height.

While the experience did not re-kindle thoughts of a sea life, it certainly proved to be a remarkably pleasant way of "discovering" Kariba. In fact it was the only way to do so.

The first thing which surprised me upon arrival at Kariba's Carribea Bay Marina, was the boat itself. There is nothing cockleshell about the Wild Goose!

There was a fridge on the bridge to keep drinks cold, another a floor below in the saloon, and a third in the galley further below, which was remarkably luxurious and spacious with a freezer, microwave oven, twin-aluminium sinks, storage cupboards, ample work space, and a regular gas cooker.

Fore and aft there were twin-bed cabins with air-conditioning, built-in cupboards, chest of drawers, overhead lighting and reading lamps, and ensuite showers, handbasins and toilets. There were fans everywhere.

Wild Goose.

To add to the general air of luxury there was a captain, Cosmos Zulu, and a good chef, Fanwell Mugwanda. We towed a twin-engined speedboat (Wild Goose 2) from which one could fish, view game or birds, or simply generally doodle.

I never got round to asking for the boat's vital statistics although I was told it could do 12 knots and was one of the fastest on Kariba. Certainly it was very spacious, much more than I really needed, although I was grateful for its size and stability.

Early the first morning at dawn we set off for Bumi Hills across the lake some four and a half hours away.

The first thing which struck me was the brilliant red glow of the sunrise only to be rivalled by the sunsets at the end of the day. A smoke haze from burning onshore fires hung over the lake making the sunrises and sunsets spectacular.

Just out of harbour we began to encounter the first kapenta fishing boats (or rigs as they are more correctly known). They are certainly more like large pontoons rather than proper boats, with a crew of two, a rudimentary wheelhouse, a none too powerful engine, and a vast circular net to catch the kapenta.

Kapenta rig heads for home.

Kapenta, a freshwater sardine best likened, although not related to, whitebait, were experimentally introduced to Kariba from Lake Tanganyika, where they had been central to an extremely healthy African fishing industry for many years.

Zambia, independent and African ruled, took the lead in introducing the kapenta, much against the wishes of the Southern Rhodesian Department of National Parks. But, because of the prevailing winds and nutrients, it was to be the Southern Rhodesian whites who first reaped the rewards, to the great irritation of the Zambian Minister.

The kapenta boats fish at night, the fish being drawn to their arc-lamps, and then into the net which scoops them out of the water. At dawn the boats head onshore where the fish are sun-dried and then marketed.

About 27,000 tonnes of kapenta are netted annually in Kariba by an unknown number of boats operating on the lake, their night-lights and generators looking and sounding like a floating town.

Apart from the Wild Goose and kapenta boats, all manner of other boats ply the lake. We passed a group of stately yachts, their sails picking up the light wind, innumerable boats ferrying tourists to the shore resorts, and houseboats, sort of cumbersome floating homes, making for the lake's many inlets.

Out on the lake we encountered Tonga fishermen in squat, metal, puntlike craft hauling in their nets. The lake that day was mirror flat and as we watched a fishermen pulled in first a bottlenose and then a squeaker, so named because it actually squeaks.

My second serious reservation about Kariba was, and remains, the heat. In Kariba town locals had told me in awed tones that in November 1994 CNN had reported a satellite reading showing that Kariba was the hottest holiday destination on earth that day.

No one could quite agree what the temperature had been, whether it had been in the sun or shade, and what part of Kariba the report referred to. It was in fact 57 degrees C - 130 degrees F - in the sun!

Kariba is certainly hot and even tour operators agreed that except for those used to heat it is advisable to suggest visitors stay away in October and November. October however, is when the world's tiger fishermen gather at the lake hoping to catch this ferocious fish and tell those stories fishermen tell.

Lone elephant at dusk.

Hungry lionesses scan the plains.

A third problem I had about Kariba was that I had a somewhat jaundiced view about game viewing having just completed a Guide on the Hwange District (*Hwange: Elephant Country*, an Into Africa Travel Guide). Having spent hours in Hwange looking at, photographing, pouring through reference books, and writing about wildlife, what more could Kariba possibly offer?

I was in for a surprise. Whereas in Hwange there is little open country other than in the *vleis*, in Kariba there are miles of open foreshore where it is easy to see animals.

True the stately giraffe are absent as are wildebeest, white rhino, bat-eared fox and black-backed jackal.

But some animals, such as lion, which more or less every tourist demands to see, rhino, and certainly hippo, are much easier to see at Kariba than elsewhere in Zimbabwe. Beyond that elephant, some tragically suffering from "floppy trunk" syndrome, impala, known locally as Zambezi goats, buffalo and zebra, are common.

At Fothergill Safari Lodge they almost guarantee lion for the visitor and on both days I went out I saw lion prides. "This is the lodge in the

11

Guide, Graeme Lemon, and visitor.

country for lion. We can almost guarantee them", said manager Brian Lemon. His guides gulped — the pressure to find lion is on them.

Cheetah are also sighted fairly regularly while leopard, as elsewhere, remain rare and a matter of luck.

Steve Edwards, who headed the National Parks rhino anti-poaching unit, specialises in tracking black rhino and these pre-historic animals are frequently seen by visitors accompanying him on Musango Safari Camp walking tours.

On my second visit to Musango an Australian television crew were filming the endangered black rhino, and for good measure they had brought with them former Australian cricket captain, Alan Border, and his children.

A further love of Steve Edwards is palaeontology and he can talk for hours about *Vulcanodon karibaensis,* a dinosaur exposed by the retreating lake on a Kariba island, other fossil finds, and the Stone and Iron Age tools he has picked up during walks.

From the nearby Bumi Hills Safari Lodge I have never failed to see elephant drinking, playing and grazing on the plains below, where there is also an abundance of waterbuck, and likely the lone hippo bold enough to venture out in daylight.

Gently pottering along the foreshore in the speedboat in the early mornings and late in the day, I saw scores of waterbirds — cormorants with their wings hanging out to dry, raucous Egyptian geese with goslings, various herons, gulls, and waders.

Hippo watched our boat warily, diving when we got too close and then re-surfacing, noisily exhaling air. A small crocodile beadily eyed a heron on a sandbank but made no discernible movement.

Kariba has many crocodiles, but locals insist it is quite safe to swim in the middle of the lake which is croc, hippo, and bilharzia free.   I still give such a dip a miss.

As I explored Kariba I realised that irrespective of my earlier doubts, the lake and surrounds have probably more to offer the visitor than any other single destination in Zimbabwe. The secret is to pick the right time of year for a visit.

Beyond that I came to realise another thing which sets Kariba apart. At Kariba, much more than at Hwange, guides tend to specialise. On the foreshore, and in the Matusadona Range behind, walking safaris are much more common than at most other destinations.

Within these walks a degree of specialisation occurs. If you want to see rhino then Steve Edwards or Graeme Lemon are the people to go with. If you want to see lion then the Fothergill area "guarantees" them. Bumi is excellent for elephant and hippo are everywhere.

Zimbabwe Sun Hotels are putting together in Kariba an impressive specialist team involving some of the country's top guides with expertise in a number of safari areas, as well as an in-depth knowledge of all the components which go into the industry.

A hippo pod (group). What you see is only a third, the rest are under water.

13

GEOLOGY

Lake Kariba lies within a rift valley, the Gwembe Trough, with boundary faults to the south marked by the face of the Matusadona Range, across the lake from Kariba town, and in Zambia to the north.

Due to the imposition of the mass of Lake Kariba on the earth's surface, the Kariba area is subject to very mild earthquakes, which can be similarly felt near Chipinge in the Save Valley in the extreme southeast of Zimbabwe.

But, so mild and infrequent are the earthquakes, which are more akin to tremors, that Kariba town residents will tell the visitor that they read about them in the press but do not feel them. Only occasionally do they even rattle tea cups.

The Kariba area is divided into three geological regions.

These are the fault bounded, sediment-filled, Gwembe Trough, the older gneisses of the Matusadona Range and the eastern end of the lake, and the ridges and valleys of the Makuti terrain through which the visitor approaches Kariba from the main Harare to Chirundu road.

The Matusadona Range and the hills of Kariba itself are underlain by Precambrian metamorphic rocks over which the relief is strongly influenced by complexly folded strata.

The third geological region reflects the linear topographic features of the Makuti terrain which are crossed by Kariba Gorge and which give way southwards to the older gneisses along the abrupt escarpment edge marked by the Tsororo River. These are a diverse sequence of metamorphic rocks dated at 830 million years old.

The Zambezi River, flowing through the Kariba Dam and gorge, and on through Mozambique to the Indian Ocean, takes with it waters flowing in from seven other rivers which flow into Lake Kariba. The Sanyati, which enters as a gorge through the Matusadona Range from the south, is the major tributary to Kariba.

PALAEONTOLOGY

A mong the many — and increasing as the lake recedes — Kariba islands, No. 126/7, nicknamed "padded bra island", was little more than yet another blob of land until 1969.

But that year the wave-eroded northern face of the island (known locally as Dinosaur Island), somewhat west of Katete Safari Lodge, revealed a secret which at least made it more than a number on palaeontologists' maps.

In July 1969 a Kariba resident and fisherman, Mr Alec Gibson, spotted large bones on the island. What he saw were the remains of a dinosaur, which became known in 1972 as *Vulcanodon karibaensis,* who had died at least 180 million years earlier.

Professional excavations rapidly followed revealing the pelvis, sacrum, a hind leg, part of the tail, and other fragments. From these it was possible to reconstruct that the dinosaur died, probably trapped in a quicksand, the right way up. The presence of pillowed lavas and crossbedded sandstones indicate a local oasis environment in the otherwise desert terrain then prevailing.

Vulcanodon had a long neck and tail, was about 6.5 metres from its nose to the tip of the tail, and fully extended probably stood some 4 metres in height.

The remains of *Vulcanodon* were found in sandstone between two flows of pillowed basalt dating it around the Triassic-Jurassic boundary. Dinosaurs, for reasons still unknown, died out at the end of the subsequent Cretaceous period, 65 million years ago.

Vulcanodon was related to two important groups of dinosaurs, the *Prosauropods* and *Sauropods,* and was originally thought to provide the "missing link" between these two. Now, however, it is thought *Vulcanodon* was an evolutionary dead-end and not a link.

After the discovery of *Vulcanodon,* several other searches in the area

15

were made without any major new find. However, since the fall of the lake to its lowest level since it was flooded, new finds of detrital bone are being made and it is possible that another amateur palaeontologist will stumble upon something which will once again bring the professionals flying to the scene.

Some of the latest finds include a tooth crown from a carnivorous *thecodontian* (the group which preceded dinosaurs) or an early meat-eating dinosaur, the teeth of *crocodilians* or *prosauropod* dinosaurs, the possible teeth of crocodile-like reptiles which were previously unknown in the region, and several other items which could not be identified.

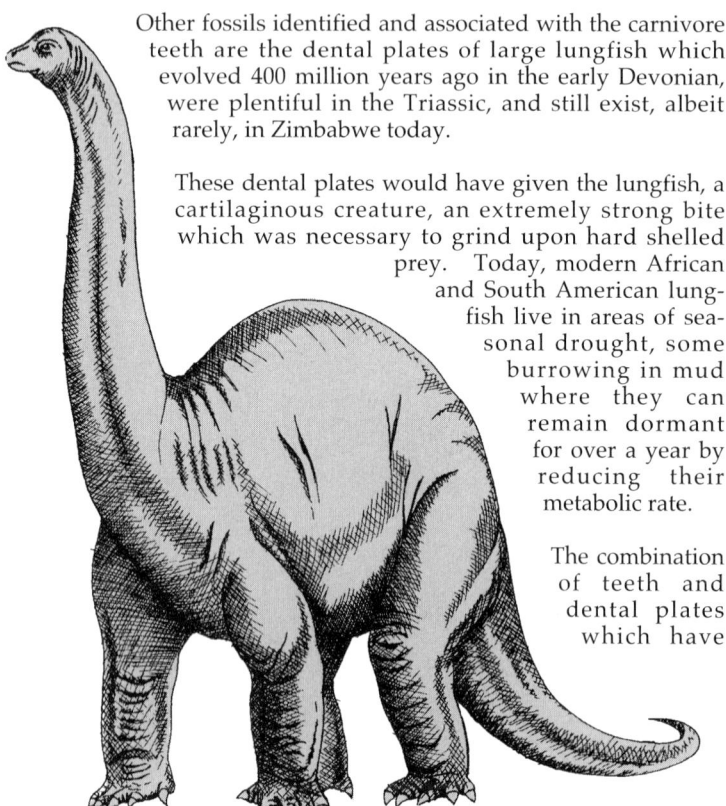

Other fossils identified and associated with the carnivore teeth are the dental plates of large lungfish which evolved 400 million years ago in the early Devonian, were plentiful in the Triassic, and still exist, albeit rarely, in Zimbabwe today.

These dental plates would have given the lungfish, a cartilaginous creature, an extremely strong bite which was necessary to grind upon hard shelled prey. Today, modern African and South American lungfish live in areas of seasonal drought, some burrowing in mud where they can remain dormant for over a year by reducing their metabolic rate.

The combination of teeth and dental plates which have

An artists impression of *Volcanodon Karibaensis*.

16

been discovered suggests a feeding orgy in just such a palaeo-environment.

Apart from *Vulcanodon*, at least four other types of dinosaur have been found in the Triassic and Jurassic strata of Zimbabwe's Zambezi and Limpopo valleys. These are:

Syntarsus, a small scavenging *coelurosaurian* found in the Nyamandhlovu area in 1963 and also later discovered in the Zambezi Valley. This animal lived on the edge of the barren desert which existed in southern Africa over 200 million years ago in the late Triassic Period. It is thought to have been covered with feathers to protect it against harsh, extreme desert temperatures, but this is not proven.

Massospondylus, Zimbabwe's commonest dinosaur. It walked on all fours, or occasionally its hind legs, was three to five metres long, and lived in deserts in the late Triassic. Remains of these have again been found in the Nyamandhlovu area, on Sentinel Ranch near Beitbridge, and in the Chewore Safari Area of Hurungwe District.

Allosaurus, a monstrous Jurassic carnosaur, probably preyed on large *sauropods*. The massive footprints, the longest and best preserved bipedal trackway in Africa, also found in the Chewore Safari Area, are thought to be those of an *Allosaurid*.

Brachiosaurus, like *Vulcanodon*, was a quadriped (walking on four feet), a herbivore, and was one of the planet's largest and heaviest dinosaurs. It existed from the Jurassic into Cretaceous times when dinosaurs became extinct. Remains of *Brachiosaurus* were discovered in 1965 near the Kadzi River in Dande Communal Lands and are also known from near Gokwe. Its presence in Africa and the northern continents is evidence for the continuity of the Laurasian land mass prior to the splitting up of Gondwanaland.

Petrified or silicified wood, known as *Dadoxylon*, is a common fossil remain in the red Triassic sediments of the Kariba lake shore. When Kariba first filled in the late 1950s, observations were made on the swamped mopane woodlands of the basin to see how rapid this silicification process was.

Also preserved in the shales and mudstones of the early Triassic strata are the fronds and impressions of seed ferns of the *Dicroidium* genus. Rare seedpods are named for their discovery location as *Karibacarpon*.

ARCHAEOLOGY

A number of rocks and other items lie in a basket beside the dining room at Musango Safari Camp. To the untutored eye they look like a collection of just that — rocks — which have been picked up randomly in the bush.

But on closer scrutiny their real meaning emerges. These are Stone Age tools which Steve Edwards has collected in the bush during his walking safaris through the area.

Stone Age chopper.

Just how rich the Middle Zambezi is — or was — in Stone Age tools, which reveal the extent of occupation in those distant days, may never be known. The bulk of them are likely to be buried under the waters of Lake Kariba.

In the dry season of 1950, when the building of the Kariba Dam was still in the discussion phase and before Kariba was subsequently flooded, a partial survey of the area was done to determine its geological and archaeological history.

Bounded (and isolated to a degree) by the 2,000 metres high escarpments on either side of the Zambezi River, those who lived in the Gwembe Valley had evolved their own forms of culture which, with local variants, were divorced from external influences.

The researchers in 1950 found evidence that the valley had been occupied since the Early Stone Age, placing the earliest known human habitation in the area as 250,000 to 500,000 years ago. However,

Zimbabwe's Rift Valley does not contain sediments or volcanic ashes which preserve the remains of early hominids such as those in East Africa.

While, geologists say, the occupation was initially sporadic, there was a considerable increase during San occupations as is always the case with hunter-food gatherers. Even so their occupation was sparse.

The Sangoan people initially lived in dry, then increasingly wet, conditions as the environment of the valley changed. Initially the tools they employed were made from large rocks, most popularly river pebbles and silicified sandstones, free from natural weaknesses and fractures.

As the San's material culture evolved, the tools became smaller and less unwieldy, reaching their final expression of the Stone Age in the *Magosian* industries in which the cores and flakes measured no more than three-quarters of an inch in diameter.

These tools were shaped with a hammerstone which chipped the core stone, and not surprisingly, the greatest number of stones found at Stone Age sites are the waste flakes chipped off the core stone by the hammerstone. Some of these flakes were also used.

Pebble choppers are the earliest known manmade stone tools. They were rudimentary and used for cutting and skinning. They were comfortably held in the hand and fashioned as handaxes, picks and choppers.

In the Middle Stone Age tools became much smaller and projectiles, such as throwing spears with a light stone point, began to appear. These were followed by arrowheads, the greatest invention of the Late Stone Age.

Because the use of bows and arrows proved a safer and more efficient way of hunting, the San now found time to paint their magnificent legacy of rock art. However, in the Middle Zambezi area, because of the absence of granite, these type of paintings are absent although they exist in large numbers elsewhere in the country.

It should be noted that the collection of fossils and artefacts is not permitted in Zimbabwe. All finds should be reported to the Museum of Natural History in Bulawayo or the Museum of Human Sciences in Harare, together with accurate grid reference and description. They will then help in identifying the find.

CLIMATE

Climatically Kariba is a place of extremes. Zimbabwe's Meteorological Office puts the highest temperature recorded at Kariba as 45.6 degrees C. American CNN says a satellite has recorded 57 degrees C.

Either way Kariba is a very hot place. The maximum temperature recorded at Kariba Airport in 1995 was 35.1 degrees C in October. June and July were the coolest months with the temperature dropping to a mere 26.3 degrees C.

At the other end of the scale the highest minimum temperature was 23.4 degrees C in November 1995 while the lowest temperature of 11.1 degrees C was recorded in July.

For those who like it hot Kariba is idyllic. But for those who do not it is as well to heed the advice of safari operators and stay away in the very hot October and November months.

Over a 30-year period from 1961 to 1991 Kariba recorded some rainfall every month. But in four of those months, it was one mm or less. And during June to September 1995 inclusive, not a drop of rain was recorded.

Apart from being the hottest place in the country, Kariba also holds the record for windspeed in a thunderstorm squall — 85 knots or 157 km/h. Sudden lake storms/waves can occur from August to October. Thereafter the rains follow from December through March.

In July the wind speed is an easterly 7-8 knots at 8am averaging up to 14 knots from the southwest in the afternoon. In October the wind in the morning is a northeasterly 14 knots and in the afternoon the exact opposite.

HISTORY

The Tonga, a proud, egalitarian, and matrilineal people without a paramount chief, believe in decentralised, paternalistic and persuasive rule, a rare attribute in much of today's world where coercion is so often used.

The Tonga inhabit both banks of the 400 km Middle Zambezi Valley, including Lake Kariba, from the Kariba Dam wall to Mlibizi.

Interestingly, given the divergence of views among historians as to whether or not there was a Bantu migration, the Tonga have no oral history of migration.

Nyaminyami

Nyaminyami, the river god, is believed by the Tonga and several other tribes, to control life in the Zambezi Valley. To them Nyaminyami is not a legend or fictitous being but the personification of a supernatural power. Before anyone scoffs at such primitive beliefs it is as well to remember the thousands of people who visit Lochness in Scotland, the supposed home of "Nessy", the Lochness Monster.

Both tourists and locals claim to have seen Nyaminyami. But hard evidence remains elusive. Some say he is like a whirlwind. But the majority say he is dragon-like with a snake's torso and a fish's head.

Legend holds he once lived happily in the Zambezi with his wife. But while she was downstream the Kariba Dam was built separating them. Infuriated, Nyaminyami is accredited with the collapse of part of the dam wall during construction and deaths of several workers. Today, it is believed, he swims the lake brooding, awaiting the opportunity to destroy the dam and be re-united with his wife.

Meanwhile, as at Loch Ness, the Nyaminyami legend has become the focal point of a thriving tourist artifact industry with elaborate Nyaminyami walking sticks sold to visitors and locals alike.

The earliest known Tonga or proto-Tonga originated in the northern part of Zambia's Southern Province and the Kafue Valley — not far from the Zambezi River - in the late 11th century.

Slowly they spread down the Gwembe Valley, which stretches from Kariba Dam to Victoria Falls, and across the Zambezi River into today's northern Zimbabwe. It is probable their domain once stretched further south and that they were pushed back by Shona northerly migration and conquest.

Tonga, on the northern and southern banks of the Zambezi River, formed cohesive political and social neighbourhood communities *(cisi)* with little significant difference between them.

Early explorers recorded encountering cases where local Tonga rulers *(mwami)* had people who farmed on either side of the river. Communication between them was by dug-out canoes.

The Tonga existed in a large number of small, scattered, independent political units, each headed by a *mwami*. The average size of these units was six small villages. But, where good soils existed near the Zambezi, the villages were significantly bigger with populations of over 1,000 people.

Tonga women smokes traditional pipe.

The name, Tonga is thought to have been applied to the people of the Middle Zambezi Valley and the southern Zambian plateau from the mid-18th century.   Prior to that they are believed to have used the name of the particular locality where they lived.

This word is thought to be of external origin, probably bestowed on the people of the Gwembe Valley by their neighbours, because the Tonga were "chiefless" and did not recognise a paramount ruler.

Such elitism as prevailed derived from the inhabitants of the Gwembe Valley, who considered themselves "purer" and less mixed than those from the east of the area where cultural fusion with the Shona was occurring.

Their language, the main one of five in the Zambezi region and the third largest in Zimbabwe, is more related to the languages of northern Zambia and Zaire than to those of Zimbabwe.

In Zambia, Tonga is the main one of the five language groups and it has seven principal dialects — Ila, Lenje, Leya, Soli, Twa, Subiya and Totela.

Each neighbourhood community *(cisi)* was headed by a *mwami* who had no political authority over neighbouring communities. If he overstepped the boundary, so to speak, he would have been sharply rebuffed, which might have resulted in inter-neighbourhood battles. But such incidents were rare.

Political authority was rooted in religion among the Tonga. The *cisi* rulers were the lineage spirit custodians *(basikatongo)* with the Tonga believing the *mwami* embodied the spirit/soul of the clan founder.

The constant communication of the lineage head *(mwami)* with the ancestor-*mwami* enhanced the living incumbent's political authority. This, however, was the sole factor which set him apart for the Tonga believed all men are equal.

As a result the powers of the *mwami* were extremely limited. Land belonged to the *cisi* and was vested in individual members with full title over its use, sub-division and disposal. The *mwami's* only authority over land was as an arbitrator in cases of dispute. As such, Tonga rulers have been described as "ecclesiastical jurists" whose chief role was to pass judgement on matters of ethnic law and its spiritual associations.

23

Thus, the Tonga's egalitarian ethic, coupled with the limitation of the *mwami's* powers, forced the incumbent to rule through persuasion rather than coercion.

The *mwami* also had specific spiritual functions in his *cisi* regarding rain-making ceremonies, the ritual planting of the first seed, and in the ceremony to mark the harvest of the first fruits. Similarities here are to be found in western culture, particularly harvest festivals.

The *mwami* was responsible for sending his representative to the spirit mediums *(basangu)* for rain-making ceremonies. A *musangu* (singular) was the ritual go-between linking the departed spirits and their living ancestors.

Every Tonga extended family had its own *musangu*, although the stature of some may have been greater than others and those who were regarded as having special powers could be approached by members of other *cisi*.

The *musangu* was given gifts — a black fowl, black beads, tobacco, and

Iron age Tonga hoe head.

in some cases black cloth, to bless the seeds and to bring good rains and a good harvest.

Once blessed the seeds were returned to the *mwami*. Thereafter all the people of the *cisi* gathered to assist in the ritual preparation of the *mwami's* land and planting of the blessed seeds. Then they tilled their own fields.

When the first crops were harvested no one was allowed to eat them until an offering has been made by the *mwami* to the spirit medium.

The Tonga believed in the immortality of the soul and in the existence of the spirits of the dead and their ability to work evil on the living.

Illnesses, no matter how trivial, were attributed to the spirits having been offended by the behaviour of the sick person.

The graves of the ancestors were considered to be sacred and revered. This caused serious problems when Lake Kariba was flooded.

Drowned forest.

Water forest

Virtually everywhere one looks near the Kariba shoreline, leafless trees, officially "drowned" some 30 years ago, jut into the air above the water-line or lurk below it threatening the unwary mariner.

Over 90 per cent of the trees are mopane, a hardwood. The remainder are leadwood.

The trees were "drowned" when Kariba was flooded from 1959. But the minerally-enriched water with its high silicone content began hardening the trees as silent sentinels increasingly emerging from the deep.

Today Kariba is only about 20 per cent full, some eleven metres below its high water mark. Optimists hope it will re-fill one day. Others simply observe the increasing number of trees — and new islands — emerging from below the water.

The trees pose a hazard for boats. But birds, butterflies and other insects, as well as lizards, find in them a new home and haven. And the new islands offer safer sanctuary from predators for such mammals as elephant and buffalo who swim across to them.

Much care was lavished on the graves. Before the price of ivory rose in the last century to meet European demand, the largest available pair of elephant tusks were mounted at the head of a grave forming an arch, or the grave was enclosed in the choicest ivory.

The biggest difference between the social system of the Tonga and that of most other Zimbabweans is that the Tonga trace descent and inheritance matrilineally through the mothers' family.

As a result Tonga succession descends through the female line to the senior nephew of the dead *mwami*. A man, therefore, can only succeed to his uncle's position as *mwami*, not his father's. Women however, cannot become *mwamis*.

Despite the diffuse nature of Tonga society it was nevertheless highly integrated with kinship links from *cisi* to *cisi*. Kinship, despite the lack of centralised authority, knitted the neighbourhood communities together thereby transcending boundaries. The Tonga, as explorer Dr David Livingstone remarked in 1860, displayed a "strong clannish feeling".

In descending order, and prior to the arrival of the tsetse fly in the 1830s and the *mfecane* (a Zulu word literally meaning the crushing), the Tonga sustained themselves economically through agriculture, livestock, hunting, gathering, fishing and manufacturing.

Tonga subsistence agriculture was primarily based on the cultivation of cereals with the society adapting their methods to suit local conditions.

The Tonga cultivated two types of fields, one near river banks to take advantage of silt deposited on the floodplains, the other on poorer soils in nearby hills away from the river.

On the alluvial floodplain soils, every family, and then each individual in that family, had a smallholding neatly divided by reed fences. Where population levels were high mile after mile of these fenced smallholdings were a common sight.

The alluvial plots required no fallowing, rotation, or manure. They could be cultivated twice yearly, during the rains and then the dry season after floodwaters receded. The scale of flooding determined field sizes in the latter case.

The two-crop cycle provided the Tonga with a form of insurance. If the summer (rainy season) crops failed because of drought or pests, they could replenish their granaries with the winter (dry season) crop.

Away from the floodplains, on poorer soils in the hills, the Tonga practised shifting cultivation. These fields were cultivated in October/November just before the rains.

The wide range of crops included maize, bulrush millet, finger millet, sorghum, water-melons, pumpkins, sweet-potatoes, ground-nuts, small-leaf tobacco and cotton. The staples were bulrush millet *(nzembwe)*, sorghum *(maila)* and maize *(zipopwe)*.

Bulrush millet was the most extensively cultivated crop, growing readily in poorer soils, ripening faster than maize or sorghum, and being easier to pound into flour than maize. But, its yield was lower per hectare than maize.

Sorghum was valued as a drought resistant crop thereby reducing the dangers of harvest failure. The Tonga maize was small and short-cobbed but relatively little was grown and then only on the floodplain smallholdings.

On these smallholdings the Tonga usually planted tobacco before planting maize. An early form of dry-season planting was employed with seedlings watered until the rains arrived. Green mealies were available from these fields as early as August.

Other crops on these alluvial plots included pumpkins and water-melons. In 1862 an early explorer recorded that "fine, long-stapled cotton" was also being grown.

Riverine cultivation and unpredictable rains exposed the crops to flooding and drought. But the neighbourhood nature of communities ensured that a community in deficit was able to barter goods with another community which had a surplus.

A further hazard was crop damage from marauding animals such as elephant, hippopotami, buffalo and smaller species. Look-out platforms were erected in fields and guarded day and night, while a loosely hung rope carrying tin cans filled with pebbles served the dual purpose of waking sleeping guards and driving off the animal that tried to invade the field.

Fires were also lit to scare off animals, particularly hippopotami, while pit-traps were dug for buffalo. Elephants were a different matter with spears and battle axes employed.

Another problem was the swarms of grain-eating birds, probably queleas. These were sprayed with poisonous chemicals from the 1960s. Scarecrows were the most effective way of chasing the birds away. Locusts posed yet another difficulty. While it is not clear how far back this problem dated, it was not until the 1930s that spraying was employed by the Southern Rhodesian government.

Yet, and despite these many hazards, agriculture remained the Tonga's principal activity. Grain stores existed in every village although these were ravaged by weevils sometimes exhausting supplies before the next harvest.

Faced with a shortfall before the next harvest the Tonga could fall back on one of their other sources of food, domestic livestock in particular.

Apart from the dietary importance, livestock were also of social importance. Cattle were used in marriage transactions *(lobola)* and the number owned reflected social status. The tsetse fly infestation in the 1830s ended the role of cattle as a social symbol. They were replaced by goats and sheep which, along with fowls, were now used for food or barter.

The Tonga were noted as fearless and skilled hunters, unafraid of elephant or hippopotami which they speared from trees or harpooned from their dugout canoes. Other animals, including buffalo, were hunted on foot.

Bows and arrows were used, sometimes with dogs in support, to corner an animal. Spears, often tipped with a poison taken from the *chenyami* bulb, were another method of hunting, while spring traps and concealed game pits were also used.

This economic pursuit, which served a dietary need and kept the tsetse fly at bay, was severely curtailed by the enactment of restrictive game laws in 1906.

The uncertainty of agricultural crops, and particularly the threat of deficit, forced the Tonga to supplement their diet by gathering leaves, roots and grasses.

The range of forest produce gathered by the Tonga in the Zambezi Valley is one of the widest ever studied in Africa. Among these were *muntili* (a tuber and important famine food), the roots of the *madadi* and *ntebe* plants, beans and berries from trees such as *miyunga, muchibi* and *mugoma,* and grasses such as *munga, shonde* and *ntombolo.*

Dr Livingstone noted several species of trees with edible fruits and nuts along the Zambezi which his party ate. No one ever died from hunger in the valley, said the Tonga porters.

Insects also supplemented the diet, particularly when the crops failed. These included locusts, flying ants, and caterpillars *(mashonja).* But gathering these remained a peripheral activity.

Fishing, despite the proximity of the river, was regarded as less important for protein supplement than animal husbandry and hunting.

Various methods, depending upon the season, were used to catch fish. During the floods, reed barriers were constructed across tributaries. As the floodwaters receded, fish were trapped behind them and scooped out.

Tonga fishermen ply their trade.

The bean of a *munyunka* tree was used to poison waterholes in the dry season, stupefying fish which floated to the surface. Fish traps, allowing entry but denying exit, were extensively used by the Tonga as were multi-barbed spears and barbed fish hooks like those in use in Europe at that time.

Archaeological, oral and documentary evidence from eyewitnesses between 1850 and 1898, shows four main types of industry — iron working, salt production, cotton and tobacco.

The Tonga were noted as skillful iron-workers; their blacksmiths produced the heads for hoes, axes, knives, as well as the keys for the *mbila* musical instrument. The weapons manufactured included battle axes, stabbing spears with a ferocious spike at the base of the shaft, lightweight throwing spears, and a fishing spear with barbed hooks. They also manufactured tin products.

Salt was produced from salt pans through a method involving evaporation dissolving the saline earth in water, filtration to separate the salt and earth, and boiling to allow the salt to again crystallise. The salt was brown in colour and traded in the area.

One place where salt was collected was at Masikele spring in what is now the Chizara National Park. Dating from thousands of years ago a well-worn footpath in the sandstone ridge leads to the site. The Tonga left an offering of pots at the site and today there is what is described as a "mountain" of pieces of pots at Masikele.

Explorers reported cotton growing in the Gwembe Valley and Dr Livingstone recorded that Tonga men (locally referred to as *baenda-pezi,* meaning "go-nakeds") wore no clothes. This was a cultural choice rather than evidence of a shortage of clothing.

However, the Tonga method of weaving was slow and time-consuming with a single blanket taking up to a month to manufacture. As a result animal skins were also widely worn prior to the arrival of European mass produced exports in the late 19th century.

Ripe tobacco leaves were picked, hung and sun-cured, before being processed and manufactured as snuff or pipe tobacco which was traded in the region, the Ndebele being large consumers.

Labour was divided within households. Men cleared the bush, cutting and burning trees. Women and their daughters cultivated the land.

Men cut and carried poles to construct a house which they thatched. Women collected the *daga* (mud) and plastered the walls.

Men produced domestic items such as mortars, pestles, cooking sticks, spoons and bowls. Women produced basketry and pottery household items such as pots, brewing vessels and salt boilers.

In polygamous households each wife was responsible for her own field, with women and children guarding the fields by day and men at night. Animal husbandry, hunting dangerous game, collecting wild honey, were all male preserves.

In some cases, such as hoeing, weeding, reaping, threshing and fishing, work parties were drawn from more than one *cisi*, and men and women worked together. Among men this also occurred on hunts.

Overall, production and consumption generally coincided, with little surplus either way. The arrival of Portuguese traders, the *mfecane*, missionaries, explorers, hunters, and finally the settlers, was to change dramatically and irrevocably the Tonga way of life.

COLONIAL HISTORY
The Portuguese established themselves on the Mozambique coast in the 16th century. By the end of the following century they had begun to make their way up the navigable 800 km Lower Zambezi River stretch which was to be their first commercial highway.

Dugout canoes were used to transport goods such as beads, cloth and guns, which were traded for very cheap ivory, which then had no monetary value to the Tonga who only used it for burials.

Recent evidence also shows that the Portuguese were involved in the slave trade, albeit on a lesser scale than other European nations. This greatly reduced the Tonga population. They eventually purchased back slaves in return for ivory when slavery was officially abolished.

The speed of the river and rapids made entry from the Lower to Middle Zambezi impossible for all but the most intrepid Tonga fishermen and posed the very real danger of merchandise being lost from an overturned canoe.

As a result, the penetration of the 400 km Middle Zambezi was slower and traders were forced to use overland routes, transporting their goods using slave porters along the river banks.

Slaves.

There is evidence that agents of the earliest Portuguese traders reached Chireya, a plateau north of Gokwe, by the 1780s. Thereafter the Portuguese established temporary settlements (*feiras*, meaning market places) which served as trade bases. The westernmost *feira* was located at what is now Zumbo in Zambia.

Such trade from the east continued throughout the 19th century with little or no discernible impact on the economies, political structures and material culture of the Tonga.

Ivory (see *Hwange: Elephant Country*, an Into Africa Travel Guide) was in high demand in Europe and it is estimated that as many as two million elephants may have been slaughtered to provide piano keys, billiard balls, knife handles and ornaments to satisfy the demand created by the European industrial revolution's new wealth.

The settlers in South Africa, having decimated their own elephant herds, pushed their ivory frontier north with the years 1860 to 1880 marking the heyday of elephant hunting in northwestern Zimbabwe and along the Zambezi. By 1880, elephants had become scarce.

The Gwembe Valley, however, remained comparatively well-stocked with elephants, and ivory trading continued until towards the end of the 19th century.

The increased demand for ivory, and its subsequent rise in value brought about significant changes in Tonga society. The most visible change occurred in burial practices. No longer were tusks used to adorn graves; they were sold instead.

By as early as 1862 the practice of placing tusks on the graves of ancestors was in decline. In 1875, an explorer recorded, worthless elephant milk teeth had replaced tusks on graves. The market-driven value of ivory had replaced the respect previously accorded to deceased rulers.

The rise in demand and in the price of ivory coincided with the official ending of the slave trade. Children had been sold to slave traders by the Tonga on the Zambezi River banks for a few coarse beads; ivory was kept for more substantial goods.

The formal ending of the slave trade by European nations brought a reversal in the trade. Tonga *mwami,* needing to replenish their followers depleted by the slave trade, began to buy back slaves in return for ivory.

A further change was the availability of European manufactured goods which undermined and destroyed the slow and inefficient Tonga cotton industry, which was purely internal, and cotton cultivation.

The trade in firearms introduced another important element to the Tonga area. While they were used in defence against Ndebele raiders, the major reasons for their acquisition were crop protection and hunting, making the latter pursuit safer.

Guns, traded for small livestock, skins and grain, were supplied by the Portuguese from their bases. This trade greatly increased the ability of the Tonga to resist would-be invaders, and added a potentially lethal new dimension to battles.

The introduction of firearms in turn led to the introduction of new industries such as making gunpowder and bullets as well as servicing the firearms.

Only a few firearms existed when the Ndebele raids began in the 1850s and by 1862 these raids had severely dislocated many Tonga polities.

Lobengula.

Once densely-populated country was abandoned as people fled to the comparative sanctuary of the hills. Many crossed the Zambezi River into present day Zambia.

The Ndebele King, Lobengula, laid claim to all land north of Bulawayo to the Zambezi River and described the Tonga (along with the Nambya and Shangwe) as his vassals. Eyewitness accounts confirm this was largely the case.

The Ndebele raids and subjugation were finally brought to an end in 1893 when the Ndebele were defeated by the forces of the British South Africa Company (BSAC) in the Anglo-Ndebele war.

By then the Tonga had suffered a plague of tsetse fly, been integrated into the world economic order at the cost of their own industries, and been overrun by the Ndebele. But worse was to follow.

The arrival of South African traders and hunters in northwestern Zimbabwe from the early 1860s introduced an element of competition into a market which hitherto had been solely a Portuguese preserve.

This brought about an important change in Tonga society, transforming it into a migrant population servicing South Africa's mines and buying cloth, beads and firearms from its wages.

But the Europeans arriving from South Africa with colonial intentions realised the dangers of allowing Africans to accumulate firearms and by the late 1880s guns had dried up from this source.

Unlike the Nambya and Shangwe, who lived in relatively tsetse fly-free areas, the tsetse was to prove an ally of the Tonga ensuring the newly arrived white settlers did not want their land.

Five Tonga reserves were demarcated in 1911 and 1914/15 but the greater part of the Tonga land remained unalienated. Because of the fact that the settlers had little interest or design on the area, African education and health facilities were not created.

Tonga relations with their new invaders, the white settlers, got off to a bad start in 1894 with the introduction of a hut tax. Each head of household was to pay Shs 10 per hut in his homestead and a further Shs 10 per hut for each wife if he was polygamous.

This touched off a protest migration, with Tonga refusing to pay, and instead crossing to the north bank of the Zambezi River. The Tonga migrants settled in Gwembe District in Northern Rhodesia (now Zambia) and the hut tax introduced there in 1904 was lower than that in the area they had abandoned.

The hut tax in Southern Rhodesia was changed to a poll tax in 1904 with every male above 16 years of age required to pay £1.

The objective of these taxes and changes was not solely to raise revenue but was intended to force Africans to work on European owned farms and in industries, which they were boycotting because of exploitative wages, poor conditions, and the more popular migrant labour option.

However, those who had not crossed into Northern Rhodesia to avoid the taxes sold their livestock instead, enabling them to pay the taxes. This resistance defeated the Rhodesian settler objective of creating a local labour reservoir, forcing them to recruit cheap labour from other countries in the region.

The Southern Rhodesian government initially tried recruiting the Tonga *mwamis* to act as their agents. When this failed they resorted to replacing recalcitrant chiefs with more pliable people. Again this had limited impact and Tonga resistance to the settlers continued.

A Southern Rhodesian Native Commissioner had noted of the Tonga that they were " suspicious, and with a strong desire ... to place obstacles in the way of, and passively resist, all outside interference with themselves and their country".

This resistance was made easier by the white settlers' indifference towards the Tonga. In 1912 the only three whites in the area were Native Department officials. By 1945 the European population was about 40, the smallest white population anywhere in the country.

While the settlers had promulgated reserves in the Tonga areas, the Tonga ignored them with little more than 3,000 moving into these designated areas out of a population of over 30,000.

By 1923 as much as 60 per cent of the Tonga adult male population had migrated to South African mines to seek salaried employment. In 1943 extensive tax patrols in the area found Tonga villages inhabited almost entirely by aged males, women and children.

Colonial laws restricting the possession of firearms, hunting, vegetation preservation in reserves, and migrations, conspired in the rapid spread of the bush, the return of wild animals and the resulting increase in tsetse fly and sleeping sickness.

Over a 17-year period from 1896 to 1913 the tsetse fly belt from Manzituba *vlei* increased by 28.2 per cent. By 1930 tsetse infestation in the northwestern part of Southern Rhodesia covered an area of 54,390 square km. By then the fly was expanding its territory at an astounding 2,590 square km a year!

Having created the conditions for the spread of tsetse fly through legislation, the settlers now resorted to forced removals of Tonga from infested to non-infested areas.

Tonga resistance, coupled with settler indifference to the Tonga and their land, paved the way for the next step in the unfolding tragedy — the building of Kariba Dam and the flooding of the lake.

KARIBA

The Federation of Rhodesia and Nyasaland brought together Southern Rhodesia, Northern Rhodesia and Nyasaland (now Zimbabwe, Zambia and Malawi respectively) in a loose political and economic grouping. It lasted from 1953 to 1963 and was opposed by black nationalists.

This short-lived and ill-fated mixed marriage was settler-driven, coinciding with demands by their industries for the development and generation of more electricity.

Nyaminyami carving and Kariba Dam wall.

In 1963 the Federation collapsed in the face of black nationalist opposition. Northern Rhodesia and Nyasaland became independent the following year, becoming Zambia and Malawi. In Southern Rhodesia black nationalists and white settlers were to fight a bloody war before Zimbabwe's birth in 1980.

During the Federation, Kariba was born. It could be "...considered as THE (and perhaps only) success story of the Federation" is the view of a white fisheries research officer and author, Dale Kenmuir.

The Tonga had a quite different view. In this decade the Kariba Dam was built and the lake flooded, forcing some 57,000 of the Tonga peo-

37

Kariba facts	
Dam wall	built between 1955/59
Height	128 metres
Crest	617 metres long
	13/24 metres wide
Concrete used	1,032,000 cubic metres
Spillway	six flood gates
Cost	£122 million
Site deaths	86
Built by	Impresit, Italy
Designed	Andrew Coyne
Lake	280 km long
	32 km at widest
Ave. depth	20 metres
Deepest	120 metres
Shoreline	2,000 km

Tourists photograph elephant.

ple to leave their ancestral homes in the Gwembe Valley.

Kenmuir provides an insight into the thinking at the time of white Southern Rhodesians in his book, *A Wilderness Called Kariba: The Wildlife and Natural History of Lake Kariba.*

"Foremost in the minds of the men concerned with planning were the possibilities of large-scale commercial fisheries — something entirely new and exciting in land-locked Rhodesia. Secondly, was the equally exciting prospect of having an inland sea with all the interesting possibilities for tourism that arose — boating, fishing, yachting, hotels, motels, boatels, game reserves on the shore, and so on.

"Little wonder then that the impending Kariba injected enthusiasm and vigour into the otherwise dull routine of normal government life. Nothing on so grand a scale had ever happened in the world before, let alone in Rhodesia."

Kenmuir goes on to list a host of committees charged with various tasks. None of the committees he lists was specifically tasked with the desirability or otherwise of the project insofar as the Tonga were concerned.

He does concede: "In view of the impending commercial fishery, a question of great interest and concern to the authorities was to what extent were the Tonga people fisherman, and to what extent were they

Salted fish drying at Tonga cooperative.

Fishing Cooperative

Fifteen Tonga fishermen employed by a company which was having difficulty making the transition from Rhodesia to Zimbabwe, set up the Luyando Gillnet Fishing Cooperative Society in 1986.

Previously they were being paid one Zimbabwean cent (US$0.0001) for every fish they caught irrespective of the size of the fish. Today they can earn over Z$1,000 per month.

A daily tally is kept of the catch from their seven boats, and monies split up on a pro-rata basis according to the kg caught. The catch in August 1996 was 3,073 kg and over Z$6,000 was paid out to the members.

A further Z$4,000 was retained to buy boats, nets, floats, twine, account books, stationery, and finally ice to preserve the fish and salt to dry it. The cooperative sells its catch in Kariba where they have purchased a freezer.

Cooperative chairman, Cephas Mabalani, beamed broadly when asked if life was better now. "Much", he said.

familiar with fishing practices to enable them to live on or close to the shores of Kariba and fish commercially for a living? Did they in fact fish at all, and if so, what methods did they employ?"

Certainly, the Tonga were fishermen, although their methods were rudimentary and fishing was not among their priority occupations.

"Early prospects of the Tonga being suitable fishermen for the new lake were not optimistic," writes Kenmuir. "...although the Tonga were acquainted with fish and fishing this activity was subsidiary, and developed only to a subsistence level. They were not familiar with the modern-day practice of fishing for commercial return, and neither were they familiar with modern fishing gear".

While that may have been true it avoided the real issue, for the Tonga could have been trained in modern fishing methods and gear.

The fact of the matter was that the Tonga were not a serious consideration because disease made their land undesirable and inhospitable for white settlers, lacked apparent mineral wealth, and they had proved a continual irritant to the settlers.

Because so few whites had moved into the Tonga area there was no one to speak for them or against the Kariba project and, in those days, black voices of protest went unheeded.

So the Tonga's fate was sealed. European manufactured goods had destroyed their industries, the ivory trade and slavery had changed their values. Now they were to be uprooted, their ancestral homes flooded by the waters of Lake Kariba.

The Federal government took the decision to build Kariba in 1955. The damming of the Zambezi River in the Kariba Gorge between the Lower and Middle Zambezi would create a 5,180 square km lake submerging the Zambezi Plain, lower courses of the tributaries feeding into the river, and the lower lying surrounding hills.

The forced removal of the Tonga from their lands below the 488 metre elevation was implemented from 1956 to 1958. The Simuchembu people were moved the furthest, 161 km from their ancestral home.

There was to be further Tonga resistance during these forced removals. Sinatatenke and his people refused to move until the lake's rising floodwaters threatened to engulf their homes.

Settler indifference to the Tonga, and ignorance of their customs, was again illustrated in these forced removals. Some were moved to heavily tsetse fly-infested areas while others created further overcrowding in already marginal agricultural areas.

Of even greater long-term significance were the social consequences. Inter-dependent and cohesive neighbourhood communities were broken up separating lineage-mates and other kin links which transcended formal *cisi* boundaries.

Some villagers who had been neighbours in the Gwembe Valley now found themselves re-settled almost 100 km apart. Once cohesive neighbourhoods disintegrated, and the former close bonds between the river Tonga who lived and farmed on both banks of the Zambezi were irrevocably shattered as they were moved to higher ground to the north and south away from the emerging lake.

In effect the lake created two Tonga nations, one now in Zambia, the other in Southern Rhodesia.

The loss of the sacred graves was probably the most serious factor, impossible to measure in material terms, or to compensate. The Tonga in general, and the *basikatongo* in particular, feared the resettlement would bring the wrath of the shades *(mizimu)* of their dead upon them.

The powers of the *mwami,* already based on persuasion, were further eroded by the resettlement because their spiritual domain had been extinguished. While the *mwami* attempted to adjust, "the adjustment [was] proving too severe a test and they [had] deteriorated into confused, often discontented people, and ...[had] resorted to alcohol as an escape from the realities of their lives" a subsequent study showed.

Economically the loss of the valued alluvial river fields, which had played a major role in staving off famine for generations, was to effect seriously the marginal Tonga land tenure system.

Rigidly maintained Tonga land tenure lineage rights were lost and this particularly affected Tonga women. New resettlement land, to be cleared and tilled, over which previous title did not exist, was allocated only to men by the Southern Rhodesian government.

OPERATION NOAH

While the fate of the resettled Tonga was largely ignored, the plight of the animals threatened by Kariba's rising floodwaters, received international publicity and initial material support.

On 3 December 1958 the two sluice gates at Kariba Dam through which the Zambezi River flowed were closed. In the first 24 hours thereafter the lake rose by six metres. By September 1959 it had risen almost 60 metres.

The mammals sought temporary refuge on the emerging islands, and Operation Noah, which struck an emotive chord, was launched to rescue them before the lake reached its height in September 1963.

Operation Noah rescuers.

Some animals were shot on the islands after attacking would-be rescuers. Others, surprisingly including birds such as robins, waxbills and babblers, remained on the submerging islands drowning in their emaciated condition as the water engulfed them. Others swam or flew to the mainland or other islands.

When Operation Noah came to an end in June 1963, the Southern Rhodesian team had rescued nearly 5,000 animals while on the Northern Rhodesian side, where game was scarcer, some 2,000 animals had been rescued.

The cost of the animal rescue operation was immense, certainly greater than the amount spent on translocating 57,000 Tonga. The external publicity generated by Operation Noah can be counted in millions and laid the foundation for today's commercial and game fishing, as well as the tourist industry at Kariba.

MATUSADONA

The 1,407 sq km Matusadona National Park is on the southern shore of Lake Kariba with the Ume River to the west, Sanyati River and gorge in the east, and the dirt road from Binga to Karoi partially running along the southernmost boundary.

Matusadona was declared a wildlife area in 1958 while the Kariba Dam was being built. Thereafter it was designated as a non-hunting area, as a game reserve in 1963, and as a national park in 1975.

There are several ways of accessing Matusadona, the preferred ones being by boat across the lake from Kariba to Tashinga and Sanyati camps within the park. Lake Navigation must be notified of all boat movements and there are movement and mooring controls along the Matusadona shoreline.

Some visitors fly into the park and surrounding camps by fixed wing charter or float plane while advance permission is needed from the Department of National Parks to land at the Tashinga airstrip.

The third, and roughest, means of reaching Matusadona is by land.

Float plane takes off.

From the Binga-Karoi road you turn north roughly 150 km west of Karoi formally entering through the Vulunduli Entrance Gate on the east of the Ume.

You can reach Fothergill and Spurwing, which have ceased to be islands because of the fall in the lake level, by this route. But four-wheel drive is strongly recommended and even then at the height of the wet season this route is best avoided unless you want to risk a night bogged down.

Matusadona is generally regarded as one of Zimbabwe's loveliest parks and the lion density in the park competes with that of northern Tanzania. Rhino, while not exactly common, are more likely to be seen in specific areas than in many other places in Zimbabwe.

The Matusadona shoreline and flatlands behind are well known. But few realise this is only one-third of the park with the remainder lying in the Matuzwi-a-donha hills which rears up from the landscape forming part of the Zambezi Escarpment and southern extremity of the Zambezi Valley. For ease of reference these three distinct areas are dealt with separately.

Shoreline
The first important thing to remember about the shoreline is that you are in a living museum only 30 years old. The births of many of its living residents in fact pre-date the park.

Ecological changes are still taking place. These are, unfortunately not being fully studied. At the same time the Matusadona puzzle is developing new complexities as the lake falls.

The first thing the visitor will notice are the "drowned forests", mile-upon-mile of hardened, leafless, mainly mopane trees which jut above the lake surface.

Fish eagles nest on them, cormorants settle on them to spread their wings to dry and replenish their oil cover, woodpeckers nest in holes, many other birds use them as perches, while yet others search them for grubs and other food.

The "drowned forests", set against a spectacular red sunset, maybe with an elephant or some other large mammal in the frame, are permanent reminders of Kariba and Matusadona.

But there is a down side to the "drowned forests". Under Cautionary Notes, the Kariba Navigator's chart warns: "There are thousands of trees still standing in the lake and although most of them are well below the surface there are those which are hazardous." Extreme caution should be exercised when approaching the shoreline, the warning concludes.

Kariba sunset.

The second thing to notice about the shoreline is the large expanse between the water-edge and the first leaf-bearing green trees. The proliferation of grasses has attracted grassland bird species not previously recorded at Kariba such as the Pinkthroated and Yellowthroated Longclaw.

Before the lake fell 11 metres, this whole area was under water. Now hardened mopane trees stand as mute leafless sentinels across these open areas.

For the large herds of buffalo, elephant, impala, waterbuck and zebra, these plains afford grazing areas. But in most areas predators, particularly lion, lurk beyond the tree line as a constant threat to the unwary.

In one incident which Kariba guides still talk about, a pride of lions were responsible for the deaths of 12 buffalo in one attack. Seven buffalo, malnourished from drought, simply collapsed and died while fleeing, five others were killed by the pride.

In virtually every creek and inlet along the shoreline one will find a resident or even a family pod of hippo. Less easily seen, except when sunning themselves, and certainly less vocal, are crocodiles of whom it is estimated there is one for every 200 metres of the Matusadona shoreline, with concentrations in most creeks, rivers and bays.

One of the greatest pleasures of Kariba is taking a small boat into an inlet at dawn. Turn off the engine and just sit quietly as Africa arises.

A myriad of waterbirds, some with long delicate pink legs begin their daily preening and search for food. Geese raise their raucous voices, Blacksmith Plover bully any other species they can, Openbilled Stork perch and peer, Ibis, and many other birds, complete an unrivalled bird-watching experience.

This is the area between the shoreline and escarpment beyond. Mainly it comprises mopane scrub and woodlands interspersed with "jesse bush" (thicket mostly comprising of *combretum/holmskioldia*), and is typical of the Zambezi Valley floor before the birth of Kariba.

Along water courses the visitor will see ebonies, leadwoods, which make up about ten per cent of the lake's "flooded forest", and tamarinds, with a very few ilala or vegetable ivory palms standing out conspicuously.

Elephants have considerably and conspicuously modified the vegetation, notably the mopane coppiced woodland. This has led to an emotionally charged debate for and against culling with those opposed, largely foreigners, in the ascendency.

Lone baby zebra on plains.

Meanwhile, trees apart, the principal victims of the elephants are the African villagers living in the communal lands to the east, west and south of the park.

"The first night elephants invade they destroy the crops. That is next year's school fees gone", said an elephant expert who refuses to be drawn into the culling debate insisting it is a management decision.

"The next night they wipe out what they have missed on the first night. That destroys what the villagers might have used to buy clothes that year. And on the third, they destroy everything else".

The Camp Fire communal lands management programme for indigenous resources has endeavoured to prevent poaching through harnessing the wildlife as a resource from which the villagers derive an income from the tourist industry.

But some communities remain openly sceptical and hostile to these alien endeavours. Tourist operators believe such scepticism will remain until monies are disbursed direct to the local population, by-passing councils who retain a considerable amount of the take.

When one considers that the end-user price for rhino horn is around US$66,000 (some Z$660,000) and that the annual income of a villager living in the communal lands is around US$30 (Z$300) it is — and disregarding age old practices — easier to understand economic imperatives, particularly the need to eat.

Meanwhile, elephant damage and poaching notwithstanding, the uneasy alliance between humans and animals continues, awaiting a formula which will ensure the harmony, prosperity and survival of both.

The evidence suggests that both species, with a few animal exceptions, are undergoing a population explosion. Zimbabwe's human population growth rate is around three per cent per annum bringing with it ever-increasing demand for land.

The populations of lion, elephant, buffalo, hippo, crocodile, impala and waterbuck have also increased, possibly at an even greater pace. And the birdlife on the lowlands, where some 400 species have been recorded, remains spectacular.

Escarpment
The Matuzwi-a-donha hills (Matusadona Range), comprising of pre-Cambrian granites and gneisses which are in marked contrast to the lowlands, rise starkly from the haze to the south of the park.

Impala in front of Matusadona Range.

Deciduous lowland and escarpment *brachastegia* woodland, which does not grow at lower valley altitudes, covers the bulk of the area extending into the drier tree savanna towards the Sanyati Gorge to the east. Mountain acacias will be found on the ridges.

The plateau, some 400 metres above the lake, is the park's principal watershed. It is a highly scenic area and definitely backpacking, walking country, free from roads and camps.

The rare black rhino may be found on these walking safaris and Steve Edwards at Musango Safari Camp specialises in tracking rhino from his camp just outside the park near the mouth of the Ume River.

His collection of Stone Age tools reveals how neatly they fitted into a hand to be used as an axe or for cutting. There is also a hoe head, although whether this particular one was manufacturered at a Tonga foundry or sold by Portuguese or South African traders in return for ivory, remains unknown.

Nearby are skulls and horns which have also been picked up in the bush. Just by looking at the skulls one swiftly realises the massive size of hippopotamus canines and the ferocious, jagged teeth of a crocodile.

MAMMALS

With a few exceptions, the visitor to Kariba is likely to see most of Africa's mammals, and the lucky one is more likely to see the Big Five (elephant, lion, leopard, buffalo and rhino, sometimes substituted by cheetah according to locality) here than anywhere else in Zimbabwe.

Where one sees specific animals at Kariba tends to be area-related. On the foreshore, particularly below Bumi Hills Lodge, elephant are generally commonly found. There is an absence of predators, and plains game abounds.

Fothergill "guarantees" lion, and there are large herds of buffalo to be found in the area. Rhino can be found on a guided walk in Matusadona National Park and environs, particularly in the Ume River area. Hippo and crocodile exist everywhere and you may see monitor lizards who prey upon the crocodile eggs.

CARNIVORES
Almost 30 carnivores — those who feed on other animals — from the supposed King of the Jungle, the lion, to the tiny mongoose, have been identified at Kariba.

But, with most visitors spending only a few days in the area, it is most improbable that they will see all of them.

Lion
Africa's largest carnivore, the lion, tops virtually all visitors' lists as the animal they most want to see on their African safari.

This demand by visitors puts considerable strain on the guides. They know in advance what the visitor wants and, until lions have been sighted, everything else tends to be rather secondary. Once lion are found the guide — and the visitor — visibly relax and begin to enjoy the fullness of their surrounds.

In sub-Saharan Africa, where the largest concentration of lion survives today, their range has gradually been reduced as that of humans has

49

Maned lion at Matusadona.

expanded. Once they were common in South Africa's Cape Province. Today, outside zoos and reserves, they have vanished.

Very occasionally, lions, who are notable wanderers and opportunists, turn up in Kariba town, on Zimababwe's central plateau, or in its eastern districts. But these are transitory migrants, often driven from drought areas in search of water and game which has moved ahead of them.

Lions are predominantly nocturnal and it is at night that they do most of their hunting and moving. At Kariba their roaring may be heard often, particularly after a kill, followed by the sound of hyenas.

Lions are lethargic animals rarely exerting themselves except when intent on a kill. Even then they are highly inefficient with their kill ratio being much lower than that for hyena or hunting dog. Buffalo herds frequently bear the morning-after scars showing where lions have hit and missed.

Usually the visitor will find lions lolling about or asleep in the shade, often in prides, sometimes in small all-male groups. But, despite their apparent passivity, they can swiftly become aggressive if unduly disturbed, wounded or otherwise threatened.

Unlike most carnivores they are distinctly social animals, living and hunting in prides which can number a dozen or more and which may embrace several generations. At Fothergill a pride of 27 has been seen.

Prides tend to be found in areas where there is abundant game, frequently buffalo, zebra and impala. The lioness is the nucleus of the pride although there may also be a dominant male. Fights between rival males for a pride can result in the death of one of the combatants.

Male lions become sexually mature at about two years old but usually have to wait another three years before mating. Females become pregnant for the first time at around the age of four and will produce litters every two years until they are around 15.

The act of copulation between lions is notable for its foreplay and frequency. Courtship is initiated by either sex with the pair remaining closely together, the male following the female at all times.

51

Copulation occurs about every 15 minutes, lasting around a minute, over a period of several hours. During breaks the lion and lioness will lie beside each other or walk short distances before the next mating session.

The male may gently stroke the female on the shoulder, neck or back with his tongue to encourage submissiveness; he may seize her by the scruff of the neck (a painless, largely symbolic act) during copulation, and the lioness can be heard purring.

Fertility from all this protracted effort is low and the number of cubs an impregnated female produces averages only 2.6. Cubs suckle for six to seven months and have a very high mortality rate — as high as 60 per cent in some recorded areas — due to scarcity of food, abandonment, disease and other predators.

An adult male lion's average weight is around 190 kg with females averaging 126 kg. Adult males, who stand 1.25 m at the shoulder, reach their maximum weight in seven years, females in five or six years.

The colour of adults is sandy or tawny on the upper body and white underneath. The backs of the rounded ears are black in stark contrast to the body colour. The tail, roughly half the length of the combined head and body, can be black tipped.

Adult males have a mane up to 160 mm in length which, with advanced years, can be black. The mane of younger males tends to be sandy or tawny although, in common with many species, climatic variations can affect colouring. Maneless male lions are rare.

Lions have five digits (toes) on the front feet and four on the rear. Each toe is equipped with very sharp, scimitar-shaped, retractable claws. Those claws and the formidable lower jaw are the main killing weapons.

Male lions rarely participate in the hunt, leaving this to the lionesses. But once a kill is made they take first priority with the female having to wait until the male has eaten his fill.

Nothing feels safe with lions around. Lions may kill baby elephants with the elephant herds reacting strongly to their presence. Other smaller animals - even mice and larger birds such as ostrich — are forced to be ever alert, to run at the least hint of danger.

Leopard.

Leopard

No two leopards, either in markings or colour, are alike. But as you are likely to see very few if any of these powerful, secretive and largely nocturnal animals, you are unlikely to notice the differences.

Generally, however, they have black spots on the limbs, flanks, hindquarters and head, with irregular broken circles covering the remainder of the body.

They are Africa's largest spotted cats with an average male weighing 60 kg and a female a little over half that amount. In common with other cats they have five digits (toes) on the front feet and four in the rear and their spoor is more compact and circular than a lion's.

Leopards' ears are small and rounded, white whiskers particularly long, and their eyesight and hearing extremely keen enabling them to avoid obstacles in the dark.

Unlike lions they are solitary animals except during mating and post-birth periods. They are much more efficient and painstaking hunters, and have withstood human encroachment much better with their range encompassing almost all of sub-Saharan Afica, the Middle and Far East, and Siberia.

Very rarely, they may be seen moving around during the day.   More commonly they lie up during the hotter hours in dense cover, the shade of rocks or caves making them difficult to see. They may be heard making a hoarse rasping, coughing sound, growling when under stress or threatened, and purring after food.

Their prey tends to weigh no more than their own body weight, usually being killed after a relatively short chase. Impala and warthog are the preferred victims although different leopards appear to have dietary preferences and have been known to eat fish, reptiles and birds, which they pluck before eating.

Leopards tend to move at a slow, almost casual pace. But when disturbed, they instantly switch to a bouncing gallop which when they no longer feel threatened, gives way to a fast trot as they head for the nearest thicket.

Whilst cheetahs chase down their prey, leopards, body crouched close to the ground, stalk their quarry before pouncing.

Cheetah
These svelte, graceful animals, built like greyhounds but physically resembling leopards, although with more distinctive spots and longer legs, are seen occasionally in open grass savanah country and light bushland.

They are the fastest animals on earth reaching speeds of over 100 km/h over short distances. Only one species of cheetah exists in southern Africa and they are genetically uniform and susceptible to diseases.

Cheetahs' bodies, unlike those of the stockier more powerful leopard,

are slender and held high off the ground on long thin legs. Their heads are much more rounded, muzzles shorter and ears smaller.

The colonisation of Africa, leading to demand for cheetahs' skins,

Cheetah.

over-emphasis on their predatory impact on domestic stock and, less frequently, the demand for them as pets, has led to the shrinkage of their range and even their disappearance in many places.

They became extinct in India by 1952 and they have disappeared from countries they once inhabited bordering on the eastern Mediterranean. But they may still be found in northern parts of the Arabian Peninsula, Iraq, Iran, Afghanistan and Baluchistan.

Cheetah, which disappeared from Kariba when the lake filled, have been re-introduced in Matusadona and are seen reasonably regularly around Fothergill, although there are indications that lions are preying on them.

Cheetah do most of their hunting in daytime mainly around sunrise and sunset, and in common with lion and leopard, often lie-up in the hotter hours of the day on an elevated site, warming themselves before moving into shade.

Cubs remain with their mothers for about a year, dispersing before another litter is born; males may form cohesive bachelor groups. They have very large, sometimes over-lapping, home ranges which can cover hundreds of square km.

Unlike leopard, cheetah are averse to swimming and are infrequent tree climbers. Their call is bird-like resembling a chirrup when excited and they may purr, growl, snarl, hiss or cough depending upon whether they are content or feel threatened.

They prefer to attack stragglers in prey groups, approach their intended victim openly, pausing only if it shows signs of nervousness, and then running the victim down with a short burst of no more than 400 metres.

Painted Hunting Dog
There are few more beautiful, efficient and caring species in Africa. But, largely as a result of ignorance and disinformation, the hunting dog, which was once common throughout Africa, is today a severely threatened species.

Painted Hunting Dog have been shot on farms, even in national parks, and continually run over by speeding motorists. Between 1956 and 1961 a total of 2,674 were shot in Southern Rhodesia, as vermin.

They are seen occasionally at Kariba. One of the area's classic wildlife

Wild dog looks right before crossing.

pictures is of a pack swimming across the Sanyati Gorge, an area where they were not previously known to have existed.

The dog is a predator and in Zimbabwe approximately 98 per cent of its diet consists of impala, kudu and duiker. These dogs are extremely efficient hunters, killing their prey in seconds.

The home range of packs is enormous, some 750 square km. They are capable of top speeds of 70 km/h and trot at 15 km/h.

They are deeply caring when it comes to their pups. Only one pair breeds annually within a pack and the whole pack participates in feeding, protecting and rearing the young. Unlike other predators such as lions, the pups eat first on a kill.

Visitors may see a number of other carnivores including hyena, aardwolf, caracal, African wild cat, serval, civet, genet, side-striped jackal, honey badger and mongoose.

HERBIVORES
Herbivore means a plant-eating animal such as a cow, a horse, or many animals you will see in the wild including buffalo, zebra and wildebeest. They are characterised by having teeth adapted for grinding plants (chewing the cud in the case of cows).

But, as with most definitions, there are variations and exceptions. Some animals are omnivores eating both animal and vegetable matter.

A further differentiation not made here is that between grazers (grass eaters) and browsers (shrub and tree eaters). Impala, to give one example, do both depending upon availability.

Elephant
Whether in family groups, including small calves, bull herds, or singly posing against a red sunset for the camera, elephants are an integral part of Kariba.

While Hwange National Park, with over 20,000 elephants, is Zimbabwe's most noted destination for this giant mammal, it is possible, particularly after the rains when they are dispersed, to visit Hwange and not see a single elephant.

At Kariba, where they number around 1,500, I have never failed to see elephants. Indeed, I have watched them a few metres away from my hotel room balcony in Kariba town drinking and bathing in the lake, and there are abundant tales of them chasing residents of the town.

The elephant's earliest known forebear, a small pig-like creature called *Moeritherium*, lived 50 million years ago. Today only two species of the family *Elephantidae* — the African and the Indian elephant — survive.

The bulk, shape, and gnarled appearance of the African elephant makes it one of the continent's most readily identifiable mammals. Sparse hair covers the grey to brownish-grey body although water, dust and mud can obscure the true colour.

Layers of cartilage in the feet act as shock-absorbers and, when standing, the elephant will often place its bulk on two legs while resting the others.

The trunk probes the air like a radar antennae continuously checking for danger, and it is employed with extreme dexterity to shovel vast quantities of food into the mouth and to exhale water into it.

The ear flaps move continuously to control body temperature; the green-to-hazel eyes are watchful, and secretion occurs through the temporal glands beneath them revealing how much an animal is under stress.

Elephants weigh up to six tonnes. They can live for around 60 years in the wild. Their permanent tusks are elongated incisor teeth which are rarely if ever the same size.

Early in the 19th century elephants ranged freely through southern Africa. But European demand for ivory, and the economic imperatives of new white settler communities led to the slaughter of well over one million elephants.

By 1900 Southern Rhodesia's elephant population was estimated to be no more than 4,000. Today it is around 70,000 and, with increasing

Floppy trunk

Elephant with "Floppy trunk" syndrome.

Visitors to Fothergill, Spurwing, and the mainland Matusadona National Park may see elephants suffering from a mystery ailment colloquially known as floppy trunk syndrome.

It is not yet classified as a disease, the cause remaining unknown and the subject of great speculation. But the 30 odd elephant victim, all bulls, are condemned to a lingering death from starvation.

The syndrome is progressive and irreversible. Paralysis starts at the tip of the trunk and gradually moves up. The trunk becomes flaccid or "floppy" as the 150,000 muscle units in the trunk progressively fail.

Initially the elephants may become dangerous as they try to comprehend and deal with their infirmity. Gradually they adapt using their feet to loosen tufts of grass they would have previously freed with their trunk. But the nourishment increasingly becomes insufficient.

The syndrome or disease appears to attack the nerves in the brain with the paralysis being selective, in this case confined to the trunk, which the elephant relies upon to eat, breath, drink, touch, communicate and scent.

Various theories, such as fighting between bull elephants, have been considered and discarded. The current prevaling view is that plant toxins combined with a nutritional deficiency are the cause. But that remains in the realm of speculation and sadly very little scientific analysis is being done.

pressure for land for development, the elephant are once again under severe human pressure, their future uncertain.

Elephant graze and browse and the damage they have done to vegetation along the Matusadona shoreline is self-evident. Daily a fully grown bull eats about 170 kg and drinks around 100 litres of water.

They are gregarious animals with family groups dominated by a matriach, while younger males upon puberty (about 12) join bull herds. Bulls, normally aged over 30, join the female herds during mating.

Elephants are deeply caring mammals with herds guarding against predators when one of them gives birth, or physically trying to carry away another elephant which has been killed or tranquillised.

Females carry their calves for 22 months, give birth in secluded places, preferably near water, and are highly protective of their calves.

Buffalo

Those familiar with the bush are probably more wary of this very large, heavily-built animal than they are of any other. Adult males stand 1.4 m at the shoulder and weigh 800 kg. They move remarkably quickly, as anyone who has been chased can testify.

To support the massive body the legs are strong and stocky. The front hooves are larger than the hind to carry the huge head and neck. Older adult males are black, females a dark reddish-brown and juveniles distinctly reddish-brown.

Their muzzles are short, hair-fringed ears large and hanging like domestic cattle, eyes ever watchful and baleful. Adult males' horns can be massive atop a heavy boss with which they persistently pound victims.

You may well hear your guide refer to an aged male bull as "the old *daga* boy" because the buffalo wallows in mud *(daga)*.

Buffalo bathe, graze and scratch.

Buffalo, sometimes in herds numbering several hundred, are a common sight on the Kariba foreshore. Sometimes one, or a handful, will be seen on islands to which they have swum in the misplaced belief they will be safe from lion.

Known as Savannah Buffalo (as distinct from the related, smaller horned, West African Forest Buffalo), their habitat must include plentiful grass, water and shade. They drink regularly, usually twice daily, graze and seek shade in the same area, and wallow as a means of controlling their temperatures.

They are inquisitive as well as aggressive. They may advance, nose outstretched, to examine a vehicle. If disturbed they race to rejoin the herd which is quick to stampede in all directions. Wounded they are highly dangerous, sometimes circling and charging the unwary hunter from close range in thick bush.

Rhinoceros, Black
Today the number of this extinction-threatened species is an official secret. After the poachers' onslaught in the late 1980s and early 1990s, and the attendant media coverage, it was decided publicity attracted poachers.

Unique picture of mating Black Rhino.

The best one can get from tight-lipped parks officials is that the rhino are "maintaining themselves".

One sympathises with this secrecy. De-horning the rhino, stepped-up anti-poaching patrols with a shoot-to-kill policy, aerial patrols and all manner of methods were tried to save the remaining rhino.

Whilst these met with some success, it was found that poachers who had tracked a de-horned rhino shot it anyway so they would not waste their time tracking a hornless animal next time.

Today most of the surviving rhino are closely guarded. In Matusadona only the black rhino still exists and they are heavily protected. Six white rhino were introduced in the early 1980s but they all died within three months because they were not resistant to tryosomiasus spread by tsetse flies.

But disease aside, unless the demand ceases by the end-users for rhino horns for their supposed medicinal properties, this species, which traces its ancestry back some 20 million years, faces little future.

Colour, may not distinguish the white and black rhino, particularly if they have been wallowing or in dust. The colour of both is grey anyway. What will distinguish them, however, is the square lip of the white rhino as opposed to the hooked lip of the black rhino.

The horns are composed of a mass of keratin (the same substance as that found in finger nails, horns and hooves) filaments similar in substance to hair and are not bone at all as many suppose. While the white rhino is a grazer, the black rhino is a browser. The calves of both weigh about 40 kg at birth and the gestation period is around 15 months.

Hippopotamus

The hippo is one of the animals the visitor to Kariba cannot fail to encounter. Most inlets seem to have at least one resident. Elsewhere, in shallow water, family groups (pods) exist. Sometimes they will be found grazing on the foreshore in daylight.

Through their somewhat beady eyes; their heads break the lake's surface; small, upright ears thrust forward, watching and listening.

If the viewer gets too close they will submerge, re-emerging a few minutes later near the same spot with a mighty blast as they empty their lungs. Immediately their eyes and ears are once again focused on the intruder.

Somehow hippo seem like very large pets. Indeed, they can be tamed and a friend has taken a photograph of one in a kitchen near Masvingo in central Zimbabwe to prove the point.

Baby, live, not stuffed, sits in kitchen.

But they can also be extremely dangerous in the wild. It is thought that hippos account for more deaths in Africa than any other single animal, including lions and crocodiles.

The hippo's full name is of Greek origin and means "water or river horse". In Afrikaans they are called *"seekoeie"* or sea cows because of their association with river estuaries.

Hippos are recogisable by their vast bulk — one to two tonnes in the case of a large male — barrel-shaped bodies, smooth, bare and frequentally scarred skin, and short, stout legs supporting the large frame.

Their heads are broad and very heavy, with the eyes and nostrils mounted high on the head. They have wide, very large jaws, and fierce tusk-like canines and incisors which they use to telling effect in fights and on the unwary who venture too close.

The tail is short and flat with sparse bristles towards the end. It is used in a flailing motion, rather like a farm dung-spreader, when the animal defecates, often under water.

Their body colours are greyish-black tinged with pink, pinkish-yellow in the folds of the skin and around the eyes, inner nose, and ears. The gape of the mouth is flesh-coloured.

Battle scars are common. Bulls, such as those found in most inlets, maintain definite territories, sometimes throughout their whole 20 to 30 year life.

These territorial bulls (recognisable by their larger heads and thick necks) may be challenged depending upon local population density and climatic changes. Fights between neighbouring territorial bulls tend to be more ritualistic than real with splashing of water and urinating demarcating territorial boundaries.

Much more serious fights take place for territory with the bulls slashing at each other's flanks with their large lower canines. These fights, sometimes between fathers and sons, can result in serious injuries, even death. The sight of a badly scarred hippo is not uncommon.

Like humans, the hippo has milk teeth which are replaced by permanent teeth. In the second set of teeth, the larger, lower jaw, canines continue to grow and may reach 700 mm of which 300 mm will be above the gum. The upper jaw canines are shorter but also very sharp.

Hippo occur widely throughout the sub-continent. Some 350 years ago they existed in what is today central Cape Town. They are great wanderers and serious crop destroyers whose meat and fat are locally sought for cooking, the hide for the manufacture of sjamboks (a whip decreasingly used), and teeth as curios.

The travels of "Hubert" (re-named Huberta after her death when it was discovered "Hubert" was a female), from Natal to the Cape Province in South Africa, showed she covered almost 1,800 km in a three year period.

Hippos' habitat requirement is sufficient water in which to submerge themselves. They prefer shallow water near sandbanks on which they can stand and bask in the sun. Nearby grazing is a further requirement with hippo normally emerging from the water as the sun sets and travelling several km in search of grass, of which they eat around 40 kg a night.

Among ungulates, hippo are the only truly amphibious animals, feeding nocturnally on dry land and spending the daylight hours in the water where mating and calving also take place.

During daylight hours they are to be found in social groups of varying sizes while the solitary animals the visitor may encounter are either territorial bulls or females about to calve.

These social groups break up at night when the animals come ashore to graze. Then the hippo may be found singly or in mother-calve groups with the cow accompanied by as many as four calves in descending order, the youngest always remaining closest to the water.

While on dry land they may appear ungainly, hippo can move with remarkable speed when threatened, and it is very advisable not to get between a hippo and its water sanctuary.

On dry land hippo tend to use established routes where the ground eventually becomes bare. They bulldoze clearly definable exits from their water sanctuaries, which create channels permitting freer water movement, and their trails are marked by a higher central ridge where the grass remains intact.

In deep water they walk along the bottom tending to use the same clearly defined submerged paths.

Adult hippos can remain under water for five to six minutes, juveniles for shorter periods. Before submerging they fill their lungs with air, and their muscles close the nostrils and ears to prevent water entering.

On returning to the surface they empty their lungs with a loud blast and bubbles may show where they have exhaled under water.

They cannot float, but in deep water push themselves to the surface with their hind legs. When swimming on the surface they propel themselves forward in a jumping manner. Normally associated with fresh water, they have also been recorded several km out at sea.

Hippo, especially females with calves, can become aggressive. Open mouths, displaying fearsome canines, and short charges, may signal an attack which can result in a boat being overturned and its occupants bitten to death. While they live in shallow water with crocodiles, the latter normally give them a wide berth.

Deep roaring grunts from a hippo, followed by four or five shorter similar sounds in quick succession, are not threatening but part of Africa's twilight melody.

Mating takes place under water, with the female only emerging at intervals to breathe, while the male's head is not submerged. Gestation is 225 to 257 days with births occurring throughout the year.

Males reach puberty at about seven years old and females have their first calves around the age of four. They find a solitary place to calve, usually in secluded shallow water, and a calf weighing around 50 kg emerges hindlegs first.

Like adults, the youngsters cannot float, but they are capable of going into deep water within minutes of birth. After about two weeks the mother and calf rejoin the group with the youngster staying close to the waters-edge while its mother feeds.

Often calves will rest their heads on adults' backs because their legs are too short to reach submerged sandbanks. Sometimes they will sit on their mothers' backs in deeper water.

In water the calves are prone to predation by crocodiles. These however, are easily chased off by attentive mothers. On land they can be the victims of lion and hyena although, once again, the mothers can sometimes successfully defend them.

Zebra

While no two zebras are marked alike, this is one of the easiest mammals to identify. They occur throughout the area, being seen most frequently in open grassland and woodland where they graze.

Their distinctive black and white markings may have shadow stripes underneath depending upon the sub-species. They are stockily built with forward protruding ears, a mane, and they have the overall look of a stocky work pony.

They live in family groups consisting of a stallion, one or more mares, and foals. Surplus stallions rejected by the group form bachelor herds.

Fighting zebra.

They are timid and shy animals, particularly when approaching water, where they can be seen deferring to other species. Larger predators prey upon zebras with adult zebras vigorously defending their foals by kicking and biting. Under stress they bark (kwa-ha-ha) excitedly.

Female zebras and donkey stallions once mated freely and such semi-domesticated hybrids were used in the early white settler days to pull Zeederberg coaches from South Africa. The hybrids were known as Zebdonks, retained some of the pure zebra's markings, and were employed in tandem with pure donkeys in the 1950s to pull milk carts in Bulawayo.

Warthog

This is one of the most captivating and busiest mammals to be found in the bush. Warthog are predominantly grazers, frequently kneeling when feeding, and they run with their black tufted tails held erect.

Those less attracted to warthogs than this author have variously described them as "incarnations of hideous dreams" and "the most astonishing objects that have ever disgraced nature". Such views fail to give this extraordinary animal its due credit.

Heavily tusked warthog.

Warthog are widespread, most commonly found in open grass or woodland, and they are most active during the day.

The mud they have wallowed in may distort their normal greyish colour. The snout is pig-like, head elongated, the canine teeth develop into long curved tusks (sometimes used as beer mug handles), and the shaggy mane on the back is raised when the animal is stressed.

Boars have "warts" (in reality skin growths and not pure warts) behind the eyes and above the tusks; on the female there are only warts behind the eyes. Their legs are short and slender for their body mass with an adult male weighing 100 kg.

Warthog live in disused burrows developed by other species adapting them to their needs. These burrows protect them against the climate and predators, their greatest enemy. Piglets enter the hole nose first, adults backwards, even when pursued, in a cloud of dust.

They occur in family groups, also known as "sounders", usually comprising an adult male, female and offspring. They are generally sociable, with piglets normally born in the burrows early in the rainy season.

Bushpig
This smaller, more pig-like mammal is easily distinguished from the warthog when running. Whereas the warthog runs with its tail pointed vertically upwards, the bushpig holds its tail downwards.

Several other features also set these two species apart. The bushpig's body is hairier with lighter hair on the face than on the body and a longer snout ending with a distinctive nostril patch. It is largely nocturnal, found in thickets or forests.

Aardvark

This mammal resembles no other, looking rather like a pinkish, long-snouted, cartoon pig with outsize ears and a kangaroo tail. Wrongly referred to as an antbear, its habits and appearance bear greater resemblance to a pig.

The aardvark is the only survivor of a now extinct mammal order. It is almost entirely nocturnal and rarely seen. Its diet consists of ants and termites and it favours overgrazed well-trodden areas where it finds it easier to locate its food.

Baboon

There are two sub-species of baboon in southern Africa, chacma and olive. In Kariba you will only see the chacma in troops numbering up to 100, usually in open country near water, and will hear their bark.

The colour of individuals in a troop varies widely depending upon age, sex and geographical area. Generally they are light grey to dark grey-brown, have dog-like heads, brooding brown eyes and sit on their haunches.

Adult males will assiduously avoid eye contact with humans — which makes them feel threatened — turning sideways or totally away. Females carry their young, who are extremely playful, slung under their bellies.

Baboon avoids eye contact.

ANTELOPE

Seventeen species of antelope have been recorded in the Kariba area. Some, such as the delicate impala and waterbuck, are common. So too are the tiny common duiker (if you have sharp eyes). Some antelope, such as roan, will only be seen in the hills.

Sable

With their sweeping scimitar horns, deep black satin-sheened bodies (in the case of adult males), pure white hair beginning on the muzzle and extending along the belly ending under the tail, this is one of Africa's most photogenic animal.

Sable makes eye contact.

Sable are more frequently found in open mopane woodland in the vicinity of water. While predominantly grazers they are also known to browse.

An adult bull weighs around 230 kg. While the bulk of his coat, including the vertical standing mane, will be black, younger males, females and juveniles tend to be reddish-brown.

Territorial bulls, through intimidation or actual fighting, defend their territories vigorously. In serious fights the bulls drop to their knees and slash at each other with their lethal horns which can result in serious injuries or death.

The nursery herds normally have a dominant female concerned primarily with welfare. She determines the herd's movements, leads the way to water or feeding, keeps watch for danger and directs the herd's flight.

During sexual foreplay males approach and scent females. If the scent is promising he will raise his head and draw back his lips exposing his gums and teeth.

Then he will approach the female gently tapping her hindlegs with his foreleg. If she responds by standing still the act of consummation follows. If she moves off his overtures have been premature.

Impala
This is the most commonly seen antelope at Kariba. It has a shiny reddish-fawn uppercoat, paler sides and white chest, belly, throat and chin.

Its legs are long and slender and both buttocks have a vertical black stripe. Only the males have harp-shaped horns sweeping back from their heads before bowing and ending in sharp points.

Their preferred habitat is lightly wooded grassland with water nearby. They are to be found in herds which increase in size to 100 or more during the wet season and early dry season. Males are only territorial during rutting, with the normal social structure being confined to breeding and bachelor herds.

Mating is in Zimbabwe's autumn and is influenced by the lunar cycle occurring during full moon. Calves are born during November to January after a gestation period of roughly 200 days.

Duiker

These tiny antelope earned their name from the Afrikaans word *duik* meaning "dive", on account of the way they duck and dive in a series of plunging jumps when disturbed.

Duiker.

They are small, easily hiding in tall grass. Grey-brown to reddish-yellow in colour with white insides on their underparts, limbs, inside the tail and ears, and dark brown to black on the facial blaze and forelegs, they are easily identifiable when they keep still.

They are normally solitary animals although they pair up during mating and females can be seen with their young. They will lie up, jumping up at the last moment literally at one's feet, and disappearing swiftly with plunging jumps in a zig-zag course for the nearest cover.

Kudu

To many, this elegant animal ranks among the most handsome of the antelope species. It was once described as the "acme of Nature's efforts to attain perfection of type".

Adult males stand 1.4 metres at the shoulder and weigh 250 kg. Their body colour is fawn-grey with up to 14 unevenly spaced vertical white stripes running down the sides of the body from the neck to the rump.

Facial markings vary enormously. But generally these tend to consist of a V-shaped white band beginning just below the eyes and ending part way down the nose which is darker than the body colour. The lips are edged with white hair.

The kudu's ears are distinct and rounded, the tail bushy and like a white powder puff on the often exposed underside. The bull is adorned with large corkscrew horns which continue to grow throughout his life. From the number of spirals in the horns the age of the bearer can be fairly accurately assessed. Females and juveniles are a more cinnamon colour.

Eland
This is the largest African antelope with fully grown males standing 1.7 m at the shoulder and weighing up to 700 kg. Females are smaller at 1.5 m and weigh about 450 kg.

Eland occur in the wild from Uganda southwards but in South Africa they are confined to the Kruger National Park and environs. They were once widespread in Zimbabwe but now only occur in the northwest, southeast and parts of the eastern districts.

Colouration between the northern and southern eland in the subregion varies with Zimbabwe being a meeting place. They are generally dun-coloured with older eland darker because of hair loss with the skin colour showing through.

Adult bulls have a patch of dark, coarse hair on the forehead, a short mane down the back, and the lengthy tail ends in a pronounced tuft of black hair.

Bushbuck
This is a shy, medium-sized antelope, the Chobe bushbuck is Bambi-like in appearance, with the rump appearing somewhat higher than the shoulders. Regional colour variation occurs.

Generally in Zimbabwe bushbuck are a rich chestnut to dark fawn, with patterns of vertical white lines and spots on the flanks giving a highly distinctive look. The tail is bushy, dark brown above, white below. Only rams have horns.

Waterbuck
This large, stocky antelope with its shaggy grey-brown coat, is easily recognisable by the distinctive white circle on its rump. The most

common explanation for this unique marking is that it is so placed for the animal behind to follow easily.

Waterbuck also have a white collar around the throat, white markings below the eyes and around the nose, and the hair on the legs tends to be darker than that on the body.

Males stand 1.2 m at the shoulder and weigh over 250 kg. As the name suggests they are usually to be found near water in small to medium size breeding or bachelor herds, although on the Bumi foreshore they exist in unusually large numbers.

Only males carry horns which rise from the top of the head and sweep forward in a single curve. They are smooth at the tips and heavily ringed over the first three-quarters of the distance from the head.

They have a strong goat-like smell and can often be smelt before they are seen. They are territorial and the males adopt a "proud" posture with head and body erect, the whites of their eyes prominently displayed, as a means of intimidating intruders. Should this fail serious fighting ensues with waterbuck tending to fight more than other ungulates.

Waterbuck, mother and daughter.

REPTILES

Crocodiles, with an evolutionary lineage of 200 million years, are the last remnants of the great age of reptiles. They are contemporaries of the dinosaurs, were mentioned in the writings of Pliny and Aristotle, and figure prominently in African legends.

Among living vertebrates, crocodiles are most closely related to birds and not, despite the superficial resemblance, lizards.

Birds, a British paleontologist has suggested, evolved from *crocodilians,* an order which includes crocodiles, alligators, and other extinct related forms. However, most experts believe birds descended from small carniverous dinosaurs.

Twenty-two species of crocodiles remain in the world today. All are

Mature crocodile shows his teeth.

endangered and protected. In Africa only one of the three living families, *Crocodylidae,* survives and three species of this are to be found on the continent.

The crocodiles the visitor will see at Kariba are known as Nile Crocodiles. Exceptionally large ones can weigh a tonne and measure almost 500 cm. More usually they are 250 to 350 cm in length.

Their jaws are long and they have prominent uneven teeth with which they tear their prey. The eyes, as is the case with hippopotamus, are set high on the head as are the valved nostrils, and they have no lips, only a flap to avoid swallowing water.

Juvenile crocodile shows his colours.

Young crocodiles are greenish in colour with irregular black markings on the back and sides. The belly and throat are straw-yellow. Adults are darker, sometimes black, with crossbands on the tail and body, although river crocodiles can be yellow.

Their diet varies according to age. Juveniles eat insects, spiders, frogs, and probably snakes, lizards and other small vertebrates. Fish form a substantial part of the diet of middle-sized crocodiles while very large adults will eat antelope, zebra, buffalo, domestic animals — and humans — as well as scavenge.

Adults seize their intended prey with a fast, sideways swipe of the head. The tail may also be used to knock over vegetation and dislodge intended prey. The victim is then pulled into the water and drowned.

Predation on the eggs is also high. Mongooses, honey badgers, baboons, otters, warthogs, bushpigs, hyenas, Marabou storks and, particularly, monitor lizards, are all a threat. Humans also threaten the nests, through fires or raiding them to kill the unborn crocodiles.

For those who survive the clutchling phase, a whole new list of predators are waiting. These include mongoose, genets, even leopards. Among Avian predators are herons, egrets, ibis, storks, eagles, kites, owls and vultures. Lake predators in Kariba include catfish and tiger fish.

For those who have survived all these traumas and reach adulthood, the chances of survival become distinctly brighter. For the adult crocodile there is little to fear — other than their peers and humans.

Nile or Water Monitor
Of the 30 species occurring worldwide only two — the Rock or White-throated Monitor, and the Nile or Water Monitor — occur in southern Africa. At Kariba you are most likely to see the latter.

The Rock Monitor has a more bulbous snout and is more usually found in savannah and arid areas whereas the Water Monitor has a more elongated snout and is found in water.

The Water Monitor, or *leguaan,* as it is most commonly known locally, is officially classified as a lizard and is Africa's largest, growing to a maximum size of over two metres, but more usually being in the range of 100 to 140 cm.

Its body is stout and lithe, limbs powerful, and claws extremely strong. The skin is tough, covered with small, bead-like scales, head/snout elongated, eyes placed high on the head as with other aquatic species, and nostrils midway between the eyes and end of the snout. It has a long, retractile tongue, like a snake, but is not poisonous.

The laterally compressed tail, which is not shed, with its low dorsal crest, is longer than the body which in adults is greyish-brown to dirty olive-brown with scattered darker blotches and light, broken, yellow bands on the head, back and limbs.

Monitors are extremely well camouflaged and even when your guide spots one, usually sunning itself on a rock, you will have difficulty seeing it. They are extremely good swimmers, using their tails like a rudder.

Monitors when cornered can be extremely fierce, defending themselves by biting and lashing out with their tails which can break legs. The world's largest monitor, the Komondo Dragon found in Java, can grow to over 3 metres, and is capable of killing a deer and occasionally even humans.

Other reptiles
Like the remainder of Zimbabwe and Africa, Kariba has more than its fair share of reptiles some of which, although very rarely seen, can be extremely dangerous.

No detailed inventory of snakes at Kariba has been done as is the case at Hwange (see *Hwange: Elephant Country*, an Into Africa Travel Guide). But, those present at Kariba will be similar.

A total of 45 snakes has been recorded at Hwange. Of these 80 per cent are non-venomous. But as few people can differentiate between the species, they are all left well alone in the unlikely event they are even seen.

There are also scorpions, some of which are capable of giving a very nasty sting, and a few poisonous spiders. But they are extremely uncommon and in 35 years in the region I have never seen a scorpion, which is more common at night, in the wild.

Finally, and distinctly more viewer-friendly, there are brilliantly coloured lizards, frogs and tortoises.

Fish
Of the more than 40 species of fish recorded in Lake Kariba, two, kapenta and tiger, are particularly associated with this vast, manmade, inland waterway stretching from Mbilizi to the dam wall. Kapenta were introduced while tiger occurred naturally.

Nobody seems to know for sure just how many kapenta boats, or rigs as they are better known, fish from the Zambian and Zimbabwean shore of Lake Kariba. One guesstimate puts the number around 280, another at +/- 500.

Statistics compiled biennially by the joint Zambia-Zimbabwe Southern African Development Community (SADC) Fisheries Project shows the steady growth in kapenta catches (and rigs) from 488 tonnes in 1974 to 28,483 tonnes in 1993.

Figures for 1993 show that September before the hot season is the best catch month with November and December the lowest months. But because of poaching and theft of fish and equipment, the statistics may not be complete.

In contrast to the highly commercial kapenta operations, tiger fishing is a major sport.

In October every year, as the Kariba temperature soars to its peak, a vast armada of tiger sports fishermen span out across the lake to do battle with each other and the ferocious tiger fish.

Their boats form a ragged line on the lake at Charara on the outskirts of Kariba town for a waterborne race, the starter's gun fires at 6 am, and around 1,500 fishermen from around the world are off. It is, according to the *Guiness Book of Records,* the worlds biggest freshwater angling competition.

The tiger fish has steely black eyes, fierce sabre-teeth, is bony and tasty but a problem to cook other than minced. It has a distinctly bloody-minded temperament which belies its sparkling silver colours and the lovely flashes of orange on its fins.

It is aptly called the "water dog" and among fish it is the pitbull of the species. Hooked, it virtually jerks the rod from the fisherman's hands, thereafter tearing at the trace with its razor-sharp, crocodilian teeth, eating swivels, snagging lines, surging in differing directions, and tail-walking as it tries to shake the hook free.

Many fishermen insist that no other fish has anywhere near the fight (certainly in weight terms) of the determined tiger which, even when landed, can bite off a finger. The largest caught on Kariba (in the 1960s when the lake's nutrient level was higher) weighed in at 15.87 kg (35 lbs). But fishermen continue to believe an even larger one awaits them.

The tiger fish is part of Kariba's cycle of life and death, its food web. The tiger feeds off the kapenta, and the fish eagle, whose mournful calls reverberate through Kariba's inlets, in turn eats the tiger.

Larger fish, such as tiger, feed on the smaller fish. Other predators, such as the fish eagle and mammal predators, feed on the tiger fish.

Fish caught in Kariba are divided into three catagories. In 1993 a total of 10.3 tonnes of tiger fish were landed, 28,483 tonnes of kapenta and a further 2,476 tonnes of inshore (gillnet) fish.

Inshore fisheries are in depths of less than 15 metres and, although the regulations are different in both countries, the inshore species caught number 18 in both Zambia and Zimbabwe.

Zambia has 278 registered fishing villages with a population of over 2,000 people while Zimbabwe has only 41 such villages in which fewer than 300 people live. Bottlenose, squeakers, Zambezi parrotfish, catfish and bream are among the fish caught.

The size of annual catches and rainfall in the catchment areas are related, with the peak catches in Zambia and Zimbabwe in 1987 and 1988 following good rains, and the poorest catches following the droughts in 1985, 1990 and 1992.

There is concern that Kariba is being over-fished, particularly for kapenta. Zambia formally halts fishing for four months a year as a conservation measure while Zimbabweans fish all year round. Greater harmonisation between the two countries remains desirable but elusive.

Tonga fisherman holds bloodied Bottlenose.

BIRDS

For myself, and many others who are not professional ornithologists — or even advanced "twitchers" — a Kariba highlight is to take a small boat into one of the lake's many inlets at dawn and watch the waterbirds.

The first thing to do is carefully select your inlet. Between the lake and the foreshore it should ideally have a flat, marshy area which attracts many species. Hardened trees nearby provide ideal roosts for other birds.

When you get to your selected inlet firmly moor the boat to a convenient tree stump to minimise movement, particularly if the lake is choppy, and cut the engine.

Then just sit back for two or three hours. Africa's birdlife, in astounding shapes, hues, and numbers, will simply come to you if you remain quiet and still.

Yellowbilled Stork and African Spoonbill.

Like people, Africa's birds greet the dawn fitfully. First, many bathe or preen. Larger birds seemed to make themselves immediately more evident, but that could have been because of their size and decible level. And, once the morning toileteries are finished, the earnest work of the day — feeding — begins.

The first thing one realises — which is not unlike land mammals — is the vast range of competence level.

Pied Kingfishers, outer-wings upturned, eyes and beaks pointed firmly downwards, hover as if standing, metres above the water. Then, something spotted, they dive dartlike into the water. But rarely, or so it seemed, did they emerge with a catch.

Tiny, misnamed, Malachite Kingfishers, displayed much greater success diving from branches in search of a carefully chosen morsel without all the preamble.

But much the most efficient avian predator I watched was a Greenbacked Heron. At first I could not even see him in the marshy flat 20 metres from the boat. Only when he made a tiny movement was he visible, hiding behind a detached piece of water hyacinth.

With infinite patience he waited watching the water beside him. Then, in a blur of movement, he pounced plunging his head into the water and striding away with a six inch fish in his beak.

More so than any other birds, one is conscious of the pervasive presence of geese. Standing at the water-edge, a pair busily prepared themselves for the day, apparently oblivious to the threat of crocodiles.

Then, their dark-brown and white wings in stark contrast to the blue morning sky, they noisily cackled their way to nowhere in particular, finally returning to the area they had recently vacated.

Much more quietly, and with much greater dignity, a lone Saddlebilled Stork gracefully crossed the sky while Greyheaded Gulls quarrelled on the foreshore. Blacksmith Plovers intimidated any other bird they could, while a pair of Whitecrowned Plovers ignored everyone, concentrating on finding food.

An African Spoonbill happily co-habited with a Yellowbilled Stork while an elegant, long-legged White Stork moved searchingly across the marsh, head ever-poised.

Grey Herons, cormorants with wings spread to dry, mournful-looking storks, Sacred Ibis and many oth-

Whitefaced Duck.

79

ers all put in their almost ritualistic appearance, but as the day lengthened, the larger birds seemed to give way to the smaller species.

African Pied Wagtails searched the trees for insects, sandpipers walked through the shallow water, a group of Carmine Bee-eaters briefly joined the throng, and innumerable LBJs (little brown jobs) made their entry.

Then, in a hole in a tree only a few metres away, a black-crowned head appeared — a female Cardinal Woodpecker who had made a nest in one of the lake's many "drowned" mopane trees.

Minutes later the crimson-crowned male with its streaked breast arrived, initially clinging perilously on the outside of the tree, before disappearing into it. Then, with blurring speed, the female emerged, flying towards the nearby foreshore.

Throughout it all a pair of African Fish Eagles, distinguished by their white upper bodies and heads, watched us like sentries from a safe distance perched on leafless trees. Occasionally they would throw their heads back emitting their hauntingly mournful call.

Kariba and the African Fish Eagle have become inseparable. That makes it an even greater pity that most of the pictures of the beautiful bird swooping onto the water and emerging with a fish in its talons are, in reality, "pictorial forgeries".

Many boatmen will offer you such a forgery. First you catch a bream from the lake, gut it, put a cork in its stomach, and then, when a fish eagle is around, throw it over the side and focus your camera on the floating fish. The eagle will do the rest — swooping to pick up the fish and providing the photographer with an apparently brilliant wildlife shot.

African Fish Eagle calls its mate.

Finally, and reluctantly, as the birds dispersed, it was time to untie the boat, re-start the engine, and leave our own very personal aviary — until tomorrow morning.

BUTTERFLIES & INSECTS

One of the many topics on which would-be Zimbabwean guides may be examined on are the country's butterflies and insects. But lepidopterology remains an area where very few guides have expertise.

Some recognise 15 worldwide butterfly families, of which nine occur in southern Africa.

Pennington's *Butterflies of Southern Africa,* which is far too bulky to carry on safari, and which is regarded by many as the region's definitive work, recognises five butterfly families occurring in the Kariba area as follows:

Nymphalidae This is a vast family occurring worldwide although the preponderance is to be found in the tropics. They are commonly known in southern Africa as Monarchs or Milkweeds, Browns or Ringlets, Charaxes, Brush-footed butterflies and Snout butterflies.

They are medium-sized to large and often very colourful. They include several poisonous species such as the African Monarch and the Acraeas whose bright red colours warn predators to stay clear. The toxicity is derived from the milkweed toxin-laden diet of the larvae.

The more flamboyant and robust Charaxes may be seen flying past at great speed, with opportunities to view their cryptic colours limited to when they settle on animal scats (droppings), urine, or the sap of trees.

Lycaenidae Blues, Coppers and Hairtails are the common names for this family which is the largest (47 per cent of all butterfly species) and most complex in southern Africa.

Most members of the species are small and are referred to as "flying jewels" with their brilliant blue, violet, orange and red colouring. Many, in a symbiotic way, are associated with ants which feed on the sweet larvel secretion, with the caterpillars in turn being protected by the ants.

81

Pieridae These include common whites, sulphurs, yellows, as well as those with orange and purple tips to their wings, which occur in confetti-like profusion at certain times of the year.

Papiliondae This distinctive family embraces the conspicuous Swallowtails and Swordtails which are very robust and extremely fast.

The Emperor Swallowtail, a Zimbabwe "Eastern Highlands Special", is the largest butterfly found in southern Africa and is readily recognisable by its yellow and black markings.

Commonly found around Kariba is the slightly smaller, tail-less Citrus Swallowtail which can be seen in the early and late rainy season, and is often found feeding on flowers or mud.

Hesperiidae This is the Skipper family which includes such bizarrely named species as the One-pip, Two-pip, Spotless, Striped and Red-tab Policeman. They are not regarded as "true" butterflies, are considered "primitive", are particularly robust, and have an extremely rapid wing beat.

The identification of insects remains elusive. The dragonfly landed on the end of a fishing rod on the boat I was using at Kariba. Its brilliant wasp-like black and yellow body colours immediately caught the eye.

Frequently, over swimming pools and any other water, one will see dragonflies hovering, sometimes briefly settling, and then travelling at high speed. Specifically identifying them is at best difficult.

The black and yellow Kariba insect, after considerable research, would appear to be an Emperor Dragonfly, the largest to be found in Zimbabwe. It measures some 127 mm from wing-tip to wing-tip. But that is definitely puny when compared to a known fossil dragonfly which had a wingspan of 685 mm.

Dragonflies are predators, eating other insects. They are the fastest fliers in the insect world with speeds of 50 km/h recorded. They are extremely agile and can even fly backwards enhancing their capacity to catch other insects while in flight.

Their eyes are extremely large for their body size, their spiny legs are adapted to hold their prey, and their wings, set on top of the body and interspersed with veins, resemble those of an aeroplane.

WHERE TO STAY

This section is inserted as a service to would-be visitors and not by the individual establishments mentioned. It is therefore not definitive. Most places have pools and other features. Details of these can be obtained direct from the establishment mentioned or through travel agents.

Caribbea Bay Resort and Casino
[PO Box 120, Kariba, Tel (161) 2453/4, Fax 2765, Telex 41295 ZW]
Has Mediterranean-style *casitas* sleeping four or five people as well as deluxe twin rooms and suites. All accommodation has ensuite facilities and air-conditioning.

Cutty Sark Hotel
[PO Box 80, Kariba, Tel (161) 2321/2, Fax 2575, Telex 41298 ZW]
Accommodation consists mainly of twin rooms with private bathroom, radio, telephone, fans, and some with air-conditioning. Doubles and family rooms are also available.

Kariba Breezes Hotel
[PO Box 3, Kariba, Tel (161) 2433/4, Fax 2767]
Kariba Breezes is a 2-star family hotel with air-conditioned rooms. A full marine service is available for boat owners. The hotel hires boats, fishing rods and guides.

Lake View Inn Hotel
[PO Box 100, Kariba, Tel (161) 2411/5, Fax 2329, Telex 2329 ZW]
Overlooking Lake Kariba this hotel has 39 rooms which are all lake facing, with air-conditioning and ensuite facilities, a restaurant, bar, putt putt course and pool.

Most High Hotel
[PO Box 88, Kariba, Tel (161) 2964]
This Christian mission hotel has lake views from all 20 air-conditioned rooms, swimming pools, table tennis, darts and video entertainment. Game drives, cruises and boat hire are arranged.

Tamarind Lodges
[PO Box 1, Kariba, Tel (161) 2697, Fax 2697]
Tamarind has two lodges sleeping four and six people. They are semi-serviced, completely self-catering, with fans and braai areas. Basics provided.

Mushuma Bush Camp
[Top of the Range, 3rd Floor, Travel Centre, cnr 3rd/Jason Moyo, PO Box 5290, Harare, Tel (4) 700911/2, Fax 722872]
Situated 35 minutes drive from Kariba Airport on the Charara River. Access by 4x4 vehicle. Has six twin-bedded walk-in safari tents under thatch with ensuite toilet and shower.

Kaburi Wilderness Camp Site
[PO Box 275, Kariba or PO Box HG 996, Highlands, Harare, Tel (4) 726089]
The camp is wild and isolated but offers those who are interested in the environment a chance to help the Wild Life Society protect the environment by staying at this camp.

Gache Gache Lodge
[PO Box 66293, Kopje, Harare, Tel (14) 734043-6, Fax 708119]
Overlooks Gache Gache Estuary and adjoining the Charara Safari Area. The lodge is 45 minutes by boat from Kariba. Accommodation is in open-fronted, thatched cottages.

Sanyati Lodge
[PO Box 66293, Kopje, Harare, Tel (14) 734043-6, Fax 708119]
The lodge is on the shoreline of Lake Kariba, 300 metres from the Sanyati Gorge. Accommodation facilities consist of well spaced stone and thatch chalets, all with ensuite facilities.

Spurwing Island
[PO Box 101, Kariba, Tel (161) 2466, Fax 2301]
Accommodation consists of eleven tents, six cabins and three larger chalets with ensuite facilities. An electric fence surrounds the camp ensuring the safety of guests.

Fothergill Island Safaris
[P Bag 2081, Kariba, Tel (161) 2253, Fax 2240]
Fothergill Island is approximately 400 ha cradled at the base of the Matusadona Mountains. The safari lodge consists of 14 thatched chalets with showers open to the stars.

Matusadona Tented Safaris
[P Bag 2081, Kariba, Tel (161) 2253, Fax 2240]
Experience living in the wild with enough luxury to make it a memorable safari. Because the road network within the Matusadona National Park is limited, this camp emphasises walking safaris.

Matusadona Water Lodge
[PO Box 288, Victoria Falls, Tel (113) 4527, 3371/3, Fax 4224]
Accommodation consists of four twin-bedded houseboat-styled rooms with a central leisure area including a dining room. Guests commute from their rooms by boat.

Musango Safari Camp
[P Bag 2019, Kariba, Tel (61) 2899, Fax (4) 795301]
The camp is tented, with each chalet covered by an A-framed thatched roof, and solar power. Every chalet has ensuite facilities. No children under 12 are catered for.

Water Wilderness Safari
[PO Box 41, Kariba, Tel (161) 2353/2439, Fax 2354]
This floating camp in the Ume River has four twin-bedded self-contained houseboats with solar power, hot and cold water, showers, chemical toilets. Meals in separate mother-houseboat.

Tiger Bay
[PO Box W41, Waterfalls, Harare, Tel (161) 2569 or (14) 708714/792211, Fax (14) 792617]
Offers a choice of thatched chalets or tented accommodation on the Ume River. This camp offers the usual fare: game cruises and drives, boat hire, canoeing and guided game walks.

Kiplings
[PO Box 3, Kariba, Tel (161) 2433, Fax 2767]
Located at the mouth of the Ume River facing Matusadona National Park it has ten thatched chalets. Morning walks and game drives into Matusadona and afternoon canoe trips up the Ume River.

Bumi Hills Safari Lodge
[PO Box 41, Kariba, Tel (161) 2353/2439, Fax 2354]
The ten luxury lodges overlook Kariba with ten standard rooms behind them. Caters for up to 40 adults and 20 children. Big Five possible, elephant almost certain. Cultural tours to Tonga villages.

Katete Safari Lodge
[PO Box 41, Kariba, Tel (161) 2807/8, Fax 2892]
Has 16 twin-bedded lodges with period furniture. All lodges are ensuite. Situated five km west of Bumi Hills Safari Lodge. Facilities include a separate dining room with silver service.

Elephant Point Tented Camp
[PO Box 6485, Harare, Tel (14) 795841/5, Fax 795845/6]
In the Omay Communal Lands overlooking Sibilobilo Lagoon approximately 20 km from Bumi. Access by boat, plane, or 4x4. Accommodation consists of eight large East African style tents.

Senkwe River Lodge
[PO Box 159, Victoria Falls, Tel (113) 2001, Fax (113) 4349]
Situated in the Chete Safari area this lodge has rustic but comfortable accommodation in A-framed chalets. All but one have ensuite facilities.

Sijarira Lodge
[Touch the Wild/Nagamo Safaris, P Bag 5, Hillside, Bulawayo, Tel (19) 74589, Fax 229986]
This lodge has Batonka style individual lodges on stilts. Accommodates a maximum of 16 persons in eight thatched chalets with ensuite facilities. Good fishing by boat or the lake shore.

Chizarira Wilderness Lodge
[PO Box 6485, Harare, Tel (14) 795841/5, Fax 795846]
Located 80 km from Binga it can be accessed by charter or by road with 4x4 vehicles recommended during the rains. Has seven large twin-bedded chalets constructed of stone with thatched roofs.

Mlibizi Hotel
[PO Binga, Tel (115) 271]
The hotel has 26 rooms with en-suite facilities. There is a separate bar and restaurant. Fridge facilities for fisherman, safe parking for cars and buses. There is an airstrip five km away.

Mlibizi Zambezi Resort
[PO Box 1511, Bulawayo, Tel (19) 65061, Fax (19) 77842]
Accommodation consists of self-catering chalets with four to eight beds. Linen supplied, fully equipped kitchens, bedrooms with overhead ceiling fans, and chalet attendants for basic household chores.

FACILITIES

National Parks
[Bookings for all National Parks facilities are done by the Central Booking Office, PO Box CY 826, Causeway, Harare, Tel (4) 706077, Fax 726089 or through the Bulawayo booking agent, PO Box 2283, Bulawayo, Tel (19) 63646]

Charara Safari Area
Charara has a network of gravel roads suitable for 4x4 vehicles only, stretching over 1,700 sq km from the outskirts of Kariba Village. National Parks have a camp at Nyanyana which has 35 camping and caravan sites. The camp is 28 km from Kariba. The turn-off to the camp is 56 km from Makuti, followed by 5,5 km of dirt road. There are ablution blocks, a slipway for boats, and firewood can be purchased.

Matusadona National Park
The park headquarters are at Tashinga which is situated on the Ume River. There is an airstrip at Tashinga and the road distance from Harare is 468 km. Basic camping facilities and hot water are available at Tashinga and another camp at Sanyati West. Changachirere Camping Site is exclusive to a party of up to a maximum of ten persons. It has a mini ablution block and a shelter. There are also two undeveloped camp sites at Jenje and Kanjedza. Exclusive 12-bedded camp sites are Ume, Muuyu and Mbabala. Camping equipment can be hired at the Tashinga Park office.

Chizarira National Park
Chizarira is Zimbabwe's third largest park. With seven different ecological zones it is the most diverse National Park in the country. The ecological zones range from Lowveld Valley vegetation (mopani woodland and baobab) to Highveld broad leaf woodland.

The National Parks headquarters is at Manzituba in the west, where there is an airstrip. There are six exclusive camping sites within the Park at present. Each camp is limited to one party up to a maximum of 12 persons. Kaswiswi Bush Camp is situated 6 km from the Park headquarters. No sleeping shelters have been constructed although there is an ablution block and kitchen area. Kaswiswi II Camp Site is 500 metres from Kaswiswi 1 and situated on the confluence of the Kaswiswi and Rwizilukulu rivers. This site has no facilities and is only accessible in 4x4 vehicles. Mobola Bush Camp is also 6 km from the Park headquarters situated on the Mucheni River below the Manzituba Spring. This camp has no sleeping shelters but kitchen and ablution facilities are available. Busi Bush Camp is situated on the Busi River 35 km from the Park headquarters. Facilities consist of two sleeping shelters, one dining shelter and a cooking area. Road access is very rough and only 4x4 vehicles should attempt this. Mucheni Gorge Camp is approximately 3 km away from the Park's headquarters situated near the Mucheni Gorge on the escarpment. The site comprises sleeping shelters, a braai stand and Blair toilet. There is no water available at this camp site. Mucheni View Camp Site is on the edge of the escarpment overlooking the valley. Facilities include a cooking area, blair toilet and a shaded area. Again, there is no running water available at this camp.

Boating

As far as we could ascertain there is no central point which provides information about all the boats for hire on Kariba. The South African magazine, Getaway, carries a large number of advertisements for boats of all descriptions and your travel agent should know what is available.

Many of the Getaway advertisements do not disclose the prices of boat hire. But judging by one from the Boating Association of Zimbabwe, boat hire is not cheap.

The mid-season all-inclusive daily rate for the Grade A+ Concorde, which can take 18 passengers, is shown as US$2,550 while the bottom of the range Grade C boats, which take eight to ten pasengers, go for between Z$3,190 and Z$5,000 daily. This may partly account for the sight of so many cars pulling their own boats on the road between Harare and Kariba.

Other advertisers include Kariba House Boats, Kariba Ferries, Hungwe Tours and Safaris, Blue Horizon Lake Safaris, Zambezi Adventures and a number of advertisers who appear to be single boat operators. Still others are Zambezi Hunters, Impexo, River Horse Safaris and Philadelphia Houseboat Charter.

The best advice we can offer if you want to hire a boat is to check with your travel agent and shop around. And be careful to check the boat's facilities.

Kariba Ferries

[PO Box 578, Harare, Tel (4) 614162/7, Fax (4) 614161]
The Sea Lion and Sea Horse car and passenger ferries operate between Kariba's Andora Harbour and Mlibizi. The one-way journey takes 22

hours, half in daylight, with four sailings weekly from Kariba. Bookings should be made in advance.

United Touring Company
[PO Box 93, Kariba, Tel (161) 2662 and 2411/2, Fax (161) 2329]
UTC offers a number of tours including one of Kariba town's highlights, morning and afternoon game drives in the Kaburi Wilderness, siesta and sunset lake cruises, full day cruises and charters, 15-minute flights over the town, gorge and lake foreshore, 45-minute flights over the lake, private boat and launch hire, as well as ground transfers. Hotel receptions have details of UTC timetables, car hire and other activities.

Safari Operators
There are a number based in Kariba such as Graeme Lemon (Kariba fax 2792). Details of these specialist operators can be obtained from your travel agent. Simpson Cruises offers cruises on the lake.

Camping and caravan sites
The Kariba Publicity Association, located above Kariba and well sign-posted, can answer many of your questions. From here good pictures of the dam wall and lake beyond can be taken. Its address is PO Box 86, Kariba, Tel (161) 2328.

M.O.T.H. Cottages offer camp and caravan sites as well as cottages in Kariba, while Mopani Bay Camp site also offers camping and caravan space, but without power.

Kariba town
While many visitors to Kariba have booked through operators and therefore have minimal requirements, and others arrive self-contained, the town nevertheless is able to meet most requirements. There are a number of petrol stations, places where ice, cool drinks and provisions can be purchased, film and other camera equipment for sale, and rods and tackle for hire. Embroidery and carvings, notably ornate Nyaminyami walking sticks and Nyaminyami sculptures, can be obtained in a number of places.

Health advisory
Anti-malarial prophylactics are strongly advised. Swimming, certainly near the lake shore or in still water, is to be avoided. The telephone numbers for Kariba District Hospital are 2263 and 2382. Kariba Pharmacy is located at 1 Msasa Ave, tel 2596.

CHECKLIST OF THE MAIN MAMMALS OF KARIBA

This mammal list is not a d definitive guide to all the mammals occurring in the Kariba basin area. 70 species of mammals have been recorded within the area since the 1960's. The mammals that occur under the uncommon and rare headings have been sighted infrequently in the Kariba area. This list has been compiled by Steve Edwards of Musango Lodge, P Bag 2019, Kariba (Tel: 263 (61) 2391)

Abundant
Elephant
Hippopotamus
Warthog
Cape Buffalo
Waterbuck
Impala
Baboon
Vervet Monkey

Common
Zebra
Kudu
Bushbuck
Duiker (Common)
Spotted Hyena
Sidestriped Jackal
Leopard
Lion
Serval
Wildcat
Civet
Rusty Spotted Genet
Slender Mongoose

Large Grey Mongoose
Banded Mongoose
Dwarf Mongoose
Bush Squirrel
Antbear
Yellowspotted Dassie
Scrub Hare
Porcupine

Uncommon
Caracal
Bushpig
Eland
Klipspringer
Sable
Sharpe's Grysbok

Rare
Hooklipped Rhino (Black)
Roan
Reedbuck
Cheetah
Striped Polecat
Painted Hunting Dog

CHECKLIST OF THE BIRDS OF KARIBA

All numbers used are taken from Robert's Guide to Birds of Southern Africa. This list was compiled by Dr Kit Hustler of Wild Horizons, PO Box 159, Victoria Falls, Zimbabwe (Tel: 263 (13) 4219) and Mr Peter Ginn of Peter Ginn Birding Safaris, PO Box 44, Marondera, Zimbabwe (Tel/Fax: 263 (79) 23411). This is not a definitive list of birds found in the Kariba basin area but a general guide to what can be seen.

No.	Bird Name	No.	Bird Name
008	Dabchick	064	Goliath Heron
055	Whitebreasted Cormorant	066	Great White Egret
058	Reed Cormorant	067	Little Egret
060	Darter	069	Black Egret
062	Grey Heron	071	Cattle Egret

No.	Bird Name	No.	Bird Name
072	Squacco Heron	298	Water Dikkop
081	Hammerkop	302	Threebanded Courser
088	Saddlebill Stork	304	Redwinged Pratincole
089	Marabou Stork	315	Greyheaded Gull
090	Yellowbill Stork	339	Whitewinged Tern
095	African Spoonbill	347	Doublebanded Sandgrouse
099	Whitefaced Duck	352	Redeyed Dove
102	Egyptian Goose	353	Mourning Dove
108	Redbilled Teal	354	Cape Turtle Dove
114	Pygmy Goose	355	Laughing Dove
115	Knobbilled Duck	356	Namaqua Dove
116	Spurwinged Goose	358	Greenspotted Dove
121	Hooded Vulture	361	Green Pigeon
123	Whitebacked Vulture	362	Cape Parrot
124	Lappetfaced Vulture	364	Meyers Parrot
125	Whiteheaded Vulture	368	Lilian's Lovebird
126	Yellowbilled Kite	371	Purplecrested Lourie
127	Blackshouldered Kite	373	Grey Lourie
132	Tawny Eagle	375	African Cuckoo
138	Ayres Eagle	377	Redchested Cuckoo
140	Martial Eagle	381	Striped Cuckoo
141	Crowned Eagle	382	Jacobin Cuckoo
142	Brown Snake Eagle	384	Emerald Cuckoo
143	Blackbreasted Snake Eagle	385	Klaas' Cuckoo
146	Bateleur	386	Diederik Cuckoo
148	African Fish Eagle	390	Senegal Coucal
160	African Goshawk	391	Whitebrowed Coucal
163	Dark Chanting Goshawk	392	Barn Owl
169	Gymnogene	396	Scops Owl
170	Osprey	398	Pearlspotted Owl
189	Crested Francolin	399	Barred Owl
196	Natal Francolin	401	Spotted Eagle Owl
199	Swainson's Francolin	402	Giant Eagle Owl
203	Helmeted Guineafowl	405	Fierynecked Nightjar
213	Black Crake	408	Freckled Nightjar
223	Purple Gallinule	409	Mozambique Nightjar
238	Blackbellied Korhaan	421	Palm Swift
240	African Jacana	423	Bohm's Spinetail
248	Kittlitz's Plover	426	Redfaced Mousebird
249	Threebanded Plover	428	Pied Kingfisher
258	Blacksmith Plover	429	Giant Kingfisher
259	Whitecrowned Plover	431	Malachite Kingfisher
261	Longtoed Plover	433	Woodland Kingfisher
264	Common Sandpiper	435	Brownhooded Kingfisher
266	Wood Sandpiper	437	Striped Kingfisher
269	Marsh Sandpiper	441	Carmine Bee-eater
270	Greenshank	443	Whitefronted Bee-eater
295	Blackwinged Stilt	444	Little Bee-eater

No.	Bird Name	No.	Bird Name
447	Lilacbreasted Roller	631	African Marsh Warbler
449	Purple Roller	635	Cape Reed Warbler
450	Broadbilled Roller	638	African Sedge Warbler
451	Hoopoe	643	Willow Warbler
452	Redbilled Wood Hoopoe	648	Yellowbreasted Apalis
454	Scimitarbilled Wood Hoopoe	651	Longbilled Crombec
		653	Yellowbellied Eremomela
455	Trumpeter Hornbill	657	Bleating Warbler
457	Grey Hornbill	664	Fantailed Cisticola
460	Crowned Hornbill	672	Rattling Cisticola
463	Ground Hornbill	683	Tawnyflanked Prinia
464	Blackcollared Barbet	689	Spotted Flycatcher
470	Yellowfronted Tinker Barbet	691	Bluegrey Flycatcher
		694	Black Flycatcher
473	Crested Barbet	701	Chinspot Batis
474	Greater Honeyguide	710	Paradise Flycatcher
481	Bennett's Woodpecker	711	African Pied Wagtail
483	Goldentailed Woodpecker	714	Yellow Wagtail
486	Cardinal Woodpecker	716	Richard's Pipit
487	Bearded Woodpecker	728	Yellowthroated Longclaw
505	Dusky Lark	737	Tropical Boubou
507	Redcapped Lark	740	Puffback
515	Chestnutbacked Finchlark	741	Brubru
518	European Swallow	743	Threestreaked Tchagra
522	Wiretailed Swallow	744	Blackcrowned Tchagra
527	Lesser Striped Swallow	748	Orangebreasted Bush Shrike
529	Rock Martin		
530	House Martin	751	Greyheaded Bush Shrike
531	Greyrumped Swallow	753	White Helmet Shrike
538	Black Cuckooshrike	754	Redbilled Helmet Shrike
541	Forktailed Drongo	761	Plumcoloured Starling
543	European Golden Oriole	763	Longtailed Starling
544	African Golden Oriole	769	Redwinged Starling
545	Blackheaded Oriole	772	Redbilled Oxpecker
548	Pied Crow	787	Whitebellied Sunbird
554	Southern Black Tit	791	Scarletchested Sunbird
560	Arrowmarked Babbler	792	Black Sunbird
568	Blackeyed Bulbul	793	Collared Sunbird
569	Terrestrial Bulbul	797	Yellow White-Eye
574	Yellowbellied Bulbul	799	Whitebrowed Sparrow Weaver
575	Yellowspotted Nicator		
576	Kurrichane Thrush	801	House Sparrow
580	Groundscraper Thrush	804	Greyheaded Sparrow
599	Heuglin's Robin	805	Yellowthroated Sparrow
600	Natal Robin	811	Spottedbacked Weaver
613	Whitebrowed Robin	814	Masked Weaver
617	Bearded Robin	816	Golden Weaver
628	Great Reed Warbler	819	Redheaded Weaver

No.	Bird Name	No.	Bird Name
821	Redbilled Quelea	857	Bronze Mannikin
824	Red Bishop	860	Pintailed Whydah
829	Whitewinged Widow	862	Paradise Whydah
834	Melba Finch	863	Broadtailed Paradise
839	Redthroated Twinspot		Whydah
841	Jameson's Firefinch	865	Purple Widowfinch
842	Redbilled Firefinch	867	Steelblue Widowfinch
844	Blue Waxbill	869	Yelloweye Canary
846	Common Waxbill	870	Blackthroated Canary
852	Quail Finch	884	Goldenbreasted Bunting
855	Cutthroat Finch	886	Rock Bunting

CHECKLIST OF TREES AND SHRUBS OF KARIBA

This list was taken from the Kariba and Mana area section of "Key to the Trees of Zimbabwe" by Meg Coates-Palgrave, PO Box 4643, Harare, Zimbabwe (Tel: 263 (4) 742 765 Fax: 263 (4) 742 800)

TREE/SHRUB NAME	BOTANICAL NAME
Baobab	*Adansonia digitata*
Bean-Tree	*Markhamia zanzibarica*
Bird Plum	*Berchemia discolor*
Crocodile-Bark	*Diospyros quiloensis*
Crystal-Bark	*Crossopteryx febrifuga*
Diamond-Leaved Euclea	*Euclea divinorum*
Duikerberry	*Pseudolachnostylis maprouneifolia*
Eared Bloodwood	*Pterocarpus brenanii*
Ebony Dalbergia	*Dalbergia malanoxylon*
False Marula	*Lannea schweinfurthii*
Four-winged Pteleopsis	*Pteleopsis anisoptera*
Glossy Combretum	*Combretum apiculatum*
Kirkia	*Kirkia acuminata*
Knob-Thorn	*Acacia nigrescens*
Large Jesse-Bush Combretum	*Combretum elaeagnoides*
Large-Fruited Combretum	*Combretum zeyheri*
Large Sourplum	*Ximenia caffra*
Large-Leaved Sterculia	*Sterculia quinqueloba*
Long-Pod Cassia	*Cassia abbreviata*
Marula	*Sclerocarya birrea*
Monkeybread	*Piliostigma thonningii*
Mopane	*Colophospermum mopane*
Mukwa	*Pterocarpus angolensis*
Munondo	*Julbernardia globiflora*
Northern Dwaba-Berry	*Friesodielsia obovata*
Purple Cluster-Pear	*Cleistochlamys kirkii*
Purple-Pod Terminalia	*Terminalia prunioides*
Red Bauhinia	*Bauhinia galpinii*

TREE/SHRUB NAME	BOTANICAL NAME
Rosette-Leaved Terminalia	*Terminalia stenostachya*
Round-Leaved Bloodwood	*Pterocarpus rotundifolius*
Sausage Tree	*Kigelia africana*
Scented-Pod Acacia	*Acacia nilotica*
Shaving-Brush Combretum	*Combretum mossambicense*
Sickle Bush	*Dichrostachys cinerea*
Silver Terminalia	*Terminalia sericea*
Single-Leaved Commiphora	*Commiphora glanulosa*
Small Caterpillar Pod	*Ormocarpum kirkii*
Small Sourplum	*Ximenia americana*
Smooth-Leaved Paddle-Pod	*Hippocratea parvifolia*
Snowberry Tree	*Flueggea virosa*
Spiny Monkey Orange	*Strychnos spinosa*
Splendid Acacia	*Acacia robusta*
Tail-Flower	*Strophanthus kombe*
Tamarind	*Tamarindus indica*
Tick Tree	*Sterculia africana*
Wild Rubber	*Diplorhynchus condylocarpon*
Willow-leaved Boscia	*Boscia salicifolia*
Wing-Pod	*Xeroderris stuhlmannii*
White-Leaved Combretum	*Combretum obovatum*
Zambezi Coca Tree	*Erythroxylum zambesiacum*
Zambezi Oak	*Triplochiton zambesiacus*
Zambezi Vitex	*Vitex petersiana*
Zigzag Terminalia	*Terminalia stuhlmannii*

INDEX

95

14548468R00329

Printed in Poland
by Amazon Fulfillment
Poland Sp. z o.o., Wrocław

Books in The Heku Series

Book 1 : Heku

Book 2 : Valle

Book 3 : Encala

Book 4 : Equites

Book 5 : Proditor

Book 6 : Ferus

Book 7 : Eternity of Vengeance

Book 8 : Ancients and Old Ones

Book 9 : Banishment

Other Books by T.M. Nielsen

Dimension Shifter (Book 1 of the Dimensions Saga)
Paragoy Dimension (Book 2 of the Dimensions Saga)
Shadowmere (Book 3 of the Dimensions Saga)
After the Dimensions (Book 4 of the Dimensions Saga)

Coming Soon by T.M. Nielsen

Return of the Encala

\

Ancients and Old Ones

Book 8 of the Heku Series

T.M. Nielsen

Find us at

www.hekuseries.com

For information about special discounts for bulk orders or to schedule
book signings in Northern Utah, please e-mail us at:

info@hekuseries.com

Copyright © 2011

Manufactured in the United States of America

ISBN 978-1-4611-2457-3

Table of Contents

Chapter 1

"You spoke in front of the entire Council just last month. Why not now?" Chevalier asked. He watched from beside Emily as she stood in the council chambers and scanned the Council.

Quinn smiled. "We just want to hear it from you."

Emily looked up at Chevalier. He realized that her silent innocence made his heart melt, and he had to remember that she would have to start speaking again before they could fully help her recover.

"Lori feels that if you were to tell the Council exactly what was said about them, it might help you realize that it was all a lie," Chevalier explained.

"It's obvious to us all that you only feel comfortable with Chevalier and Kyle," Zohn told her. "It's important to us as a faction that you trust the entire Council."

"It'll be easier now that Dustin is gone," Kyle told her, and then smiled.

Emily sighed and looked up at Chevalier again. He smiled and marveled at her green eyes as he waited for her to speak. As most heku had dark eyes, her vibrant green was just another charming characteristic that set her apart from the immortals she lived with.

"Maybe we should start with a question," Akili suggested.

"Good idea," Quinn said. "Let's start with this... did Salazar specifically talk about the Chief of Finance?"

The Chief of Finance frowned. "Why would he?"

"We're just asking," Zohn told him.

Emily again looked up at Chevalier and ever so slightly nodded.

"What did he say?!" the Chief of Finance yelled.

She gasped and grabbed Chevalier's arm.

"Would you not!" Quinn yelled at him.

The Chief of Finance's eyes grew wide, and he nodded. "I'm sorry, Elder."

"What was said about him?" Kyle asked her.

Emily leaned up and whispered in Chevalier's ear.

"Yes, he's from Uintah Coven."

"He spoke badly about my coven?" the Chief of Finance asked.

She again whispered to Chevalier.

He sighed, "Yes, I guess Salazar was right about that, but that was a long time ago."

"What did he say?" Zohn asked.

"He just told her about how Uintah Coven was the last Ancient supporting coven and how they fought to keep their Coven Lord alive when orders were sent out to destroy them."

The Chief of Finance was getting angry. "That was thousands of years ago."

Kyle nodded. "I completely understand how that can make you leery of him. We all know that you've had numerous run-ins with Ancients. However, the Uintah Coven is probably one of the more mortal friendly covens that I know. They make huge donations to local charities and almost entirely fund a high-profile children's hospital."

Three hours later, most of the Council had been covered, but she still held tightly to what she was told about the Records Keeper, Jerry.

"It's amazing how much he knew about this Council," Kyle said. "I mean, he had information… true information, about each of us."

"I still want to know what I did that's so bad she won't say," Jerry said.

Quinn studied Emily for a moment and couldn't help but notice that she was still visibly uncomfortable being with the Council. "I don't suppose you would just tell Chevalier everything in private, and he can relay it?"

Emily looked at him and then began to wring her hands again.

Chevalier smiled. "Let's take a break. I think we've done enough for today."

Jerry sighed, "I still don't know what he said about me."

Chevalier nodded. "I'll try, but she's still not very chatty, even with me."

She looked up at him.

He smiled. "You want to go back to the room?"

Without a word, she headed for the door quickly.

"Do you want me to walk you up?" he asked as she disappeared out the door. "Or not."

Kyle chuckled as Chevalier returned to his seat.

Emily hurried up the stairs with four members of the Cavalry behind her. They didn't know her well, so they followed her in silence, something she preferred with strange heku. Suddenly, she remembered she was going to go to the infirmary to get some cough drops. She'd had a sore throat for a few nights.

She opened the door and then smiled when she saw two heku in a loving embrace. Silas turned suddenly and let go of Lori, his eyes wide. Emily backed out and started to shut the door, but Lori came and held it open.

"I'm… I'm sorry… we…," she stammered.

Silas looked nervous. "Em, we can explain…"

Lori glanced nervously at the Cavalry standing behind Emily, but they were too busy talking among themselves.

"It's… I'm sorry," Silas said softly.

Emily smiled broadly and then hugged him.

"I'll take it that this isn't upsetting you then?" Lori asked skeptically.

Emily moved over and hugged Lori and then stepped out of the infirmary and shut the door.

She smiled all the way to her room and then pet Devia as she stepped in and shut the door. Chevalier was already in the room and sitting in a chair by the fire.

"I heard...," he told her, and she could tell he was waiting for a reaction.

Emily moved over and sat on his lap, then leaned back against his chest.

"Are you upset about it?" he asked as he wrapped his arms around her.

She shook her head and gently ran her nails along his forearms.

"We were afraid to tell you. I guess we were wrong."

"Why?" she whispered, and then looked up at him.

"To be honest, we aren't sure what will set you off."

She frowned and then crawled off of his lap.

"Don't be mad," he said, gently taking her hand, so she wouldn't leave. When she pulled against him, he sighed and let her go. She walked into the bathroom and shut the door behind her and then locked it.

Emily ran a hot tub and then crawled in. She was freezing from being in the cold council chambers all day and irritated that Chevalier made it sound like the entire palace was walking on eggshells around her.

She'd just put a cold rag over her eyes to calm her headache, and as she turned on the jets, she heard a knock on the door. Without waiting for an answer, Chevalier came in.

He sat down beside the tub. "I don't think that came out right."

"I'm not as frail as you all seem to think," she whispered. She found it easier to talk with her eyes covered but wouldn't tell that to Chevalier, or he would involve Lori.

"It's really hard to see that when you won't talk."

She shrugged.

Chevalier moved to the head of the tub and began rubbing her shoulders. "You just aren't quite... well... you yet. Until you come completely out of your shell, we still fear that something will put you back into it."

"You don't have to coddle me," she whispered.

He kissed the top of her head. "I know that. The others may not, but it'll all work out in the end. I promise."

After a few minutes of silence, Chevalier spoke, "It'd really help if you would talk to Lori in a regular session."

"No," she whispered, and then adjusted the washrag on her eyes.

"Tell me why you won't talk to the Council, and when you're near them, your fear level goes so much higher."

She shrugged.

"I'm feeling emotions now, but every emotion has fear under it, and I worry about that."

"I'm fine."

"Then what are you afraid of?" he whispered, and moved so he could look at her face.

Again, she shrugged.

He sighed, "It's just strange. When you're out horseback you feel free and alive but fearful. When you're sleeping you are afraid. I just can't help but worry."

Emily pulled the wash rag off of her eyes and looked tearfully at him.

"Tell me."

"They... aren't like you," she said, soft enough that no sound came out.

"Who are they?"

She shrugged.

"Do you mean all heku?"

When she didn't answer, he whispered, "Or is it the Council that's not like me?"

"Kyle is."

"I think most of them are, if you knew them better." He frowned when he noticed her hands shaking. "The Council is worried about you. They care about..."

"No"

"No to what part?"

She turned her swimming green eyes up to his. "If you were gone..."

"If I was gone, they would still keep you here and watch over you."

She shook her head.

"Yes, you're my wife... but I've told you, you're important to this faction, and each member of that Council has become quite attached to you."

"No"

"Yes, besides, Kyle wouldn't let anything happen to you if I wasn't around."

"He's not..."

"What?"

Emily reached over to add more hot water to the jetted tub.

"Don't mistake his calm temperament for weakness. If Kyle's mad, no one will mess with him. Not even me."

"The Valle…"

He waited for a moment before asking, "What about them?"

"They will use you to get to me," she said, her voice cracking.

He smiled. "No, they are too afraid of you to do that."

"Something's going to happen."

"Like what?"

She shrugged.

He reached over and kissed her lightly. "Things will be okay. They always are."

***

"Good morning," Chevalier said, smiling.

Emily looked up at him and then curled against his chest.

He softly kissed the top of her head. "I ordered you some breakfast, but now I have to go to trials."

She nodded slightly and pulled the covers up over her shoulders.

"It'd be nice if you would start ordering your own breakfast."

Without a word, she shut her eyes, and he smiled and left for the council chambers. Once seated, Zohn called for the first prisoner to be tried.

When Derrick opened the door, a gray and withered Valle was escorted in by two Equites prison guards. Once he was on his knees, he looked fearfully up at the enemy Elders.

The Court Reporter grabbed a file and then read, "We don't know his name. He was caught in the trees west of the city, and we suspect there were others with him at some point, as the smell of the Valle was pretty strong. We've not gotten a lot out of him other than he was waiting to talk to… well… looks like he wants to talk to Mark."

Zohn frowned and looked down at the Valle. "Why did you want to talk to Mark?"

"I don't have to tell you," he scowled.

Chevalier smiled. "Do you honestly think we're going to let it go at that?"

"I'm very much aware of what I have coming. I also know it's nothing compared to what I would get from Elder Sotomar if I do tell you," he said bluntly.

"Sotomar's a pussycat compared to Chevalier," the Chief of Staff said, laughing.

"Still not telling."

"Fine, Mark?" Quinn called out.

Within just a few seconds, the General came in and looked down at the kneeling Valle. "Yes, Elder?"

"Take him into interrogation and see what he's doing in our trees."

Mark nodded and then hauled the Valle out of the council chambers by the collar on his gray shirt.

"Now what?" Chevalier asked, looking down at the others.

"We have three turnings waiting for approval," the Records Keeper said. "One here, one in Johannesburg Coven, and one in Galwait Coven."

"Isn't the one in Galwait still waiting for medical clearance?"

"No, he cleared."

"Okay then, stats on Galwait's mortal?"

"He is a 78-year-old, former school teacher. Lord Galwait's reasoning is that he also did some metallurgy on the side."

Zohn frowned. "Why does Galwait need a metallurgist?"

"They didn't say, sir. That was just what the petition said as a reason."

"No other reasoning?"

"No, Elder."

"Denied then."

Chevalier nodded. "Denied."

Quinn looked down at him. "State reasons as insufficient purpose. There's no way a metallurgist can benefit the Equites."

"Yes, Elder," he said, and then pulled out another file. "Johannesburg Coven's petition is for a 67-year-old female. She was a psychiatrist."

Chevalier sighed, "Why is it, that since Emily needed a psychiatrist, every coven thinks they need one?"

Zohn chuckled. "Because they want their psychiatrist to cure Emily to get on our good side."

"Denied, we have enough psychiatrists in the faction now."

"Denied," Quinn said.

Zohn shrugged. "Fine, tell them insufficient purpose."

The Records Keeper nodded and pulled out the last file. "Sierra and Arion from here in the city want to turn a 72-year-old male. He was a TV repairman but is former Air Force. He's a pilot with experience in mechanic work on both helicopter and airplanes."

Chevalier nodded. "Now that we do need. Since Crocker moved back to his coven, we only have the two mechanics."

Zohn nodded. "Agreed."

"It's unanimous. Get him set up," Quinn said.

"When is Kyle due back in?" Zohn asked.

"He sent word last night that he's almost finished," Chevalier explained. "I'd say he'll be back by tomorrow night."

"Shall we get our morning Valle report?" Quinn asked.

Zohn sighed, "Let's get it over with."

"Copko Coven was attacked by 14. The Valle were driven off and only two were killed," the Records Keeper said. "DRV Coven killed 11 attacking Valle. Malay Coven lost 14 and drove off 152 Valle, with only two Valle dead."

"They're just being pests," Chevalier growled.

"We could go ahead with the plan to send Powan and Thukil to Wright Coven. It's the Valle's largest, but we would outnumber them," the Chief Interrogator suggested.

"Tell them to get ready. I plan on sending Emily to Thukil during the turning, and we'll send them to attack after that."

"Yes, Elder."

"We actually can turn him this Friday," the Records Keeper said.

"Schedule it then," Zohn said. "You attend. I don't think any Elders are warranted."

He nodded and then called out for the next prisoner on trial. A heku was brought in, scowling at the Council. He had the signature tattoo of the Encala. As he was forced to kneel down in front of the Council, he growled slightly. Derrick smiled at the Council and then returned to his post.

The Records Keeper opened a file and turned to the Council. "This fine Encala was staking out Powan."

"Why would you do that?" Chevalier asked him.

"I do what I'm told," he snapped.

"Who told you to spy on Powan?"

The prisoner grinned evilly. "I'm not going to tell you that."

Chevalier shrugged. "Kill him then."

Zohn shook his head. "I vote for banishment."

"Five hundred years, as soon as Kyle returns," Quinn said.

"We can't kill everyone," Zohn said to Chevalier.

"Why not?" he asked, grinning.

***

"It's only for a week and then we'll send for you, okay?" Chevalier said when Emily looked at him fearfully.

She didn't speak or nod but looked at the heku in the helicopter with her.

"Em... talk to them. You can trust Lord and Lady Thukil and Captain Darren."

Emily started to crawl out of the helicopter, but Darren took her arm gently and kept her from leaving.

Chevalier motioned for the pilot to leave and then watched as one of the Thukil Captains shut the helicopter door, and the helicopter took off for Texas.

Kyle smiled. "She's not going to say a word to them."

"Nope," Chevalier chuckled. "I trust her more with Thukil though."

Kyle looked back toward the door. "We better go. Farlane Coven is causing problems."

Kyle and Chevalier sat down just as the Lord of Farlane was screaming at the Council. "It's unacceptable, and if it were up to me, you would all be replaced!"

"Do not talk to us like that!" Zohn growled, and then called for the Cavalry. Lord Farlane turned and glared as all 102 of the Cavalry filed into the trial area.

"It's things like this that point to new leadership in this faction," Lord Farlane yelled, after turning back to the Council.

"New leadership?" Chevalier asked angrily. "Who's going to replace us? You?"

"I would be better than any of you."

The Chief of Defense blurred into the room and shouted, "Clear out the Elders! Get the Council out of here."

"What's going on?" Zohn asked, standing slowly.

Lord Farlane grinned. "I told you. It's time for new leadership."

Two of the Cavalry took Lord Farlane into custody, but a loud explosion was heard from just outside of the palace. Chevalier was the first to disappear from the council chambers, so Zohn and Quinn quickly blurred to the waiting helicopters.

Kralen jumped into the pilot seat and then turned with wide eyes. "Get into Equites 2. This one's not starting up."

When it was discovered that Equites 2 had also been compromised, plans were made to take the fastest Equites cars to get the Council out of the city. When the Council entered the garage, they were met with over 600 heku waiting for them.

Zohn growled, "Do not do this!"

"It's too late," the nearest said. "It's way past time for new leadership, and as we're one of the closest covens, it's our duty to do that."

***

Captain Darren blurred into the Thukil's conference room. "They banished General Skinner and have taken over Powan."

"Damnit," Lord Thukil growled. "That means we're next."

"Not if we show support to the new Council," one of the Thukil Captains said.

Darren sat down. "We also need to consider Emily. She doesn't know that Chevalier has been banished."

Lord Thukil nodded. "I wonder if the new Council knows she's here."

"No one's notified us," Lord Thukil's secretary said. "So do I call them to show our support?"

Darren sighed, "If we show our support, they are less likely to attack and find Lady Emily here."

Lord Thukil shut his eyes and nodded. "Do it."

"We have to protect her at all costs," Lady Thukil said through tearless sobs. "From what I've heard, she's going to try to get to Chevalier."

"Agreed," Darren said, "but we have to tell her. It's the only way to explain why she can't go back to Council City."

"That poor child is going to be lost," Lady Thukil said with a cracked voice.

"She's closest to you," Lord Thukil said to Darren. "Talk to her, and let her know why we've pledged our support to the new Council."

He nodded. "I'll try. She's been here for three days and hasn't spoken."

"Do what you can."

Darren nodded and then stood slowly and walked out of the conference room. Tensions in the main house were high, and it was obvious that a dark pal was over the entire coven. He knocked lightly on Emily's door and then stepped in.

Emily looked up at him and smiled.

Darren shut the door and sat down beside her in a chair. "I really need you to listen to me and trust me on this, okay?"

She watched him silently.

"Can you at least nod or something? Let me know you understand? It's important."

Emily smiled.

Darren sighed, "There's been… there's been a hostile takeover of the Council…"

Emily tensed and stood up.

Darren quickly stood to block her from the door. "Lady Emily, it's more important than ever that you listen to me."

She looked up at him, and he could see the panic in her eyes.

"A new Council is now in place, and they've taken over Powan." Darren took her hand when she tried to get around him. "Please, listen to

me. You can't go running back to Council City. We suspect that they will be looking for you."

Emily tried to pull her hand out of Darren's grasp.

"Thukil has pledged our support to the new Council…"

She gasped and glared at him.

"Hear me out… we did it to protect you. If we don't show our support, then we will be taken over too. By sending our blessings to the new Council, it will keep them out of Thukil. We can't have you falling into the new Council's hands."

Emily reached into her pocket and pulled out all of the rank pins. Darren studied them. "The Elders and Chief Enforcer have been banished. The members of the Cavalry are imprisoned. Except for Mark, he's been banished also."

She slowly sunk down onto the floor.

Darren knelt down beside her. "You are safe here as long as we keep it a secret. This has happened before. The entire Council was replaced around 540 BC, all except Chevalier that is. Things will calm down and return to normal. Chevalier will be un-banished in 600 years."

Emily looked up at him with pained eyes.

"I know that sounds like a long time… but we'll keep you safe. I swear."

She shook her head and stood up.

"Lady Emily, no," he said, blocking her way. "Please, trust me. You need to stay here. Nothing can bring them back now."

She tried to step around him, but he blocked her.

"You're not giving me a choice. I'm going to have to put guards on you."

Emily glared at him.

"It's complicated. Only the new Chief Enforcer can un-banish them now."

"The Valle will," Emily whispered harshly.

Darren shook his head. "I doubt the Valle will want to even get involved in this. They would tell you to wait it out here and not get involved."

She turned suddenly and sat down to face the fire.

"The new Council is made up of heku that are well known as being mortal haters. You need to swear to me that you'll stay here where we can protect you."

When she didn't answer, he nodded. "You're safe here."

Darren hesitated and then turned and left. By the time he got back to the conference room, there were four members of the Thukil Cavalry at Emily's door and two more outside of her window.

"How did she take it?" Lord Thukil asked.

Darren sat down. "As well as can be expected. She's going to try to get to them."

"You explained how dangerous that is?"

"Yes, sir."

"She's not known for her patience though. I see how we're going to have a hard time containing her."

"I don't think she'll turn the coven to ash. However, if the rumors are true and she can wipe the memory of a heku, then she can escape without us knowing until it's too late."

"Those are just rumors though," Lady Thukil said.

"Well, just in case… we have to make her understand how dangerous it will be for the Equites if the new Council gets a hold of her," Lord Thukil said.

"I tried," Darren explained. "I don't think she sees anything but Chevalier's banishment."

One of the Thukil Generals broke a few minutes of silence. "I don't think they'll kill her if they get her. However, I do think she would be forced to do their bidding."

"The Elder told me she won't turn anyone to ash," Darren said. "He explained that a fear was implanted that if she's to pass out, she would be buried again."

"Then I would assume she would be taught obedience and discipline."

Darren nodded. "I don't know how much she can take. She's still pretty fragile from the capture. I don't know even a fraction of what happened to her, but what I do know… let's just say she shouldn't be sane at all."

"Our number one priority will be to prove our loyalty to the new Council to keep them out of Thukil," Lord Thukil said. "We need a backup plan to get Emily to safety if we are attacked."

"I have a home in Berlin," the General said. "If we can get her out of the city, I can get her to Berlin, and we can wait it out there. No one knows where that home is."

Lord Thukil thought for a moment and then nodded. "Fine… you have permission to use the underground exits."

The General nodded.

"Sir?" one of the servants said after being told to enter.

Lord Thukil looked up at him, not sure he could take any more bad news.

"Lord Samuels has been banished, and Samuels Coven is now under the control of the Council."

Lord Thukil nodded and then whispered, "Thank you."

"We've shown our support. That's all we can do, but I suggest we

reinforce, just in case," Darren said.

"Make it so."

***

"Get in," Darren said from inside of his car. Emily lowered her thumb and looked in at him. "Get in, please."

Her shoulders fell, and she got into the car. Darren drove back to Thukil in silence. He understood her drive to get to Chevalier but was frustrated that he couldn't make her see how dangerous her mission was.

Before passing into Thukil, Darren finally spoke, "I understand. I truly do... but I need you to understand how dangerous it is if you go back. I know you think you can get to the banished, but you aren't going to make it into the palace without being accosted."

He waited for her to speak, something she hadn't done but once in her two weeks with Thukil. "Once the new Council has you, there's no telling the horrors they would put you through. You know as well as I do that you aren't the most loved Equites. This Council doesn't like mortals and aren't going to allow you to stay in the palace. I'm imagining you would be kept in the prison until they need someone wiped out."

Darren pulled into the Thukil garage and stopped the car. "Is it that bad, thinking you will spend a few hundred years here with Thukil?"

When Emily spoke, her voice was barely above a whisper, "I can't leave Chevalier to suffer."

"He would want you to stay here where you'll be safe."

Darren escorted Emily back into her room, where she sat on the bear-skin rug in front of the fire.

"Do you need anything?" he asked finally.

Emily turned and looked at the door and then back to the fire.

Darren nodded and then sighed, "Very well. I'll leave you alone."

When he left, Darren headed down to talk to Lord Thukil.

"You found her?" Lord Thukil asked.

"Yes, sir. However, there's something strange."

"Like what?"

"Her scent is off."

"Maybe the child is getting sick," Lady Thukil suggested.

Darren thought for a moment. "I don't know of a single mortal doctor in Thukil."

"Try Woody."

"Well, I guess a vet is better than nothing," Darren said before heading off to find the old Veterinarian. Less than an hour later, Darren and the Veterinarian, Woody, stopped at Emily's door.

"Rumor has it that she doesn't like doctors," Darren warned him.

He smiled. "I'm not a doctor."

"True"

One of the Cavalry guarding Emily's door knocked and then waited a few seconds before opening the door.

Darren walked in and smiled. "Lady Emily?"

She turned and looked over at him from a chair by the window.

The Captain shifted nervously. "This is Woody. He's... well... a vet."

Emily didn't say anything but turned to look out the window.

"I'd appreciate it if you'd let him take a quick peak at you."

This time, she looked at him and frowned.

"I couldn't help but notice your... your scent is off some. I thought maybe you might be getting sick."

Emily's eyes grew wide, and she watched him.

Woody tipped his old cowboy hat. "Nice to meet you. You're quite famous around here."

"She's not talking much," Darren explained when she didn't say anything.

"I don't mind looking at you a bit," Woody said with a smile. "I don't know your normal scent, but it's... quite interesting."

"A lot of that is Winchester, but there's something faintly different."

Emily slowly shook her head and kept a close eye on them.

Woody smiled. "I guess it's okay if I don't. I wouldn't know if you were sick anyway."

Darren thought. "Any pain?"

She just watched him.

"Cough? Sore throat? What else... headache?"

Emily turned to look out the window, but the heku heard her heart race.

"I guess you'll tell us if you think you're getting sick."

As soon as they left, Emily looked around the room quickly, trying to decide what to do. She understood the dangers of going back to Council City, but she couldn't imagine leaving Chevalier and Kyle to suffer. She put her odd scent to the back of her mind. It didn't surprise her, though she'd hoped it was just a coincidence.

Knowing she didn't have a choice, Emily dug through her bag and took out her wallet. She had only a little bit of money with her. There was no real need for cash on a vacation to Thukil.

Emily went to the window and looked down at the two Cavalry members stationed there. She could see the trees just past the Thukil gates and knew she had a better chance of escaping once she got there.

Breathing one quick sigh, she opened the window and looked down the ten feet to the horses below.

"Lady Emily?" one of them asked, seconds before gripping his chest in agony. Once they were unconscious, Emily dropped carefully to the grass below and ran for the trees. Anyone she encountered, she knocked unconscious or erased their memory, and she was soon in the trees.

The interstate was busy as she wrote the location of the city outside of Council City on a paper and then held her thumb up. It wasn't long before a semi-truck driver pulled up. She handed the address to him, and he smiled.

"I can't take you the entire way, baby. Get in and I'll go as far as Akron," he said, opening the door.

Emily hesitated and then crawled into the truck. Once buckled in, the driver took off. He spoke about his wife and kids for most of the drive, but when Emily fell asleep, he grew quiet and drove slowly closer to Council City.

On the outskirts of Akron, the driver used his CB and arranged for another truck to take Emily farther north. The new truck driver was a lot quieter, and she was thankful for the time to think. She realized her first task would be to get into the city unseen and make sure that Alexis and Dain were safe. She'd been to Alexis' house in the city numerous times, and she knew she could get to it easily.

Emily smiled as she crawled out of the truck, and the driver looked up the dark road. "You sure you're okay here?"

She nodded and then shut the door. Once the semi was out of sight, she turned and headed up the unlit road that led a few miles up to Council City. When she could see the gates, she noticed unfamiliar guards and thought before walking up toward them.

"Stop there!" the closest shouted before turning to ash. Emily ran past the two piles and into the city. She quickly made her way to Alexis' house and knocked softly on the door.

Garrett gasped when he saw who was at the door and quickly ushered her inside.

"Mom!" Alexis whispered.

Dain stood up and looked, shocked, at his mom.

"Lady Emily, you have to get out of here. The entire faction is looking for you," Garrett told her.

She swallowed hard and then forced herself to speak, "Listen to me… get Alex and Dain to Palau."

"I'm not leaving you, Mom. Come with," Alexis said.

Emily looked at Garrett. "I'm still a member of the Council, and I'm ordering you to take these two out of here. Don't come back until myself or Chevalier gets you."

"Mom… Dad's been…," Dain started.

Emily nodded. "I know, but I'm going to get them out."

Garrett immediately began packing a bag. "Do you know how to get to where we're going?"

Alexis looked at him tearfully and nodded. "Yes."

"Do not come back," Emily stressed.

"Mom, come with us, please," Dain said. "We aren't sure what the Council wants with you, but they've put all resources into finding you."

"I can't let your dad suffer. I have less than a year to revive him."

Alexis quickly hugged her mom. "They may hurt you."

"I can take it."

"But…"

"Go, now," Emily said to Garrett. Without another word, he opened the door and the three blurred away, keeping a slower pace with Alexis.

Emily sat down on a chair to think out a plan.

Chapter 2

"Tell the former Captain if he doesn't stop demanding to see us, he'll be banished along with the rest of the departed Council," the acting Elder said to Derrick.

Derrick nodded and stepped back out to his post. He shut the door and then his eyes grew wide when he saw Emily standing before him.

She looked at the door, and Derrick moved closer and whispered, "Get out of here... run."

Emily shook her head and put a hand on his shoulder, then smiled at him.

"You don't understand. They are mean, and they want you."

She nodded and then walked to the door.

Derrick sighed before opening the door. "Lady Emily wishes to see you."

There was a rumble of talking between members of the Equites Council and then a stern voice sounded, "Show her in."

Derrick stepped aside and let Emily in. She walked in and scanned the new Council carefully. It was obvious that they were afraid of her and shifted nervously in their chairs.

"You, my dear, are in quite a bit of trouble," one of the new Elders said.

Emily put her hands on her hips and watched him.

"We've had the entire faction looking for you. Where were you?"

When she didn't answer, he yelled for Derrick.

"Yes, Elder?" Derrick asked, though Emily could hear the hint of sarcasm.

"Make her speak."

"She hasn't spoken to anyone since her captivity with Salazar," he explained.

"Well, she'll talk to me when I tell her to."

Derrick glanced at Emily and then returned to his post.

"So, I suspect you're here to get your beloved Council back."

Emily glared at him and scanned the Council again.

"It won't happen, and as you're a possession of the Equites, we'll watch over you."

"What do we do with her?" the heku sitting in the Court Reporter's seat asked.

"For now, put her in her room," he said, and then called for members of the palace guards.

Emily didn't recognize the guards. They escorted her out of the council chambers. She smiled reassuringly at Derrick as she passed but could tell he was worried.

Once in the bedroom, Emily immediately began packing a bag. She took out four large bottles of a clear liquid and encased them in layers of clothing, so they wouldn't break. She sprayed herself with a bottle that was partially full and then wrapped it up also.

She turned when someone walked in and saw the acting Elder she had been talking to earlier. He shut the door behind him and motioned to the chair. "Please, have a seat."

Emily got up and hesitantly sat down, watching him closely.

He smiled and sat down. "I don't want any surprises, so let's go over this carefully, okay?"

When she didn't answer, he continued, "No one on the Council likes you. We don't feel you should be in the palace of the heku, so you will be moved out to the overseer's room in the stables. You will not turn anyone to ash unless told to do so by the Council. Any disobedience will be dealt with, with physical punishment. Do you understand?"

She watched him but made no indication that she understood.

"You will be heavily guarded, and we as a Council expect full compliance with anything we order you to do. No selfishness, whining, or complaining. You are the property of the Equites, nothing more."

Emily fought to keep her face neutral. She knew she had to show compliance and wait for a chance to get to the ashes of the true Council.

The Elder looked over at the bag. "Good, you've packed. Take that, and your guards will show you to the stables. You aren't to set foot into the palace unless called by a member of the Council. You aren't worthy to live here."

She stood up and grabbed her bag and then turned to the Elder.

"Good, so far you've done well," he said, smiling. "We'll have three meals a day brought out to you but expect to hear nothing from you unless spoken to."

Without waiting for her to respond, he opened the door and ordered her guards to take her to the stables. When she got into the cold overseer's room, she unpacked her suitcase, careful to hide the bottles of liquid where they wouldn't easily be found.

***

"The Council wants you," a gruff heku said. He glared at her with disdain and snarled as he spoke.

Emily watched him carefully as she walked out into the stables, and she winced when she saw the horses in unkempt stalls. Derrick let them into the council chambers, and Emily moved up to stand beside the heku in the trial area.

"My dear," one of the Elders said. "Our Chief Enforcer has gone

out for a bit, and we need this heku turned to ash immediately."

Emily looked over and into the eyes of Lord Dexter from Okanogan coven, Kralen's home coven. She saw the fear in his eyes as she turned back to the Council.

"Do it now," the acting Chief Interrogator said.

She crossed her arms and watched them. The Chief Investigator suddenly appeared behind her and slammed a thick stick into the back of her knees, sending her in agony to the floor. She caught her breath and looked up at him.

"Turn him to ash, now," he growled.

Emily defiantly stood up, ignoring the growing pain in the back of her knees, and she faced the Council.

"Your punishments will increase until you do as you are told," the Chief of Finance said.

"Turn him to ash," the Elder said again.

She crossed her arms and watched him.

"It's okay," Lord Dexter said. "Don't take punishment for this."

Emily ignored him and glared at the Elder.

He nodded. "I see that it's going to take more to get you to be compliant."

The Chief Interrogator appeared in front of her and backhanded her to the floor. She looked up as blood dripped from her mouth, and she glared at him.

"Do it," he hissed.

Emily stood slowly and faced him as her eye began to swell shut.

"I will not tolerate disobedience!" the Elder yelled. "Do as you are told!"

Very slightly, she shook her head.

When the Chief Interrogator hit her again, she felt her head slam against the cold dirt floor of the trial room, and blackness engulfed her vision.

Once Emily began to wake up, she felt the cold cot beneath her and heard a soft voice, "Em... wake up."

She took a deep breath and slowly sat up as her head began to spin. She couldn't see out of her left eye, and her mouth was sore and swollen.

"Em, can you hear me?" she heard Silas say.

Emily was finally able to look around and saw that she was in the palace prison.

"Listen to me," Kralen whispered. "You need to get out of Council City. Leave the former Council and get out of here. Ash them all if you have to."

Emily swallowed and ignored the taste of blood in her mouth as she whispered, "I can't."

"You have to. They are going to use you as the main disciplinarian of the faction."

"I have to get you out of here," she whispered.

"No, even Chevalier would want you to get out of the palace."

Emily laid back on the cot and put her arm under her head. She knew that Chevalier would tell her to leave, but she couldn't live while he suffered in the cold, dark ground.

"Em, you have to trust us," Silas said. "Next time they let you out, you have to ash them and get free."

"No," she whispered, and then rolled onto her side.

It was two days later when a harsh guard opened her cell. "Get out, Winchester. The Council wants to see you again."

She sat up slowly and followed him out, still sore from sleeping on a cot. As she passed Silas, he caught her eye and nodded slightly, then sighed when she turned away from him.

"I caught that, Emily," Silas called to her.

Emily started to feel fear as she ascended the steps to the palace. She knew what Silas meant and was afraid others might catch it too. Her masking scent was still tucked safely in the overseer's room.

Derrick was no longer at the door, but a stern looking female was there and opened the door when they came close. "You may go in."

The heku escorted Emily in, and she stood before the full Council.

"We've been debating, and we feel it's best to just banish you and put you with the others," the Elder said. He turned and nodded at the acting Chief Enforcer, who grinned and headed down toward Emily.

She frowned slightly, not quite sure she'd heard right. When a drop of his blood hit her arm, she wrinkled her nose and wiped it off on her shirt.

"She apparently can't be banished," the Chief Enforcer said to the Council.

"I was afraid of that," the Elder said.

Emily rolled her eyes and then watched them.

"Are you going to be obedient now?" he asked her.

She didn't respond but watched him.

"Very well. I just wanted to mention that if you attempt to retrieve any of the banished from the former Council... we will be forced to scatter their ashes to prevent them from being brought back prematurely."

Emily tensed but kept quiet.

"I'm going to take your silence as a revered silence, done to show respect," he said, and the others nodded. "Remain in your room until further notice."

Emily turned and followed the heku guard out of the council

chambers and finally began to relax when she got back into the overseer's room. As soon as she reapplied the masking scent, she sat down to decide what to do.

She knew her main goal was to free the Council and then she planned to take them to the Valle for revival. She figured they owed her after she set them free following a coup of the Valle's leadership. Now that the threat stood though, she had to be sure that when she reached the former Ancient's room, she wouldn't get caught.

Chevalier's words kept ringing through her head that she wouldn't be buried if she turned heku to ash, but she still hesitated to turn the palace's current inhabitants to ash to set the Council free. If she did fall unconscious doing so, she would be at the mercy of whoever found her.

There was some consolation knowing that Alexis and Dain were safely out of the eye of the Council. She hoped to get word to Allen soon, so he could meet the others in Palau and wait for her and Chevalier to arrive.

It was two days later when she saw a heku other than those who sporadically delivered food to the stables. He slammed the door open and then stepped aside. Although he didn't speak, it was obvious that he wanted her to follow.

After marking her place in her book, she stood up and followed the silent heku into the palace. He stopped at the third floor foyer and pointed toward the Elder's offices.

Emily shrugged and walked down, not sure which of the three offices she was going to. It became obvious when one of the heku standing at the door opened it and stepped aside. It was surprising to see that the new Elders each had a guard at their door. She hadn't seen that before.

"Emily," the Elder said with a smile. "Come, child. Have a seat and talk to me."

Emily hesitated and then sat down across from Chevalier's mahogany desk.

The Elder leaned back in his chair. "I think we got off on the wrong foot. I know it's disturbing to have your husband banished, but you have to understand that it was for the good of the Equites. It's well known that, even though mostly mortal, you consider yourself an Equites, so I figured you would understand."

She watched him, silently wishing he would suddenly fall over dead.

"It's important to the new Council that you learn to obey and do as you're told. You're a valuable asset to the Equites, but only if you follow instructions and be obedient."

He smiled when she didn't answer and then he continued, "I

understand that the former Council allowed you a lot of free reign and were very lenient with you. We don't feel that that is what's best for the faction. However, we also understand that you can wipe out this entire city, us included."

A small smile escaped as she thought about what he was saying.

"What you don't understand, is that once a Council is replaced, every member of the faction swears their allegiance to the new Council. If you try anything, you'll have the entire Equites faction after you."

She frowned, and her hands tightened on the chair.

"We've been discussing ways to discipline you without seriously injuring you. Obviously, you heal some, but not nearly as fast as a full heku, so we have to be careful and not incapacitate you for any length of time. First, we want an odd scent looked into. Of course, I don't catch it now, but earlier this week you had an odd, enticing aroma to your blood."

Emily made sure to hold her face neutral.

"Dr. Edwards is waiting for you in the infirmary. Just know that we have ways of punishing you for disobedience, and it's very important that we don't have to use them. Trust me, Emily, your life will be easier if you accept the new Council," he said, and smiled again.

A heku guard opened the door, and Emily stood up, spun, and walked out with him. She stepped into the infirmary and saw Dr. Edwards waiting. He looked nervous, and she had a feeling that he had been threatened. The door shut behind her, and she sat down on the table and looked at him.

"We'll start with a routine physical," Dr. Edwards said in an official voice. It was obvious that he was going to stick strictly with procedures.

After taking her blood pressure, he listened to her heart and lungs, and wrote everything in a journal. "Lie back, dear."

Emily sat still and watched him.

Dr. Edwards frowned. "Emily, lie back on the bed please."

Again, she didn't move.

He sighed and his eyes were pleading. "Please, don't cause trouble right now."

Emily nodded and then laid back on the cold medical bed. Dr. Edwards began pressing against her stomach and when he hit her lower abdomen, his shoulders fell.

He looked over at her, and she nodded slightly. Dr. Edwards swallowed hard and then helped her sit up. "I don't see any reason for the odd scent, and I don't detect it now. I will send a report to the Council."

She moved to him and wrapped her arms around him. It was comforting to feel the caring arms of a heku she trusted. He hugged her

briefly and then stepped back. "I think the Council wants you in your room."

Emily opened the door and the heku looked down at her. "The Council wants to see you first. Follow me."

When she was once again standing before the Council, the Elder she had spoken to earlier stood up. "Now we test your ability to behave. Where are your children?"

Emily looked up at him but didn't answer.

"Fine then… start with Alexis. Do you know where she is?"

A rumble ran through the Council when she refused to answer.

The Elder sighed, "Very well. Move up here to the Council stand."

Emily stepped forward and looked up at the Elder.

"Put your hands on the desk."

Not quite sure what he was doing, she did as she was told. Emily cried out softly when he smashed a wooden stick against her hands numerous times. She looked up at him and glared when he told her to step back. She glanced down at her hands and saw they were bloody and bruised.

"As a boy, that was one of my punishments. We are pulling from what we knew as humans. Be forewarned, that's not the worst of it," he said, sitting back down. "Where are your children?"

Fighting back tears from the pain, Emily slowly shook her head.

"Do not tell us no!" the Chief Enforcer screamed. "Tell us the location of your children, or you will have to be punished."

Emily crossed her arms and watched the Council.

The Chief Interrogator nodded. "I do believe she's familiar with lashings."

She looked over at him and glared.

"Then so be it," he hissed.

***

Emily rolled over and looked at the window. The sun was shining onto newly fallen snow. The room was cold, and the one blanket she had was insufficient. She pulled the blanket higher on her shoulders and wondered what the Council had in store for her today.

In the last week since Dr. Edwards saw her, she'd been questioned every day on the whereabouts of her children. She wasn't sure where Allen was but was comforted that the Council didn't know either. Allen and Miri had disappeared from Island Coven shortly after the hostile takeover of the palace.

The lashings started out slowly but became brutally more violent as her silence wore on the Council. Numerous times she had her hands

beaten with a stick, and it was now too painful to even use them. Sometimes the heku would miss, and her forearms were a mass of bruises and bloody cuts.

Emily was also getting tired of being forced to kneel. She refused to show obedience, so the Council took turns hitting the back of her knees with a steel rod to force her to her knees. There was still a strong part of her that felt the need to curl into a ball and rock, but she realized that she may be the only being that could bring back the true Council and end the tyranny of the acting one.

The door to the overseer's room suddenly flew open, and she sat up and looked at an angry heku.

"The doctor informed the Council that you have the flu. They said to bring you this," he growled, and then put crackers and Sprite on the table. He slammed the door just as Emily dove for the bathroom.

As she leaned her cheek against the cold wall of the tiny bathroom a few minutes later, she was able to hear the conversation of the guards posted outside of the stables.

"I just think it's odd is all," one of them whispered. Emily wondered why he wasn't speaking even quieter but decided to take advantage and listen in.

A female added. "The Encala had a complete Council wipe out in the 900s."

"The Equites never have though. I heard that covens aren't happy, and that's why some of the larger covens are being brought in. Their leaders are banished and replaced with select members of the Council's supporters."

"Some were excited about the change, but some of the policies coming down the line are ticking covens off, and I've heard of three that have petitioned to join the Valle," she whispered.

"Did you hear that the mortal won't do their bidding?" He sounded amused. "I really think they expected her to obey them and scare the covens into behaving. Rumor has it that she won't talk to them or do anything they ask. Not sure how long before they just kill her."

"I may not like her, but her defiance is awesome."

"She can't last long."

"Yeah, well no one's ever rescued all nine Elders from a hostile takeover either. That's pretty strong."

"True"

Emily broke the silence with another round of nausea. When she returned to the wall, all she caught was the sound of guard drills out in the snow.

She began to try to formulate a plan, some course of action that would allow her to gain entry into the Ancient's room and get the

banished Council out of Council City. Now that she wasn't deemed worthy to live in the palace, it was going to be harder. She also realized that she'd never been able to get the door open on her own, and the windows from the bar were boarded up when the banished were moved inside.

After an hour, she was finally able to crawl back out to the room and sat down against the bed with the box of crackers. It helped some, and she was able to clear her mind a little more. She wasn't sure what the Council had in store for her, but from the sounds of it, they were making a lot of the Equites covens mad.

When Emily was able to get to her feet, she decided to start her plan to rescue the former Council. She braced herself and sent waves of burning pain to the heku at her door. When they fell unconscious, she let them go and made a mad dash for the palace.

Once she wiped the memories of the door guards, she went to the garage and pulled a crowbar out of a strange truck. She couldn't help but notice that Chevalier's vehicles were no longer in the palace garage. Continuing to wipe the memory of any heku she came to, she finally made it to the Ancient's room and pried open the heavy stone door with the crowbar.

It took a painfully long time for her to find the banishment markers for the Council. She worked quickly and set her plan in motion, one that was fairly safe but could have dire consequences if the heku figured it out.

She tensed when she heard yelling echo through the palace to find her. She carefully tucked the 13 small leather bags of ash into her pockets and then listened at the door.

When the rush of footsteps passed, she sat down and used her legs to force the heavy door open. She cried out when strong hands suddenly grabbed her and roughly began to drag her to the council chambers.

Emily was pushed inside and landed on her hands and knees before the Council. She looked up at the 13 angry heku and slowly got to her feet.

"Search her," the centermost Elder hissed.

She was forcibly pushed against the stone wall as harsh hands began patting down the pockets in her clothing. Tears streamed down her face as all 13 bags were taken from her, and she turned when the heku returned to his seat.

The Elder sighed, "Emily, I warned you. You've now forced us to dispose of these ashes for the good of the Equites. If you'd have just left them alone, then in 600 years you would have had your heku back."

Emily's eyes narrowed, and she sent a flash of burning to each of the Council. She couldn't turn them to ash. Thirteen of them would

have only made the palace guards mad, and she wouldn't have gotten away.

When they recovered, Emily was immediately backhanded to the floor and then kicked painfully in the side.

"You will not do that again!" the Chief Interrogator yelled. He returned to his seat as Emily slowly got to her hands and knees, sure that he'd broken a rib.

"Scatter them," the Elder ordered, and the Chief Enforcer gathered up the 13 small bags and disappeared from the room.

"What to do with you," another Elder said as he watched the tears stream down her face.

"You made us do that to them," the Chief of Finance said. "Their death is on your head."

Emily looked down at her battered hands and let the tears flow. She expected no sympathy or understanding from the new Council and suddenly felt very alone.

"Notify the covens that because of Emily's disobedience, their former Council has been killed," the Chief Investigator said with a malicious smile.

"Now you will be hated more than even we are," the Elder said.

Emily finally made it to her feet and swayed slightly. She wiped the blood from the corner of her mouth and looked at the Council.

"How do we get obedience out of you?" he finally asked.

She stayed silent and glared at them.

He smiled. "The rumors of your temper weren't exaggerated, were they? We will have respect and obedience from you. I won't hesitate to put you in prison for the rest of your life if you don't do as you're told."

Emily smiled, and the Council gasped when the Elder turned to ash in his chair. Her mortal eyes didn't catch the movements of the other Elders, but suddenly, she was thrown down onto the ground with a tight hand around her throat.

She gasped for air and clawed at the strong hands as she fought to breathe.

"Learn now or things will become very difficult for you," he screamed at her. She saw him grin just as her oxygen ran out, and she lost consciousness.

***

"Em, wake up," she heard Kralen whisper as a soft hand touched her face.

Emily tried to say something to him, but her throat hurt too badly to speak.

"Come on, Em. Open your eyes."

When she finally managed to look up at him, she saw that he was smiling down at her and sitting on the side of the bed in the overseer's room.

"Stay down," he whispered when she tried to sit up. "The Council let me in here because I told them I can talk you into behaving. We have limited time, so you have to listen to me."

She nodded slightly and took his hand.

"You have to stop fighting back. Do you hear me? They will kill you."

Emily tried to speak again, but he shook his head. "Don't talk, okay? You aren't going to be able to hide it much longer, and when they find out, you need to be on good terms with the new Council."

She shook her head, and he sighed.

"I know what happened with the former Council, how they were scattered. Don't let them blame you for that. That was unnecessary and not your fault."

She swallowed painfully and touched the bruises on her neck lightly.

"You have to trust me on this. Stop making trouble for yourself. Silas and I are doing all we can to get out of prison, and if we can be reinstated to the city, you won't be alone anymore. If you cause problems, that may work against us."

Emily looked up at him with frightened eyes. He smiled and touched her cheek. "Things look bad now. I know. I promise though, that it'll all calm down. It may not get back to normal, but there will be a new norm, and you won't have to put up with a lot of this."

Kralen picked up her hand and looked at the cuts and bruises across her fingers.

"I'm scared," she whispered softly.

He smiled. "I know. Trust me though. Things will be okay. I've asked the Council to let you grieve. You need to do what you can to mourn Chevalier. After that though, do as the Council asks and try to get on their good side before they find out."

She nodded as her eyes filled with tears.

"The Council has told all of the Equites that you are to blame for the scattering of the former Council's ashes. They aren't happy, so you'd be best staying away from the city and any covens, okay?"

Again, she just nodded, afraid if she spoke he may leave.

Kralen softly kissed her forehead. "I have to go back. Behave, please. The abuse is only going to get worse."

Emily watched him walk out and then turned onto her side and studied the wood-grain pattern on the wall.

A few hours later, there was a knock on Emily's door, and she

turned as the main Elder came in. He set down a plate of spaghetti and then pulled a chair up beside her.

"I want to start over, you and I," he said, and then smiled. "My name is Kirt, and I was a member of the Farlane Coven before coming to the Council."

She watched him but made no move to eat.

"I realize we started off on the wrong foot, and I apologize for that. I see now that continual threats and punishment may not be how to gain your obedience. I've spoken to two of your former guards, who suggested a softer and kinder approach."

Emily's eyes fell to his Elder's pin and realized it had once been Quinn's.

"It's not in heku nature to try a soft approach, so this will be a learning experience for us both. I know you have the flu, and now you also need time to mourn your husband. We'll give you three days and then we'll meet again, just you and I, and we'll see if we can work out an arrangement."

Emily watched as he looked around the tiny room.

"We'll also see if we can get you back into the palace where it's warmer. I didn't realize how cold it is out here."

She fought back the repulsion and the urge to turn him to ash again, and simply nodded.

He smiled. "Good, then do what you need to, and we'll talk in three days. If all goes well, we may have you back in the palace before long, without so much violence."

Again, she nodded and watched him leave the room. Even though her stomach lurched at the smell of garlic, she managed to eat some and then laid back down to try to get some sleep. She realized she would need all of the strength she could muster to gain the confidence of the new Council.

Chapter 3

"Come, child," Kirt said, motioning Emily forward.

She stepped toward the Council and watched them closely.

"We understand that you are feeling better?"

Emily nodded slightly.

"Good, that was a long flu. We're glad that after two months, it is over."

She didn't reply but watched him.

"Are your palace accommodations acceptable?"

She again nodded and wondered at the patronizing tone in his voice. It seemed to her as if he was pretending to be sweet and caring, but there was a definite undertone of the harshness of reality beneath it.

Kirt smiled. "Well, we have done all we can as a Council to make sure you're well taken care of."

"Now though, we want a show of obedience from you," another Elder said to her.

"Emily, this is Neal. He's also an Elder."

Neal looked down at her. His scrutinizing glare made her shift uncomfortably.

"To show the Council that you are willing to do your part, we ask that you turn a heku to ash. He was caught trying to join the Valle and is being banished for 400 years, but our Chief Enforcer is off dealing with a coven and cannot do it," Neal explained.

Emily turned and saw a terrified heku brought forward. He was forced to his knees.

"Please... don't do it...," he whispered.

She didn't recognize him, and following Kralen's advice, she instantly turned him to ash.

"Good, child!" Kirt said, clapping. "We're very proud of you."

Neal nodded. "Fine, then she's showing obedience. However, will it continue?"

"I'm sure it will," Kirt told him. "She seems very willing to assist the new Council."

"Then why isn't she speaking?"

"Dr. Edwards told me it's part of the psychological abuse imposed on her by Salazar."

"Well, get over it," he snapped at her.

Emily's eyes grew wide, but she kept silent when Kirt began to yell, "Leave her alone! She's doing as we ask, and we have no right to punish or demand more from her."

She watched with some amusement as they began to quarrel among themselves. As she watched, she realized that this Council wasn't nearly

as strong as they thought and was only a mere fraction as good as the former Council.

Finally, the argument ended and Kirt smiled at her again. "We were told that you enjoy swimming. Would you like to go?"

Emily thought briefly. She knew that she was already showing, but it was hidden by the baggy overalls that she'd started wearing again. As the swimsuit would surely show off her growing form, she shook her head.

"Very well. We were advised that you are the peace keeper," Neal said. "You mediate meetings with other Councils?"

Emily nodded.

"The Valle want to speak to us then. Stand back against the wall and stay silent, unless they threaten us."

She stepped back and put her back against the cold stone walls.

Valle Elder Ryan and their Faction Liaison Officer entered and walked up to the trial area. With her scent masked, they didn't even notice Emily hiding in the shadows behind them.

"Why have you asked to see us?" Kirt asked.

"It's time we meet the new Equites Council," Ryan said. He looked along the row of heku. "I don't recognize any of you."

"No, you wouldn't. However, we are the ruling body of this faction now, and you've met us. So get out of this city."

Ryan sighed, "We want to know where Emily is."

Kirt smiled. "She's standing behind you."

Ryan spun and instantly caught sight of her. His keen heku vision picked up scars along her hands and dark circles under her eyes. "Come out where I can see you better."

"She's fine where she is," Neal hissed.

Ryan turned back to them. "There are crimes against the Valle that we wish to hold her accountable for."

"There are crimes against this faction also. We will not let her go."

"What crimes?" the Valle's Faction Liaison Officer asked.

"None of your concern."

Ryan glanced back at Emily again and then turned to the Equites. "The Valle will see holding her as an act of war."

"We have a right to hold her."

"And we have a right to fight to get her into custody for crimes against my faction!"

"No," Kirt said sternly.

"We are demanding immediate release of our former Chief Interrogator, his officer, Solax, and Emily."

"You may have your former Chief Interrogator and his officer. For that we understand he should have been turned over to you immediately.

You may not, however, have Emily," Neal said calmly.

"You'll back your decision with a war?"

"Yes, we will. Just because we're new, doesn't mean we can be pushed around."

Ryan turned suddenly to Emily. "Turn them to ash, and we can ensure your safety."

She gasped just as Kirt stood up. "Get out!"

"Come with us," Ryan said, stepping closer to Emily. "We'll protect you."

Emily wanted to go with him badly. Even with Sotomar mad at her from before, she truly believed that they would be nicer to her, and she would again be around friends. When members of the palace guard came and forcibly removed the Valle, Emily fought back the tears and waited for the Council to calm down.

Once things were quiet, Kirt smiled at her. "I'm very proud of you. You could have gone with the Valle. We know they are friends of yours."

When she didn't reply, he nodded. "Well, we have business to attend to. Your things have been taken to the Elder Guard's quarters, as it's one of the few with human amenities. Please stay there until you are needed."

She nodded slightly and then followed palace guards up to Kyle's old bedroom. Once alone, she quickly started the fire and tried to warm up. She'd been cold for too long, and her entire body ached.

Emily was finally able to do what she had been wanting to. She sat by the fire in a tight ball and buried her face in her arms, then slowly began to rock. The slow movement calmed her down, and she felt the slightest bit less afraid and alone.

Late that night while she slept, she heard a commotion outside of the bedroom door and suddenly her room was flooded with lights. She shielded her eyes and watched Kirt come in. He was obviously furious.

"Get dressed! You're heading out immediately to take care of a coven. You are to wipe out the entire population and report back here at once," he yelled, and then left and slammed the door.

When he was gone, she hurried out of bed and threw on the old overalls and a large sweater to help hide her tummy. Once dressed, she stepped out of the bedroom and was pulled up the stairs by an angry heku who didn't say anything to her.

Equites 1 took off with Emily and four palace guards. No one spoke, but tension was high and Emily wondered who she was going to be forced to wipe out. If Kralen was right and the entire faction blamed her for the death of the former Council, she could only imagine how mad they would be when she began to discipline them also.

The flight gave her time to consider what she was going to do. She wasn't sure wiping out the entire coven would make things any worse in the faction, but she did know that not doing it would earn her punishment. By the time the pilot announced they would be landing in five minutes, she'd decided to go along with the Council to buy her some time.

Emily looked out the window and gasped as the helicopter descended into the lush ranch lands of Thukil Coven. The Cavalry was already lined up and ready. It was obvious they were there to prevent what was going to happen. Darren was at the head, and she could tell he was furious.

"Don't give us any problems," the highest ranking heku in the helicopter yelled at her. "Just take them out."

Her heart sank when the helicopter landed, and the deafening sound of silence filled the area as the heku watched her, and she looked out the window and into the eyes of her friends.

Darren didn't seem surprised to see her, and he nodded slightly when she met his eyes.

"Do it," one of the heku ordered.

She nodded and then crawled out of the helicopter alone. As she walked toward Darren, she could tell he was waiting for her to attack.

Emily stopped and put her hand against his horse's neck. "I…"

"I know why you're here," Darren said angrily. "We know you caused the former Council's death and have started doing the dirty work for the new Council. So get on with it."

She frowned and swallowed hard.

"We expect no loyalties from you anymore."

Emily was finding it hard to breathe as she looked down the long row of heku she considered friends and saw that they all watched her, scowling.

She turned without a word and walked back to the helicopter.

"What are you waiting for?" the closest heku snapped.

Darren watched, not sure what was going on. All of Thukil was ready to stand by their decision to defy orders from the new Council and were ready to turn to ash for it.

As the helicopter took off, the entire Thukil Cavalry saw Emily backhanded to the floor and then the helicopter disappeared on the horizon.

"She's going to get punished… for us," one of the Generals said, still in shock.

Darren nodded. "I think we were wrong."

"We still have to be ready for a fight. The Council isn't going to let this go."

"Keep the coven locked down. I'll go talk to Lord Thukil."

***

"I thought we'd worked this out," Kirt said as Emily was tied to the rack. "You were going to behave... what happened?"

Tears streamed down Emily's face. She couldn't turn all of Thukil to ash, not after all they'd done for her. It was hard to breathe as she waited for the stretching pain to begin, something she'd experienced before at the hands of Exavior.

Kirt sat down beside the rack. "I'm disappointed in you. I thought you claimed to be an Equites. Equites do as they're told and honor the wishes of the Council."

She screamed as the Chief Interrogator turned the crank and stretched her limbs painfully.

"Stop!" Kirt yelled, and then stood up and looked down at her. As her body stretched, he noticed the slight bulge in her lower abdomen, and his eyes narrowed.

"What?" the Chief Interrogator asked.

"You kept this from us?!" Kirt yelled at her.

Emily was in too much pain to answer, and only a slight groan escaped her lips.

"How far along are you?" he screamed.

The Chief Interrogator looked over and finally saw what the Elder had. He turned the crank back and loosened the ropes that were pulling at her limbs.

"Answer me!" he yelled.

She screamed when the Interrogator again tightened the ropes and stretched her body.

"You will stop defying the Council!" Kirt screamed. His eyes showed exactly how furious he was over Emily's secret. "Hang her up until she decides to talk."

The Interrogator nodded and untied Emily from the rack. She was in too much pain to fight back and within only a few minutes, was hanging from shackles high on the wall.

"You can stay there until you talk," Kirt said, and stormed out of the interrogation room.

"Sir, Silas wants to speak to you," one of the prison guards said to him.

Kirt nodded and walked over. "What?"

"Please, let me talk to her. I can get her to tell you," Silas said. He was panicked to get to Emily. Her screams echoed across the palace, and he needed to tell her to get away and never come back.

"She'll talk without your help," Kirt snapped, and then left the prison.

"Why isn't she taking off?" Kralen whispered to Silas, who was in the next cell.

"I don't know. I thought when Chevalier was scattered, she would disappear."

"They don't have the kids... nothing's holding her here."

"Unless she's hoping to save us."

"Which is why we need to get to her. She has to get out of here, or they'll kill her."

Silas nodded. "I know."

"Damnit," Kralen hissed when the strong smell of Winchester blood filled the prison. As the prisoners began to throw themselves against the bars, fighting to get to the source of the scent, Silas sighed.

"Why the hell is she still here?" Kralen whispered as he sat down on the hard cot.

Silas was too upset to answer.

***

Barely able to move, Emily was dropped to the floor of the council chambers. She was finally able to prop herself up with one elbow and look up at the heku with her one good eye.

"The staff is acclimated," Kirt said, irritated. "You are now confined to the council chambers during our regular hours."

As he spoke, Emily's left ankle was shackled to the wall with a thick chain.

"When we are not in here, you are confined to your room. You are no longer trusted by the Council and will be treated like nothing more than a broken weapon."

"You will do as you're told," the Chief Investigator said calmly.

"No more disobedience will be tolerated."

Emily's strength gave out, and she laid back against the cold dirt floor. The rest of the trial day, she stayed there and ignored the boring trials and faction business. The hard floor was making her back ache worse, pain that started with the rack and grew continually more severe as she hung from the shackles.

When the Council began to leave, Kirt stood up and called for the door guard.

"Yes, Elder?" he asked.

"She's too weak to walk. Get her to bed," Kirt said, watching Emily with disgust.

The heku snarled and then roughly picked her up and blurred her to

the tiny room she was assigned. This one had a partial bathroom installed in haste and was her new living space. Once he dropped her onto the bed, she rolled onto her side and pulled the blanket up to her shoulders.

She couldn't help but let the tears stream down her face. She felt lost and alone in a place now set out to do nothing more than order her around and hurt her. The world seemed a lot larger, more cold and desolate. Even though she still had plans, she wondered if they would work or just cause even more suffering.

The baby moved slightly and brought a new round of tears. After a few hours, she finally cried herself to sleep.

"Get up." Emily jumped when the gruff voice sounded in her dark room. She turned and looked at a strange heku. "I said, get up."

Ignoring the pain as best she could, she sat up and then stood, still dressed in blood-drenched clothing from the night before.

"We need the Grand Hall floor scrubbed," he said, and turned toward the stairs.

Emily nodded and followed him down. He left her in the massive room with a bucket of hot, sudsy water and a tiny sponge. She knelt down and immediately began to clean. She didn't mind hard work, but the soapy water stung the deep cuts on her hands, and her knees and back still ached from the rack.

Her arms started to ache almost immediately as she scrubbed. She'd been hung in the interrogation chamber by shackles for nearly 12 hours, and she was still feeling the effects of that. The soap continued to sting her hands, but she let her mind wander to good memories to try and escape the new horror she found herself in.

No one came in all day, and by nightfall, she was scrubbing the second corner of the massive room. As she sat back on her feet to look over the floor, the Records Keeper came in and looked closely at her work.

"That'll do I guess… we can't expect much more from a pathetic little mortal," he said, faking sadness.

He turned and held the door, then looked at Emily. She forced herself to stand and followed him out. The next two weeks was spent the same, scrubbing floors and walls throughout the castle, while her nights were spent in various forms of punishment by the Council for minor infractions.

After having her hands beaten again with a wooden stick, Emily sat down on her bed to see if she could nurse her wounds at all. The new cuts were over the top of old scabs and older scars. It was getting too painful to even bend her fingers. The new fun by the Council was to force her to kneel by slamming a baseball bat against the back of her legs

and thighs.

Today, the Chief Enforcer had crossed the line, and it took every ounce of control for her not to turn the entire Council to ash. When asked again where her children were, the Chief Enforcer followed up her silence with a brutal stomach punch, one which left a vicious purple bruise across her expanding middle.

Emily had also begun to suspect that the Council planned on getting rid of the baby as soon as she had it, because it belonged to a former member of the Council. She figured that's why they wanted her children too, to dispose of them and erase Chevalier's very existence.

Her heart sank when she remembered the terrified look on Dr. Edwards face when the Chief Enforcer banished him right in front of her. The Council realized that he'd known about the pregnancy but had kept it from them. The all-too brief sound of his scream echoed through her mind as she sat in the dark and looked around the small room.

The Council had refused to let Emily change clothes, and she'd already outgrown the once baggy overalls. Each night she scrubbed them with weak hands and then hung them on the door knob to dry. They were getting too tight though, and it made it hard to even walk.

While replaying thoughts of her time on the Island with Chevalier, she finally fell asleep but was woken up before dawn again.

"Get up! You've slept too much," the Chief of Staff yelled. Emily was curious why they assumed telling her something wouldn't work unless they screamed it at her. She hurried and dressed and then followed him down, wondering what needed scrubbed now.

She tried not to react when he opened the door to the game room and stepped back. "Clean it all."

Emily nodded, hiding the excitement in her face. She cried out slightly when the Chief of Staff's foot connected with the middle of her back and sent her flying. She crashed into the pool table and heard him laugh as she fought to catch her breath.

Once she'd calmed down, she rubbed her sore tummy and looked around the game room. One of her eyes was completely swollen shut, and the other was puffy enough it was hard to see. She finally found the bucket and tiny sponge and knelt down to begin scrubbing.

She had to be careful not to rush, not to hurry, even though her pulse raced and the excitement grew. Taking extra time to clean behind the one bar, she finally got the courage and tilted the mirror slightly. She wasn't even sure it still worked, but the fast whoosh of the spinning door threw her into the hidden bar and then shut tightly behind her.

Emily looked around the dark bar. Now that the windows were boarded up, no light was coming through them. It took a few minutes for her eyes to adjust, and she immediately wedged a chair into the door so it

wouldn't spin. She suspected no one in the palace even knew of this room, but she wanted to be safe.

After stacking two tables and then putting a chair on top of it, she finally managed to crawl onto the ledge and started pulling at the boards. She'd almost given up hope when her fingers dug into the crack on a board, and it pulled away from the others slightly. Tugging as hard as she could with painful hands, she managed to pry open the board and looked down into the abandoned Ancient's room and onto the banishment sites of hundreds of heku.

Emily braced herself and then jumped down the ten feet to the hard ground below. She managed not to scream when she landed, and the jarring sent a painful stab up her legs and back. Once she was sure no one heard her, she immediately began moving around the room and digging up the tiny leather bags under the banishment markers of well-known Equites' criminals.

When the bags were safely hidden in the baggy legs of her overalls, she dug up the crowbar she'd buried and listened at the door. She heard several heku walk past and then waited a few minutes before she used her legs to open the heavy stone door.

By the time Emily got to the garage, she'd only had to turn 12 heku to ash. None of the cars looked familiar, but she'd managed to learn a lot about cars in her years with the heku and chose to steal what looked like a brand new Bugatti Veyron.

When she peeled out of the garage, she sped past numerous heku that tried to jump and stop her, but she flew past them and then winced when she hit the two gate guards that tried to step in front of her. She knew the damage to the Veyron would be substantial and that they were sure to immediately get police on her tail, so she kept with the plan to get to Exavior's old house and see if her car was still there.

Emily skidded to a halt outside of the mansion's garage and left the Veyron only after checking carefully around her. No heku came at her from the house, and she began to wonder if the Equites had just abandoned it when they thought she was dead.

The lights in the garage took painfully long to turn on, and she sighed when the only thing in there was her Harley. Emily immediately lifted one of the rear compartments and saw the money that Chevalier insisted she carry with her when she went out. It was enough to get a few tanks of gas and some food.

After grabbing her helmet, she slipped it on and was soon out on the Interstate with the Night Rod special pegged as she moved farther west. When she left the Interstate for less conspicuous back-roads, she finally began to relax. She had what she needed. Now she just needed to make it to the nearby Banks Coven to get help.

Chapter 4

"Well look at this," one of the massive heku said from the gates of Banks Coven.

"Seems the Council sent us a traitor to deal with," another said.

Emily took a step back, and her eyes grew wide when she saw the anger in their features.

"Someone needs to pay you back for what you've done. Know what we do to traitors in this Coven?" the first one asked as he roughly grabbed her arm.

"She even let one of them knock her up... shows how far she's fallen."

Emily tried to speak but fear gripped her, and she felt a sudden sense of loss. Banks Coven was going to help her. They were going to be her safe haven while they found someone to revive the ashes. Now they were angry, and she wasn't sure who to turn to next.

"Little bitch, let's go," the first one said as he pulled her into the Coven.

Heku came out and watched as they passed the tiny row of houses and headed for the mansion in the center. Most snarled and hissed at her, and some shouted curses and accusations. Her heart was dropping. She didn't want to turn them to ash, but she had to get to safety.

Lord Banks met them at the entrance to the mansion, and any hope Emily had that he would help her vanished when he glared at her. "It's our duty as Equites to seek revenge for the scattered."

Emily gasped and shook her head, then finally managed a whisper, "I didn't..."

"Don't speak!" he shouted, and she was immediately gagged with a thick cloth. "You deserve nothing more than pain and suffering for eternity for what you did. Betraying the faction and killing your own husband... it's disgusting."

She shook her head and tried to speak, but the cloth prevented it.

"Maybe you'll meet Chevalier in hell," he growled, and the guards pulled her down into the prison. Once she was thrown into a cold cell, they locked the doors and she finally untied the gag.

"Please, help me," she whispered. "I didn't..."

"Shut up!" the guard yelled. "Nothing you can say will help you now."

One of the guards grinned. "She's all bruised up. Seems someone else already punished her some. It'll get a lot worse for you... maybe we'll have to cut out that baby of yours."

Emily gasped. "I didn't get them..."

"Shut up," he said, and both disappeared.

She didn't see anyone again until the next morning when one of the Banks guards threw a t-shirt in at her. "Get out of that filthy get-up and put that on."

Emily looked down at her blood covered clothing and quickly put on the t-shirt. It was obviously from one of the guards and came all the way to her knees.

"Lord Banks thinks you need to suffer before we finally kill you," another heku said as he unlocked the door. She wasn't surprised to see he was wearing a menthol mask. "We have an idea that'll label you as the traitor you are."

"They aren't scattered," Emily whispered. "You have to believe me."

"Believe you?" he hissed, stepping toward her. Emily gasped when she saw a knife in his hand, and she tried to run past him. A second heku spun her around and painfully slammed her into the rock wall of her cell.

"Traitor it is...," one of them said. Emily was held down, and her screams filled the mansion as the word 'Proditor' was carved into her back above the Equites Crest. Other prisoners began to hiss and call for her as the scent of her blood filled the prison.

When the heku let go of her, she fell to her knees. The pain had drained all of her energy, and she slumped down and leaned against the wall.

"We're not done," the other grinned evilly. "You'll learn not to mess with the Equites."

"They aren't scattered," she said softly, and then cried out when one of them kicked her in the hip.

"Just shut up," he growled, and again, she was left alone. She could feel the blood dripping down her back as she finally managed to stand.

Emily sat on the bed and shut her eyes, fighting to clear her mind, so she could figure out how to get out of this. She finally felt the baby move and was relieved that the last few days hadn't done as much damage as she feared.

It was only an hour later when another mask wearing guard appeared. "Lord Banks wants you interrogated."

The second he opened the cell door, he fell to ash, and Emily rushed out of the prison. She wiped the memory of any heku she came to and was soon back at her motorcycle. She'd hidden it in the brush with the 13 bags of ashes hidden in the seat. After catching her breath, she sped off into the night.

Island Coven was much farther than Banks, but she decided it was going to be the safest. If she could explain to Storm what happened, she was sure the Island would help her. The ride seemed extremely long, and she couldn't help but check over her shoulder constantly.

Each time she got gas, she wondered if heku were going to attack her from behind, and by the time she got to the ferry, she was shaking and on the verge of a breakdown. The Captain glared at her but set off for the Island. After four hours, Emily had a plan formed on what she would tell Storm. She believed Captain Darren's thoughts that the Valle wouldn't help her, so she hoped to get the ashes to the Encala.

"What the hell are you doing here?" one of the pier guards growled at her. His dog's hackles were raised, and he was pulling on the leash to get to her.

"I need help," Emily said, fighting the internal fear she had of speaking.

"You'll get no help from here."

"I need you to listen to me," she said. "They weren't scattered..."

"Shut up!" he screamed. "Get back to the mainland and leave this coven alone."

"Let me talk to Storm."

"Storm's been banished," he hissed.

"Then Walen?"

"Go away! Island Coven no longer belongs to Chevalier, and you're no longer welcome here."

Emily pulled out a small bag with the name Damon on it. "This is..."

"You bitch! You're really going all out aren't you? First, you get your own husband killed. Now you want help for another traitor?"

"No..."

The Pier Guard grabbed her arm tightly and threw her back onto the ferry, then signaled for the Captain to take her to the mainland. She watched the island fade from view and her heart sunk further.

She relaxed slightly when she was off of the interstate again and on a smaller road. She recognized it and put her next plan into action, which was going to Clark Coven. She didn't know Lord Clark well and had only seen him while making a V.E.S. visit. She hoped that a smaller coven might not have heard as much about her as the larger ones.

The looming house was dark when she pulled up and hid the motorcycle in the trees again. As she pushed the wrought iron gate open, a dark form appeared.

"What do you want?" Lord Clark asked.

Emily looked up at him. "I need help... I have..."

"You aren't welcome here."

"Please, listen to me. I have the..."

"No! I won't be brandished a traitor to listen to your lies."

When he slammed the door, she went back to the motorcycle.

Now Emily wasn't sure where to go. She had been confident that if

she could get to an Equites Coven, they would help her and all would go back to normal. After fueling up and ignoring the odd glances at the pregnant woman wearing a blood-stained t-shirt, she finally decided that her best bet would be with William.

Just outside of the gates to the Encala's main city. Emily again hid her motorcycle but put the ashes into a leather satchel and then walked barefoot up the gravel road toward the gates.

"Stop!" one of the guards yelled when they saw her. He blurred to her and looked down. "What do you want?"

She looked up at him with her good eye and her voice cracked. "Please... I need to see William."

The guard crossed his arms. "Why should I bother Elder William for you?"

Emily looked behind her at the long gravel road and then back at the Encala. "I don't have anywhere else to go."

"Well, you aren't coming in here. We've heard that you turned traitor to the Equites."

"What did you find?" a familiar voice asked.

Emily was relieved when Lt. Andrew appeared, and his eyes grew wide when he saw her. "Oh my God."

"I need to see William," she said again, barely above a whisper.

Lt. Andrew took a step back. "We're not acclimated to you."

"I've masked it," she whispered. A tear fell as she swallowed hard. "I need help."

She saw indecision creep across his face. "I'll have to go ask."

Emily turned tear filled green eyes toward him. "I was afraid you were dead."

"Your Equites opted to banish me, not kill me."

She nodded, and he disappeared. The gate guards watched as she shifted nervously and waited for Lt. Andrew to appear. A few minutes later, William appeared and pulled Emily into a tight embrace.

"I've been worried about you," he said as he set her down and looked her over. "Did the Valle do this to you?"

She shook her head and then took his hand when he extended it.

They walked toward the palace in silence for a bit before passing through the front door guards and into the council chambers of the Encala.

"Let's meet in the Elder's conference room," William said. He then led Emily out from the watchful eye of the Encala Council and into a more private room.

A servant brought Emily a glass of ice water, which she drank in one long drink.

William sat down and motioned to the two other heku in the room.

"This is Elder Iuna and Elder Patrick."

She nodded to them and put the water down.

"Who did this to you, child?" Iuna asked.

Emily shrugged and fought back the tears.

"It's okay," William said, smiling. "We're glad you came here. You can rest, and we can talk later. There's a mortal doctor in the city. We can have him come look at you."

She shook her head and watched them.

Iuna looked at her. "We don't understand what you want."

"They told us she's non-verbal," Patrick reminded them.

"She spoke to Lt. Andrew though."

William's eyes narrowed. "Did the Equites do this to you?"

Emily frowned and then nodded slowly.

"The Council or covens?"

Again, she nodded.

"You can stay here as long as you'd like. They put out an APB on you country-wide, saying you're an escaped mental patient," William told her.

She looked down at the leather satchel and then put it on the table.

"We also were alerted that the Equites Council is blaming you for having to scatter the former Council," William said, and took her hand. "Don't let them blame you for that. It was their choice, and I'm sorry they did that to you."

"You can stay here though, and we'll keep it from the Equites," Patrick said. "We still aren't strong enough to fight them."

Emily pushed the satchel closer to them.

"Do you want us to go through this?" Iuna asked her.

She looked at the satchel and then nodded.

William took the leather bag and opened it, then gasped. "Oh my God! Who is this?"

"What?" Iuna asked, and then looked into the bag, and his eyes grew wide.

William pulled out a small bag and read it. "This is Damon."

"Samuel, Ingram, Selhman," Iuna read from the bags.

"Let's see… there's a David, Vaughn… is this the former Encala?"

Emily shrugged and watched them go through the ashes.

"Wow, Dustin is here, and the doppelganger we put in for their Records Keeper," Patrick added.

William looked up at Emily. "Why did you bring us these?"

She sighed and whispered, "It's the Council."

He frowned. "We were told the Council was scattered."

"I switched them."

Iuna was shocked. "The entire former Council is here?"

She nodded.

William smiled slightly. "It's against heku laws to bring them here."

"Please, revive them."

Iuna looked over at William. "We can't. It's against ancient customs to revive a banished member of the Council."

"It's never been done," Patrick said.

A tear escaped her swollen eye. "I'm afraid, William."

He sighed and put the ashes down. "I know. I realize how scary this all is, but this is how heku Councils work. If the covens feel a new Council is needed, it's their job to replace them."

"Please, help me."

William rubbed the bridge of his nose. "It's breaking too many laws."

When she spoke, her voice showed her desperation, "I can go to the Valle."

Emily stood up and began returning the bags of ash to the satchel.

"How far along are you, Em?" William asked, taking her hand to stop her from re-packing.

"Help me. I beg you."

He studied her hand and frowned. "My God, what did they do to you?"

Emily pulled her battered hand out of his and put the ashes back in the satchel. She sat suddenly when she started to feel dizzy.

William blurred to her side and knelt down. "Tell me what's wrong."

She looked at him, and the pain in her eyes made his heart pound. "I haven't felt well since the rack."

"The Council interrogated you?"

Emily nodded and stood up again with the satchel. "I need to go."

William stood up also and glanced down at the back of her legs. "What did they do there?"

"Before night falls," she whispered, and started for the door.

"Let us discuss this," William said. "Go to your room and get some rest. I'll ask the Council, and we'll decide."

"The Valle won't help you and more than likely, will hold you prisoner," Iuna said.

She stopped at the door and thought before turning and nodding. "Okay."

"Let me take them," Iuna said softly.

Emily pulled the bag farther from him.

"We won't do anything bad with them," William promised. "I wouldn't do anything to hurt you."

The bag slowly slipped to the floor. "I'm so tired."

William reached down and tenderly picked her up. She started to protest but then leaned her head on his shoulder. It felt good to feel safe again, and she was exhausted from the last three months. He walked up the stairs slowly and laid her down on the bed the Encala kept for her.

Before the Elder left, a servant brought in a bowl full of muffins and fruit, and a pitcher of ice water.

"You have food?" Emily asked, looking at the table.

William smiled. "We always keep fresh food, in case you come to visit."

He watched her for a moment before shutting the door and going down to the council chambers.

He sat down just as Iuna was explaining, "So we told her we'd talk about it."

"Are you certain she is telling the truth?" the Chief Enforcer asked.

"No one has ever dug up members of a banished Council," the Records Keeper said.

William smiled. "This is Emily. She doesn't know heku traditions and just follows her heart."

"So re-banish them here," the Court Reporter suggested. "When their 600 years is over, they will be in our custody."

"I promised her we wouldn't hurt them," William told him.

"They all but obliterated our faction."

"I know, but Emily has always been a friend to the Encala."

"Except when she had Frederick hostage."

William shrugged. "That entire situation got out of control. I do believe she's been punished enough for that mistake."

"You can't seriously be thinking about bringing them back!" the Chief of Staff gasped.

"They would owe us."

"They would be outcasts. You know as well as I do that once a banished is revived, they are factionless."

"That's not up to us," William said. "If we revive them, they would simply be unfactioned."

"We can't do this," Iuna said. "I know that Emily is your friend, but this breaks too many laws."

"Does it?" William asked. "Is it in the law books that a mortal can't come to an opposing Council and ask for revival?"

The Records Keeper shook his head. "No, I'm imagining no one ever thought we'd need that rule."

"The Equites have made it very well known that nothing we do would ever align us again," Patrick said.

"It's no secret that the Equites Council is considering finishing what Chevalier started and wiping us out," William said. "If we can reinstate

the former Council, that may not happen."

"So we tell the Winchester that the revival didn't work and then we offer to let her stay here. She can wipe out any army they produce," the Chief of Defense suggested.

"It's too risky," William said. He looked down at the bags of ash. "We don't even know who is who."

"My vote is no," Iuna said. "I don't want to bring back the very Council that wiped us out not seven years ago."

"I say we do it. They can't help but owe us after this," William said. "Plus, not only would it infuriate the Valle, it would bring Emily back in as an ally."

Patrick was deep in thought.

"It's your call then, Elder," the Chief of Staff said to him.

Patrick nodded. "I know… I'm trying to decide."

"This is absurd! We cannot bring back a banished Council," the Records Keeper said. "It's never been done for a reason."

William sighed, "That child was ripped from her ranch because of heku attacks. She found comfort and protection on Island Coven with Chevalier. Once comfortable, she was torn from her home again and thrown into a palace full of heku that disliked her."

"This isn't our fault," Iuna said.

"She aligned the factions for the first time ever and protected this very faction on numerous occasions."

"She also wiped out this city once."

"Now she's pregnant, scared, abused, and God only knows what she's been through over the last three months. She risked her own life to bring back the heku she cares about."

"We can't do this," Iuna said.

"If we keep her here, she'll be in hiding for the rest of her life. If we let her go back to the Equites, they will continue to abuse her."

"William…"

Patrick squeezed his eyes shut. "Do it."

"No! We can't do this!" Iuna screamed.

"The Elders have voted," the Records Keeper said. "I will log what happens. This has never been documented because it's never been done."

"We should go to the ceremonial room," Patrick said. "It may help in whatever we find."

William nodded. "Let her sleep. This may not work."

The Chief Enforcer stood up. "Let's bring in the palace guards. The Equites aren't going to be happy when they are revived and will first attempt to fight us."

The entire Encala Council was dressed in blue robes except for the

Chief Enforcer, who wore black. Palace guards lined the outside walls of the ceremonial room.

"We will do one at a time. When each is calmed, we'll do another," William said.

The Chief Enforcer nodded and poured out the bag marked 'Damon'.

"What do we do if that is really Damon?" Iuna asked.

William shrugged. "Then re-banish him."

The Chief Enforcer nodded. He pulled the dagger from his pocket, checked to make sure all were ready, and then let one drop of his blood fall to it. The screaming started immediately, and as Quinn formed, he took a defensive posture and scowled at the Encala.

"Listen to us," William said. "We didn't do this to you."

Quinn hissed and scanned those gathered.

"Think back," Iuna said. "You were overpowered by Equites and banished for 600 years."

Quinn tensed and then stood up. "It's been 600 years?"

"No, it's been three months," William explained.

He frowned. "I don't understand."

"Emily brought you to us, at great risk to herself."

"Emily did?"

"Yes"

"Where is she?"

Iuna smiled. "She's resting in her room."

"And the others?"

The Chief Enforcer held up the satchel. "I'm not certain, but I think we have the entire former Council."

"We will explain when we're done," the Chief Interrogator said as he handed Quinn a robe. He slipped it on and then turned just as the Equites Court Reporter was revived and ready to fight.

Kyle was the last of the Equites that was revived. He immediately flew at Iuna and was pinned to the floor by Chevalier and Zohn.

"Calm down," Zohn said to him.

He snarled and fought to get away from him.

"They didn't do it," Chevalier told him, straining to hold Kyle down.

It took a few minutes for Kyle to finally start to calm down, but he was still glaring when Chevalier helped him to his feet and handed him a robe.

"This will be easier in the conference room," William said, and led the way out of the ceremonial room. The 13 revived Equites watched around them carefully, still not sure what was going on.

They all sat down, and it was obvious that the Equites were

confused and leery of their revival.

"So start from the beginning," Zohn said.   "Farlane Coven attacked… with…"

"It was Wells and White River Covens," Quinn said, nodding.

"Yes, well, you were all replaced and banished for 600 years," William explained.

"But it's not been 600 years?" Kyle asked.

"No"

"Where's Emily?" Chevalier asked him.

"We'll get to her," Iuna said. "Equites began to revolt against the new Council, which, of course… is normal when an entire Council is replaced."

"Who were residually banished then?" Zohn asked.

"General Skinner was the first. Thukil decided to back the new Council, so they were safe for a while. The Lords from Harris, Fischer, and Ozark Covens were banished within the first week and replaced with members of Farlane Coven."

Quinn nodded. "Thukil would have shown support. They had Emily."

"Had being the main word there," Patrick told them.

"So where is she?" Chevalier asked again.

"I'm getting there," William said. "Lots of new laws began to come down from the Council, one of which was that your children were to be immediately killed. However, the Council couldn't find them or Emily, for that matter."

"The Equites began to get furious when more and more rules and strict regulations came from the new Council," Iuna explained. "Then… Emily showed up."

"Damnit," Kyle hissed.

"The first we even knew the Equites Council had her was when word came down that because she attempted to steal your ashes, the Council was forced to scatter them because of her."

"Wait… scatter us?" the Equites Chief of Staff said, shocked.

"Yes, you'll have to ask her… but from what she said, Emily had switched you so the new Council no longer worried about her taking you," William said. He smiled softly. "She broke all heku traditions and brought you here to us."

"Why did you revive us?" Chevalier asked.

"Several reasons. First, because she's my friend, and she asked us to."

"And?"

"Fine," Patrick sighed. "The new Council has decided to finish what you started and wipe out the Encala completely."

Chevalier nodded. "Where is she?"

"You have to understand that she came to us like she is," William told him. "We haven't hurt her."

"What do you mean like she is?" Kyle asked.

Quinn sighed, "I can only imagine what she went through to get us out of Council City."

William looked at Iuna and he nodded, so he turned to Patrick, who stood up. "We'll take you to her. We slipped some sleeping pills into her drink to help her sleep. We should be able to talk in the room. The doctor is in there now."

Chevalier's eyes narrowed. "Why does she need a doctor?"

"You understand we didn't hurt her?" Iuna asked.

Chevalier nodded. "Yes, we'll all go see her."

William stood up. "Okay, I'll take you."

A strange heku met them at the door.

"How is she?" William asked.

The heku looked at Chevalier. "We okay to talk here?"

"Yes, he's fine," William told him.

"I don't know how she is. I've never seen a mortal that badly beaten."

"What?!" Chevalier growled.

"We asked her if the Council or Covens did it," William explained. "She just nodded."

"She's not speaking?"

"She spoke some to Lt. Andrew and a little to us."

Chevalier stepped forward and opened her door. He immediately saw her cuddled up against a pillow as she gripped it tightly in her arms. The covers were pulled up to her shoulders, but he was able to see numerous bruises and cuts across her face.

He knelt down and studied her face. "Her scent is gone."

"She told us she's masking," William said. "Go ahead, Doctor. Let them know."

The Encala doctor pulled the blanket down to the foot of the bed, but she didn't stir. "You can see her face. There are many levels of bruises."

Kyle hissed as Chevalier looked her over.

"What I've not seen before are the bruises behind her knees," the doctor said. Quinn and Kyle looked closely at the deep purple and blue bruises. "I've also not seen what happened to her hands."

Chevalier pulled one of her hands away from its grip on the pillow and frowned. "What in the hell happened?"

"I don't know. There are scars, scabs, and fresh lacerations and bruises. It travels up her arms a bit," he explained. "The word proditor

is etched into her back along with the initials B.C., and she has a shoe print bruise on her back and another on her hip."

"Etched?" Kyle whispered. The doctor lifted her t-shirt a bit to expose the word. "Damnit, did the V.E.S. get her again?"

"They wouldn't know what proditor means," Quinn said, slowly getting angrier.

The doctor sighed, "Okay... so... there's something else."

"What?" Chevalier asked softly. He was too busy studying her injuries.

William nodded at the doctor and then gently tugged the pillow that Emily was grasping. When he removed the pillow, her pregnancy became obviously.

"Oh my God," Chevalier whispered.

"Did you know?"

He shook his head.

The doctor swallowed hard. "There's a large bruise across... her stomach."

Chevalier didn't care any longer who saw as he lifted her t-shirt slightly, revealing her bulging middle and a deep black bruise.

"I want to see if the baby's okay," the doctor said.

Chevalier nodded and took Emily's battered hand in his. He studied it carefully while the enemy doctor listened to her stomach.

"I can hear the heartbeat, so whoever hit her didn't kill the baby," the doctor said. "There's no telling if they did damage though, not until the birth."

Chevalier kissed her hand softly and then pulled the covers over her after looking at the bruises behind her knees. "Get ice on her eye."

The doctor nodded and disappeared.

"Who is still supporting the former Council?" Quinn asked William.

"No one that we know. You were scattered, remember?"

"Thukil will back us," Kyle said.

"As will Banks and Samuels," the Chief of Staff said.

"We may get Powan to revolt against their new leader."

"True"

"Never, in the history of our species, has a banished Council reclaimed their position," the Records Keeper said.

"There's a first time for everything," Chevalier said.

"We'll back you," William told him.

"We can't ask that," Zohn said. "You've done enough, and we're thankful that you broke the laws and brought us back."

He smiled. "I didn't do it for you."

Chevalier sat on the side of the bed. "I want to stay with her until she wakes up. Let's contact every Level 3 coven and above, and send

out feelers. Don't tell them we're back. Just have them meet us at our secondary hangar."

Kyle nodded. "I'll start the calls with Thukil."

When the other heku left, Chevalier lowered the blankets again and looked over Emily's injuries himself. He lightly touched her stomach and felt a soft kick against his hand.

He curled up next to her and pulled the blankets up, then shut his eyes and pulled her close. He smiled when he caught a brief glimpse of emotions from her dream, but it didn't escape him that there was a strong fear surrounding her still, stronger than he'd felt before and somewhat masked by a deeper level of aloneness.

Just after noon the following day, he felt her begin to stir, and he lightly kissed the top of her head. Emily's eyes flew open and she jumped out of his grasp, got tangled in the blankets, and fell to the floor.

"It's me, Em," he whispered, and looked over the edge of the bed at her.

Emily's eyes grew wide, and she lunged into his arms and buried her face into his chest. "You're back."

He nodded and held her tighter. "Thanks to you."

Chevalier held her while she cried against his chest. The horrors of the past several months finally came to a close, and she felt safe again in his arms.

She began a frantic rambling against his chest, "You were... they ashed all... you were..."

"I know. It's okay."

"But then no one helped... then William said no... then I'm here and ashes everywhere..."

"Shhh," he whispered, and kissed the top of her head again. "It's okay. I'm back."

Finally, she looked up at him with her one good eye, and he took her hand again and kissed it softly.

"Who did this to you?" he asked, brushing the hair away from her face.

She hugged him again but didn't answer.

"There's going to be a big fight," he told her. "We want our positions back."

Emily nodded.

"I don't want you near the fight, okay?"

He was surprised when she nodded again.

Chevalier smiled softly. "No one has ever stolen the banished ashes of a former Council."

Her green eyes pierced into his soul as she watched him.

"Course... never has anyone ever taken the ashes from a Council to

an enemy for revival."

She frowned.

"It's okay, no one's mad... well... okay, so maybe the new Council." His eyes narrowed when she stiffened. "What did they do?"

When she looked down at her hands, he took one in his and flipped it over to see the bruises along her forearms. "I can't imagine what you've been through for the past three months."

There was a soft knock at the door, and Emily gripped tightly to Chevalier's arm.

"Enter," he called out. The former Equites Council all came in. Kyle pushed past them and pulled her into a tight embrace.

She wrapped her arms around him.

"Way to go, kid," he said, smiling.

Emily started to turn back to Chevalier but ended up being hugged by each of the revived members.

"Leave it to you," Quinn said, hugging her a little too tightly.

"Enough... enough...," Chevalier chuckled. Emily walked over and sat down on the bed beside him.

"Are we going to have to separate you two?" Zohn asked, looking at Emily.

She glanced down at her expanding middle and shrugged as a blush rose to her cheeks.

"I'm starting to think that birth control may not work against a heku," Quinn said as he sat down on a chair in the room.

"Now you tell us," Chevalier sighed, but then grinned.

Zohn sat down and took one of Emily's hands gently in his. "We need to know everything about the Council that you know. I realize it's hard for you to talk, but we have to know what we're up against."

Emily nodded.

Kyle sat beside her on the bed. "The Encala don't know much, so this is all going to rely on how much you can tell us."

"Let's start with who the acting Elders are," Zohn said.

Emily swallowed hard and then spoke in hushed tones, "Kirt and Neal."

"No third?"

"Yes, he sits by Neal, but I don't know his name."

"What does he look like?"

She smiled crookedly. "He's tall and muscular, brown hair, beard and mustache."

Quinn chuckled. "She just described 2/3 of the heku."

"Wait," Emily said, and she shut her eyes to concentrate. "He has a tattoo... or maybe it's a scar... on his nose that runs under his left eye."

Kyle nodded. "That's Lenol, from Nova Coven."

"Do you know any of the other Council members?" Quinn asked as he leaned forward on his elbows.

"Not really."

"Do you know if anyone is unhappy with the new Council?"

"Yes, lots are."

Quinn sighed, "Do you know who has been banished?"

Her chin quivered slightly. "Mark..."

Kyle smiled. "We'll get him back."

She nodded and then thought. "General Skinner has been, Lord Dexter, and the Ozark Lord, Sand or Sandy something, and another that starts with an L."

"Litation maybe?"

"Yes, that's it. They have all been banished. Dr. Edwards too because he..." Emily turned pained eyes to Chevalier. "He was trying to protect me."

Chevalier nodded. "It's okay. We'll get him back."

"We're a little confused as to why the entire heku population thinks we were scattered," the Chief of Staff said.

Emily sighed, "The Council warned that if I ever tried to get the banished former Council out of Council City, they would be forced to scatter the ashes. So I went in and switched you all with prisoners I knew. That way, when I was caught and they were scattered, they wouldn't suspect that I would still try to free you."

Kyle smiled. "That's brilliant."

"Who did they scatter then?" Zohn asked.

"Well, Ingram and Selhman, Damon, David, Vaughn, Samuel, Dustin, and a few others that I have heard you talk about," she said. "Am I in trouble for them being scattered?"

"No, it's okay," Quinn said. "What did they do to your hands?"

Emily looked down at the massive cuts on her hands and then simply shrugged.

"What about the back of your knees?" Kyle asked softly.

She didn't look up but whispered, "I can't..."

"It's okay," Chevalier told her. "We'll work all of that out later."

"We'll wait for you down stairs, Chevalier," Quinn said as the Council left.

Chevalier nodded and then turned back to Emily. "I want you to do me a favor."

She looked up at him.

"Promise me you'll stay here with the Encala until I come for you, okay?"

Emily nodded.

"This fight is going to be nasty, and I don't want you involved in

any way."

"I know."

He smiled. "You'll be okay here. The Valle have no idea where you are and neither does the current Council."

She kissed him softly, and he touched her cheek lightly before leaving her alone and heading down to the others.

"So far we have Banks, Island, Thukil, Powan, Yearings, Miller, and Pilot Covens coming. They believe that they are coming to protect Council City from a Valle attack," Kyle explained.

"How did you get by Powan?" Quinn asked.

"I spoke to General Skinner's next in command and told him if they can get away from their current Lord, we may hand the General back to them."

Zohn nodded. "We won't know if the people from the city will help the current Council or not. They are going to be too confused at first."

William, who sat silently until now, stepped forward. "They will back you. The current Council is vindictive, demanding, and selfish. From what we've heard, the city wants nothing to do with them and is just biding their time until someone replaces them."

"The Equites covens are also very angry at Emily," Elder Iuna added.

Chevalier frowned. "Why is that?"

"She had you scattered, and it was rumored that she was doing the punishments for the new Council."

"She must not have been if they labeled her a traitor," Kyle told him.

Iuna shrugged.

"It is rumored that your entire Cavalry has been imprisoned," William said. "It might behoove you to let them free."

"Let's head out," Quinn said. "The Encala have lent us a vehicle, and we should be at the staging location by tomorrow morning."

Chapter 5

"They didn't say anything but to wait here," Thukil's Captain Darren said to the hundreds of gathered heku.

The highest ranking from Island Coven sighed, "Great."

Tensions were high. No one wanted to be there to support the new Council, but it was their duty as Equites to serve whoever was leading.

Lord Banks turned toward the road. "I hear them coming. It's odd that they ask to meet us here."

"Yeah it is," Darren said. "Line up!"

The heku formed perfect rows of 50 and were standing full at attention when Chevalier appeared before them.

"Oh my God!" Lord Banks gasped.

"It... how?" the Island Coven General whispered, shocked.

Chevalier put his hands up. "Listen to me before you decide to attack us."

Kyle joined him, followed shortly by the other 11 members of the former Council.

"We were told you had been banished and scattered," Lord Banks said, still in shock.

"You were told what the Council thought," Kyle said. "Emily risked her life to get us out of Council City, and now... we want our places back."

"She did?" Lord Banks whispered.

Chevalier's eyes narrowed at the nervous way Lord Banks spoke. "Yes, she did. If it weren't for her, we wouldn't be here, and you'd be stuck with those idiots running things."

Captain Darren smiled. "Let's go then."

"We need to know what the city has for defenses," Chevalier said. "Does anyone know?"

"They imprisoned your Cavalry," one of the Powans said. "They were replaced by the entire coven from Orion Coven."

"Orion... little experience but a lot of them," the Records Keeper said.

Chevalier nodded. "This is not going to be a good fight. It's not often that we have to do battle with our own."

"Those aren't us...," one of the Powans hissed. "Let's take care of them and return General Skinner."

"Why don't we bring Lady Emily in to wipe out the entire palace?" a Thukil Lieutenant suggested.

Chevalier sighed, "Not only is she very pregnant, but she's been severely abused and beaten. Right now, I want her to stay safely away from the fight."

Lord Banks took a step back and watched the ground.

"We need one team to focus on getting the Cavalry out of the prison," Kyle called out. "I want Banks Team 4 to do that."

"Yes, Elder," one of Banks' Captains called out.

"We can't banish the current Council until their Chief Enforcer has fallen," Kyle reminded them. "As much as I hate to say this... kill them."

Moods lightened, and an excitement replaced the earlier tension.

"Do we have any covens completely against us?" Zohn asked them.

"Farlane, of course. Nova is also," Darren reported. "I heard that Ontario and Glenwood Covens have already been accepted into the Valle, but I suspect they will return when you do."

Chevalier nodded. "We'll deal with that later. We're going to re-work the laws on a lot of this."

Darren smiled. "Sounds like Lady Emily already did."

Chevalier chuckled and then turned to Zohn.

"Alright, who has a level Omega reconnaissance team?" Quinn asked.

A Powan Commander stepped forward. "We do, Elder. They are all here."

"Then you go in first."

The Commander nodded.

Chevalier looked over the hundreds of anxious faces and then nodded. "Let's go."

***

Chevalier bent low and looked over at the gates to Council City. "I don't know them."

Zohn shook his head. "I don't either. I'm guessing they are from Farlane."

"Kill them," Kyle ordered. Within seconds, Powan had quickly disposed of the four gate guards and then immediately fallen back into the protection of the trees.

"We don't know what's going to happen when we get into the city," Zohn reminded them. "Listen for orders and kill as few members of the city as you can."

Chevalier held up one hand, and as he slowly lowered it into a fist, the entire army with the former Council began to move en masse into Council City.

The city alarm sounded shortly after they began blurring through the streets. They met little resistance and weren't shocked to find that very few of the city members even acknowledged they were there. What

guards they came across were young and inexperienced, and easily dispatched.

When the hundreds came to the palace lawn, they were met with an ominous looking army of angry looking heku.

Elder Kirt stepped forward, obviously furious. "How have you returned?!"

"You were outsmarted by a mortal," Zohn said with a grin. "Now it's time to hand us back our places."

"We will not! You have been banished and are therefore no longer Equites!"

"Wanna bet?" Kyle asked, and rushed at him. The second Kyle and Kirt began to fight, the rest of the heku blurred into a cloud of furious fighting.

Growls and snarls filled the night, and as heku began to fall in bloody heaps, no one was sure who was winning. The noises caught the attention of the city, and from what the former Council could tell, most of them had joined their side and were fighting the current Equites leadership.

"Tous pour un!" Kralen yelled as he dove head-first into the fight.

Chevalier chuckled and then slammed his elbow into a heku at his back. As the heku fell to the ground unconscious, Chevalier quickly removed his head and then grabbed his torso and threw it hard at several heku attacking Silas.

Zohn, Quinn, and Chevalier met up after almost an hour of fighting to ascertain what was happening. From what they could see, their side had pulled far ahead, but the current Council could no longer be seen.

"A helicopter did take off," Zohn said, scanning the skies.

"It's just odd to leave after joining a fight," Quinn told him.

"They are cowards. What can I say?"

Chevalier blurred quickly over to help a member of the Cavalry who currently had four heku on him at once. The Elder grabbed the closest one and slammed his head into another one, sending both unconscious to the ground. Once there, he quickly dismembered them and then turned to fight another but found only allies.

Zohn looked around. "None are left?"

Silas blurred up. "Permission to take a team into the palace?"

"Granted," Quinn said.

Silas, Kralen, and 50 members of the Cavalry disappeared inside. The others waited for word on what was left, and it was an hour later when Kralen returned.

"No one's in there but servants," he said. "We've gathered everyone into the Great Hall... oh... and Kyle, this is yours."

Kralen handed the Equites dagger over. "Seems their Chief Enforcer

left it at his desk when he fled."

Kyle smiled and slipped it back into his pocket. "I'll need that."

"Just make sure Em didn't mix up anyone else, or you could revive the entire banished population," Zohn said with a grin.

"Where is she?" Kralen asked, suddenly very serious.

"She's okay," Chevalier said. "She's with the Encala right now."

Silas' eyes fell. "She was…"

"We know… well… most of it. We'll find the rest later."

"The baby then?" Kralen asked.

"We don't know. Someone hit her in the stomach pretty hard, but a doctor said we won't know until after the birth if anything happened."

"Did you know?"

Chevalier shook his head. "No, I didn't."

"Let's go deal with the servants," Zohn said.

"I really don't know if I can start reviving," Kyle said. "What if she mixed up more ashes?"

"Take Silas and Horace," Chevalier said. "Revive Mark first, and if it's not Mark, re-banish and we'll wait for Emily."

"Sounds like a plan," Kyle said as he headed inside with the two heku following.

Chevalier's blood was pumping as he walked in to face the servants. The rest of the Council was tense and ready, alert for anything amiss. They knew it was going to take time to weed out who supported the new Council and who might have helped with their banishment.

As the Council took their seats, Quinn grabbed a baseball bat from beside his chair and held it up. "They played baseball?"

Zohn shrugged. "Who knows."

Chevalier picked up a thick iron rod. "What is this?"

The Chief Interrogator looked over. "That's an odd thing to have in here."

"See those?" the Court Reporter asked, and then looked over at shackles on the wall.

Chevalier shook his head. "We have a lot to learn."

"Let's hope we can find someone who knows something," Zohn said.

Kyle came in a few minutes later. "We've had to re-banish Boris. He was buried in Mark's banishment sight."

Quinn nodded. "We'll talk to Emily later and find out her method."

"We did find Derrick though," Kyle said, and turned when their door guard walked in.

Quinn studied his stiff movements. "How long were you with the new Council before being banished?"

Derrick bowed slightly. "Only a few weeks."

"What is this?" Chevalier asked, holding up the metal rod.

"I don't know, Elder."

"This?" Quinn asked, motioning to the baseball bat.

Derrick sighed, "That was used by the Council to force Lady Emily to kneel."

"How?"

"They hit the back of her knees with it."

Kyle hissed, "That explains the bruises there."

"Make a full written report of everything that happened," Zohn told him.

Derrick nodded and then disappeared.

"How do we find out about the servants?" the Chief Investigator asked.

"We have a problem," Chevalier said. "It is heku rule that they had to serve the new Council. How can we punish them for following heku tradition?"

"We can't, really," Zohn said.

"Same thing with the covens."

"Except for those that abandoned the Equites and joined the Valle."

Quinn nodded. "Even though we agree with why they did it, we need to take into consideration that it was traitorous to do."

"So, we don't punish the servants for doing as they are told to do from turning," Zohn said.

Chevalier shrugged. "I guess I agree. I do want to know if they helped with the takeover though."

"True"

"Right now, I suggest a complete coven lockdown," the Chief of Defense said. "Until we can ascertain which covens are stable and which are going to fall apart over this, we need to lock them down to prevent rumors and panic."

"Do it," Zohn told him. "Lock down every coven until further notice."

The Chief of Defense nodded and disappeared.

Quinn's nose wrinkled and he looked around. "This room stinks."

"It kind of does. How odd is that?" Zohn asked, looking around.

"It has a different feel."

"That too."

Kyle stood up. "I'm going to call Em and see if I can find out her pattern in the banishment room."

When Quinn nodded, he disappeared.

The Records Keeper shook his head. "These new laws passed down are insane. They forbid any Equites from going into donor bars. They said it's beneath an Equites to beg for food."

"Since when is a donor bar begging? We pay them," Chevalier said.

He shrugged. "They also can't petition to turn a mortal until that mortal has lived in the coven for a year."

Quinn gasped. "We have mortals living with our covens?"

"I don't show any have done it yet."

"Anything else come down from them?"

The Records Keeper kept looking through files. "Lots of little stuff. Those are the only big things."

The Court Reporter frowned. "I have some death warrants."

"Do we even want to know?" Quinn asked.

"I guess it's no surprise that Allen, Alexis, and Dain are on the top of the list."

"Not surprising at all," Chevalier said. "I wonder where they are."

"I bet Em knows."

"Thukil was set to be wiped out."

"Anyone else?"

"Looks like Lady Kim was on the chopping block, and Lord Jay."

"What did Lady Kim do?" Quinn asked.

"Kim Coven refused to answer a call from the Council for the entire coven to move to Council City and become new staff servants."

"Forced?"

"Yes"

"Okay, what else are you reading in there?" Zohn asked.

The Court Reporter thumbed through papers. "Lord Dexter was banished. Says here that Emily was supposed to do it, but she refused."

Silas led 92 members of the Cavalry into the trial area. "This is all that's left, other than Mark."

"What happened to the rest of you?" Chevalier asked.

Horace stepped forward. "Most were killed during the initial attack, defending the Council."

"Buried where?"

"Mass grave out back," Horace explained. "We were told they were to have no services."

"Rebury them with honors in the graveyard."

"Yes, Elder."

"For now, I want you out in the city," Zohn said. "Put the city into lockdown. No one is to set foot out of their homes until we re-secure our positions here."

"Yes, Elder," Horace said, and then left with the Cavalry.

"Silas, Kralen, wait," Zohn said.

They all looked over when Kyle walked in. "Okay, Emily told me her pattern, and I should be able to start reviving."

"Take Silas and Kralen, just in case."

Kyle chuckled and walked out with them.

"I need to go get Em back here," Chevalier said, standing up. "I don't trust her with the Encala."

Zohn looked up at him. "It could still be too dangerous."

"Let's wait a week," Quinn said. "At least make sure there are no skirmishes."

Chevalier sighed, "You're right. I'll call them."

"They won't hurt her."

"I know. I just want her with me."

***

"Sir?" Mark asked, looking back at Chevalier.

"It's okay," he said. "I can understand why they are nervous."

Mark nodded and watched as the Encala palace guards surrounded them. "Keep an eye on the Elder."

The twelve members of the Cavalry nodded and fell into formation.

When they were escorted into the Encala council chambers, Chevalier walked up. "We've come to take her back."

William nodded and turned to an Encala General. "Take him up to Emily. She's in the middle of a massage."

"Massage?"

"Yes, we've given her a team of heku to make sure she's taken care of."

"Interesting," Chevalier said as he followed the General out. Mark tried to go too, and after a brief argument, was allowed go to with while the rest of the Cavalry waited in the council chambers.

Outside of a door on the third floor, the heku knocked softly and Lt. Andrew stepped out. "What?"

"Elder said he can see the Lady," the General said.

Lt. Andrew scrutinized Chevalier. "She's asleep."

Chevalier frowned. "We won't wake her."

Lt. Andrew nodded and then stepped aside. Chevalier and Mark walked in and looked around the room. Emily was asleep face-down on a massage table with a bulky female masseuse massaging the muscles in her back.

Chevalier walked over and saw the shoe print bruise on her back was fading, and the carved 'proditor' on her back was covered with bandages. Her elbows, wrists, knees, and ankles were all bound with braces, and her hands were tightly wrapped with bandages.

"Elder?" Mark whispered.

Chevalier looked over at a bath tub set into the floor and frowned. "What is that?"

"Mud," Mark said, amused.

Chevalier scanned the room carefully and then studied everything he found. Off beside the mud bath was a pedicure and manicure station, a miniature hair salon, and small fridge full of juice.

When Chevalier turned back, he noticed Lt. Andrew standing beside Emily's bed, and his hands were tightened into fists.

"She shouldn't be on her stomach," Chevalier whispered to the masseuse.

"It's a maternity table," she said as she moved up to Emily's neck.

Chevalier nodded and then looked over when the door opened. It was obvious that the heku was waiting for Mark and Chevalier to leave.

They both followed the palace guards down to the council chambers and stepped in.

"That's an interesting room," Mark said.

William shrugged. "She needs a lot of help right now, and we felt it best to get a team over her care. Things in her room were suggested by members of the team."

Chevalier crossed his arms. "Why exactly does she need a team?"

Elder Patrick looked at him. "It started with the need to address some of her physical concerns."

"Such as?"

"Such as recovery from after-effects of time on the rack."

Chevalier frowned. "Who put her on the rack?"

"Equites did."

He growled slightly, so Mark spoke, "What else?"

"Our psychiatrist said she's still mentally frail, and the incidents with the Equites made things worse. We have taken precautions to make her as comfortable here as possible," William explained.

"I want to see this... team," Chevalier said.

William nodded and called out. "Bring in Lady Emily's team, please."

Chevalier watched as eight heku entered and stood beside them in a neat row.

"Introduce yourselves," William said.

"I'm a physician," the first heku said. "I've overseen her injuries and am consulted on everything the others do."

The second heku stepped forward. "I'm an Obstetrician. I've been making sure we're doing all we can to help the pregnancy."

The Masseuse nodded. "I'm Lady Emily's Masseuse. Right now, I'm working on relieving pain from her time on the rack and hanging from shackles."

"I'm the chef," another said. "That one is straight forward, but I worked as a nutritionist, and we are focusing on pregnancy friendly

foods."

Chevalier just watched them closely when another heku stepped forward. "I'm the Physical Therapist. She has a lot of pain in her joints from the rack, but she was pushed around a lot and has residual muscular-skeletal trauma."

"Which is where I come in," a shorter heku said. "I'm a Chiropractor and work with the Physical Therapist."

"I do facials, manicures, and pedicures," a younger heku woman said with a smile. "I also do her hair when she allows."

"She's said yes to that?" Mark asked.

She smiled broadly. "Yes, almost every day."

"That's odd," Chevalier mumbled.

"I'm her tailor," another heku said, and glanced over at William before falling back into the line.

Mark frowned. "This is all necessary?"

Elder Iuna nodded. "Yes, it is. We have done all we can to alleviate any pain or emotional trauma."

Chevalier's eyes narrowed. "This is all of her team?"

"No, Lt. Andrew has been reassigned to her."

Chevalier turned to Elder Iuna. "Why?"

"He has one single task… to protect her."

"So he's just a guard?"

"No, there's more. If the Encala is ever attacked or taken over, Lt. Andrew's job is to get her to safety and stay with her, so she's never alone."

"He's become close to her, and once we forbid him from telling anyone anything she said, even the Council, she opened up to him and has told him about her three months with the new Council."

Chevalier glared. "I want to know."

"No, she needed someone to talk to that she can trust. We won't betray that by telling you what she said to Lt. Andrew in confidence. He never leaves her side."

The psychiatrist waited for permission from the Elder to speak and then stepped forward. "She's comforted by his presence."

"She's changed," Elder Iuna said.

Mark looked at him. "How so?"

"She's quiet, reserved, almost timid."

He nodded. "Yes, we knew that."

"She's relaxed a lot over the two weeks with us," William explained.

"She's awake," Iuna said. "When she's dressed, she'll come down to see you."

They waited in silence, and it wasn't until bare feet padded

unevenly against the stone stairs that they turned to the door of the trial area.

Chevalier gasped when he saw Emily. She peeked out around Lt. Andrew, and he saw her red hair was pulled away from her face and cascaded down her back in soft ringlets. When she stepped into the room, the heku were silent and her bare feet were all that could be heard.

Mark watched, shocked, as she appeared in a floor-length red babydoll made out of layers and layers of soft, flowing material which accentuated her growing middle. A richly embellished ruby necklace was around her neck, and she looked up at Lt. Andrew before following him into the trial area.

Emily moved forward and into Chevalier's arms. He looked questioningly over at Mark, who just shrugged, not sure what was going on. Emily's team of specialists moved out of the room, and she pulled away and looked back at Lt. Andrew.

Chevalier reached down and gently took a bandaged hand, but Emily gasped and didn't even see when Lt. Andrew blurred into Chevalier and pushed him back.

"Don't touch her hands!" he yelled.

Chevalier snarled and blurred toward him, but Emily stepped between them with her back to Lt. Andrew and her hands out to Chevalier.

Members of the Council descended into the trial area and restrained both of them.

"Don't tell me how to treat my own wife," Chevalier hissed.

"Then don't hurt her," Andrew yelled back, still struggling to get out from the tight grasp of the heku.

"Calm down!" William shouted.

Chevalier and Lt. Andrew both looked up at him.

Lt. Andrew angrily shrugged off the hands of the Council and walked over to stand behind Emily. She looked over at Chevalier and then back at Andrew before walking over to him.

Mark frowned and moved closer to his Elder.

"Lt. Andrew has taken her safety personally," Iuna explained. "It'll be best if everyone calm down, and we start over."

Chevalier looked down at Emily. "Are you ready to go home?"

She looked over at Lt. Andrew when he spoke, "I'm not sure she wants to go back."

"How would you know that?"

Lt. Andrew shrugged. "Just saying."

"Do you not want to go back?" Chevalier asked her.

Emily looked along the Encala Council and shrugged.

"Why not?"

"She's more than welcome to stay here for as long as she needs," Patrick said.

"Why don't you want to go back?" Chevalier whispered.

Emily leaned her head against his chest and looked at Mark.

"If I were her, I wouldn't go back either," Lt. Andrew snapped.

"Shut up!" Mark yelled, and then tried to get to Lt. Andrew but was held back by two palace guards.

Lt. Andrew looked him in the eyes. "Just saying that if you knew what I know… you may not even want her back among the Equites."

"Meaning?" Chevalier asked.

He shrugged. "Take it how you will."

"Dear, your lunch is ready," the Chief of Staff said to Emily.

She looked up at Chevalier, and he smiled. "Go eat. It's okay."

Lt. Andrew moved in behind her when she left the trial area.

"Is there some reason she's dressed like that?" Chevalier asked angrily. "She hates being what she calls heku Barbie."

"She has many clothes to pick from," William explained. "I don't know why she chose that, but she's pretty much chosen dresses during her stay. That's something else we realize has changed."

He frowned. "She chose that?"

"Yes"

"Was she offered anything else?"

"Yes, she has many jeans and overalls… she chose the dress."

"Jewels too?"

"That was a gift from Lt. Andrew," Patrick said.

Chevalier's eyes narrowed. "When she's done eating, we're taking her back with us."

Elder Iuna tapped a pen against the desk. "Unless she doesn't want to."

"If she doesn't, it's because you've done something to make her fear the Equites."

"We did nothing. The fear was there before she came to us," William said.

"Why would she fear the Equites? The Council that caused all of this is gone."

William shrugged. "I don't know that either. Lt. Andrew is the only one she's told."

"Then order him to tell me."

"I won't do that. Emily needs a confidant that she can trust."

"Right," Chevalier said, irritated. "Someone who won't leave her alone."

"She was terrified," William said softly. "She came to us completely hopeless and fearful. She was alone with the ashes of her

loved ones, and she was utterly lost."

Chevalier could feel her emotions, and his heart sank at how much less her fear was with the Encala than when she lived with the Equites.

"Where is she?" Chevalier asked.

"She's in her room eating."

"With Lt. Andrew?"

"Yes"

"Back him off. I want to speak to my wife alone."

William nodded. "We can arrange that."

Chevalier headed out with a palace guard, with Mark following.

Lt. Andrew met them at the door. "Don't upset her."

Chevalier's eyes narrowed. "Are you falling for her?"

Lt. Andrew glared at him and took up a post outside of her door. Mark watched him and stood to his side when Chevalier went into the room.

He shut the door behind him and was immediately attacked by two puppies, one pulling on each pant leg. He looked down and shook off the dogs before walking over to Emily, who was at the table.

Chevalier sat down. "Cute dogs."

Emily looked over at the two puppies and nodded.

"You've been talking to Andrew?"

She nodded again.

"Why do I get the silent treatment?"

"You don't," she whispered. When she set down her fork, she relaxed her bandaged hands on the table.

Chevalier very tenderly took her hand. "What did they do to your hands?"

"It doesn't matter," she said, pulling her hand out of his.

"It matters to me."

Emily picked up his hand and pressed it against her cheek. "I don't know where to go."

"Why can't you come back with me?"

"I can't."

"Tell me why."

She shook her head and then kissed his hand softly before putting it back down on the table.

Chevalier reached down and picked up one of the puppies that was chewing on his pants. He held up the white and brown ball of fur and looked it in the face. "What is this?"

"St. Bernard"

"And the other one?" he asked, looking over as the other puppy collapsed on a rug by the fire.

"Bulldog"

He nodded and put the St. Bernard down. "So you've decided to stay with the Encala?"

"No"

"What do you want to do?"

"I don't know," she said, looking around the room.

"The hostile Council is gone."

She nodded.

"They hurt you. We know that."

Emily looked at him.

"Did others?"

"Chev," she whispered. "It's not worth it anymore."

"If it's keeping you away from the Equites, then it's worth it to tell me."

Emily looked down and a tear fell down her cheek. "They thought I killed you."

"Yes, the former Council made sure the covens hated you."

"They were my family."

"Were? Em, tell me what happened."

She put her bandaged hands on the table. "This was the Council."

He nodded. "That and the bruises when they forced you to kneel."

Emily nodded.

"The foot bruises?"

She swallowed hard and looked up at him.

"The hand bruise on your arm?"

She shook her head.

"So tell me why you don't want to come back to the Equites then. The Council is gone."

"Please, let me stay here for a while."

"Just tell me why."

"It's over."

Chevalier lifted her chin, so she was looking at him. "You really want to stay here?"

"For a while."

"Are they being nice to you?"

She smiled and nodded.

He reached down and again pulled his pants out of the St. Bernard puppy's mouth. "How about I give you a week, so you can think things over and then you come back to Council City."

Emily thought for a moment and then nodded. "Okay."

He smiled. "You look amazing."

She looked down at her dress and then lightly touched the ruby necklace.

"He likes you," Chevalier said.

Emily shook her head. "Not like that."

"Watch him."

"He's my friend."

Chevalier kissed her softly. "I'll be back in a week."

She nodded and then picked up the St. Bernard, though even as a puppy, she had a hard time carrying his weight.

"Em," Lt. Andrew hissed, and took the dog from her. "I told you, Sebastian is too big for you to carry."

Mark smiled at her. "Coming home, kiddo?"

"She's staying for another week," Chevalier said, closely watching her with Lt. Andrew.

It was obvious the Lieutenant was checking her over carefully for new injuries, which infuriated Chevalier. Mark saw the interaction and took the Elder's shoulder. "Let's go."

Chevalier growled softly and then left with Mark. He gunned the rental car, and they were soon taking off in Equites 1.

"Something happened," Chevalier said to Mark.

"Something the Council did?"

"I suspect something else… maybe city residents or palace guards."

"She said that?"

"No, she's pretty open about what the Council did. However, there are more injuries that aren't accounted for."

"Proditor?"

"That… and I am going to Banks when we get back."

"You think the carved BC is for Banks?" Mark asked.

Chevalier shrugged. "I'm not sure. I do know Lord Banks was acting strangely when he first saw us."

"What do you do if he did do something to Emily?"

"I don't know. If what she was accused of was true, she would be a traitor."

"If," Mark said, irritated.

Chevalier sighed, "I'm afraid we're going to find out that most of our loyal covens tried to avenge us."

Mark nodded. "Which is their right, I guess."

"Five minutes, Elder," the pilot called back.

Chevalier nodded, and as soon as the helicopter was set down, he walked past the line of gathered guards and into the palace. When he sat with the Council, he turned to the Court Reporter. "Have Lord Banks come to the palace immediately."

He nodded and disappeared to make the call.

"Is Em up in the room?" Kyle asked, standing up.

"No, she's staying with the Encala," Chevalier replied. It was obvious that he wasn't happy about the idea.

"Why would she stay?"

"She's not saying, and Lt. Andrew isn't divulging what she's telling him either."

"She's talking to him?"

"Yes, apparently he knows everything that happened. She's completely opened up to him."

Quinn frowned. "So, have their Council force him to tell you."

"They won't. Her psychiatrist said she needs a trusted confidant."

"They got her a psychiatrist?"

"Doctor, psychiatrist, obstetrician, tailor, manicurist, pedicurist, beautician, chef, masseuse…"

"We get the idea," Kyle said. He sighed, "So she fell for it, and she's staying?"

"Something Andrew said has me curious," Chevalier told him. "He said that if I knew what he does, I wouldn't want Emily back with the Equites either."

The Court Reporter sat down and frowned before turning to the Elders. "Lord Banks was already on his way. His secretary said that he, Lord Clark, and a representative from Island Coven are all on their way to turn themselves over to the Council."

"Why?" Zohn asked, shocked.

"She didn't say. They should be here any moment though."

"Who from Island Coven?" Kyle asked.

"Marsden"

"You revived Storm, right?" Chevalier asked.

"Yes, she was banished after only a few days… when the Council went looking for Allen," Kyle explained.

"Did you ask her where the kids are?" Zohn asked.

Chevalier shook his head. "No. I want to find out why she's afraid of the Equites before I push for the kids' location."

Derrick stepped in. "Sir, Lord Banks, Lord Clark, and General Marsden are here to speak to you."

Zohn turned to face the trial area. "Let them in."

The Council watched the three heku come into the room and stand nervously in front of the Council.

"We came for punishment," Lord Banks said with lowered eyes.

"Why exactly would we punish you?" Quinn asked.

Lord Clark looked up. "Because of what we did to Lady Emily."

"We're ashamed of what we did," Marsden said. "We should have known better and not…"

"Let's just get it out in the open that Emily isn't talking right now, and we have no idea what all was done to her other than what the former Council did," Chevalier explained.

Lord Banks sighed, "I'll start then."

"Go ahead."

"Lady Emily came to Banks Coven on her motorcycle. We... we were told by the Council that it was her fault you were killed and then we heard that she had started to do the Council's bidding in punishing heku."

"So she came to you for what?" Quinn asked.

"She asked us for help," Lord Banks said softly.

"Did you help her?"

"No, Elder. We... we imprisoned her and... well we... proditor was us," he said, barely above a whisper.

Chevalier nodded. "So the B.C. was you. What else?"

"My guards threatened to cut the baby out of her because..."

"They what?!"

"Sir... we thought she had... we... we didn't know the baby was yours."

Chevalier growled low, and when he started to stand, Zohn put a hand on his shoulder. "Let's hear this."

"Go ahead," Quinn said.

"She was pushed around a bit before she turned some to ash and got away," Lord Banks explained.

Marsden addressed Chevalier, "That's when she came to Island Coven."

"What did you do?" Chevalier hissed.

The heku looked up at his Coven Lord and swallowed hard. "She came to seek help. When the pier guards saw she held the ashes from Damon, one of them threw her back onto the ferry and ordered the Captain to return her."

Kyle hissed, "Island Coven has always been a safe haven for her."

"Well, we were told the same as Banks Coven. We told her that Chevalier was no longer the Coven Lord, and therefore, she was no longer welcome," Marsden said.

Lord Clark stepped forward. "I believe that's when she came to me."

Chevalier nodded, deep in thought.

"She said again that she needed help. Tried to tell me that you hadn't been scattered, but I called her a traitor and told her we wouldn't listen to her lies," Lord Clark said.

Kyle sunk his head into his hands. "The faction turned on her."

Zohn watched the Coven Lords. "She's shown nothing but devotion and loyalty to this faction, yet one rumor and she's immediately brandished a traitor and an enemy."

"That must be why she went to the Encala," Kyle said, irritated.

"Why even try another Equites coven when three that she felt would help her all turned her away."

Chevalier nodded. "We already know that Thukil wasn't exactly mean to her but did assume she would turn them to ash and were rude. By this time, she didn't know any other covens to go to."

"Elder…," Lord Banks whispered. "I'll take the punishment. We thought she had turned on you."

The Coven Liaison Officer finally spoke, "I don't see how we can punish them for this. They did nothing more than what is done traditionally in this incident."

Chevalier nodded. "I know that. It's just hard because now… the faction she's always considered herself a part of, proved Salazar's point that we would turn on her eventually."

Kyle spoke angrily. "We punish them! She came to them for help, and as part of this Council, she should have been granted the common courtesy extended to all of us!"

"She was a traitor," Zohn told him. "At least, that's what they were told."

Chevalier shook his head. "How can I ask her to come back now? She's always told me she was afraid what would happen if I were to die. I assured her that the Equites would take care of her, even if I weren't around."

"It wasn't just your death," Lord Clark said. "We were told that she was being used by the Council to turn innocent heku to ash."

Quinn's voice was sharp as he spoke, "They tried… she was severely beaten for refusing to banish Thukil. Servants said she refused to turn Lord Dexter to ash and was punished for that also."

"We didn't know."

"My own Coven," Chevalier whispered as he watched his hands.

"We're out of the picture for a month and you turn on the Coven Lord's wife!" Kyle screamed. "I'm ready to banish all of you and start over!"

Marsden gasped. "We…"

"We know," Chevalier told him. He turned to the other Elders. "I can't ask her to come back here."

"We can't leave her with the Encala," Zohn said.

"Why not? They have taken better care of her than we did! She has an entire team dedicated to making sure she has everything she could ever want. She's comfortable enough with them to dress feminine again."

"She is?" Kyle asked, surprised.

"Yes. She has puppies and a friend that she can confide in. A friend who is assigned to make sure if the Encala are destroyed, that

she's not alone."

"She was very much alone," the Chief Interrogator said. "I can only imagine how isolated she felt when the Equites not only refused to help her but threatened and abused her instead."

"We will take the punishment," Marsden said. "We've come to turn ourselves in."

"Go back to your covens," Quinn told them. The three bowed and left the trial area.

"I don't know what to do," Chevalier said, looking over at Kyle.

"I wouldn't come back either!"

"It's not their faults," Zohn told them.

"It is! They didn't have to threaten to cut her apart, or hit her, or cut her... if they had just listened, they could have saved us themselves without involving the Encala."

"I wouldn't come back either. She's always trusted us and considered us friends. Now though... now we've turned on her," Chevalier said.

"She's not going to want to be away from you though," Zohn said. "So she's not going to stay with the Encala, no matter how comfortable her life is there."

Chevalier was deep in thought for almost an hour before he nodded. "Get Exavior's old house cleaned up and livable."

"Good idea," Quinn said, nodding.

Kyle added. "Replace her Rubicon and Dodge Ram. Put them in the garage. Hell, even replace that ugly Aero."

"It'll be a bit before we can get it ready," the Chief of Staff said. "I'll send a team over. It's been boarded up for almost seven years."

"Do it," Chevalier said. "They have a week to make it ready for Emily to move into."

"Do we get her a team?" Kyle asked.

"No, just bring Lori back from Dover, and we'll resume her panel," Chevalier said.

"Have we revived all of the missing?" the Chief Investigator asked.

Kyle smiled. "No, we're still missing Lord Dexter. She assures us she can find him when she returns."

"Does Powan know that Dustin has been scattered?" the Coven Liaison Officer asked.

"No, I see no reason to tell them."

"We're still missing Garrett," Kyle said. "Silas said that he wasn't on the roster because he was away with Alexis for a while. The new Council didn't know he was Cavalry, so he was ordered to stay with Alex."

"So where are they now?" Quinn asked.

"No one knows."

"I do feel better knowing that Garrett is with her," Chevalier said. "He's new and inexperienced but still a trained guard."

"I would imagine Emily knows where they are."

"Let's hope so."

Chapter 6

"Yes, we'll tell her you're here," Patrick said to Chevalier.

He nodded and waited for someone to bring Emily. He glanced at Kyle and Mark and then back to the Council.

William took a message and then looked at Chevalier. "She'll be a moment. She was out bowling with some of the guards and wants to change."

Kyle's eyes grew wide. "She was out in public, bowling?"

"No, we have a bowling alley in the main guard house."

Chevalier frowned. "She's in the main guard barracks?"

"She'll be okay."

"Should she even be bowling?" Mark asked.

William shrugged. "Her team was consulted, and she was approved. Their only concern was her hands, but we were assured she wouldn't put her fingers in the bowling ball."

"Bowling?" Kyle asked Chevalier.

He shrugged.

"She's speaking freely again," William told them.

"She is?" Chevalier was shocked.

"Yes, she and Andrew had a conversation about her silence, and she's begun to open up more and even speaks freely with this Council."

When Emily finally came in, she shocked them by wearing a fitted, floor-length, black slip dress. She was again wearing black jewels, and her hair was curly and fell softly around her face.

She moved quickly and wrapped her arms around Chevalier as he hugged her but watched Lt. Andrew, who came in with her.

"Can we have a private conference room?" Kyle asked the Encala Council.

"Yes, Lieutenant, show them please," Patrick ordered.

Lt. Andrew nodded and then walked out the door, followed by Emily and the Equites. When the Equites sat down, they were surprised when Lt. Andrew sat down beside Emily.

"This is private," Kyle told him.

Lt. Andrew nodded. "I can keep a secret."

Emily watched them glare at each other before she spoke softly, "I want him to stay."

Chevalier put his hand out to stop Kyle from arguing. "It's okay."

Lt. Andrew sat back and watched them carefully.

Emily smiled and took Chevalier's hand. He noticed that she was starting to be able to bend her fingers some.

"We wanted to tell you that we've talked to the Equites covens, and we know what they did when you came to them for help," Kyle told her.

Emily frowned and looked nervously at Lt. Andrew. He sat forward and put his elbows on the table.

Chevalier ignored him and smiled at her. "We decided it might be best if you and I moved into your house... Exavior's old house."

She nodded.

"We can have privacy there, though there will be guards. We can work through what the Equites did and do it at your own pace."

Emily looked over at Lt. Andrew.

"He needs to stay with the Encala."

It was apparent that Lt. Andrew didn't want her to leave. "You can stay here, too. No law says you have to go back to the Equites."

"Hey," Kyle snapped.

Emily looked down at her ring and then smiled at Lt. Andrew. "Can I visit?"

He smiled. "Any time, Em."

She nodded and then turned to Chevalier. "Can I bring my puppies?"

"You can bring whatever you want."

"Dr. Edwards will call your team," Kyle explained. "He'd like to get information on anything you need."

She nodded.

"Out," Chevalier ordered. Kyle and Mark both stood, and watched Lt. Andrew until he finally stood and they all stepped out.

Emily looked up at him.

"I'm not going to force you to leave here. I've always sworn to you that in my absence, the Equites would protect you, and now I see that I was wrong. I want you home. I want you with me, but I'll understand if you want to stay here," he said, watching her green eyes.

Emily smiled softly. "They were good to me."

"I know."

"I missed you."

"So are you coming home?"

"To my house?"

"Yes"

She looked around the tiny conference room before speaking again, "The other Council?"

"They took off. We'll find them though."

She nodded. "I'll get my things."

Chevalier turned to the door and then back to Emily. "Your team has already packed for you, and they are conferenced into Dr. Edwards and Lori in Council City."

"Let me say good-bye to the Council," she whispered, and then stood up and brushed her dress down. It was odd to Chevalier how

differently she was acting. Before he was banished, she wore nothing but ugly overalls and fatigues, now she comfortably wore dresses and was well manicured and had her hair done.

Chevalier opened the door and was met face-to-face by Lt. Andrew, who stepped to his side to see Emily. Mark glared at him and started for the Encala, but Kyle held him back and whispered for him to leave them be.

Lt. Andrew gently took Emily's hand and led her to the council chambers. It was irritating to the three Equites how openly she met with the enemy Council and how she didn't seem nervous at all.

"We're going to miss you," William said, smiling.

Emily nodded and then let go of the Lieutenant's hand to walk onto the council stand. Kyle held Chevalier back when she reached down and hugged the enemy Elders.

"Come back and visit, okay?" Patrick said.

She smiled and nodded again. Mark and Kyle each took a puppy, and soon, they were in a black Tahoe, headed toward Council City.

Emily fell asleep shortly after they left and didn't wake up until they were almost half-way to the city.

Chevalier smiled and looked over when she sat up. "Are you hungry?"

She shook her head and then reached down and picked up the sleeping Bulldog puppy. He curled up on her lap and fell asleep again as she pet him.

"So Sebastian is the St. Bernard?" Mark asked as he played with the fat puppy.

Emily nodded.

"What's the Bulldog's name?"

"Quiesco"

Mark chuckled. "He does seem to sleep a lot."

"We've moved Devia over to the house," Chevalier said. "He's kind of bored, but we figured you'd want him. There will be 25 members of the Cavalry around the house at all times. At least until we find the hostile Council."

Emily shrugged slightly. "Devia needs to be on a ranch."

"So you want us to take him back?"

She nodded. "He can stay with Kralen."

Chevalier smiled. "We can't find the kids."

Emily laughed a little. "Alex and Dain are in Palau."

"And Allen?"

She frowned. "I don't know."

"Kralen knows where they are then," Chevalier said. "We'll send him to go get them."

"Only you or I can get them."

"That's fine. I'll call them when Kralen gets there."

She nodded and watched out the window.

"So how far along are you?" Mark asked after a few minutes of silence.

Emily looked at him and smiled.

"Not going to tell me?"

She grew serious and looked out the window.

"We know that Banks thought a member of the new Council was the father. We know that's not true."

Kyle glanced back in the rear-view mirror. "They are sorry. It's hard to explain, but what they did was fairly commonplace when a member of the Council is replaced... let alone the entire Council."

"Where is he?" Emily asked as she watched out the window.

Chevalier glanced at Mark, not sure if he should say that the Valle had regained custody of Salazar.

"The Valle have him in their prison now," Mark said. "We may try to get him back though."

They arrived at Emily's house late that night. When they stopped at the front doors, Silas and Kralen were waiting. The lights in the house were on and there was smoke pouring out of the chimney.

"Anything?" Mark asked them as he walked up.

"No, sir," Silas reported.

Chevalier carefully scanned the trees around the house and then opened the door for Emily with one hand while he cradled the sleeping Bulldog in the other. The St. Bernard waddled into the house and was immediately met by Devia, who began looking over the hyper puppy.

Gifford, the new member of the Cavalry from Thukil, was inside the house at the foot of the stairs. "Welcome back."

He bowed to Emily, but she didn't say anything to him as she skirted around him to get into the kitchen. Silas shrugged at him and then followed her.

Emily got a glass of orange juice and turned around when she heard someone come into the kitchen. She gasped and then ran into Dr. Edwards arms when she saw him and Lori in the kitchen.

"I'm sorry," she whispered as he hugged her tightly.

"Not your fault, dear," Dr. Edwards said.

"It was... I should have told them."

"No, you did what you should have."

Lori smiled. "None of that was your fault."

Emily looked over at the psychiatrist. "Are you okay?"

"Yes, I was sent back to Dover is all."

Dr. Edwards sat down at the table. "We've been talking to your

Encala team. I'm pleased at how well your injuries are healing."

She nodded and set the cup down.

"So your hands are all that's still really bad?"

"Some"

"The Records Keeper is trying to find a masseuse in the Equites to help with leftover aches from the rack."

Emily ignored the soft hiss from Silas and shrugged. "I don't need one."

Dr. Edwards shifted nervously. "I don't suppose I can give you a quick exam."

She frowned slightly and was about to answer, when her phone rang. She picked up the phone and listened but didn't speak.

Finally, she smiled. "I'm okay."

There was a pause before she glanced around the kitchen. "Lots of them."

"Who is that?" Silas whispered.

Emily turned away. "Please don't…"

Suddenly, she gasped and ran into the other room when they heard Chevalier's cell phone.

"Chevalier here," he said, and then moved when Emily tried to grab his phone. "Excuse me?!"

She reached for his phone again, but he held it higher, so she couldn't reach it.

Kralen gently pulled her away from the Elder when it became obvious that he was becoming furious.

"I don't care what your Council said! You stay away from her and mind your own business," Chevalier yelled, and then slammed his phone shut.

Emily sighed and watched him.

Chevalier turned to Emily. "How close did you get to Andrew?"

She shrugged and watched him with wide eyes. Kralen moved closer to stand by her side.

Chevalier took one step toward her. "How close?"

"Elder," Kyle whispered, and touched his shoulder. "She didn't do anything."

Emily reached down and picked up the St. Bernard, then hauled him up the stairs, ignoring Chevalier's angry expression as he watched her. The Bulldog puppy looked up from his spot on a rug and waddled up the stairs after them.

"He's in love with her," Chevalier snapped, and turned to Kyle.

"I figured."

"He has no right calling here to say that we should clear out this house, so she can be alone!"

"I know."

"Why don't we go get Alex and Dain?" Kralen suggested.

Chevalier's eyes narrowed. "You go, now. I'm waiting for Andrew."

"He's on his way?" Kyle asked, shocked.

"No, but he will be."

Kralen nodded and then disappeared.

"Calm down, okay?" Kyle whispered. "She's still uncomfortable enough without you yelling around her."

Chevalier glared at him and then stormed up the stairs.

Lori sighed, "She can't help that heku are drawn to her."

Silas nodded. "He will see that when he calms down."

"It's curious how much more comfortable she was with the Encala."

Kyle looked over at her. "It just proves that Salazar didn't plant anything about them."

"We need to get him back."

Silas nodded. "I heard that Zohn is working on that already."

***

"You will do as you're told!" Salazar roared. Emily looked up at him from inside the cage, and fear emanated out from her dream.

She nodded, and he struck the cage with a heavy, metal bar. "You're nothing! Do you understand me? The Equites don't even want you. No one wants you."

Chevalier opened his eyes and watched her. There was no outward appearance that her dream had turned bad. When he shut his eyes, he had to fight from jerking back.

Salazar swung the metal bar and slammed it into Emily's hands. She cried out softly and looked down at the blood pouring from her battered fingers.

"Stop it!" Lt. Andrew yelled.

Salazar looked up and gasped at the massive Encala.

Lt. Andrew stepped forward and cracked his neck as he tightened his hands into fists. "Why don't you pick on someone your own size for once?"

"This is no concern of the Encala!" Salazar yelled.

"Besides, you can't take us all on," former Elder Kirt said, grinning as blood dripped from his chin.

"Wanna bet?" Andrew hissed. As they blurred into a fight, former Elder Neal appeared and began to drag Emily into the trees where she saw hundreds of Valle waiting for them.

Emily screamed and fought against his hands.

Chevalier looked over at her again and wondered why she wasn't thrashing or screaming like she used to. He also wondered why no Equites came to her rescue in her dreams.

Deciding to stay awake, he watched her sleep, occasionally glancing at the snoring Bulldog puppy by the fire. The noise began to wear on his nerves but hadn't woken Emily, so he decided that wasn't a fight he wanted to get into.

Just after dawn, Emily began to stir and finally sat up and looked around.

Chevalier smiled. "Good morning."

She yawned into her hand and then patted the bed. The St. Bernard puppy jumped up, and she began to pet him.

Chevalier looked over the edge of the bed and saw the Bulldog puppy pacing back and forth along the side of the bed. When Chevalier looked over at Emily, she was watching him and raised her eyebrows.

"You seriously want me to pick him up?" Chevalier asked, though he already knew the answer.

Emily smiled, and he shook his head and picked up the heavy puppy. He was surprised how solid the little dog was, and he realized why he couldn't hoist himself onto the high bed with his little legs. The puppy waddled over to Emily, and she began to pet him also.

"We're going to have to start you a zoo," Chevalier said when he realized that he couldn't hold Emily while the dogs were in the way.

She laughed and then rubbed her face in the long hair of the plump St. Bernard.

"Your team on the Encala," he said, and then waited for her to look over. "They felt you needed all nine of them?"

She nodded and watched him.

"Did you?"

She shrugged.

"Why the silent treatment?"

"Nothing to say yet," she said as the Bulldog puppy waddled over and leaned against Chevalier's leg before yawning and resting his head against the heku's knee.

Chevalier frowned slightly and then looked up at Emily. "I would give you a team of 100 if you need them."

"I don't."

"What part of that team do you need?"

She shrugged.

Chevalier's nose wrinkled when he realized the Bulldog puppy was drooling on his uniform pants.

Emily smiled when she saw the wet spot but didn't move the puppy.

"Fine, you have Dr. Edwards and Lori, so that takes care of two of

them."

She nodded.

"An obstetrician would be nice, obviously."

"Dr. Edwards is fine."

"He's not an obstetrician." When her eyes narrowed, Chevalier sighed, "Fine… do you need a masseuse?"

"No"

"Hair stylist?"

"No"

"You have a tailor… though he may be making you the wrong things if you're now going to wear dresses."

"I'm not."

He thought for a moment. "Manicurist? Pedicurist?"

She shook her head at each of them.

"Physical therapist?"

"No"

Chevalier studied her. "Are you still in pain from the interrogation?"

She just watched him.

"I'll have to take that as a yes. Again, you have a chef… I can find a chiropractor."

"No"

"What about Andrew? He was someone that was forbidden to talk to anyone so you could confide in him?"

"Yes"

"He was also to take you away in times of danger and to ensure you'd never be alone?"

She nodded and then looked down at the dog.

Chevalier's voice softened. "I never meant to leave you alone."

"I know."

"I'm sorry."

Emily looked up at him. "I had nowhere to go."

"I don't blame you for going to the Encala. I'd actually prefer that over the Valle. The Valle wouldn't have brought us back."

"Why?"

"Rules… the Encala broke a very sacred rule."

She thought and then looked at him. "Why did they?"

Chevalier smiled. "For you."

"I tried to," she whispered and then looked over at the fire.

"Tried what?"

"To bring you back."

He studied her face. "How?"

She shrugged. "Concentrated, I guess."

"Those were rumors from hundreds of years ago."

"I had to try."

"I'm sorry about what the Equites did to you."

Emily smiled and looked over at him.

"What?" he asked.

"They tried to banish me."

He gasped. "The Council?"

She nodded. "Got blood all over my arm."

He leaned his head back and laughed.

"The baby's yours," she whispered, and watched him carefully.

He stopped laughing and looked at her with a slight frown. "I know that."

"Some don't."

"Lord Banks is very sorry," he said. "They explained everything they did to you, including cutting your back."

She buried her face in her arms. "They were going to kill it."

"I know," he told her, and put a hand on her back. "The Council is trying to come up with a plan to stop this in the future."

She looked over at him and rested her head against her arms. "The entire faction turned on me."

He fought to control the anger in his voice and simply nodded.

Emily pulled the covers up high against her chest when someone knocked.

"Enter," Chevalier called out.

Alexis was the first to burst through the door. She immediately sat on the bed and threw her arms around Emily. "I was so afraid they were going to kill you."

Emily nodded and wrapped her arms around Alexis.

Chevalier looked over at Allen and Garrett as they stood beside the door. "I owe you my life."

Garrett simply nodded, but Allen sighed, "If I had known she was going to come after you, I would have returned to Council City. When I got to Palau, I really thought she would already be there."

"I don't blame you."

Dain came in, looking a little uncomfortable, and stood beside the fire.

Alexis gasped and let go of Emily, then looked down. "Oh my God, Mom!"

Emily just shrugged.

"Seriously, Dad?" Dain said, and rolled his eyes.

"It wasn't on purpose," Chevalier said, though his eyes narrowed at his young son.

"You do know how that happens, right?"

Garrett hurried and grabbed Dain's arm and pulled him out of the

room.

Alexis was studying Emily's hands. "What did they do?"

"I'm okay," Emily whispered, and pulled her hands away from Alexis.

Allen sat down beside them on the bed. "Why didn't you come to Palau with them?"

She looked over at Chevalier. "I had to get to your dad."

"We could have helped you. Garrett and I are both trained. Alexis and Dain could have helped. Had you come to Palau, you could have avoided the beating," Allen told her, obviously irritated.

"I wasn't going to risk you getting hurt."

Allen started to argue, but Chevalier held his hand up. "Don't start. It's over."

Alexis sighed, "How far along are you?"

Emily looked at Chevalier and then back at Alexis.

"Still not talking much?"

"I do," she whispered.

Alexis crossed her arms. "So you did all of this, knowing you were pregnant?"

"It didn't change anything."

"It should have! Allen was right. It was stupid and reckless of you to…"

"I'm still your mom," Emily whispered harshly, and glared at her daughter.

"She's been through enough without you two getting on her case," Chevalier snapped at them. He picked up the Bulldog when he'd completely covered his pants in drool. "Must he be on the bed?"

Emily took the Bulldog and sat him in her lap.

"It's disgusting," Chevalier said as he disappeared into the bathroom with a clean pair of pants.

"More dogs, too?" Alexis asked as she began to pet the St. Bernard.

"The Encala gave them to me," Emily said softly as she rubbed the Bulldog's tummy.

"How far along, Mom?"

"Doesn't matter."

"What happened to your hands?" Allen asked.

She looked down at the bandages. "Punishment."

"From the Encala?"

"No," Emily said, irritated. "The Encala were nice to me."

"The other Council?"

She sighed and then looked over when Chevalier came back in. "That dog drools more than any animal I've ever come across."

Emily smiled. "He's cute."

"Well he snores, he drools, and all he does is sleep."

"He's still cute."

"Elder?" Garrett said from the doorway. When Chevalier looked at him, he stood at attention. "The Council is requesting your presence. They said it's an emergency."

Emily gasped and stood up quickly.

"Not that kind, ma'am," Garrett told her.

"Sit, Mom, it's okay," Alexis said.

"I'm sure it's nothing big," Chevalier said as he headed for the door.

Garrett smiled at Emily. "Horace and I are out here if you need us."

Allen quickly followed Chevalier out the door.

"So... want me to call Dr. Hayden?" Alexis asked.

"No," Emily said, sitting back down.

"Not going see him?"

"No"

"Going to see anyone?"

"I'm fine."

"I just..." Alexis stopped talking when Emily's phone rang.

Emily picked up the phone but didn't talk.

"Em? It's Andrew," he said.

"Good morning." Alexis was surprised when Emily smiled and spoke to someone on the phone.

"Are you okay?"

"Yes"

"Did they finally back off and leave you alone?"

Emily looked toward the door. "I'm not sure, actually."

"If you need anything, call me. I can be there in a few hours."

"I know, but I'm okay."

"It's too boring around here without you," he chuckled.

"I bet it's nice and quiet."

"I'm actually worried."

"About me?"

"Yes, I don't trust the Equites with you."

She sighed, "Neither do I."

"I can come stay with you. I'm sure Elder William would grant me a TDY."

"I'm sure he would, but I'm fine."

"I'll call later, okay?"

"Sure," Emily said, and then said her good-byes and hung up.

Alexis studied her. "Who was that?"

"Andrew"

"The Encala?"

"Yes"

***

Chevalier sat down and studied the Valle in the trial area. "What's up?"

"They're protesting our return to power," Zohn explained.

"You know as well as I do, that you were banished and cannot return to your former positions," Valle Elder Randall said.

"We understand it's never been done before, but we're not stepping down."

"It's against all heku tradition!"

Chevalier smiled. "We can't find any rules against a mortal taking and reviving a banished Council."

Randall glared at him. "That's because it's preposterous."

"It may be... but it was done."

"We'll deal with the Encala's infractions later."

"What did they do?" Kyle asked, leaning forward.

"Don't be stupid. We know that Emily took you to them to be revived," the Valle's Chief Investigator snapped.

"Nope," Zohn said, sitting back in his chair.

Randall rolled his eyes. "Oh, then the mortals have the ability now?"

"She was a very nice old lady," the Chief of Finance said.

"This isn't the true Council."

"Yes, it is."

"No, it's not! You are unfactioned that have taken over a factioned Council against heku laws."

"If that were true," Chevalier said, leaning forward, "what would you do about it?"

He glared. "Then I'd gather the loyal Equites, and they would band with the Valle to exterminate you."

"Try it."

Kyle smiled. "I could use a good fight."

Randall smiled. "We also want Emily, now not only for crimes against the Valle but for crimes against all heku."

"What crimes?" the Court Reporter asked.

"Prematurely reviving members of a banished Council."

"There's no law against a mortal doing that!"

"She's 51% heku... the law stands."

Chevalier shrugged. "You know perfectly well that we're not handing Emily over."

Randall smiled. "Then you shouldn't be sitting here while we take her from her home."

"Guards!" Zohn yelled when Kyle and Chevalier disappeared and

called for the Cavalry.

Palace guards filed into the trial area. "Take them to prison."

Kyle and Chevalier pulled into the mansion's drive, followed by the Cavalry. Dark plumes of smoke rose from the mansion, and before Kyle even stopped the car, Chevalier was out the door and walking toward the remains of the house.

Pieces of heku were lying around the front of the house. Some of them burned with the front face of Exavior's old mansion, while others were torn apart and scattered.

Chevalier spun toward a sound off to the side, and he saw Dain and Horace helping Allen to walk. The Elder blurred to them. "What happened?"

"Valle attack," Horace said, still healing himself.

"Where's Em?"

Dain shook his head. "When the attack started, Garrett grabbed her and took off."

"Alex?"

"She's back helping some of the wounded," Horace said.

Mark helped Allen sit down and then looked over the bite wounds that covered his body. "Lay down. You'll heal."

Allen nodded and leaned back against the cold grass.

Chevalier looked around carefully. "I'm not catching her scent."

"She's still masking," Kyle said after coming around the back of the house.

Horace looked over. "They've been gone almost a thirty minutes."

Alexis walked around the house and ran into Chevalier's arms. He held her tightly. "Are you okay?"

She nodded. "There were so many of them."

"Did you get any?"

"Some," Alexis whispered.

Chevalier watched as the wounded were brought to the front lawn and members of the Council began to arrive.

"What are the losses?" Zohn asked, looking around.

"There are five dead Valle," Mark explained. "We lost Johnston, and there's still no sign of Garrett."

Chevalier nodded and knelt down by Alexis, who was tending to the wounded. "Where would Garrett take her?"

"I don't know. It all happened too fast."

He stood up and walked over to Quinn and Zohn. "We need to consider the Valle have her."

Zohn nodded. "I agree. Garrett would have turned up by now."

"Not necessarily," Alexis told them as she walked up. "Garrett once told me that he considered her one of the greatest Equites treasures, and

if in his care, he would do all in his power to protect her."

"So you think he's still out in hiding?"

She shrugged. "I would guess so."

"How do we find him?"

"He doesn't have his phone," Alexis said. "So I suggest we wait."

"Was she hurt?" Kyle asked.

Horace looked over at Allen. "Did you even see her?"

Allen shook his head. "No, the only thing I saw was the Valle."

Alexis frowned. "I didn't see her either. I just heard Garrett call out for her."

Chevalier growled, "Wait! So no one saw Garrett with Emily?"

Horace turned and called out to his troops, then looked back at Chevalier. "No, Elder. I guess no one did."

Dain angrily stormed off into the nearby trees.

***

Emily sighed and rolled over in bed, clutching the pillow to her tightly. When she didn't feel Chevalier in bed with her, she opened her eyes and then gasped and sat up as she looked around the bedroom. She immediately recognized the Valle bedroom that Exavior once prepared for her.

She looked over at the window and saw metal bars blocking it. There was French toast on the table and steaming hot coffee beside it. Emily crawled out of bed, still in her nightgown, and walked over to the door and knocked.

An Imperial Guard opened the door. "Yes?"

She glared at him and crossed her arms.

He smiled. "Elder Sotomar would like to see you."

Not seeing as though she had a choice, she followed the Imperial Guard while three others fell in behind them. The council chamber door guard opened the door for them, and Emily stepped in to face the Valle Council.

Sotomar smiled. "Step forward, dear."

She scowled at him and moved forward.

Elder Ryan nodded. "We know you're mad, but hear us out."

Without a word, she looked at him.

"We feel you'll be safer here than with the Equites or the Encala. The true Equites Council is here with us until we can restore them to their positions. You belong with the true Council, and not the unfactioned former one."

The Chief Enforcer stood up. "Now we are going to try you for crimes against the heku species."

Emily watched him.

"You are hereby charged with breaking heku tradition by stealing banished members of the Equites Council and taking them to the Encala for premature revival," he explained. "How do you plead?"

She set her jaw and sent a flash of burning pain at him. He growled and blurred toward her but was stopped just short of hitting her by Sotomar and the Valle's Chief Interrogator.

"Do not do that!" the Chief Enforcer screamed.

Emily glared at him.

"Calm down," Sotomar told him. He turned to Emily. "I suggest you keep your abilities to yourself if you want to stay in comfort here."

Once everyone was settled back in their chairs, the Chief Investigator stood up. "We are still waiting for your plea."

The entire room grew silent as the Valle Council waited for Emily to speak. A few minutes later, Sotomar shook his head. "Fine, we'll take that as a guilty plea. You are hereby sentenced to life on house arrest here at the Valle palace."

She shrugged and watched them.

"How you are treated here will depend on how cooperative you are," Elder Ryan explained. "Keep your abilities to yourself, and we'll make sure you have everything you need."

"When the baby is born, because it will be born within our walls, we will raise it as a Valle," Sotomar said.

"Oh good, Dr. Graham," Ryan said when a strange heku entered.

Emily's eyes narrowed at the doctor and then she turned back to the Council.

"He's here to be your personal physician and to see you through this pregnancy," Ryan told her.

"How far along are you, child?" Dr. Graham asked her.

She ignored him and glared at the Council.

Sotomar smiled. "There is a psychiatrist coming in from Hogge Coven. She's not speaking much since her confinement in Salazar's care."

"I see," Dr. Graham said, and it irritated Emily that he seemed to be looking her over. "What is wrong with your hands?"

The Council looked down at her bandaged hands and wrists and then waited for an answer that didn't come.

"May I look?" Dr. Graham asked after a few minutes of silence.

She shrugged and held out one hand. He moved forward cautiously and unwrapped the bandages.

"Who did this?" he gasped, and looked over the bruises and scabs of healing wounds.

"It was a punishment by the Equites Council," Ryan explained.

"She can be quite stubborn."

Dr. Graham carefully wrapped her hands back up and then looked at the Council. "Might I suggest we come up with something not quite so violent? It's okay to do this to a heku, but a mortal can't sustain injuries like that."

Sotomar smiled. "We won't physically hurt her."

Dr. Graham nodded and studied Emily's tummy. "Well... she's pretty small, and as the father's rather large, I'm just going to have to guess that she's about six months along."

Sotomar thought. "According to Equites Elder Neal, her scent didn't start until three months ago though, so that would put her a lot less than that."

"This would really help if you would just tell me," Dr. Graham said to her.

She ignored him and looked nonchalantly around the Valle's council chamber.

"May I?" Dr. Graham asked her. She looked over at him and saw he'd pulled a stethoscope out of his bag. When he moved to put it against her chest, she ripped it out of his ears and tossed it at his head, but he caught it and smiled slightly. "I'll take that as a no."

"She's never allowed doctors to get near her," Elder Ryan explained.

"Yet she keeps getting pregnant," the doctor commented, seconds before turning to ash.

"Emily!" Sotomar shouted. "Stop it!"

She shrugged and then started for the door.

"You have not been excused," the Chief of Staff said.

Emily opened the door and came face-to-face with a massive member of their Imperial Guard. She looked high up into his face and then took a step back.

"You may now leave," Sotomar said as he nodded to the guard. Emily followed him out.

Elder Ryan smiled. "She's going to keep us on our toes."

"We'll be lucky to keep her for a week," the Chief of Defense said.

"Are we ready for an Equites attack?"

Sotomar nodded. "Yes, I think we are. Everyone is in place out in the city."

***

"Still no word from Garrett?" Kyle asked when he sat down at his chair.

"No word from them or the Valle," Quinn explained. "Zohn is there now trying to find out what's going on."

"Hope he returns."

"So do I."

Chevalier sat down a ledger. "I'm still just getting annoyance from Em. I don't think she's being mistreated."

"That's better than last time at least," Kyle said.

"How is Alexis holding up?" the Chief Investigator asked.

Chevalier frowned. "Not well. She knows the Valle won't kill Emily. Garrett, however, is another story."

***

Emily looked up from her book when someone knocked. "Go away."

Sotomar smiled and walked in. "You cannot tell an Elder to go away."

She watched him closely.

"Come, I want to show you something," he said, and held out his hand.

Emily set her book down and watched him. "Why are you doing this?"

"Crimes against..."

"Bullshit... why?"

Sotomar nodded and then shut the door behind him before sitting down. "The Equites can't properly care for you."

"Yes, they can. That's a cop out. Tell me why."

"You belong here."

"Are we playing the Ulrich card again?"

"You are Valle by blood."

Her eyes narrowed. "If you say by marriage also..."

"I won't."

"You're risking your entire faction by keeping me here."

"I know," Sotomar said. "However, I also know that you've not used it much since your return from... anyway. We can better care for you."

"I'm tired of being a pawn between factions. Who can keep Emily the longest? I'm not a toy, I'm not a weapon, and I'm most certainly not a Valle."

Sotomar smiled. "It's deeper than that."

"Tell me."

"It's been well known for centuries that any faction having a Winchester would be stronger than the rest."

"It has to be more than that."

"It is... you're also a friend to the Valle, and we don't feel that it's

good for the Equites to have you around."

She sighed and looked out the barred window. "Even knowing that you can't keep me here?"

"This time, I suspect we can."

"Just because I may not ash your city, doesn't mean Chevalier's going to sit back and watch this."

"We're ready for the attack," Sotomar said. He watched her for a moment and then stood up and put his hand out. "Come, I still want to show you something."

"No"

He smiled and pulled her to her feet. "You still can't tell an Elder, no."

She rolled her eyes as he gently pulled her out of the room. Four Imperial Guards fell in behind them, and Emily jerked her arm away from Sotomar and followed them down to the council chambers.

The door guard bowed and opened the door for them. When Emily stepped inside, she gasped at the sight of a bloody Equites lying in a heap on the floor.

She rushed to him and knelt down beside him. She gently turned him over and then became furious when she saw that it was Garrett. She looked up angrily at the Council.

Sotomar took his seat. "It's simple. He's ours now, and how he's treated will depend on how you behave."

Emily's eyes narrowed. "Let him go."

"No"

She looked down at Garrett and then took his hand. "I'm here Garrett. It's okay."

They all watched the Equites heal, and after a few minutes, he was able to sit up with Emily's help.

"Let him go!" she screamed at the Valle Council.

"No," Ryan said.

"Listen to me," Garrett whispered, though it was obvious he was still in a great deal of pain. "Turn this city to ash and get out of here. Just leave me. I'll be okay."

"Actually, you would be dead," the Chief Interrogator said.

"I can't leave you here," Emily told him.

"You're too important. You have to get out of here."

"Again… leave and he's a dead heku," Sotomar told her.

She smiled and squeezed his hand. "I'm not going to leave you here alone."

"Smart girl," the Chief of Defense said with a smile.

Emily looked up at Sotomar. "You won't beat him?"

"Not if you do as you're told."

"He'll feed?"

"Yes"

When Garrett finished healing, Emily helped him stand and they both faced the Council.

"Fine," Emily said, crossing her arms. "I'm behaving."

"Please, Lady Emily...," Garrett started. With one nod from Sotomar, he was roughly pulled from the room before he could finish.

"You said you'd be nice to him!" Emily screamed.

Sotomar nodded. "We will be."

"That wasn't nice."

"He's heku. He's fine."

Emily pointed at him. "Be nicer, or I walk."

He smiled. "We need to get on with trials."

She spun on her heels and walked out. When she was safely in her room, the Imperial Guards escorted Chevalier, Mark, and Kralen into the Valle's council room.

"I'll just preempt this," Sotomar said, watching them. "The answer is no."

"Don't you think this is getting a little old?" Chevalier asked. "Can't you just leave her alone?"

"No, we can't," Ryan said. "If she wanted to be with the Valle, then the Equites would kidnap her. She's valuable beyond anything the heku have ever had."

"She's my wife."

"That's irrelevant."

Mark growled, "You're willing to back that up with a war?"

Elder Ryan nodded. "Yes, we are."

"If you hurt one hair on her head," Chevalier hissed.

Sotomar's eyes narrowed. "We care about her too much to harm her."

"Taking her from us right now is harming her!"

"She is fine here. We have provided what she needs."

"Then prepare," Chevalier whispered harshly.

"Where is Garrett?" Kralen asked.

"He's our bargaining chip with Emily," Ryan said. "You may go."

The Equites left angrily, knowing that the Valle wouldn't hurt Emily, but they fully planned on attacking to get her back.

As much as it angered Chevalier, Randall was returned to his faction. It was against heku tradition to imprison an enemy Elder for such a small crime.

***

The Valle doctor smiled. "I think we can do without these bandages now."

Emily looked down at her scarred hands and shrugged.

He sat back with a notepad. "Let's try these questions again, alright?"

She watched him but didn't speak.

"How far along are you?"

Emily shrugged.

"Do you not know, or are you just not saying?"

She grabbed her book and sat back, but he tore it out of her hands and then calmed down and set it beside her.

"I can figure that out on my own," he explained. "Any pains?"

"Just you."

He smiled. "I see... any headaches?"

Emily reached for her book, but he pulled it out of her reach.

The doctor sighed, "Let me just put this right out for you. If you don't cooperate, I'll be forced to tell the Council and your dear guard may suffer for it."

She frowned.

"How far along are you?"

Emily felt the panic begin.

He put a hand on hers. "You can trust me. I just want to help you."

She looked around the room but saw nothing that could save her.

"I will call in Imperial Guards if you don't cooperate," he whispered softly.

"I...," she started, but then pressed her hands into her eyes to stop the strong headache that was getting stronger by the minute.

"What's wrong?"

When blackness began to creep into her vision, she fought to keep focused. Sounds around her became far away, and suddenly, she lost control and fell unconscious.

"What's going on?" Sotomar asked as he blurred into the room. The Valle doctor was just lying Emily down on the bed.

"She passed out," he said, quickly digging in his bag for a blood pressure cuff. The other two Elders came in and watched him as he put a stethoscope to Emily's chest.

"So?" Randall asked.

"Her blood pressure is way too high."

"Fix it."

"I can't just fix it," he explained. The doctor took her pulse again and then turned to them. "It takes time and a calm environment to bring it down."

"So we stop threatening her?" Ryan asked.

"We'll have to see if that works. High blood pressure is the second most cause of maternal death."

"Death?" Sotomar gasped.

"Yes, and it's very well-known that she has pre-eclampsia when pregnant."

"You can't do anything about it?"

"Birth is the only fix we know of. Right now, all we can do is lessen her stress."

Sotomar nodded. "Do what you can to calm her down when she wakes up."

"We'll be in the council chambers," Ryan said. "It won't help if she wakes and sees us here."

Four hours later, Emily slowly opened her eyes and looked around the room. She squinted at the bright sunlight, but someone quickly shut the thick curtains.

"How are you?" the doctor asked as he sat down beside her on the bed.

Her head hurt too badly to speak, so she pressed her palms into her eyes to try to stop the small flashes of light in her vision.

"Drink this," he said softly, and then helped her sit up. She took the drink in her hand and drank the cold orange juice. "Good girl."

Emily laid back down and looked up at the doctor.

"Does your head still hurt?"

She nodded and shut her eyes.

"Do you see light flashes?"

"Yes," she whispered.

"I know it's hard for you to do right now, but you have to try to calm down. If your blood pressure keeps getting high, it can hurt you and the baby."

She nodded. "Let me go."

"I can't. You'll be safe here if you'll just calm down, okay?"

"I miss him," she said with a cracked voice.

The doctor put a cool rag on her forehead. "I know, child."

When she fell back to sleep, the doctor headed down to the council chambers to give them a report. The trial area was cleared, and he was let in immediately.

"How is she?" Sotomar asked.

"Her blood pressure is dangerously high, so she has bad headaches."

"Caused by?"

"Stress, mainly, though when I first heard of the Winchester having pre-eclampsia, I theorized that it was due to having a baby that was only partially of her own species."

Sotomar nodded. "That sounds right."

"We may not be able to bring down her blood pressure."

"No medication can do that?"

"Some can help, but the only way to completely fix it is to deliver the baby."

"So let's just take it early," the Chief of Staff suggested.

The doctor frowned. "It's too early for the baby to survive."

"So we remove the fetus to save her life."

Ryan shook his head. "That's not a bad idea."

"Do you not remember when the Encala did something like that?" the Chief of Defense said. "She wiped out their palace and half of their city."

"That's true," Sotomar said.

"We may have to return her to the Equites to save her life and the life of the baby," the doctor said.

"That's not an option," Ryan told him.

"There's just not much I can do."

The Elders turned and spoke in private for a few minutes before turning around. "Do what you can."

The doctor nodded and then left the trial area. He spoke to the Chief of Finance in the hallway and ordered medical supplies before returning to Emily's room. She was still sound asleep, so he took the opportunity to study her more to try to determine how far away she was from delivering.

Emily dreamt of having a headache, and when she woke up, her head was pounding, and she had a hard time even opening her eyes.

"It's okay," the doctor whispered as he took her hand.

"Where's Chev?" she asked softy.

"You're still with the Valle, but you're going to be okay."

She felt something on her face and tried to pull it off, but the doctor held her hands down.

"It's oxygen. Leave it on," he told her.

"My head," she whispered, and squeezed her eyes shut.

The doctor replaced the rag with a new, cold one and then dimmed the lights in the room.

"Please, Emily. Tell me how far along you are," the doctor said. "If you get sicker, we're going to have to take the baby, and I need to know when it's safe to do that."

A tear fell from her eye. "Four and a half months."

He nodded but inwardly cringed. "Thank you."

"I'm so tired," she whispered.

"It's the magnesium sulfate in your I.V."

She frowned.

"I'm trying to keep you from having a seizure because of your high

blood pressure."

Emily couldn't fight when she felt the heku restrain her hands to the side of the bed but moaned when she felt the pinch of a needle.

"What are you doing that for?" Sotomar asked softly when he walked into the room.

The doctor stood up with a syringe full of blood. "I need to test her kidneys to make sure they aren't failing. Magnesium Sulfate is pretty hard on them, and if they give out, she could die."

"You have her on a medication that can kill her?"

He turned to his Elder. "It's all there is to control this."

Sotomar sat down on the side of the bed and checked Emily's wrist restraints to make sure they weren't too tight.

"Can you stay with her while I run this?" the doctor asked.

Sotomar nodded and adjusted the cold rag over Emily's eyes.

She sighed, "Kyle, please get Chev."

"You're with the Valle," he told her softly.

"Why?"

"We're going to keep you safe."

***

"Not even a day!" Lt. Andrew yelled.

"We'll get her back," Chevalier told him from his seat on the council stand.

"It's pathetic," William growled. "How can you lose her the same day she returns from the Encala?"

"Valle attack, plain and simple," Zohn said. "It's obvious that you have an informant. They knew as soon as she left."

"We do not!"

"Calm down," Quinn said. "We'll get her back."

"Maybe the Valle are right, and you aren't fit to have the Winchester in your care," the Encala's Faction Liaison Officer said.

Chevalier glared at him. "Get out of my palace."

"No, I want to go to the Valle with you," Lt. Andrew told him.

"Well that would be awkward," Zohn said, smiling slightly.

Lt. Andrew growled softly.

William sighed, "We want to help. Emily is our friend too, and I don't like that she's back under the Valle's influence after what Salazar did to her."

"You don't even know what you're talking about," Quinn said.

Lt. Andrew's eyes narrowed. "She told me what he did."

Chevalier snarled. "She did?"

He nodded and then smiled. "Don't even ask."

"We'll get her back, and we don't need the Encala's help to do it," Zohn said, trying to break the tension.

William scowled and then turned and left with the rest of his faction.

Quinn looked over at Chevalier. "Still sick?"

He nodded. "Yes, I'm afraid she's very ill. I can tell she's not alone, but that's all I'm getting. It's pretty vague."

"Kyle should be back soon with a report on the attack," Quinn said. "We'll see how they like being attacked while they're busy."

Chevalier nodded.

"Do you really think she told him?"

"I don't know."

"She may have," Lori said from the doorway. "Sorry, I overheard."

"You think she would tell him?" Chevalier asked.

"Salazar didn't plant fear about the Encala. It's actually healthy for her to be able to get it out and speak to someone about it. When William forbid him from telling anyone what she said, he gave her the opportunity to let loose."

"I just wish it had been one of us."

Lori nodded. "I know, but I'm quite pleased that she told him."

"But we'll never know."

"Maybe"

"Here's Kyle," Quinn said, turning to the door.

Kyle came in and sat down, then turned to them. "It's done. We wiped out the entire Wright Coven."

Chevalier nodded. "Now we wait for them to come talk to us."

"What were our losses?"

"Thukil lost four, Powan four, and Council City lost 12," Kyle reported.

***

"Emily?" Sotomar said, sitting down on the bed beside her.

She looked over at him and then pulled at the restraints on her wrists again.

"We can't let you go. You have to keep your oxygen on and your I.V. in."

She sighed and looked toward the window.

"How can we convince you to trust us and calm down?"

"I don't feel well," she whispered, and squeezed her eyes shut.

Sotomar looked up at the monitor the Valle recently purchased and saw her blood pressure spiking again. "Please calm down. We're not going to hurt you."

"I want to go home."

"I know."

A tear fell from her eyes as she looked at him. "Please, let me go."

"We can't. I wish you could see how much better you are here."

"Go away," she said, and then turned her face away from him.

"We've decided not to leave you alone," he explained. "We're hoping you will be more comfortable if you aren't alone."

She swallowed dryly and pulled harder at the restraints. "My head."

"I know. That's why you need to calm down."

She frowned. "My leg hurts."

"Your leg?"

Emily nodded and tried to readjust her position while Sotomar pulled the blanket back and looked down. "Which leg?"

"Left," she said, groaning softly with the pain.

He reached down and felt her leg. "It's hot."

She cried out when he squeezed her calf lightly, so he jerked his hands back and called for the doctor.

"What's wrong?" the Valle doctor asked.

"Leg pain, it's hot too," Sotomar said, stepping aside.

The doctor felt her leg and then cursed. "She has DVT."

"Meaning?"

"Meaning she has a blood clot in her leg... she's going to die if we can't get her well enough to get up."

Sotomar looked down at her. "Do something."

He began digging through his bag. "I don't think I have what we need."

"Name it."

"It's all still new... I'd say Heparin and Tinzaparin."

"I'll get it," Sotomar said, disappearing.

The doctor turned back to Emily and smiled. "We'll fix it."

"I'm scared," she said as her lip quivered.

"I know."

***

Chevalier frowned and looked over at Mark. "Something's wrong."

Mark shook his head and studied the roster. "I don't see anything wrong with this."

"No, Em... she's scared."

Mark's eyes narrowed. "What did they do to her?"

"I don't know."

***

"Help her!" Elder Randall roared as Emily's body stiffened.

"I'm doing all I can," the doctor said as he held her down.

Emily's eyes rolled back in her head, and the doctor studied the monitors. "We're going to have to take the baby."

"We can't," Ryan told him.

"We either take it or we lose her."

Randall growled, "We don't have an option! We are going to have to take her back."

"Randall, we can't," Ryan said.

"It's better if they take the baby. Let her wipe out their city and not ours."

"This could be our last chance…"

"I know!" Randall yelled. "Steal a van and bring Garrett to me."

Ryan sighed and called out the order.

Emily finally relaxed back on the bed, and the doctor sat down. "She may not make it to the Equites."

"Once she's in the van and on her way, she's out of our hands," Randall said sadly. "I don't know what else to do."

"Take her by helicopter."

"We can't risk them keeping the pilot."

The doctor frowned. "You're risking her life over a pilot?"

He nodded. "I realize that Sotomar would send her and risk the heku, but he's not here, and both Ryan and I agree that she's going by van."

"You're sending the last Winchester in a stolen van," the doctor hissed. "Even if she does make it, there's a chance they will get stopped on the way."

"Then it will be Garrett's fault," Ryan said, turning when the Equites walked in.

"What did you do?!" Garrett yelled, and then placed himself between Emily and the Valle.

"We've stolen a van and are equipping it with medical equipment. The doctor will sedate her long enough to get her to Council City," Randall explained when he walked in. "Once you're out of our gates, she's in your care."

Garrett hissed, "You're sending her away in a stolen van?"

The doctor sighed, "I'll have her sedated. She'll have oxygen and an I.V. I have notes here for the doctor in Council City."

"What if something happens while I'm driving?"

"She's out of our hands," Randall said.

Garrett growled and then began loosening the restraints. The Valle didn't attempt to help as he picked her up gently and started for the door. The doctor was the only one that followed him down.

Once Emily was on the floor of the van, the doctor hooked her I.V. to the ceiling, adjusted it to a slow drip and then put on her oxygen.

He turned to Garrett, looked around, and then whispered, "Get her there fast. I can't guarantee that she's going to make it. I suspect she'll recover some when she's in her own home."

"I'm going to just take her to a hospital."

"In a stolen van? She has no I.D., and she's still traumatized from captivity. They will surely put her back in the psychiatric ward. She's still listed as an escaped mental patient," the doctor said. "Your best bet is to just get her there."

Garrett nodded and shut the back doors. "I could use a phone."

"No, just go."

He thought for only a moment before crawling into the front of the van and taking off. As he left the gates of the Valle's city, he heard the sound of alarms and the city gates shut tightly behind him.

***

"Nothing," Chevalier said, and looked down the row at Kyle.

"What's that mean?"

"It means she's... I don't know. If she's asleep, I get feelings. I would guess she's sedated."

Quinn frowned. "Why would they sedate her?"

"I don't know."

"I'm almost ready," Zohn said as he signed another paper in a stack.

"I still think I should go," Chevalier told him.

"Let me take the Cavalry and see if we can get to her."

Quinn smiled. "I agree. Let Zohn go."

The Court Reporter returned from a phone call. "The Encala are still insisting that they join us, and we take out the Valle's main city."

Chevalier's eyes narrowed. "I vote yes."

"No!" Quinn said, frowning. "We can't give in to that."

"They have her and she's hurt."

"I know, but let Zohn try."

Zohn sighed, "I vote no also."

The doors in the trial area burst open and Mark came in.

"What are you...?" Zohn started to yell, but Mark quickly spoke to Chevalier.

"Garrett called. He's on the way in from the Valle with Emily. They're in a stolen van and have been surrounded by Valle."

"Where?" Chevalier said, standing slowly.

"Only about two hours outside of Council City. He said Emily's pretty bad, and the Valle doctor said she may not make it."

Kyle disappeared from his chair as Chevalier called out orders for the entire Cavalry to get into cars and meet up with Garrett.

Chevalier hadn't replaced his vehicles the previous Council had gotten rid of, so he jumped into the first Veyron he saw and took off toward the Valle. He impatiently tapped his fingers on the steering wheel as he topped 280 mph, followed shortly by almost 30 cars full of Equites.

On speakerphone, Mark gave more of a report. "They left the Valle palace yesterday in a silver Dodge Caravan. Emily's in the back hooked up to medical equipment, and Garrett said he was told she probably wasn't going to make it."

After a brief pause, he continued, "I guess when the Valle found out about Wright coven, they sent scouts to find the van and bring Emily back to them."

"Silver Dodge van?" one of the Cavalry asked.

"Yes"

"Got it!" he shouted, and Chevalier rounded a corner and saw the older silver van surrounded by 12 sleek sports cars.

"Team 4 get around that van and see them into Council City," Mark ordered. "Everyone else cut off one of those cars and take care of the Valle inside."

Chevalier growled and pulled away from the rest of the Equites. He whipped around and ended up behind the van but ahead of the Valle. For one brief moment, he caught Garrett's eye and saw determination.

Chevalier quickly hit his brakes and two of the Valle's sports cars slammed into the back of his car, sending parts flying in every direction. Before the sound of the wreck calmed, he was out of his car and walking angrily toward recovering heku.

All around him, Equites were slamming into Valle and sending cars flying in a blaze of sparks and shattered metal.

Garrett gasped at the wreckage behind him but saw five of the Equites surround the van. He finally began to relax before he called back to Emily. "Hang on, we're almost there."

He could hear the beeping of her heart monitor, the only sign he had that she was even alive. The rhythmic tone was comforting some, but he was deathly afraid it would stop.

The silver van blew past the gate guards, and Garrett finally slid to a stop at the doors to the palace, where Dr. Edwards, Quinn, and Lori were waiting.

Before Garrett even got out, Dr. Edwards had the back door open and had crawled into the van beside Emily. He checked a few things while the others watched and then picked up a chart and started reading quickly.

"Can we take her inside?" Quinn asked after a few minutes.

"Not yet," Dr. Edwards said. "I need to know if she needs to be hospitalized."

"We can't though," Lori reminded him. "They will institutionalize her."

"Better institutionalized than dead," Dr. Edwards said, crawling back out of the van. "I think we can give her some time here. If she doesn't improve though, we won't have a choice."

Quinn nodded and then gently picked Emily up out of the van while Garrett and Dr. Edwards grabbed the medical equipment she was hooked too. Lori had the bed turned down and waiting for them when they arrived.

Quinn laid Emily down and began looking through the medical charts, checking the monitors often.

"So?" Lori asked.

"Pre-eclampsia, though I've never seen the onset this early," Dr. Edwards said to them. "Also looks like DVT because she's been bedridden for a month."

"Damn," Lori sighed. "Two major causes of maternal death."

Quinn frowned. "Is she that bad?"

Dr. Edwards nodded and then took a blood pressure to compare with the monitors.

After only two hours, Chevalier blurred into the room.

"What happened?" Zohn asked. He was called back from the Valle when Garrett first called.

Chevalier sat down and took Emily's hand. "No Valle left. We took care of them all."

"So they were trying to get her back?"

"Yes, the Valle changed their minds after our attack and decided not to send Emily back. Apparently, Sotomar was gone and was furious that the other two Elders sent her away."

Dr. Edwards sat down beside Chevalier and went over her entire chart, page by page.

Chevalier sighed when the doctor finished. "So now what?"

"If we can't get her blood pressure down, we'll have to take the baby early."

"Can it survive?" Lori asked.

"Not this young, no."

Chevalier nodded. "I won't risk her life…"

"I know," Dr. Edwards said. "I won't let it get that far. I suspect the Valle were afraid they would have to make the choice and decided to make us do it."

"Why is she unconscious?"

Garrett cleared his throat. "They sedated her for the trip."

"It was in her I.V.," Dr. Edwards explained. "I've turned it off. I'm hoping she wakes up soon."

Chevalier studied the beeping monitor. "What is a mortal's blood pressure supposed to be?"

"120 over 80."

"So hers is…"

Dr. Edwards pointed to a place on the monitor. "196 over 150."

"Is that way high?"

"Yes"

"That's come down," Garrett said. When Chevalier looked at him, he straightened up and continued. "I stopped for gas, bought a phone, and checked on her. The monitor read 198 over 165."

"When was that?" Dr. Edwards asked, frowning.

"I would say about four hours ago."

He nodded. "Then it's coming down. That's good."

Emily sighed softly, and the heku looked over at her. Quinn quickly shut the heavy blinds, and Garrett stepped back out of the way.

Chevalier took her hand, frowning at the restraint marks and then gently touched her face. "Em? You're home now."

She opened her eyes briefly and then fell back to sleep. They watched her through the night as Dr. Edwards wrote down any change on the monitors and changed out the I.V. when it was needed.

The only sound during the night was when the Bulldog puppy began to snore softly from the rug in front of the fire place. Garrett picked him up quickly and left, shutting the door quietly behind him.

Kyle returned just before dawn and sat down opposite Chevalier. He smiled and gently took her hand while Chevalier took her other.

Dr. Edwards was just checking the monitors again when Emily looked up at him. He smiled at her. "Welcome back, dear."

Emily looked around the room and swallowed dryly. "I'm back?"

"Yes," Chevalier said, then kissed her forehead lightly.

"Can you drink something?" Dr. Edwards asked her.

She nodded and Quinn ordered some juice, then took it from the servant and walked up to the bed. Chevalier helped her sit up but continued to hold her hand while Quinn helped her drink some.

When she laid back down, she looked around. "Where's Garrett?"

"He's here too," Chevalier said.

"How is your leg?" Dr. Edwards asked as he pulled the blankets away from her left leg.

"Just sore."

"I've put white stockings on you that'll help. Please leave them on."

She nodded and then tried to get her hand away from Kyle. "Let me go."

"I can't."

"Let me go," she said again, pulling harder.

"No," Chevalier told her. "You're leaving the oxygen on and the I.V. in… just this once."

Emily sighed and then looked at the heku in the room. "How did I get free?"

"They thought you were dying, so sent you home with Garrett," Kyle explained.

She frowned. "I don't feel like I'm dying."

"Things are actually looking pretty good," Dr. Edwards said. "Since waking up your blood pressure is a lot better, though still high."

Chapter 7

Emily's nose scrunched. "Did he really say that?"

Alexis nodded. "Yes… but you know Dad. He's a lot meaner sounding than he really is."

"Well, I don't care what he said. I'm not spending the next four months in bed."

"I figured," Alexis said as she pet the Bulldog puppy.

"Who's outside my door?"

"I don't know their names… four Cavalry."

Emily thought. "Okay, let me free then."

Alexis smiled and then reached over and unfastened the soft leather restraints on Emily's wrists. Emily promptly tore out her I.V. and oxygen, and looked up at the monitors.

"If I take these off, that thing's going to freak out, and the room will fill with heku," Emily said.

Alexis shrugged. "More than likely."

"So let's turn it off."

"Then they'll hear silence. You know Dad. He's listening to that beeping."

Emily took a deep breath and thought. "Okay then. I'll put it on you."

"Me? Why?"

"Because I'm thinking our hearts beat about the same."

"Yes, but I'm trying not to get myself into trouble too," Alexis explained.

Emily smiled. "How fast is the heartbeat on that puppy?"

Alexis moved her hand to the puppy's heart. "Faster than yours."

Emily reached down and removed the tight white stockings Dr. Edwards put on for the blood clot.

"Why don't you just do as they ask this once?" Alexis asked.

"Because I'm not going to sit here for four months."

"Why not? What if it's better for the baby?"

"Baby's fine… you all forget I've done this before."

"True"

Emily smiled slightly. "I think it's time I get fixed."

"I think it's about one kid too late."

"Well, it'll stop at four though."

"Unless you heal."

Emily frowned. "How can I heal from that?"

Alexis shrugged. "I don't know. I'm just commenting."

"You know what? I'm an adult, damnit," Emily said, crawling out of bed. "I can do what I want."

"Whatever you say, Mom," Alexis said as she picked up the Bulldog and put him on the floor.

Emily quickly tore off the electrodes on her chest and then went into the bathroom to get dressed.

Alexis looked over when Chevalier and Kyle blurred into the room.

"Where is she?" Kyle asked, scanning the room.

"She's expressing her adulthood," Alexis said, and then smiled.

Chevalier sighed, "I was waiting for this."

"Yes, well… she's not going to sit here for four months."

Kyle frowned. "It's for the good of her and the baby."

"Tell her that. I'm sure it'll work."

The heku looked over when Emily stepped out in jeans and a t-shirt. She wasn't watching them but was braiding her hair.

"Em…," Chevalier sighed.

"Don't say it," she told him as she wound a rubber band around the base of the braid. "I'm fine."

"Look though," Kyle said, pointing to the monitor. "Your blood pressure is still high."

"I'm sure it is," she said as she dug around in the closet. "It'll be the same here as it will be outside in the sun."

Kyle looked at Chevalier, and he shrugged before walking over. "It's not safe."

Emily stood up and slipped on her cowboy boots. "I can't sit here. The Cavalry is out training, and I'm just going to go watch."

Chevalier reached down and picked her up from under her arms and lifted her, so he could look into her face directly. "It's too dangerous."

She sighed, "I can't sit here anymore. I've been good and stayed in bed for two weeks. Now though, I'm bored, I'm anxious, and I need to get out of here."

He set her down gently. "Then take Dr. Edwards with you."

"No"

"No?"

"You heard me," she said as she headed for the door.

Chevalier looked down as the St. Bernard puppy pulled at his pants, and then he looked at Kyle. "Now what?"

He shrugged. "I guess we let her go."

Alexis smiled and pulled the puppy off of her dad. "She'll be okay. Hold on too tight and she'll explode, remember?"

"I know," he said, and then headed back down to the council chambers with Kyle.

Emily smiled and turned her face up toward the sun as she walked to the stables. The Cavalry was all out on the hills above the town, except for the four trailing her. When she slipped a bridle onto her

stallion, the one closest to her gasped.

"You're getting on a horse?" he asked with wide eyes.

Emily looked over at him. "Yes, so?"

"It's… the… well, the Elders said no horses."

"They aren't my Elders," she said, and slipped onto the horse.

The other four blurred around the stables and came out on their horses. She smiled and kicked her stallion into a nice, slow walk toward the gates.

"What the hell!" Kralen growled when he saw them coming.

Mark sighed, "Nice."

Emily stopped her stallion beside them and smiled. "How's it going?"

"What are you doing out of bed… and on a horse?" Kralen yelled.

"Stop it!" she said angrily. "I'm not sitting in that bed anymore."

"The Elders said…"

"Need I remind you that I am not, nor have I ever, listened to the Elders."

Cavalry members around her tensed and looked nervously at Mark as he shook his head. "You know it's dangerous."

"No, what's dangerous is forcing me to stay in bed for another four months. I've had babies before. I think I have this down."

"Do you have a headache?" Mark asked.

"Yes"

"Flashes of light?"

"Yes"

"Then you should be inside!"

"No, I shouldn't!" Emily yelled, irritated. "Now either get on with training, or I will."

Silas, silent up until now, grinned. "You're going to train them?"

She looked over at him. "Yes."

"That should be interesting."

"You think I can't?"

"Oh, I know you can."

Her eyes narrowed. "Do I detect sarcasm?"

"Not at all," he said, smiling broadly.

"Fine," Emily said, and then turned her horse toward where the Cavalry was doing training. "Listen up, heku!"

They all turned, unsure, and looked at her.

She smiled. "Time for some Emily training."

"Oh God," Mark sighed, and rolled his eyes.

She glared at him and then turned back to the Cavalry. "I don't care how you tackle a heku or bite your donors… what I care about is how well you ride your horse."

"You don't what?" Horace asked, not sure he heard right.

She smiled. "I'm going to see how well you maneuver through trees."

"How exactly are you going to do that?"

"Easy, divide up into Cavalry from before my death… and then Cavalry that joined after. Gifford stays with the seasoned though."

The Cavalry leaders watched as they divided up and then turned to Emily.

"New guys," Emily said, and turned her horse to face the woods on the other side of Council City. "In those woods is a broken down Durango. Under the passenger seat's floor mat is a compartment with a diary in it. I want it."

Before she'd even fully finished, the new Cavalry members took off across the field toward the opposite side of the city.

"And the others?" Mark asked, looking at the seasoned members of the Cavalry.

She turned around. "Beat me through the trees… and I'll go back to bed and tell Chev that you're the one that talked me into it."

There was a gasp seconds before Emily kicked her racing stallion and disappeared through the trees.

"Screw it. I want that," Mark said, kicking his horse into a gallop after her. He could hear the others close behind him as he slowly lost sight of Emily. He growled when Kralen passed him on foot, and he suddenly ditched his horse and blurred toward them.

Emily had a big grin as she flew through the trees, easily guiding the racing stallion through her chosen path. She gasped though when a blur passed her, and she realized the heku were cheating. While the racing stallion could easily beat them out in the open, he was severely compromised by the twists and turns of the dense forest.

When she came out of the trees, she came face-to-face with over half of the seasoned Cavalry. "You cheated!"

Mark smiled. "Nope, we didn't."

"Yes, you did. You were supposed to race me on horseback."

"You didn't say that," Horace told her. "You said we had to beat you through the trees."

"No!" Emily yelled. "You still cheated. You know what I meant."

"I won," Silas said, smiling.

"You didn't win anything," she said, turning her horse back for the trees.

He suddenly appeared on the horse behind her. "I'll walk you back."

"Hey!" she yelled when he took the reins from her hands.

"Don't forget. The Elder knows I did it."

"Yeah… the Elder will know you cheat."

By the time they got back to the hills outside of town, the newer Cavalry had returned, and one rode up to her and handed her the old diary.

"You are?" she asked, thumbing through it.

"I'm Jeremy."

"Did you read it?"

"No, ma'am."

"Okay," she said, and then tucked the book into her saddle bag.

"Let's head back," Silas said, kicking her horse.

"Wait," Mark called out, and then he turned toward the city. "The previous Council is causing problems."

Emily glared. "I'll take care of them."

"No," Kralen told her. "You stay out of the way and let our Council handle this."

"I owe them."

"No," Mark said.

"Silas, take Team 8 through the cemetery," Kralen said. "We'll go meet up with the Council."

"Wait, no!" Emily yelled when Silas headed for the cemetery. She angrily crossed her arms when he kept heading for the cemetery's entrance.

Everyone fell silent when they entered the cemetery. There was always a hushed reverence in the ancient burial ground, and only the sound of hoof beats could be heard.

"Wait," Emily whispered, and started to slide off of the horse.

"What?" Silas asked.

"I want to see my grave."

He frowned but let her down and watched as she walked over and pulled off the black cover.

"Not sure this is proper," Silas grumbled.

Emily knelt down and ran her fingers over the etched stone. Next, she examined runes that were carved into the marble. "What are these for?"

"That'd be a question for the Elders," Silas said.

Emily stood up quickly and looked toward the back of the cemetery that was gated off. It was dark and gloomy in that area, and she'd never bothered to go there because it was restricted. "Did you hear that?"

Silas looked over. "No."

"Voices… like a whisper."

"That's abandoned."

"What's over there?" she asked, taking a step closer.

One of the members of the Cavalry looked over at the unkempt area. "Those are the dead. No retirees over there, no banished, just those that

were killed without honor."

"So, like a criminal graveyard?" she asked, trying to see over the fence.

"Sort of," Silas said. "No one worth anything is buried over there, and it's restricted."

Emily got on her tiptoes on one of the metal bars and looked over the railing. "I still hear whispers."

Silas appeared beside her, though he didn't have to stand on the railing to see over the fence. "I don't hear anything."

She studied the broken down cemetery with its crumbled headstones and dead grass. "This place is creepy."

"All the more reason to get you inside."

"No, I hear voices."

"So now what?"

Emily looked down the fence and saw the gate. "Do you know the code?"

"No, I'm not authorized to be in there."

"Who is?"

"The Elders," Silas said. He grabbed her ankle when she began to crawl over the fence. "Oh no ya don't."

"Let go. I want to go see."

"No! If I'm not authorized to be in there, neither are you."

"I'm a member of the Council."

He sighed and let her go. "Chevalier's going to kill me."

Emily jumped over the metal spikes and landed on the dead grass. "The voice is louder in here."

"Just one?"

"Yeah, thought it was more, but from in here I can hear just the one."

Emily knelt down and put her ear to the ground.

"Hear anything?" Silas asked.

"No"

"So let's go."

"Hello?" Emily called out, but the vast cemetery remained silent.

"Come on, Em," Silas said.

"Wait," she whispered, and cocked her head to the side.

He watched her closely.

"What's ego sum promptus?" she asked, turning to Silas.

He frowned. "It's... well... pretty much *'I'm ready'*."

"What are you ready for?" Emily yelled toward the back of the cemetery.

"Seriously, come out, or I'll have to call for the Elder."

She sighed, "I guess... though I want to know who is talking."

"Maybe Chevalier will know. He's the only one that comes in here."

"Why?"

"Something about being an Old One."

Emily crossed her arms. "That doesn't make sense."

"Well that's all I know."

"What?" Emily asked, turning suddenly back toward the cemetery. "What?"

"What's vuol dire quisnam es?"

"Get out!" Silas roared, and jumped the fence just as Emily took a step forward and disappeared into the ground with a scream.

Emily stopped screaming and fought to grab onto something. She was quickly sliding down a metal tube, deeper into the earth, and she couldn't find any way to stop her momentum. It was too dark to see, but when the metal disappeared from beneath her, she screamed again and landed hard against the cold ground, slightly twisting her ankle in the process.

She got to her knees and looked around, but her eyes wouldn't adjust.

"Did you hurt yourself?" a soft voice said from the dark.

Emily screamed and crawled away from the voice frantically.

***

"Get out of there!" Chevalier yelled.

Silas turned with wide eyes. "Emily... she... fell..."

Chevalier appeared by his side. "In here?"

He nodded. "I was trying to get her out. She kept hearing voices... and then she just fell."

Silas watched as Chevalier cleared out the exact spot Emily fell and looked down a tiny hole. "Are you sure she fell down here?"

"Yes, Elder. Right where you are."

"Damnit, Emily'd be the only one that would fit down there too."

"What's there?" Mark asked, appearing beside them.

Zohn and Quinn appeared, and Quinn was outwardly angry. "No one is supposed to be over here!"

Silas straightened up and saluted. "Sir... I was trying to get Emily to return."

"Emily came over here?"

"Yes, sir."

"Then where is she?"

"She fell down the portal," Chevalier said, looking up at him.

Zohn gasped. "She did? That's so tiny."

Quinn sighed, "So is Emily."

"Has he said anything?" Zohn asked Chevalier.

"No, nothing yet."

"Clear out!" Quinn ordered.   The members of the Cavalry immediately disappeared from the restricted cemetery.

"Emily?" Chevalier called down the metal lined hole.

***

Emily wasn't sure where she was, but she knew it was cold. "Who are you?"

She turned quickly when she heard someone behind her. "It's been thousands of years since I saw another," the voice said softly.

Emily covered her neck instinctively and whispered, "Who are you?"

"You ask my name?"

"Are you heku?"

"I am... yes. I am a heku," he said, sounding unsure.

"Well bite me and I'll ash you," she said, spinning around when she heard a sound behind her.

"You will do what?"

"Turn you to ash."

"Fascinating"

Emily backed into a wall and then used it to stand up. "Is there a light down here?"

"A light?" he asked. His voice was soft and comforting, but she fought against its sincereness and kept on guard.

"Yes, I can't see."

"You are interesting," he said, and she could tell he was closer by the sound of his voice.

"Oh?"

She heard him inhale and braced herself for an attack, but it didn't come. "You are not mortal... yet you are not heku."

"I'm... well... about half and half."

"Half and half would be a mortal though."

"So it's more like 51 / 49 I guess," she explained and then moved along the wall until she came to a corner. She turned and put her back to the cold stone walls.

"It's more," he said, sounding concerned. "Are you an Old One?"

"No"

"You carry the scent of an Ancient."

"My father... was an Ancient."

"Interesting"

Emily jumped when a light shone suddenly, and she saw a dark form light an old lantern. When he turned, he was withered and gray, his face full of deep wrinkles, and his eyes shone silver in the light.

***

Chevalier stood up and looked around the cemetery.

Zohn broke the silence. "Even as Elders we are told very little about this place."

"It's for Old Ones only," Chevalier whispered.

"Where did she fall to then?"

"The vaults," Chevalier said, looking over at them.

"The Equites vaults?!"

"Yes"

"Guarded by an Ancient?"

Chevalier nodded. "Yes, one which can communicate only with Old Ones and other Ancients that are above ground. That's why he was put down there."

"Emily's with another Ancient?" Zohn whispered.

"Yes"

"But Silas said she heard a voice."

"Somehow, she heard him. It's about time for a delivery, and he calls out to me when it's time," Chevalier said.

"How can she hear if only Old Ones and Ancients can hear him this far up?" Quinn asked.

"I don't know."

"So we dig," Zohn said.

***

"Did you injure yourself in the fall?" he asked, studying her carefully.

"No"

"Which is an untruth," he whispered, and then smiled. "Might I have a look?"

"What is this place?" Emily asked as her eyes began to adjust, and she saw the tall rows of books.

He cocked his head slightly to the side. "That is confidential."

"Is there a way out?"

"No"

Emily limped over to a chair and sat down, then looked at him. "How long have you been down here?"

"I have always been down here."

"You're an Ancient?"

"Yes"

"Then why weren't you banished with the rest?"

He frowned. "Were the Ancients banished?"

"Just some of them," she said. She wasn't quite sure what to say to him and was still waiting for an attack.

As he walked, he limped slightly, and it looked like it pained him to move. "I haven't seen another in thousands of years."

"Why are you down here then?"

"To protect what is ours."

She looked over at the books again and got the feeling that the underground expanse of books was massive.

"You are with child?"

Emily looked at him but didn't answer.

"I am sorry. That is intrusive," he said, and then sat down carefully.

"Are you hurt?" she asked him.

He thought and then looked up at her. "I am not."

Emily jerked when a loud thud sounded. The Ancient stood slowly and hobbled over to a small container. He opened it and then unrolled a parchment.

"You are Emily. Are you not?" he asked, re-rolling the paper.

"Yes"

"They are looking for you above."

She nodded. "I would think so."

"I have been rude. Are you needing nourishment?"

"You have food down here?"

"Yes, it is how I stay alive."

"I don't drink blood though," she told him.

He looked at her and frowned slightly. "You don't?"

"No"

"No, you wouldn't, would you. No one that can carry a child is a natural blood drinker," he said as he sat back down.

Finally, she sighed, "I'm sorry if this sounds rude... but... you're not going to bite me, are you?"

"Bite a mortal?" He sounded confused.

"It's... what do you eat?"

With great effort, he stood up and disappeared down one of the many dark corridors made by the towering shelves. When he returned, he had a small squirming animal in his hands.

"I do believe it's courteous to offer food to guests first," he said, holding out the animal.

Emily smiled slightly. "No, thank you."

She grimaced when he tore the small animal's head off with his

teeth and then drained it into his mouth with loud slurping sounds. When he was done, he tossed it back down one of the rows.

"How can I get back up to the top?" she asked when her stomach settled down.

He frowned. "To the surface?"

"Yes"

"There is no way."

"I can't stay down here."

"Why not?"

"I'm mortal."

"You are?" he asked, sitting down again.

Emily frowned. "Are you okay?"

"Yes... now can I look at your ankle?"

She sighed and then held it out. "I think I just twisted it."

His cold hands carefully gripped her foot as he pulled off her cowboy boot and lifted her pant leg, then looked at the dark bruise forming. "Why have you not healed?"

***

"Insane?" Zohn asked, frowning.

"Yes," Chevalier said. "The Ancients found him insane, and he was sent below ground for it, destined to forever guard the documents for the Equites."

"How insane?"

"I'm not sure he was insane at all. He was the only mortal supporting Ancient, so they deemed him insane."

"So there's hope?" Quinn asked.

"I don't know. I've never met him," Chevalier said. "He was already below ground when I was turned."

"Does he have an ability?"

"No." Chevalier stood up and sighed.

Zohn frowned. "How does he feed?"

Chevalier smiled slightly. "Off of small earth animals."

Quinn's nose wrinkled. "If he's been living off of animals, Emily has no chance."

"I don't know," Chevalier said, and then turned toward the portal and cocked his head to the side. "He is asking where she is to be filed."

"Filed?" Zohn asked.

"Maybe he is a bit insane."

"So she's alive at least?"

"Yes, now we just have to figure out how to get her out of there."

"Well she fit down the portal," Zohn said. "Let's just pull her out."

Chevalier turned and called for Kyle to bring a rope to the restricted cemetery.

***

"It does not appear to be broken," the Ancient said before sitting down.

Emily studied him. "Why are you down here?"

"I am protecting."

"I know… it just seems like almost a punishment to be stuck down here for eternity."

"It's an honor."

"I see," she said, and rubbed her hands along her arms to warm up.

"Are you cold?" he asked, looking at her oddly.

"It is kind of cold down here."

"I hadn't noticed," he said, and looked awkwardly around the area. "Who did you say you are again?"

She smiled. "Emily Winchester."

"Oh, that's right. You want information on Miles Winchester."

"Yes, that's right."

"Let me see now." He thought for a moment before walking down a dark row and disappearing.

Emily looked over when she heard something in the tube she'd fallen down, and she saw the end of a rope appear.

"Here we go," the Ancient said when he came back. He had a group of files bound together with old twine.

"What's your name?" Emily asked as she sat down beside him.

He looked up and his brow furrowed. "My name?"

"Yes, what's your name?"

"My, my," he sighed. "I do have a name."

"Do you remember it?"

"Yes, my child. Heku remember all things," he said as he started to look through files. "What part of this did you want to see?"

"First, do you have a piece of paper I can write on?"

He took a slip of paper from inside the file and handed it to her. "Here you go. This is recorded twice."

"Do you have a pen?"

He looked up curiously. "A what?"

"Something to write with."

Without a second thought, he dug a long, sharp nail into his wrist and held his bleeding hand out to her.

"Umm," she said, trying not to gag.

He looked at his wrist. "What's wrong?"

"Nothing, just… is that all you have to write with?"

"What more do you need?"

"It's okay. That will do," Emily said as she pulled a tiny root from the wall, dipped it into the Ancient's blood and then scribbled out a small note on the back of the paper. Once done, she tied it to the end of the rope and tugged on it a few times. When it disappeared up the shaft, she sat back down with the Ancient.

"It is most odd that you came here," he said, still looking through records.

"Why is that? Don't others come?"

"No, no, you are the first."

"What if they need a record?"

"Then they must dig to the door," he said. He looked over, and Emily followed his gaze to a stone door built into the wall.

"No one's ever come down?"

"No, dear," he said, and handed her a file. "Is that all you came down for?"

She smiled. "Yes."

"Good, good, would you like something to drink?"

"No, thank you."

The Ancient disappeared down another dark corridor and Emily turned to the file.

***

Chevalier sighed, "She said she's visiting and will be a moment."

Kyle gasped. "She's… she's visiting?"

"Apparently"

"With the Ancient?"

"He's the only one down there."

Quinn chuckled. "Well, she must be safe."

"I still don't like her down there with him."

Quinn looked at the note. "What's that paper?"

Chevalier flipped it over and read it. "It's information on the Miles Winchester home."

"So she went down to find out about her history?"

"I doubt it. Silas said she fell down there."

"Is that written in blood?"

Chevalier chuckled. "Yes, that's what the Ancient writes in. I'm sure he helped her."

Zohn studied the hole. "How did she even fit?"

Chevalier shrugged.

"So let's send Alexis down to get her."

"I'm not sure even Alexis would fit down there."

"So send a note down and ask her to please come back up," Quinn suggested.

"You two have this handled. I'm going to go back to the Council," Zohn said, then blurred away.

Chevalier wrote on a note and dropped it down the hole, followed by the rope.

***

The Ancient looked up and saw the paper slide down into the room. "Curious."

Emily looked up. "What is?"

"Another note."

She smiled. "It might be for me."

He stood up slowly and limped over to the note. He read it several times and then turned it over in his hand. "I'm not sure who it is for."

"What does it say?"

"It's for Emily."

She smiled. "That's me."

He looked up at her. "Oh, well… this note is for you then."

Emily took the note from the Ancient and read Chevalier's request that she come back up immediately.

She looked over at the door again. "So heku can dig down to this door and come in for records?"

"Yes"

"Chevalier can dig down here and get us?"

"Who is Chevalier?"

"He's my husband."

He frowned. "Is he heku?"

"Yes"

"Are you?"

"Sort of," she said, and tried the door knob. The door didn't budge.

"Is he an Ancient?"

"No, he's an Old One though."

The Ancient thought. "No… no, I know all of the Old Ones, and he's not one of them."

Emily turned to him. "Chevalier isn't?"

"No, he is not."

"Everyone says he is."

"I know them all."

She thought for a moment. "You know the entire Equites Council?"

"Yes"

"Who is on it?"

He thought. "That… you may not be permitted to know."

She smiled. "It's okay. I'm an Equites."

"You are?"

"Yes"

"Are you heku?"

"Yes," she said, finally giving in.

"Oh, well okay. So there's Aulus, Titus, Appius, Equitis, Amintah, Haemon, Elpidios, Yorgos, Zenon, Aalis, Barhan, Sevar, and Khalid."

Emily shrugged. "I don't know any of those."

"But you are Equites?"

"Yes"

"Curious"

"Do you know Sotomar?"

He thought and then shook his head. "No, I do not."

"He's another Old One."

"No, the Old Ones are Ariadne, Diocletian, Himerius…"

Emily smiled. "That's okay. I'm sure he's not among them."

"I can name them all."

"Yes, I'm sure you can."

When the Ancient didn't speak again, Emily started reading through the file on Miles Winchester. She was shocked to learn that he was attributed to killing over 100,000 heku from all three factions.

"You have an odd scent," the Ancient said after almost an hour of reading.

She nodded. "I've been told that."

"You must be careful around the heku."

"I am. I promise."

"There is very little control among the species."

Emily laughed. "Yes, I know."

"Hmmm," he sighed, and sat in silence when she turned back to the file.

Finally, she looked up. "Would you like me to get you out of here?"

He cocked his head to the side. "Away from the vault?"

"Yes"

"There is no way out."

"You said the heku could dig down to get records."

"Yes, but then they stay."

She gasped. "What?"

"That is our way. If they need records that badly, they dig down, but then they stay."

Emily looked quickly around the vault. "Is anyone else down here?"

"No, no one has ever done it."

She frowned. "That makes no sense. Why keep precious files if you can never access them?"

"You can. You simply dig down to my door," he explained.

"I see... so what was your name?"

He smiled. "I do have a name."

"Yes, but what is it?"

"No one's asked me my name in thousands of years."

Emily watched him as he stood up slowly and limped down a dark row, then disappeared. When he returned, he had another file. He handed it to her and then sat down.

Emily opened the file and thumbed through old parchments full of names. "Are these all your names?"

"Mine? No... they are Equites."

She smiled and put the file down. "I need to send another message to the surface."

He nodded, bit his wrist and then held it out. Using the same root, she wrote Chevalier a note and sent it up with the rope.

***

Chevalier sighed and hissed slightly.

"What?" Kyle asked as he studied the ground.

"She said she can't leave him down there alone."

"Of course she did."

Chevalier smiled. "She said he's not all the way there."

"Meaning?"

"Meaning, he is insane."

"Then she's not safe down there."

He shrugged. "She must be, or she wouldn't casually be writing to us."

"True, but he could still turn on her."

"Rumor has it... I'd say from about 4,000 years ago, that he'd lived on animals for so long, that he no longer wanted human blood," Chevalier explained.

"Well that's lucky for her," Quinn said.

"Now to figure out how to get her back up here."

"Just tell her that's his job to stay there."

Chevalier looked at him oddly.

Quinn chuckled. "Yeah, that'd never work."

"If he is insane and somehow makes it up here..."

"We'd have to kill him," Quinn said. "Tell her that. That'll change her mind."

"I'm not going to bring that up to her."

***

"It's Emily," she said, smiling.

"Oh what a pretty name," the Ancient said as he sat down. "What can I do for you then?"

She smiled broadly. "There are secrets down here, right?"

"Well, I suppose there are."

"Like what?"

He frowned. "You're mortal though."

"No, I'm heku."

"Oh, okay then. Well, there are things such as how to bring one out of retirement, the retirement incantations, or… well there's even a way to un-turn a heku."

"There is?!" she gasped.

"Well, yes, though I've never heard of it done. It can only be performed by an Ancient, but the Old Ones know about it."

"What about…" She hesitated. "The Yisolatara ritual?"

He nodded. "Yes, yes, that's down here too."

"What else do the Old Ones know that Ancients only can do?"

"Summon each other, of course," he said, smiling. "You're an Old One though, you should know that."

She nodded. "I did… so what good is it to summon each other?"

"That's how we communicate across vast differences."

"I see… and Old Ones can do that?"

"Well, no… Ancients can do it, call other Ancients and those with Ancient's blood." He fell serious and looked into her eyes. "You said you're an Ancient?"

"Yes," she said, leaning toward him.

"The summons was going to be used with the Aboleo," he whispered.

"What would that do?"

"You remember when rumors started that the Old Ones were trying to arrange to have the Ancients banished?"

"Yes"

"This would take care of the Old Ones. We would summon them and then Aboleo. They would be ash."

"It would destroy the Old Ones?"

"Yes, then we would start over. The main meeting place for the Ancients was in what is now called Wiltshire, England. A central location, yet a neutral location where the Ancients could gather long enough to make decisions before going their own separate ways."

She thought. "Wiltshire, England? I've heard of that place."

"Yes… we also have an incantation to incapacitate a mortal. That made it easier to feed in small tribes. If the mortal screamed, it woke up the others, so we had to knock them unconscious first."

She smiled. "I'll have the files on the things you just mentioned."

The Ancient nodded and then shuffled down a dark corridor. When he got back, he had a stack of files that he handed to Emily.

She sat back and began to read each of the files as the Ancient sat patiently and watched. When she came to an interesting incantation, she entered the information into her phone for later use. It was hours later before another note was dropped down with the rope.

"Ahh, a message," the Ancient said with a smile. He picked up the note and read it.

"Is it for Emily?"

"Why, yes it is… not sure who that is though."

"I'll take it," she told him. She read the note, a brief request for her to take the rope and return to the surface.

The Ancient moved to the portal and cocked his head to the side, then turned to Emily. "Your presence is requested by the Council."

"I'm sure it is," she said, changing files.

He lifted her up by her arm. "You musn't keep the Council waiting."

She stood up and put the files down on a table. "I don't want to leave you here alone."

"Why not?"

"It's not right."

He smiled. "It is my job."

Suddenly, an image flashed through her mind of Dustin tearing Nicholas' head off right in front of her. She frowned and watched as the Ancient began putting away the files.

Emily sighed when she realized that the heku would kill him the second he did anything that they deemed insane. She herself had told Chevalier that he wasn't with it, and her heart sunk. She gave him the ammunition to kill the Ancient the second he saw him.

"Oh, hello," the Ancient said when he saw Emily. "What can I get for you?"

She looked around the cold, dark room and then turned pained eyes toward him. "I don't want to leave you here alone."

He smiled. "I'm not alone. You are here now."

"I am supposed to go back up to the surface."

"Yes, Equitis is calling for you."

"Who?"

"Equitis, from the Council."

"Is he the Old One?"

"Yes"

She nodded and then remembered that most heku had had many names.

"I told him no one can leave the vault," the Ancient said.

"You know Equitis well?"

"Yes, I do."

She smiled. "Tell me about him."

"Oh, he was a prized possession when he turned. As a mortal, he was one of the strongest leaders and was sought by all three factions," the Ancient said, and then sighed. "He didn't want to turn though, so the Ancients gathered and came up with a plan to use Ephraim."

Emily leaned forward to listen.

"As a mortal, he was sought out from great distances by every father with a daughter. Everyone wanted him as their son, so he could produce noble children. He often said that no woman would be worthy to carry his children though, so he remained alone. Women were weak and feeble, and he was strong and powerful."

She frowned.

"Once turned, he hated the mortals, despised them, I should say. So now he hated Ephraim for turning him, yet Ephraim took him away from the species he loathed. I've never seen any... well except for the Ancients, who hated mortals as badly as Equitis does."

"Hates mortals?"

"That may not even be a strong enough word. The Ancients were so proud to have turned him and had him share their beliefs on the mortals. Do you know that Equitis got mad at a small clan of mortals so badly, that he wiped them out without a drop of blood hitting the ground?" the Ancient said, smiling.

"Equitis did?"

He nodded. "Yes. I've never seen such loathing for a species that was once his own. It just made the Ancients prouder, the more he hated them. That also earned him a spot on the Equites Council. He was the first non-Ancient on the Council and was made Chief Enforcer because of his hatred."

"But the Chief Enforcer protects mortals."

"Not back then. Back then, they punished mortals for wrongdoing against the heku."

Emily just nodded, but her heart sank.

"Just stay away from Equitis, child. You will be safer."

"The baby is his though," she whispered.

The Ancient frowned. "Equitis is the father of your child?"

She nodded.

"That's very peculiar. What special traits do you have that sets you apart from other mortals?"

"I'm half heku."

"That makes you a mortal, dear. Though I do detect some Ancient in you. Very odd."

"My father was an Ancient."

The Ancient gasped. "That can't be!"

"Why not?"

He stood up and disappeared back down a hallway, then returned with a file. "It's in the heku laws. Ancients were very careful not to produce children with the lowly mortals… just in case one became lax, their children and the mothers were to be killed immediately."

"Why is that?" She was finding it hard to breathe.

He smiled. "No mortal is worthy to carry the blood of an Ancient."

"I see."

"So Equitis knew you were half Ancient, and that deemed you worthy?"

"He didn't know."

"He didn't? Are you certain?"

"Actually, no, I'm not. How many mortal women did he turn down?"

"Thousands, the great Equitis was very picky. He said no woman would ever be worthy of his children. I guess the one thing he despised worse than mortals, was their women."

Emily frowned. "Why is that?"

The Ancient shrugged. "I don't know. He used them and then left, making sure never to leave tracks."

"Used them?"

"That's enough about him, dear. He's not going to like you, nor will he want you as a wife, so you best just leave him be."

Emily fought back tears. "Can… can you go get me something to drink?"

"Oh, yes… guests must drink. It's polite," he said as he disappeared down a dark passage.

Emily walked over and wrapped the rope around her forearm and then tugged it a few times. The ride up the tiny tube was fast, and soon, she was back in the dark cemetery.

"Are you hurt?" Chevalier asked when he saw the tears.

She shook her head and looked down the hole. "He's all alone."

"He doesn't know any different."

Emily looked up at him and glared. "And you… stay away from me."

"What?" he gasped as she limped off.

"What did you do to her?" Kyle asked.

"Em," Chevalier called out, following her.

"Stay away from me!" she screamed, and stormed into the palace.

Kyle walked up by Chevalier and frowned. "What'd you do to her?"

"I didn't do anything!"

He shrugged. "Sounds like you did."

Chevalier glared when Kyle walked into the palace.

"I didn't see you do anything," Quinn said, and followed Kyle. Chevalier finally calmed down and went into the palace, then took his seat at the council chambers.

"What did you do to Em?" Zohn asked him.

"I didn't do anything!" he roared.

Zohn's eyes grew wide, and he sat back.

"Next," he growled and then turned to the trial area.

***

Emily sat on the bay window and looked out over the lush green lawns of Council City. She started to wonder if the Ancient was too crazy and maybe even misunderstood who Equitis was. It finally dawned on her who she could find out from.

She pulled out her cell phone and dialed the Valle Council.

"What?" Elder Randall yelled.

"Stop yelling at me," she hissed.

"Emily?" Sotomar asked, shocked.

"Who is older, you or Chevalier?"

"Excuse me?"

"Age… who was turned first, you or Chevalier?"

"That's not proper to ask."

"I don't give a rat's ass about proper," she said, irritated. "It's an easy question… who is older?"

Emily could tell that Sotomar had picked up the phone, and taken her off of speakerphone. "Why do you ask?"

"I want to know about him when he first turned."

Sotomar sighed, "That was a long time ago."

"So you do remember him?"

"No, actually, I'm a couple hundred years younger than he is."

"Can you give me the phone number of a Valle Old One who is older than him?"

"Not right off hand. You're going to be hard-pressed to find anyone older than Chevalier that's not retired."

"Did you know him?"

"I met him shortly after I turned, yes."

"Was he a mortal hater?"

There was silence for a few minutes, and when Sotomar spoke, he

sounded pleased. "Yes, he was."

"Was it the Chief Enforcer's job to protect mortals?"

"No, it was not."

"He hated mortals then… especially the women?"

"Yes, why the questions? Did something happen?"

Emily answered him by hanging up the phone. She thought for a moment and then picked up the St. Bernard puppy and headed down to the trial area.

"Good evening, Lady Emily," Derrick said, smiling.

"I need to talk to the Records Keeper."

He opened the door. "Go on in."

Emily walked in and then turned when Kyle blurred to her and tried to take the heavy puppy. "Go away."

"You shouldn't be carrying him," he said, and finally took the puppy from her.

She glared as he moved off to the side a bit.

"Can we help you, Em?" Chevalier asked, unsure if she was still mad.

Emily walked up to Jerry, the Records Keeper. "I need the phone number of an Old One who is older than Chevalier."

"What? Why?" Chevalier asked, surprised.

She ignored him and addressed Jerry. "Can you give me that?"

"Might I ask why?"

"No, you can either tell me, or I'll call William next."

"Next? You called the Valle?" Zohn asked.

Emily glanced at him and then crossed her arms and turned to Jerry. "So?"

Jerry looked at Chevalier, who finally nodded, exasperated with the entire situation. "The only two I know of are both retired."

"Out in our cemetery?"

"Yes"

She turned to leave but then sighed when Quinn called her. She turned slowly. "What?"

"Why do you want to know?"

"None of your business."

Quinn smiled slightly. "I'm not accustomed to being told no."

"Then get used to it," she snapped, and stormed out of the room.

Kyle looked at Chevalier. "She's not calling you Chev."

"I noticed that."

"Do you think the Ancient said something to her?"

"I'll go find out," Chevalier said. He disappeared from the trial area and returned twenty minutes later.

"Did he help?" Kyle asked.

Chevalier sighed, "He doesn't recall a mortal being down with him."

Zohn smiled. "Nice."

"An Ancient with no heku memory?"

Chevalier shrugged. "He's been down there longer than I've been a heku."

Emily walked out to the cemetery and looked around at head stones. She finally realized she didn't know the names of the Old Ones, so she decided to just yell the incantation and wake them all up.

Pulling out her phone, she scrolled down to the incantations marked 'Revive Retired'.

Not knowing what she was actually saying, she called out the words on her phone in an unknown language. "Audite mihi."

She stumbled when the ground shook beneath her feet, then she looked around and frowned. Once she was sure the small earthquake was over, she turned back to the cemetery. "Ego dico vobis…"

Emily grabbed the iron fence when the earth shook again.

***

Mark blurred into the council chambers. "E… Emily… she's trying to… revive the retired."

Chevalier sighed, "Only Elders and Ancients can do that."

"Well… she seems to know the words."

"How?" Kyle asked, frowning.

When the ground shook again, Chevalier disappeared from the council chambers, followed shortly by the rest of the Council. By the time they arrived, Chevalier had Emily pinned to the ground as he straddled her thighs, and his hand was firmly over her mouth.

Emily was pulling at his fingers and fought to get up.

"Elder…" Kyle said softly. "Calm down."

"What were you thinking?!" Chevalier yelled at her.

Quinn nodded at the Chief of Defense and the Records Keeper, and they fanned out to see if any of the heku had been revived.

Zohn reached down and put a hand on Chevalier's shoulder. "She didn't know. Let her up."

He removed his hand from her mouth and then stood up and held a hand down to help her up. She batted it away and then stood up and turned to him, glaring.

He took a deep breath. "I'm calm…"

"I'm not!" she yelled. "Do not touch me!"

"You can't revive them all."

She crossed her arms. "I just want the Old Ones."

"Why?"

All she did was glare at him.

"None were successfully revived," the Chief of Defense reported in.

"How can you even know how to do that?" Zohn asked her.

She smiled. "You'd be amazed at what I found in the vault."

The heku all gasped and looked at her with wide eyes.

"Like what?" Quinn asked in a cracked voice.

"I'm not going to tell you. I may need it someday."

"That ritual takes an Elder or an Ancient to perform," Zohn explained.

Emily shrugged. "It was worth a shot."

Kyle looked at them. "The ground shaking then?"

Chevalier looked up at the sky. "That's what happens when an Ancient revives a bunch of retired heku."

"The ground shakes?" the Chief of Staff asked.

He looked at Emily. "Yes."

"Let's all move back into the council chambers," Quinn said calmly. "Apparently, we need to discuss a few matters."

"I'm not going anywhere with him," Emily said, looking at Chevalier.

"Why is that?" he asked.

Her eyes narrowed. "Don't let this mere mortal woman keep the great Equitis from his trials."

"What?" he growled, and then followed her when she stormed off.

Zohn and Quinn each took an arm to keep him from following her. Quinn finally spoke, "Let her go. We need to meet as a Council."

Chevalier nodded. "Okay."

Once the Council was seated in the Council's conference room, Kyle stood. "It shouldn't surprise us that she has some of the Ancient's abilities."

"She's never shown any of that before," the Chief of Staff Said.

Quinn shrugged. "We've never given her the opportunity."

"What else do you suppose she knows?"

"There's no telling," Chevalier said.

Kyle shrugged. "I can talk to her."

***

"Emily, it's good to hear from you," William said, sounding pleased that she called.

"Thanks, I have a question though."

"What is it?"

"Do the Encala have any Old Ones that are older than Chevalier?"

The Encala's Records Keeper spoke, "That's hard to say. I'm not sure how old he is."

"Is your oldest Old One retired?"

"No"

"Can I call him?"

William sounded amused. "Might we ask why?"

"Sure, I want to know about Chevalier when he was turned."

"We'll send him over with Lt. Andrew."

"That's not necessary. A phone call will do."

"We insist. Expect them tomorrow," Iuna said.

"Okay, thanks," she said, and then hung up. After a few minutes, she heard a knock. "Who is it?"

"Alex"

"Come in," Emily said, and turned toward her daughter.

Alexis sat down and looked out the window. "Need to talk?"

"You heard, huh?"

"No, I just know the Council is meeting in private about something you did."

"Just do me a favor, Alex," Emily said, taking her hand. "Stay away from your dad until I figure something out."

Alexis frowned. "Like, avoid him?"

"Yes"

"Why?"

"Just for me, please."

Alexis sighed, "Okay, though I wish you'd tell me why."

"I need to do some research."

"Oh, the Council is calling for me."

Emily nodded. "Just tell them no."

"I can't tell them no."

"Yes, you can."

Alexis stood slowly and smiled. "Just this once, for you."

Emily watched her leave and then turned back to the window. Alexis walked down and smiled at Derrick.

"They're waiting for you," he said, reaching for the door.

"Actually, Derrick," she said, and stopped his hand. "I'm not going to answer the summons."

He frowned. "You're not?"

"No, please tell them that as a favor to Mom, I'm not to speak to Dad," Alexis said, and then smiled at him. He nodded and watched her walk down the stairs.

Clearing his throat, he stepped in.

"Is she almost here?" Zohn asked.

He sighed, "Miss Alexis said that as a favor to Emily, she's not

coming in."

"A favor to Em?" Chevalier asked.

"Yes, Elder. She said she can't speak to you."

"Why?"

"She didn't say, sir."

Chevalier sighed and looked at Kyle. "Your turn."

Kyle smiled slightly and blurred from the room. He lightly knocked on Chevalier's bedroom door and then opened it when he didn't hear a response. Emily was curled up on the bay window, asleep.

He hurried back down to the council chambers. "She's asleep. Go see if her dreams tell you."

Chevalier disappeared before any could see the Old One move.

Quinn turned to the others. "Now that he's gone, we need to discuss what happens if Emily has the abilities of an Old One or even of an Ancient."

"I find it hard to believe that she could have any of the abilities of an Ancient, and none of us have noticed in the last 30 years," said the Chief of Defense.

Kyle shrugged. "We've never really tested it. It's not like she knows a bunch of incantations."

Quinn turned to him. "How can we test it?"

"I thought we just did," Kyle said. "She almost woke up the entire cemetery, and she heard what only Old Ones and Ancients can hear."

Chevalier watched Emily sleep in the bay window. It was obvious that she was dreaming, even though she didn't move or jerk like she used to. Her hands were tightly gripping the blanket, and her breathing was fast.

Careful not to wake her, he reached out and touched her shoulder, and was immediately thrown into her dream. Suddenly, blackness invaded his vision, and he couldn't breathe or move. He began to thrash, trying to free himself until he moved back and let go, breaking contact.

He panted as he caught his breath and then watched as her knuckles turned white from gripping the blanket.

Not quite sure what he'd seen, he touched her again and found himself completely restrained and unable to move in the dark. The tight binds kept him from taking a deep breath, and he was instantly panicked.

Again, his thrashing broke contact from his hand, and he looked down at her. Deciding he was ending it, Chevalier sat beside her in the bay window and whispered to her. "Em… wake up."

Emily stirred slightly and then looked over at him. "Why did you wake me up?"

"Do you remember your dream?"

"No"

"It was bad…"

"Like you care," she said, and turned away from him to look out the window.

"What do you mean by that?"

"You're just not the man I thought you were."

He stood up and frowned. "Explain yourself."

She sighed, "I may be wrong. I'll know tomorrow."

"What happens tomorrow?"

She looked over at him. "Tomorrow, I'm told the truth."

Furious, Chevalier decided to leave before his violent urges lashed out at her. Once seated, he glared toward the trial room door.

"Did you catch her dream?" Zohn asked when Chevalier didn't speak.

"Yes"

"What was it?" Kyle asked.

"Darkness, restraint, panic, torment…"

"Is she okay?"

He looked at Kyle. "She doesn't remember it."

"So why are you mad?" Quinn asked.

"She said I'm not the man she thought I was."

"Meaning?"

"She won't tell me!" he yelled, and slammed his fists on the desk. "She's infuriating."

To help Chevalier relieve some frustrations, Zohn called for six prisoners that were to be tried together. After a long interrogation session that lasted through the night, Chevalier and the Chief Interrogator returned to the council chambers and sat down.

"Before we bring in the accused," Zohn said. "The Encala have representatives here."

"Why?" Chevalier asked.

"We'll have to ask them."

The Council turned when William, Lt. Andrew, and another heku stepped into the room. Chevalier stood angrily and appeared in front of the heku.

"Why are you here, Tiberius?" Chevalier's hands balled into fists.

"I go by Ovidius now," he said calmly.

"I don't care what you go by!" Chevalier yelled. "You have no business here, and if you don't leave, I'll be forced to repay you for Londinium."

"That? That was thousands of years ago."

"You don't deserve forgiveness."

He smiled. "I'm here by request though."

"Who requested you?"

"Your wife did."

Chevalier growled and was instantly restrained by Zohn and Kyle.

"Hold off, Elder," Kyle said. "We'll get him… let's find out what's going on."

Ovidius snarled. "If it's an Old One fight you want, bring it on Equitis."

The Chief Interrogator joined Zohn and Kyle as they pulled Chevalier away from the Encala.

William finally spoke, "If we can just see Emily, then we'll be on our way. She did request we bring him."

"How does she even know you?" Chevalier yelled.

Lt. Andrew looked over at the enraged Elder. "She doesn't know him. She asked to see the eldest Encala Old One."

"Bring Emily," Quinn called out to Derrick. "Also get 12 of the Cavalry in here."

Lt. Andrew and William each grabbed onto Ovidius when he lunged at Chevalier, hissing.

Emily stepped in and gasped at the standoff. She moved to stand between them, though their glares were far above her head.

"Chevalier, stop it!" she yelled.

He looked down at her with enraged eyes. "Why did you summon him?"

"None of your business," she said, and then turned to Ovidius. "You're the Encala Old One?"

He answered her by struggling against William and Lt. Andrew to get to Chevalier.

William smiled, though strain showed on his face. "Yes, he is."

She nodded. "Let's go out on horses for a bit."

"No!" Chevalier roared. "You are not going out with them."

Emily glared at him. "You can't tell me what to do."

Quinn sighed, "You may talk to them, but you have to take guards."

"No, I don't," she said to him. His eyes grew wide and then he calmed quickly.

"You have to be protected."

"I'm sure the three Encala can keep me safe," she said, heading for the door.

"I meant safe from them."

She ignored Quinn and left the council chambers, followed by the three Encala while the Equites held Chevalier back.

Emily was quiet while she led them out to the stables, watched closely by the curious Cavalry. William couldn't help but watch them carefully, as they were the ones that destroyed his faction.

Once everyone had a horse, Emily and Ovidius mounted the horses

quickly, and watched as William and Lt. Andrew struggled a bit before settling down in the saddles.

When they started out for the gates, Emily turned to William. "For someone as old as you are, I'd think you would have been on a horse or two in your day."

William smiled. "Carriages."

"Wimp"

"Wimp?"

Lt. Andrew chuckled. "Only the poor rode horses. The wealthy had carriages."

"Even to go to war?"

"I didn't go to war," William said.

Emily frowned. "Why not?"

"I was the Coven Lord."

"Not following."

"I stayed to make decisions while those below me fought."

She thought about that until they reached the green hills to the east of the city.

"Now, do you want to tell us why we're here?" William asked.

Emily looked over at Ovidius. "You're an Old One?"

"Yes"

"Older than Chevalier?"

"No, I'm a few centuries younger."

She sighed, "Is no one older than him?"

"Only the Ancients and a few that are retired."

"Fine then... I want to know everything you know about Chevalier's early days as a heku."

Ovidius's eyebrows rose. "You do?"

"Yes"

"What's up?" Lt. Andrew asked.

She looked over at her cherished friend. "I spent some time with an Ancient..."

"Recently?"

"Yes"

His eyes narrowed. "The Equites have revived an Ancient?"

"No, he's in the vault."

William gasped. "How did you get into the vault?"

"I fell."

"You can't fall into a vault."

"I did."

Ovidius shrugged. "So what did the Ancient say about me?"

"He didn't talk about you... he spoke about Equitis."

"Right, what did he say exactly?"

Emily checked the hills for any sign of an Equites and then turned back to Ovidius. "He said that Chevalier hated mortals... like really hated them."

Ovidius nodded. "He did."

"How bad?"

"Pretty bad, why?"

"As Chief Enforcer, he punished mortals for messing with the heku."

"Right"

"When did that change?"

William shrugged. "That had to have been around 400AD."

"The Ancient said that Chevalier hated mortal women more than the men."

Lt. Andrew moved his horse closer to Emily. "Did Chevalier do something to you?"

"Did you know your Elder was an Ancient?"

"Yes"

"And my dad?"

"I didn't know that until you came to the palace," Lt. Andrew said.

"What are the chances that Chevalier knew for a long time?"

"I don't think he did," William said. "We kept the Ancient from the factions, and we didn't even know he was your father."

"Tell us what's going on," Lt. Andrew said.

Emily sighed, "The Ancient showed me a rule that if an Ancient knocked up a mortal, both the baby and the mother were to be killed immediately."

Ovidius nodded. "I remember that rule."

"When was it repealed?"

"I don't think it was."

William smiled. "Are you afraid that because you're the daughter of an Ancient, that we're going to kill you?"

"No, I can defend myself."

"Then what's the problem?"

"The Ancient said that for Chevalier to be with me, he had to have known I'm different... because the great Equitis didn't even like mortals, despised them, especially the women."

"I've never seen any heku, other than the Ancients, that hated mortals as badly as Equitis did," Ovidius said.

"He slaughtered innocent humans," she whispered, and looked out over Council City.

Ovidius nodded. "Yes."

"When did he change his views?"

Ovidius looked over at William, who cleared his throat before

speaking, "I don't know when he changed exactly. Once Chief Enforcers were set to punish the heku instead of mortals, he kept his hatred but enjoyed the kind of torture a heku could take."

She looked him in the eyes. "Why is he with me?"

"That's hard for us to say."

"Would he be if I were 100% mortal?"

"I don't know," Ovidius said. "He turned down many offers from what I've heard. Rumors were that he was a fierce warrior and a demanding leader, and that no woman was fit to carry his children."

"We were all pretty shocked when we heard that he'd bonded with a mortal," William explained. "Then when your heritage came out, it made more sense."

"I don't even know him," she whispered softly. "He's caring and kind..."

"No, Em, he's not," Lt. Andrew said. "He's famous for his brutal nature and harsh ways. He's one of the most vicious heku known to our kind."

She looked at him and frowned. "Because of what he did to the Encala?"

"No, because of how he tortures for fun."

"He does?"

"Yes, I think all of the Equites do. He's just better at it."

"How do I not know all of this?"

"We keep things from you," William said. "You're... well soft and frail... our ways would hurt you too badly."

She ignored the insult and continued to watch the city.

Lt. Andrew finally broke the silence, "If you're afraid of Chevalier, you can stay with us."

"Chevalier has always been rock steady. He's logical, and his actions are well thought out. He protects mortals, doesn't hate them, and he cares a lot about his family," Emily said, mostly to convince herself.

William watched her. "Things change, Emily. I'm sure even if he once loathed the mortals, that's all changed."

"Has it?" she asked, looking at him. "Or am I just not mortal enough to feel that wrath?"

"What are you going to do?"

"Maybe I'll turn him back into a mortal."

William chuckled. "That's not possible."

Emily looked over at Ovidius and caught the surprise in his eyes.

She looked him in the eye and saw the anger building, so she decided not to push that. "I don't know what I'm going to do."

Lt. Andrew gently took her hand. "Come back to our palace and give yourself time to think about it."

"He's not going to hurt me. I just need to find out if he knew I was half Ancient, and if he's still a mortal hater."

"You sure he's not going to hurt you?"

"Yes. I do have another question though."

"Okay"

"When an Ancient performed rituals, did the ground shake?"

William frowned. "Excuse me?"

"You know… like an earthquake almost."

"Sometimes… it depends on how big the ritual was."

"Like what?"

"Well, when he put the rune on your thigh, the ground didn't shake. That was a small ritual, and no one even noticed."

"What if an Ancient attempted to revive an entire cemetery full of retired heku?"

"Yes, that would cause the earth to shake," William said, amused.

"Why would an Ancient even do that though?" Ovidius asked, watching her closely.

She shrugged. "Just asking. So little things they could do in private, but big things let everyone around them know?"

"Yes, but it wasn't to let everyone know," William explained. "When an Ancient did something big, it went against nature and caused things to become disturbed. They didn't do rituals like that often."

"Were there things Old Ones could do that other heku couldn't?"

Lt. Andrew spoke after a few moments of silence. "You're starting to tread on information that's restricted."

She smiled. "You're Encala… who cares if it's restricted?"

"True," he chuckled.

"So?"

"Yes," William said. "There were things that the Old Ones could do that we can't. They usually kept the information to themselves though, so even I don't know most of them."

"But you do?" she asked Ovidius.

He nodded.

"What are the chances that I could do them too?"

"Why would you be able to?"

"My father was an Ancient."

Ovidius shrugged. "I still doubt you could. It's no secret that you, aside from percentage, are mostly mortal."

"It's getting cold," she said as a cold breeze came from the north.

William nodded. "Let's go back then. I can hear them calling the Cavalry to come check on us."

She nodded and silently followed the Encala back into town. As they passed through the city, residents shut up their houses and peered

out at them from behind locked doors.

Chevalier and Kyle were waiting in the stables when they rode up. Chevalier carefully watched Ovidius and the tension was strong.

"Are you okay?" he asked, helping Emily down off of her horse.

"I'm fine."

"What's up then?" Kyle asked before handing Emily's stallion off to a member of the Cavalry to take care of.

When she didn't answer, William smiled. "She just had some questions is all."

"Like what?"

"Like private questions."

Kyle glanced at Chevalier and then held his hand out. "Come on, Em. I'll take you in for dinner."

She looked back at William and smiled and then took Kyle's hand and left for the palace.

Chevalier glared at Ovidius. "What did you tell her?"

He smiled. "Just what she wanted to know."

"Lies?"

"No, I told the truth."

"About what?" Chevalier asked, moving to stand directly in front of the smaller heku.

"If she wants you to know, she'll tell you," Ovidius snapped.

Chevalier shoved the other Old One against the stable door, and they immediately blurred into a fight that even the other heku couldn't see. Mark saw the initial push and called for the entire Cavalry.

The Cavalry fell back to the walls of the stable and watched the Encala to make sure they didn't interfere with the fight. Zohn and Quinn joined when they heard what was going on.

"Saw this coming," Zohn said, watching the blur of the fight.

"Wish I could see what was going on," Quinn said.

"Just keep Emily out of here."

Mark nodded. "She's with Kralen, and he knows to keep her out of the stables."

"I should go back and talk to the Valle," Zohn said, smiling. "This is much more interesting though."

"Need Cavalry in there?"

"No, the Council can handle them."

"What the hell?!" Sotomar growled as he stepped into the stables. His eyes were the only ones that could catch every aspect of the brutal fight.

Mark looked at him. "Stay out of it."

Sotomar looked over at Zohn. "They're going to kill each other. If you want to keep your Elder, I suggest you stop this."

"He's losing?" Quinn gasped.

"Well… no… but they are pretty evenly matched."

"I don't want to stop them," Zohn said.

"Me either," Quinn agreed.

"Well I sure as hell can," Sotomar said, stepping forward. Mark appeared in front of him.

"No," Mark said.

Suddenly, Cavalry was surrounding the Valle.

"Would you two at least act like Old Ones!" Sotomar yelled. "It's disgusting how juvenile this fight is. Get over it!"

"You know what this is about?" Zohn asked him.

"Yes, and it's childish to still be mad about it."

"What was it?"

"I'd rather not say."

The heku all turned back to the fight when it stopped suddenly, and Chevalier had Ovidius pinned to the straw floor with a hand around his neck. Both were beaten and bloody, with torn clothes and vicious wounds across their bodies.

"Kyle," Chevalier hissed, still out of breath from the fight.

Kyle appeared in the stables, and his eyes grew wide at the bloody mass. "Yes, Elder?"

"No!" William yelled. "You cannot banish him."

"Do it," Chevalier growled.

Kyle stepped forward with the dagger, and Lt. Andrew moved to block him. "No."

"He's already been punished for that," Sotomar told Chevalier. "You can't do it again."

Chevalier tightened his grip, cutting off Ovidius' airway until he fell unconscious. Once the Encala's body lay motionless, Chevalier fell back against the straw, gripping his side as he fought to catch his breath.

"Grow up," Sotomar hissed.

"Damn," Chevalier groaned as the bites across his body healed slowly.

When Ovidius regained consciousness, he moaned in pain and rolled way from where Chevalier was recovering. "I hate you."

"Likewise," Chevalier hissed.

"Pathetic," Sotomar mumbled, and then turned back for the palace.

Mark smiled and walked over to Chevalier. "Feel better?"

He chuckled, though still in pain. "Yes."

"Get him," William said, starting for the door. "Let's go before they decide to go at it again."

Lt. Andrew helped Ovidius up, and soon, the Encala were out of Council City. Chevalier slowly made it to his feet but stumbled and

Mark caught him.

Quinn shook his head and returned to the council chambers while Zohn stayed behind with Chevalier.

"You're going to let Emily see you like that?" Zohn asked when Mark helped the Elder out of the stables.

"Damnit, no," Chevalier said. "Take me to the barracks."

Mark nodded and disappeared with Chevalier.

"Don't you have something to do?" Zohn asked the Cavalry that was still in the stables. They disappeared, and Zohn returned to the council chambers.

Chapter 8

"Are we sure we want to do this?" Quinn asked after Derrick left to get Emily.

Chevalier nodded. "We need to find out what's going through that head of hers."

"My guess is hormones," Kyle said. "Remember, she always gets moody."

"This is beyond moody though."

He shrugged. "I think it's normal."

"She also had time alone with the Encala again," the Chief of Defense said. "That's not safe, nor is it allowed."

"I just think that this may be a matter that Chevalier needs to deal with and not this Council," Quinn explained.

"She won't talk to me though," Chevalier reminded him.

"Kyle then."

"She won't talk to me about the Elder. She thinks I'll tell him," Kyle said.

Quinn smiled. "She knows us too well."

"Do we get to know what Ovidius did to deserve being beaten to a pulp?" the Chief Interrogator asked.

Chevalier shook his head. "No, you don't."

"Old Ones never have liked each other," the Chief of Finance said.

"This seemed to go way past that," Zohn said.

Chevalier chuckled. "Oh it does."

Emily finally came in, though it was obvious that she didn't want to. The Council was shocked at how big the baby had grown over the last couple of weeks. She seemed off center and extremely grouchy.

"What?" she asked, crossing her arms.

"Em, we want to know what's going on," Chevalier said.

She ignored him and watched Quinn.

Quinn smiled. "We're just worried."

"About?"

"You seem particularly upset with… well… everything lately."

Her eyes narrowed. "Yeah, and this little meeting is helping."

"Are you mad at the Council?"

"No"

"Just the Elder then?" Kyle asked.

Emily glared at Chevalier. "Equitis knows damned well why I'm mad."

"Stop calling me that!" Chevalier said angrily.

"Once a heku abandons a name for a new one, it's not proper to use the former name," the Records Keeper said.

"Good, then I'm abandoning Emily," she said, watching him.

He grabbed a ledger and began to write. "Okay, so what's your new name?"

"Em...," Chevalier sighed.

"My new name is KissMyAss... that's one word," she told him.

The Records Keeper smiled and put the ledger down. "I'll just hold off on that one."

"We're also concerned that you were in the presence of three high-ranking Encala for almost an hour by yourself," the Chief of Defense said.

"Oh?" Emily glared at him.

"We'll... no, we're not doing that now," Zohn said. "We just want to know what happened to make you so angry with us all."

"Let's just say that I learned quite a bit from your little Ancient that's hidden away in the vault."

"Such as?"

She smiled. "Such as the words to some of your rituals."

The Chief Investigator gasped. "What kind?"

"Obviously the retiree revival," Kyle said.

"I'm apparently able to do them too. According to the Encala, the little earthquake was my doing," she said, pleased with herself.

"We don't know to what extent though," Quinn said. "We aren't even sure if that would have entirely worked."

"One way to find out."

He smiled. "That would make for a lot of very angry heku."

"Besides, that doesn't explain why you are so mad," Zohn said.

"Ask Equitis," she said smugly

"Stop it!" Chevalier growled.

"What else did you learn?" Kyle asked, trying to get their attention off of each other.

"I learned the Renovare..." Before the word was even out of her mouth, Chevalier and Emily disappeared from the room.

Quinn sighed, "Where did they go?"

Zohn shrugged. "I don't know. He must be angry though. I didn't even see him move."

"What's Renovare?"

"Never heard of it."

"Course, there were a lot of rituals around before I was turned. Ones that only the Old Ones know about now."

"Old Ones and Emily, apparently," the Chief Interrogator said. "She purposely said it in front of Chevalier to catch a response."

"She got one," Kyle said, frowning. "I wonder where he took her."

***

Emily felt like she was in a tunnel, a vacuum that pressed against her skin and made her unable to talk. When she stopped moving, she was in a small stone room with no windows and only a heavy door. Chevalier let go of her and stepped back.

She looked up at him with wide eyes and took a step away from him. He was more furious that she'd seen him, and it was obviously directed at her.

She was barely able to whisper, "Chevalier…"

He stepped angrily toward her. "How dare you even say that ritual."

"I didn't…"

"You're messing with something you can't handle."

Emily backed up again but found the cold wall at her back. "Calm down."

"No! You've overstepped, and code says I have to kill you."

She gasped. "What?"

He growled low in his chest. "You've gone too far."

"I…" She barely managed to choke out.

"Did you say that to Ovidius?"

Emily shook her head.

"This entire time with the heku has taught you nothing, has it?" he yelled. "You cannot overstep in this society, or you have to pay the consequences."

"You're going to kill me?" she asked, terrified.

"No." She got the strong suspicion that at that moment, he wanted to.

"Chevalier… I didn't mean…"

"It doesn't matter what you meant to do! You spoke a word that is reserved only for Old Ones and one that the others can't even know about! By the code, I should not only kill you but every one of the Equites Council."

Emily was finding it hard to even breathe. The rage in his eyes was fierce and unnatural. "Please, Chevalier, I didn't know."

His hands balled into fists, and he instantly disappeared from the small stone room. After a few minutes, she tried the door, but it was either locked from the outside, or too heavy for her to move.

As she looked around the unheated room, she began to panic. There was nothing in the room, just the cold stone walls and the heavy, unmovable door. She slowly slid down the wall to sit on the freezing cold floor, too numb to feel the dampness of the air.

For the first time, Emily felt that her drive to know more than she should took a terrible turn. Not only was her life in danger but she'd

endangered the lives of the entire Council. One word had completely changed her life, and she wasn't sure how to get out of it.

After a few hours, Chevalier returned but moved too quickly for Emily to see anything more than blurry movements. He hurriedly stocked the room with a bed, dresser, couch, clothes, and linens. Without a word, the blurs stopped, and she found herself alone again.

Knowing she didn't have a choice, Emily began making the bed. She was now freezing, and she hoped the blankets were warm enough that she could get comfortable.

***

"Where is she?" Quinn asked. "It's been a week."

Chevalier looked over at him angrily. "She's safe."

"We're just worried," Zohn said. They were alone in the Elder's conference room because tensions between Chevalier and the Council were high.

He turned his menacing eyes toward the other Elders. "She's safer where she is."

"I'm sure she's scared. You tore out of here without a word. She has to be terrified," Quinn said, choosing his words carefully.

"I haven't hurt her."

"You don't have to hurt her to scare her. You took her out of her home and away from everyone."

Zohn sighed, "We understand that she said a word forbidden by anyone but Old Ones. We also understand that because of her father, she may be able to successfully perform those rituals. However, she didn't know that the Ancient told her things she shouldn't know."

"She's fine," Chevalier stressed.

Quinn watched him. "Fine... but we're also wondering why you've put the Cavalry into the council chambers, and why no member of the Council is allowed out of the palace."

His eyes narrowed. "My orders have never been questioned before."

"You're right... though we should have when your doppelganger was around, and we've learned not to take your anger as a reason to let things slide."

"What you heard..."

"Just tell us," Quinn said when Chevalier hesitated.

"It's my responsibility as an Old One to..."

"What?"

"Kill you," Chevalier said, and looked up.

Zohn hissed, "For hearing the name of a ritual we know nothing about?"

He nodded.

"But…"

"If the others come, I can't protect you."

"Others?" Zohn asked.

"The other Old Ones, if they heard it, felt it, then they'll come to do what I couldn't," Chevalier explained.

"How could they have heard?"

"There are spies all over this city."

Quinn frowned. "Then we should evacuate."

"No, this will suffice," Chevalier said. "I doubt anyone knows, but I'm taking precautions just in case."

"And Emily?"

"I should have killed her too," he said softly.

Zohn leaned back and looked at the ceiling. "She didn't know."

"I know."

"What happens to you if they find out you didn't kill us?"

"If the Old Ones find out, those that are staunch into the old ways of the Ancients…, then I'll be banished and scattered."

"What can we do?" Quinn asked.

"Just stay protected until I figure out what to do."

"Do we even get to know what the ritual is?"

"No"

"Does Emily know?"

Chevalier pinched his nose between his thumb and finger. "Yes."

Zohn's voice broke slightly. "Did you kill her?"

"No!" Chevalier growled. "She's just out of view of anyone who might tell the Old Ones."

"Sotomar won't kill Emily either," Quinn said. "I would imagine he would stop the Valle."

"He can't stop that many."

"Let's think here… how many Old Ones are there not in retirement?" Quinn asked, deep in thought.

"Eighty nine," Chevalier said.

Zohn looked at him. "How do you know that?"

Chevalier looked at him oddly, and Zohn just shook his head.

"Ovidius knows," Chevalier said sadly.

"Are you sure?"

"Yes"

"Why didn't he kill her?"

"I don't know."

Quinn looked over at Chevalier. "Let's tell William. He'll kill Ovidius before Ovidius has a chance to get to Emily."

Chevalier smiled. "I already did."

"Is he dead?"

"Not yet, but he's being watched by Lt. Andrew."

Zohn nodded. "Now back to Emily. Can she get out of wherever you have her?"

"No"

"So if something happens to you, we may not be able to find her."

"No, you won't… but nothing's going to happen to me."

"Well you get to tell Kyle," Quinn said, standing up. "He's furious with you."

"He'll survive," Chevalier said as they left the private conference room.

***

"Chev?" Emily whispered.

"It's me," he said as he locked the door behind him. Emily ran to him and wrapped her arms around him. "It's okay."

"I kept hearing noises," she said, pulling tighter against him.

"No one's around here," he said as he set her dinner down and wrapped his arms around her. "I promise. You're safe here."

She nodded and stepped away from him.

Chevalier led her over to the table and sat down when she sat and started to eat. "Did the electric blanket help?"

"Yes, and I like the generator. It's too quiet down here," she said, digging into the lasagna.

"Kyle's pretty mad at me."

She nodded but continued to eat.

"I think three weeks is enough," Chevalier said. "I haven't heard from a single heku about the ritual, so at the end of this week, you can go back to the palace."

Emily looked up at him and frowned. "Are you sure?"

"No, but you can't stay down here. It's not healthy. If it was, you'd be down here permanently."

She nodded and then stood up from the table.

"Is that all you're going to eat?"

"Yeah, I'm not feeling all that hot," she said as she crawled back into bed and slid under the covers.

He frowned. "That's another reason we need to get you back to the palace. I like that Dr. Edwards can keep an eye on you, and I still hope to get you to Dr. Hayden."

"He retired."

"You called him?"

"Yes"

"So we'll find another."

She shook her head. "I did… and I wanted to talk to you about that."

"What about?"

"I want to get fixed."

"Fixed?"

"Yes, no more kids," she said, watching for a reaction.

He smiled. "It's your call… I just don't think you realize how long eternity is."

"What do you mean?"

"I mean… yes you're done having kids… four is enough, but what about in 300 years?"

She frowned. "You still want me having babies in 300 years?"

"That's not what I mean. I mean don't do anything drastic. You don't know what's going to happen in 300 years. You may want another by then."

"I doubt it," she mumbled.

Chevalier smiled. "You'd be amazed at how many new heku do things like get tattoos and then regret it a few hundred years later."

"I can't keep getting pregnant."

"Quinn thinks your birth control may not work against a heku."

"I have my own theory."

"Let's hear it," he said, leaning back in the chair.

"I think my body heals… and then fixes what the birth control pill did to prevent it."

He nodded. "That sounds about right too."

"Then we go to raincoats."

"Do what?"

She watched him until it sunk in and then he shook his head. "No."

"So getting fixed is the only way."

Chevalier moved over to sit beside her on the bed. "I really don't think during pregnancy is the time to decide this."

"Why not?"

"You're hormonal."

She glared at him. "What?"

Chevalier chuckled. "You can get mad at me all you want. You are hormonal and emotional. You always are when you're pregnant. Now's not the time to make life-changing decisions."

"The doctor said though, he can take the baby by c-section and do the hysterectomy at the same time. One surgery," she explained.

He lightly kissed the top of her head. "Just wait… for me."

She glared at him. "You do want more kids!"

"No…"

"Yes, you do! Is that why you married me?"

Chevalier sighed, "Are we back to that?"

"Back to what?" she grumbled, and pulled away from him.

"Back to calling me Equitis and being mad… I still want to know what I did to deserve that."

She shrugged and stared at the bare rock wall.

"Why won't you tell me what the Ancient said about me?"

"Because"

"Oh, that's helpful," he said, getting frustrated.

She looked over at him. "When you first met me… if you had known that my father was an Ancient, would you have killed me?"

"No, I never did agree with that rule."

Her eyes narrowed. "You would have, then."

"I just said I wouldn't."

Emily reached up and began to rub her belly, and her breath caught slightly.

"What's wrong?" Chevalier asked, suddenly alarmed.

"Go away."

"No, what's wrong?"

"Just little pains."

"That's it. We're going to the hospital," Chevalier said, standing quickly.

"No, we're not," she said as she laid back down on the bed.

"If you're in pain, we have to."

"No, we don't! This isn't my first baby. You keep forgetting that."

She saw him start to get angry. "How far along are you?"

Emily just glared at him.

"Damnit, Em! Why do you have to be so stubborn about this?"

"Go away."

He crossed his arms. "Yeah, I'm going to leave while you're in pain."

"I'm not in pain anymore."

"So it is labor…"

"No, it's not! Now go away."

He growled and then stormed out of the room, slamming the heavy stone door behind him.

Emily tried to relax and take deep breaths. Her head started pounding when Chevalier first started arguing about the hysterectomy.

***

"I don't want to go," Emily said as Chevalier grabbed her bag.

"You can't stay here forever."

"Why not?"

He smiled. "No. You talked me out of an extra week, and I think four weeks is long enough to be in this room."

"What if they come for me?"

"I think they would have come for me by now if anyone was going to get attacked."

"I don't know," she said, watching the door.

He put his hand out. "Come on. Besides, if I don't prove to Kyle that you're not dead, he may come after me."

She rolled her eyes and took his hand. "Fine."

Chevalier stopped at the door and pulled a scarf out of his back pocket.

"What?" she asked, eyeing him suspiciously.

"You can't see where this is."

"Why not?"

"You just can't," he said, trying to put it over her eyes. She ducked away from him.

"I didn't have a blindfold when you brought me here."

"I was mad. I'm considerably faster when I'm mad."

"No, I walk out."

"No, I carry you."

She backed away from him when she saw the twinkle in his eye. "Don't even…"

He became a blur, and the first Emily could fight back was when she was already blindfolded and gripped tightly in his arms. Somehow, hers were held at her sides as the wind flew past her.

When Chevalier set her down gently, she immediately began swinging and caught him on the chest a few times before he moved. She quickly pulled the scarf from her eyes and ran at him, pounding him on the chest. It infuriated her more when he started to laugh.

"Em…"

"Don't do that!" she screamed, still swinging.

"Em…"

"What?!"

Chevalier reached out and spun her around to face the Council, and she could hear him still laughing behind her.

She glared at them and then turned and hit Chevalier in the stomach. "I don't care if they see me beat the crap out of you!"

Chevalier turned his side toward her when she tried to punch him in the groin. "Stop it before you hurt yourself."

Just before her fist connected with his chest again, Kyle gently pulled her away from Chevalier. "Calm down."

"Don't… touch… me," she screamed, and accentuated each word

with a hit to Kyle. He blocked her easily and couldn't help but laugh some.

Quinn shook his head and appeared behind her, then quickly restrained her, making sure she didn't head butt him. "Emily, calm down before you hurt yourself."

"Let me go!"

"Not until you're calm."

Kyle and Chevalier met up and were laughing behind her as she glared at the Council.

When she stopped struggling, Quinn looked up at Zohn. "We safe?"

Zohn shrugged. "Hard to tell."

"I'm letting go. Just stay calm," he said to her, and let go. Emily spun and slapped him as hard as she could and then stormed out of the room.

Quinn chuckled and returned to his seat. "A tad moody is she?"

Chevalier just grinned and sat down. "She didn't want to leave."

"She didn't?" Kyle asked, frowning.

"No, she knows how badly she messed up, and it scared her."

"Do we know for certain that no one's after her?"

"No, I don't," Chevalier said. "Which is why I've upped her guards to six, though she doesn't know it."

"How are you going to hide that?" Quinn asked.

Chevalier chuckled. "Easy... two will always be asking Mark for help with something when she's around."

"That'll never work."

"She didn't want to come back."

"Is she anti-Council City again?"

"No, she just felt more protected where I had her."

"Which was where exactly?"

He smiled. "I'm not telling you that."

"She doesn't feel safe here?" Kyle asked.

"Not really. I suspect she's not honestly felt safe since Salazar had her, but that room somehow gave her an added protection that she's needed," Chevalier explained.

The Council looked toward the doors when they heard Emily walk down the stairs quickly.

"Good morning, Lady Emily," Derrick said.

"Bite me," she grumbled, and continued down the stairs.

Chevalier chuckled. "Just a tad moody?"

"Okay, so extremely so," Quinn corrected.

Emily walked out to the stables, hoping to find the Cavalry. She hoped watching them beat each other up might help her mood. Once saddled, she used a bale of hay to climb up onto her stallion and then

rode out toward the city gates where training was being held, followed by six members of the Cavalry, though she didn't really notice the extra two.

"Welcome back," Silas said to her when she rode up.

"What's going on?" Emily asked. She saw Mark, Silas, Horace, and Kralen but no Cavalry.

"Are you sure you should be on a horse?" Mark asked, frowning.

She glared at him, and he moved his horse back a bit.

"We're just waiting for the Cavalry to get back," Kralen said, trying to take the pressure off of Mark. "We hid items in the trees, and they have to sniff them out and bring them back."

"Great... turned the Cavalry into drug dogs," she grumbled.

Silas grinned behind her back.

"Where were you?" Horace asked.

She shrugged. "Grouchy won't tell me."

"Grouchy?"

"Yeah... the royal pain in the ass."

"The Elder," Silas told him, still chuckling.

Suddenly, all four heku looked south, and before Emily could ask what was going on, they all kicked their horses into a dead run down the road. Emily shrugged and did the same.

She pulled her horse to a hard stop when she saw a face-off between 12 members of the Cavalry and a group of strange heku. One of them looked up at her, and his eyes narrowed.

"There she is. Get her," he growled.

Emily gasped as the Cavalry moved forward and blurred into a fight with the strangers. She turned her horse hard and raced back for the city.

"Get help!" Emily yelled at the gate guards. Within seconds, the rest of the Cavalry appeared and headed down the road to the sounds of fighting. She barely caught sight as Chevalier blurred past her to join them.

Kyle appeared at her side, and she could tell he was ready to either fight anyone who came at her or grab her if she tried to go to the fight.

"What's going on?" she whispered as she watched the mass of blurring.

"I'm not sure exactly."

"Who are they?"

"Heku from all three factions," Kyle said, frowning.

"Equites too?"

"Yes"

His eyes grew wide, and he quickly mounted behind Emily on her horse. She didn't have time to react before he kicked the stallion, and they rode rapidly toward the stables.

"What's going on?" she asked.

Kyle didn't answer, but when they arrived at the stables, Quinn and the Chief of Staff were waiting. Emily turned to ask Kyle again, but he was gone.

She looked over at Quinn. "Tell me what's going on."

He sighed, "The Old Ones are attacking."

"They are?" she gasped.

"Yes, let's get inside."

"No! I can help."

The Chief of Staff looked up at her. "Seeing you fuels their anger and makes them stronger. We're better off letting the guards handle it."

She frowned and then nodded and climbed down off of her horse. One of the palace guards came and took the stallion from her, and she followed Quinn back inside.

They all sat down in the council chambers, with Emily in Chevalier's chair. It was less than an hour later when they heard the Cavalry come back in. Emily watched breathlessly to make sure everyone was okay.

Chevalier and Kyle were the first inside. They were both covered in blood, and their clothing was torn, but they didn't seem injured.

Chevalier kissed Emily on the top of the head and then picked her up, sat down, and put her on his lap.

"So?" Quinn asked, looking over at Kyle.

"It was what we were afraid of. Twelve Old Ones came to take care of Emily."

"Where are they?"

"They got away."

"We held them off," Chevalier said. "It's not over though."

Emily frowned. "Then I should go back to the room."

"We can't risk that now. If we leave, we risk being followed."

"So now what?" she asked, frustrated.

"We wait... and watch," Kyle said, looking over at her.

"No, I need to go away, or they will come after the Council. You weren't supposed to hear what I said," Emily told them as she pressed her palms into her eyes and leaned back against Chevalier.

"We're well protected here," Zohn said, smiling. "There are only 89 Old Ones, two of which won't attack you... maybe three."

"You're sure?"

"Yes," Chevalier told her, and kissed the back of her head. "Do you need to go lay down?"

She nodded and then stood up and wobbled slightly. Chevalier stood with her and walked her up to the bedroom. She was only slightly surprised to see Dr. Edwards waiting.

"How are you, dear?" he asked as she laid down.

"Peachy"

"Headache?"

"No"

"Yes," Chevalier countered.

"May I please just check your blood pressure?" Dr. Edwards asked as he began to dig in his bag.

Emily nodded, shocking both of them. She held her arm out, and Chevalier frowned when she didn't even complain as the doctor took her blood pressure.

"It's too high," Dr. Edwards said softly.

"I figured," she mumbled, and rolled away from him.

Chevalier's eyes narrowed. "You're not going after them."

"After who?" Dr. Edwards asked.

"Emily, did you hear me?"

She nodded but didn't answer.

"Stop protecting the heku!"

"They're after the Council because of me," she whispered.

"Get out," Chevalier snapped at Dr. Edwards. His eyes grew wide, and he disappeared from the room. Chevalier turned back to Emily. "No..."

"I'm not going to do anything until I feel better."

"I'm doubling your guards."

She sighed, "You know they can't stop me."

His eyes narrowed. "Stop being stubborn! You can't take on a group of Old Ones."

"I just need a nap, Chev," she said softly.

***

Emily rolled over and took her cell phone from the table. She thumbed through some of the saved notes and read again how to summon and how to abolish the Old Ones. She couldn't let them torment and eventually kill the Equites Council all because of something she did.

The Ancients had worked out all of the details and meticulously took notes, notes Emily had already read. They knew their lives were in danger and were planning on getting rid of the Old Ones before they were all banished.

Faking a nap, Emily laid for hours and had a plan formulated in her mind. Her main concern was how to avoid hurting Chevalier, Sotomar, and Ovidius once she called the Old Ones to her. She already had a good location. Now she just needed to set her plan in motion.

She knew she couldn't risk sleeping. Chevalier loved to watch her

dreams, and she was afraid of giving away her plan. When night fell, she sat up and looked sadly around the room. It was time to stop the Equites from being punished for her being there.

"Chev?" she whispered softly.

It only took a second for him to appear, and it was obvious he'd calmed down. "What's wrong?"

"I'm sorry," she said, watching him.

"For what?"

He turned to ash suddenly, and within only a few minutes, she had scooped him into a bag and hid the ashes in her pockets. After knocking the six guards unconscious, Emily started for the garage.

"Where are your guards?" Zohn asked as she passed him on the stairs. Without a word, she turned him and Derrick to ash, leaving them in front of the council chamber doors.

Emily took her new Rubicon. It had never been driven. She'd had no desire to leave the palace, and as she drove out of Council City, her heart sunk. She was shaking as she drove toward the East.

"Sir, the Winchester is here," the Valle's door guard said.

Sotomar smiled. "Let her in."

Emily came in and stood before the Valle Council.

"You've returned."

"Sort of. Can I talk to you for a second please?"

"Go ahead."

"In private."

Sotomar nodded and then walked down to the trial area. He and Emily walked out together. "What seems to be the problem?"

"Just sit in my car with me for a second, please," she said, and her seriousness wasn't lost on him.

He sat down beside her in the Rubicon and frowned. "Why do I smell the ashes of two heku?"

Before Sotomar even looked up at her, he'd turned to ash, and Emily took off out of the Valle city. She now had Chevalier, Sotomar, and Ovidius. It was lucky that Ovidius Coven was near the Valle's main city. While driving, she'd made the plane reservations she needed and immediately headed for the airport.

At the airport, Emily walked up to a young attendant. "I have an offer for you."

He smiled and turned to her. "What might that be?"

"Want to make an easy $10,000?"

Suddenly, he became serious. "What did you have in mind?"

Emily held out a box, inside were the ashes of the three Old Ones. "Take this box with my mother's ashes to an address I give you. Tell them Emily said to pay you $10,000 for it."

He was obviously skeptical. "I take this box and get $10,000?"

"Yes"

"If they don't pay it?"

"You have my mom's ashes. They'll pay."

He thought for a moment. "When do I have to deliver this?"

"In three days."

"Jeff!" the kid yelled. When another boy joined him, they spoke for a second and then he turned to Emily. "Sure, we'll do it."

She smiled and handed the box over. After giving the address to the farmhouse with directions, she headed inside and within a few hours was over the Atlantic heading for Heathrow Airport.

Chevalier tightened his grip on Emily and focused in on the finer parts of the dream. He was aware that she had already worked out the details and was only replaying them in her sleep because of the time spent working on them.

She spent the entire flight to London reading the incantations she'd put into her phone; one to summon the Old Ones, and one to then abolish them. She watched out the window as the airplane landed in Heathrow Airport. From there she caught the bus to Amesbery.

Emily was the only one that got off of the bus at Amesbery, and it was already nearing dusk. She watched the bus leave and then started the two mile walk to Stonehenge.

When she arrived, the last batch of tourists were just leaving and dark clouds were rolling in. Emily wandered among the massive stone structure and waited for darkness to set in.

Lightning cracked high above her as she pulled out her phone, took a deep breath, and began the incantation to call the Old Ones.

"I summon you," Emily said, and then braced herself with the ground began to shake. "Come to me where the Ancients meet."

Chevalier frowned. Those weren't the ancient verses used to summon.

She felt a rush of power run through her as her voice echoed through the dark night. Excitement grew. She could almost feel the Old Ones in the world frowning and wondering who dared to summon them.

Emily wasn't sure how long it would take. They had to come from all over the world but most had private jets. She sat down to wait, hoping they would all arrive the following night. She pulled her coat around her and wondered if the ashes had been delivered yet.

Back in Council City, the farmhouse guard appeared at the door to the council chambers with a box in his hands.

"What do you need, Dwight?" Derrick asked.

"I need to see the Council."

Derrick nodded, announced him, and then opened the door. "Go

in."

"*Come, Dwight,*" *Quinn said, motioning him forward.*

"*What do you need?*" *Kyle asked.*

The farmhouse guard held out the box. "*This was just delivered by two mortals from New York.*"

"*What's in it?*"

"*I detect three sets of ashes.*"

Kyle gasped. "*Bring them to me.*"

Dwight handed up the box and then stepped back. "*I had to pay them. They said Lady Emily told them they would be given $10,000 for the delivery.*"

Zohn nodded and watched Kyle open the box. "*Return to the farmhouse.*"

The guard nodded and blurred from the room.

"*Three bags,*" *Kyle said, looking into the box.* "*Chev, Soto, and Ovi are written on them.*"

Quinn sighed, "*Call the Encala and Valle and let them know that Emily has returned the members of their factions that she took.*"

The Court Reporter nodded and left to make the call.

"*Just bring Chevalier back,*" *Zohn said.* "*We'll let them revive their own.*"

Kyle nodded and had Chevalier revived a couple minutes later. He growled deeply when the pain subsided and then looked around. "*Where is she?*"

"*We aren't sure,*" *Quinn said.* "*We believe she's gone to Europe.*"

"*Why?*"

Quinn looked nervously at Zohn and then turned to Chevalier. "*Did the Ancients have a way of summoning Old Ones?*"

Chevalier's eyes narrowed. "*The summon called Old Ones and Ancients.*"

"*We've had to imprison both Dain and Alexis,*" *Kyle said.* "*They were trying to answer the summons of an Ancient.*"

"*And Allen?*"

"*I notified Storm and she has Allen restrained.*"

Chevalier frowned slightly. "*What does an Ancient summons have to do with Emily though? She left before the summons was sent, or I would have heard it.*"

"*We suspect she's doing the summoning,*" *Zohn said.*

"*She couldn't...*"

"*We don't know that.*"

Emily moved to the center of the stone monoliths when darkness came on the second night. She suspected the Old Ones would start showing up, and she had to be ready.

"What is this?" a stranger hissed from behind her.

Emily spun and looked at him. "Come any closer and you'll be ash before you get to me."

His eyes narrowed. "Who summoned us?"

"Us?" Emily turned when she saw another shadow and realized there were almost 20 heku standing around the stone structure.

"Only an Ancient can summon us," he said angrily. "Where is he?"

"I summoned you, and you'll stay where you are… last warning."

"The Winchester summoned the Old Ones?" an angry female growled.

"Yes, I did."

"What do you even want?" a shorter heku asked from the shadows.

"You'll know when the rest get here."

"The rest of us?" another heku said. Emily turned to him and saw even more heku approaching. "There are only three of us missing."

Emily took a deep breath and nodded. "Fine then."

She heard another hiss and turned to a female that was glaring at her. "This better not be a waste of our time."

"It won't be," yet another said. "If all else fails we get to destroy the Ancient's offspring, which we should have done years ago."

Emily smiled. "You'll not get the chance."

"You're going to turn us to ash?" a haughty heku asked as he took a step forward.

Emily felt the power within her arms as she flipped through her cell phone and then began to chant in a foreign language.

Chevalier growled softly when most of the words for the incantation were correct. She either mispronounced or missed some of the words, but it was troublesome how much she memorized.

Screams filled the night and Emily braced herself as the ground again began to shake. Black clouds rolled in and obscured the moon as the Old Ones began to fall to the ground, writhing in pain. Emily noticed how similar it was to ashing but without the burning smell.

Emily gasped when the gathered Old Ones only partially fell to ash and continued to writhe in pain, screaming into the night air. She watched, horrified, as they reached out to her for help, but their partially formed bodies soon fell to the ground, unable to hold themselves up.

"Help us," one of the Old Ones whispered and then he screamed as the lower half of his body fell to ash and pulled away from the formed upper half.

"Oh my God!" Emily screamed, and stepped farther away from them.

One of the heku clawed forward, using bloody fingers against the

ground as she inched away from Emily frantically. She left trails of ash behind her, and her terrified screams faded as she fell unconscious.

Emily took a step back from the horror and ran into someone. She spun suddenly and came face-to-face with her Ancient father.

"You're only half Ancient, Emily. You cannot expect to be as powerful as I am," he said, smiling as he watched the suffering heku.

"Help them," she said, and turned away from the terrifying images.

Emily sat up suddenly and grasped her chest to calm her breathing. She looked over at Chevalier as he sat up.

"No," he said sternly, and looked at her. His body was tense, and she moved away from him a bit.

"What?"

"I saw your dream… I know what you're planning."

She swallowed hard. "I'm not planning anything."

He growled and blurred her phone from the table. In a few touches, he relaxed some and handed the phone back to her.

Emily looked at it and yelled. "You factory re-set it!"

"Yes, I did," he said, moving toward the door. "I'm not going to let you try to take on the Old Ones with a ritual the Ancients came up with."

She glared at him as he left and shut the door. Finally, she smiled and then began to retrieve her documents that she had backed up on the web.

Chevalier moved quickly to the council chambers and sat down. He was deeply troubled by Emily's plans and how much of the ancient incantations she knew.

"You okay?" Zohn asked, studying his face.

"Emily plans on ashing me, Sotomar, and Ovidius… then summoning the Old Ones using an incantation the Ancients came up with. Once summoned, she's going to use a forbidden incantation to abolish them."

Quinn smiled. "Is she just going to make this stuff up?"

"No, that's what's disturbing. She had the incantations on her phone and had partially memorized one of them."

Zohn gasped. "She did?"

"Yes. I re-set her phone though and erased them," Chevalier said as he pulled out a ledger.

Kyle thought for a moment and then called for Silas.

"Yes, Chief Enforcer?" Silas asked, bowing slightly.

"The Elder found things on Emily's phone that shouldn't be there. He re-set it to factory settings," Kyle explained. "You're the most technical, is there a way for her to still retrieve them?"

Silas nodded. "Yes. Most smart phones come with an automatic backup in case the phone is damaged or accidentally erased."

"What?!" Chevalier growled.

"Get me that phone," Kyle whispered.

Silas nodded and disappeared. He reappeared a few seconds later with the smart phone and handed it to Kyle. Kyle gave it to Chevalier, who began pushing buttons.

"Damnit!" he growled. "They are all back on here."

Silas turned to him. "They will keep coming back until the backups are erased."

"Can you do that?"

"Yes, Elder."

"Would you see what the files are?"

"Probably"

Chevalier sighed, "He can't see those incantations."

Silas smiled slightly. "I can tell you how to erase them."

The Council all turned when the doors flew open and Emily stormed in, still in her nightgown. "Give me my phone!"

Chevalier held it up. "No. I'm not going to let you take on the Old Ones."

"You have no right treating me like a child," she said, stomping angrily.

"You have no right knowing those incantations, let alone threatening to use them," he explained calmly. "We realize that as half Ancient, you may be able to do them, but we don't know that for certain."

"Then let me try."

"No, it's out of the question."

"I have as much right to those incantations as you do."

"Calm down," Kyle said to her.

"No, you don't," Chevalier said. "Only Old Ones know the names to those. The rest of this Council doesn't even know those."

She shrugged. "Then maybe I'll tell them so it won't be such a secret."

Chevalier growled softly. "Do not overstep."

"Calm down," Zohn said again. "Emily, this Council doesn't want to know the information you threaten to tell us."

"Threaten?" she asked, glaring at him.

"Yes, it's a threat," Quinn explained. "If you tell us information we aren't to know, then it is the responsibility of the Old Ones to destroy us."

Emily shook her head. "You have one screwed up society! The Ancients are banished, the Old Ones are gripped in delusions of grandeur, and you are all afraid of words."

"Gripped in what?" Chevalier yelled, standing up.

Kyle and Zohn both appeared at his side, ready to grab him if he lunged for Emily.

Emily glared at him. "Give me my phone."

Chevalier slammed the phone onto the table, shattering it into hundreds of pieces. "You will get a new phone."

She crossed her arms and glared at him.

"Sir," Silas said, stepping away from Emily. "She can still retrieve those documents from a new phone."

"What?! Why?" Emily screamed at him.

Silas sighed, "You shouldn't have those."

He nodded. "Then go pick her out a new phone."

"She can get them from the Internet too."

Chevalier glared at her. "You put them on the Internet?"

She shrugged. "They're secure."

He turned to Silas. "Fix it."

Silas nodded and disappeared. Emily stood and glared at Chevalier, with her arms crossed above her expanding middle.

Kyle sighed, "You both need to calm down."

Chevalier sat down. "You have no idea what you're messing with."

"I won't be treated like a child!" she screamed. "Until you start treating me like an adult, I'm going to stay with the Encala."

Emily turned and stormed out. Chevalier stood to follow her, but Zohn put a hand on his arm.

"She won't get out of the palace, but you need to stay here," Quinn said.

"Have we at all considered that not only is her body not aging but her mind as well?" the Chief of Staff asked.

Chevalier growled at him, and he sat back.

The Council looked up when they heard Kralen call for Dr. Edwards immediately. Chevalier and Kyle both disappeared and suddenly appeared in the bedroom. Emily was lying on the bed, and her entire body was stiff. Kralen had her head cradled as he watched her eyes roll back into her head.

Dr. Edwards appeared and immediately began hooking her up to the monitor the Valle had sent with her. He studied the readouts as she relaxed and fell asleep.

"Damnit," he growled. "We have to get her to a hospital."

Chevalier nodded and Kralen immediately grabbed his phone to summon an ambulance to the farmhouse.

***

Chevalier sighed and began to pace. Kyle watched him as he sat in

the waiting room.

"Maybe we should send her back to the Encala," Chevalier said. "She seemed less stressed there."

"She wasn't stressed until recently though," Kyle said.

"Yeah, until we argued... again."

"Now that we know the Old Ones are after her, we can't leave her protection up to the Encala."

"True"

"Okay, she's ready to go," the young nurse said to them. "Did the doctor talk to you?"

"Yes," Chevalier said as he signed the release forms.

Kyle followed them both back to Emily's room where she'd spent the last ten days. Emily was just slipping on her coat when they walked in. Things were still tense between her and Chevalier, so the Elders had ordered Kyle to go along.

"Ready, Em?" Kyle asked, smiling.

She nodded but kept a close eye on Chevalier.

The nurse smiled. "Just keep that baby cooking for at least another 13 weeks."

Emily nodded and then sat in the wheelchair the nurse was holding for her. They all walked out, and Kralen looked over from the driver's side of the Humvee. Emily smiled at him when he winked, and then she stood up and got into the vehicle, ignoring Chevalier's hand when he offered it.

Kyle climbed in beside her as Chevalier got into the passenger seat next to Kralen. The ride to Council City was silent, and it was obvious that Emily and Chevalier were both still mad at each other.

Dr. Edwards was waiting at the door to the palace and opened the door when the Humvee stopped. "Welcome back."

She smiled. "We'll see."

He attempted to pick her up, but she squirmed out of his arms. "You aren't supposed to be on your feet."

"I'm walking," she grumbled, and started inside.

"Did he at least tell you how far along you are?" Dr. Edwards asked as he followed behind her.

"I already knew."

"So?"

"So what?"

"How far along are you?"

"Go away," she said, and then slammed the door in his face.

"It's going to be a long 13 weeks," Kyle said from behind him.

Dr. Edwards turned. "I'm assuming you looked at her chart?"

Chevalier chuckled. "She's right at 24 weeks."

"Wow, that is a big baby then."

"Right, so they want her to hit 37 weeks and then immediately induce."

"She's asked for a c-section with tubal ligation," Kyle said.

Dr. Edwards nodded. "She's mentioned that before."

"Make that a complete hysterectomy," Chevalier said, and then smiled slightly. "I mentioned that she may heal from tied tubes."

Kyle sighed, "Nice."

"Well! I didn't realize there was another option."

"A drastic one," Dr. Edwards said. "What if she wants more children in the future?"

"She doesn't see it that way."

Derrick came up to them with a box in his hand. "There was a delivery for Emily at the farmhouse."

Chevalier took it and looked at the box. "It's from the cell phone company."

"I thought you gave her one," Kyle said.

"I did... but it wasn't a smart phone."

"You mean... it's a phone?"

Chevalier nodded. "She's going to be mad when she realizes that an ally with the Valle was able to break into her account and erase the backup files."

Kyle started to walk away. "Yell when you need revived."

Chevalier followed him. "I'll give her time to get settled."

"Dad," Dain said, running down the stairs.

"What?" he said, turning to his son.

"I want to go train with Allen."

"Have you asked your mom?"

Dain shrugged.

"Get your mom's permission, and I'll agree," Chevalier said, starting down the stairs again.

"You're the Elder. Why do I have to ask Mom?"

"Stop being afraid of talking to your mom."

"I'm not afraid," Dain growled.

"Then why don't you talk to her anymore?"

"Nothing to say."

"Get her permission, and I'll agree," he said again, and then disappeared into the council chambers.

Dain sighed and looked up the stairs, then headed down to the barracks where he'd been hanging out lately.

Chapter 9

"Is she speaking to you yet?" Zohn asked Chevalier.

He shook his head. "Nope, not a word since she got back last week."

"What does she do all day then? I know she's not really leaving her room either."

Kyle chuckled. "Don't ask."

"Why not?"

"Because she spends her days talking to the Encala on her laptop," Chevalier hissed.

Quinn sat back to avoid looking at the angry Elder.

"How does one talk on a laptop?" the Chief of Finance asks.

"With a webcam," Kyle said. "They can see each other and hear each other that way."

"Why don't we have that in here?" the Chief of Staff said. "We could outfit the covens, and when we need to speak to them, we can see them."

The Chief Interrogator's face lit up. "That's not a bad idea! I can tell if they are lying."

Chevalier looked over at Kyle. "Do you know enough to start that?"

"Well... no... but I can ask Em."

"She's not going to help the Council," Quinn said.

"I bet she will. As long as Chevalier doesn't get involved," Kyle said, and then quieted down when Chevalier glared at him.

Zohn looked up when he heard Emily's soft feet on the stairs. "Ask her in please, Derrick."

"Good afternoon, Lady Emily," Derrick said. "The Council would like to see you."

Zohn winced when the footsteps didn't stop and then Derrick called out. "Okay... well... I'll just tell the Council to take a rain check."

Quinn chuckled and turned back to his paperwork.

Emily slowly walked toward the city gates, ignoring the questions from Kralen and the five members of the Cavalry with him. They'd gotten into an argument earlier about why she always saw six guards instead of her normal four.

"We're leaving the city?" one of the Cavalry asked when they neared the gates.

Emily didn't answer but stopped at the gates and looked out.

One of the gate guards bowed slightly to Kralen. "Can we help you, sir?"

"I have no idea," he said, irritated. "Em... why are we here?"

She didn't answer but continued to watch out. The heku all turned

when the sound of an approaching motorcycle could be heard. Emily was the last to hear it, and she smiled and waved when the rider stopped.

Lt. Andrew pulled off his helmet and smiled. "I told you not to meet me here."

"Grouchy won't let you in, I'm sure," she said, walking forward to greet him.

Lt. Andrew looked over at Kralen. "He shouldn't either. You could have sent word though."

"I'm fine," Emily said, sighing. "Stop treating me like I'm about to die."

He grinned. "Sure thing. You ready to get going?"

"Sure," Emily said, and then stepped back when he got off of his motorcycle. He pushed it over to the side of the gates as the Equites watched him carefully. After grabbing a duffle bag from the back, he started for Emily, but the gate guards and Kralen blocked him.

"We have to have Council permission for you to come in here," Kralen told him.

Emily pulled on his arm. "I'm on the Council, and I invited him."

"You know that doesn't count," Kralen said.

Emily smiled, and Lt. Andrew disappeared from behind her.

"How did we get out here?" Kralen asked, looking over at the gates.

"I'm just out for a walk," Emily explained. "Now I want to go to the training room for a bit."

He shrugged and followed her, glad that she'd finally spoken. She turned at the doors to the out-building. "I'm alone from here."

"Why?" Kralen asked, and then sniffed at the air. "Why do I smell an Encala?"

"They gave me this sweater," Emily said, looking down.

"Fine, but I post at the back door too."

She nodded and headed inside.

Lt. Andrew shook his head when she walked into the padded training room. "It's scary how you do that."

"They'll remember in an hour or so though," she said as she slipped off her shoes.

"Let's get going then," he said, and handed her the bag. "As requested, the Encala tailor made you some workout clothes."

"I hope it covers this huge belly," she said, frowning at her growing tummy.

He smiled. "No, it doesn't. You can't comfortably do this if you're restricted."

"Fine," she grumbled, and disappeared into the pool room to change. Debating changing back into her pants and sweater, she finally just shook her head and changed into the sports bra and yoga pants.

Emily avoided looking at the mirrors as she passed and then stepped into the training room. Andrew had set out yoga mats and was leaning against the wall watching for her.

He smiled. "You actually look pretty hot."

Emily blushed. "Stop it… let's get going."

"Fine, come on over."

One thing Emily had discovered, was that Andrew was a yoga instructor before turning and kept up with it to stay flexible. He offered to help her learn some yoga poses to see if she could lessen stress and help her during labor.

"Stand on the mat and just relax," he said, and then stepped up behind her. He took her wrists and held them out to her sides as his chest gently touched her back. "Relax and breathe in through your nose, and out through your mouth."

Emily started taking deep breaths, not even realizing the closeness of the enemy.

"We're going to start with the warrior pose," he whispered. Gently, he lifted her arms above her head. "Step forward with your right foot and bend your right knee."

Emily did as instructed and looked over as he demonstrated. His muscles stood out as he stretched into the pose. Andrew grinned when he realized she was watching him.

Emily hurried and turned back to the front.

"Here, let me help you," Andrew said. He moved so he was standing directly behind her, then reached up and put his hands on each side of her right thigh. "Your thigh has to be parallel to the floor."

She nodded and adjusted, suddenly feeling the muscles in her left leg stretch.

"Very good," Andrew said softly, and then brushed the hair off of her neck.

Emily smiled and pushed farther into the pose.

"Now, let's move your hands. Stretch one out in front of you and one out in back," he said, and then took her hands tenderly and moved them into position.

She stretched forward again and felt the pull on her thighs.

"This is Warrior II," Andrew explained as he ran his hands down the length of her arms. "You'll have to be careful, because as the baby grows, it'll be harder to stay balanced."

Once they switched sides and Andrew returned to the same stance beside her, they moved into the two poses and Emily felt the stretch in her right leg.

"You're doing great," Andrew told her. "I didn't realize how flexible you are."

Emily smiled and looked over at him.

"Now lay down on the floor," Andrew said.

She nodded and laid on her back. Andrew reached down and picked up her ankles and then stretched her legs up, pinning them against his chest.

"Don't forget to take deep breaths," he reminded her. "Now grab my ankles."

Emily reached down and took a hold of his ankles as he stretched her legs upwards.

She felt her back stretch pleasantly. Andrew took her feet and pulled them so her toes were pointing. He stretched her feet while she relaxed her back. For the first time in months, her back was no longer aching.

"This is really nice," she said, smiling up at him.

He smiled. "I knew it'd help. Now we go into the bridge pose."

Andrew lowered Emily's feet, and she bent her knees and put them on the floor.

"Lift your bottom up," he said, and gently pushed on the small of her back as her back arched and her tummy rose higher.

"This is just... weird," Emily said. Her bare tummy was now fully exposed and sticking up to the sky.

Andrew chuckled. "It's good for your back. Push your hips up farther toward the ceiling."

She nodded and pushed farther.

"Keep your feet parallel," he whispered, and gently moved her feet for her. She wasn't sure, but it felt like his hands traveled up her leg a bit before he moved back to her head and smiled.

When her strength gave out, she lowered her back to the floor and took a deep breath.

"Good, do it again," he said, and helped her lift her hips toward the ceiling. After a few minutes, he smiled. "Now relax."

Emily dropped her bottom back to the floor and smiled. "That actually does feel pretty good."

"Then let's keep going. Sit up now," he said, helping her sit. "Bend your knees and bring the soles of your feet together. Make sure you keep your back straight."

Emily did as she was told, and Andrew did the same thing right in front of her so their knees were touching.

"Shut your eyes and relax," he said, watching her. "Take deep breaths and feel the air going in and out of your lungs."

She thought it felt amazing as she took relaxing breaths. She could already tell that her blood pressure was coming down, and her headache was markedly improved.

"Stretch here," Andrew said, and lightly touched her inner thighs.

Emily gasped slightly but relaxed again when he moved back into position. She started to think it was a completely innocent touch.

"In and out," he whispered softly.

Once she was so relaxed she felt herself falling asleep, Andrew's voice made her jerk. "You awake?"

She smiled. "Sort of."

"Stand up, let's stretch your back more," he said, and then nimbly jumped to his feet.

Emily watched as he spread his feet wide and then turned his right foot to point forward. He reached his left arm upward and put his right arm down on the floor.

Andrew looked up when Emily attempted the pose and then chuckled and moved over to her.

"Your shoulder has to be straight up from the other, and your hips have to do the same. Then look up at your left hand," he said, and helped her into position.

Emily almost fell over but he put a steadying hand on her back, and she finally was able to hold the position on her own.

"This stretches your side," he said, and softly ran his hand down her side and onto her hip, where his hand stayed as he spoke. "This opens your chest and shoulders, and also stretches the legs, groin, and hamstring."

Emily nodded and continued to breathe deeply.

After a few moments, Andrew helped her stand. "How was that?"

"Awkward"

He chuckled. "It'll get better."

"My headache is gone though."

"So it's working," he said. "Now face away from me."

Emily turned her back to him and looked over her shoulder.

"Move your feet apart."

Again, she did as instructed.

"I'll help you with this. I want you to bend at the waist and put your hands on the floor."

"I don't have a waist," Emily said, and then started to laugh.

He smiled. "I said I'll help."

She leaned forward, and Andrew grabbed her waist and gently lowered her hands to the floor.

"Walk your hands backwards as far as you can go."

Emily laughed again and then moved her hands backwards.

"I'm going to help you stretch a bit," Andrew said. He leaned up against her and bent over with his thighs pushing against her butt. He reached forward and put his hands on her shoulder, then pulled back

softly.

"That's too hard," Emily groaned when she felt the muscles in her thighs burn.

"You'll get used to it and then you'll be able to stretch farther," he said, applying more pressure to the back of her legs with his body as he bent over her and grasped her shoulders.

His weight suddenly disappeared as a growl sounded through the once quiet room. Emily had to struggle to stand up, and when she did, all she saw was the blur of fighting. She started forward to stop them, but Kralen took her arm.

"Chev, stop it!" she screamed.

"Let him do this, Em," Kralen said. "Andrew overstepped."

The fight stopped suddenly when Chevalier fell onto his back and clutched at his chest.

"Em, stop it," Kralen said sternly.

Andrew walked up to her and took her face in his hands. "It's okay."

She looked up at him and let Chevalier out of pain. Kralen called for Mark and Kyle just as Chevalier tackled Andrew again.

Within just a few seconds, the fight stopped and Chevalier had Andrew on the floor with a hand around his neck.

"Let him go!" Emily screamed.

Andrew looked up at him and croaked. "You win. I won't hurt you, because that would hurt Em."

Chevalier growled.

"Hurt him and I'll leave you!" Emily yelled.

Chevalier looked over at her with wide eyes, then slowly let go of the Encala.

"Grow up!" Emily yelled. "He's helping me and you have no right to attack him for it."

"He was…," Chevalier hissed.

Kralen let go of Emily, but then grabbed her arm again when she slapped the Elder.

"It's okay, Em," Andrew said as he leapt to his feet. "I'm sure that looked bad."

"Yes, it did," Chevalier told him.

"I feel better than I've felt in weeks," Emily said, pulling away from Kralen. "My back feels better. My headache was gone…"

Chevalier sighed, "How bad is it?"

"Funny, it came back with a vengeance the second you attacked my friend!"

"He… was…"

Emily stopped him with a glare. "Get out and let Andrew get rid of

my headache again."

"If it was harmless, then he won't mind if I stay."

"I don't mind at all," Andrew told him.

Chevalier crossed his arms and watched.

Emily frowned. "I'm not going to be involved in a spectator sport when I'm all hanging out."

Andrew smiled. "You're the only one that cares."

"I don't care," she said to him.

Chevalier turned and ordered her guards out of the room. Emily looked up when it was just Chevalier, Andrew and her.

She sighed, "I'm too tense for this now."

"Let me see," Andrew said, and blurred to her back. He put his hands on her shoulders and began to massage. "You are tense."

"Get your hands off of her!" Chevalier yelled.

Andrew stepped back. "You should trust her more."

"I trust her implicitly… it's you I don't trust."

"Or like."

"That too."

Emily sighed, "Chevalier, get out."

"Why?" he asked, frowning at how she used his full name.

"Because I'm barely dressed and in poses that make it worse."

"I'm your husband. I can see you barely dressed."

She glared at him. "Just get out."

Andrew stepped up. "Calm down, okay? He's just concerned for your welfare."

"Yeah, I guess."

"Let him stay."

She looked down at her exposed belly and frowned, "No."

Chevalier sat down in the corner. "Go ahead. Forget I'm here."

Andrew smiled. "Em, you're the only one that thinks your figure is repulsive. As heku, we rarely see it, and honestly, you can't be any more feminine than you are right now. It's kind of nice."

"Hey," Chevalier growled.

Emily blushed and smiled at Andrew. "It is?"

He nodded. "Come on, back to work."

She was still blushing when she spread her feet and reached back down for the floor. Again, Andrew put his hands on her waist and ignored the hiss from the corner as he gently set her hands on the floor.

"Walk them back again," he said, and then stood to the side as she brought her hands closer. "Now shut your eyes and just take deep breaths. Let's get back to the relaxed state we were in earlier."

Emily shut her eyes and then mumbled, "Stop staring at my ass."

Chevalier chuckled and then leaned against the mirrored wall to

watch.

***

"How much longer?" Zohn asked.

"I don't know," Chevalier told him. "I don't think he planned on staying, but Em called the Encala Council and asked if he could."

"They, of course, agreed."

He nodded. "I hate to admit it, but it's really helping her."

"How?" Kyle asked, still fuming that the Encala was allowed to stay in the city outside of Council City and visited every day with Emily.

"Her headaches have backed off, and she said it's helping her back a lot."

"I'm sure we can find a yoga instructor in the Equites," Kyle grumbled. "I could just go turn one."

Quinn smiled. "Just let her have her friend. Chevalier is there during the yoga sessions, and it is helping her mood too."

Kyle mumbled under his breath. "No, let's not kill him... let's banish him and make him suffer."

Chevalier chuckled and turned back to the ledger.

***

Andrew thought for a moment and then moved his chess piece. "Check mate... I won, and you promised."

Emily frowned. "I lied."

"No, now let's go."

"The Old Ones are out there waiting for me."

"I told you, we'll have your Equites guards."

Emily looked over at Kralen, and he smiled. "As much as I hate to admit this... I agree with the Encala."

"They're out there."

"We can handle them," Andrew said, and then stood up and put his hand out.

"It'll be fun," Silas said from beside Kralen.

Emily sighed, "How many are going?"

Kralen grinned. "I don't know if I should say."

"Why not?"

"If the number's too high, you won't go. If the number's too low, you won't go."

"I just don't see why I'd risk my life for pizza and a movie," Emily said, glancing from Kralen to Andrew.

"Because you have to get out," Andrew told her. "I won the darts

match, the pool match, even the roulette wheel. Stop stalling and let's go."

She shrugged. "It'd help if I had my phone."

"No, it wouldn't," Silas told her. "We deleted those backup files."

Andrew chuckled. "There's no ancient incantation that works better than brute force."

Kralen nodded. "True... so let's go. The movie starts in 45 minutes."

"I thought we were leaving," Dain said from the doorway.

"She's stalling."

"Come on, Mom. We're all ready."

Emily finally resigned herself to movie and a pizza. She stood up and followed them out to the black Suburbans, where Chevalier and Kyle were waiting for them.

"It's about time," Chevalier said with a smile.

Emily just glared at him and got into the front seat of the first Suburban.

He reached in and kissed her on the cheek. "Stop holding grudges."

"Just get in," she grumbled.

"I'm not going."

She looked up at him. "Why not?"

"I have something I need to do here. You're way overprotected," he said, smiling reassuringly.

"You're turning someone?"

"Yes," he said, and shut her door. "Now be good and listen to Kralen."

"We'll call you tonight from the hotel room," Kyle said as he stepped back.

"What hotel room?" Emily asked as Silas drove away from Council City.

Andrew reached up and began rubbing her shoulders. "They need us away for the night."

"So no one thought to tell me?"

"I honestly thought you knew."

Emily turned to look at Silas, and he grinned. "We knew it'd be easier once you were already in the car."

"Way to build trust!"

"It'll be fun," Andrew said as he leaned back in his seat. "A fiery red head, an Encala, and 17 Equites."

Emily couldn't help but smile. "Interesting."

"What movie did you all pick, anyway?" Andrew asked. "I'm hoping it's not some chick-flick, political message carrying, mystery turned snoozer."

Kralen chuckle. "We have tickets to see Blood Dragons Die."

"Nice." He seemed impressed.

Emily's nose wrinkled. "I don't want to see that."

"You're outvoted," Silas said, smiling.

"Oh, I see how tonight's going to be," she said, acting mad.

"You could just wait in the car."

"Now that's an idea."

Kralen sighed, "Don't even offer that."

"So I get to go watch a blood and guts movie, surrounded by 18 overprotective heku, who will, no doubt, be watching the movie and not me?"

"How do you get overprotective and unobservant out of the same heku?"

"Very easily."

Andrew just sat back and smiled as they pulled into the movie theater.

Emily frowned and looked at the empty lot. "I think they're closed."

"Nope," Kralen said, and then cleared his throat. "The Elder bought out the building."

"He did not!" Emily gasped.

Andrew nodded. "It's safer."

She huffed and then turned to Kralen. "You promised me pizza. I'm starving."

"It's catered."

"Of course it is."

Silas appeared at her door and opened it. "You're the only woman I've ever met that has anything she wants and still chooses pizza."

"Meaning?" Emily asked, standing slowly.

"Meaning you could have the most expensive meal in town, Kobe Steak... but you chose pizza."

"I like pizza," she said as they moved toward the door. Emily couldn't help but notice that every heku was carefully scanning the area. "Relax, we're not going to get attacked in an empty building."

"We're just being unobservant," Horace said as he held the door for her.

"Ha-ha"

The entire building was silent and immaculately clean. One lone usher came to greet them, and he smiled broadly. "Mr. Jones, I presume?"

Kralen nodded and shook his hand. "Yes, we're all here."

The usher looked at the hulking heku. "You did say... one pizza, right?"

"Yes, one will be enough."

"Right this way," he said, and showed them to the large double doors.

"Need one?" Silas asked. Emily turned and then glared at him as he grinned and stood up with a booster seat in his hand.

"Maybe I do," she said, and grabbed it from him. He barely had time to dodge when she swung the booster seat at him.

"Come on, children," Kralen said from inside the theater.

"But Dad, he started it."

"Sit"

Emily walked past him and then took a seat front and center. The large IMAX theater was massive and seemed even more so with only a handful of them there.

Before the movie started, the usher returned with a rolling cart full of candy and drinks, and topped with a hot pizza.

"Who gets the pizza?" the young man asked as he plated two pieces.

"I'll take it," Emily told him, and then took it. She was starving and it smelled amazing.

"I brought candy. In case you get hungry."

Emily almost choked on her first bite of pizza as the heku began calling out candy orders. The young usher began to toss them what they ordered and soon everyone had something to eat and a drink. He returned with a bag of popcorn for each of them and then assured them the movie would be starting shortly.

She shivered slightly, as they were sitting right under the vent, so Andrew slipped off his red jacket and put it over her shoulders, ignoring the glares from Silas at her other side. She wondered if the usher thought it was weird that the big men had formed a barrier around her three heku deep in each direction.

Emily sighed as the lights dimmed, and she resigned herself to two hours of senseless violence and wanton bloodshed. She couldn't help but grin, because that thought was a brief representation of her life.

It wasn't very long into the movie that she saw the heku really enjoying themselves, and she smiled and leaned back in the chair. It wasn't often she saw them actually having fun, and it was nice to see. She ignored the idiotic movie with its narrow plot and shallow characters, and focused on the camaraderie between the Equites. Andrew sat motionless at her side but smiled when he saw her look over at him.

"Are you okay?" she whispered.

"Yes, why?"

She shrugged and turned back to the movie. It was so boring, that even though she enjoyed watching the heku, she was starting to find it harder and harder to stay awake. Figuring she had nothing to lose, she

picked up a small piece of popcorn and tossed it into the row ahead of her.

One of the heku turned and smiled, but she shook her head and pointed at Andrew. She felt him chuckle from beside her. After feeling around and finding a bag of M&Ms Silas had given her, she tossed it to the front row again.

"Would you behave?" Horace asked with his hand against where the M&M hit him in the back of the head.

She shrugged and again pointed at Andrew.

"You trying to pick a fight?" Andrew asked, amused.

"Want me to?"

"Not really."

"You can't take this many Equites?"

He grinned. "I'm sure I could… but it would get blood all over the theater, and that's a big mess to cover."

When he turned back to the movie, she realized that he was really into it, and she leaned back in the chair. Soon, she was leaned up against Silas' shoulder, deep asleep.

"Em?" Andrew said as he touched her shoulder lightly.

She looked up. "Is it over?"

"Yup," Kralen chuckled, and quickly looked around the room.

"Next time, I pick the movie."

Andrew followed her as they left the theater. She began wondering during the movie if she was being purely selfish keeping him in Council City. He was away from his Encala and in the middle of heku that watched his every move and often shot him evil glares.

It was silent until they pulled up to a posh hotel, surrounded by tall trees and scantily clad women running around an Olympic sized pool.

"Look, Em, you can go swimming," Kralen said when he opened the door.

Emily watched as a tall man in Bermuda shorts tackled a tan blonde in a thong bikini, and she sighed, "Right, they can use me as a raft."

Silas sighed, "Are we playing the fat game again?"

She ignored him and walked inside. Andrew waited beside her as Silas checked in, and she couldn't help but notice how he watched one of the swimmers as she gracefully dove off of the high board.

"Put your tongue back in your mouth and let's go," she snapped, and walked over to the elevator after Silas.

Andrew took one more look behind him and followed them up to the penthouse.

One of the heku put Emily's bags in the bedroom and then walked out as the rest surveyed the penthouse and searched for bugs or cameras.

Emily knelt in a tall window and looked down over the pool.

"Just go swimming, Em," Kralen said, joining her at the window.

"Not with Barbie down there."

He rolled his eyes and went over to turn on the TV.

Emily finally went to the couch and sat on her knees, facing Andrew, who was sitting on the edge of the couch.

He smiled and looked at her. "Can I help you?"

"Do you want to go home?"

"Are you kicking me out?"

"No, but I wonder if you miss being at home."

He smiled. "I'm needed here, so I'll stay."

Silas huffed but quieted down when Emily glared at him.

"I think I have the yoga down if you want to go."

"Prove it," he said, and then stood up and held his hand out.

"No"

"Yes"

"No, I'm not going to do that in front of everyone."

"Wimp," he said, smiling.

"Maybe"

"They aren't going to care, and I can tell you're tensing up again."

She sighed, "Then let's go into the bedroom alone."

"No," Silas, Kralen, and Horace all said at once.

Emily turned away from them and watched out the window. She wasn't sure but felt like the heku were arguing where she couldn't hear it.

"Okay, we agreed on the bedroom, but Kralen and Silas get to watch," Andrew told her.

She looked over at him. "Do you have a girlfriend?"

He was slightly taken back. "What?"

"Do you?"

"No"

"Have you had one?"

His eyes narrowed. "I'm not sure this is appropriate."

"She doesn't care," Kralen chuckled.

Andrew shifted uncomfortably. "It's... well... no."

"Never?"

"No"

"How old are you?" Emily asked, turning more toward him. The others in the room all turned to watch the interaction.

He smiled. "Older than any in this room I'd imagine."

"And why the Encala?"

He gasped, and Kralen stepped between them. "Em, it's not nice to ask."

She shrugged. "I'm just curious."

"That's something he's not going to want to divulge in front of us."

"Well, I'm bored. Why not find out more about him?"

Andrew smiled. "Because your Equites could not care less about me."

"So why did you join the Encala?"

"Em…," Kralen hissed.

"Were you always an Encala?"

He shook his head. "No, I was unfactioned for a while."

"How does that happen?"

"It happens when those that turn you aren't factioned."

She thought about that and then nodded. "Okay, so how long were you unfactioned?"

"Four hundred years."

"Then you… wait…" She turned to Silas. "Wouldn't the Encala be untrusting of an unfactioned if he came knocking and asked to join?"

Silas frowned. "Drop it."

Emily bit at her bottom lip as she watched the nervous way the heku looked at each other. "Okay, so you went to the Encala, and they met you with open arms?"

"Not quite," Andrew said, and then leaned back on the couch.

"How did you convince them to accept you in?"

"When are you going to tell them?" he asked, motioning for the Equites.

Kralen's eyes narrowed and he crossed his arms. "Tell us what?"

Emily turned pale and watched Andrew. "What?"

"I told you… they need to know."

"No," she said in a soft whisper.

"Tell us what?" Silas asked.

"It's time for me to go to bed," she said softly and then stood up slowly.

Andrew frowned. "Your back is really hurting you."

"Back," she mumbled, walking into the bedroom, "hips… arms… knees… feet…"

Kralen turned to Andrew when the bedroom door shut. "What is she keeping from us?"

"It's not my place to say."

"But you feel we should know?"

"Yes, I do."

"Then tell us."

Andrew smiled when Emily called for him. "Again… not my place."

Silas followed Andrew into the bedroom, where Emily was sitting on the edge of the bed in a thick white nightgown.

"You called for me?" he asked, standing in front of her.

She nodded and glanced at Silas before speaking. "Can you help my back and hips?"

He smiled and put his hand out. "Of course."

Emily stood up slowly with his help, and Silas frowned. "How badly are you hurting?"

"He can fix it," she whispered, obviously in pain.

"How are you injured, Em?"

"Why don't you ask your overly gargantuan Elder?"

Andrew helped Emily get into the Warrior pose easily, and her breathing slowed. Silas watched closely, ready to tear Andrew's head from his body if he put one foot out of line.

"Just take deep breaths," Andrew said as he brought her arms down slowly to Warrior II. "Watch the balance."

Silas hissed when Andrew put his hands on Emily's hips, but the Encala ignored him. "You're favoring your left side. You need to put your weight forward."

Emily shifted slightly and winced.

"Relax, you're too tense," Andrew said softly. He lightly brushed the hair away from her shoulders and adjusted her arms slightly.

"Do you have to touch her?" Silas asked under his breath.

Andrew nodded. "Yes, I do."

"Do what?" Emily asked, tensing again.

"Just relax."

She shut her eyes and took deep breaths, already feeling her hips and legs begin to relax.

"Okay, turn and face away from me but keep your feet apart," Andrew whispered.

Emily did as she was told, and knowing what came next, she took a deep breath and slowly lowered her hands to the floor. When the baby got in the way, Andrew put his hands on her waist and lowered her gently to the floor.

"That's enough!" Silas hissed.

"Walk your hands back," Andrew told her, ignoring Silas.

"God, this feels good," Emily sighed as her back began to relax.

"Good, just stay there for a bit then."

"You aren't going to stretch my legs?"

Andrew looked over at Silas. "He may attack me if I do."

"Please, it feels so good."

Silas hissed, "Do it."

Andrew moved up behind her, and when his thighs touched her back side, he bent over, took her shoulders, and gently pulled her back against him.

"What the hell....," Silas growled.

"Shut up, Silas," Emily whispered. When her back quit hurting, she stood up with Andrew's help and sat on the bed.

"Better?"

She nodded. "Yes, thanks."

"Is the pain getting worse?"

"Sort of."

"From what?" Silas asked, stepping up beside Andrew.

"The baby's too big and puts pressure on her spine, which in turn puts pressure on her hips, legs, and back," Andrew explained. "Yoga helps stretch them and relax them. She'll have to do those when I'm gone."

Emily looked up at him. "It is time for you to go, isn't it?"

He sighed and then nodded. "Yes, when we get back tomorrow I'll pack and then it will be time to return."

* * *

"Your breakfast is here," Kralen called through the door.

Emily came out of the bedroom freshly showered and sat down with a plate of pancakes.

Kralen sat down beside her. "Silas checked us out. We're good to go back any time."

She nodded. "Turnings are done?"

"Yes"

"Do you still have to leave?" Emily asked Andrew.

"Yes, it's time."

"Why don't you just join the Equites?"

"Emily!" Kralen gasped.

"Too stuck up and stiff for my taste," Andrew chuckled.

Emily nodded. "I hear ya... I've always said I'm more Encala."

"What?" Kralen asked with wide eyes.

"Oh the Elders know already."

"Then you should join us," Andrew said, smiling broadly.

Emily finished eating in silence while Kralen and Andrew had a silent staring match that ended when Emily yelled at them to grow up. One of the heku took her bags, and they all headed down to the waiting Suburbans.

She wasn't aware that it had snowed that night, and she pulled her coat tighter around her as the wind lashed at her. She was glad for the warmth of the Suburban and fastened her seatbelt after turning up the heater.

"Trying to cook us?" Silas asked. Snow plows hadn't been by yet,

so the Suburbans cut fresh tracks into the nearly 12 inches of new snow.

"It's cold," she said, and turned to look out the window.

The Suburban fell silent as Silas drove slowly back toward Council City. Emily was staring blankly at the snow when Silas cursed and slammed on the brakes.

She turned toward the road as the Suburban began to fishtail and slide right toward a dark figure in the road. Emily screamed and grabbed the steering wheel as the Suburban hit the guard rail and came to a rest.

"Are you okay?" Andrew asked frantically when Emily grabbed her head.

"Did we hit him?"

"No"

Emily looked up just as Silas disappeared from the Suburban, and she saw that the Equites had surrounded the man standing in the road.

"Who is he?" she whispered.

"I don't know," Andrew said, watching them closely. "Just a heku I guess."

"But he's not hurt?"

"No... who's Alec?"

Emily's eyes grew wide. "Is that Alec?"

"Yes... come back!" Andrew growled when Emily bolted from the Suburban and walked unsteadily toward Alec. Her light shoes had been fine yesterday, but in the deep snow, they made her feet freeze.

She pushed past the Equites and walked up as Kralen and Alec screamed at each other.

"I don't know what stops me from ripping you apart, right here," Kralen yelled.

"Emi," Alec said, turning to her when she walked up.

"What do you want, Alec?"

He smiled. "I see another Winchester is on the way."

"I'm sure you knew that already."

"It's true... you're looking good."

"What do you want?"

"I want to talk to you, in private."

"No!" Silas and Kralen yelled together.

Andrew walked up to stand beside Alec, and he stood a good nine inches taller than Alec. Alec looked up at him nervously. "The Equites have an alliance with the Encala now?"

"No," Andrew said, crossing his arms.

"Em, you need to get back in the truck," Silas told her. "It's too cold out here."

Alec smiled at Emily. "So it's you that has an alliance with the Encala."

"What do you want, Alec?" she asked, yet again.

"Please, let me talk to you for just a moment."

"Start talking," Kralen hissed, squaring his shoulders at the smaller heku.

He sighed and took Emily's hand. "I've made a lot of mistakes over the last ten years."

She just watched him.

"I want to make it up to you."

"How?"

"By doing what you've always asked... by joining the Equites."

Emily gasped. "You do?"

"Wait," Silas said, watching him. "It's not going to be that easy."

"You really want to join me in Council City?"

He smiled. "Yes, I miss my family. Pat and his wife don't want me living there. I've left the Valle for good, and you're the only family I have."

Emily suddenly wrapped her arms around him. "I've missed you, Alec."

Andrew's body tensed as she hugged the Valle.

"Em," Kralen said softly. When she looked at him, he continued. "This has to go through the Council. He's done too many things against the Equites to simply be welcomed in."

"I will face them," Alec said, and then smiled at Emily. "It's going to be okay."

Emily sighed and glanced at Kralen before speaking to Alec. "I love you. You're my family and always will be. I can't, however, forget that the Valle have done nothing but torment me since I came to the heku. I also can't forget that you followed Exavior, even knowing what he did to me."

"If you're going to be alive forever," Alec said softly. "You're going to have to learn to forgive."

"You're going to have a harder time getting the Elder to forgive," Kralen told him.

"We'll take you to the Council though. Get in," Silas said as he took Emily's arm and led her back to the Suburban. She crawled in and put her freezing feet under the heater.

Kralen made sure Alec was surrounded by Equites before taking off for Council City, followed by Silas and the other Suburban full of Cavalry.

Emily reached down as best she could and tried to get her hands close to the heater by her feet.

Silas frowned. "You're going to get pneumonia, and the Elder is going to kill us."

"She's a slippery thing," Andrew said from behind them.

"I wanted to talk to him."

"You should have waited in the warmth."

Emily rolled her eyes and then sat back in the chair. By the time they reached the palace, the Council had been alerted, and palace guards were waiting for Alec's arrival.

Andrew got out first and took Emily's arm when she started for the palace. There was ice under the deep snow, and it was hard to keep your footing.

"Are you okay?" Chevalier asked when Andrew led her into the council chambers. It was obvious he was worried about her.

"Just cold," she said, shivering slightly.

One of the servants appeared with a heated blanket and slippers, so she slipped off her wet shoes, and the warm slippers felt amazing against her feet. Andrew put the warm blanket over her shoulders as the Council watched him carefully.

"Em, move up here while we talk to Alec," Quinn said, motioning to the chair by Chevalier.

She started up and then turned to Andrew. "Coming?"

He smiled. "To the Equites Council stand? No."

"You may move back by the wall," Chevalier told him.

Andrew chuckled and moved into the shadows.

Silas and Kralen both came in, followed by Mark, who had been filled in on their encounter with Alec. They stopped in the trial area.

"What's he saying?" Chevalier asked.

"He wants to join Emily with the Equites," Kralen said.

Silas sighed, "We were notified that the Valle are here also. They weren't aware he defected."

Chevalier's eyes narrowed. "This all seems like a set up."

Quinn nodded. "Agreed… let in Alec first."

Alec was led in with his hands restrained behind his back and four members of the Cavalry around him. He smiled warmly at Emily and moved up to the trial area beside Mark.

Chevalier hissed, "I'll just get this out in the open. We don't believe you and think this is all a ruse."

"I understand, but Emi's my family, and I miss her. I don't fit in with the Valle," Alec said. "I never planned on being a Valle."

"Right, you were determined to start the Ferus."

Alec just looked down at the ground.

"We don't trust you around Emily," Zohn said.

"I wouldn't hurt her."

"We don't believe that either. Right now, she's not able to protect herself and adding you into the mix is too dangerous."

"I can too," Emily said, eyeing Zohn. She frowned when she heard Andrew chuckle.

Alec looked back at the Encala and then toward the Equites Council. "So you'll allow her to be around an Encala, one that single handedly wiped out an entire Equites Coven?"

"You did?" Emily asked him with wide eyes.

He glared at Alec. "Watch it, Valle."

"Well? Did you?"

"It was a long time ago."

Alec shrugged. "I just find it hard to believe that you'll allow an Encala to be alone with her, but not her uncle. I have loved Emily since I first set eyes on that beautiful red headed baby."

"We trust him more than we do you," the Chief Interrogator said.

"Put him in a cell," Quinn said. Once Alec was removed from the trial area, Quinn turned to Emily. "What do you want?"

Emily looked like she was on the verge of tears. "I don't know."

"We care about what you think about this. He's your uncle."

"I know… but he's done so much."

Chevalier nodded. "Let's hear the Valle out then."

"Derrick!" Quinn yelled when he heard the door guard growl moments before a fight erupted.

Mark and Kralen disappeared to stop the fight, but then it sounded to the Council like they joined in instead of trying to end it.

"Silas… go," Chevalier sighed.

After a few minutes, Derrick came in, obviously mad and still breathing hard from the fight.

"Was that necessary?!" Quinn yelled.

"Let's see what you think," Derrick hissed, and then turned when Sotomar and Salazar entered the council chamber.

Chevalier stood up and started to hurdle the desk when Zohn and the Chief of Defense each grabbed an arm.

"Let's hear them out," Quinn said to him.

Emily stood slowly, her breathing coming in gasping bursts.

Andrew appeared beside her while the others tried to restrain Chevalier.

"Calm down. We won't let him get to you," Andrew said as he gently took her arm.

Without a word, Emily began to walk backwards but ran into Andrew, her eyes still locked on Salazar. He was staring directly at her with the hint of a smile on his lips. "Salve infans."

Chevalier finally calmed enough to see the fear on Emily's face. As Andrew softly whispered to her, Chevalier moved between her and Salazar.

"Em… we're not going to let him touch you," he said softly.

Emily looked up at him, terrified. Her piercing green eyes watched him, and he was aware that she was moments from running.

"Calm…"

Suddenly, Emily spun on Andrew and tried to get past him. He grabbed her shoulders and dodged a few of her attacks. When she managed to elbow him in the groin, he groaned softly but still maintained a grip on her. His fast movements were all that kept her quickly fighting hands from hurting himself or her.

Finally, Chevalier spun her around and was able to lock her eyes quickly. Her body stayed tense, and he spoke softly to her as she tightly gripped his shirt. The rest of the Council kept a close eye on Sotomar and Salazar, making sure they did nothing to heighten the situation.

"Sleep," he said at last, and she crumpled into Andrew's arms as he lifted her gently. Chevalier smiled slightly at Andrew. "Are you okay?"

He chuckled. "She's harder to hold onto than you'd think."

Chevalier nodded and returned to his seat as Silas ushered Andrew out of the council chambers, still carrying Emily.

Mark and Silas were both crouched behind Salazar. One word from the Council and they would easily rip him to pieces.

"Care to explain?" Zohn asked Sotomar angrily.

Sotomar glanced casually at Salazar before addressing Zohn. "He's our new Winchester expert."

"Meaning?"

"Meaning… we're using him to learn about Emily's ways and behaviors, so we can more easily keep her next time we have her."

Chevalier growled and stood up, ready to fight. "He's not leaving this palace."

"Yes, he is," Sotomar said. "We have the ability to add members to the Council, and he's in as an interim expert until a position opens."

"Get him out of my sight!"

Mark and Silas pulled Salazar out of the room. He went with them but watched his Elder nervously as Sotomar made no attempt to stop them.

"This is low, even for a Valle," Quinn hissed.

Sotomar put his hands up. "We don't agree with what Salazar did, but we need to learn more about Emily, and he's our best bet."

"So you can kidnap her again…"

"No, so we can convince her to return to her true family."

Chevalier tried to jump the desk again, but Zohn and Quinn held him back. They turned suddenly when the Chief Investigator and Chief Interrogator grabbed a hold of Kyle when he tried to get to Sotomar also.

Sotomar smiled. "When Emily is safely in our care, the reign of the

Equites will finally end."

"Calm down," Zohn said to Chevalier. "Let us handle this."

The Chief of Defense glared at Sotomar. "The reign of the Equites?"

"Yes, it's no secret that with Emily's ability, the other factions are kept at bay. While I see that the Encala have gone the route of attempting to become an ally, the Valle want to end any thoughts of supremacy."

"You're not getting Salazar back," Zohn said when Chevalier had calmed enough he could be released. "His crimes against this faction are too great, and he was taken without approval."

Sotomar smiled. "As you aren't the true ruling body of this faction, and the Council gave him to us... he is ours."

"Since when are we not the true ruling body of this faction?"

"Since you were replaced."

"We were also reinstated by the faction as the ruling Council."

"That cannot be done," Sotomar said. "You were replaced, fully within heku tradition."

"Then reinstated," Quinn told him.

"The true Council will come back into power, and you will return to the ground where you belong."

Kyle scowled at the enemy. "But only after you get Emily?"

"Yes, I will admit that she's standing in our way."

"She's not a pawn!" Chevalier yelled. "Leave her alone!"

"We can't," Sotomar told him, patronizingly calm.

"Why are you even here? What would possess you to bring Salazar here where Emily is?" Kyle asked. "You know what he did!"

"We felt hiding his addition to our Council would not be beneficial."

"No, you brought him here to intimidate Emily!"

"Possibly"

Kyle stood suddenly but was again restrained. "You can't just leave her alone, can you?!"

"No, we can't. Now I'll expect Salazar to be returned to me immediately."

"No!"

"Calm down," Quinn said to Kyle. His eyes narrowed, but he finally sat down in his chair.

Sotomar turned to Chevalier. "Have you ever seen a banished Council returned to power?"

"No," he replied bluntly.

"Then what makes you think we're going to stand by and watch it happen?"

"Because you don't have a choice."

"The Valle have taken it upon ourselves to right this wrong, and we do feel that to do so would mean getting Emily out of the picture."

"That sounds like a death threat," Chevalier hissed.

"No, we don't want her dead. We do want her obedient to the Valle though."

The Coven Liaison Officer chuckled. "From what I've seen, good luck."

He smiled. "Salazar had compliance…"

"He tortured her!" Kyle yelled.

"If that's what it takes."

Chevalier stood up. "I'll not stand here and listen to you threaten my wife."

"You know the Old Ones aren't going to let her go. If the Valle can show that she's under our control, they may back off."

"No"

"You're going to stop them?"

"Yes"

"Return Salazar then, and I'll be off."

The Chief of Defense frowned. "You came only for that?"

"No, I also came to inform you that you will be re-banished imminently."

"Very well… the message is received," Quinn said.

"Return Salazar."

"No, you may go."

"He has diplomatic immunity," Sotomar told them.

"No, he doesn't."

"He's a member of my Council!"

"Not holding a valid position," Zohn reminded him.

"Neither are any of you!"

"You may go," Chevalier hissed. It was obvious that he was seconds from breaking heku tradition and doing away with the Valle's Elder.

Sotomar spun suddenly and stormed out of the council chambers. Once he was gone, Derrick stepped in with Andrew.

"I have to be going," Andrew told them. "Emily is still asleep."

"You're leaving without telling her?" Chevalier asked. He wasn't sure he could take the pain in her eyes from a betrayal.

He smiled. "She knows."

"Very well," Zohn said coldly.

Without another word, Andrew turned and left.

Chevalier looked over at Kyle. "Even though she knows… she's not going to like that."

They turned to the trial area door when Lori came in. "Silas just told

me about Salazar."

"We aren't sure what to expect when she wakes up," Chevalier said to her.

"I'm not really sure either," Lori said, deep in thought. "I mean, she's come out of that a lot... but she hasn't actually seen him lately."

"Stay close."

Lori nodded and left.

Quinn smiled. "They're getting bonded."

Chevalier chuckled. "I figured."

"Em's okay with that?" Kyle asked.

"Yes, actually. She was pretty happy for them."

"Well at least no more yoga sessions."

Chevalier's face fell. "I hated those... but they did help her a lot."

"Well we can do that, as well as he can."

"Can we?"

Kyle's eyes narrowed. "I'll go take a class if I have to."

Chevalier tapped his fingers on the desk. "Since Andrew started hanging around Emily, her fear level has decreased significantly."

"She has guards though," the Chief of Defense said.

"I know, but for some reason, she felt safer with him."

"As safe as she does with you?"

"Not quite that safe," Chevalier said, smiling slightly and shrugging.

"So maybe until the baby comes you should stay with her."

"That's still a couple of months away."

"Are you sure?" Zohn asked. "She's... well... huge."

Chevalier nodded. "Yes, I'm sure. I checked her chart."

"You do make'em big, don't you?"

Chapter 10

Emily rolled over and looked at the clock. It was only 3am, and she couldn't sleep. She'd still been doing yoga since Andrew left two weeks before, but it wasn't doing quite as well, and her back was aching. She also had a dream that she didn't fully remember but felt that the Council may be in trouble.

"Chev?" she whispered, and sat up in the dark room. The fires were dying down, and it threw the room into shadows. As she crawled out of bed, she felt an odd burning on her back but figured she must have slept weird.

After grabbing a robe, she stepped out of the room and looked up at her six guards.

"You okay?" Kralen asked, frowning.

She nodded. "Can't sleep."

"Do I smell blood?"

"Not from me," she said, and headed down the stairs.

"What's wrong?" Derrick asked, rushing to her as she came down the stairs.

"Nothing, is Chev in there?"

Derrick took her arm and led her over to the trial room doors. "No, he had to run over to Banks for a bit."

"Is the Council in there?" she asked, frowning slightly.

"Yes, do you need to see them?"

She nodded and then walked in when he opened the door.

"Em, what's wrong?" Kyle asked, looking up from a thick folder.

She walked up awkwardly to stand before his desk. "When will Chev be back?"

"He'll only be gone a few hours. What's up?"

She shrugged and looked along the Council. When she saw the Chief of Staff missing, she frowned. "Where's the Chief of Staff?"

Kyle glanced at Quinn briefly before answering. "He's been banished."

"What? Why?" she gasped.

"It's part of the natural Council process," Quinn explained. "Do I smell blood?"

"No, believe it or not I'm not always injured."

"What's wrong with your wrists?" Kyle asked, leaning over the desk.

Emily looked down and saw light bruises forming around both of her wrists. "I'm not sure."

His eyes narrowed. "What's going on?"

"Nothing, I'm just going to go make pancakes," she said as she

started for the door.

"I still smell blood."

"Then plug your nose." As she disappeared through the door, Kyle sighed and looked over at Quinn.

"We'll just have to assume she has a minor injury and let it go."

"We should tell Chevalier."

"We will, when he returns."

Emily started down the stairs and dismissed the chef that had been summoned when she first woke up. He bowed and then left while she gathered what she needed for pancakes.

"Why are you cooking?" Mark asked, sitting down on a chair by the stove.

She looked over. "I'm perfectly able to cook."

"I'm sure you are."

"Why were you called in? It's 3am."

"It's unnerving when we smell blood."

She shrugged. "I'm not bleeding."

Mark watched as she stirred the pancake batter, and he easily saw the bruises forming around her wrists. "Let me see your wrists."

"No"

"No?"

She smiled. "No."

"Why not?" Mark asked, suddenly tensing.

"Because nothing's wrong, and I like to see you squirm."

Mark smiled. "You do, don't you?"

She nodded and plated the pancakes, then sat down to eat. "So when are you going to tell me why I have six guards instead of four?"

He flipped the chair and then sat in it backwards, facing her. "Two of these are in training."

"Right... and the two last night were just talking to Kralen. Then the two yesterday were asking Silas something..."

Mark smiled. "I told the Elder that wasn't going to work."

"So spill it."

"Easy enough. Old Ones are stronger than most heku. If they're going to target you, then we have to up your security."

Emily shrugged. "Whatever floats your boat."

Mark leaned forward a bit. "You have a mark on your neck?"

"So?" she said, and then stood up to put her plate in the sink. As she poured a glass of milk, Kralen moved closer to her and leaned down to look.

"It's a welt," he said, looking over at Mark.

Emily pushed against his arm. "Stop inspecting me."

He smiled and stood up. "Then stop getting hurt."

"I'm not hurt!" she hissed, again surprising the guards as to how many heku traits she exhibited.

"Good morning," Dr. Edwards said as he walked in.

Emily turned and glared at Mark. "Seriously?"

He shrugged. "You're up at 3am… you smell like blood and have bruises on your wrists. What was I supposed to do?"

"Let's see… I'm pregnant and had the munchies… that can happen at 3am without needing medical advice. I'm accident prone and probably cut myself trying to shave legs that I can't even see."

Dr. Edwards chuckled. "True."

"I also don't have bruises on my wrists." She looked down at the yellowing color. "I'm guessing it's from the fact that I'm swelling so bad that my coat cut into my wrists."

"Swelling's bad?"

She looked at him. "So?"

"That's not healthy."

"Go away."

"Let me just look you over," Dr. Edwards said as he pulled his stethoscope out of his bag.

Emily smiled. "As a member of the Council, I'm ordering you to go away."

"Hey," Mark snapped.

Dr. Edwards thought for a moment and then left.

Emily smiled. "That's kind of handy."

"Can't just let him look, can you?" Kralen sighed.

"I can… but I won't," she told him as she headed for the door. They followed her in silence as she went up to the game room and picked out a movie.

"You're not even going to try to sleep?" Mark asked, watching her settle down on a large pillow.

"No"

"Why not?"

"Go away."

Mark smiled. "You can't pull that on me."

She huffed and then turned around to watch the movie. Almost an hour into it, she turned to Mark again. "Did you see that they banished the Chief of Staff?"

"Former Chief of Staff… yes, I did."

"Why?"

"I'm not privy to that information."

"Privy?"

"It means that they don't tell me."

She frowned. "I know what it means… it's just… British is all."

He chuckled as she turned back to the movie.

"It's freezing in here," she mumbled as the credits began to roll.

"No, it's 72 degrees."

"Which is freezing."

"Thirty two degrees is freezing," one of the newer members of the Cavalry informed her.

She glared at him. "Don't be so literal."

"Yes, ma'am."

"And don't call me ma'am!"

His eyes grew wide and he looked at Mark, who just grinned.

"Em, what's wrong?" Chevalier asked as he walked into the game room. He ignored the Cavalry as they bowed slightly at his presence.

She turned to him. "Why did they banish the Chief of Staff?"

His eyebrows rose. "It was time. Why do I smell blood?"

"Oh my God!" she yelled, and then stood up with much effort. "Why don't you all just go away?"

"Well why?" he asked, following her out of the room. "And why are you even up this early?"

She rolled her eyes and walked up the stairs.

"Em?"

"What?"

"Why are you up?"

"Damn! I was hungry, okay?"

Chevalier stifled a grin. "So everything's okay?"

"Peachy," she grumbled as she walked into the bedroom and shut the door before any heku could enter.

Mark chuckled. "She's also on to the six guards."

"I figured she would be soon enough," Chevalier said, turning to Mark. "She has bruises on her wrist."

"Not if you ask her."

"Is she upset about the change in Council?"

"She seemed more frustrated."

Chevalier nodded. "Okay, call if you need me."

Chevalier watched the door for a bit before heading to the Council. As he sat down, the other Elders turned to him.

"So?" Quinn asked.

Chevalier nodded. "He'll be here this afternoon to take his place as Chief of Staff."

"We'll have the coronation tonight then."

Zohn leaned in. "Did you see her?"

"Yes," Chevalier whispered. "I saw the bruises on her wrist and the mark on her neck. That could be a scratch though."

"I thought it looked like a welt."

"Maybe"

Emily tossed and turned for a couple of hours before resigning herself to being up for the day. She stepped into a hot shower and sighed as the steaming water began to loosen the tight muscles in her back.

When she stepped out of the shower and wrapped in a heated towel, she noticed the burning in her back again and turned to look in the mirror. She gasped as she saw the darkening bruises of strap marks across her back.

Emily jumped when Chevalier knocked on the bathroom door. "Em?"

"I'll... be right out!"

"You okay?"

"Yes," she said, checking out the bruises on her back again. Now she wasn't sure how to get out of the bathroom. He was certain to see the bruises if she walked out in a towel.

After a few minutes, he came to the door again. "Are you okay?"

"Sure"

"Then why are you just standing there?"

She sighed. It was irritating how much the heku could hear. "Because."

"Oh that's helpful," he said, amused.

"I'll be out in a bit."

"Okay... I have your dress ready for the coronation tonight."

"Damnit, I don't want to go."

It irritated her how he found that funny. "We need you there."

She silently mimicked him behind the door. "Go away."

"Fine, but the dress is here," he said, chuckling and then left the room.

Once he was gone, she peeked out into the room to make sure it was clear and then quickly dressed in a long-sleeved sweater to hide the darkening bruises on her wrists.

She glanced once at the dress and saw that, even though maternity cut in the front, the back was plunging, and she didn't know how to hide the bruises. Emily spent a few hours in front of the bay window watching the snow, trying to figure out how she could get lashed without even knowing it and who had done it.

Not knowing what else to do, she called Andrew.

"Em! How are you?" He sounded honestly pleased to hear from her.

"Okay," she whispered.

"What's wrong?" His voice suddenly turned concerned.

"Something weird happened."

"Tell me."

"When I woke up this morning at like… 3am…"

"You're hesitating… you can trust me."

"I have bruises on my wrists and lash marks on my back," she whispered even softer.

"What?!" he screamed.

"I don't know how they got there."

"You don't know or you don't want to tell me?"

"I honestly don't know."

"So someone controlled you long enough to erase it!"

She thought before speaking. "No… I can't be controlled like that. I'm not sick."

"I saw Chevalier control you completely when Salazar came," Andrew reminded her.

"I allowed that."

"Oh, that's right. I forgot you can do that."

"I don't know what to do. Chev had this ridiculous dress made with a plunging back for tonight. I can't hide this."

"Em, don't hide it… tell the Council," Andrew said. "You're obviously being beaten!"

"No, I'm not!"

"Are you protecting the heku who did it?" Andrew asked, sounding angry.

"No!"

"I can see you doing that."

She frowned and hung up the phone, then turned back to the snowy window and watched the heku and their wolves patrolling the palace lawn.

Emily didn't answer when a knock sounded. Mark waited a few seconds and then walked in. "Em?"

"Yes?" she said, not looking over at him.

"Lunch is here."

"I'm not hungry. Just take it back."

She felt a hand on her shoulder and fought a wince when Mark's hand brushed one of the lash bruises. "Please, tell me what's wrong."

"Nothing's wrong. I just don't feel all that hot," she told him. "Tell Chev I'm not going to make it to the coronation."

Mark sat down beside her. "There's more."

She fought back the tears. "I'm okay."

"Tell me."

She turned to him with flowing green eyes. "Please, tell him I can't go."

He studied her before nodding. "I will, but he's going to want to know why."

"Tell him I'm just sick."

"Are you?"

She nodded.

"I'll see what I can do."

Mark stood up and then helped her stand. She walked over and watched him leave before pulling off her robe and sliding into bed. If she was going to be convincingly sick, she had to stay in bed.

***

"Are you sure you can't go?" Chevalier asked as he sat down on the edge of the bed.

Emily nodded and pulled the covers up around her shoulders more.

He studied her for a bit and then nodded. "Okay. I wish you could though. It's seriously breaking tradition for you not to be there."

"I'm sorry," she whispered, and looked up at him.

He saw confusion in her gaze and mistook it for illness. "I'll explain it to the others. Get some rest, okay?"

She nodded and rolled onto her side as he left. Emily wasn't sure what to do. She was starving but was supposed to be too sick to eat. She was also tired of lying in bed all day but couldn't get up, or she'd be asked again to go to the coronation.

After hours of tossing and turning, she finally fell asleep. When she woke up, it was still dark outside, and she could hear the sounds from the coronation reception coming up the stairs. As she went to burrow deeper into the warm covers, the blankets brushed her back, and she fought back a scream.

Moving slowly to lessen the pain, she reached over and turned on the bedside light, then inhaled sharply when she saw that her wrists were now black with small amounts of blood seeping out of what looked to be fresh wounds.

Knowing she had to move fast or she risked Mark coming in, Emily jumped out of bed and ran into the bathroom, locking the door behind her. She heard Mark peek into the room and then shut the door behind him when he didn't see her.

When she was sure no one was going to check on her. She pulled up her night gown and looked into the mirror, wide eyed. The lashes that were light yellow bruises were now deep, black and blue welts. Some of them were cut slightly, and she had dried blood on her nightgown. She changed her nightgown and then looked around the bathroom, as if to find something to explain the late-night lashings.

Unsure what to do, she went back into the bedroom, crawled into the closet, and called Andrew.

"Why are you up this early?" he asked without saying hello.

"It happened again," she whispered.

"The lashings?"

"Yes, but it's really bruised this time and bloody."

"Who did it?!" he yelled.

She shook her head and fought back tears. "I don't know."

"How can you not know?"

"I don't remember it happening. My wrists are bruised more now too."

"Then it's the Council."

"They wouldn't do this."

"They would."

She sighed, "Even if they did, I'd remember it."

"Not if they controlled you."

"They didn't!"

"I'm not going to let this happen," Andrew said, irate. "I'll stop it."

"No!" Emily gasped. "Don't come here and accuse the Council of anything."

He sighed, "A heku needs to intervene."

"Let me figure this out first."

"You can't hide it."

"I can try," she whispered, and hung up the phone.

"Em?" Chevalier said from in the bedroom. "Are you in the closet?"

"Well… yes," she said.

"Taking a break?" he asked, sounding unsure.

"No"

"Then come out."

"No"

"What? Why not?"

"I'm… I don't know why."

He sighed, and she could tell he was now at the doors to the closet. "You're not making sense."

She racked her brain trying to think of a reason to be sitting in the closet. "I saw a mouse."

"There're no mice in the palace."

"You don't know that."

"I can smell them… I know there aren't."

"Oh well then, I guess I thought I saw one?" She didn't mean to make it a question, and she winced when it came out as one.

Chevalier opened the door and looked down at her. "Come out."

She hadn't realized that her wrists were covered by her robe, and she was afraid if she stood up they would be exposed. "I'm fine here."

He crossed his arms and looked down at her as she sat in the closet and watched him.

Chevalier finally shook his head. "Fine… I'll have your breakfast brought in."

She nodded and then smiled slightly when he shut the closet door before leaving. After she heard her breakfast delivered, she finally crawled out and sat down to eat, making sure her robe covered her wrists in case anyone came in.

***

"Is there some reason I haven't even seen you in four days?" Chevalier asked through the bathroom door.

"Nothing I can think of," Emily said as she studied the deep black welts on her back, thighs, and arms. The lash marks were getting worse, and now she sported a bruise on her cheek that was starting to swell into her left eye.

"You're just acting strangely. Is it the weight thing?"

"No"

"Then why can't I see you?"

Emily pulled on the thick velvet robe with its high collar and long sleeves and then sat on the edge of the tub. "I'm just going to bathe."

"I'll join you then."

"No"

He sighed, loud enough she heard him through the door. "Fine."

Emily didn't know how not to make him mad. She knew it wouldn't take a heku but a second to smell the dried blood on her back, and she didn't know how to hide it. The only thing she could think of was to try to avoid any contact until she figured it out. The problem was, was it wasn't going away, and every time she slept, it got worse. She was tired from being up in pain most of the night, but the slightest sleep made things worse.

Chevalier sat down in his spot and looked over at Kyle. "She's now hiding in the bathroom."

"It has to be the weight thing again," he said. "She knows how big the baby's gotten."

"Still… no one's seen her in four days. Not even her guards have actually seen her."

Quinn frowned. "So go see her."

"I don't want to just break into the bathroom while she's bathing."

Derrick stepped into the room. "The Encala have representatives here."

"Why?" Zohn asked.

He smiled. "They didn't say."

Chevalier shrugged. "Whatever, let them in."

It was obvious from how Andrew and William entered that they were furious.

"What brings the Encala here?" Zohn asked, frowning.

"I won't sit by and let you beat her!" Andrew yelled. William put a hand on his arm to stop him from advancing on the Equites Council.

"Excuse me?" Kyle asked angrily.

William silenced Andrew with a glare. "We want to see Emily."

"She's being a tad elusive at the moment," Quinn said. "I'm sure she won't see you either."

"She'll see me," Andrew hissed.

"I'm still trying to figure out why you think we're beating her," Chevalier said, irritated.

Andrew glared at him. "Let me see her."

"She's not letting any heku see her right now," Kyle told him.

"Just Equites!" Andrew yelled.

Chevalier stood up and growled, his body ready to attack.

"Derrick," Zohn called out. When the heku entered, he motioned to Andrew. "Please escort Andrew to the Elder's bedroom, so he can speak to Emily. If she refuses, don't let him in."

Derrick nodded and moved back so Andrew could pass by. Once at the door, Derrick knocked and waited for an answer.

"Who is it?" Emily called through the door.

The six guards watched Andrew carefully.

"It's Derrick. Andrew from the Encala is here to see you."

They were surprised when she went into the bathroom, shut the door, and then called for Andrew to come in.

Andrew stepped in and shut the door behind him. Once shut, Emily came out and looked over at him. She was pale and had dark circles under her eyes. One cheek was bruised, and her eye was swollen shut above it.

He studied her and noticed the deep black bruises on her wrists and the strong smell of dried blood. "What did they do?"

She shook her head. "No one's done anything."

He continued to look over her to ascertain her injuries.

She turned to the mirror. "I don't know what's going on. No one's doing this."

He moved to her and hugged her tightly. "Someone is... you don't have to protect them."

It felt good to be held. She was too afraid to let Chevalier see the injuries, but she needed to feel the protection of a strong embrace.

"Elder William is here," he told her. "We'll take you back to the

Encala. No one will hurt you there."

"No one's hurting me here. I don't understand."

"Can I see?"

She nodded and turned around. Andrew lowered the back of her nightgown slightly and hissed.

"How bad?" she asked. Even with mirrors, it was awkward to see.

"Your back and neck are covered in welts."

She nodded.

He turned her around and took her shoulders gently. "Tell me what's going on."

She looked into his eyes. "I don't know."

He looked toward the door. "Let's get you out of here."

"I can't let them see."

"Why not? It's obvious an Equites is doing this."

She shook her head. "No one's doing this! I would ash them if they tried."

He smiled softly. "You know as well as I do that you wouldn't."

"No one is lashing me."

"You can't stay here," he said, moving to the door.

Emily looked down at her bruised wrist. "It doesn't make sense."

"Get dressed and pack a bag. I'll go talk to the Council, and we'll get you to safety."

She finally nodded and then turned to the closet when Andrew left. He stormed down to the council chambers and threw open the door.

"She's packing," Andrew growled at them.

"Why?" Kyle asked as Chevalier stood up.

"Don't act stupid with me! You can fool her, but I'm not going to let this happen."

"Let what happen?"

"Again… I wasn't turned yesterday! I'm taking her to the safety of the Encala palace."

William watched him and then turned to the Equites. "It's pathetic how you abuse a pregnant mortal woman."

"Em's not abused!" Chevalier hissed.

"She saved this entire Council at great risk to herself!" William yelled. "She's shown never before seen loyalty to this faction and what does she get? Flogged?"

"Calm down," Quinn said sternly. "No one's flogging Emily."

"What the hell?!" Derrick yelled from the other side of the door.

The Council looked up as Emily opened the door and stepped in with a bag grasped tightly in her hand.

"Em…," Chevalier gasped when he saw the dark bruise on her cheek and her swollen eye. The smell of dried blood hit the Council, and

bruised marks were prominent against her neck.

She looked up at the Council and then turned to leave, but William blurred and took her arm gently. "We'll protect you."

He led her over to the Council, followed by her six heku guards that all looked confused and afraid they might get blamed for this.

Chevalier appeared beside her. "Who did this?"

"You have no right talking to her!" Andrew said, pushing Chevalier back slightly.

William and Zohn dove into the fight that ensued and pulled the two heku apart.

"You disgust me!" Andrew growled at Chevalier.

"Did you do that?" Chevalier yelled back.

"Calm down!" Quinn roared. Both heku looked at him. "The Equites are not abusing Emily."

"Who did this to you?" Chevalier asked her softly, fighting back the rage.

She looked up at him. "I don't know."

"How can you not know?" Kyle yelled.

She flinched and then looked over at him. "No one's doing this!"

The Chief of Defense and Chief Interrogator grabbed a hold of Kyle when he started forward.

"I want to see your back," Chevalier told her.

She looked at the heku, all staring at her, and shook her head. "No."

"You cannot tell an Elder no," the new Chief of Staff said.

Emily glared at him, but her lip quivered. "I can too."

"Shut up," Kyle yelled at the Chief of Staff.

Dr. Edwards and Lori both came into the council chambers when summoned. Dr. Edwards hissed and moved up to Emily immediately. She sighed and let him study her face.

"This cheek bone might be broken," he said as he shined a bright light into her eyes.

Chevalier pulled out of the restraining grasp and then took her arm gently and pulled her aside. "Who did this?"

"I told you, no one hit me," she told him.

"Em…"

"Don't Em me! No one is hitting me."

"You have marks on your neck," he said softly.

Emily left him and walked up to Richard, the Chief Interrogator. "Have at it."

He glanced at Quinn. "I need permission."

"Wait!" William yelled.

"Granted," Quinn said to him.

Chevalier watched Richard closely as the Interrogator left the room

with Emily following.

"He cannot interrogate her," William said, "or is that what's going on here already?"

"He won't do anything more than ask her questions," Zohn assured him. "He's only taking her to the Elder's conference room for privacy."

Emily shut her eyes against the pounding in her head as she sat down in the private conference room. She looked up when Richard dimmed the lights.

"Thanks," she said softly.

He smiled. "Don't be so nervous."

"I'm not."

"Then stop wringing your hands."

She looked down. "Oh."

"You know me and trust me, right?"

Emily nodded.

"Then don't mask… I can recognize that."

Again, she simply nodded.

Richard reached out and gently took her hands. "You'll tell me the truth?"

"Yes"

He smiled softly. "Let's start simple. Who is lashing you?"

"No one."

"No one or you don't know who it is?"

"I don't think anyone is."

He studied her face and then nodded. "Okay, when did it start?"

"When I woke up five nights ago."

"Is it getting worse?"

"Yes"

"Your back and neck only?"

"Yes"

He squeezed her hands softly. "Try that again."

She frowned and looked down at the table.

"Look at me, please." She was surprised by how much he seemed to care and how calmly he asked about the injuries.

Emily looked up at him, and it was obvious she was thinking about lying.

"You're too easy to read. Tell me the truth. Where are your injuries?"

"Back and neck…"

"…and…"

"… arms and the back of my legs."

"Same, lash marks?"

She nodded.

"Yet you don't know who is doing it?"

"Not just that… I don't know if it's even being done."

"Okay, who hit your face?"

"No one."

"The bruise just appeared?"

"Yes"

"No one hit you?"

"No, I know no one believes me," she said, her voice cracked.

He smiled. "I do."

"Then help me. The Encala are blaming the Equites. The Equites don't know who to blame. If everyone will leave me alone, I can figure it out."

"We can't just let it go. You're pregnant and vulnerable."

She frowned. "I'm what?"

Richard looked into her eyes again. "There's something else you're not telling me. Is it another injury?"

"No," she whispered.

"Is it a bruise?"

"No, I'm not hiding anything."

"Pain?"

"No"

"Where is it?"

Her eyes began to swim, and she tried to pull her hands away from the Chief Interrogator. "That's enough."

Richard held tightly to her hands. "Just tell me where the pain is."

"Don't," she whispered, starting to panic.

He concentrated on her eyes, and she turned away from him and tensed.

"Stop"

"I'm sorry," Richard said softly. "Now please, tell me."

"I can handle it."

"You don't have to do this alone."

"No one's doing this to me, Richard."

"May I ask a few more questions?"

She nodded and looked into his eyes.

"Do you have an idea about how this is happening?"

"No"

"Did you do it to yourself?"

"No!" she gasped.

Richard smiled. "I had to ask."

"I didn't do it."

Finally, he let go of her hands and stood up. "Do you want to go back in there?"

She looked at the door. "They'll fight if I don't."

"Not what I asked."

"No," she sighed, and looked up at him.

"I'll tell him that you have a headache and are going to retire for a bit."

"Thank you."

He smiled and swept out of the room. As he sat down, he saw that Quinn and William were ending a heated argument, and both of them were glaring at each other while Andrew watched Richard.

"What did you do with her?" Andrew asked.

"I didn't do anything to her," Richard explained. "She has a headache and has gone to lie down."

"Or she's dead and you're covering."

Richard ignored him and turned to the Elders. "She honestly doesn't know what's going on. She can't even say that she doesn't know who did it, because it's not being done. She does have a pain she won't talk about, then the lashing marks are across her neck, back, legs, and arms."

Zohn nodded. "You got nothing?"

"She only tried to hide the mysterious pain."

"Was it in her forearms?" Andrew asked.

Chevalier turned to the Encala. "You know about that?"

"Yes"

"What is it?"

"She doesn't want you to know... is the pain there?"

Richard shrugged. "She didn't want to say, and I didn't push the issue. She was starting to panic."

"We have this under control now that we know," Quinn told the Encala. "You may go."

"No," William said, crossing his arms. "I'm not convinced you aren't abusing someone you should be treating like royalty for saving your asses."

"We're not abusing her," Chevalier said again.

"That remains to be seen. I want to bring our Chief Interrogator here."

"We've already questioned her."

William just watched him.

Kyle sighed, "She has really bad luck with Interrogators. I'm surprised she even agreed to speak to ours."

"Ours has never hurt her."

"He threatened her once," Mark reminded them from the back of the room.

"The former one... this one has never said anything to her," Andrew told him.

"I don't feel comfortable having my wife interrogated by an Encala," Chevalier said angrily.

"Yet you allow her to be flogged?" William snapped.

"See them out," Zohn said to Mark as he helped hold Chevalier back.

Mark called for the closest Cavalry and soon had the Encala escorted out of the city.

"How do we handle this?" Quinn asked Chevalier when she sat down again.

"Nothing at all?" Chevalier asked Richard.

"Nothing. She honestly doesn't know."

"How can she not know? It looks like she's been repeatedly flogged over the last few days," Kyle said.

"So for now, we don't leave her alone at all," Richard suggested. "If she's not alone, she can't be harmed."

Chevalier stood up. "Starting now. Until we figure this out, I don't want her alone. If I can't be with her, it should be Kyle or Mark."

Kyle nodded. "Understood. When Mark gets back I'll talk to him."

"One thing though," Zohn said, and then called for the doctor.

Dr. Edwards came in and bowed. "You called for me, Elder?"

"Yes, I want you to find out any torture used in our history that can cause forearm pain."

He frowned. "Okay… do I have more to go on?"

"No, you don't."

Dr. Edwards nodded and disappeared.

Chevalier called for food and then headed up the stairs. He eyed the six members of the Cavalry closely as he walked into the room. Emily looked over from her seat by the bay window. It was obvious that she had been crying.

He pulled up a chair and sat down beside her. "I wish you would have told me."

"Told you what? How I'm being abused by nothing?"

"About the lash marks."

"I didn't know how, and I didn't want everyone to freak out."

"So you told Andrew?"

She shrugged and took his hand when he put it out.

"I'm not mad. I just wish you had told me."

"There's so much going on right now with the Old Ones and the baby coming, then the Valle and Alec, and Andrew left…"

He turned and watched the Bulldog puppy stretch out in front of the fire. "Where's the other one?"

"Outside, I think. Garrett took him out earlier."

Chevalier took her wrists gently in his hands and held her arms out,

soft side up. "Where's the pain?"

"I can handle it."

He lightly kissed her forearms. "Where?"

"My..."

"Please," he whispered, looking into her eyes.

"My arms and... behind my knees."

He studied her arms and saw no sign of injury. "Can I see your knees."

"There's nothing there."

Chevalier turned and told the servant to enter when he heard a knock. The servant seemed tense with the slight smell of blood in the room, and he set the tray down quickly, then blurred away.

"Pleasant fellow," Emily said, wrinkling her nose.

"You smell like dried blood."

"Oh, I can go shower."

He smiled. "Why don't I go with you?"

***

Chevalier watched her sleep. He was amazed at how still she slept and how she never cried out with nightmares. He was afraid to touch her tonight though, so he just watched her sleep and marveled at her beauty and strength.

As the light of dawn trickled into the room, Emily stirred slightly and lifted her hand from under the cover. Chevalier frowned and studied it, as it now had a deep purple bruise forming along her fingers. That hadn't been there the night before, any trace of it and his keen vision would have seen it forming.

Moving slowly, so not to wake her, Chevalier pulled the covers off of her, and as he went to look at her other hand, he noticed a dark bruise showing on her side through the light nightgown. That bruise was new also.

"Em," he whispered, and touched her shoulder gently.

A loud, angry voice yelled in his mind. "Get out!"

Chevalier let go of her and stood suddenly, watching her. She hadn't moved or made any indication that she heard the loud voice. He caught his breath and then reached out to touch her again. This time, Emily jerked away from him and almost fell out of bed.

"Don't do that!" she yelled, clutching her chest.

He watched her with wide eyes. "What were you dreaming?"

"What?"

"Just now... what were you dreaming?"

"I don't know," she said, half yawning. She gasped when she saw

her hand and then held both up. There were dark bruises across her knuckles, and her fingers were beginning to swell.

"Your side too," he told her.

Emily peeked into her nightgown and saw the bruise forming. She looked up at Chevalier and frowned. "What happened?"

"Nothing," he told her. "I was here all night."

"It's okay," she said, hiding the pain in her hands.

Chevalier called out for ice and then walked closer to her. "I heard a voice."

"In the room?" she asked, looking around at the dark shadows.

"No, in your dream."

"Well if you were seeing my dream, why did you ask what I was dreaming about?"

"I didn't get that far. The voice caught me off guard, and I let go. It yelled at me to get out."

Emily sat down and pulled the hem of her nightgown out of the Bulldog puppy's teeth.

Chevalier took an ice pack from a servant and then sat down beside Emily and held it against her hand. "I don't understand how this happened."

Emily looked up when Chevalier told someone to enter and then Dr. Edwards came in.

"Chev," she said, frowning.

"He has to look," Chevalier told her. "Something's wrong."

Dr. Edwards knelt down beside Emily and took her hand. "What happened?"

"Nothing happened... again," she explained.

Dr. Edwards looked up at Chevalier and then sighed, "May I talk to her alone?"

"No," he hissed.

"Please, just for a moment."

"No!"

Zohn and Quinn both came into the room. "Chevalier..."

He turned to them and frowned. "What is this?"

"Just come talk to us," Zohn said.

"I didn't do this."

"For a moment," Quinn said, stepping aside.

Chevalier growled and walked out with the other two Elders. He saw Kyle walk into the room, just as they started down the stairs.

Emily looked up at Kyle and then back to Dr. Edwards. "Nothing happened. I told you."

"Let me see your side," Dr. Edwards said, lifting her nightgown slightly. Emily gasped and turned to Kyle, but he was conveniently

watching out the window. "This looks pretty bad. It's a fist."

"What?" Kyle hissed, turning around.

Emily tried to pull her nightgown down, but Kyle blurred to her side and bent down to look. "That is a hand bruise."

"Who hit you, dear?" Dr. Edwards asked her, lowering her nightgown.

"No one!" she said, frustrated. "No one is hitting me."

He took her hands and began looking at them closely. "These look like lash marks on your hands too."

"Did he hit you?" Kyle hissed.

"Kyle… no," she said sternly. "Chev didn't hurt me."

"He was the only one in here."

"That's it!" Emily screamed. "Get out!"

"We aren't to leave you alone," Kyle said, squaring off. He was ready for this fight.

"I don't really care. Get out."

"No, enough."

"Get out!" she screamed louder and then stumbled slightly and sat down.

"Em!" Kyle gasped, kneeling beside her as she pressed her hands into her eyes.

"Please… go away."

"I can't."

Dr. Edwards took her battered hand. "It's not safe to leave you alone."

"It's not safe to be in here either, apparently," she said.

"How bad is your head?"

"I need to be alone."

"Let us help you," Kyle said softly. "If it's Chevalier, Elder or not, we can help you."

"Get out!" she screamed again.

Dr. Edwards stood and left quickly, while Kyle pulled a chair up beside Emily. He took her hand after lowering the blinds.

"I'm sorry, okay?" Kyle whispered. "I don't mean to accuse him, but he was the only one in here last night."

"He didn't do anything."

"Do you know what's happening?"

"No," she said softly, and then looked up at him. "I just wake up and it's worse."

"So, it's only when you're sleeping?"

"Yes"

"You're sure?"

She nodded. "I've not had so much as a scratch while I'm awake."

"I'm just trying to figure this out. Why don't you take something for the headache?" he asked, brushing the hair away from her face gently.

She sighed, "Because I'm not going to sleep for a while. I can't handle any more of this."

"You can't stay awake for long."

"With enough coffee I can."

He tenderly touched the deep bruise on her cheek. "I don't understand this. Maybe if we had several of us in here while you slept."

"I'm not going to sleep with an audience."

He smiled. "Why not? It's fascinating."

She looked at him crookedly. "Sleeping is?"

"Yes"

"What are Quinn and Zohn doing to Chev?"

"Probably questioning him."

"He didn't do anything."

"It just doesn't look good. He's the only one that was in here last night, and you have more injuries."

"The other nights though he was on that stupid trial," she reminded him.

"Yes, but he came up here to check on you several times."

"He does?"

Kyle smiled. "Yes, he's very protective, remember."

Emily sat up straighter and turned toward him. "Fine then... control me and ask."

"You're going to allow that?"

"Yes"

Kyle nodded and then sat down on the bay window beside her. She looked up at him and suddenly let control go. As her breathing matched his, Kyle looked deeply into her eyes and easily got her under his control.

"I want you to relax and listen to me," Kyle said calmly. He immediately felt her entire body relax, and he held her shoulders, so she didn't slump down into the bay window seat. "You have to trust the Council and listen to what we say about the injuries. Do you understand?"

She gasped softly but didn't speak. Confused, Kyle tried again but got no audible answer. He was in full control, could feel her wielding under his power, but got no compliance.

He waited a few minutes to make sure she was firmly locked. "Emily, who is hitting you at night?"

She inhaled sharply and began to shake.

"Talk to me... anything...," he ordered, but she started to breathe

quickly. Although he felt no loss of control, he wasn't getting a reply.

When he heard her pulse race, he quickly broke control and then caught her when she fell forward slightly.

"Are you okay?" he asked, sitting her up to look at him.

She nodded. "Just really tired."

"It didn't work."

"I allowed it though."

"I know, but it didn't work. I've never seen that."

Emily leaned back and pulled a blanket over her shoulders. "Then I have to figure this out on my own."

"No, you don't. We'll keep trying," he said, and then watched her. He could tell she was fighting sleep. "Why don't you just take a nap. I'll stay here."

She shook her head. "No. If Chev can't stop it, no one can."

"Maybe…"

"No. Please go get Chev out of whatever it is they're doing to him."

Kyle thought and then nodded. "Okay."

She watched him leave and then ordered some strong coffee as she leaned back against the wall and looked over the bedroom.

Kyle knocked on the Elder's private conference room, knowing that was strictly against the rules.

"Enter," Quinn said angrily. He frowned when he saw it was Kyle. "You knocked?"

"I'm sorry, Elder. I felt it was important."

"Come then," Zohn said, still eyeing Chevalier. "You're not supposed to leave her alone."

"I don't think it matters if she's alone or not," Kyle said. "She allowed me to control her."

"She did?" Chevalier gasped, shocked.

"Yes, and I got nothing."

"So she told you she didn't know…"

"No, she wouldn't speak. I had full control at all times, but she wouldn't answer me," Kyle explained.

"How can that be?" Quinn asked. "Maybe she held back."

Kyle smiled slightly. "I've controlled enough mortals to know when I have a full lock, sir."

"It just doesn't make sense."

"She still swears to me that Chevalier didn't do it."

"I didn't," Chevalier said. "I watched her all night, and she didn't so much as flinch."

"I've been thinking about that," Zohn said. "Emily's always been restless… why since her capture has she been quiet?"

"I'm not sure."

"You've seen dreams though, right?"

"Yes"

"Normal?"

"Pretty much," Chevalier said. "I don't see anything different, nothing that would keep her as still as she is."

"Ever notice she always seems tired too?" Kyle asked. "I've suspected that since her return, she doesn't sleep well."

"She's never slept well while pregnant," Quinn added. "If I remember correctly, that's common."

"It's not just lately though."

Chevalier nodded. "I've seen that too. I wish we could interrogate Andrew."

"Figure out why her forearms are in so much pain?" Zohn asked.

"That... and see if there's anything we don't even know about."

"I suggest we have three or four of us in her room while she sleeps tonight," Kyle said. "If she sleeps tonight. She's ordered strong coffee and told me she's not going to sleep."

"I wouldn't either," Chevalier sighed. "She's getting abused in her sleep."

"The voice has me concerned... the 'get out' voice," Quinn said. "Yet it didn't sound familiar?"

Chevalier shrugged. "It's a disembodied voice. It could be anyone."

"Allen used to hear the Encala's Ancient. Maybe we should call him to see if he hears anything coming in."

Chevalier looked at Quinn. "That's not a bad idea."

"We could just use Dain or Alex," Kyle said.

"They're all on such different levels though," Quinn said. "I mean... Alex is barely heku, Dain is full, and Allen is mostly... we may need his mostly to hear it."

"Bring Allen immediately," Chevalier called out. Within minutes, the sounds of a helicopter taking off shook the palace.

***

Emily sat back in bed and glared at the heku in her room. Chevalier, Kyle, Quinn, and Allen were standing around the bed.

"No, I'm not going to sleep with an audience," Emily said, frowning.

Chevalier sat down and took her hand. "You've been awake for three days straight. You can't keep this up, and we're all here to make sure nothing happens."

Emily looked at Allen. "Then why bring Allen in?"

"The voice I told you about. We want to see if he catches an outside

influence."

"No, it's too dangerous for him."

Allen sighed, "Stop trying to protect me. I'll be fine. A voice can't hurt me."

"You don't know that."

"Well it's not going to work," Allen said, crossing his arms. "I'm staying."

"Fine by me," Emily snapped. "You can visit with me while I stay awake!"

Allen looked over at Chevalier, so did Emily, and her eyes narrowed.

"What did you do?" she asked as a wave of fog began to sweep over her.

"You can't stay awake," Chevalier said. "So I … well I spiked your coffee."

"You what!" she screamed. She looked at the heku and started to panic. "How could you?"

"Trust us," Quinn said, and then smiled when she started to sway slightly.

"Relax, we'll be here," Kyle said softly.

Emily frowned and then laid down, feeling light headed. "No. I can't take the pain right now."

"We're here, Mom," Allen said. Emily looked up at him and was surprised how much he acted like Chevalier. She smiled slightly as she drifted off to sleep.

"She's out," Chevalier said, and then pulled the covers off of her. "You have where to watch. See if we can actually see the injuries happen."

The heku positioned themselves around the bed and watched her sleep.

"Damn, she'd been pissed," Allen chuckled.

Chevalier smiled. "That's why we're not going to tell her how closely we watched."

As night drew on, the heku watched Emily sleep and kept a close eye out for the sign of any injuries.

"Dad," Allen whispered, shocked. Chevalier looked over and saw that Emily's wrist had begun to bleed around a darkening bruise.

"Here," Zohn said quietly, and bent down to study a new welt that had just appeared across her shoulder.

"Are you getting anything, Allen?" Chevalier asked.

"Nothing"

He thought for a moment and then reached down to touch her arm. He tensed when the sound of the voice screamed in his mind. "Get out!"

"Let go!" Quinn said quickly, not bothering to be quiet.

Chevalier let go and looked up at him, then down to Emily. "Oh my God."

"It got worse when you touched her," Zohn said as he dabbed at a bloody gash on her forehead.

"Wake her up before she dies," Allen said, starting to panic.

"We can't. We drugged her."

"Then don't touch her!"

"I won't," Chevalier said, ignoring Allen's ordering tone of voice.

"What is that?" Quinn asked, bending to look at her forearms. He frowned as he watched the muscles contract independently of each other.

"I'm not sure," Chevalier said, and then called for Dr. Edwards.

When the doctor came in, he went to Quinn and watched her arm. "What the hell...?"

"What is that?" Quinn asked him.

"I've never seen anything like that." Dr. Edwards reached down and touched her arm. "It's hot too, but her skin's not burning."

"Damnit... damnit...," Quinn hissed, and then picked up Emily's hand. As they watched, her nail beds depressed beneath her nails and began to bleed. "How the hell is this happening?"

"Ship Salazar out to Powan," Chevalier said. "I want to know if he's doing this somehow."

Quinn nodded and called out orders to Mark.

"I'm waking her up," Dr. Edwards said as he dug through his bag.

"We drugged her though."

"I can counteract that." The doctor filled a syringe and then exposed Emily's battered thigh long enough to inject her. He stood back, and within just a few minutes, she began to stir.

Allen called out for coffee and then covered her with the blankets. When she woke up enough to move, Emily groaned slightly and ran for the bathroom, slamming and locking the door behind her.

Allen frowned and looked at the bathroom door. "Wow, she's sick."

"Everyone out," Chevalier said. "She doesn't need listeners."

They all nodded and left the room as Chevalier went and knocked on the bathroom door. "Em, you okay?"

"Go away," she mumbled.

"I want to see your forehead," he told her, remembering the fresh gash that appeared while she slept.

"I'm begging you to go away."

When he heard her voice crack and realized that she was crying, he sighed, broke the lock, and walked in anyway. Emily was on her knees beside the toilet, and curled up into a ball with her arms wrapped around herself.

He knelt down and touched her back lightly. "We'll figure this out."

"I'm being punished," she whispered, and began to rock slowly.

"By who?"

"Salazar"

"He can't punish you," Chevalier said. "He's locked in the prison... well now he's on the way to Powan."

"He is punishing me."

"For what?"

She sniffled slightly. "He told me that if I ever got pregnant from anyone but him... he'd punish me. Now he is."

Chevalier grabbed a cool rag and laid it across her burning neck. "He can't punish you though."

"I don't know how he is... but he is."

"I've sent him away. If he was doing this somehow, it'll stop."

She shook her head. "No, it won't. He told me no matter where he was, he'd punish me. I wouldn't..."

"Wouldn't what?" he asked softly.

"I wouldn't give him one."

"I know."

"He was dead set that it had to be consensual."

Chevalier nodded.

She looked up at Chevalier with tear filled eyes. "I didn't want another baby."

"I'm sorry."

"He's going to punish me until I either have this baby or I die."

"How though? He's not been up here. We watched the assault happen right before our eyes last night, and you didn't so much as flinch in your sleep."

"I hurt everywhere," she whispered, and returned to her tight ball as she rocked.

"I'm going to take Kyle and Mark to the Valle and find out what's going on," Chevalier hissed.

When Emily didn't answer, he called for Silas to come into the room and then he left and went to the council chambers.

Zohn looked up when Chevalier entered. "Is she okay?"

"No, she's not. Kyle, Mark, you're with me," Chevalier said, and then turned and disappeared from the room. When all three were in the helicopter, they headed out for the Valle.

"Em?" Dr. Edwards asked from the door. She'd managed to crawl into bed and was curled up under the blanket, staring at the darkened window.

"Go away," she whispered.

"I can help with the nail pain."

Emily looked over at him. "How?"

He smiled. "Not even medicine. May I show you?"

Hesitating, she finally put one hand out to him. Her knuckles were bloodied and swollen, and there were dark bruises on her nail bed. Dr. Edwards sat down beside her and gently took her hand, then applied firm pressure to the nails on her exposed hand.

"Is that better?" he asked, watching her.

Emily nodded. "Yes, thank you."

"He'll figure this out."

"Maybe"

"I believe he will."

"How early can we take this baby?"

"How early?"

"Yes"

"Well… we try to get to 37 weeks. That's another ten weeks from now."

Emily turned and looked out the window.

Dr. Edwards softly patted her hand. "I have an idea. Are you okay here alone?"

"Go"

He left, leaving her door open so the six guards could see into the room. She glanced at them and then turned back to the window.

Emily wished Chevalier was there with her. Although she didn't know how the assaults were happening, she felt utterly alone. She wanted nothing more than to have the baby and get on with her life. She wanted to go horseback riding through the snow or try the new Rubicon Chevalier had bought her and tricked out.

"Why don't you go swimming?" Kralen said from the doorway. Emily looked over at him and then thought before nodding slightly.

He smiled. "We'll clear the out-building."

She got up and grabbed her swim suit before heading into the bathroom to change. After much complaining, she'd managed to get a decent maternity swim suit that covered her entire tummy.

As she turned to leave, she saw the black welts across her back and arms and then pulled on a robe to hide them. She glared at her growing middle and left. The guards were overly alert as they walked around her toward the out-building. The door guard met her with a heavy Parka and snow boots, which she slipped on without complaint.

"We'll just move quickly… unless I can carry you," Kralen told her.

"I'll move as fast as I can."

He nodded and then opened the door. The fierce winds blew fresh snow into the main foyer as they all trudged out to the building with the pool. Several minutes later, Emily was stepping down into the water

alone.

She had to admit, it felt really good to have the soothing water against her battered skin. She leaned back and began to float, then shut her eyes when she heard nothing more than the sound of her own heart beat and the gentle hum of the filters.

***

"Let him in," Quinn said when Derrick announced that Dr. Edwards needed to see the Council.

He came in with a heku that seemed angry to be there.

Zohn smiled. "Dr. Alona, it's good to see you again."

"Do I have a choice?" he asked, a little snappy.

"Watch it," Derrick hissed at him.

The doctor sighed. He'd sworn when Emily had Alexis with his help that he wouldn't attend another Winchester birth. The traumatic ending with the close death still made him nervous.

"We'll discuss your choice to be here when we know why you are here," Zohn told him.

"What's up?" Quinn asked Dr. Edwards.

"I suspect that Emily is going through a depression. We obviously can't take her to see an Obstetrician, so our only option was to bring in Dr. Alona."

"Why is that exactly? Why can't she see Dr. Hayden like she did with Dain?" he asked, glaring at Dr. Edwards.

Zohn nodded toward Dr. Edwards. "You're correct. We can't involve mortals in this."

Quinn smiled at Dr. Alona. "For now… you're here on orders."

He nodded. "Fine… I can give her anti-depressants and then return to my coven."

"It's more than that," Dr. Edwards said. "Even for the birth we can't take her to a hospital… not unless we get the current situation cleared up before then."

"Situation?"

"I'll take him," Richard said as he stood slowly.

Quinn looked up at him. "Do you still want information from her?"

"No, but I want her to keep trusting me, and I'm going to do that by trying to stay on her good side," he said, grinning slightly as he left with the Obstetrician.

Dr. Edwards watched them go and turned to the Council.

"Why do you suspect that Emily is depressed?" Zohn asked.

"Something she said, about wanting to take the baby as early as possible," Dr. Edwards explained. "I think it's compounded. She was

kidnapped and subject to tortures, and was just barely coming back to reality when this Council was banished, and she found herself pregnant and alone."

"Go ahead…," Quinn said when he hesitated.

"She was clear about not wanting another baby, and I know we switched her birth control to a stronger dose to try to stop it. Now with the assaults happening, I think she's overwhelmed and needs some help."

"I can see that."

"Emily has always been very protective of her offspring though," the Chief of Defense said. "I'm surprised she'd be willing to let a doctor take the baby early."

Dr. Edwards frowned slightly. "This one's different. It's making her feel more vulnerable, and now that she is being beaten uncontrollably, it's worse."

"He obviously doesn't want to be here," Zohn said to Quinn. "Yes, we can force him, but if Emily's fear of doctors gets to him, it could cause more stress."

"Let's wait and see how things go."

An hour later, Richard returned with Dr. Alona, who seemed more relaxed and less angry about being called back to Council City.

Richard smiled and sat down. "She was calmer than I expected."

"What are your recommendations?" Quinn asked Dr. Alona.

He stepped forward. "Other than stopping the abuse as soon as possible? I agree that she needs anti-depressants and a lot of TLC."

"TLC?" the Chief of Staff asked.

"Something foreign to our kind, normally. She's extremely fragile right now and on the verge of reverting back to what Lori calls her post-recovery stasis."

"So we have to be quiet, not make sudden movements, and try our hardest to make her life easier," Dr. Edwards said.

"So Lori has also been advised?" Quinn asked.

"Yes, she's out with Emily now."

"Emily's allowing that?"

Dr. Alona smiled. "Her psyche is reaching out for someone to understand."

"But Lori will be gone in two days on a honeymoon."

"Silas and Lori have both agreed to hold off for now," Dr. Edwards said. "We haven't told Emily that. We don't want her to think she's interrupting their lives or being a bother."

"When Elder Chevalier returns," Dr. Alona said. "I suggest we give him and Emily time alone, and that we do not allow her to feel abandoned for even one second."

"She's not abandoned," Zohn told him.

Dr. Edwards frowned. "Lori said she is feeling abandoned because the three heku she's closest to are away."

"They want answers from the Valle."

Dr. Alona smiled. "They need to stop being heku, for Emily's sake."

"Stop being heku?" Quinn asked, not sure he heard correctly.

"Yes… it's our way to confront problems face on. Show no fear, show no mercy… however, if one of them were here right now, Emily wouldn't be crying in the pool."

"She's crying out there?"

Richard nodded. "Yes, it was obvious when we walked in that she'd been crying for some time."

Zohn thought about it and lightly tapped his fingers on the desk.

Quinn finally nodded. "Very well. We'll talk to Chevalier when he returns about what's been said here."

"Should we call her in?" Zohn asked when the Council heard Emily return from the out-building.

Richard smiled. "No, let her be."

"But she's alone."

"We've called Alexis in for a visit."

***

"Come in," Emily said as she looked over from the bay window seat.

"Mom?" Alexis asked, walking into the dark room.

"By the window."

"Why are you sitting here in the dark?" Alexis asked when she walked over to the window seat. She bent down and picked up the Bulldog puppy on the way and then sat down beside her mom. She had been filled in on what was going on, and she knew that Emily didn't want to be alone.

"I don't know," Emily said, looking around the shadowed room.

"Well, Garrett's out on patrols tonight and I'm bored."

"Or did the Council call you in so I'm not alone?"

Alexis smiled. "That too."

"Damnit, I don't need my daughter to babysit me."

"I know that. It doesn't take the Council to elicit a visit. Let's turn on the lights and do something."

"No"

Alexis looked around and then began to play with the puppy as he nipped at her knuckle.

"Do you want this baby?" Emily asked her after a few minutes.

Alexis looked up. "Do what?"

"This baby, do you and Garrett want it?"

"I'm not going to take your baby, Mom."

"Why not? Or do you not want it?"

Alexis sighed, "You know I want a baby more than anything, but I can't just take yours."

"Sure you can."

"I know you're having a hard time right now. When things calm down, you're going to want the baby."

Emily shrugged and looked out the window.

"Besides, I don't think Garrett wants to be a dad."

"Why not?" she asked, looking over at her daughter.

"He just sounded weird about it when I suggested we adopt."

"Heku adopt babies?"

"No, it's against the rules... but I'm not a heku... well, not fully."

"I tell you, you can have this one."

Alexis smiled. "Let's do something fun."

"Like what? Count the lash marks on my back?"

"Stop feeling sorry for yourself. Let's go for ice cream."

Emily raised her eyebrows. "You hate ice cream."

Alexis stood up and put the puppy down on the floor. "I don't hate it... it's just not as good as blood."

"Ew," Emily said as Alexis pulled her to her feet.

Alexis gasped and then turned around with a mischievous smile. "I have an idea."

"What?" Emily asked, not really sure she wanted to know.

"Let's play a prank on the Cavalry. They aren't expecting it. It's perfect."

"Like what?"

"You tell me... you were the one with all the ideas."

Emily walked past Alexis. "Let's just go get something to eat."

Alexis shrugged and followed her to the kitchen, followed by six members of the Cavalry. Alexis sat down and watched Emily make a pot of coffee.

"I thought we were eating," Alexis said as Emily put in three times the scoops of coffee she normally did.

"I'm not really hungry."

"Are you on a sleeping strike?"

"Maybe"

Kralen frowned. "Em... you need food."

"I'll eat if you do."

Kralen glanced back at Silas and then smiled at Emily. "I go find a donor, and you'll eat."

"Nope," Emily said, sitting down. "You eat a grilled cheese

sandwich, and I will."

His eyes grew wide. "No."

"See"

"I will," Silas said, sitting down beside her.

"You cheat."

"I don't cheat... I'll eat it."

"I'm just not hungry," she said, sipping the tar-like coffee.

"You have to sleep, too," Alexis told her.

"I'm the mom!" Emily yelled.

"Fine"

"If you want to go babysit, go watch Dain."

"I can't... he's on the Island."

"Doing what?" Emily asked, frowning.

"I don't know. I'm not his keeper," Alexis snapped.

"He went to help Allen build a garage onto his house," Silas told her. "Nothing bad. I promise."

"Right, I'm not stupid. He's out there training with the bloody guard staff," Emily grumbled before taking another drink.

Everyone fell silent until she winced slightly and rubbed her tummy.

"You okay?" Kralen asked, moving a step closer.

"No, I'm tired of getting kicked in the ribs... baby must be full heku," she said, and then slammed her coffee cup down and started to make another pot of coffee.

Silas tried to hold the amusement from his voice. "I wouldn't hold the species responsible for the actions of a fetus."

She turned and glared at him until he had to turn away to stop from grinning.

"Lady Emily?" a timid voice said from beside the door.

Emily spun to look at him just as Silas and Kralen pinned the heku against the wall.

"You do not talk to her!" Silas hissed, grasping the heku's neck too tightly for him to speak.

Kralen tore a package out of the terrified heku's hand just before Silas threw him out of the kitchen. Two members of the Cavalry that were guarding Emily followed the heku out and slammed the door after them.

"Very nice," Emily sighed.

"He knows better," Silas said, sniffing the package. He then grinned slightly and handed it to her. "Think this is yours."

She took the box, looked at it briefly, and then started for the stairs. "I'm done here."

"What's in the box?" Alexis asked as they all followed her out.

Emily looked up when she heard the helicopter arrive. "It's for

Chev… is that him?"

Silas nodded. "Yes, that's him."

"Good, let's go give this to him," she said as she started slowly up the stairs. She kept rubbing her tummy as they walked up and heard the three heku coming in from outside.

Mark, Chevalier, and Kyle met them on the sixth floor.

Chevalier smiled. "A welcoming committee."

"Yes, with gifts," Emily said, handing him the box. "I bought this for you."

His smile widened. "You got me a gift?"

"Yup, enjoy," she snapped, and then turned and walked down to the bedroom.

Kralen chuckled. "She's grouchy today."

"Well the baby keeps kicking her," Alexis explained to Chevalier when Emily and her guards disappeared. "She also tried to give the baby to me."

Chevalier nodded and then opened the box and started to laugh. "My God, Em."

Kyle looked over at him. "What?"

Chevalier handed Kyle the plain brown box, and he looked in and chuckled. "Nice."

"What is it?" Alexis asked.

Kyle handed her the box, and she looked in and a deep blush rose to her cheeks. "Oh… well…"

Mark looked over when she blushed and peeked into the box also. He grinned, shook his head, and started down the stairs to get a report from Kralen.

"I want to go fill the Council in on what happened," Kyle said, heading down the stairs also.

Chevalier took the box from Alexis and went down to his room.

"Dr. Edwards and Dr. Alona need to speak to you," Silas told the Elder when he arrived.

"Dr. Alona is here?"

"Yes, Dr. Edwards brought him in."

Chevalier nodded and then went into the room and shut the door behind him. He looked over at Emily, who was sitting in the bay window. "Seriously, Em? Condoms?"

She turned to look out at the night. "Get used to them."

"Yes, well, I'm not sure if I'm more offended by the size you bought or the amount."

"Size issues, Chev? Isn't that beneath you?"

He fought back a grin. "These'll never fit."

She shrugged.

"Not to mention… there're only four of them."

"Sounds like enough to me."

Chevalier put the box down and sat beside her in the window. "Wanna talk about it?"

"No"

"Want to know what the Valle said?"

"No"

"What do you want, exactly?"

She looked over at him. "I want this baby out, now… and I want to give it away."

He thought for a moment before speaking. "I'm afraid if you do give the baby to Alexis, you're going to regret it."

"Doubt it."

Chevalier cocked his head to the side when he was asked to come to the council chambers.

"Go," Emily said without even looking over at him.

"We'll talk about your… gift… later."

"Whatever"

He smiled and walked out. When he sat down, Kyle was still laughing about the gift.

"I'm surprised you would return," Chevalier said to Dr. Alona when he saw him standing in the trial area.

Dr. Alona bowed slightly. "I don't believe I was given a choice."

Chevalier looked over at Kyle. "You're still laughing?"

"I'm sorry," he said, fighting back another round of laughter.

He smiled. "I know. It's kinda funny."

"The size…"

"She and I are going to discuss that later."

"What's so funny?" Richard asked, smiling at how hard Kyle was trying to control his laughter.

"Emily bought me a small… very small… gift," Chevalier said with a grin.

"Interesting," Dr. Alona said. "I can only imagine."

"So why are you here?" Chevalier asked.

"Dr. Edwards brought me in under suspicions that Emily is going through a depression."

"That's no surprise. Can you fix it?"

"Some… first though, we have to get her to agree to pills."

"She won't do it. Dr. Hayden gave me some once that were tasteless though, and we just slipped it into her food."

Dr. Alona nodded. "We can do that… if she'll eat."

"Damnit, is she not eating again?" Chevalier asked, looking over at Quinn.

He shook his head. "No, and she's drinking coffee to stay awake."

"I seriously hate that stuff."

"What is being done about the abuse?" Dr. Alona asked. "That's making the depression worse."

"I thought you filled them in," Chevalier said to Kyle.

Kyle grinned. "Sorry, I was going to when I could do it without laughing."

He chuckled. "Fine then... the Valle didn't seem to know what was going on, then accused the Equites of actually assaulting Emily to pin on them."

"They have to know! Who else is doing this?" Zohn asked.

"The Encala wouldn't do it. They are too afraid of us," the Chief of Defense said.

"Has to be Salazar, without their knowledge," Chevalier told them.

"Well he's in Powan now," Kyle said.

"Now we just need her to sleep so we can see if it happens again."

"And if it does?"

"Then I'll have to touch her, voice or no voice... blood or no blood... and see if I can see what's going on in her dreams."

"No more sleep medication though," Dr. Alona said. "Any chemical imbalance can only make the depression worse."

"She tried to give the baby to Alexis," Chevalier told Zohn.

He frowned. "I can't imagine her doing that."

"It's not her. It's the depression," Dr. Alona explained.

"What besides pills can we do?" Chevalier asked.

"We've discussed it with the Council and have decided that you may need to step aside on out of town business and stay in the palace. She's feeling very alone, and you're the best bet we have in keeping her from dropping further into depression."

He nodded. "I can do that. I just wanted to confront the Valle about this."

"We need to minimize stress and try to make her feel as safe as possible."

"Which is hard while she's repeatedly beaten."

"I've been thinking about that," Zohn said. "If moving Salazar out of the city doesn't help, I want to make a team."

"Doing what, exactly?"

"I've batted around the idea of a team... finally I came up with myself, Richard, Team 6 of the Cavalry, and Dain. We would start digging to see if we can find what's happening to her."

"Why Dain?" Kyle asked.

Zohn smiled. "To keep him out of trouble."

"Now what's he doing?" Chevalier asked, cringing.

"He's following around your Island guards. Allen called because he's not authorized but won't stop. He wanted permission to intervene."

"Damnit, what did you tell him?"

"I told him to hold off for now. We don't need the two sons of an Elder destroying his coven."

***

"Do not make a sound or this will get worse!" Salazar screamed at her.

Emily hung from shackles in his bedroom. Her wrists throbbed from the weight of her body on them, but her feet didn't reach the carpeted floors of the now burnt-out mansion.

"I told you that you would be punished," he said as he drew an X on her back with an orange-hot poker from the fire.

She groaned softly, fighting back the screams that threatened to erupt. Even when he put the poker into the fire, her back burned, and she was finding it hard to breathe. She wasn't pregnant, and her fevered skin was being slowly ground on as she hung against the rough rock wall.

"I said no noise!" he screamed again, and then grabbed a leather strap.

When the leather strap hit the burns across her back, she felt like she would pass out from the pain. She bit her lip to stop from screaming. It infuriated him further. With only four lashes, he stepped back to admire his work.

Emily hated this almost more than the beatings. This was his time to stand back and study the damage done to her and to berate her for getting pregnant by what he referred to as 'a heku willing to give his seed to any loathsome mortal that allowed it.'

She leaned her forehead against the rough rock and tried to catch her breath. Her back was so tender that even the movement of air as he walked past her caused the pain to intensify. She couldn't pass out. Doing so made Salazar mad, and she would pay for it dearly.

Emily jerked when Salazar yelled. "Get out!"

He followed his command by grabbing a knife and cutting a deep gash into her cheek, just under her swollen eye. She opened her mouth in a silent gasp, and he suddenly pressed his face against hers.

"Did you say something, baby girl?" he whispered.

Emily shook her head, reeling at the feel of him touching her.

"Emily," she heard Chevalier say. She was afraid to answer, afraid to make a noise but was surprised when Salazar didn't react.

Salazar wrapped his rough hand around her neck and slowly began

to squeeze until her airway was cut off. She tried to pull away from him, but the shackles kept her from moving more than an inch.

"Don't fight me," he whispered into her ear.

"Emily, wake up," *Chevalier said sternly.   His voice echoed through the room.*

Emily fought to breathe. Her lungs began to ache at the lack of air, and she began to feel dizzy.

"You defied me… and I warned you," Salazar whispered, tightening his grip. Emily was suddenly afraid he would tear her head off.

He forcibly turned her face toward him and kissed her hard as his hand continued to cut off her air. "I shouldn't have given you the choice. I won't make that mistake next time I have you in my care."

"Emily, wake up, now!" Mark yelled. She couldn't understand why Mark and Chevalier didn't stop Salazar before he killed her. She could feel the life draining from her body as her lungs screamed in agony.

Finally, her body relaxed as her oxygen deprived brain gave up the fight, and her thoughts turned to black.

"Damnit, breathe," Dr. Edwards growled before giving her another breath.

Chevalier watched, too stunned to speak. He had watched the burns appear on her back, followed by deep lashes across the burns. He then watched helplessly as a hand bruise formed around her neck, and she slowly quit breathing.

After Dr. Edwards gave her a sixth breath, Emily gasped in a breath of air and began to cough.

"Good girl," Dr. Edwards said as he helped her turn onto her side.

Mark was visibly shaken and stood beside Chevalier, watching her recover.

"You got nothing?" Mark whispered.

Chevalier shook his head. "Just the voice. I didn't see anything."

Dr. Edwards looked up at him. "Don't do that again. The abuse became worse."

"I know that!" he growled.

Emily finally managed to croak. "My back…"

"It's burned," Dr. Edwards said to her. "Dr. Alona has gone to get something to help."

"He's going to kill me," she said, and dropped her head to the floor.

"I want a watch on Salazar," Chevalier ordered. "Tell General Skinner, he's to have two sets of eyes on him at all times. I want to know if anything changes when Emily is asleep."

"I can't sleep again," she murmured from the floor. "I can't take it."

"Come, let me see your back better," Dr. Edwards said as he gently lifted her from the floor. He sat her down on the bed and pulled her shirt

up and tucked it onto her shoulders.

Chevalier hissed at the sight of the third-degree burns across her back in an X. The lash marks on top of it were minor compared to the harsh reality that she was again abused in front of heku who couldn't stop it.

Dr. Edwards took a salve from Dr. Alona and carefully began to apply it to the burns.

She gasped. "Stop!"

"Let me do this. It'll help."

"No," Emily said, trying to stand. Mark appeared in front of her and held her down as he pressed her face against his stomach. "Let me go."

"Not until he's done," Mark said, fighting back his anger.

She struggled against him and screamed when the pain became unbearable.

Chevalier turned toward the fireplace as his hands balled into fists. He wanted to go kill Salazar, but he'd agreed to stay with Emily until this ended. As an honorary member of the Council, it was against heku tradition to harm him, but Chevalier didn't care.

"Silas!" Chevalier hissed.

Silas appeared at his side. "Yes, Elder?"

"Kill him."

Silas nodded without even having to ask who. "Yes, Elder."

"We can't kill him," Dr. Alona said. "He's our only chance of ending this."

"I can end it, now," Silas told him.

"Unless it's not something he's doing… what if it's something he's done, and only he can end it?"

Silas looked over at Chevalier.

"Fine! Don't kill him… but find out what he's doing."

Silas disappeared and called for his team before leaving the city.

Emily screamed again when Dr. Edwards began applying another layer. She fought against Mark, but he held her firmly, and his jaw tightened as his shirt became wet with her tears.

When the doctor was done, he moved back away from Emily, and Mark let her go. Chevalier went and sat down beside her, and she curled against his chest, trembling from the pain.

"Please…," she whispered.

Chevalier kissed her lightly on the top of the head. "Anything."

"Kill me."

His heart ached. It was the second time she'd asked him that. "We'll figure this out."

"I can't take it," she said, shaking her head. "Just please…"

"Em, I won't kill you."

She looked up at him with pain filled eyes. "It's been three weeks. I can't take it."

Dr. Edwards spoke too low for her to hear. "Anti-depressants can only do so much. We need to consider putting her on suicide watch."

"Agreed," Dr. Alona said, watching her pleading for Chevalier to end the pain.

"Get masks on the staff," Mark whispered toward the door.

"Masks?" Dr. Alona asked.

"She's masking her pregnancy scent," Mark explained. "The best way to kill herself would be to stop doing that or to cut herself. It'd be strong enough to bring any heku to her without a second thought."

The heku in the room heard Zohn's order to distribute menthol lined masks immediately. Emily was breathing in short gasps to lessen the pain and held tightly to Chevalier's shirt.

Dr. Alona touched her hand lightly. "We can get rid of the pain at least."

"No!" she said, sitting up suddenly. "No, it'll put me to sleep. I can't sleep."

"Not if we give you enough."

"Won't that hurt the baby?" Chevalier asked.

"No, we can give her safe ones... enough she won't dream," Dr. Alona explained.

"No!" Emily said fervently. "This isn't happening in a dream. I'm not dreaming at night."

"You're dreaming... we can see it."

"I'm not either. I remember my dreams, and I'm not having them."

"Stop arguing with her," Chevalier hissed.

Dr. Alona stepped back and nodded. "Maybe a cool bath would help?"

Emily looked over at him. "That's... that's not a bad idea."

"I'll run it," Mark said before blurring into her bathroom.

Within a few minutes, Emily was relaxing into the cold water as Chevalier stood against the counter and watched her. She was sitting in as tight of a ball as she could and was rocking slightly with her forehead against her knees. Her back was a mass of blisters, bruises, and gashes.

"The only way I can think to stop this is if I can see into your dream," Chevalier told her. "However, when I try, you seem to get punished for it."

"Yes, I do," she whispered.

"It may be worth it though... if I can stop it."

"If... if not, then it just gets worse."

"We may not have a choice."

"Yes, we do," she said, looking over at him. "Take this baby and turn me."

"We can't turn you."

"You've never tried."

"We saw what happened when Exavior did though."

"I think it'd work if I had a choice," Emily told him. "So we'll go to a remote location, just me and 13 of you... then if I knock everyone out, it'll only be a handful."

Chevalier moved over and knelt down by the bathtub. "We can't turn you."

"Then end it," she said, watching his eyes.

"I'm not going to kill you either."

"Then go away." Emily returned her forehead to her knees.

"I've decided you can't be alone."

"You've decided?"

"Yes"

"Surprised it wasn't a Council decision."

He smiled. "I can make some decisions on my own."

"I doubt that."

"Go ahead, pick a fight. I'm not falling for it."

"Go away!"

"You're kind of sexy when you're mad," Chevalier said with a grin.

Emily quickly splashed him with as much cold water as she could. He stood up, wiped his face off with a towel, and then looked down at her. "See..."

"God, I hate you," she said, glaring at him.

"I know," he chuckled, and moved back to the counter.

"I'd rather have Dustin standing in here than you," she mumbled, and ran her hands under the cold water.

"I can have the rest of his ashes brought up if you'd like."

"Damnit, Chev. Go away or I'll ash you."

"No, you won't."

"Maybe four condoms were too many."

Chapter 11

"I hate that I don't know what's going on," Chevalier said as he paced back and forth along the foot of her bed. Emily had been asleep for eight hours, and no injuries were happening. She'd been assaulted every time she slept for the last six weeks.

"There has to be an injury here," Zohn said, inspecting her arms closer.

"Nothing I've seen," Dr. Edwards said as he watched out the window. "Maybe she has a break tonight."

"She's not had a night off in six weeks," Chevalier said. "I don't buy it for one second. Something's going on."

"Touch her and see," Kyle suggested. He'd been watching her closely for the entire eight hours and hadn't seen any injuries either.

Chevalier nodded and touched her hand slowly. He jerked back when he heard the loud voice scream and then he looked at Emily, but there was no change.

"Did you hear it?" Zohn asked.

"Yes, any injuries?"

"There are injuries we can't see," Dr. Edwards said. "There could be injuries happening internally."

Chevalier looked down at Emily as she slept. "How do we find out?"

Dr. Edwards walked over to Emily as he watched Chevalier. When he saw that he wasn't about to get attacked, he lifted her nightgown above her expanding middle, careful to replace enough sheet to cover her discreetly but expose her middle.

"I'd think there would be bruises or red marks... swelling...," he said, studying her closely.

"There's nothing," Chevalier said, replacing the blanket.

"Maybe she's sleeping," Zohn said again. "Truly sleeping."

Chevalier shook his head. "No, something's happening."

"I don't see...," Kyle started, but then gasped when everyone heard a harsh grinding sound.

"What was that?" Chevalier asked, wide eyed.

Dr. Edwards frowned. "I'm not sure exactly."

"Her hands are turning white," Zohn said, and looked up at Dr. Edwards.

"No... no...," Dr. Edwards chanted as he tore her nightgown at the neck and brought it down to her chest. "Damnit!"

"What?" Chevalier asked, moving closer.

"Her shoulders are dislocated."

"What?!" he growled. Turning suddenly, Chevalier threw a chair

through the bathroom door, shattering it to pieces.

"I'm going to try to put them in before she wakes up," Dr. Edwards said as he grabbed her upper arm. "It'll be too painful if she's awake."

"Do it," Zohn said when Chevalier didn't answer.

Kyle disappeared just after Dr. Edwards popped Emily's shoulders into place and relaxed her arms onto pillows. The doctor looked up when the door slammed open and then turned back to Emily.

"Her circulation is back in her hands," he said, covering her with a blanket.

"It's the pendulum?" Chevalier said to the wall.

Zohn sighed, "That's my guess. It looks a lot like what I've seen."

"The pendulum?" Dr. Edwards asked.

"We would... restrain someone's hands at their back and attach them to a pulley. If they didn't tell us what we wanted to know, we'd raise them slowly, lifting them by their arms," Zohn explained. "It's for interrogation though, not normally for sheer torture."

"Commonly used by Interrogators," Chevalier hissed.

"Maybe she's reliving something Salazar did while she was with him," Zohn said. "Can her mind do the damage?"

"It's been said that the mind can do things like that," Dr. Edwards said, "but her mind would have to think it's happening now. Memories shouldn't do this."

"Call Kralen, see if he saw anything," Zohn said toward the door. Within minutes, Mark came in and looked down at Emily as he spoke.

"Kralen said that Salazar hasn't moved or done anything in almost two days."

"I say kill him," Chevalier said. "Kill him now..."

Mark looked at Zohn. "Elder?"

"I'm thinking," Zohn said. "I'm still afraid he's the only one that can stop this."

"We've tortured him! He says he can't stop it, doesn't know what it is."

"He lied about not knowing what it is though," Zohn reminded him. "Richard said he knows what's happening but can't stop it."

"Oh, I can stop it," Chevalier hissed.

"He may be the only one... damnit, there he goes," Zohn sighed when Chevalier disappeared.

A couple of hours later, Emily's sudden screams pierced the quiet palace. Dr. Edwards immediately sat beside her as he dug through his bag.

Kyle burst through the door. "What happened?!"

"Her arms," the doctor said, giving her an injection of pain medications. "She just woke up."

As the medication slowly worked, Emily's screams turned into agonizing groans and finally fell down to soft sobs.

Kyle finally calmed enough to sit down and talk to her. He took her hand gently. "Em? Can you hear me?"

"Help me," she whispered hoarsely, and then looked up at him fearfully.

"Chevalier's gone to kill Salazar."

"No!" she gasped, and then tried to sit up, but the pain from her shoulders made her scream again.

Kyle gently pushed her back onto the bed and propped her arms up. "We haven't, until now, because you don't want us to. It's too late. We have to stop this, and this is the only way we know how."

"It'll get worse," she said as tears streamed down her face.

"It can't get worse if he's dead."

"Yes, it can," she whispered, and turned her head away from him. "It will get worse."

Kyle bent down and gently kissed her bruised hand and then looked up at her. "We'll stop this, and this is how we're going to start."

"What happened to my arms?"

Dr. Edwards sat down beside Emily. "We think he used an old Interrogator's torture called the pendulum. It often resulted in dislocated shoulders."

"What information did he want?" Emily's voice was barely above a whisper.

"We don't know."

"I want to be alone."

Dr. Edwards nodded and then left, but Kyle stayed beside her on the bed.

"He's gone," Kyle told her.

"You too."

"I can't leave you alone right now."

Emily finally looked over at him. "Do you care about me?"

"Of course I do. What kind of question is that?"

"Will you do anything for me?"

He gently wiped the hair away from her forehead. "Yes."

"Kill me."

He sighed, "I should rephrase that. Anything but that."

"I can't do this."

"You're stronger than you even know. Look what you've been through already and survived."

"Not this… I can't do this."

Kyle looked over when Emily's cell phone rang from across the room. "Do you want me to get that?"

She nodded and watched as he answered her phone.

"Kyle here."

He smiled. "Yes, I know whose phone this is."

After a short pause, he shrugged. "Okay, hold on."

Kyle turned to her. "Andrew wants to talk to you."

Emily tried to reach out for the phone, but the pain in her shoulders sent sharp stabs down into her chest, and she cried out softly.

"I'll hold it," Kyle said, and put the phone on speaker before sitting down. "Andrew, you're on speakerphone. Emily can't hold the phone."

"Why not?" he asked skeptically.

Emily sighed, "He broke my shoulders."

"Who did?!"

"Salazar"

"He's free?"

"No"

There was a pause. "I don't understand."

"I don't either, but he's going to kill me," she said, her voice cracking.

"Then kill him!"

"That's what I mean. Chevalier is killing him, and I'm going to pay for that."

"He can't kill you if he's dead," Andrew said.

Emily glared at the phone. "Yes, he can, and he will! I told them not to kill him."

"I know you're upset," Andrew told her. "I realize this is bringing back a lot of what happened… but killing him has to stop it. If he's the one hurting you, then he can't do it from the grave."

"Yes, he can!" she yelled. "Why won't you heku listen to me?!"

"Calm down, okay? I am listening. I just don't understand how you can think he's going to kill you when he's dead."

"How is he beating me from prison?" she asked. Kyle could tell she was on the verge of breaking down again.

"I don't know how you're certain it's him and not some Equites," Andrew growled.

"It's not us!" Kyle hissed.

"Yeah right, she's in your care. No one else is even around, yet she seems to keep getting injured."

"Stop it," Emily whispered, but both of the heku grew quiet. "Andrew, I need a favor."

"Em…," Kyle sighed.

"Name it," Andrew told her.

"I need you to come and get me."

"What?!" Kyle hissed.

"I'll be right there," Andrew said.

"Wait!"

"What?"

"She just wants you to kill her," Kyle said.

"Em?" Andrew asked.

She nodded but could only manage a soft whisper. "Please…"

"I'm not going to kill you."

"I can't do this. Why won't you all help me?"

"We are helping you, Em. No one wants you dead," Kyle said.

"Fine! You're both are about as loyal as the Valle," she snapped, and then started to cry softly.

Andrew sighed, "When you feel better and this is all over, you'll see our side."

"Hang up," Emily said, and then watched Kyle disconnect and put the phone back on the table.

Kyle sat down. "By now, Salazar is dead."

"Unless Chev decided to torture him first."

"I don't think he did. He was too mad."

Suddenly, Emily gasped and her eyes grew wide.

"What?" Kyle asked, wondering what she'd thought of now.

"Go away," she whispered as her body tensed.

"No, tell me what… what's that smell?" he asked, frowning. "Are you bleeding?"

"Go away!" she screamed.

"I said no! Tell me what's wrong!"

Emily sent a quick flash of burning to him, and he stood suddenly, grasping his shirt. Her eyes widened when his body tensed, and he growled as his hands tightened into fists.

"Silas!" Emily screamed when the rage crossed Kyle's face.

Silas appeared almost immediately. "What's… Chief Enforcer, no!"

Kyle lunged at Emily just as Silas dove for him, knocking him back into the table. It shattered as the two began to fight, and the room suddenly filled with Cavalry and members of the Council.

Richard was the first to turn to Emily. "What's that scent?"

She looked up at him and masked her emotions. "Get everyone out of here."

"It's part blood," he said, inhaling deeply.

Richard looked down at her with predatory eyes, and Emily tried to scramble out of bed but her arms were no longer under her control. Zohn and Quinn appeared in the fray with more of the Cavalry. They began quickly putting menthol lined masks on those fighting.

Silas and Kralen finally got control of Kyle and pulled him out of the room.

Richard gasped when he regained control. "Oh my God, Emily. I'm so sorry."

"Last warning... everyone get out!" she screamed.

Zohn ordered everyone to leave, and the room quickly cleared out of heku, except for Quinn and Zohn.

"You too," Emily said to them.

"No, what's that scent? I caught it briefly," Quinn asked.

"My God, get out!" Before he could respond, she squeezed her eyes shut tightly and took a slow, deep breath.

Zohn frowned and watched her. When she looked up at him, he sighed, "Are your shoulders hurting again?"

"I swear, get out or I'll ash you two."

"We promised Chevalier that you wouldn't be alone."

Quinn smiled. "We also don't think you'll ash us... just tell us what's going on. If your shoulders are hurting again we can call for the doctor."

"No!" Emily said frantically.

"I'm sorry," Kyle said, walking calmly into the room with his mask. "I didn't mean to."

"We know," Zohn said. "Did you catch that scent?"

Kyle nodded.

"Kyle, no!" Emily screamed. "Get out!"

"No, and I've already called Dr. Alona."

"I hate you," she hissed.

Kyle smiled. "I know. I've also called Chevalier back, and Alexis is on her way in."

"For what?" Zohn asked.

"Her water broke. That's why she's trying to get everyone out of here."

"Isn't it too early?" Zohn asked, frowning.

Kyle was still watching Emily. "I've suspected for a while that the doctors had the date wrong, and she knows it."

Emily huffed and watched the window as another pain started and shot through her back. She hated nothing more than being watched and had hoped to avoid a heku audience for this birth.

"What's the problem?" Dr. Alona asked as he and Dr. Edwards casually stepped into the room. With their menthol lined masks, neither could catch any scents in the room.

Kyle smiled as he watched Emily glare out the window. "Em's water broke."

"Hm, it's a bit early," Dr. Alona said. Another pain hit Emily, but she didn't react and just braced herself and watched out the window.

"The baby could be underdeveloped," Dr. Edwards told the Elders.

"We can't exactly take it to a hospital without explaining where the mother is."

"So, we stop the labor somehow?" Zohn asked.

Dr. Alona shook his head. "No, we can't. Once the amniotic sack ruptures, we have to take the baby."

"How far away is Chevalier?" Quinn asked Kyle.

"Only about 20 minutes."

"Mom?" Alexis asked, stepping into the room.

Emily didn't answer.

"Do you all need to be in here? This isn't a spectator sport," Alexis said. She tensed briefly when it dawned on her that she'd spoken to the Elders like that.

Quinn nodded. "She's right, let's go."

"You too," Zohn said to Kyle as he passed.

"What? Why? I've been there for all of them."

"If Chevalier decides you can be in here, then you may return," Quinn told him, and disappeared from the room.

"Oh, don't give a damn what Emily wants... if Chevalier wants it...," Emily grumbled.

Kyle sighed and followed Zohn out of the room.

Alexis sat down. "How bad is it?"

"It's not, yet," Emily told her, and then turned and glared at the two doctors. "Get out. Alexis can call when we need you."

"It's customary for the doctor to stay in during labor though," Dr. Alona told her.

"It's also customary for me to ash your asses if you don't get out!"

Dr. Edwards thought and then stepped out of the room.

"That's a start," Emily said. She started to say more, but another contraction hit.

Alexis looked over at him. "Do you absolutely have to be in here for this part?"

"Well... no... but if something goes wrong..."

"You're a heku. If something goes wrong, I'll call for you."

He sighed and then nodded. "Very well. I'll clear out the palace."

Alexis smiled and turned back to Emily when it was just the two of them in the room. "There, no more audience. Would it help to sit up?"

Emily sighed, "I can't move my arms."

"Why not?"

"Salazar dislocated my shoulders."

Alexis gasped. "When was that?"

"In my sleep. He's going to kill me."

"I thought Dad killed him."

"Doesn't matter," Emily said, and her last word turned into a slight

groan from pain.

"Can I get you anything?"

"Take the baby, Alex."

When another pain hit, Alexis got a cold wash cloth from the bathroom and laid it across Emily's forehead. "Things will work out."

Both looked over when the door flew open and Chevalier blurred into the room. He shut the door while watching Emily and then sat down on the bed opposite Alexis.

"Did you do it?" Emily asked him.

He nodded. "Yes. That should stop it."

"You've killed me then," she whispered.

"He can't hurt you now that he's dead."

***

"It's a girl!" Dr. Alona said with a smile. He handed the screaming baby over to Kyle, who wrapped her in a warm blanket.

Chevalier smiled and brushed the hair off of Emily's sweat covered forehead. "It's a girl, Em."

She turned her face away from him and shut her eyes.

After a few minutes, Chevalier looked over at Dr. Alona. "So?"

He smiled. "She's doing well. Not a lot of bleeding this time. Enough she'll be tired though. I'm happy with the eight-hour labor. That's better."

Chevalier took Emily's hand and kissed it softly. "How are you feeling?"

She didn't answer but kept looking away from the heku in the room.

Alexis took the baby from Kyle and smiled. "Mom, she's beautiful. She has red hair and green eyes, just like you."

Dr. Alona finally lowered the sheet and stood up. "Why don't you try to feed her."

"Get it a bottle," Emily said, and rolled onto her side away from them. Her arms screamed in that position, but she didn't want to face any of them and was just hoping they would leave.

Chevalier frowned. "You hate bottles."

When she didn't answer, Alexis took the baby out of the room and ordered supplies to feed her.

Dr. Alona, too softly for Emily to hear, explained to both Chevalier and Kyle about post-partum depression.

"Em?" Chevalier asked softly, and touched her arm.

"Go away."

"I know you don't want the baby now... but you will very soon, and I think if she's bottle trained you'll regret it."

"If you want it nursed so badly, you do it. Let it make your nipples bleed and wake you up in the middle of the night," Emily mumbled.

"Well at least she's being rational," Kyle whispered, and then smiled slightly.

Dr. Alona chuckled. "Let me give you a pain medication and then you can get some sleep."

She shocked everyone in the room by nodding. Still surprised, he gave her a shot hesitantly, fully expecting her to change her mind and turn him to ash in an instant. Eventually, her breathing slowed down, and she relaxed.

"I can't believe she agreed to that," Kyle whispered.

Dr. Edwards came in with the baby and a bottle in his hand. "She won't take it."

"Let me try," Kyle said, and took the baby from the doctor. He expertly rocked the newborn, but she began to scream when her lips hit the hard rubber nipple. "Well…"

Chevalier looked over at Emily. "She's knocked out… just… do it."

Dr. Alona gasped. "We can't do that."

"Why not?"

"I'll get her to feed," Kyle said, and left the room before the baby woke Emily up. The infant's screams soon filled the palace.

Zohn came into the bedroom. "Another screamer?"

"She's just hungry," Chevalier assured him.

"So feed her."

"We're trying! Emily doesn't… well… we have a bottle, but she won't take it."

Dr. Alona sat down beside sleeping Emily and listened to her heart and lungs. "Think she'd go for an I.V.?"

"No," Chevalier said bluntly. "Why?"

"She didn't lose a lot of blood, but she did lose enough that I don't like her color."

"Then do it while she's knocked out."

Dr. Edwards disappeared and returned with supplies. He watched Emily sleep while Dr. Alona put in an I.V. and started a fresh supply of blood.

"At least she's resting," Dr. Edwards said. He then smiled. "Getting rid of the attacker must have helped."

"I don't trust it," Chevalier said, watching her closely. He reached out and pulled the covers down to the foot of the bed. "I just want to know if she's being attacked again."

"Touch her," Zohn suggested.

Chevalier reached out slowly and wrapped his hand around her ankle.

"Get out!" the voice screamed at him.

Chevalier fought the instinct to jerk his hand away, and he looked quickly around the room. It was unfamiliar to him, but the gray banner above the door said enough.

"I said, get out!" Salazar screamed at him. He was holding a leather strap in his hand. Emily was hanging from high shackles, facing the wall as blood trailed down fresh marks on her back. He could tell from her breathing that she was in a great deal of pain.

Chevalier couldn't move in the dream. His entire body was frozen, and he watched in horror as Salazar brought Emily down from the shackles, looked at Chevalier, and then sent Emily flying with a strong backhand.

Chevalier opened his eyes when he felt Emily's ankle leave his grasp. He spun away from the empty bed, and the entire room was a blur. In an instant, Emily flew across the room and landed hard up against the rock wall. Her head smash against the stone, but as she fell, Kyle appeared and caught her before she could hit the floor.

He gently laid her down on the floor as the doctors blurred around her, checking for injuries. Chevalier watched, in shock, as a bruise formed on her cheek and quickly spread into her eye, swelling it shut. A small trickle of blood appeared from the corner of her mouth.

Once the doctors were sure that Emily didn't have a head or neck injury, Dr. Edwards picked her up carefully and gently laid her in bed. He then stepped back and looked over at the Elder. "What did you see?"

Chevalier found it hard to even speak, and when he did, his voice was malicious, "It is Salazar. He's beating her in her sleep."

"You killed him!" Kyle gasped.

"He's still doing it somehow."

"We have a problem," Dr. Alona said. The other heku looked over at him. They hadn't noticed he was examining Emily.

"What's wrong?" Chevalier asked, taking a step closer.

Dr. Alona looked up at Dr. Edwards. "She's bleeding internally."

"Get more B positive!" Dr. Edwards yelled before pushing on the I.V. bag to make it faster.

Zohn frowned slightly. "You said she wasn't bleeding badly."

"She wasn't until she was thrown up against a wall," Dr. Alona snapped. He shut his eyes and then looked over. "She's dropping fast. Her heart rate is too fast."

As Chevalier focused in on Emily, he heard her heart racing, and her breathing was fast. She'd broken out in a sweat and was losing her color.

While Dr. Edwards pushed against the bag of blood, he explained, "Labor and delivery is traumatic. That's why the long recovery. Everything inside of a woman is pushed up during pregnancy and then is

assaulted and slowly moved back into place after delivery. By slamming her into a wall, he further damaged already irritated organs and tissue."

"Her hands are mottled," Dr. Alona said, and then looked up at Dr. Edwards. "We need to get her to a hospital before she bleeds out."

"Can't you do that here?"

"No, I'm not a surgeon. I can do C-Sections, but I can't locate and then fix a major bleed."

"She's beaten," Dr. Edwards reminded him.

"I'll take the fall for that," Chevalier said. "Let's get her to a hospital."

"What's going on?" Alexis asked as she rushed in with the still screaming baby.

"Wait," Dr. Alona said. He leaned down and put his ear against her chest. "It's slowing some."

Dr. Edwards quickly hung up another bag. "Just as long as it doesn't keep slowing."

"Hand her over," Chevalier told Alexis. He took the infant and expertly began to rock her. She soon settled down against his shoulder.

"She wouldn't feed at all?" Dr. Edwards asked.

Alexis shook her head. "No. We... well don't tell Mom, but we even tried a little blood."

"She didn't drink that?" Chevalier asked her.

"Did you hear her start to scream?" Alexis asked, smiling.

"Yeah, let's keep that from Emily."

"What do we do about the abuse then?" Kyle asked, still watching Emily, afraid if he turned away she might quit breathing.

Chevalier was deep in thought as he gently bounced the baby.

"What I don't understand is how the marks are showing up on her body," Kyle said. "How does an assault in a dream throw her across the room?"

"The body is an amazing thing," Dr. Edwards said. "If her mind truly believes the assault is happening, it will react with injuries. It's entirely possible."

"So how do we stop the dreams?"

"That I don't know."

"Well she can't take this much abuse, or any at all, this close to delivery." Dr. Alona stood up and disappeared into the bathroom to wash his hands.

"If it's her mind doing the damage, maybe we need to call in Lori again."

Dr. Edwards nodded. "I'll do that. At least we'll run it by her and see."

Emily sighed softly, and everyone turned to watch her. The baby

seemed to sense it and immediately started to scream again.

"She needs to feed," Dr. Edwards said. "Infants have to feed soon after being born, to help maintain energy."

"First of all," Alexis said, crossing her arms. "She doesn't need to feed. She needs to eat... she's mortal as far as I can tell."

He rolled his eyes. "Semantics."

"Will she be in pain from the internal bleed?" Chevalier said as Emily began to move slowly. Her eyes opened briefly but then quickly shut again.

"Some, maybe. It'll be masked by pain left over from the delivery," Dr. Alona said.

"Can you give her pain medications that won't knock her out?"

He nodded and quickly administered another shot before Emily was awake enough to complain.

Chevalier sat down when Emily began to look around. "Em?"

She looked over at him, still only partially awake.

"The baby needs to eat."

Half in a daze, Emily tried to sit up and then cried out when the pain hit. Although muted by the medication, she still broke out in a sweat and moaned softly when she relaxed again.

"I'll help you," Chevalier said before ordering the room cleared out. He glanced at Alexis when she opted to stay and then he helped Emily feed the baby.

The shrill screaming that filled the palace died down as the baby settled down to nurse. Emily watched Chevalier oddly, her mind still foggy and confused.

He smiled. "She's beautiful, Em. She looks a lot like you."

Emily looked down and reached out to touch the baby's soft red hair but stopped just short of physical contact and then turned to watch out the window.

When the baby fell asleep, Chevalier gently laid her against his chest and began to rock her again. Emily stayed watching the window.

"I believe you," Chevalier said to her.

She looked over at him.

"That it's Salazar and that killing him didn't work."

She nodded slightly.

"I saw him in your dream."

"I don't dream anymore."

"You do, and in that dream, he's beating you. We'll figure this out. I promise."

Alexis smiled and sat down. "What do you want to name the baby?"

Emily shrugged. "I don't really care."

"You will, Mom. You need to consider that soon, you'll be happy

to have her."

"Just take it with you. I don't want to hear it scream. I don't want to hold it. I just want it gone."

"Enter," Chevalier said when a knock sounded.

Kyle came in smiling. "I brought lunch."

Emily looked up and then watched him lay the tray on the bedside table. He went over and gently took the baby's fist. "Wow, she looks a lot like you, Em."

After a few minutes of awkward silence, Alexis grabbed a sandwich from the tray and handed it to Emily. Her arm shook with pain as she took a few bites and then handed it back.

Alexis smiled at Chevalier and Kyle. "Might I suggest you step out."

"Why?" Chevalier asked, patting the baby's back gently.

"Please, Dad..."

"Fine, for just a few minutes. If she falls asleep, I want to know immediately," he said as he walked out after Kyle. Kyle glanced into the room and then shut the door.

"Now that you don't have an audience, I'll help you eat," Alexis said as she picked up the glass of orange juice. She was glad they thought to put a straw on the tray. Emily didn't respond but allowed Alexis to help her eat. She wouldn't admit it, but she was starving after the long labor.

"Thank you," Emily said when she was done eating.

Alexis smiled. "Now I think you need to name the baby."

"Chev can name it."

"You also need to stop referring to her as an it."

"Stop telling me what to do," Emily snapped.

"Contrary to how the heku treat you, you are a rational person," Alexis said. "You have to see that someday soon, you may actually want and love her. If you force a bottle on her, or call her it, or even let that unimaginative heku of a father name her, you'll regret it."

Emily couldn't help but smile. "He is unimaginative isn't he?"

Alexis rolled her eyes. "My God. The entire species severely lacks imagination."

"I don't want to name it... her... whatever. I just don't care."

"I realize that... however, Dad may name her something in Latin. Do you want a baby named Filia?"

"What's that?"

Alexis smiled. "It means daughter."

"Fine, name it that."

"I'm not going to name her. You are."

Emily looked up at her daughter with tear filled eyes. "I don't want

her."

"I know," Alexis said, and then turned and called for ice.

"You want a baby, Alex. You want one badly. Just take it."

"Her," Alexis reminded her. "I do want a baby, but I'm not going to raise my sister."

A servant delivered an ice bag, and Alexis held it to her mom's swollen cheek. She decided not to mention when tears began to stream down Emily's face. After almost an hour of silence, Emily cried herself to sleep, and Alexis called for her dad.

Chevalier came in with the baby asleep against his shoulder. "Did you make any progress?"

"Not really. You may have to name the baby."

"Did she even hint at a name?"

"Nope. I threatened to name her Filia."

Chevalier chuckled. "I'm game."

"No, we're not giving that poor child a Native word for a name!" Alexis said, trying not to laugh. "If you absolutely can't come up with a name, then just wait until Mom feels better."

"Let's just wait," he said, watching Emily closely. "Take the baby. I need to be ready for an assault."

Alexis gently took the baby and kissed her on the top of the head before settling her down against her shoulder. "If it's her mind doing this, can't you control her and stop it?"

"That's what we were talking about in the hallway. We're going to try it, but your mom may have to allow it. I don't know how strong she is right now."

"She may allow it to stop the assault."

"Maybe"

Alexis watched Emily sleeping peacefully.

"I hate this part," Chevalier whispered. "Waiting to see what injury appears next."

Alexis smiled. "It's so nice to add another Winchester. It gets old being one of the few."

"I would imagine."

"How are you two going to control this though?"

"Oh, your mom has ideas."

"I bet she does," Alexis said, laughing.

Chevalier looked over when the Bulldog puppy started to snore from in front of the fire. "I hate that dog."

"Why? He's cute."

"He snores. He drools. He's lazy..."

"And the Encala gave him to Mom."

"That too."

"Where's Sebastian?"

"Who knows," Chevalier said as he sat down by the fireplace. "Seems random members of the Cavalry take him out."

Alexis sat down beside him. "Have you considered going into Mom's dream and killing Salazar there?"

"I have, but the one time I fully saw into her dream, I couldn't move."

"Did she?"

"Move? No, I don't think so."

"I wonder if that's why she sleeps so soundly, she's paralyzed."

Chevalier frowned. "I hadn't thought of that."

Alexis watched Emily sleep for a while and then sighed, "Her hands..."

"I see," Chevalier hissed. Thick bruises were appearing along the top of Emily's fingers as she slept.

"The fake Council did that too."

"I know."

"Did you kill him or banish him?"

"Salazar? We killed him."

"So I vote that you go in and get rid of him."

"I told you, I can't move in her dream."

Alexis thought for a moment. "There has to be something."

"I know that!" Chevalier yelled. He winced when the baby on her shoulder jerked and then began to cry.

"Nice, Dad," Alexis sighed.

"Damnit, bring me a bottle."

Within just a few seconds, a servant came in with a bottle of warmed formula. Chevalier laid the baby across his arm and tried to get her to take it, but her screams grew louder.

Alexis smiled. "She doesn't just look like Mom..."

Chevalier looked over at Emily when her eyes opened. She looked at Chevalier and the screaming baby and then tried to get onto her side. Alexis stood up and helped her roll over and then returned to her seat.

When the baby refused to calm down, Chevalier carried her over and sat down. "Em?"

She looked up at them and sighed, "Again?"

"Yeah, sorry."

With reluctance, she finally positioned the baby on the bed and nursed her without having to roll onto her back. She shut her eyes and soon fell back to sleep.

***

"Let her in," Zohn told Derrick.

Derrick turned and opened the door so Lori and another heku could enter.

Both heku bowed once they got to the trial area in front of the Elders. Lori smiled when she saw that Chevalier had the week-old infant against his shoulder.

"Who are you?" Kyle asked the heku beside Lori. The entire palace was on edge from the nightly beatings and their inability to stop them.

"My name is Mitch, sir," he said, bowing toward Kyle.

"Okay, why are you here? We're busy."

"I suggested he come," Lori explained.

"Why is that?"

"I'm a trained hypnotist," he said.

This caught Chevalier's attention. "Why do we have a hypnotist in the faction?"

The new heku shifted nervously. "I was inducted because I have extensive knowledge of Civil Engineering."

"Okay, then why do we need a hypnotist in this palace?"

"Lori has told me about Lady Emily…"

"What?!" Kyle growled.

Lori held her hand up. "Mitch is a good friend, and I sought his counsel when I had some suspicions about what's happening to the Lady."

"Keep going…," Chevalier said, obviously not happy with Lori going to outsiders.

Mitch stepped forward. "Lori suspects that Salazar hypnotized Emily, and it took nothing more than a trigger word by him to start the assaults. Killing him won't stop what he's already planted, and her body thinks the assaults are real and is showing that through injury."

Chevalier's eyes narrowed. "You think she's hypnotized?"

"Not now, no. However, if it was planted while she was hypnotized, it would explain the sleeping assaults."

Chevalier looked over at Kyle. "Kill them."

"No! Listen to us!" Lori yelled when Kyle stood up.

"Let's hear them out," Zohn said, amused. Kyle sat down and turned back to the trial area.

Lori put up a calming hand. "What he says is widely believed in the psychiatric industry. Salazar had every opportunity to hypnotize her and plant things we haven't even seen yet."

Quinn sighed, "For one moment, let's pretend that you're right. How can we prove it and fix it?"

"We can prove it by letting me hypnotize her," Mitch explained.

"She'll never allow that."

"If she can be controlled, we can use that relaxation to force it."

"I still vote to kill them both," Chevalier said.

Lori smiled when the baby started to kick from his shoulder and soon began to scream in anger.

Chevalier began to rock her.

"Would you like me to take her to Emily and see if I can help?" Lori asked. Chevalier was surprised, twice in the last few minutes, he'd ordered her killed, yet she still had a genuine offer to help.

Kyle shrugged. "She needs to fee... erm... eat again."

Chevalier nodded. "Fine... if you can get Em to feed the baby, I'll re-think killing you both."

Lori reached up and took the baby, who only screamed and kicked harder with the change of hands. "I'll be back."

Mitch watched her leave and then turned nervously to the Council.

"How, exactly, do you know how to hypnotize someone?" the Chief of Defense asked.

"It started out as a party trick and turned useful."

"How?"

"It's a lot like controlling a mortal now, but it took more time and cooperation. Its uses to control smoking... or weight loss... are invaluable."

Kyle thought briefly. "You're certain that the sleeping assaults can be done through hypnosis?"

"Positive. When Salazar last saw the Lady, did he say anything out of the ordinary?"

"Not really. He just said 'hello child'," Zohn said.

"Actually," Kyle said. "He said salve infans."

"Same thing."

"Not when talking to Em... she doesn't speak Native."

Zohn nodded. "That's true."

"That could have been a trigger word," Mitch explained. "He had the idea planted, and all he needed was the trigger word."

"That would explain why he wanted to even come here after the torture Chevalier inflicted on him," the Chief of Staff said. "It was his revenge."

Lori carried the screaming baby up to the bedroom. She smiled at Silas, who was upset that Chevalier had ordered her killed.

"He's just upset," Lori told him. "He'll calm down."

Silas just growled softly as Lori knocked. The baby was turning red from screaming in Lori's unfamiliar arms.

"What?" Emily called out.

Lori walked in, and Emily sighed when she saw the baby. "She can't be hungry again."

"I tried to tell her that..., but she disagreed."

Emily's eyes narrowed. "Don't patronize me."

"I'm sorry… however, she is hungry," Lori said as she held the baby out. She focused in on Emily and how she unconsciously turned her body slightly away from the baby.

"You're a shrink… get her to drink from a bottle."

"She wants you."

Emily finally took the baby and laid her down to nurse, though Lori noticed no loving caresses or attention was given to the infant.

Lori pulled up a chair. "May I stay?"

"Sure"

"How are your arms?"

"They hurt, but not as bad as the fresh burns across my back."

Lori winced slightly. "The baby is beautiful."

Emily looked down at the infant. "I guess."

"She looks a lot like you. I was surprised that her eyes are green. Your other three have black eyes, do they not?"

"Allen has green eyes too."

"Would you like something to drink?"

Emily sighed, "Stop with the mindless chatter. Why are you here?"

"I brought a friend… a heku who thinks you might have been hypnotized."

"Hypnotized?"

"Yes… if Sa… if he hypnotized you, then he could have planted these assaults."

"That's stupid. I'm not hypnotized."

"Not right now, no."

Emily pulled her book out and started to read while the baby ate. When she was done, Lori took the baby and began to rock her gently.

"What?" Emily asked, looking up.

"Don't you want to burp her maybe?"

"No, you can do that."

"What's her name?"

"I don't know, ask Chev."

Lori nodded. "Okay, well if you need anything, let me know."

Emily nodded and ignored the psychiatrist when she left the room with the baby. The baby was sound asleep by the time Lori entered the council chambers.

"Did she eat?" Chevalier asked, taking the baby from her.

"Yes, without a lot of coercion… Emily's post-partum depression is severe."

"Yes, we know."

Chevalier gently patted the baby's back. "We've spoken to Mitch, and the idea is intriguing. We don't want to go against Emily's will

though, and she may not agree to be hypnotized."

"It may be the only way to stop the attacks," Mitch said. "If we wait for her to allow it, it could be too late."

"She thinks he's going to kill her," Zohn said to Chevalier.

"I know… he's already tried."

"Let's go with plan B then," Quinn said.

"Plan B?" Lori asked.

"Yes… have Chevalier go back into her dream and stay there. We want to see if he can break free of whatever's restraining him and see if he can destroy the Salazar image."

"What do you mean break free of restraints?"

Chevalier looked at her closely before speaking. "When I'm in her dream… I can't move."

Lori frowned. "That doesn't make sense. You're not actually in her dream but simply watching it. How can you not move?"

"I don't know… what do you mean I'm not actually in her dream?"

"I mean you may not be able to interact with, nor destroy, Salazar from inside the dream. You're an observer, nothing more. Dreams come from her mind, and unless you can influence her mind, you can't influence her dreams."

"Well damn," Chevalier sighed.

"However, I would still think you might pick up on subtle clues about not only the assaults but about her entire capture," Lori explained.

"It's not worth the risk for me to go in there just for information," Chevalier said. "Whenever I do, she's assaulted worse. When Salazar backhanded her across the room, he'd seen me, and it was obvious it was in retaliation for me being there."

"Hypnosis is our best bet then," Mitch said. "If I can get in there and erase the scenes, it would stop."

"Can't I do that by simply controlling her then?"

"No, being controlled by a heku is deeper than hypnosis. Two separate levels of psyche are involved."

The Council paused when Silas notified Chevalier that Emily was asleep.

Chevalier sighed and stood up. "I hate this. I wonder what abuse she'll endure."

"Let me see if I can help her," Mitch suggested.

"No, I'll go in one more time."

"Just remember you can't influence the dream. You move if her mind moves you… you talk if her mind tells you to," Lori said.

Chevalier handed the baby off to Kyle and then disappeared up the stairs.

"She just barely fell asleep," Silas said.

Chevalier motioned to Silas and Horace. "You two come with me."
They nodded and followed him into the room.

"I'm going to look into her dream again. If you see injuries, call for
Dr. Edwards. Position yourselves to catch her if she flies off the bed
again."

"Yes, Elder," both said as they stood around Emily's bed.

Chevalier watched her for a moment while she slept and then
reached out and grasped her wrist tightly. He was hoping he might be
able to hold her on the bed if Salazar tried to throw her against the wall
again.

"Get out!" Salazar screamed as he looked in Chevalier's direction.

Chevalier attempted to move or speak but couldn't.

*Salazar turned back to Emily. "You... I heard a small noise. You
will learn to be quiet when I tell you to."*

*Emily was panting as she stood up against the wall. She leaned her
forehead on the stone and readied herself for more pain. Her back was
exposed, and deep burns were visible on her back and neck.*

*"I told you to get out," Salazar said, glaring at Chevalier.
Chevalier tried to answer, but no sound came out.*

Suddenly, Salazar smiled. "Come, child..."

*Emily turned toward him, covering her chest with her arms. He
reached a hand out to her, but she pulled back.*

*"You will obey me!" Salazar screamed. He roughly grabbed her
arm and pulled her into an adjacent room. "I'm tired of these games...
and you will pay for your Elder ignoring my commands."*

*Emily started to struggle when Salazar pulled her toward a bathtub
filled with ice water. She started to scream, but Salazar let go of her arm
and punched her in the stomach, knocking the wind out of her.*

"This is for defying me," he said, and grabbed a handful of hair.

*As Chevalier watched, horrified, Salazar dunked Emily's head into
the ice water and then looked over at Chevalier. Emily's body struggled
to get to the surface, but the Valle held her down.*

*Salazar finally lifted her head, and she gasped for breath as she
clawed at his hands.*

*"I'm done," he whispered menacingly, and then pushed her head
beneath the water again.*

Chevalier opened his eyes and shook her. "Wake up, Em."

"What's going on?" Silas asked. He'd heard Emily's heart rate pick
up, but her breathing stopped.

"Emily!" Chevalier yelled.

"Get help in here!" Silas called out. He watched as Emily's lips
began to turn blue.

"Wake up!" Chevalier said as she shook her.

Dr. Edwards, Dr. Alona, and Lori all appeared in the room as Chevalier began to pull Emily off of the bed.

Dr. Edwards put a hand on his arm. "Be gentle…"

Silas immediately fell to his knees and began CPR on Emily when her heart stopped.

Lori gasped. "What's going on?"

Chevalier's voice sounded ominously through the room. "He's killing her."

Dr. Edwards dropped down and began helping Silas with CPR. Slowly, Emily's eyes opened and stared fixed on the ceiling, unmoving.

Lori watched breathlessly and took the baby from Kyle when he appeared. Kyle froze in the bedroom and watched the heku as they fought to get life back into Emily.

"Come on, damnit!" Silas growled before giving her another breath.

The heku watched helplessly as Dr. Edwards and Silas continued CPR, fighting to save her life, and suddenly, her heart began to beat slowly.

"She's back," Lori whispered, and knelt down beside him.

Silas looked up at her and then over to Dr. Edwards. He nodded. "Keep breathing for her. Let me intubate."

Within ten minutes, Dr. Edwards had Emily hooked up to a respirator that breathed slowly for her. The heku watched as she breathed in sync with the machine that was leftover from Emily's three month long coma.

"She's sedated," Dr. Edwards said to Chevalier. "We'll keep her sedated until I know she'll breathe on her own."

Chevalier nodded and then ordered everyone to leave. He turned when Zohn and Quinn reappeared.

Zohn calmed down and then pulled a chair toward the bed. "We want to talk about what to do when she wakes."

Chevalier sat on the bed beside her. "I wonder if the assaults will stop now that he's almost killed her once."

"They may."

"Or they may not," Quinn said. "We suggest letting Mitch have a try."

"I can't believe Lori spoke to him about my wife," Chevalier growled. "As a member of the Council, she had no right to break that privacy."

"We'll talk to her about that later. Right now, we need to decide how to handle it if the assaults continue."

Chevalier thought for a moment as he watched Emily. "If the assaults continue, then I'll control her and see if I can erase it."

"She'll allow that?"

"I suspect that after this... she may."

"Then what?"

"Then if that doesn't work, we'll allow Mitch to hypnotize her, but I will be there."

Zohn sighed, "I wonder how long she'll have to pay for what that sadistic sonofabitch did."

Quinn smiled slightly. "Lori said that the baby won't calm down."

Chevalier called out for Lori and then took the baby when she came in. The infant instantly calmed in her dad's arms, and he gently rocked her against his shoulder.

Zohn smiled and bent down to look at her. "Amazingly like Emily."

Chevalier nodded and watched Emily's motionless body as he silently willed it to take a breath.

"I know she's healing. It's just disturbing," Quinn said as he looked out the window.

"I know. Now how to feed you...," Chevalier said when the baby started to kick. He lifted her, so he was looking into her innocent green eyes. She saw him, and her bottom lip started to quiver, moments before her cries filled the palace.

"Now what?" Zohn asked, standing up.

Chevalier ordered a bottle and then tried in vain to get her to eat. "This is going to be a long process if she won't eat."

"Let me try," Quinn said, and held his hands out. Chevalier shrugged and handed her over. Quinn tried to get her to take the bottle, but she seemed even more upset to be out of Chevalier's arms.

"Try Alexis?" Zohn suggested.

"She's tried."

***

"Em?" Chevalier whispered as he sat on the bed beside her. The Elders had sat vigil over her bed for three days as the respirator breathed for her. Dr. Edwards finally consented to remove the breathing tube, and she immediately began breathing without it.

Emily moved slightly, but her eyes remained shut and her breathing was uneven and strained.

"Get the doctor in here," Chevalier said.

Zohn called for him and Dr. Edwards came in. "Did she wake up?"

Chevalier nodded.

Dr. Edwards listened to her heart and lungs and then sat back. "She has pneumonia."

"Great," Chevalier sighed.

"At least she's breathing."

"So now what?" Quinn asked.

"Antibiotics," he replied, and dug in his bag. He quickly gave her an anti-biotic injection before she fully woke up. He smiled when she groaned as the needle punctured her skin.

"Bring the baby," Chevalier whispered. Because of her incessant screaming and refusal to eat from a bottle, she was kept away from Emily's bed.

Lori came in a few minutes later with the baby, who was beat red from screaming and covered in sweat. She angrily kicked as Lori handed her over.

"Out," Chevalier said.

The other heku stepped out of the room and met up with Alexis.

"Did she wake up?" Alexis asked, worried.

Zohn nodded. "She's sort of awake. She has pneumonia, but she's breathing."

Suddenly, an eerie silence filled the palace, and Alexis smiled. "Finally."

"She has to be starving."

Within just a couple of hours, Emily's guards reported to the Council that she was talking with Chevalier now and was awake enough to make sense.

Chevalier sat down with the baby. "It's all we can come up with right now."

Emily's voice was dry and cracked. "I don't want to be hypnotized."

"I know, but he's dead… how else can we stop this? He tried to kill you."

She nodded and watched the baby.

"Do you want to hold her?"

"No"

"Do you want to name her at least? We can't keep calling her 'the baby'."

"You name her. I don't really care."

"How can you not care?"

"Let Alexis and Garrett have her. They can name her."

Chevalier sighed and gently rocked the infant. "I still feel like you'll change your mind in time."

Emily's coughing stopped the argument that was about to start, and when she stopped coughing, she laid down in bed and shut her eyes.

Chevalier watched her sleep but called for Alexis to take the baby when dark purple welts began to appear on Emily's arms and legs.

Watching more bruises form, Chevalier called for Kyle.

"What now?" Kyle asked, examining the bruises.

"We have to let Mitch try."

"She agreed to that?"

"No, but do we have a choice?"

"Not really," Kyle whispered. He turned when Lori and Mitch came in, followed by Mark, Zohn, and Quinn.

Chevalier looked at Mitch. "You can try it without her permission, but if we tell you to stop... you end it. If the assaults get worse, we'll have to think of another way."

Mitch nodded and tensed when a gash appeared on Emily's cheek and began to bleed.

"Damnit," Kyle hissed, and pressed a clean cloth against the wound.

"Do it now, before he kills her," Chevalier ordered. He asked that all stay and watch for signs of duress.

Mitch sat down, glanced nervously at the Elder, and then called Emily.

Emily sighed softly in her sleep, but the second she opened her eyes, Mitch locked her gaze. Listening closely to everything he said, the heku in the room watched Mitch take her from heku control, over to hypnosis.

"Emily, can you hear me?" Mitch asked.

"Yes," she said, almost dreamily.

"You are hypnotized," Mitch whispered. "This state you are in now, have you been there before?"

"Yes"

"When was that?"

Her body tensed, and her breath caught.

"No one here will hurt you. Do you believe that?"

"Yes," she said, but her voice was somewhat strained.

"Now take a deep breath."

She complied slowly.

"Tell me when you have been in this state before."

"He did it," she said, almost silently.

"Salazar did?"

"Yes"

"When did he do that?"

"I don't know."

"How often?"

It was obvious that she was starting to panic as her heart rate rose quickly.

"Emily, calm down, okay? Salazar can't hurt you now," Mitch said calmly. He softly placed a hand on hers, and she settled some. "How often?"

"Buried," she whispered.

He frowned slightly and kept focused on Emily while Chevalier

explained the burials.

Mitch finally nodded. "Did Salazar hypnotize you while you were buried?"

"After…"

"When he hypnotized you, what did he say?"

She frowned. "He wanted a baby."

"Right… so in the hypnosis he tried to get you to agree?"

"Yes"

"But you didn't."

She slowly inhaled. "I'll be punished."

"Salazar is dead. He can't punish you."

"He will."

"When will he do it?"

"If I ever give another heku a baby."

"So if you ever get pregnant, he'll punish you?"

"Yes"

"He'll start the punishment by saying what?"

"I don't know what it means."

Mitch smiled. "I know, but what were the words."

"Salve infans," Emily whispered.

"What were the words that would make him stop?"

"Words?"

"Yes, what words will he say to stop the punishments?"

"I don't know."

"He didn't give any?"

"No"

Mitch looked at Chevalier and frowned, then turned back to Emily.

The heku were surprised that the hypnosis lasted through the night and most of the next morning. Emily laid out detailed and orderly plans explaining the punishments down to the minute detail. Each punishment was then erased by Mitch's soft voice and continual reassurance.

Any time it became too tense, Mitch walked Emily through relaxing imagery with scenes of her out on her horse or walking among herds of cattle that grazed in lush fields. When she felt comfortable again, he would continue undoing what Salazar had planted.

Toward noon, when Mitch couldn't find any more hidden punishments planted by hypnosis, he asked one final question for Chevalier. "Emily, you're still doing really well. Can we ask one more question?"

"Yes," she said. She was lying perfectly still and relaxed as the heku watched.

"Salazar had a punishment that involved your forearms."

He paused when her breath caught.

"Do you know which one I mean?"

"Yes," she whispered, and a tear streamed down her face.

"Can you tell me what the punishment entails?"

She inhaled sharply as her back arched, and she groaned loudly.

"End this!" Chevalier growled when he realized that in her hypnotic state, she was reliving the torture.

"Emily, we're going to come out now," Mitch whispered. He ignored the way the muscles in her forearms began to bubble and bulge as she broke out in a sweat.

"Now!" Dr. Edwards yelled.

"He has to bring her out slowly," Lori explained. "Too fast and what he did may not hold."

"You won't remember what we've gone over," Mitch said, almost chanting. "The punishments by Salazar will stop. You will fall asleep when we're done and rest peacefully."

Emily screamed when her forearms began to turn red.

"End this or I'll stop it myself," Chevalier hissed.

"On the count of three you'll wake up," Mitch said louder, so she could hear above the painful cries.

When Mitch reached one, Emily relaxed on the bed, opened her eyes, and then rolled over and was almost immediately asleep.

Mitch stood up and looked at the Elder. "Now we wait."

Dr. Edwards knelt by the bed and looked over Emily's forearms. "Damnit, what does this?"

Chevalier bent over to look. "I still want to know. It's bad enough that even Sotomar won't tell us."

"Then I suggest we find Equites that have been held by the Valle and ask them," Quinn suggested.

Zohn nodded. "I'll go ask the Valle prisoners. Someone has to know."

Mitch frowned. "I've never had anyone under hypnosis react like that."

"Let her sleep," Dr. Edwards said. "We'll talk to her when she wakes up."

"I'm staying. I want her guards in here and silent," Chevalier ordered. "If there's any sign of injury, I want to know."

"Elder?" Lori said from the doorway. When he turned, she sighed, "Alexis can't get the baby calmed down."

Chevalier nodded and blurred down to the makeshift nursery on the second floor. Alexis was frantically rocking the screaming baby.

Chevalier took the infant from his daughter, and she nuzzled against his neck and almost immediately calmed down.

Alexis smiled. "Ahh, a Daddy's girl."

"Yes, well… Daddy can't feed her."

"She'll come around."

"I hope so."

Chevalier stayed with the baby until Emily woke up almost 12 hours later. Silas called the Elder when she was just starting to stir. Chevalier handed the baby over to Alexis, and she started to turn red as he walked out of the room. Before he got to the fifth floor, her screams rang through the palace.

"Anything?" Chevalier asked from the doorway.

"No, Elder," Silas reported. "We don't see any sign of injuries."

"Out then."

When Chevalier was alone with Emily, he ordered breakfast and then sat down. "Em?"

She yawned into her hand and then rolled onto her back and looked at him.

"How are you feeling?"

"Okay," she said, and then sat up with help. Her shoulders felt better every day but weren't yet strong enough to lift herself.

Chevalier took her wrists and pulled out her arms, so he could see the damage to her forearms. She tried to pull them away from him but couldn't manage.

"Let go," she whispered.

He sighed and did as she asked. "I wish you'd tell me what that is from."

Emily shifted. "Where's the baby?"

"Screaming down with Alexis."

"Bring her up here."

He smiled. "You want to hold her?"

"No, but if she doesn't eat, I might just explode."

"Oh, right," he said, and called for the infant. He was hoping Emily would finally attach to her, but obviously, it hadn't happened yet.

Chevalier watched the way Emily fed the baby without showing any attachment or interest. As the baby didn't seem to care and ate hungrily, he hoped there was no lasting rift between them.

Chapter 12

"No sign of it still?" Zohn asked.

Kyle shook his head. "No, since Mitch hypnotized her, she's slept through the night with no injuries. As it's been two weeks, I suspect it's over."

Quinn smiled. "Wonderful news. I just kept waiting for it to start again."

"She still won't say what that torture is though," Kyle said. "It's driving the Elder crazy."

"I'm curious too," Richard, the Chief Interrogator said. "Maybe if we knew, we might adopt it also."

"Chevalier tried explaining that to her… she stuck with her thoughts that no one, no matter how bad, should have that done to them."

Richard smiled. "Which only makes me want it the more."

Zohn glanced at the door. "Is she really dead set on doing this? It's so soon, and her arms aren't even fully healed."

"Yes, she is," Kyle said. "Chevalier is up there right now trying to talk her out of it."

The Chief of Defense shrugged. "Maybe she needs it. She's always felt better out on horseback."

"Is she taking the baby?" Quinn asked.

Kyle sighed, "No…well… McIntock is taking her per the Elder's orders."

"How is he doing with his assignment?"

"Really well. He's the only member of the Cavalry that had children, so he knows what he's doing."

"Was Silas mad?"

"I think he was at first. He was the personal guard for Alexis and Dain…, but we explained we thought a Newlywed had more things to think about than a tiny charge," Kyle explained.

Zohn nodded. "There they are."

Chevalier came in through the trial area and shrugged after shutting the door. "They're just going out for a casual ride."

"With six guards at least?" Quinn asked.

"Mark's taking out three teams."

"I wonder if the Old Ones are still even after Emily."

Chevalier sat down at his chair and turned it toward the others. "Yes, they are."

Emily glanced at McIntock as he settled the baby against his shoulder and then the group slowly headed their horses out to the hills. It was still cold out, and the horse's breath shown in the crisp morning air.

"Are we training, sir?" Kralen asked as he rode up to meet them.

Mark glanced at him. "Nope, just a casual ride."

Kralen nodded and fell in beside Emily. "How are the arms?"

"Okay, I guess."

He looked forward, and they rode in silence for a few minutes before Emily sighed, "What?"

"I didn't say anything," Kralen told her.

"That's the problem… let me have it."

"Let you have what?"

"The same thing everyone else has been asking for the past few weeks."

He smiled. "I have no idea what you're even talking about."

"Sure you don't."

Mark looked over at McIntock when the baby started to fuss. Even though she was wrapped up in blankets, he suspected that she was still getting too cold.

McIntock pulled her closer and wrapped the blanket around her, then shrugged at Mark.

"Em?" Mark asked.

She looked over at him.

"We don't put out the body heat you do, and the baby's getting cold."

"Then take her back inside. I told Chev she shouldn't be out here."

"She likes it when you hold her."

"Drop it!" Emily snapped.

Mark ordered McIntock to return to the warmth of the palace and then kicked his horse when Emily took off across the field. Soon, they were all heading into the trees and had already lost Emily. The sound of hooves was all that rang through the dense forest as the Cavalry fought to be the first to catch up to Emily on the racing horse.

Mark frowned when he saw Emily pull her horse to a sudden stop, and it reared angrily, but she managed to hold on.

"What's wrong?" Kralen asked when he pulled up alongside her. Her eyes were fixed deep into the trees, and her breathing was fast.

When she didn't answer, Mark surveyed the trees. "Did you see something?"

Emily couldn't breathe as she slightly nodded.

"What?" Mark asked.

"Go," Kralen whispered to the Cavalry off to his left. They took off toward where Emily was looking.

"Em, breathe," Mark told her. He studied her closely and saw that her body was tense, and she was gripping the reins so hard her knuckles where white.

"Him," she managed to whisper.

Kralen watched the Cavalry disappear into the dark trees. "Who?"

Without another word, Emily pulled her horse and banked him in a hard right causing him to whinny angrily. As soon as she faced the palace, she kicked him hard, and he jerked forward and flew back toward the city.

Mark cursed and took off after her, knowing that his horse couldn't catch up to her. He could hear her saying something, but she was too far away to make out anything more than it was frantic and not very clear.

Kralen turned when he saw Mark take off after Emily and then led the rest of the Cavalry out into the trees. He stopped when he saw a lone figure talking to four of Emily's guards.

Kralen got off of his horse and walked forward to the heku. "What's going on?"

"Sir!" the heku said, panicked. "I need moss... I swear. That's all."

"What's your name?"

"Magnus, sir."

"I've seen you in the city," Kralen said, walking around him. "Did you see Lady Emily?"

"Yes, sir. She looked afraid, so I left. I don't want to scare her."

He nodded. "Damnit, you look a lot like Salazar."

"Sir?"

"Never mind, carry on."

The heku nodded and walked away, still not sure he wasn't going to be brought in to the Council for this encounter.

"Mount up," Kralen said. "Let's go."

Kralen kicked his horse to speed up when he saw Mark and Emily's horses at the palace gates, untethered.

"Where did they go?" Kralen asked the gate guards.

One of them pointed down the road. Kralen followed them after telling the Cavalry to get their horses back to the stables and notify the Elder. Only a quarter of a mile away, Kralen slid off his horse when he saw that Mark had Emily pinned to the snow-covered ground.

He walked up quietly when he realized Mark had Emily's gaze locked and was whispering gently to her.

Kralen looked over when Chevalier blurred up.

"What happened?"

"We were racing, and Emily came across a heku from the city that looks alarmingly like Salazar," Kralen explained.

Chevalier sighed and focused in on the comforting words Mark was whispering to Emily as he looked deep into her eyes.

"She took off and Mark went after her. That's all I know."

Chevalier nodded and waited for Mark to finish. Finally, Mark told Emily to sleep and gently picked her up off of the frozen ground. He

turned to face the others.

"She was in a blind panic," Mark explained. "I don't think she knew where she was going. She was just running away."

Chevalier nodded. "Get her inside. I still need to talk to her about going away for the weekend."

Mark nodded and started inside, followed by Kralen and Chevalier.

"Elder… are you sure I can't go with her?" Kralen asked.

Chevalier shook his head. "I don't want to send her to the island either. We need the ranking Cavalry here though."

"I know, but she doesn't know the Cavalry you're sending with her."

"As soon as she gets to the island, she'll be with friends… Allen and Dain are already there."

"Maybe we should send Alexis too."

"Can't, she has plans."

Kralen thought for a moment. "So the baby will go?"

"We have to send her away too. We don't know if she'll affect the turnings."

Mark was just laying Emily in bed when they walked in. A servant was stoking the fires, and a warm lunch was on the table.

"Out," Chevalier whispered. When the room was clear, he sat down and took Emily's hand. "Em? Wake up."

She stirred slightly and then tensed and sat up, looking around.

"It wasn't Salazar," he said, and pulled the blankets over her legs.

Emily looked over at him. "It… it looked like him."

"Yes, he does resemble Salazar. You have to trust us that he's dead."

She pulled her knees up against her chest and looked into the fire. "Didn't seem to stop him."

"I think we have that under control."

Emily nodded.

"We have an important ceremony this weekend where we turn a group of mortals."

She frowned. "How many?"

"This weekend is 12."

"Why so many?"

"It doesn't happen often, but we're turning a squadron of U.S. Marines. When they know each other and have worked together, we try to turn them at the same time."

"So I'm getting sent off to a hotel?" Emily asked, and looked over at him.

"Allen and Dain want you to come to the island."

She shrugged. "Fine."

"I don't want to send you away, but I don't see as though we have a choice."

"No problem. I'm used to getting kicked out."

He studied her. "Are you taking your pills?"

"No"

"Why?"

"I don't want to."

"We've explained that you're still depressed."

"Then back off!" she snapped, and then stood up to pack.

"I wish you'd see that I care about you, and I'm only trying to make you feel better."

"I wish you'd see that I'm fine."

"Will you take them for me?"

Emily turned toward him with tear filled eyes. "I don't like those."

"Please," he said softly, and then moved so he could hold her. She buried her face in his chest. "Just try them."

She nodded and took one of the anti-depressants. Within the hour, she was in Winchester 1 with the baby and four members of the Cavalry. The ride was in silence because she didn't know them, and the baby was asleep. She didn't want to wake her, or she'd be hungry again.

A sudden jerk made Emily cry out, and the engine in the helicopter began to whine.

She looked over just as a black helicopter appeared beside them.

"What's going on?" she asked, starting to panic. Memories of being in a helicopter wreck flashed back to her.

"They're trying to down us," one of the Cavalry growled. He unbuckled, grabbed the baby, and handed her to Emily. She cradled the baby and looked out as another black helicopter appeared at their other side.

"We're going down!" the pilot yelled back.

One heku opened the door, and Emily saw the tops of trees appearing. She screamed when one of the guards grabbed her and jumped out of the helicopter just as it hit the trees. They landed moments after a loud crash sounded, and an explosion rang through the dense forest.

They looked up when a plume of fire rose above the evergreens.

Emily finally took a breath and looked around the small, snow covered clearing.

"Are you okay?" the heku asked her. She nodded and then her eyes grew wide when she saw a circle of heku surrounding them.

The member of the Cavalry with her crouched toward one of them. "Stay back!"

"Or what?" one of the intruding heku asked. "You alone are going

to take on over 100 Old Ones?"

Emily gasped and held tighter to the baby. Three of the Old Ones came forward with the other three members of the Cavalry in their grasp.

After a very brief fight, the last of the Cavalry was restrained, and Emily found herself surrounded by a hundred angry looking heku.

"Get back," she whispered. As much as she wanted to sound angry, terror had taken over.

One of the heku smiled. "Or what? You'll turn all 100 of us to ash? Fall unconscious and then be destroyed? You, my dear, forced us to awaken more Old Ones just to deal with you."

"Which faction are you?"

"When something threatens the way of the heku... factions don't matter."

"What do you want, then?" she asked. The others had stopped walking toward her, and she was aware that there was no escape. She was angry enough that ashing them wouldn't be a problem, but she wondered if it took more energy to ash a mass of Old Ones. If so, she risked falling unconscious and freezing to death. A sudden feeling of protectiveness swept over Emily, and she clutched the baby tighter.

"You are an abomination. The second Chevalier found out you are the product of an Ancient and a mortal union, you should have been killed."

Emily frowned. "That's not my fault."

"It doesn't matter. You're the first known offspring of an Ancient, and you shouldn't be allowed to live."

She took a step back. "So you're here to kill me?"

"Yes, we are. We've watched you closely, to see if you were going to push the limits of what a mortal should know. By simply speaking the name of a ritual banned from anyone but the Old Ones, we decided you've overstepped and have to be destroyed."

"I'm not going to stand here and let you kill me."

He smiled and looked at the baby. "Your children will have to be killed also. They have too much Ancient blood to live."

"No!" Emily screamed. "You stay away from my kids."

"You have to see that you are bad for the heku as a whole," he said, smiling evilly. "We won't stand by and see our species destroyed all because one Ancient did what he was banned from doing."

"I won't use the stuff I know! I swear to it."

"It doesn't matter. It was pushing our limits when we discovered that you negatively affect the turning process... but when you spoke the name of a forbidden ritual and then attempted to perform another, it became clear that it's time for your existence to end."

"Chevalier won't stand for this."

"I'm sure he'll attempt to destroy us. However, he's one of the eldest Old Ones, and deep in his heart, he knows you should have been destroyed at birth and not allowed to walk the earth."

"We will make it painless, child," another Old One said. He stepped forward, and his hands were tensed into tight fists.

Emily shook her head and pulled out her cell phone. Even though Chevalier had the files erased, she had the foresight to make copies beforehand for emergencies.

"You're going to call for help?" he asked, laughing.

"No, I'm not," Emily whispered. She quickly pulled up the ritual the vault Ancient let her read and took a deep breath before speaking. "Please work…"

"What?" he asked, stepping back some.

Emily smiled suddenly and then shut her eyes and started to chant. "Ego voco sanguinem…"

"What are you doing?" one of them gasped.

"Ego ordo vos somnium dimittere," she said, and the ground again began to shake.

"Stop her!" the closest heku roared.

"Aboleo heku ex vestrum somnium."

Four Old Ones began to move toward her but were thrown back onto the ground of the forest, writhing in pain, along with the heku in the trees.

"Ego voco aboleo," she whispered, watching as they screamed in pain.

***

Zohn turned suddenly when Chevalier's chair fell back and smashed against the ground. His back was arched, and the veins in his neck stood out as he groaned.

"What's going on?" Kyle asked, kneeling beside the Elder.

"I don't know," Quinn whispered.

Chevalier's body was wracked with intense pain. Every muscle bulged, and he began to convulse.

***

"Find out!" Valle Elder Ryan screamed.

The Valle's Chief of Staff knelt down beside Sotomar as their mortal watched, horrified. The round ceremonial room had grown silent when Sotomar fell and began to writhe in pain in the middle of the turning ceremony.

"Do something!"

"I don't know what to do," the Chief of Staff whispered.

***

Emily felt exhausted when she spoke the last word. "Perago."

She looked around the clearing, and the silence sent chills up her spine. The Old Ones were unmoving, and blood drenched the snow beneath them. She wrapped her coat around the baby tighter and kissed her lightly on the head when she started to fuss about her confinement.

"Lady Emily?!" she heard one of the Cavalry yell. She jumped at the sudden sound that broke the eerie silence.

"Over here," she said, still watching the unmoving heku.

The four members of the Cavalry came into the clearing as she put her phone back into her coat.

"What happened?" one of them asked as he knelt down beside one of the Old Ones.

"They were going to kill us," she said, and a tear fell from her eyes.

"Did you... did you try to turn them to ash?"

"Yes"

"What happened then?"

Emily's voice gave away her terror, "I think I did something bad."

One of the heku moved forward quickly and began making a fire to keep Emily and the baby warm.

"Are you hurt?" one of them asked.

She shook her head and looked around at the Old Ones. "Are they dead?"

"I don't know."

Emily hadn't noticed, but the fourth guard was off to the side of the clearing on the phone. She looked over when he shut his phone and turned to her with wide eyes.

"What did the Council say?" the closest heku asked him.

He watched Emily closely. "Elder Chevalier... he's also unconscious."

"What?!" Emily yelled.

"Elder Zohn said that reports are coming in from Equites around the world... the Old Ones are all unconscious."

"Oh my God," Emily whispered. She was finding it hard to breathe.

"They are sending someone to get us," the heku said, but kept a safe distance from Emily.

Emily sat down beside the fire and pulled the baby out from under her coat. She squirmed slightly but fell asleep once the heat from the fire warmed her.

It was four hours later when Equites 2 landed only a mile away. Mark, leading 12 members of the Cavalry, appeared in the clearing and looked around at the unconscious heku.

"Are you okay?" Horace asked, kneeling down beside Emily.

She nodded but watched Mark.

"Four of you stay here," Mark said. "A transport helicopter is on the way, and we'll take them all back to Council City."

"Mark?" Emily whispered, and began to tear up again.

He looked over at her.

"I'm sorry."

He frowned slightly. "I'm not to discuss this with you. You are to go back to the Council immediately."

She nodded and turned back to the fire.

"Let's go," Horace said when Mark was done giving orders.

Emily looked over at him and then followed silently as they walked back to Equites 2. She was surprised that none of them attempted to pick her up, but they instead walked with her the mile to the Blackhawk.

When they arrived at the palace, guards formed a line into the palace, and Emily followed Mark silently. When McIntock tried to take the baby, Emily shook her head and put the infant against her shoulder as she slept.

Derrick opened the door. "They will see you now."

Emily walked into the council chambers, and her heart dropped when she saw Chevalier's empty chair.

"Is he okay?" she asked, barely above a whisper.

Zohn nodded, obviously furious. "Yes, unconscious, but he is alive. What happened?"

Emily let the heku pilot explain to the Council about how the Old Ones downed the helicopter and restrained the heku while they spoke to Emily. He then explained how the Old Ones restraining the Cavalry suddenly fell into pain and finally fell unconscious.

Zohn sighed and looked at Emily. "What did you do, exactly?"

"I'm sorry," she whispered as a tear fell from her eye.

"Just tell us, so we can fix it."

"Back before the Ancients were banished by the Old Ones," Emily explained, "the Ancients were also forming a plan to banish the Old Ones and start the heku over with more loyal followers."

"They were?" Quinn gasped.

Emily nodded and continued, "The Ancients had a ritual that would summon the Old Ones to Stonehenge and then ash them all with a single incantation."

"My God," Zohn whispered, too shocked to speak louder.

"I wrote down the words to those… in my phone…"

"Chevalier destroyed those."

"Chevalier doesn't know technology well enough to have completely done that," Emily said. "I was afraid that if I turned the Old Ones to ash out in the forest, that I'd fall unconscious and the baby and I would freeze to death. So…"

"So you pulled out that incantation and said it?!" the Chief of Defense screamed.

Emily jumped slightly and then nodded.

"What's the incantation?" the Chief of Staff asked. "If we know the words, we can maybe undo it."

"No!" Quinn shouted. "Those are for Ancients and Old Ones only. Just because those authorized to know that are unconscious or banished, we have no right to hear the words."

Zohn watched Emily angrily. "Only Ancients and Old Ones know what you spoke… maybe not even the Old Ones. You've now forced this faction to revive an Ancient in hopes they can reverse it!"

"I didn't mean to…"

"You are messing with something older than humankind… what did you expect to happen?!"

She fought back the tears. "They were going to kill the baby."

"I don't care! That's a small crime compared to killing every Old One in existence. We don't even know if you've affected the banished ones too."

"Calm down," Quinn said to Zohn. "She put them in this state. We may be able to figure out how to have her reverse it."

"Then get on with it," Zohn growled.

Quinn turned to Emily. She could tell he was furious but holding back as he spoke, "Go up to your room, and read the incantation backwards."

She nodded and then left with the baby. The heku throughout the palace wouldn't look at her, and some even stepped farther away as she passed. Once in her room, she laid the baby on the bed and then sat down with her phone.

Softy, she read the words backwards. When she finished, she sighed. The ground hadn't moved, and she suspected it didn't work when Derrick slammed open the door without knocking.

"Get back down to the Council," he snapped, and then stood aside.

Emily walked into the trial area. "I have an idea."

"No more of your ideas!" Zohn yelled.

She sighed, "I'll ask the vault Ancient how to fix this."

Quinn shook his head. "No, you've done enough. We've contacted all three factions and discovered that all of the Old Ones are unconscious. There were 12 Old Ones not at your gathering, and we've

found out that the ones that attacked you had revived others out of retirement just to come after you."

"Let me talk to him…"

"No!" Zohn yelled. "You are to follow this Council's instructions and do as you're told."

She nodded slightly and held tightly to the baby.

Quinn took a deep breath. "You're to stay in your room while we revive an Ancient and see if it can be reversed."

"Where's Chevalier?" she whispered.

"It's none of your concern," Zohn hissed. "Now do as you're told and get back to your room."

When Emily left, Zohn turned to Quinn. "I still say Thutmose is our best bet."

"Why not just bring up the vault Ancient?"

"Chevalier said he's no longer completely sane. It will have to be Thutmose."

Quinn nodded. "I concur. He'll be less likely to take off when revived."

Kyle tapped his fingers impatiently against the desk. "So bring him here."

Zohn ordered four of the palace guards to go to Thutmose's banishment sight and to feed him, then bring him immediately to the Council.

Quinn turned to Kyle. "Are you going to need restrained?"

Kyle frowned. "Why?"

"Because Emily will need punished for this…"

"She didn't know!"

"It doesn't matter," Zohn told him. "She stepped way out of bounds this time and risked the entire species because she meddles with things beyond her status."

Kyle sighed, "No, I don't need restrained."

The Council turned when four members of the palace guard came in restraining a furious Ancient.

The Ancient hissed, "What is the meaning of this?!"

Quinn studied him and then answered, "We need your help."

"You banish me to the ground for thousands of years, and now you ask my help?"

"Yes"

His snarl turned into an ominous grin. "What have our minions done to themselves that warrants breaking our banishment?"

Quinn glared at him. "We know that the Ancients were planning on banishing the Old Ones right before you, yourselves, were banished."

The Ancient answered with only a growl.

"The incantation you came up with to destroy the Old Ones was used."

The Ancient started to laugh. "That's great! So there is an Ancient free that spoke the words... it was long coming."

"No, it wasn't spoken by an Ancient," Zohn said.

He frowned. "Then it wouldn't have worked."

"It was spoken by a half-Ancient."

"Explain yourself."

Quinn took a deep breath. "There's a child among us... who is, to put it simply, 50% Ancient, 49% mortal, and 1% heku."

"He should have been destroyed then!" the Ancient yelled.

"She," Zohn said, "is a special case... and the Old Ones decided to let her live... until she showed signs of having some of the Ancient's abilities."

"Then kill her," he hissed.

"It's not that simple..."

"Yes, it is!" the Ancient screamed. "The Ancient who produced her should have immediately killed the infant."

"Yes, he probably should have, but he didn't and now she's in our care."

"Bring her here. I want to see her."

Quinn and Zohn spoke briefly before they turned back to the Ancient. Zohn sighed, "Bring Emily here."

Quinn looked at Thutmose. "She has a unique blood scent that will be hard for you to resist."

Thutmose scowled. "I'm an Ancient..."

"Who hasn't fed regularly for 2,000 years," Kyle said. "You will have a hard time, so watch yourself."

Derrick escorted Emily into the room. She wrapped her arms around herself and walked forward, not sure if she was in trouble.

"Emily...," Quinn said before sighing.

Thutmose turned feral eyes toward her and crouched slightly as a hiss escaped his lips. Seconds later, Mark and Kralen appeared in the trial area and restrained him. Emily watched with wide eyes as he fought to get to her.

"Control!" Quinn yelled. "Thutmose we warned you..."

After a few minutes, Thutmose closed his eyes and then stood up, still trembling from the intense thirst that ran through is body. "I'm okay."

Mark and Kralen let go of him and stepped back, staying close in case he decided to attack Emily.

Emily watched, tense, as the Ancient circled her.

"This is the half-Ancient?" he asked, studying Emily as he walked

around her.

"Yes," Quinn said.

"She's puny… weak…"

Emily frowned but stayed silent.

The heku in the room didn't catch when the Ancient blurred to Emily, took her wrist, and inhaled deeply. The first they saw him move was when he touched his nose to her wrist. She gasped and pulled her hand away from him when Mark and Kralen dragged him back to the center of the trial area.

"I see Arrianus is to blame," Thutmose said. He didn't struggle against the guards but watched Emily closely.

Quinn nodded. "Yes, he is her father."

Emily was shocked. She hadn't heard his name before.

"Figures, he never was a bright one," Thutmose said as he turned to the Council. "I still have no reason to help you. I've suffered for thousands of years below the ground because of you."

"The three Councils agree that if you help us, we will let you stay," Zohn told him.

"Intriguing," he said, and turned to look at Emily again. "You, mortal, why is your scent different?"

She looked over at Kyle, and he cleared his throat before speaking, "Emily is the only member of a family known as Dulcris Cruor. She not only has the scent, but she can turn a heku to ash."

"This tiny thing can?" Thutmose walked around Emily again.

"Yes"

"Another reason why she should be destroyed."

"She's bonded to an Elder, Chevalier," Quinn explained.

Thutmose frowned and turned to him. "Equitis bonded to this thing?"

"She's not a thing," Kyle snapped.

Thutmose smiled. "I see…"

"What's that mean?"

"It means you are all infatuated with her. She is beautiful but still scrawny."

Emily'd had enough. She put her hands on her hips and turned to him. "Let's just get this straight! I'm not puny, weak, tiny, or scrawny. I can turn you to ash before you can blink, so I suggest you stop with the insults!"

Thutmose frowned. "The mortal dares to address me?"

"I'll do more than address you," she said, and started for him. Kralen appeared at her back and stopped her with strong hands on her shoulders.

"She has no right to speak to me!"

"Calm down," Quinn told him. "She's a member of this Council and has every right to address you."

"A member of this Council?" Thutmose laughed. "Pathetic."

"Will you help us or not?!"

Thutmose glanced at Emily and then crossed his arms. "If the price is right."

"Name it."

He smiled. "You've already agreed to let me stay above ground."

"Yes"

"But I stay in the palace."

"Why? You're not a member of the Council."

"That's the deal."

Quinn's eyes narrowed, and Kralen hauled Emily out of the room when she tried to give her opinion on the matter.

"Calm down," Kralen said when he put Emily down in her room.

"I don't have to put up with that!" she screamed at him.

"I know, but he's our best chance to get the Old Ones back."

Emily sighed and sat down. Kralen watched her for a few minutes and then left and shut the door. After feeding the baby, Emily grabbed her laptop and sat down. She gathered what she needed and made the call.

"Cornwall Construction," the secretary answered.

"I need to speak to whoever is in charge."

"One moment."

After a few minutes of waiting, a gruff man answered. "Rayburn here."

"Rayburn, my name is Emily Winchester, and I have a proposition for you. What I need has to be kept confidential and has to be done exactly as I specify," Emily told him.

"Keep talking…"

"If you do as I ask, it will be very much worth your time."

"What, exactly, are we talking?"

"I own property here in the city, but the mansion burned down. I need blueprints drawn up to replace the building and then I need it built within the next three months."

"I see… let's meet to go over specifics."

"That's a tricky one. This has to be over the phone and through e-mail only."

"Why's that?"

"No questions, Rayburn," Emily said.

"Fine, but there's no way to get any large structure done in three months."

"No way at all? I'll pay well."

"It's just not possible, not without working my guys 24 hours a day, seven days a week without breaks."

Emily sighed, "Okay, thanks anyway."

She hung up and then thought for a moment before dialing again.

"Emily?" William asked.

"Yes, it's me."

"Are you okay? You don't sound well."

"It's been a rough week."

"I know… we have Old Ones who are unconscious also."

"Are you mad?"

"No, not mad," William said.

"I need a favor then."

"Name it."

"Do you have the ability to have a mansion built in three months?"

There was a pause before he spoke, "Yes."

"I'll pay."

"You want a mansion?"

"The Valle burned down Exavior's old house…, and I need to move out of Council City."

"You can live here," William said, sounding expectant.

"No, I just want my own house."

"So you need one built in three months?"

"Yes, I can put up with house arrest for that long."

"You're under house arrest?!"

Emily sighed, "Yes. I just need that house."

"We'll do it… what exactly are you looking for?"

She then outlined specifics for the new mansion that included a heku-proof panic room, several hidden passages and corridors, and a host of other amenities that she might need in an eternity of living.

Emily hung up with the Encala and smiled at the baby. "It's time we give you a name."

The baby immediately stuck her fingers into her mouth like Alexis used to.

"I've been thinking about something your dad said when he named Dain. What do you think about Megara?"

The infant simply watched her mom.

Emily smiled. "That's it then, Megara. We'll have a birth certificate drawn up when your dad gets back."

She picked up the baby and rocked her gently before turning to the door when she heard a knock. "Come in."

Derrick stepped in. "The Council needs to see you."

"Tell them no."

"I can't tell them no."

"Why not?"

"No one tells the Council no," Derrick reminded her. "You're in enough trouble without making it worse."

"I don't want to see them."

"Do what they ask. It'll be easier."

Emily sighed and then repositioned the baby and followed Derrick down to the council chambers. She stepped in and walked around Thutmose before standing in front of Quinn.

"Thutmose will need your help in reviving the Old Ones," he explained.

"What kind of help?"

"He needs to know what was said but without any heku hearing it."

Emily nodded and pulled out her phone. She opened it to the incantation and then hesitated before handing it over to the Ancient. His eyes bore into the sleeping baby and made Emily uncomfortable.

"Does the infant belong to Equitis?" Thutmose asked her.

"Yes"

"Willingly?"

Emily frowned. "What kind of question is that?"

The Ancient shrugged. "Surprising is all."

Thutmose read the phone and then looked over the device closely before handing it back to Emily.

"You shouldn't have said this. No wonder it didn't entirely work, this is Ancient only."

"I know that now."

"Have you been punished?"

Her eyes narrowed. "Try it, Gramps."

Thutmose leaned his head back and laughed before turning angry eyes toward her. "You need to learn your place."

"She will be punished," Zohn told him. "Seth will show you to your quarters."

A heku appeared and opened the door for Thutmose. He glanced again at Emily and then strode haughtily out of the room.

"Come forward," the Chief of Defense said to Emily. She held the baby tightly and stepped forward.

"You've gone dangerously overboard this time," Quinn said to her softly. "As much as this Council owes you, even for our very lives, we can't let this go."

Emily nodded.

"We tried to come up with something that would teach you about staying out of things you know nothing about," the Chief of Finance said.

Kyle sighed and avoided looking at Emily. She was sure he wouldn't have put up with this if he had a choice, but she didn't want to

risk his life by calling him on it.

"Get on with it then," she said, clutching the baby tightly.

"We feel that house arrest would be the best thing here," Zohn told her. "We can't express enough how displeased we are with what you have done."

"And you have no idea how displeased I am that nothing I can do is good enough for this Council," Emily whispered. She caught the direct eye of each member of the Council before sighing. "I've always been assured that even with Chevalier out of the picture, I'd be taken care of and would unfailingly be an Equites…"

"We're not removing you from the faction," Quinn said. "We also aren't saying that we don't appreciate what you…"

"Stop, that's enough," Emily told then. "I'm not your property to toss into jail when you see fit. I'm not a child who can be chastised, and I'm tired of it."

"Meaning?"

"Meaning, I'm gone," she said, and started for the door.

"Emily," Quinn sighed.

She didn't turn around. "When Chevalier wakes up, call me."

"We can't let you leave the palace," the Chief of Defense said.

Emily turned and fought back the tears. "I trusted you."

"We're still your friends," Quinn said.

"No, you aren't."

"This isn't permanent. Just stay in your room until we figure out what to do."

"The Ancient has moved into the palace?"

"Yes, but that doesn't…"

"Yes, it does matter," Emily said, and walked out.

Zohn sighed, "Now what?"

"Mark, keep her from leaving," Quinn called out.

Kyle turned to them. "How did you not see this coming? How much does she have to go through for us? I mean… she's risked her life for this Council."

"She verbalized an Ancient only incantation…"

"One an Ancient gave her."

"An insane Ancient."

"She didn't know… the Old Ones had her cornered."

"Enough," Zohn said. Kyle sat back and wondered what Emily was going to do. She had been too afraid to leave the palace without guards, and as far as he knew she didn't have anywhere to go. He briefly wondered if Chevalier even mentioned that he'd sold her house in Georgia when they thought she was dead.

***

"Has she said anything to you?" Zohn asked Kyle.

Kyle shook his head. "No, Elder. As far as I know, she hasn't spoken since she threatened to leave."

Quinn thought. "That's been almost three months ago."

"How much longer does Thutmose need?" the Chief of Defense asked. "This would be easier if Chevalier were awake."

"He said any day now."

"Maybe the Lady realized how badly she messed up and then decided to take her punishment," the Chief of Staff suggested.

Kyle looked at him. "You just don't know her well enough. She's up to something."

"Have you asked Dain? I still think it's odd that she asked him to return," Zohn said.

"I did, and he won't say."

"So she is up to something…"

"Yes, she is. Dain's part of it but reminded me that, even though an Elder's son, he's not sworn his allegiance to the Equites."

Quinn frowned. "He said that?"

"He's just upset," Kyle explained. "He's still very protective of Emily, and with Chevalier in… stasis… I think he's taken her safety upon himself."

"It's just…" Quinn's voice suddenly cut off. Kyle looked up and gasped when he saw that the Council had been turned to ash. He blurred out to the garage when he heard the Aero start up.

"Please…," Emily whispered when Kyle stepped in front of her car.

"You can't take him, Em," Kyle said, looking in at Alec.

Alec smiled and sat back as Dain brought the Rubicon up behind the Aero.

Kyle sighed, "Where are you going?"

"To my house," Emily told him. "Tell the Equites that I ash anyone that comes near me… except Chevalier."

Kyle looked up at the ceiling and then nodded. "Fine… but knock me unconscious."

Emily cringed when he fell to the floor, writhing in pain. He relaxed after he fell unconscious, and Emily spun out and headed to her new home, followed by Dain with the baby.

Chapter 13

"Mom, where do you want this?" Dain asked as he carried in a large box.

Emily looked up. "Oh, umm… put it in my room."

He nodded and left after glancing out the window. The Equites had stayed away from Emily's home since she'd warned them two weeks prior. Dain kept a close eye out, and Alec was always on his guard as he tried to fix the relationship between him and his niece.

"Emi?" Alec said from the doorway. Emily turned and smiled at Megara as she nuzzled against his shoulder.

"What's up?"

"Alexis called and she's on the way…"

"Okay"

"With Garrett."

Emily sighed, "That's pushing it… but I'll let him come in with Alex."

"Want some help?"

She looked over at the dishes. "No, I'm almost done."

Alec sat down and began playing with Megara. He stood up when he heard a knock on the door.

"Mom?" Alexis said, walking into the house. "This house is great! I love the colors."

"Thanks. It's about time you came to visit," Emily said, smiling. Her face fell when not only Garrett came in but Kyle also.

"Please don't turn me to ash," Kyle said to her. "I'm worried about you."

"Come on, Garrett," Alexis said, taking his hand. "Let's go check out the rest of the house."

Garrett got a nod from Kyle and then left the kitchen.

Emily sat down and handed the baby a toy. "I won't ash you."

"How are you?" Kyle asked, standing by the door.

"I'm okay. Any word on Chev?"

"Thutmose thinks it'll be pretty soon."

"He's going to be furious."

"Not at you," Kyle said, and finally sat down.

"Yes, he will be."

"He's going to be too mad at the Council."

She sighed, "I can't win with them."

"They don't know how to handle you."

"They don't have to handle me… they just have to treat me like an equal."

"It's hard though."

"You do."

He smiled. "I've known you longer, and I've not been on the Council for as long as most of them."

She shrugged. "Doesn't matter, Chev's going to be mad at me still."

Kyle caught the baby's toy when she dropped it and then he put it back in front of her. "Have you named her?"

"Yes"

"Not going to tell me?"

"I'm okay here," Emily said, looking into his eyes.

"I know. Chevalier's going to want you back at the palace though."

"I'm better off here. There's an Ancient living there now."

"Why Alec, Em? How can you trust him?"

"I don't. He's watched."

"By who?"

"It's okay."

Kyle looked around the large kitchen. "The house looks good."

"Thanks"

"Em?" Lt. Andrew called out from the front door.

"Damnit, Emily," Kyle whispered.

"In the kitchen," Emily yelled.

Andrew came in a few seconds later and eyed Kyle suspiciously. "Everything okay?"

"Yeah, Alexis came for a visit."

Andrew spun a chair and sat down in it backwards, still watching Kyle.

"You're staying here?" Kyle asked.

"He's keeping an eye on Alec for me," Emily explained.

Andrew smiled but said nothing.

"Maybe I can stay here too," Kyle suggested.

Emily shrugged. "There's room."

"You're letting me?"

"We don't need more help," Andrew said.

Kyle's eyes narrowed. "Chevalier is going to have issues with you being here."

"I'm sure he will."

"Come to think of it, I have issues with you being here," Kyle said, standing suddenly.

Andrew stood also and Emily jumped forward and placed herself between them. "No fighting here!"

"We've been doing fine without Equites help," Andrew hissed.

"You have no right moving in here!" Kyle yelled.

"Dain!" Emily screamed when the two blurred into a fight around her.

Garrett, Alec, and Dain all appeared and dove into the fight. Emily watched, as slowly, the fight broke up with Garrett and Alec holding Kyle back, and Dain restraining Andrew as best as he could.

"Both of you, sit!" Emily screamed, pointing at the two chairs.

Kyle glared at Andrew and finally sat down, followed by Andrew, who sat across from him.

Emily was the last to sit down, and she turned to them. "This is my house... and as owner, I declare it factionless! There will be no fighting, no power struggles, and no heku egos. Is that understood?"

"Em..." Kyle started.

"No! Do you understand?"

"Yes," Andrew said, watching Kyle.

Kyle nodded.

"Good, now you better act like friends or you both can leave," Emily told them.

"It's more comp...," Andrew said, and then stopped talking when Emily glared at him.

"No faction crap in this house!"

"Sorry, Em," Kyle said.

"Yeah, sorry," Andrew whispered.

Alec disappeared from the room and returned with Megara. Emily took her and rocked her gently as she turned green eyes to the heku.

"So what is her name?" Kyle asked.

"Megara"

He thought for a moment. "Like Creon's daughter?"

"Who?"

"Never mind, I like it."

Alexis came in a few minutes later. "This house is beautiful!"

Emily smiled. "Thanks."

"You designed it?"

"No, I had a contractor do that."

Alexis sat down and picked up Megara. "I'm amazed at how much she looks like you."

Emily leaned her elbow on the table, put her head in her hand, and nodded.

"Are you sleeping?" Kyle asked, studying her.

"No"

"Why not?"

"I just can't," she said, and got up to get a drink.

Alexis watched her and then whispered to Garrett before turning back to Emily. "Mom, why don't you let me stay here tonight and watch the baby while you sleep?"

"You can't feed her," Emily reminded her, and then sat down with a

glass of Coke.

"I can do the rest though, maybe give you some rest."

"I'm fine, Alex."

Suddenly, everyone in the kitchen except Emily turned toward the front door.

"What?" Emily asked, and stood slowly. She gasped when the entire room emptied out.

The door to the kitchen flew open and Chevalier walked in, his features dark and menacing.

"Chev!" Emily yelled.

"Where is Kyle?" Chevalier hissed.

She swallowed hard, suddenly afraid for Kyle. "Why?"

Chevalier inhaled and turned to Emily with his hands balled into fists. "I smell an Encala."

She nodded and then whispered, "Andrew is here."

"Where is Kyle?"

"I don't know."

"Kyle!" Chevalier roared. He turned to the door, but the house was unnaturally silent.

"Chev, what's wrong?" Emily asked softly. She wanted to run into his arms, but he was obviously furious.

"Did they kick you out?" he asked, turning to her.

"No, I left."

"But they did something…"

"They… they put me on house arrest again."

"Anything else?"

"No, I waited until the house was done and then I moved out. I won't live in the same place as an Ancient, not with the baby a Winchester too."

His features softened slightly. "You're okay?"

She nodded and then took a step toward him. He gently pulled her into his arms and held her tightly as she buried her face in his chest.

"I was afraid you wouldn't wake up," she said. "I'm so sorry."

"You didn't know," he said, and kissed the top of her head. "We'll talk later about that, okay?"

After a few minutes, Emily stepped back. "Why do you want Kyle?"

She stepped farther away from Chevalier when he turned furious again. "They had no right! How dare they punish you for that!"

"It's over."

"I don't care. They're lucky I don't replace all of them… I've done it before," he growled, and then walked out of the kitchen.

"You replaced the Council once?"

He nodded. "Yes."

"This Council doesn't need replaced over this. I'm okay here, and I like this house."

"Kyle!" Chevalier yelled.

"It wasn't Kyle's fault. He didn't go along with them."

"He didn't?" Chevalier turned toward her.

"No, but he kept most of his opinions to himself at my request."

Emily took his hand and gently smoothed it out of a tight fist.

"After all you've done for this faction... I'm out of the way for a couple of months, and they treat you like this?"

"I know," she whispered. "It's just time to stay away from the Council."

"I need you at the palace," he told her, and kissed her softly.

"I can't..."

"I understand." Chevalier looked around. "When did you start this house?"

"The same week you went unconscious."

"They finished that fast... for mortals."

Her nose scrunched slightly as she considered telling him.

His eyes narrowed. "Who built it?"

She sighed, "The Encala."

"Why?"

"Because I was tired of house arrest and needed the house faster. I called a contractor, but he couldn't do it in that time frame. William was my only hope to get out of that palace faster."

He nodded and looked up when he heard the baby talking. Emily followed him up the stairs to the nursery, and when he walked in, the baby smiled broadly at him and held her arms out to be picked up.

Chevalier picked up the baby and kissed the top of her head. "She's grown so much."

Emily nodded.

"Did you ever name her?"

"Yes," she said, amused. "I named her Megara."

"After Creon's daughter?"

"Who the hell is Creon?"

"Never mind, I like it." Chevalier held Megara and watched Emily for a few minutes.

She shifted nervously. "What?"

"How are you and she getting along?"

Emily smiled. "We're doing fine."

"No more trying to give her away?"

"Nope," she said, laughing slightly.

Chevalier held up the baby, so he could see her better, and looked

into her familiar green eyes. "She looks so much like you."

"I've heard."

He moved her close against his chest and looked around the nursery. "So how long is Andrew going to stay here?"

"I'm not sure. He's helping keep an eye on Alec."

Chevalier gasped. "Alec is here?"

"Yes"

"You trust him?"

"Nope… that's why Dain and Andrew are here."

He nodded and then thought for a moment before putting the baby to his shoulder. "So show me around the house."

"Do you just want to see, or are you checking for security risks and scrutinizing the Encala's work?"

He smiled. "Just show me."

Emily turned and walked out into the hallway on the third floor. "This is just for bedrooms."

Chevalier went down the long hallway and looked into each room as he expertly cradled the baby. When he came back, Emily's eyebrows rose.

"See any security risk?"

"Nope… pretty empty though."

She shrugged and started down the stairs. "No use filling them all. Not sure why they are there, actually. I asked the Encala for eight bedrooms and ended up with 16."

Chevalier smiled. "Sixteen is better."

"Not if you have to clean them." Emily stopped on the second floor. "This floor has offices for each of us…"

"Me too?"

"Yes, though it's empty. I don't know what you want in it."

He nodded. "Okay, what else?"

"There's a game room, a home theater system, and a playroom for when Megs grows up."

"Nice"

"There's also a billiards room, but I haven't filled it yet."

"You asked for a billiards room?"

"No, actually, I didn't," she said as she started down to the ground floor. Chevalier chuckled from behind her.

"The first floor is pretty simple. There's a kitchen, pantry, butler's pantry… I don't even know what that's for, and I don't have a butler. There's also a study, library, music room, sun room, sitting room, and a dining room."

"Wow, it's bigger than it looks."

She shrugged and started across the grand foyer. "There's a little

garden off of the kitchen, so I can keep fresh herbs on hand."

Chevalier stopped in the hallway and looked closely at a blank wall.

Emily frowned. "How do you even see that?"

"What is it?" he asked, running his hands along an invisible line.

"It's my panic room."

He smiled and turned to her. "You have a panic room?"

"Yes, a heku-proof one."

"Interesting"

Emily opened up a double door and headed into the basement. "Down here is a wine cellar, hot tub, the laundry with an attached maid closet..."

"You have a maid?"

"No, I do the cleaning."

"We can get you a maid."

"I don't want one. The house stays pretty clean. It's nice."

He nodded and looked around. "Cells?"

"No, I specifically said no prison, no torture room, nothing heku-ish."

Chevalier chuckled and smiled at the baby when she looked up at him and smiled.

Emily opened a door and walked into a sizeable sitting room with a bar in one corner and a large TV on the wall. Hundreds of DVDs lined the walls in neatly organized shelves.

"I'm surprised you don't have a pool," Chevalier said as he sat down on one of the plush couches.

Emily sat beside him on her knees and looked around. "I may put one in eventually."

"Or just use the one in the palace."

"Not with an Ancient running around."

He sighed, "I'll take care of that. Contrary to what the Council told him, we can't keep him around."

"He wants me destroyed."

"Yes, I would imagine he does."

"He refers to me as a 'thing' and thinks I'm weak and puny."

"Ancients don't like mortals... I told you that."

Her eyes narrowed. "Apparently, neither do you."

Chevalier looked over at her. "Why did I deserve that?"

"Oh, I've heard... the great Equitis hates mortals."

He sighed, "That was a long time ago."

"I know what the Chief Enforcer's original job was."

"Again... a long time ago."

She shrugged. "We'll see."

"I don't hate mortals."

Emily reached over and took the baby from him. She immediately reached out for her dad and then started to cry when Emily kept her in her arms.

"I don't hate mortals, Em." Chevalier stood up and looked at her. "You've known me for how long?"

"I'm not fully mortal."

"I didn't know that at first."

"You knew it before taking me to Colorado."

He sighed, "Yes, but I didn't know the extent."

Emily turned and headed back up the stairs, with Chevalier following silently.

Alec, Kyle, Dain, and Garrett met them in the foyer.

Chevalier looked over, irritated. "Where have you been?"

Garrett bowed. "Elder, we were patrolling outside."

"Avoiding me…"

"No, sir."

"You and I need to have a chat later," Chevalier said to Kyle.

Kyle nodded. "I figured."

"Where is Andrew?"

"He's outside checking the perimeter of the house."

"What's his deal?"

"He's just here to watch Alec," Emily said. She watched Kyle for a moment as he looked at Chevalier, and she figured out they were talking too silently for her to hear. "Stop it!"

"What?" Kyle asked, looking over at her.

"If you're going to talk, you might as well say it in the open."

Garrett stifled a grin.

"Megs and I are going to bed anyway, whisper away," Emily said, irritated, and walked up the stairs.

The heku watched her disappear up the stairs and then turned when Andrew walked in and shut the door.

He stopped and looked at Chevalier. "Oh good, you're back."

"No sarcasm?" Chevalier snapped.

"Not at all. Emily was worried about you."

"How long are you going to stay here?"

He shrugged. "I don't know. As long as she wants I guess… or at least until the Equites re-banish the Ancient."

"Why don't you keep out of it?" Kyle growled.

Andrew smiled. "I won't keep out of anything that poses a risk to Em."

Kyle and Alec both took an arm when Chevalier started forward. "We don't need your help."

Andrew started for the door. "If you'll excuse me…"

Alec sighed, "You didn't tell them about that."

"Tell us about what?" Kyle asked.

Chevalier hissed when over twenty Encala blurred into the mansion and immediately began to clean.

"About who actually keeps this house clean," Alec said, watching the fast workers.

"Wait... she doesn't know the Encala are cleaning it?" Kyle asked, shocked.

"Nope," Alec sighed. He watched the Encala for a few minutes and then walked up the stairs, followed by Dain.

"Well hell... just watch them," Chevalier whispered. The Equites spread out to keep an eye on the Encala workers.

Andrew came back over and crossed his arms.

"What?" Chevalier asked.

He shrugged. "Nothing."

"Why haven't you told Em about the cleaners?"

"She wouldn't allow it."

"So you did ask her?"

"Nope... but I know her well enough to know she'd prefer to clean the house herself. I also know she can't keep it clean alone."

"Well I'm back... so you can go."

"That's not up to you," Andrew said smugly, and then disappeared up the stairs.

Chapter 14

"Daddy!" Megara called out, and then ran across the trial area and up the stairs, into Chevalier's arms.

He kissed her soft cheek. "Good morning, princess."

She looked over at Quinn and smiled.

"Where is your mother?" Quinn asked, looking over at the doors.

"Simming," Megara told him, and then shied away when Zohn smiled at her.

"Did Andrew come with her?" Kyle asked the 3-year-old.

Megara shook her head. "Adrew not like you."

"Did he say that?"

She nodded and turned around to sit in Chevalier's lap. "We do today?"

"We have trials," Chevalier said, and called for McIntock.

"I can see?"

"No, you have to go for this one."

McIntock appeared before the Council. "I was summoned?"

"Yes, take Megara please," Chevalier told him.

"No," Megara yelled, and then crossed her arms.

Kyle chuckled. "So much like Em."

"You can't stay for this," Chevalier said, and lifted her over the desk and into McIntock's waiting hands.

Megara turned and frowned at Chevalier. "He bit me."

McIntock gasped.

"No, he didn't," Chevalier said, hiding a grin. "Now stop telling stories."

Most of the Council erupted into laughs when Megara mimicked Chevalier, just like Emily does.

McIntock spun suddenly and disappeared with the toddler.

"She's going to be a handful," the Chief of Staff said, still laughing.

Chevalier nodded. "Like no other... I don't doubt it."

***

McIntock appeared beside the swimming pool and put Megara down so she could play.

Emily looked up from swimming laps. "Want to swim?"

Megara shook her head and sat down with her dolls.

"Is Chev still in a meeting?"

McIntock bowed slightly. "Yes, Commander."

Emily sighed, "You've been Megs' guard for three years... when will you just call me Emily?"

He smiled. "It's not proper."

"I don't really care."

"I do."

"I thought I smelled a half-breed," Thutmose said, appearing beside McIntock.

McIntock's eyes narrowed, and he called for more Cavalry before turning to the Ancient. "You aren't to be with the Lady."

"I won't hurt her," he said, smiling at her. Emily's skin crawled when he even looked at her.

Mark, Silas, and Horace blurred in.

"Damnit, Thutmose!" Mark roared. "You are to stay away from Emily."

He shrugged. "I'm an Ancient. I can do what I want."

"No, you can't."

Silas and Horace each took an arm of the Ancient.

"I'm reporting this to the Council," Mark told him. "So I suggest you leave."

Thutmose watched Emily. "You're an abomination that shouldn't be allowed to be in the presence of heku."

Emily swam for the ladder, and her mortal eyes missed when the Ancient was taken from the room by furious members of the Cavalry.

McIntock turned to her. "I'm sorry about that."

She crawled out. "I'm just going to head home."

"Don't let him scare you off…"

"I'm not scared of him," she said, drying off quickly. "However, as long as he's here… this will be my last visit."

"The Council will deal with him…"

"Doesn't matter," she said, picking up the toddler. "We're still heading back."

Chevalier and Kyle met Emily at her Jeep.

"We heard," Kyle said when she walked up.

"I would assume the entire palace heard," she told him as she put Megara into her car seat.

"Don't go," Chevalier said softly, and touched her arm.

She looked at him. "I don't want to be around him."

"We'll put him in prison while you're here."

"Oh he'd love that."

"I don't really care what he loves. The Council has no right to keep him above ground."

"Then they can make a decision," Emily said, sitting down in the Jeep. "Either they get rid of prehistoric heku… or I stay at my house from now on."

"I'll talk to them."

She nodded and started the Jeep. "I assume you've got minions still around my house?"

"Of course."

"Tell them to keep out of my way."

He nodded. "Horace is sorry that his Cavalry rushed into the house…, but you did scream."

"I stubbed my toe on the bed."

"Still"

"Coming tonight?"

"Of course," he said, and shut her door. Chevalier and Kyle watched as she drove out of the palace garage.

"I think Richard's about to sway," Kyle said, looking over at the Elder.

"Even if he does… that's still only four to nine."

"Still… if he votes for banishing Thutmose, then others may follow."

"I hope so."

***

"Dain?" Emily yelled as she dropped her keys on the table. When she didn't hear anything, she tried another. "Andrew?"

"Where they go?" Megara asked from Emily's arms.

"Not sure… Dain?" she called out again, and then walked toward the kitchen. It was getting late and almost time to start dinner.

Emily flipped on the light and then froze when a stranger appeared before her in the hallway. She took a step back as he grinned, his teeth almost glowing in the dull light.

"Who are you?" she whispered.

"I am Cleto," he replied, and looked at the baby. "This must be the child belonging to Equitis."

Emily took another step back but ran into someone and spun toward yet another stranger. He wasn't smiling but was scowling at her.

"No half-breed can be allowed to live."

"Aharon, she is here," Cleto said, still smiling at her.

Emily gasped when another heku appeared and looked down at her. "And with the infant even. Much easier this way."

"Who are you?" Emily asked again, gripping the baby tighter.

The newest heku glared at her. "We… child, are Ancients."

"Andrew!" Emily screamed.

"Your heku can't come to your aid. You know you shouldn't be here. You should have been killed at birth," Cleto told her.

Emily struggled when arms wrapped around her, and she felt a cold

nose run along her neck. "Mmm, the scent on this one is intriguing."

"As a mortal, she is ours to play with," Aharon said. "I'm sure Equitis won't mind."

She finally pulled away from the heku behind her and put her back to the wall. "I've about had enough of you..."

"Going to turn us to ash?" Cleto laughed.

"That's right... she can turn simple heku to ash," Aharon said, nodding.

"Have you turned any Ancients to ash, child?"

Emily nodded.

The unnamed Ancient smiled. "I remember... she turned Arrianus to ash."

Aharon then reached out and gently touched the locket of ashes that hung around Emily's neck.

Cleto smiled. "I bet you can't turn more than one Ancient at a time though."

"Wanna bet?" Emily snapped, and then narrowed her eyes and concentrated.

Aharon began to laugh. "You'll hurt yourself doing that... I feel nothing more than a tingle."

"It's an uncomfortable tingle though," Cleto said, no longer smiling. "So I suggest you stop!"

Emily fell back against the wall when blood began to trickle from her nose. She was suddenly exhausted, but the three Ancients remained solid.

Aharon inhaled. "I'm first."

"No, I am," Cleto snapped at him.

"Stop fighting," the third said calmly. "We'll each get a taste."

"Andrew!" Emily screamed.

"Step away from her," Chevalier said when he appeared in the hallway. Mark, Kyle, Quinn, and Silas followed shortly and were crouched and ready to attack.

"Equitis! Good to see you, boy," Cleto said. "We were just about to snack on your wife."

Emily gasped when the hallway turned into a mass of blurred fighting. She fought against arms that appeared around her until she realized it was Mark. He set her down in front of the panic room. "Open it."

Without a word, she immediately put in the code and stepped into the tiny living space.

"No, you don't!" Andrew said, blurring into the room.

Mark slammed the door shut behind the three of them, and Emily quickly locked it. Andrew turned to the monitors and started adjusting

them to see around the house.

"Where did they come from?" Emily finally managed to ask, still holding tightly to Megara.

Mark looked over at her. "Thutmose has been reviving the Ancients."

Andrew growled, "Leave it to the Equites to revive just enough to bring back the entire population of Ancients!"

"Watch it... Encala..."

"Stop it," Emily hissed. "We need to go help them."

She started to put the code in to leave the panic room, but Mark stopped her. "The Elder said we're to stay in here until the Ancients are re-banished."

"What?! That could take ages."

"Nevertheless, we stay."

Andrew nodded. "It's not safe for you out there."

"What provisions are in here?" Mark asked, looking around the small living room.

"There's a bathroom, bedroom, kitchen, and this living room. It's stocked with enough supplies to feed a mortal for four years," Andrew said proudly.

Mark nodded. "Fine... then we stay."

Emily frowned. "No, we don't."

She swayed slightly and Mark put a hand against her back. "Sit down."

Hoping not to pass out, Emily did as Mark asked, and then sat the toddler down beside her.

"What's wrong?" Andrew asked, watching as Emily laid down on the couch.

"Chevalier suspects that she can't ash more than one Ancient," Mark said. He blurred away and returned with a warm wash cloth, then handed it to Emily, and she started washing the blood from her nose and ears.

"Why not?" Emily asked. "I ashed 3400 Valle."

"Ancients are just stronger," Andrew said, sitting down beside her. "They aren't built exactly like us heku that were turned."

"I ashed my father."

"That was one."

Mark turned to the door and cocked his head slightly to the side. Finally, he turned back to Emily. "Two of those Ancients got away. Chevalier was able to kill one of them."

"How did they get away?" Emily asked. "They were outnumbered."

"Ancients again," Andrew explained. "Chevalier, as an Old One, is more able to kill one. The other two had heku with them."

She sighed, "So now what?"

"Chevalier said we stay here until he comes back for us," Mark told her.

"As did William," Andrew said.

Emily looked around the small living room. It had a large TV on one wall with only a handful of DVDs, but the area seemed comfortable. "How long?"

"We aren't sure."

She nodded. "Fine…"

***

"I killed Cleto," Chevalier said to the Council.

"We've alerted all three factions," Quinn said. "They are all reviving the Old Ones."

Chevalier nodded. "We'll need to get the Enforcer's together again."

"Do we get to know how that was done?" Zohn asked. No heku was ever told how the Old Ones once gave themselves the ability to turn a heku to ash. It was well known that that ability was temporary and was used to banish the Ancients across the planet quicker.

"You won't know the incantation… but it takes all three Chief Enforcers," Chevalier said.

"Where is Em?" Kyle asked.

"She's in the panic room with Mark and Andrew."

"You're okay with that?"

"I wish Andrew wasn't there… but he calms Em, so we'll leave him."

"How long can they live in there?"

"According to William… about four years," Chevalier explained.

"The mortals can… what about the heku?" Kyle asked.

"We'll just have to let them out to feed."

"Equitis," a strange heku said from the trial room door.

Chevalier turned and his eyes narrowed. "Himerius."

"Why have I been awoken?"

Chevalier walked over to the Old One. "The Ancients have been revived."

"What?! By who?"

"Thutmose was revived after Aboleo was used… knocking out all awake Old Ones."

"Only Ancients can do that."

"It's a long story," Chevalier said. "Wait until we have all gathered, and I'll explain."

Kyle frowned when Himerius walked out of the room. "You're going to tell the Old Ones about Emily?"

"I don't know as though I have a choice."

"They'll kill her."

"I don't think they will," Chevalier said, returning to his seat.

"Equitis is in here," Himerius said. Another strange heku walked in, looking furious.

"Why am I here?!" the heku yelled.

Chevalier sighed, "This is going to get old."

Quinn nodded. "Zohn will be done soon, and we can explain to them all what's happening."

"You will explain now," the new heku said, scowling.

"No, I won't," Chevalier said. The others couldn't help but notice that he was about to lose his temper. "You will wait with the others."

"He always was a bossy sonofabitch," Himerius grumbled, and walked out with another newly revived Old One.

Chevalier chuckled. "This is going to be interesting."

"Where will you all meet?" Quinn asked.

"In secret," Chevalier said. "When Zohn is done, we'll take Kyle and head out."

Kyle nodded. "Yes, Elder."

The Court Reporter came into the room and took his seat. "Kralen was able to get Allen and Miri also, and they have left for the undisclosed location. Alexis, Garrett, and Dain were not happy about leaving."

Chevalier nodded. "I figured."

"They wanted to know why Emily isn't with them."

"She's going to be safer where she is."

He nodded and sat back.

Within four hours, Zohn returned after reviving all of the Equites Old Ones. He sat down and sighed, "That was not pleasant."

Chevalier stood up. "We won't be back until this is over."

Kyle stood also and turned to them.

"And the Ancients here?" Zohn asked.

"If you can restrain them... do it. Otherwise, you may have to kill them."

"That's easier said than done," Quinn sighed.

"Let's go," Chevalier said, and started for the door, followed by Kyle. Soon, they were flying across the ocean in a large jet with some of the Valle Old Ones.

"Now are you going to tell us who woke up the Ancients?" one of the Old Ones asked.

Chevalier nodded. "I will be honest with you, just to help the cause.

I have a wife…"

"Equitis, married?" one of the Old Ones gasped.

He glared at the heku. "When I married her, I thought she was mortal."

"What?! You ma…" the heku's words were cut off by another glare from Chevalier.

"I don't hate mortals anymore."

The heku just nodded, still in shock.

"My wife, Emily, is a Dulcris Cruor. She comes from a family several hundred years old that was started by Ulrich."

"Who?" one of them asked.

"Bacab"

"Oh… okay."

"Anyway, when he produced a child with this family, not only did the children have the enticing blood…, but they can turn a heku to ash."

"That family should have been killed immediately."

"I know that… anyway… Emily is the only one of that family left. It wasn't until we'd bonded and even had a child that I discovered that Emily is the daughter of Arrianus."

Another Old One gasped. "She's part Ancient?"

"Yes"

"Then she…"

"I know she should have been killed. She's my wife, and I wasn't going to punish her for something she had no control over. We didn't know until very recently that Emily can partially do some things the Ancients can… incantations, rituals…"

"How is she alive?" Himerius asked.

"She's alive because she's my wife," Chevalier hissed. The heku sat back, fearful of Chevalier's anger. "She accidentally let it known that she knew of the Renovare incantation, and some of the Old Ones sought her out for it and tried to kill her."

Kyle shifted nervously when the Old Ones began to talk among themselves.

"When they attacked her… she used Aboleo on them…, but it didn't work. They didn't turn to ash. They just went unconscious… along with every Old One above ground at the time."

"You included?" Himerius asked.

"Yes, even me."

"How were you revived?"

"The Equites Council revived Thutmose, and he returned the Old Ones. He did so under the agreement that he could stay above ground and live in the palace. What we didn't know, was that he was also reviving Ancients around the world."

"How?!"

"That we don't know..., but it's been done."

"So we are meeting in Ur?" another Old One asked.

"Yes"

Kyle cleared his throat. "It's no longer called Ur... it's now called Iraq."

"Equitis... when this is over... we will need to deal with your mate," another heku said.

Chevalier's eyes narrowed. "Over my dead body."

"This wasn't her fault," Kyle said. "An Ancient told her those incantations..."

"Which one?"

"The one in the Equites vault. He's no longer completely sane and freely gave her those incantations. She used it in self-defense."

Chevalier hated to do it but to keep Emily safe he spoke, "Emily also has the ability to create heku children."

Himerius smiled. "She can?"

"Yes, and she, herself, isn't aging."

"She's heku then..."

"No, she's not. From what we can tell, she's 50% Ancient, 1% heku, and about 49% mortal. She has mostly mortal traits, other than she doesn't age and she does heal... though very slowly."

Kyle hated to even say it but picked up on what Chevalier was trying to do. "We can't just kill a specimen like Emily. No one in the history of the heku has ever produced heku children, nor have we ever had the chance to study a mortal with these abilities."

"Her family was sought for hundreds of years before Emily was accidentally handed to me," Chevalier said.

"If she has that ability, then we must do away with her, Equitis," Himerius said. "You know that... if there are heku children, then we use them to further the line... if the line is really that important."

"Chevali... Equitis' children, his daughters, are too heku," Kyle explained. "They cannot have children themselves. Emily is unique in that ability."

"Still," another Old One said, "she is able to do things even we, as Old Ones, cannot. We can't let her walk this planet."

"She is under my care and my protection," Chevalier told him.

"Let's deal with the half-breed later," Himerius said. "For now... how many Ancients do we know have been revived?"

"There's no real way of knowing. We have to assume all of them, so 208."

"There are 215 Ancients," one of them corrected.

"Emily killed her Ancient father. I killed another just after I met

her, and we have killed Thutmose and Cleto just recently."

One of the others smiled. "Wait... that half-breed killed an Ancient?"

"Yes," Chevalier said, fighting back the urge to rip the heku's head from his body for calling Emily a half-breed.

Sotomar chuckled. "Then Equitis killed his maker..."

"Well that shouldn't surprise any of us," Himerius said, amused.

Chevalier glared at them. "Then we killed Sterling too."

Sotomar nodded. "Chevalier also killed Besinious."

"They will gather and regroup."

"We've sent several covens to the Ancient's meeting place. They cannot kill that many Ancients, but they can alert us when they begin to arrive."

"It's a long trip," Kyle said. "Let's begin planning so we have something set in motion and agreed upon before we involve the other factions."

***

"Are you two just going to glare at each other?" Emily asked, irritated. She glanced up from her book and saw Andrew and Mark sitting across from each other, their eyes locked.

Andrew looked over at her and smiled. "We're fine."

"You're pouting."

"We aren't pouting."

"Why would we be pouting?" Mark asked.

"Because you're stuck with each other in this tiny apartment," Emily said.

"Yeah," Megara said, and then smiled at Mark.

Mark grinned at her. "We don't need input from you."

Emily stood up and stretched her back before walking into the tiny kitchen.

"Do we need to work on your back?" Andrew asked.

Mark glared at him, but he ignored the enemy heku.

"May not hurt," she said, coming back out with a glass of orange juice.

Mark sighed, "Can you at least keep your hands off of her?"

"Nope," Andrew said, smiling. He walked over and pulled a yoga mat out from a storage bin.

***

The Old Ones from all three factions looked over the others. They hadn't gathered in thousands of years, and most had been retired since

the time the Ancients were first banished.

Chevalier stepped forward. "Did your faction representatives tell you why we are here?"

Sotomar nodded. "I have informed the Valle."

"Yeah, we know," one of the Encala said. "And we believe, to avoid this in the future, it's time to do away with your wife."

Chevalier hissed.

Sotomar put his hand up. "That's not going to happen. We cannot kill Emily."

"She's the cause!"

"She is not the cause," Sotomar said. "You will find thousands of heku that will fight for her."

"Enough about Emily," Chevalier said. "We'll do this the same as last time. Watch the TV for news of mortal slayings…"

"Watch the what?" one of the Old Ones said.

Kyle sighed, "We'll go over new technologies with you later."

"Very well, continue."

"We feel that they will see the attack coming from us. However, they haven't fed, aren't aware of technology, and are very much outnumbered by heku now," Chevalier said. "They will be distracted and will be fighting among themselves. Once we perform the ritual to give you all the ability to turn a heku to ash, it will again last four months only."

"Then we will be retired again?" one of them asked.

"If that's what you wish, yes."

Sotomar stepped forward. "We'll begin by dividing up into global areas. Each group will have a designated leader. They will be responsible for contacting our main point of contact, Chevalier."

"Who?" one of them asked.

Sotomar smiled. "Equitis, sorry."

"Who is making up this list?" another asked, irritated.

"Equitis already has."

"Who put him in charge?"

Sotomar sighed, "He's in charge… deal with it."

Kyle smiled. He knew the Old Ones often spoke about how the Ancients hated each other, but it was well known by the heku that the Old Ones didn't like each other much either.

Chevalier took a stack of papers from Kyle and began distributing the list to everyone he had chosen as a leader. His group consisted of three Old Ones, one from each faction. Sotomar took his group of four Old Ones, and they immediately set off for the southern tip of South America.

Kyle walked up to Chevalier's group. "I want to go."

"You are not an Old One, boy," one of Chevalier's group snapped. "I can still turn an Ancient to ash."

"You're in," Chevalier said. "We need all the help we can."

Kyle stepped up and joined in the plans.

***

Emily reached out, holding her breath, and hit the first number of the code to the door. She waited to see if the heku heard and then pushed the second number.

"No, Em," Mark said from behind her.

She sighed and turned around. "I can't stand this! We haven't heard anything in two weeks."

Mark gently took her hand and pulled her over to the couch. "We just need patience."

She sat down and put her hands under her chin. "It's boring in here."

"It's the safest place for you," Andrew said, coming out of the bedroom with Megara.

"What if he's dead," she whispered.

"You would know that already," Mark reminded her. "The last thing Chevalier needs right now is to worry about you. With you here, safe... he can put his full concentration into exterminating the Ancients."

Emily stood suddenly and disappeared into the small bedroom. She shut the door behind her.

Mark sighed, "Now she stops sleeping and eating."

Andrew looked over at him. "Why?"

"That's just what she does when she's stressed."

"She won't this time. It'll be different..."

***

Chevalier leaned toward the TV and watched the newscast on a group of missing hikers. "This isn't working."

"We've already banished two," Kyle said, sitting down. "I'm not sure what else we can do."

"Let your mate call them," one of the Old Ones said. "If she can do what an Ancient can, that is."

"She can... and no. I'm not going to get Emily involved in this."

"She started it."

"Stop it, okay?" Kyle snapped. "We're not involving her."

He rolled his eyes and turned back to the newspaper.

"Here," another heku said. "There's a report of some bodies found

in Kazym. Four so far, one found just this morning."

"Drained?" Kyle asked.

"There's some old mortal claiming it's the work of an upir."

Chevalier stood up. "Enough for me. Let's go."

The five heku piled into a Kombat T-98 and started for the remote Siberian town. It was silent until they pulled up into the dark, snow covered streets of Kazym.

"Spread out," Chevalier said after stopping the SUV. "Alert us if you catch the scent."

The heku blurred from the vehicle, and within the hour, Kyle caught the scent of an Ancient and alerted his team. Chevalier was the first to arrive, followed shortly by the others. They all immediately caught the scent and began to follow it through the abandoned streets.

"Vadim," Chevalier hissed when he saw the Ancient feeding from a dead mortal.

The Ancient stood suddenly and fell into a crouch. "Equitis..."

"How many have you killed?"

"They are mine to do with as I please."

"Times have changed," one of the Old Ones said to him. "We're here to return you to the ground."

"Try it, infants," he hissed, and immediately lunged for Chevalier.

It took the four Old Ones only a few minutes to pin the screaming Ancient to the ground. "You owe me your very lives!"

Kyle stepped forward and grabbed the dagger from his pocket.

"Stop this! You have no right... I am your past..."

"Eternity," Kyle whispered, before a single drop of blood fell from his wrist. It froze in the air before hitting the Ancient. His screams filled the snowy streets moments before falling to ash.

Chevalier stood up and looked around. "Let's get him taken care of and head out."

One of the Old Ones gathered the ashes and handed them to Kyle for safe keeping.

"What's the count?" Chevalier asked.

Kyle grabbed a small notebook and looked through it. "Fourteen."

"Total?"

"Yes, Elder."

"Damnit, we have to do this faster."

"It's not as easy as it used to be," one of the team said. "There are a hundred times more mortals now."

"Still, it's been three weeks," Chevalier growled. "How can we only have 14?"

Kyle sighed, "Maybe we should have Em summon them."

"No," Chevalier snapped.

***

"Just one bite?" Andrew asked, holding out the plate.

"I'm not hungry," Emily told him.

He looked down at the untouched spaghetti. "You can't just stop eating like this."

She shrugged.

Andrew looked up at Mark.

"Em, come on. Eat... for me?"

"I'm not hungry! Drop it."

"We can't just let you starve."

Emily glared at both of them and wrapped her arms around her knees.

"Do we even mention sleep then?" Andrew asked.

"Who appointed you my babysitter?"

Mark grinned. "Your husband kind of did."

Andrew stood up and thought before speaking. "So you don't eat for two weeks... how are you even alive?"

"She's used to it," Mark said. "It's her 'thing'."

"It's not my thing."

"Yes, it is."

"Shut up, Mark."

***

Chevalier turned and shook his head, keeping his team from ambushing the Ancient.

Kyle motioned for them all to head back to base-camp, and they all disappeared from the frozen Moscow streets.

"Why did we stop?" Kyle asked when they arrived in their tiny hotel room.

One of the Old Ones sat down and sighed, "Baltasar has the ability to summon mortals."

"So we kill him quickly."

"If he has the chance to summon mortals, we'll be surrounded."

Chevalier was at the window looking out. "We can't risk having even one mortal see us."

"So now what?" Kyle asked.

"We have to wait until he goes away from populated areas."

"How close does he have to be to summon a mortal?"

"Only a mile or so."

"They're slow... it can take them a lot of time to get that mile."

Chevalier turned to him. "We need Emily's scent."

One of the other Old Ones frowned. "What good would the scent of a mortal be?"

Kyle smiled. "You have no idea."

"Contact Council City," Chevalier said to Kyle. "Have them send Emily's pregnancy scent to us overnight. Exavior's vial is in the safe."

"Are you sure?"

"Yes, it's the best bet to lure him away from the comfort of mortals."

Kyle nodded and disappeared.

"What good is that? We're wasting time!" one of their team said angrily.

Chevalier smiled. "Just wait... my wife... the Dulcris Cruor, has a pregnancy scent that can bring down even the most controlled of us."

"It can't be any better than the simple taste of a mortal," he said. "I salivate just thinking about the flavor."

***

"You!" Emily screamed at Mark, pointing at the kitchen. "Get in there!"

"But...," Mark started, then quieted down when Emily glared at him.

"Now"

"I don't..."

"Damnit, Mark! I'm a member of the Council, and that's an order. Get your ass into the kitchen."

Mark glanced at Andrew and then sighed and walked slowly into the kitchen.

Emily spun to Andrew and his smug grin faded. "Get into the bathroom."

"What?! Why?"

"Now!"

"I didn't do..." Andrew gasped when she took a step toward him. He instinctively took a step away from her as she narrowed her furious eyes.

"Get... in... there... now."

Andrew disappeared and then shut the bathroom door when he appeared inside.

Emily sighed and picked up the baby, who watched the encounter curiously.

Megara smiled and turned her vivid green eyes to her mom. "What they do?"

"They are acting like children," Emily said as she sat down on the

couch. "So we'll treat them like children until they decide to behave."

"I heard that…," Mark said from the tiny kitchen.

"Good!" Emily yelled at him. "So you're grounded for eight hours."

"I have to stay in here for eight hours?"

"Yes"

"Damnit," Andrew growled from inside the bathroom.

"I swear…," Emily sighed.

Megara pointed at the TV. "We watch it?"

"Again, Megs?"

The toddler nodded.

"Fine, but this is the last time."

***

"We're going to have to acclimate ourselves to this," Kyle said as he began to open the package from Council City.

"You two are acting like we have no control at all," one of the Old Ones growled.

Chevalier chuckled and then turned to Kyle. "How are we going to do this? You and I aren't acclimated either."

Kyle looked at the harmless looking vial. "Not sure. Course… we'll acclimate faster. We've at least encountered it before."

"We could control the maid, and have her dilute some of it in water."

Kyle nodded and disappeared from the room. He came back in, followed by the maid, who had a blank expression on her face. He handed her the vial and then watched as she walked into the bathroom. When she returned, Kyle slipped a hundred rubles into her apron before escorting her out of the room.

Chevalier ordered the others to stay, and he slowly walked into the bathroom. A few minutes later, he called for Kyle, who joined him. Once Kyle regained control, Chevalier opened the tiny vial, and both began to shake with thirst.

It took four hours to completely acclimate the other Old Ones, and no one again doubted that this plan would work to lure the Ancient away from the city.

"Hurensohn!" one of them gasped.

Chevalier smiled. "We warned you."

"Still… you're bonded to the owner of this scent?"

"Yes"

"Lucky bastard."

"I don't feed from her."

He frowned and looked up. "Why the hell not?"

"Yeah… how can you even stop feeding from her?" another asked.

Chevalier sighed, "She's my wife… not a donor."

"But you have?"

"Yes"

He grinned. "This half-breed must be special."

"Stop calling her that," Chevalier hissed.

"Let's go," Kyle said as he came out of the bathroom with the vial. "We still need to get to Jekaterinburg by tomorrow night."

Chevalier nodded. "Head out."

An hour later, Kyle was shrouded in a cloak and walking quickly through the streets of Moscow. The cloak was doused in the enticing scent, and the Ancient was trailing less than a mile behind him as he made his way out of the city. Behind the Ancient were the Old Ones, carefully watching his every move to protect any mortal he came to.

Once out in the trees off of the Uchinskoe Reservoir, Kyle stopped and waited for the others to arrive. He heard the hiss just as the Ancient appeared in the small clearing.

Kyle lowered his hood and smiled. "Zdravstvujte."

The Ancient froze and snarled. "Kto tee?"

"You knew we were coming," Chevalier said as he appeared behind the Ancient.

"Stoj!" he hissed, and stepped back away from the advancing Old Ones.

The Old Ones formed a circle around him, but he continued to watch Chevalier.

"Kak vas za vut?" he asked.

"I was known as Equitis…" Even his name made the Ancient hiss and crouch.

"Ne delaĭte etogo!"

Chevalier smiled and took a step toward him. "Why not? Who's going to stop us?"

The Ancient growled and lunged at Chevalier. Kyle sighed as his heku eyes couldn't catch what was going on. The other Old Ones stood back and watched the blur of fighting, so Kyle assumed that Chevalier was at least winning.

When the fighting stopped, Chevalier stood up from the pile of ash with an exhilarated look on his face. He smiled at the ash. "I'll tell Sotomar you said hello."

The closest Old One began to gather the ashes into a tiny bag. "Easy enough…"

"Easy?" Chevalier chuckled. "Bastard bit me."

Kyle grinned and shook his head as he followed Chevalier through

the wintry country, toward the waiting SUV.

***

"Feel better?" Emily asked as she looked down at the recovering heku.

Andrew nodded and then grasped his side and rolled onto his hands and knees.

Mark managed to crawl to his feet but was shaky and leaned against the wall for support.

"Want to explain that?" she asked, turning to Mark with her arms crossed.

Megara looked up at Mark and smiled. "You gots owie?"

"Not really worth explaining," he said, still trying to catch his breath.

"Fine then... I'll talk. We've been cooped up in this apartment for two months... this is the fourth fight, and I'm getting tired of it!"

"Em...," Andrew said as he managed to get to his feet. "We'll try, okay?"

"No, do better than try! Megara acts more mature than you two most of the time."

"Yeah," the toddler said, and then turned back to her dolls.

"He blamed the Equites for the first Punic war," Mark said, sitting down on the couch.

"If you hadn't helped capture Messana, that war wouldn't have even started."

"Well if the Encala had let us have that stronghold!"

"Stop it!" Emily yelled when the heku again began to get angry. "I don't even know what a Punic is, so drop it."

Andrew's eyes narrowed. "Eat and we'll drop it."

Mark smiled and looked over at her.

Emily rolled her eyes. "Get over it."

***

"I think I have this one," Kyle said, stepping forward. He looked down at the heku crouched beside a tall snow bank outside of the small Russian town of Naryan-Mar.

"Please..." he whispered, and held his hands up to block his head.

"You are just having one unlucky day, aren't you?" Chevalier asked the cowering heku.

"I didn't do it... I... I came to stop whoever is killing," he whimpered.

Kyle turned up the heku's collar, revealing the symbol of the Valle. "Well, I'm not picky about only punishing Equites."

"I didn't do it. You have to believe me."

"Your little thirst problem has us off of our mission to hunt down the Ancients, and chasing good-for nothing heku," one of the Old Ones hissed.

"I... I saw an Ancient... he did it," the heku whispered.

Kyle smiled. "Nice try."

Chevalier turned to one of the Old Ones. "You're the only Valle here... how long?"

He shrugged. "For sending us out to this God forsaken ball of ice? I'd say 700 years."

"What?!" the heku gasped, just as Kyle turned him to ash and scooped him into a bag. "This'd be much easier if we could just banish these here."

"You want to dig through the frozen ground?" Chevalier asked.

Kyle smiled. "No, not really."

"Get her!" one of the Old Ones shouted, and then disappeared. Kyle turned just as the rest of them blurred out of sight almost instantly. He sighed and followed them as fast as he could.

Kyle caught up with the others on a small icy road as they stood around one of the few female Ancients.

"Fancy meeting you here, Nyx. I thought you preferred the desert," one of the Old Ones said to her.

She looked at the heku around her with silver eyes and crouched slightly with her hands balled into fists.

"Equitis...," she hissed.

"You know better, Nyx," he said to her.

She stood tall and squared her shoulders as an evil grin formed across her cracked lips. "You won't kill me, my young lover."

Chevalier's eyes narrowed. "That was a long time ago."

Nyx took a step toward him. "Have you forgotten?"

"No, I haven't. That doesn't change the fact that you're to be put back into the ground for eternity."

"I still love you," she whispered, and blurred so she was standing against him with her hands on his chest and her head resting against his shoulder. "My precious boy."

Chevalier put a hand on each side of her shoulders and pushed her away from him. "I'm not interested in you."

"You and Nyx?" one of the Old Ones asked, highly amused.

Kyle chuckled softly from behind them.

Nyx reached up and put a dry, rough hand against his face softly. "We can have it all again, Equitis. We can make love in the blood of

fallen mortals…"

"Things have changed," he said, and moved a step back.

"You haven't changed," she whispered, and gently ran her hands along his chest.

Chevalier took her wrists in his hands. "Enough."

"Would you two like a moment alone?" another of the team asked, laughing.

"No, we're good."

"One moment alone is all it would take to show you how much I love you," she whispered, and began to kiss along his neck.

Chevalier hissed, "Would you do it already?"

The Old One beside him smiled. "I wouldn't want to break up this little love fest."

"Oh for hell's sake… banish her!"

Nyx whispered softly into his ear. "I can give you pleasures that no other can."

"Oh, do tell," Kyle said, smiling.

Chevalier grabbed her shoulders and spun her around to face the others after her hands trailed lower. "Do it."

She hissed, "Do not touch me! You owe us your existence."

"Yes, we do," the Old One said to her. "However, you're no longer wanted here."

She screamed moments before the heku turned her to ash. Kyle knelt and began to gather the ashes into a bag.

"You and Nyx? Seriously?" one of the team asked. "How did I not hear about that?"

Chevalier sighed, "It wasn't something we advertised."

"Does Em know?" Kyle asked as he stood up.

"No, she doesn't."

Kyle chuckled and walked past his Elder.

"She won't know… either," Chevalier said as he followed Kyle.

"I know."

"Where to now?" one of their team asked.

"Let's check in and see how many are left," Chevalier said, sliding into the driver's seat.

***

"Em?" Mark asked as he sat down on the bed beside Emily.

She looked over at him with tear filled eyes.

He smiled. "It'll be over soon."

"It's been three months."

"I know, but we'll be out of here before you know it."

She rolled onto her side, away from Mark, and wrapped her arms around a soft pillow. He watched her until she drifted off to sleep again and then stepped out into the living area.

"How is she?" Andrew asked as he gently rocked Megara.

"She cried herself to sleep."

"Did you talk her into eating?"

"No, it won't work."

"How does she survive doing that?" Andrew asked.

Mark shrugged. "She eats just enough to keep herself alive."

"I want Daddy," Megara said softly, and looked up at Andrew.

"I know," he said, and kissed her forehead lightly.

"Where he go?"

"He went to get rid of some bad heku."

"He okay?"

"Yes, he's fine."

"Where's Alex?"

"She's safe… I just don't know where she is."

Mark turned toward the security cameras when he saw movement. "William is here."

Andrew frowned. "Elder William?"

"Yes, but we can't let him in here."

"He knows that."

A few minutes later, Andrew moved over to the door when William called through to him.

"Elder, it's good to see you."

"I was just in Council City getting an update," William explained. "There are but three Ancients left, so it won't be long."

"That's great news, sir."

"How is she holding up?"

"She's not eating anymore, barely sleeps, and she cries a lot."

"In talking to Zohn, that is normal."

"It's disturbing, sir."

"I would imagine. Just stay put until two Elders come and release you."

"Yes, sir."

Andrew turned to Mark, and he nodded that he'd also heard.

***

The Old Ones gathered again in the arid desert in Iraq. Chevalier studied the reports from the other teams, as word came of how many losses.

"So we've lost 12 in the process?" Sotomar asked, checking over

the records.

Chevalier nodded. "Seems so."

"Dion, Xenocrates, and Gaspar are all that's left?"

"We've seen no sign of them," one of the gathered Old Ones told him.

Chevalier looked over across the desert and sighed, "I suspect they're either lying low or were killed, and we just don't know it."

Sotomar looked over at one of the Encala. "They were banished by the Encala, who failed to record their location."

His eyes narrowed. "Why would we write down where we banished them?"

Sotomar just shook his head and then turned back to Chevalier. "We may have to leave these three, with outstanding orders to dispose of them if they are ever seen."

"To come this far and not finish though," Chevalier sighed. "It seems incomplete."

"What do we do? We've checked everywhere we can think of for them."

"We may just have to wait until they cave and return to their ways of tormenting and hunting the mortals."

Sotomar looked across the gathered Old Ones, and sighed, "Very well."

"First, we need to decide what to do about the half-breed," one of the Old Ones said. "I have not forgotten that she attempted to destroy us with an Ancient incantation."

Chevalier looked over at him. "She has every right to defend herself against attacks."

"Not by using forbidden incantations!"

"She can use anything in her means."

"You're too close to her," another said. "We need an unbiased representative."

Sotomar's eyes narrowed. "Representative to do what, exactly?"

"She must be studied, and if deemed a threat, she must then be destroyed."

Chevalier growled.

"We cannot have a half-breed walking this planet," another said. "It's well known that the code states she should have been killed at birth."

"Well she wasn't," Sotomar said. "If we torment that child, kill that child, then we're no better than the Ancients we just banished."

"She's a threat to the heku!"

"No, she's not," Chevalier said. "She stays with me and only does harm to heku in self-defense."

"The ability alone poses a risk."

Sotomar put his hands up. "No one is going to hurt Emily."

"Why do you care, Valle?"

He smiled. "Emily is a friend to the Valle."

"Our Elders are protective of her also," one of the Encala said.

"You just don't know her," Kyle said. The others turned to him, insulted that he dared to speak. "If you met her, you would see why heku go to war for her."

"She's mostly mortal... there's no reason to keep her alive," one of the Valle said.

Chevalier turned on him. "You'll have to get past me."

He snarled. "When did Equitis stoop to bonding with a mortal?"

Another laughed. "Unless he gets his frustrations out on her also... a little mortal abuse to clear his head in the morning."

"You should smell her," one of Chevalier's team said. "I can see why he keeps her around."

"That's not...," Chevalier started.

"It's obvious that Chevalier and Sotomar are too attached to this mortal to be unbiased. The decision should be made by the majority of the Old Ones," one of them suggested.

"Meet her first," Kyle said. "Get to know her, and you'll see that she's not a threat."

"The young one has a point... let's meet her."

Chevalier frowned. "She's not going to do that."

"Why not?"

"She knows the Old Ones are after her."

"Demand it."

Kyle grinned slightly.

Chevalier glared. "I don't order her around... but I will see what I can do."

"Let's reconvene in Council City then," Sotomar said. "We'll see if we can get Emily to come talk to you."

Ovidius, quiet up until now, smiled. "I'd like to see her again. She's a charming child."

"You know her also?" the heku closest to him asked.

"Yes, I have met her, and I agree with the young heku."

Kyle sighed. He was getting tired of being referred to as young when he was well over 1600-years-old.

***

Emily rolled over and looked at the clock. She'd tossed and turned for hours, and decided that even though it was only 2am, it was time to

get up. She checked on Megara, who was asleep in a crib beside the bed, before throwing on jeans and a t-shirt and stepping out into the living area.

She gasped and looked wide-eyed around the destroyed room. The furniture was turned over, and pieces of broken decorations were tossed around the room. The computer monitors, showing the surveillance cameras around the house, were all that was left untouched, and they lit up in the dark room.

"Mark?" Emily whispered as she braced herself for an attack.

"I'm okay," he groaned, and stood up from behind where the couch used to be.

Her eyes narrowed as she took in the vicious gash across his shirtless torso and the bites on his arm. "Were you attacked?"

"Yes," he whispered, and flipped over a chair, so he could sit down.

"Where's Andrew?"

"Dead I hope."

"I'm not dead," Andrew hissed, and slowly got to his feet.

"You two were fighting again?" Emily growled.

"It's kind of hard to explain."

"No, it's not! You two are worse than children."

"Em...," Mark said, but then turned to the cameras. "Someone's in the house."

"Who?" she asked, looking over the monitor. Nothing could be seen in the dark mansion.

"I heard it too," Andrew said, moving up to them.

Mark and Andrew both spun and faced the door to the panic room. Emily stood slowly and turned also.

"Who is it?" she whispered.

Mark smiled. "Elder Chevalier and Sotomar."

"Chev...," Emily gasped, and ran to the door. She started punching in the numbers, but Andrew took her arm.

"Wait"

"No! Let me go."

"We don't know what they want yet."

"I don't really care. Let me go or I'll ash you."

"It's okay... things are clear," Mark told Andrew. He nodded and let go of her. With shaking fingers, Emily managed to unlock the door and then ran into Chevalier's arms.

He held her tightly and lightly kissed the top of her head. "It's okay."

Her tears saturated his shirt as he listened to Mark give a report on the last three months. Andrew went to get the baby and came back out with her asleep in his arms.

Emily finally composed herself and whispered against Chevalier's chest, "Imprison both of them."

He frowned. "Who?"

"Mark and Andrew," she said, looking up at him.

"What did you do?" he asked, angrily studying them.

Mark's eyes grew wide. "Nothing! Why, Em?"

Emily took the baby from Andrew and then started for the stairs. "Just do it."

"We can't just throw Mark in jail," Chevalier said as he followed her. "What did they do?"

"What didn't they do?!" she screamed, turning toward him. "They fought, bickered, bitched, moaned, tore up the apartment, fought again, and were royal pains in the ass."

Sotomar chuckled. "We can't imprison them for being heku."

Emily glared at him and walked toward the kitchen.

"Em… there's one thing," Chevalier said as he took her arm to stop her from walking.

"What?"

He glanced nervously at Sotomar and then back to Emily. "The Old Ones want to see you."

Her grip tightened on Megara. "Why?"

"They are curious."

"No"

Sotomar cleared his throat. "It's not really an option, dear. They want you killed, and we hope if they meet you, it will change their minds."

"They still want to kill me?" she asked, looking up at Chevalier.

"Yes, but we really think if they can see you, talk to you, that they will calm down."

Her eyes turned to panic. "I'll stay hidden…"

"You can't live in the panic room. It'll be okay," Chevalier told her.

"We'll be there," Mark said.

"No, you won't," Sotomar said to him. "This would be only for Old Ones."

"I can't, Chev," Emily whispered.

"Why?" he asked, gently touching her face.

"If they… if they try to kill me and I ash them… I'll be…"

"We won't bury you again, and they won't attack."

Sotomar smiled. "Chevalier and I will be with you at all times. We've already made preparations for if there are problems."

"Well I don't like this," Andrew hissed.

"You don't have a choice," Sotomar told him bluntly.

"Chev, I can't…"

"We'll be there. I swear."

"As will I," Andrew told them as he crossed his arms. "You two aren't my Elders, and I was told to stay with Emily."

"Do not interfere here," Mark growled at him.

Andrew spun to face him. "Are you going to stop me?"

When the fight started, Emily sighed and looked up at Chevalier. "See…"

Sotomar chuckled. "They really don't care for each other, do they?"

"Will you stop them, please?"

Sotomar reached in and pulled out Andrew, as Chevalier restrained Mark.

"As much fun as that was, please refrain from killing each other in front of Emily," Chevalier said, obviously amused.

"Stop interfering with Emily's care!" Mark yelled.

"I do what I want," Andrew growled at him.

Emily sighed, "Put them in prison, and I'll go to your meeting."

"Really?" Chevalier asked, shocked.

"Yes… I can't go to a meeting if I think these two are killing each other."

Sotomar shrugged. "Deal."

"Wait! You can't imprison me," Mark said.

"You have no right to imprison an Encala!" Andrew yelled.

"That's the deal," Emily said, and grabbed a new bag for Megara before walking out into the darkness of night.

***

"Why is our General in prison?" Quinn asked when Sotomar, Emily, and Chevalier walked up to the grand hall entrance.

"I'll explain later… though he's not a criminal," Chevalier said.

Zohn sighed, "You sure we can't be in there?"

"No, things might be said that are not for your ears."

Sotomar opened the door and slipped inside before shutting it behind him. Emily tried to see inside the grand hall but wasn't able to because the lights were off.

"I'll take Megs," McIntock said from behind Emily. She handed the toddler over and then turned toward the door.

"I don't want to walk past them all," she said.

"We'll go around back," Chevalier told her as he took her hand. "Sotomar's already waiting for us up front."

She nodded and let him lead her around to the back. When he held open the door for her, she wrapped her arms around herself and walked into the dark room. The whispers stopped, and an eerie silence fell over

the large room.

Emily started to panic almost immediately when the stage lights turned on, and she saw Sotomar standing mid-stage, smiling at her.

"Come on, it's okay," Chevalier said, gently pushing her forward.

When Emily caught sight of General Meun from Samuel Coven, the heku that was brought in by Dustin to find Frederick's location, she turned suddenly and came face-to-face with Chevalier.

"No one's here to hurt you," he said, and gently took her arm. He turned her around and forced her to walk to Sotomar.

"This is how it will be done," Sotomar said. "Any break in these rules and we'll stop the questioning, and you will be required to return to your covens."

Chevalier eyed them all carefully. Emily could feel that his body was tense and ready for any hostility.

"Ovidius will be the only heku asking Lady Emily questions," Sotomar explained. "You will direct questions to him in tones too low for Emily to hear. She will not be threatened or yelled at. That's a solid order from all three factions."

Ovidius stepped forward and smiled at Emily. She tightened her arms around herself and glanced back at the door.

He frowned slightly when Emily reached up and wiped a tear away from her cheek with shaking hands.

"Dear… you're safe here," Ovidius said to her. "We just have some questions."

"They want to kill me," she whispered to him, and her voice shook with fear.

"They just want to speak to you, child."

She nodded and then checked to make sure Chevalier was close.

Ovidius stood still for a moment before speaking. "When did you first realize that you were the daughter of an Ancient?"

Emily swallowed dryly before answering. "I was 28. He was channeling through the heku to try to kill me."

"And who was that Ancient?"

"I don't…"

"It was Arrianus," Sotomar told them.

Ovidius nodded. "Was your mother aware that you belonged to an Ancient?"

"No," Emily said, starting to get a little braver. "She didn't know what a heku even was. We thought our attacks were from vampires."

There were chuckles among the Old Ones and then Ovidius nodded. "Very well. Where is Arrianus?"

Emily touched her locket slightly. "I ashed him."

Chevalier silenced the crowd when they began to talk loudly. "No

more warnings… keep it down."

"What gives you the ability to turn a heku to ash?" Ovidius asked.

Emily shrugged. "It's something about my family's blood mixed with that of a heku."

"How many heku have you turned to ash?"

"I haven't counted."

"Can we see it?"

"No!" she yelled, and took a step back.

Sotomar smiled. "Lady Emily doesn't turn a heku to ash without reason and hesitates to do so even then."

Ovidius looked at her. "But you can turn more than one to ash at a time?"

She nodded.

"How many?"

"I don't know," she whispered. She was afraid if they knew how many, they might see more of a reason to kill her.

"You are in full control?"

"Yes"

Ovidius listened for a moment and then addressed her. "Have you ever killed a heku accidentally?"

"Not a heku, no."

"But another?"

"I can't help it," she whispered.

Chevalier held up his hand to stop Ovidius. "Emily negatively affects the turning process. It's a proximity effect that kills the mortal involved."

"I see… now we want to talk about the incantation you used to put Old Ones to sleep," Ovidius said. "Where did you learn it?"

"From the vault Ancient," she said, unconsciously stepping closer to Chevalier.

"How did you converse with him?"

"I just… heard him and then I fell down the hole."

Chevalier couldn't help but smile when the heku started to laugh.

Ovidius smiled. "You are very small, dear."

Emily frowned slightly but kept her comments to herself.

"What other incantations did he tell you?" Ovidius asked. Emily again started to panic when the room fell silent.

"He… well he told me Aboleo, the one I used… and the Renovare and…," Emily said, and then stopped and looked up at Chevalier.

"What?" he whispered.

Emily reached up and whispered into his year. "He told me about Yisolatara."

Chevalier turned to the others. "He told her about one which we no

longer say."

Emily tried to slow her breathing. "Then… the retirement and waking up the retired… I think that's all."

"Anything other than incantations?" Ovidius asked.

"Yes, he told me how the Ancients were planning on getting rid of all heku and starting over."

Ovidius gasped. "They were?"

She nodded. "Yes, but then you all banished them before they could do it."

Sotomar looked out over the crowd. "That shouldn't surprise us. They were as unhappy with how we had evolved, as we were with their actions."

"Why should you be allowed to live?" Ovidius asked her. "When you are obviously half Ancient."

Emily frowned. "That's not my fault."

"It doesn't matter."

"You're half Ancient," Emily said to him, and then crossed her arms.

He smiled. "You're comparing yourself to an Old One?"

"No, not at all. It's just that I shouldn't be punished for this."

"If not punished, at least expelled from living with the heku."

"But…" she said with a cracking voice, "I'm not mortal either."

"Yet you are not heku."

"I know that… I'm caught in the middle."

"Such an abomination should not be allowed to live!" The strange voice rang out through the dark audience.

"We warned you!" Sotomar yelled. "You will obey the rules or get out."

"No, it's okay," Emily said, putting a hand on his arm. She looked toward where the voice came from. "I'm sorry that I am the product of an Ancient, but that's not my fault. No, I'm not worthy to live among the heku. I've never claimed to be. I don't know where else to go though. I'm not aging. I heal when I shouldn't, but I'm still mortal. I'm too mortal for the heku world, too heku for the mortal world."

"Do you drink blood?" Ovidius asked.

"No," she said, stepping back to Chevalier.

"Have you tried it?"

"Yes"

Ovidius nodded. "Yes, she did come back from death."

She watched as he answered what he knew.

"She does sustain injury from things we do not."

Sotomar smiled at Emily and then turned to Ovidius.

"The rate of healing is substantially slower."

It was quite a while later that Sotomar turned to Emily. "They want to know what it is you want."

"Want? What do you mean?"

"What is your purpose with the heku?"

She glanced up at Chevalier, and he nodded and smiled.

"I... the Equites have taken me in. They are my family, my friends, and my entire world," she said. Although timid, her voice carried easily to the gathered heku, "I don't know why they keep me, other than everyone's afraid of Chev."

Sotomar chuckled, and turned to the gathered. "That would be Equitis."

"My husband is Equites, and my children have sworn their allegiance to them also... except Megara, that is..."

"She's only 3-years-old," Chevalier explained.

"What do I want? I want everyone to go back to the way they were and forget about me. I want to get on with my life and not fear that I'll meet one of you in a dark alley. I want to know that my children are safe, and that you aren't going to try to kill them either. I also want to make sure that none of you will harm the Equites because I'm here."

"Em... for hell's sake... stop protecting us," Chevalier said. His words were mad, but his voice was kind and caring.

She ignored him and continued. "The Valle and the Encala are my friends, and I don't want them hurt because of that either. I'm not going to threaten you. I'm not going to hurt you or seek you out... unless you mess with someone I care about."

Sotomar turned to her, amused. "We can protect ourselves also."

"How can we protect ourselves?" Ovidius asked. "You have the ability to summon us and either turn us to ash or knock us unconscious at will."

"I do... but I'm not going to."

"How can we know that?"

She shrugged. "I don't know. I can assure you I won't be doing Aboleo again... it not only hurt the ones that were after me, but it hurt two Old Ones that I care very much about."

Sotomar smiled broadly.

"I understand my mistake, one which took an Ancient to fix... one that then caused all of this. I get into trouble a lot. That's not going to stop, but I'll stop sticking my nose into heku business."

Chevalier looked over the crowd. "Not to mention... to get to Emily, you have to get through me."

"And me," Sotomar said.

Ovidius stepped down and moved to the stage. "I stand by her also."

Chevalier's eyes narrowed when General Meun stepped up to the

platform and took Ovidius' place. Emily moved closer to Chevalier and gripped his arm tightly.

"Into trouble a lot? Why don't we address some of those issues before we all get feeling warm and fuzzy about this nuisance?" General Meun said, glaring at Emily.

"Meun...," Chevalier growled.

"Let's start by addressing Emily turning an enemy Elder to ash and then hiding the ashes and keeping them for 16 months as a punishment."

"She's already paid dearly for that," Sotomar shouted. Gasps and talking sounded through the gathered heku.

"I'm sorry," Emily whispered, and gripped tighter to Chevalier.

"Shall we then talk about how she went behind the Equites' backs and joined up with the Encala to exterminate a rogue coven?"

"Stop it," Chevalier hissed at him.

General Meun smiled. "Let them hear it all..."

"You're treading on very thin ice."

"Should we also bring to light when she threatened all three factions with an ultimatum? They were to play nice in the sandbox, or she would disappear and take the heku children with her," Meun continued. "Or how about because of an infatuation with her, a fourth faction was established... one that continually destroyed heku until we... again... had to intervene to stop it."

"This is absurd," Sotomar told him calmly. "None of this has anything to do with this gathering."

"Let him keep going!" a voice shouted from the back. "We're hearing what we need to know."

"Why do you need to know this?" Chevalier asked, obviously furious.

"To make a decision... an educated decision... on how to handle the half-breed," Meun answered.

Emily gasped and turned to run, but Chevalier took her hand and smiled at her. "I won't let it happen."

"Let them get out frustrations," Sotomar said to her. "We won't allow them to harm you."

Meun grinned maliciously. "The half-breed also played a joke on the Equites' Council that took two months of their time... two entire months."

A murmur ran through the heku.

Chevalier chuckled. "That was payment for something we did to her. There was no harm in that."

"Using Emily's abilities... the Valle wiped out many Equites and Encala covens. So she lied... she has turned heku to ash against her will."

"That's different," Sotomar growled.

"Nonetheless, she did," Meun said, pleased at the angry responses he heard from behind him. "She's too dangerous to live. Had the ancient ritual been successful, she would have been turned heku... as a monster."

Emily panicked and tried to pull away from Chevalier, but he held tightly.

Sotomar's eyes narrowed. "You cannot blame her for that. Her abilities kept it from happening so even if it's tried again, it won't work."

"Another point. Try to turn her and she massively puts heku to sleep for months! She's a danger."

"Not if heku stop trying to turn her," Chevalier said.

Meun's grin broadened. "She attempted to destroy a ceremonial room with a sledge hammer."

Irate shouts were heard among gasps and talking.

Chevalier's hands tightened into fists. "Stop it, or so help me Meun, I'll destroy you."

Sotomar stepped forward. "This is all true... What Meun is leaving out are the good things that Emily has done."

"Such as?" a voice asked from the darkness.

Sotomar smiled. "She's saved the species... the entire species... twice."

"How?"

"When the rogue fourth faction took over the Valle Council, imprisoning Elders from all factions... she risked her life to rescue us. She was in a coma for three months because of that."

"What's the second time?"

Sotomar looked at Emily with great admiration. "Emily risked her own life to infiltrate the V.E.S. and destroy evidence that the vampire exists. She then brought out the heku that were imprisoned by the cult. She's shown the heku an entirely new world... one with caring, compassion, and selflessness. She's united the three factions as no other has and brought years of peace."

"Some of us don't like peace," Meun hissed.

"She's been kidnapped and tortured beyond what even heku can imagine. She's been tormented, gone through pain and suffering, and been persecuted by heku since she found out about us," Sotomar said. "Yet this child has chosen to not only stay with the heku but has taken it upon herself to protect the species."

Meun started to laugh. "This puny being cannot protect us."

"That's not the point. Mortals hate us... they seek us out, make movies about their hatred... but this one... she's different..."

"She stays with the heku because we give her everything she wants!

She's nothing but a spoiled child."

"She takes very little," Chevalier said. "It's sometimes irritating how little she takes from me, and I'm her husband. She keeps her small bank account and uses it only. I'd love nothing more than to buy her the world..., but she won't take it."

"We give her protection..."

"She usually protects herself, much to my displeasure."

"Enough," Emily whispered. The entire room fell suddenly silent, and all eyes turned to her. "You don't have to do this. I won't stand here and watch the species fall apart because I'm here..."

"Damnit, Em," Chevalier growled. "Why do I have the feeling you're about to try to protect us again?"

"I have a home of my own now... I have money... I'll leave the heku, if you'll leave Chevalier and Sotomar alone over this," she said softly.

"No"

"Emily, don't do this," Sotomar said to her.

She shrugged. "If the Old Ones will promise to leave them alone, then I'll promise to stay in my home in the mortal city and not bother the heku again."

"No," Chevalier said again, eyeing General Meun angrily.

Meun's eyes narrowed. "That's not good enough."

"Then what do you want from me?" Emily asked him.

"Death," he hissed.

Sotomar smiled. "Seems you're out numbered."

Emily looked at him, confused. She hadn't heard anyone say anything against the General.

General Meun glared at her. "This isn't over."

The General stepped down, and Sotomar went to the front of the stage. "This questioning is over. Emily is under the protection of all three Councils. We order no retaliation against her, and no Old One will even contact her without the explicit authorization from Chevalier."

Emily looked up at Chevalier, and he was carefully scanning the heku.

"There are still three Ancients out there," Sotomar continued. "Watch for signs of them. They will surface soon enough. Retirements are set up for those that have requested it. The others may return to their covens."

Emily watched as the Old Ones left the Equites' great hall. When it was empty, Sotomar turned and smiled at Emily. "You did brilliantly, my dear."

Emily was finding it hard to breathe. The massive room began to close in on her, and she pulled away from Chevalier.

"It's okay, Em," Chevalier told her. "The ones that left here against you were minor, and General Meun is already facing the Council."

"I can't stay here," she whispered, and took a step backwards toward the stage door.

"What's wrong?" Sotomar asked. "They aren't mad at you."

Emily spun and ran from the room.

Chevalier sighed, "She takes things very personally."

Sotomar nodded. "She still thinks we're in danger for having her with the heku."

"Yes, she does."

"So will she disappear?"

"I'm not sure."

Sotomar heard the Cavalry call to the Council that Emily was out on horseback and had threatened to turn anyone to ash that followed her.

"I need to go deal with Meun," Chevalier said, and then turned to Sotomar.

He nodded. "My helicopter is waiting."

Emily flew through the trees. The only way to clear her mind was with the feel of the horse beneath her and the wind in her hair. She let the stallion lead the way as he wove in and out of the dense forest as tears streamed down her face.

She hated that the Old Ones wanted her dead. She knew most would return to retirement, but that left some, and she was afraid that they would attack the Equites to get to her.

***

Chevalier sat down, and his features let the Council know how furious he was with General Meun. The General stood in the trial area and glared at Chevalier.

Zohn turned to the General. "Okay, now. Why are you here?"

"I would imagine for picking on the little mortal," General Meun said sarcastically.

"Watch it," Kyle hissed.

"Have you forgotten who we are?" Quinn asked, glaring at him.

"No, sir, I haven't," Meun said.

Zohn turned to Chevalier. "What are we talking to him about?"

"He tried to rally the Old Ones to kill Emily."

"Why would you do that?" Quinn asked him.

Meun stared at Chevalier. "Because she needs to die for crimes against the heku."

"I'm actually quite surprised at the things you told the gathering," Chevalier said to him. "How do you even know about Emily trying to

destroy a ceremonial room?"

"Dustin told me."

"So you and Dustin were…"

"Vying to get rid of the bitch, until she died, that is."

"Interesting," Zohn said.

"I've heard enough," Quinn said. "I say 600 years."

"Ditto," Zohn said.

Chevalier kept quiet and watched Kyle banish the Old One.

"Now bring in Mark," the Chief of Staff said.

Mark came in with four guards around him and smiled sheepishly at the Council.

Chevalier chuckled. "Let him go."

"Why was he in prison?" Zohn asked. The guards around Mark disappeared and left him alone in the trial area.

"I think he and Andrew had some problems in the panic room, and Emily was irritated with that," Chevalier said.

"That heku is annoying," Mark told them. "Several times I had to put him in his place."

Zohn smiled. "I can see how that might have been needed."

"He loves her," Mark said, looking at Chevalier.

He nodded. "I figured as much. Did he act on that?"

"No"

"Then let him go," Chevalier said. "I'll tell Em we couldn't hold them just because they fought."

Several minutes later, Andrew appeared beside Mark in the trial area. "You can't hold me."

"We aren't going to," Chevalier told him. "We did as Emily asked and consider time spent in prison to be enough."

Andrew smiled. "Yes, I learned my lesson in the four hour prison sentence."

Mark chuckled.

"I'll chastise you then," Quinn said, and looked over at them. "Next time you two are alone in the panic room with Emily, please refrain from fighting."

"Yes, Elder," Mark said, stifling a grin.

Andrew shrugged. "It helped pass the time."

"Your Council has requested that you return," the Chief of Defense said to him.

Andrew nodded and then left the trial room.

Mark sighed, "Silas said she's out alone."

"Yes," Chevalier replied. "It was a rough few hours."

"What was decided?"

"They decided to leave her alone."

Chapter 15

Emily was just sitting down to make coffee when she heard the doorbell ring. She put her cup in the sink and then went to see who it was. The Cavalry only let certain people onto the property and had set up a security desk to appear as mortal security.

Alec was just shutting the door when Emily arrived.

"Who was it?" she asked.

"It's a package for you from the Encala," Alec told her, and then handed her the heavy box.

"Oh good."

"What is it?"

She just watched him as she disappeared into her office on the second floor and locked the door behind her. She'd been waiting patiently for the package William promised her, and she quickly tore it open and lifted out the massive 3-ring binder.

Emily sat down on an overstuffed chair and began going through the binder, which listed all known Ancients, their abilities, and personal things about them. She was warned by William that if any Equites caught her with the information, they would take it away, so she was in a hurry to get through as much as she could before someone found out.

The files were interesting. She was amazed at some of the abilities the Ancients possessed and how few of them had abilities. She knew most didn't, most were just powerful heku, but those that did were intensely frightening.

The hours poured by quickly as she delved through the files of the Ancient heku. She spent an extra-long time on her father's file. Because the files came from the Encala, they mentioned his time as an Elder and his encounters with Emily's mother, though there was nothing about her heritage or any information about producing children. It wasn't until the last notation that Emily was even brought into the file. She found it interesting how casually the Encala were going to accept her into the faction when they found out their Ancient had a child that wasn't immediately killed, as tradition dictated.

Emily was so engrossed in the files that she jumped when someone knocked.

After calming her voice, she called out, "Who is it?"

"It's Chevalier."

She stood up and quickly locked the binder in her small safe before going to the door and stepping out.

"Hi," she said, smiling up at him.

He chuckled. "What did you hide?"

"I didn't hide anything."

"So I didn't hear the dial on your safe?"

She sighed, "Stop being nosey."

"I wasn't being nosey. It's not my fault if I can hear that," he said, and took her hand.

"Well… yes, I hid something. Just stay out of my office."

"I will… is it dangerous?"

"No"

"Fine… come sit down in my office," Chevalier said, and then headed to the office she made for him in the mansion.

She sighed, "Am I in trouble?"

"No"

Emily stepped into the office and sat down in the overstuffed chair she'd put in there just for her use. "So what's up?"

Chevalier sat down beside her and looked into her eyes. "Want to talk about why you called the Valle?"

Her eyes narrowed. "How do you know I did that?"

"Sotomar called me."

"Did he tell you why?"

"No, he said it was personal."

"If it was so personal, why did he call you?"

"He felt it was dangerous."

Emily crossed her arms. "So you don't even know why I called but are bringing it up because Sotomar said it's dangerous?"

"Yes"

"It's not."

Chevalier smiled slightly. "So tell me why you called them."

"No, it's none of your business."

"I know you called William next."

"He told you that?!"

"No, when I called, he denied it…"

"But you pulled my phone records."

Chevalier tried to take her hand, but she pulled it away from him. He studied her before replying. "I'm worried about it."

"Don't be."

"Sotomar doesn't like me. If he told me you're in danger, then I have to take that seriously."

"Maybe he's just trying to cause problems."

"I didn't get that impression."

Emily gasped. "You had Richard listen in?"

"He's the Chief Interrogator for a reason… I needed to know if what Sotomar was saying was true."

"Don't use your little Council against me!"

"Stop, right now," Chevalier said sternly. "I'm not picking a fight.

I'm concerned, and I have to use everything available to me to find out how to protect you."

"Stop putting your energy into protecting me and focus on the Council."

"We're not...

"I know the former Council is trying to gather supporting covens..."

"How do you even know that?" he asked, getting irritated.

"I know they aren't gaining ground, which is making them mad."

"Still..."

"No, they're serious. You're looking for danger where there is none and ignoring the danger right in front of you."

"We're not ignoring it."

Her eyes narrowed. "If you don't take care of them, then I'll have to."

Chevalier hissed softly.

Emily took a deep breath. "I'm just saying that I'm fine. Stop worrying about me calling the Encala. I call them all the time."

"Yes, but you don't normally get a package from them."

"Damnit, stop it!"

"What was it?"

"Divorce papers... now go away," she said, and angrily stood up and left the room.

Chevalier followed her out but was blocked from the stairs by Alec.

"She wants to be alone," Alec said as he crossed his arms.

"Do not, ever, get in my way," Chevalier growled.

"Emi needs to be alone. If you keep pushing, she'll take off to get away from you, and you know it."

Chevalier disappeared from in front of Alec and reappeared in his office. He slammed the door shut and sat down to call the Encala.

"Encala Council," Elder Iuna said.

"What did you send Emily in the mail?" Chevalier asked.

"Why don't you ask her?" William suggested.

"No, tell me."

"I don't have to tell you."

"Was it dangerous?"

"No"

"You're sure? She has a way of making things dangerous."

William chuckled. "That I can see... but no. It's not dangerous, or we would have accompanied it with a guard."

"She's not yours to protect."

"That's not your decision to make."

Chevalier slammed the phone down and then thought for a moment before calling Dain into the office.

"Yeah, Dad?" Dain asked, sitting down across from him.

"The Encala sent your mom a package."

He frowned. "What was in it?"

"I was hoping you knew."

"I didn't even know she had a package. I know she's been in her office for a while though."

"If I get Em out of here, will you go in there and find it?"

"No"

"What do you mean, no?" Chevalier asked, irritated.

"I mean I'm not going to make her mad."

"She won't even know."

"Oh, she'll know," Dain said, standing up. "I'm not going to risk being kicked out of here. Who would watch Alec?"

"Damnit, why is everyone else always trying to protect her?"

"Because you're seldom here."

Chevalier glared at him. "Get out of my sight."

Dain shrugged and blurred away.

***

Emily was curled up with the binder when she finally came across the Ancient she was looking for. She sat up straighter and carefully read through the file on Paian, the Ancient that had the ability to reattach a heku's head and bring them back to life.

Her heart almost stopped when she read the last passage.

> *Paian seems to prefer reviving deceased heku that can cause problems with enemies of the Valle. Though never sworn in as a Valle, he seems to favor them. Just before being banished beneath the Equites Palace, Paian had just revived a slain heku that had once tried to usurp power from the Equites Council. ~Equitis, Chief Enforcer of the Equites*

Emily looked around her office as she tried to decide what to do. There was one good way for the Valle to get revenge on the Equites, and she figured it was her job to make sure Paian hadn't done it while he was revived. She'd called the Valle to see if Sotomar would tell her about the Ancient that could revive the dead, but he refused to answer her questions, including whether he had been awakened by Thutmose.

The Encala, because no Old One was on their Council, wasn't sure if he'd been awakened but finally relented in sending her all they knew about the Ancients. The binder they'd sent her was compiled by an Old One in the Valle and given to each of the factions, to be kept secret in

case the need arose to someday revive the Ancients.

Emily knew if she was going to do this, it was going to have to be now while Chevalier and Kyle were both with the Council. One of them was normally at the house with her, but the current trial was important enough that both had to be there. She also suspected that Mark was involved in the trial, as she hadn't seen him in a few days either.

Deciding it had to be done to protect herself, her family, and the Equites, Emily picked up the phone and called the Encala.

"Council," Elder Iuna said.

"Hi, it's Emily."

"Well, hello, child."

"Is William around?"

"I'm here. Are you well?" William asked.

"Yes, but I need another favor that needs to be kept from the Equites."

William chuckled. "Trying to cause tension, are we?"

"No, not at all. This is a big one though."

"What do you need?"

"I need to know the location of the coven that tried to turn me into..." She paused, knowing how badly heku reacted to the word. "Turn me into a Yisolatara."

As expected, the Encala Council burst out into angry talking.

"Please, William...," Emily said after she let them vent for a few minutes.

"Why do you need to know that?"

"I can't tell you, but I do."

"He wasn't revived."

Emily sighed when she realized William had pieced together prior requests to figure out what she wanted.

"I have to check."

"Then I'll send someone to see."

"No, it has to be me."

"Why?" Elder Iuna asked.

"I'm the only one that can stop him if he's back," she whispered.

William was no longer amused. "Stop trying to protect the Encala!"

"If he's back... I need to do this."

"He wasn't revived. The Ancient you asked about wouldn't have even heard of Exavior, let alone know that he's an enemy of yours."

"I have to know."

"It's too dangerous," William said softly.

"You said he's not been revived. How can it be dangerous to go to the cave and see?"

"That is true."

"I'll take guards. I swear."

"I guess there's no harm in it then."

Emily was relieved when he finally relented and told her the location of the caves in Wyoming. Now she just had to fulfill her promise and take guards, but she needed ones that wouldn't stop her.

She walked out of her room when she heard Megara talking to Dain in the hallway.

"It's about time you poke your head out," Dain said as he picked up the toddler.

Emily smiled, trying to hide her concern. "Sorry about that. Can you do me a favor and take Megs over to Chev for a bit?"

Dain shrugged. "I guess."

"Daddy!" Megara squealed, and then pointed at the door. "Go."

Emily smiled. Megara had always shown a strong attachment to her dad.

"I thought Dad was busy with some trial or something," Dain said.

She shrugged. "Guess he's done for a bit. I just need a few minutes alone to go over some stuff."

"Now?"

"Yes, please."

Dain sighed and then nodded. "Sure thing."

Megara was obviously excited as Dain carried her out of the house. As soon as Dain's truck left the driveway, Emily walked out of the house and locked it behind her.

"Who's out here?" she asked into the empty lot.

Six members of the Cavalry stepped out from around the building and met up with her. She didn't recognize five of them, but one was Gifford, from Thukil.

"Is there a problem?" a strange Commander asked her. He quickly surveyed the area.

"Not at all," she said, smiling. "I'm heading into town and want to take two of you with me."

He frowned. "You're offering to take guards?"

"Sure"

"Fine, I'll go with…"

"No, that one," she said, pointing to a newer member of the Cavalry.

"Me? Ma'am?" he asked, shocked.

She noticed another very new heku and pointed at him. "You… are going."

"Why can't I go?" the top-ranking heku asked.

"Because I'm a member of the Council, and I say those two go," she said, crossing her arms.

He snarled. "Fine."

Emily walked to the garage, and one guard opened the door for her. He looked at his Commander and then shut the door and got into the Jeep. She headed out of the garage and fought to keep her hands from shaking. She was afraid she'd find Exavior revived and wasn't sure she could survive an encounter with him. She knew she was willing to do whatever it took to take him out.

"I thought we were just going into town," one heku asked from the passenger seat.

Emily smiled and held out her hand. "Phones please."

"Why?"

"Don't ask me why!" she yelled. "Hand them over."

He sighed and handed his cell phone to her, as did the heku in the back seat. He wasn't at all surprised when she tossed them both out of the window.

The heku smiled when Emily looked at him but spoke too low for her to hear when she turned away. "When we get back, let's suggest to Mark that the Council do something with the phone habit."

The heku in the back seat agreed and then sat back, wondering what was in store for them.

"Where are you from?" she asked the heku in the passenger seat.

"Shaw Coven, ma'am."

"What's your name?" Emily asked after about an hour of driving in silence.

"Robin, ma'am."

She sighed, "Stop with the Ma'am thing. I quit the Cavalry."

"You're a member of the Council."

"Fine, then I order you to call me Emily."

"Can I speak openly?"

"Please do."

"Where are we going?"

"Wyoming"

"Why?"

"I don't want you to know yet," she said, and then glanced back at the heku in the back seat.

"So it's dangerous?"

"Maybe"

"Then if we're being completely open," the heku in back said. "You're going to get us banished."

"No, I won't. I've done this before, and the Council knows you don't have a choice."

"Are you just going to drop us off in the middle of nowhere?"

"No, you're going with me."

"But we won't know where," Robin said.

"Right"

"Two years on the Cavalry, and I'll be banished," the back seat one mumbled.

"What's your name?" Emily asked.

"Elliott"

"Where's your home coven?"

"Powan"

"Oh, you're a wolf?"

"You could say that."

"Good to know, may come in handy."

"How so?"

***

"That was how long ago?" Chevalier asked the highest ranking of the Cavalry at Emily's house. He shifted Megara to his other arm, so she wasn't in between him and the Commander.

"It was four hours ago, sir."

"Why did no one notify me?"

"Orders are to notify you of anything suspicious. She just wanted to go into town for a bit."

"With two guards… that she picked!"

"Nothing on their cell phones," Silas said, blurring up. "My guess is she tossed them out of the window."

"We need to stop that," Kralen hissed.

Kyle joined them on the lawn. "She called the Encala just before leaving."

Chevalier sighed, and looked around the lawn. "She hasn't taken off like this since before her death."

"I'm guessing she felt it was important."

"What did the Encala say?"

Kyle shrugged. "The usual… they said it wasn't dangerous, and they won't say."

Chevalier turned to Kralen and Silas. "Search her office."

They both bowed and then disappeared from the lawn.

Megara laid her head gently against Chevalier's shoulder and smiled at Kyle. "It's my daddy."

Kyle smiled, again amazed at how much she looked like Emily. "Yes, it is."

"He's mad at Mommy."

Kyle chuckled while Chevalier moved Megara, so she could see him. "Do you know where Mommy went?"

Megara nodded and put her tiny hands on Chevalier's face. "She went bye-bye."

"Do you know where though?"

The toddler wrapped her arms around her dad's neck and shook her head. "Just bye-bye."

Chevalier went back inside when a cool breeze came up. Megara shivered in his arms and then looked over when he stepped into the warm house.

He set her on the floor and then started for Emily's office.

"Hey!" Megara shouted.

Chevalier turned and then smiled when he saw her frowning. "What?"

She held her hands up and waited for him.

Kyle chuckled as Chevalier returned to the toddler and picked her up. She smiled at him and then went with Chevalier into Emily's office.

Her attachment to her dad was starting to worry some of the Council. He seemed intent on spoiling her and giving her anything she wanted, and Megara was turning into a demanding toddler. They suspected that Chevalier gave the 3-year-old things that he wished Emily would take and lavished her with expensive gifts and a lot of attention.

"Find anything?" Chevalier asked, walking into her office.

Kralen looked up. "Nothing yet. We're almost in the safe though."

Silas was knelt down by the safe and had one ear pressed close to the dial. Within a few minutes, he'd managed to crack the safe and opened it. He immediately began emptying its contents.

Kralen first picked up the large binder and then sighed and looked over at Chevalier. "This is a copy of the Ancient Registry."

He growled and put Megara down, despite her protests, then began going through it. "Damnit! How would she get this?"

"Encala would be my guess," Silas said as he looked over the other things in her safe.

"So much for staying out of heku business."

"What is this?" Silas asked, holding up a warped book.

Chevalier took it and couldn't help but smile. "The first time I ever saw Em, she was in the bathtub. I startled her, and she dropped this book into the water. Odd she kept it."

Kralen chuckled. "Go figure… the first time you saw her, she was naked."

Chevalier smiled and handed the book back. "What else is in there?"

"Some old, dirty, Island Coven shirt," Silas said, and handed it over to Chevalier.

He smelled it and frowned. "This is mine."

"Why would she have that?"

"Not a clue."

"My guess would be from the crypt," Kyle said. "You gave her that shirt when we found her."

"That's right. Then she dropped it to the floor though."

"She must have grabbed it one of the times she went back."

"I didn't realize how sentimental Em is," Kralen said.

"She has a bikini top in here too," Silas said, and tossed it up to Kyle.

Kyle quickly tossed it back and nervously headed for the door. "I'll go contact the Encala again."

Silas chuckled and put it back into the safe. "I thought I recognized it."

"She has our pins in here," Kralen told them, and turned to look at Chevalier.

"That's enough. Put that stuff back and lock it," Chevalier told him.

Kralen nodded and used his heku memory to put everything exactly where they found it, including the 3-ring binder. Once it was locked, they all left and re-locked her office door.

***

Emily pulled up to the dark face of the cave around midnight and shut off the Jeep.

"What's in there?" Robin asked, straining to see into the mouth of the cave.

"Hopefully nothing. Is that opening clear?"

"Yes, I can see about twenty feet back."

"Damnit, the Encala were supposed to have closed it off."

"They might have," Robin said. "There's rubble pushed off to the side."

Emily's heart pounded. "Moved recently?"

"I'm not sure."

She grabbed in the glove box and pulled out a flashlight.

"We're going in there? It doesn't look all that safe," Elliot said.

"You can stay if you want," she told him, and stepped out and pulled on a coat and then a large, empty backpack.

Her throat was closing off with fear. The thought of the dark passageways filled with dead heku was almost more than she could handle. Knowing that her final destination was a ceremonial room that brought back memories of the Yisolatara ritual, nearly sent her running.

Robin frowned and looked over at her as her pulse raced. "Are you sure you want to go in there?"

She nodded, afraid that if she spoke, the horror would be too

evident. She took a deep breath and then headed into the mouth of the cave. The entry way seemed too quiet, as if an unnatural stillness had fallen over the area. All she could hear was the thudding of footsteps from the heku behind her.

"I smell dead heku down here," Robin whispered. He looked at Elliott, and the heku nodded.

Emily stopped and looked at him. "Do you smell any live heku?"

"Other than us? No."

She used her flash light and slowly made her way through the cave, fully expecting at any moment to run into the first decapitated corpse of the Ferus guard. There was a clear path made through the rubble, and larger rocks were pushed off into side rooms. Still no bodies had been found, and after twenty minutes of heading deeper into the cave, Emily turned to Robin.

"You said you smelled dead heku?"

"Yes"

"So where are they?"

He frowned. "I don't know these caves."

"There's another smell," Elliott told her. "I don't know what it is though."

"Could it be live heku?"

"No, I don't think so."

"These walls are covered in blood," Robin told her. She moved the flashlight over, and it showed crimson stains across the wall and ceiling.

"So where are the bodies?"

He frowned and turned toward her. "Are we down here looking for dead heku?"

"No"

They walked farther in silence, Emily leading the way with her flashlight, and the heku walking behind her and staying on guard. It was hours later when they came to a heavy rock door and stopped.

Emily swallowed hard and looked at it.

"You don't want to go in there," Robin said, and put a hand on her arm.

"We have to."

"We came all this way to go into a ceremonial room?"

"This is where the Ferus tried to turn me into a Yisolatara," Emily whispered.

"What?!" Elliott yelled. "We can't be in here!"

"Why are we here?" Robin asked her.

"Open the door," she said, barely above a whisper.

"No, it's out of the question."

She turned to him. "Open it or leave, and I'll figure out a way."

"We can't go in there," Robin told her. "We all know what happened, and it's completely against all rules."

"Fine," Emily huffed, and then stuck the flashlight in her pocket. She braced herself and pulled on the door but was only able to open it an inch.

"You can't get in there without help," Elliott said.

Emily sighed, "I'm not leaving without getting in there. I suggest you open it, so we can get back to Council City."

She waited while Robin and Elliott discussed things, and it was a few minutes before Elliott sighed and opened the door.

Emily was the first to step in, and she immediately spied the thirteen bodies lying across the floor. She instinctively covered her nose but then frowned and lowered her hands. "No smell?"

"Why would they smell?" Robin asked as he touched one of the blue robed heku with his foot. The robes were covering all of the bodies, but their heads were tossed around the room.

"Decay…," she whispered and then pushed against Exavior's arm with her foot. When the robe pulled up, it exposed perfectly preserved flesh, and she screamed and started for the door.

Elliott blocked her. "Calm down… he's dead."

Emily couldn't speak. She pushed against him, and when he didn't move, she turned toward Exavior's body with wide eyes.

"Heku don't decay very quickly. It can take decades to show even the slightest sign," Robin said. He looked up at her. "You should know that."

"They don't?" she asked, not sure she believed him.

"Of course not. He's dead."

She nodded and then walked over to where Exavior's head was lying up against the wall. Sotomar had ripped his hood off at the same time, and it was still covering his head.

Emily knelt down, grasped the hood, and then tried to calm her nerves before moving it away from his face. She screamed when his dead eyes peered up at her, and she made a lunge for the door. This time, Robin stopped her.

"He's dead. I swear," Robin said, holding her tightly. He was afraid if she took off through the cave in a panicked run, that she'd hurt herself.

She pushed against the large heku and pressed her face against his chest, trying to erase the memory of Exavior's lifeless eyes. When she finally calmed down, she looked up at Robin.

"I need your cloak," she said softly. The cave was so quiet that any sound was amplified.

He nodded and unclasped it before handing it to her. Emily spun

before her nerves could prevent it and then walked over hesitantly.

"What are you doing?" Elliott asked.

"Taking his head," she whispered. She could feel the heku's eyes on her as she knelt down and carefully wrapped his head in the green cloak.

"Why?" Robin asked.

She ignored him and made sure the cloak was all around the head before shoving it into her backpack and putting it back on.

"Can we go now?"

Emily focused in on the three metal cuffs on the ground. They were situated so her body formed the Y needed for the Yisolatara ritual. She reached out and touched them lightly, then jerked her hand back when her fingers brushed against the ice-cold steel.

"Someone's down here," Robin whispered. Emily turned and saw that both of the heku were crouched toward the door.

"Who?" she asked quietly.

"I don't know the scent."

"Damn, whoever it is, is fast," Elliott said.

"Shhhh," Emily hissed.

"It's too late," Robin said as his hands balled into fists. "He's already coming for us."

"Then run," Emily told them. "I can ash them, but you two need to get out."

"We're not guarding you to run," Elliott told her, somewhat offended.

"Back up," Robin whispered. The three of them all stepped back just as Emily heard a shuffle outside of the door.

"No use hiding," Elliott called out. "Make yourself known."

There was a soft laugh before the door opened slowly. Emily used her flashlight to show who entered, but her breath caught when the silvery eyes of an Ancient peered from behind a dark cloak.

"Stay back," Robin growled.

"A mortal and two young heku... how very odd," the Ancient said as he closed the door behind him. "Were you feeding?"

"I'm not a donor," Emily said indignantly.

His eyes narrowed and he inhaled. "Why do you have the stench of Arrianus?"

"Leave her alone," Elliott said, and then stepped closer.

The Ancient smiled. "You are too young to take me on, dear boy."

"We can at least try."

"Besides... I don't need heku protection from you," Emily said.

He stepped around the heku and smiled at Emily. "I guess I should introduce myself... I am Gaspar."

"I don't care who you are," Robin spat.

"Well, I can't let you go now," Gaspar said, amused. "You know my hideout."

"Just let us go and we won't tell," Emily said.

He smiled. "You have no choice in it, mortal. Mmmm, that scent."

The instant Gaspar inhaled, Robin and Elliott moved closer to block the Ancient's path to Emily.

"You didn't answer me, child. Why do I detect Arrianus on you?" Gaspar asked.

Emily shrugged. "I have no idea."

Without warning, Robin started to laugh and then stood up out of his defensive posture.

"Robin?" Emily asked, confused.

Gaspar smiled. "Come in, Dion. Stop playing and meet our guests."

Emily watched with wide eyes as Elliott moved to the wall of the ceremonial room and sat down against it with a grin. He dug a small knife out of his pocket and started a game of tic-tac-toe with himself in the dirt.

She backed up against the wall as another Ancient appeared and smiled at Robin before turning his dull, gray eyes to Emily. "What did you find?"

"A toy," Gaspar said.

Robin sighed and laid down on the dirt floor, then began counting his fingers nonchalantly.

"Robin?" Emily asked again.

"Oh, do leave them alone. They're having fun," Dion said. He smiled and moved closer to Emily. "A succulent mortal you found, Gaspar."

"Yes, she is."

"What did you do to my guards?" she asked, watching as Elliott crossed out his game of tic-tac-toe and then began drawing stick figures in the dirt with his knife.

Dion smiled. "A little talent of mine. They're fine though… quite… well… pre-occupied."

"Very odd, she's bonded to a heku," Gaspar said when his eye caught the essence ring on her finger.

"How low… who, my dear, would bond with you?" Dion asked.

Emily's eyes narrowed. "I'm the wife of Equitis."

Dion leaned his head back and laughed. "Equitis marry a mortal? I think not…"

"Ooooh, she's not fully mortal," Robin said with a grin. He looked up at the runes painted on the ceiling and began to count them slowly.

"What does he mean, child?" Gaspar asked.

Emily fought to calm her breathing. "I have no idea. He's delusional apparently."

"Equitis wouldn't marry a mortal," Dion said, and stepped closer. "Unless he wanted his donor closer."

"I think not," Emily huffed. "Equitis doesn't feed from me."

"Pity"

"I suggest you let us go, or you'll have to face him."

Dion shrugged. "No, we won't... Equitis knows his place and won't care if we kill just one little mortal."

"She's not fully mortal," Robin sang, and then started to laugh after he cut his finger with the knife he was attempting to spin in one hand.

Gaspar's eyes narrowed. "Explain that... now."

"I told you. He's wrong," Emily told him.

"You, on the floor... is this child fully mortal?" Dion asked Elliott.

Elliott shook his head and smiled. "Nope."

"So I'm part heku. Who cares?"

Gaspar slowly walked to Emily's side, studying her. "There's more to it... but what I think is impossible."

"Let's just kill her," Dion said.

"No, let's play first," Gaspar suggested, and then smiled at Emily.

"I'm not going to let you hurt me or those two heku," Emily said.

Dion chuckled. "You're going to stop us?"

"Yes"

"How? Going to bleed on us?"

"No, but I can turn you to ash."

"You?" he asked, now amused.

She nodded, but a fear ran through her, one seated deeply, that if she were to ash the Ancients, she might go unconscious and be at the mercy of her confused guards.

"Have the young heku given you that ability?" he asked, smirking.

"In a way... Ulrich did."

"Who is Ulrich?"

"He's an Old One. He started my family and somehow gave us the ability to turn heku to ash," Emily said. She hoped they would just believe her and let her go.

"A liar, this one," Gaspar said, smiling at her. "What else can you do?"

"I'm not lying."

"Sure you aren't."

"Oh look... if you stare at the runes, they turn blue," Elliott said from the floor.

Emily sighed, "Here's the deal. I can turn you to ash... you won't be able to even scream before it's done... so I suggest you let me go, and

I'll return to Council City and forget I ever saw you."

Gaspar smiled and then inhaled. "Me first."

Emily barely had time to scream before he had her pinned to the wall, and his teeth were sunk deep into her neck. The panic disappeared too quickly and the relaxation that came from feeding hit her harder. She was only partially aware when the Ancient let her go, and she slumped to the floor.

"My God," Gaspar gasped. "She is exquisite."

"My turn," Dion said, and immediately latched onto her neck.

Emily managed a small moan before succumbing to the euphoric feeling.

"Don't kill her," Gaspar said. "With that flavor, she may be useful keeping around."

Dion let go after some time and then kissed her softly before standing up. "She's quite beautiful also."

"Tie her up," Gaspar said. "We still have to find any Ancients that are left."

Dion frowned. "You tie her up. I'm not your slave."

"Fine," Gaspar growled. He produced a thin leather tie and wrapped it around Emily's hands at her back. She managed to roll away from them and tried to pull out of the fog that came with low blood.

When the Ancient's left, still arguing, Emily whispered, "Robin?"

"Yeah?" he asked loudly.

"Shhhh, be quiet!"

"Why?"

"Because I said so... come untie my hands."

"I don't want to," he said, and then started to laugh. "It's funny how often you get tied up."

She sighed, "No, it's not. Now untie me, please."

"What'll you give me?"

"I'll tell Chev you helped me escape."

"Naw... he doesn't reward. He just punishes."

"Yeah, imagine the punishment when he finds out you let the Ancients have me."

"Oh, true," he said, but she still didn't hear him move.

"Elliott?"

"Shhh," he whispered.

"Untie me."

"What?"

"Untie my hands."

"Who's talking?" Elliott asked.

"Oh for hell's sake," Emily mumbled. It was obvious that she would have to get herself out and then try to get the two heku to obey

long enough to return them to Council City.

***

"Encala Council," William said over the phone.

"It's been three days, and Emily's not back," Chevalier told him. "I need to know where she is. She could be in trouble."

"She's not back yet?"

"No, where is she?"

William sighed, "We swore we wouldn't tell you."

"It's been too long! She could be injured."

"Can't you tell?"

"No… that's been… sketchy, since I returned from banishment."

"There's no real danger in what she's doing," Encala Elder Iuna said. "I'm sure she's fine."

"Just tell me, damnit!" Chevalier yelled.

"She's fine," William said calmly, and then hung up the phone.

Chevalier turned to Kyle. "Do it."

He sighed, "That's going to backfire on us."

"I don't really care."

Kyle nodded and disappeared.

***

"You put the lime in the coconut and mix it all up," Elliott sang. "You put the lime in the coconut and call the doctor, woke him up. I said doctor, is there nothing I can take…"

"Shut up, Elliott!" Emily yelled. "So help me, I'll pay you back for that song."

"I said, Doctor, to relieve this bellyache."

Emily tried, once again, to get out of the leather restraints. They were tied tighter than the Equites normally did, and she wasn't able to slip out of them. She'd tried numerous times to call for Chevalier but wasn't sure her messages were getting through.

She wasn't sure how long it had been since the Ancients had restrained her. They came in occasionally to remind her that she would be killed when they were done, but they hadn't fed. She wondered if they had the restraint to only feed on her occasionally, so she didn't die.

Knowing she didn't have a choice, Emily decided that the next time the Ancients came in, she would turn one of them to ash. She knew she couldn't do three, and she suspected that she wouldn't be able to do two at a time either.

"Woooo Woooo is there nothing I can take?" Elliott continued to

sing at the top of his lungs.

Emily briefly debated turning Elliott to ash but wanted to keep up her strength for the Ancients. The hard part of her plan was to catch just one of them in the room. She wasn't sure if even ashing one with another Ancient around would be harder.

She jerked when she felt a hand on her shoulder. "I do hope you've resupplied... I'm thirsty."

"Do it. I am too," the other Ancient said. Emily turned her head just as Gaspar's teeth sunk into her neck.

"Hurry up," Dion said, anxiously tapping his foot.

Gaspar looked up at Dion. "She has a wrist free... stop complaining."

"I don't want her wrist!" Dion growled.

Gaspar shrugged and re-bit Emily's neck. She was too relaxed when he released her to fight back, and within seconds, Dion took his turn. Just as she fell unconscious, she heard Elliott begin another round of his song.

Emily woke up and looked around the room. Robin was picking at the wall with his knife, while Elliott continued to sing from beside her. She sighed and studied the room, hoping to find something she could use to help her. The bodies of the thirteen heku were still strewn around the room, and her backpack, with Exavior's head inside, was sitting by the door.

"What time is it?" Emily whispered.

Elliott looked at her and then sang. "It's time to put the lime in the coconut and mix it all up."

"Great," Emily mumbled. She looked over at Robin and wondered why the room wasn't fighting him back. She took a sledgehammer to a ceremonial room, and it knocked her out. He was prying at a rune with his knife, and it left him alone. "Robin?"

"Yeah?" he asked, though he didn't stop digging at the rune.

"Stop it."

"No"

"That's an order," she hissed. "Stop it right now."

"It's an order?" he asked, and looked over at her.

"Yes"

"Don't care," Robin told her, and went back to picking at the wall.

Emily knew she needed to turn the Ancients to ash before Robin ended up getting knocked out by the room. "Hey! Ancients... guess what? I'm Arrianus' daughter."

They both appeared instantly.

Gaspar frowned. "Do what?"

"Arrianus? He's my father."

"That's impossible…"

"Is it? Then why do I smell like him?"

"I'm not quite sure."

Dion smiled. "If you were the daughter of an Ancient, you would have been killed at birth."

"Yeah, well I wasn't."

Gaspar's eyes narrowed as he studied her. Emily shut her eyes and concentrated hard. She heard screams coming from the Ancients but kept concentrating even when her head began to pound. Risking a quick glance, Emily saw that both were on their knees, and the heku had fallen silent as they watched the Ancients, shocked. Blood began to roll down Emily's lips as she continued the assault, afraid she would pass out before the Ancients fell to ash.

Relief swept over her when she saw Gaspar finally fall into a pile of ash beside Dion. She focused on the last Ancient as he writhed in pain and emitted an inhuman scream. Just when his form faded to a small pile, Emily lost consciousness.

***

"She is such a pretty child," Camber said to Chevalier. Chevalier held the toddler tightly and watched Camber, who was standing before the Council.

"Camber?" Zohn said. "Did you come here to waste our time?"

"Oh… no…," he said, and pulled a paper from his pocket. "I just wanted to submit papers for three turnings."

"Your coven is pretty small to do three turnings at the same time," Quinn said.

Camber smiled. "I know, but they are beneficial."

"Let me see," the Chief of Staff said. Camber gave him the papers, and he started going through them.

"Can you turn a heku to ash, child?" Camber asked Megara.

Megara smiled and nodded.

"No, she can't," Chevalier told him.

The toddler looked up at her dad and wrapped her arms around his neck.

"Interesting," Camber said.

"Loves my daddy," Megara said, and kissed Chevalier on the cheek.

"She seems quite attached to you," Camber said.

Kyle chuckled. "You have no idea."

"May I hold her?"

"No," Chevalier said, frowning.

"No," Megara repeated, and then smiled.

"I see no reason why any of these can benefit the faction," the Chief of Defense told him.

Camber frowned. "You're denying my turnings?"

"That's up to the Elders, of course."

"Of course," he said.

The Court Reporter took the files and then read through the first one. "First up is a 28-year-old female. She's a... she's really a Psychic?"

"Yes, she is," Camber said.

"She's too young," Chevalier told them.

"You aren't one to be talking about age," Camber said.

Chevalier glared at him. "Excuse me?"

"Denied," Zohn said quickly. "We have no use for a Psychic in the faction."

Quinn nodded. "State reasons as insufficient purpose."

The Court Reporter wrote something down and then read from the next file. "44-year-old man, who is a Crocodile Wrangler."

Chevalier chuckled. "Is your coven being invaded by crocodiles?"

"No," Camber snapped.

"Watch it," Kyle warned him.

Camber sighed, "No, Elder."

"No," Chevalier said to the Court Reporter.

"State reasons as insufficient purpose," Quinn said.

"This is ludicrous!" Camber yelled. "You cannot deny these."

"Yes, we can," Zohn said. "Next up?"

The Court Reporter flipped to the last file. "39-year-old Snake Miller."

Quinn shook his head. "Denied."

"No!" Camber shouted. "These are important to me, and I won't be denied."

"Yes, you will," Zohn said. "State reasons as insufficient purpose."

Camber crouched slightly and hissed.

"You may go," Quinn said, irritated.

Derrick opened the door and pulled Camber from the room.

The Court Reporter shut the file. "Those were insane. Why in the world would the faction need a Crocodile Wrangler?"

"He's just trying to cause problems," Kyle said.

"Now that that's over. What do we do about Emily's disappearance?" Quinn asked.

Chevalier sighed, "She's been gone for seven days. I'm not even sure which way she drove."

"The Encala..."

"Won't tell us a thing."

"Maybe we need to force it out of them."

***

"I said, Dooooooctor, is there nothing I can take?" Elliott sang.

Emily heard the singing and slowly opened her eyes. When they adjusted, she saw the two piles of ash lying among the clothes of the Ancients.

"Robin?" she whispered, unable to fully use her voice.

"Emily," he said, and then grinned. "That's a funny name... Emmmily."

"Can you focus for me, Robin? I need you to untie my hands."

"Well, who tied them?"

"The Ancients did."

"Ask them to untie them."

"They are ash. I need you to untie them."

He frowned. "Did you turn them to ash?"

Emily thought for a moment. "Yes."

"Why?"

"They fed off of me."

"I am thirsty too."

She sighed, "Don't do it, Robin."

"I've never fed from an unwilling donor," he said, and turned back to the wall.

Emily finally managed to sit up and continued to struggle against the leather binds.

"You say yah yah, ain't there nothin' I can take. I say waah waah," Elliott sang loudly.

"Elliott, shut up!" Emily yelled. She sighed when he only got louder. "Robin... can you get my phone out of my front pocket?"

Robin looked over at her and shrugged. "I'm sure I can."

"Do it, please."

He sighed and then crawled over as she knelt up higher. He stuck one hand into her front pocket and then smiled and pulled her body close against his. "You're kind of hot."

"The phone... Robin... focus," Emily said, trying to pull away from him.

He reached down quickly and kissed her, then slipped his hand out of her pocket and wound it behind her neck. She sighed and let him kiss her and then looked into his eyes when he pulled away and smiled.

"Phone now, please."

He nodded and reached into her pocket, then pulled her phone out.

"Is there a signal?" Emily asked.

He shook his head. "Nope... we're too far in this hole."

"Damnit," she whispered, and looked around.

Robin smiled and pulled her close again. "Let's do it... right here on the floor."

Emily smiled. "Sure, Robin. Untie my hands and we'll have a go."

He nodded vehemently and quickly tore the leather from her wrists. Before she could even stand, he kissed her again passionately.

When he pressed against her shoulders to lay her down, Emily pushed away from him and smiled. "Not here, Robin."

"Why not?" he asked, frowning.

"I'm mortal. It'll hurt my back," she explained, and then stood up and flexed her hands to get the circulation going again.

He stood up and nodded. "We'll find a bed."

Emily grabbed her phone and looked at it. "I need to get a signal... stupid phone has the worst reception."

Robin quickly took it out of her hand and easily snapped it in half. "Yeah... stupid phone."

She sighed, "Why did you do that?"

Robin turned and started to wander toward the door. "I need to find a bed."

Emily quickly scooped the ashes into pockets in her backpack and put it on before turning to Elliott. "Elliott, come on..."

"Dooooctor, is there nothing I can take?" he sang.

"Elliott!"

He finally looked over at her. "Don't interrupt my song."

"I had to interrupt. You've been singing forever!"

"No, it's only been nine days."

She gasped. "We've been here for nine days?"

"Now I have to start over," he said, and smiled before breaking into song again. Emily walked over and picked up his hand and then pulled until he relented and stood up, though the singing never stopped.

"I found a bed," Robin said, and then turned back for the door.

"I have a headache," Emily told him as she pulled Elliott toward the door. "Once we get into the palace, I promise."

He smiled. "I can't wait."

"I bet. Let's get back to the Jeep."

With Robin leading, Emily forced Elliott out of the caves while he sang through his song over and over. She was relieved to see her Jeep still sitting where they'd left it, and within a few minutes, they were on their way to Council City.

"She put the lime in the coconut and mixed it all up," Elliott continued to sing from the back seat.

"Stop it," Emily said, and slapped Robin's hand away from her knee.

***

Derrick blurred into the trial area, and the Council looked up at him. "Lady Emily called."

"Where is she?" Chevalier asked, standing slowly.

"She wouldn't say," Derrick explained. "She gave me a new cell phone number for you to call. One of those pay by the minute ones."

Chevalier quickly dialed her number.

"I'm sorry, okay," Emily said when she answered.

"Where are you?"

"We're okay... we're..."

Chevalier frowned. "Who is singing?"

"Elliott, shut up!" Emily yelled at him.

"To relieve my bellyache," he sang, even louder.

Kyle looked over when the Council turned toward Chevalier. Even though his phone was turned down, they could hear the singing. "Who is that?"

"Elliott, apparently," Chevalier said, and then shrugged.

"We're okay, Chev," Emily assured him. "I'll explain when I get back in the morning."

"Do I need to talk to Elliott?"

"No, we're good."

"I'll send cars to meet you."

"Chev... I'll see you in the morning," she said, and then shut her phone. She sighed when Robin immediately laid his head in her lap and smiled

"You have an amazing body," he said, and slipped his hand under her shirt.

Emily grabbed his wrist. "Nice to know."

Six hours later, Mark and Silas pulled up alongside her in their cars. She smiled and hoped neither noticed that Robin's head was still in her lap. Mark did frown when he saw Elliott in the back of the Jeep, singing at the top of his lungs.

She was trying to focus on the road when Robin tenderly touched her face. "I love you."

Emily sighed when her phone rang. "Yes?"

"What the hell is going on over there?" Mark yelled.

She took Robin's hand and pushed it back down to the seat. "Nothing."

"I saw him touch you!"

"I'll explain later."

"Pull over!" Mark screamed when Robin's hand appeared again and firmly grasped her left breast.

Emily slapped his hand. "Robin, I said stop it."

"Pull... over...," Mark growled.

"No," Emily told him. "It's not his fault."

"How is that not his fault?!"

Emily hung up the phone and glanced at Robin. "You better sit up before your General sees you."

"Mark? He won't care... I love you," Robin said, and then lightly ran his hand up her thigh.

She grabbed his wrist again. "Stop it."

Silas honked, and when Emily looked over, he angrily held his phone up to the window.

Emily smiled and grabbed for her phone, then wrestled it from Robin and finally called Silas. "Well hello."

"Pull the hell over, now!" he yelled.

"No... if I do that, then you and Mark are going to tear Robin to pieces before I can even explain."

"Tell them I love you," Robin said.

"He what?!" Silas yelled.

"We're four hours out of Council City. He can grope all he wants and then I'll explain it," Emily said. "You better go ahead and warn everyone you see that if they try to touch one hair on his head, I'll ash them before they get a chance."

Silas simply growled, and within a few minutes, pulled ahead of Emily and Mark and soon disappeared.

"Let's get bonded," Robin said, and lightly kissed Emily's hand.

"I already am, remember?"

"I'll just kill him... then you'll be free."

"Sounds like a plan, but let's wait a bit."

He nodded and then leaned toward her and began kissing her stomach.

She sighed and pulled her shirt back down.

Hours later, the gate guards let Emily through and then watched, confused, as Elliott began yet another round of singing from the back of the Jeep.

"Stop at the barracks," Robin said, finally sitting up. "I have a bed in there."

"Oh, that'd be fun with the entire Cavalry watching," she said, and passed by it quickly without stopping.

"True... we'll use your bed."

"The one I share with your Elder? Think that's a good idea?"

Emily stopped her Jeep in the garage and then looked over when the Cavalry appeared, with Silas and Mark in the lead. She gasped when Robin instantly moved to her and pressed his lips hard against hers.

Kralen blurred to the Jeep and tried to pull Robin out by his collar, but Robin tightened his grip around Emily. Kralen's strength broke her out of the seat belt, and she fell after them and landed hard on the garage floor.

"Don't touch him!" she yelled, grabbing onto Kralen's wrist when he started to break Robin's neck.

"Doctor! Is there nothing I can take?" Elliott sang as the Cavalry pulled him out of the Jeep also.

"I love her... isn't she sexy?" Robin asked, looking over at Mark with a smile.

Mark growled, but Horace put a hand on his arm. "We promised the Council that we wouldn't hurt him."

"Keep your hands off of her," Kralen hissed, and then shoved Robin toward the door.

"Fine... until we find a bed."

Emily blushed and followed them up to the council chambers. Derrick frowned at Elliott, who was still singing, so he opened the door quickly and followed the others in.

"Stop singing," Zohn said to Elliott sternly.

"Don't say that. I makes him louder!" Emily yelled over Elliott's rising voice.

"That's an order," Quinn growled.

"You put the lime in the coconut and mix it all up..."

"Stop it!"

"I said, Dooooctor..."

"Take him to a cell," Zohn said, frowning.

"No, this isn't his fault," Emily said, and crossed her arms.

"Besides, we'll still be able to hear him from there," the Chief of Defense said, loud enough he could be heard over the singing.

"What do you mean it's not his fault?" Chevalier asked.

She sighed, "We... well... Dion..."

Chevalier hissed, "You found Dion?!"

"Yes"

"Where is he?"

"In my bag," she said, and then glanced at Robin. She was thankful that he was currently preoccupied with a gash on the wall of the council chambers.

Chevalier smiled slightly. "Dion's effects will wear off in a couple of days."

"I smell dead heku though," Kyle said, and looked over as Elliott started to dance along with the song.

Emily looked over at smiled. "You go, Elliott."

"Take him to the barracks until he recovers," Zohn said. "I can't

stand that noise."

Mark nodded at Horace, and soon, two members of the Cavalry walked out with Elliot. His voice eventually trailed off, and silence filled the palace.

"Dion?" the Chief of Staff asked, looking over at Chevalier.

"He has a natural intoxication ability… it influences all heku within just a few minutes of being around him. It will wear off soon."

"Why didn't it affect Robin?" Zohn asked, and looked over at the heku.

Without warning, Robin spun, put his hands under Emily's arms, and brought her up so he could kiss her as he dropped one hand and gently squeezed her butt.

Emily squealed just as he was torn away from her, and she landed hard against the ground. "Don't hurt him!"

Chevalier stood up and was immediately restrained by Zohn and the Chief Interrogator.

"I love you," Robin said to Emily from Silas and Kralen's grasp.

"It's not his fault either," she said, standing up finally.

"You promised we'd find a bed…"

"Shut up, Robin," she whispered.

"Get him out of my sight," Quinn yelled. Kralen and Silas wrestled him away from the council chambers as he professed his undying love for Emily.

She turned to the Council, blushing. "He's sorry… I'm sure he'll be embarrassed if he remembers."

"He'll remember," Chevalier hissed, and then sat down.

"Now… what were you doing?" Kyle asked, glaring at Emily.

She sighed, "I had to go check something out."

"What?"

She hesitated and then opened the backpack and pulled out Exavior's head, still encased in the green cloak. "I had to make sure this was still there."

Zohn frowned. "I'm afraid to even ask what that is."

"It's… well…," she said, and then decided to show them. She pushed her hand into the cloak, got a handful of Exavior's black hair, and lifted his head to face the Council.

"What the hell are you doing with that?" Chevalier asked, too shocked to yell.

"I just wanted to make sure Paian didn't… you know… get to him."

"Had you asked, we would have told you that he was found in Australia, far from Exavior."

She nodded and then shrugged. "I just wanted to be sure."

"Then you ran into Dion?"

"And Gaspar."

Quinn frowned. "You encountered two Ancients?"

"Yes, they were living in the cave."

The Council didn't notice when Chevalier left his chair until he appeared in front of Emily with his hand wrapped around her head. He gently laid it to the side and studied her neck as he hissed softly.

She sighed, "It's not that bad."

"Which of them fed?"

"Let's see… you starve them for 2,000 years, and I have this blood of mine…"

"So both?" he asked, scowling down at her.

She nodded, almost too afraid to speak. "I'm not hurt."

He reached down and grabbed both of her wrists and studied the bruises forming.

"Stop it," Emily whispered, and pulled her hands away from him. "I'm not hurt."

Chevalier picked her up by her shoulders and stepped back, then dropped her into a soft recliner that was along the wall of the trial area.

"What the hell?" she gasped, and tried to stand up. In a whirl, she found her ankle shackled to the wall behind her, and she watched in disbelief as Chevalier returned to his seat.

"Bring in the next case," he called out to Derrick.

"Belay that," Zohn said, and turned to Chevalier. "Are you even going to talk to her about the chair?"

Chevalier looked over just as Emily reached down and tried to unfasten the fur-lined metal shackle around her ankle.

Emily looked up, her eyes furious. "You cannot keep me locked in here."

"Yes, I can. You do nothing but get into trouble, and now I can keep an eye on you personally."

"No!" she screamed, and then reached for her phone.

"Derrick," Chevalier whispered.

Emily gasped when her phone disappeared from her hand, and she looked up just as Derrick handed it to Zohn.

"Let me go!"

Quinn smiled at her. "This is how things need to be until we can trust you not to run off by yourself."

"You've always told me that I'm not a prisoner here."

"You're not a prisoner… but what you did was reckless and irresponsible. You could have gotten two members of the Cavalry killed, and you could have given the Ancients ammunition to stage a war," Zohn said calmly.

Derrick picked up Exavior's head on his way out of the council

chambers and then shut the door after him.

"I want that back!" she yelled at him.

"Why, Em?" Kyle asked.

"I want to ensure it can never be re-attached."

"We'll make sure he remains safely away from his head," the Chief Interrogator said, obviously having fun.

The Chief of Defense smiled suddenly. "Oh good, Emily has returned."

"Em... stop it," Chevalier said.

She shrugged and sat back in the comfortable chair. She noticed a blanket sitting across the back and pulled it over her legs.

Once the Chief of Defense had his memory back, Chevalier called for the last trial of the day.

Derrick came in without looking at Emily and forced a heku to his knees. The heku gasped and looked over at Emily, but she just crossed her arms and glared at him.

"Davis, you are... Emily!" Zohn yelled when their heku turned to ash on the trial room floor.

She didn't respond but kept staring at the pile.

"Please, we need to try him," Quinn said, and then nodded at Kyle. Kyle shook his head and revived the heku, who was immediately pushed back to his knees.

As soon as Kyle sat down, the heku again turned to ash.

"Maybe this wasn't a good idea," the Coven Liaison Officer whispered.

"It is a good idea," Chevalier told him.

"Emily, please...," Zohn said to her softly. "We'll talk about your confinement later, with just the Elders, if you'll let us handle this."

She simply shrugged, and when Kyle revived the prisoner, he stayed nearby in case he needed to revive him again.

Zohn smiled slightly. "Davis, you are hereby charged with petit treason for the attempted murder of your Coven Lord. How do you plead?"

The heku smiled. "I've already been turned to ash by a member of the Council... twice, in fact. I declare you are now treading on double jeopardy."

Emily smiled when the Council looked at her.

Zohn chuckled and looked back at the prisoner. "I'm glad you watch mortal TV, but here in this court, there's no such thing as double jeopardy."

The heku glared at him. "Then I plead not-guilty."

"But you attempted to remove his head... with a chain saw," Chevalier said.

"He probably deserved it," Emily said smugly.

The Chief of Staff ignored Emily's comment and continued, "We, the Council, find you guilty on all charges. The Elders will decide on a punishment."

"Death," Chevalier said.

"Six hundred years banished," Zohn countered and then turned to Quinn. "Your call."

The heku smiled at them. "I've already been turned to ash by a member of the Council... twice, in fact. I declare you are now treading on double jeopardy."

Chevalier sighed and looked over at Emily. "Having fun?"

She glared at him but didn't answer.

Quinn studied the prisoner and then shrugged. "I think death is appropriate for trying to kill a Coven Lord."

"See," Chevalier said, and smiled at Zohn.

Zohn shook his head. "Fine... record his fate as death."

The Records Keeper began writing while the heku stood up and blurred for the door. He flung it open and came face-to-face with Derrick. Emily hadn't seen this part of the court experience and was shocked at how angry Derrick looked as he crouched and then lunged at the heku that was trying to run.

Derrick growled low as he ripped the head off of the heku and let the body fall to the floor of the trial area. After carelessly tossing the head by the body, Derrick stood up, straightened his shirt, and then returned to his post at the door.

"Derrick!" Emily yelled, and leaned forward in her chair.

The door guard stepped back in. "Yes?"

"You... you're so sweet."

He grinned. "Around you, yes, I am."

"I didn't know you had that in you."

He bowed slightly and then stepped back to his position at the door.

"Derrick is very good at his job," Zohn said as he stood up and slipped off his heavy green robe.

"Why didn't Kyle kill him?"

"He ran... so we leave those for Derrick," Kyle explained.

"Or were you just afraid he'd hurt you?"

Kyle started to get angry but was quickly ushered out of the room by Quinn.

Zohn and Chevalier walked over to the overstuffed recliner and looked down at Emily.

"Are you ready to talk?" Zohn asked.

Emily crossed her arms. "Let me go."

"Will you remain civil?"

A slow smile crossed her face. "I'm surprised at the Council, actually."

"How so?"

"You let Derrick take the kill… which tells me everyone on the Council is a wimp, and Derrick has to cover for you and kill your prisoners."

Chevalier smiled. "Not going to work."

"What?" she asked, looking up at him innocently.

"We're not going to let you pick a fight," he said, and unfastened the chain around her ankle.

Emily stood up and started for the door, but Derrick stepped in and blocked her.

She looked up at him. "Aren't you tired of the Council pretending to be strong, when in fact, it's you that make them appear so?"

He smiled. "Go talk to the Elders."

Emily turned. "Fine, I'll talk to you… but only if Derrick comes."

"Why?" Zohn asked, frowning.

"Because I said so."

Chevalier chuckled. "Derrick… come with us."

"Yes, Elder," he said, and then followed them all out the back door and into the Elder's conference room where Quinn was waiting.

They all sat down as Chevalier explained to Quinn why Derrick was with them.

"Start talking," Emily said, and leaned back in the chair. "I want to know what right you have to restrain me to a chair."

"Why did you go after Exavior's head?" Chevalier asked.

"I told you. I wanted to make sure that Paian hadn't reattached it."

"So your only concern was that Exavior would revive and come after you?"

She hesitated and then nodded. "Yes."

"Don't lie, Emily," Zohn said.

"Stop interrogating me then!"

"We just want to know your reasoning."

She sighed, "According to what I read… Paian liked to revive heku that could benefit the Valle."

"Yes," Chevalier said. "That's true."

"Exavior would fit that profile."

"Then let me guess… to protect the Equites from Exavior's wrath, you decided to confront him if he was revived," Quinn said.

Emily lightly tapped her fingers on the table.

"So that's true," Chevalier sighed.

Zohn nodded. "Yes."

"So ultimately, you were trying to protect us."

She didn't answer but picked at her nails as the room fell silent.

"Em?" Chevalier asked. When she looked up at him, she saw the concern. "We are just concerned that you went after Exavior alone."

"I can take him."

"We know that… but it's not your job to protect the heku."

She shrugged. "Derrick can't do it all by himself."

Derrick grinned and sat back when Chevalier chuckled. "Stop trying to pick a fight with us."

"This conversation is getting old," Emily told them. "I'm apparently not going to stop protecting you, so get used to it."

"I refuse to leave it at that."

"As do we," Zohn said. "What you did was more dangerous than you can imagine… proven by your encounter with two Ancients."

"I took them out."

"After nine days though… and after how many feedings?"

"I take it by the chair, that you plan on locking me up in the council chambers every day?" Emily asked, glaring at them.

"Yes… if even the Cavalry can't keep you from running off, then we have no other choice," Chevalier told her. "You're too important for us to let you go off on dangerous missions alone."

"Then you're condemning me to be a prisoner of the Equites?"

"No…"

"Yes, you are. I won't sit there all day and be bored while you watch me… it's humiliating."

"Until you realize how important your safety is, we don't have a choice," Zohn explained.

"If Mark, Kralen, and Silas are available… we will let you go, and they can stay with you," Chevalier said.

"I won't stand for this."

"It's just until we find an alternate method to keep you safe."

"How is what I did so dangerous? I brought back two Ancients and the other… thing… I went in for!"

"After you turned the Ancients to ash… how long did you sleep?" Quinn asked.

She shrugged. "I don't know."

"Elliott said you slept for 112 hours."

"He's an idiot."

"Had you been found during that time… it could have exposed the heku," Zohn said.

Emily frowned. "But…"

"Heku aside… let's say the last Ancient had found you, or what about unfactioned."

"I just wanted to make sure he was still there," she whispered, and

ran her fingers along the wood grain on the table.

"The bad outcomes outweigh the good ones," Zohn said. "It's honestly frightening to think what would have happened if the Valle got you. When they had you before, you were used to massively wipe out our covens."

"I didn't think about that."

"That's why we want to keep you safe," Chevalier said, and took her hand tenderly. "We understand you're fueled by passion, and it will take us to keep you safe."

"I'm not fueled by passion," she mumbled, but blushed deeply.

He smiled. "It's one of the reasons I love you."

She sighed, "I'm sorry, okay? I didn't think what that would do. I honestly thought we'd find the cave completely obstructed."

"When you didn't, you should have called us."

"I don't want to be locked up in the council chambers all day."

"For now, we need you there," Zohn said. "We thought by putting a higher ranking member of the Cavalry in charge that you wouldn't get away…"

"He's not very experienced," she said softly, and then gave them a crooked smile.

"The Council will watch you for now."

"I'll behave! I'll put myself on house arrest."

"No, you will need to be with the Council."

"I apologized! Now don't keep punishing me."

"It's not a punishment," Chevalier said. "It's a safety measure until we can get a grip on your adventures."

Her eyes narrowed. "I won't do it."

"Which is why we put in the shackle," Derrick said, and then smiled broadly when she glared at him.

"You can't keep me chained up!"

"Yes, we can, Em. We have to keep you safe until we can find how to watch you better," Chevalier explained.

"Try it, vamp boy," she said, and stood up angrily.

"Sit down, please."

"No, I'm not putting up with this!" Emily spun and left the room quickly. She yelled at Mark and Silas when they fell in behind her, but they followed her anyway and then stopped her before she got into her Jeep.

"They want you to stay here," Mark told her.

Emily tried to step around him. "I don't live here."

"Em…"

Chevalier came into the garage and took Emily's arm. "Please, for now, just stay with me."

"I don't live here! I refuse to live here."

"For tonight, stay with me. We'll talk about it in the morning."

Emily jerked her arm away from him and angrily started up the stairs with the Cavalry following.   Once inside the bedroom, she slammed the door shut.

***

Mark was furiously searching the bedroom, trying to figure out how Emily got away from him.

Silas came out of the bathroom and began looking under the bed.

"She's always gotten out of here," Chevalier said as he moved aside a dresser to look behind it. "I don't blame you."

Mark growled in response and stormed into the bathroom.

Silas smiled slightly. "She usually can't ditch us."

"I know."

Kyle walked into the room and watched them searching. "No surprise. She won't come back."

"I'll go get her later," Chevalier told him. "See if you can calm Mark down."

Kyle nodded and went into the bathroom just as Mark tossed the towel warmer across the room. It shattered up against the far wall when Mark began feeling along the wall behind it.

"It's not your fault," Kyle said as he sat down on the toilet. He knew it was best to stay out of Mark's way.

"It's my responsibility to watch her and to make sure she didn't leave the palace!" Mark roared.

"Just... wait...," Kyle said, and then faced forward on the toilet and studied the wall directly in front of him.

Mark walked over. "What?"

Kyle stood up. "Sit down and look at that wall."

Mark did as he was told and then growled and moved forward. He wedged his fingers in between a few loose bricks, and the wall opened to the passageway of a long-forgotten dumb waiter.

"Elder!" Kyle said, smiling.

Chevalier came in and his eyes grew wide. "What is that?"

Mark raised the dumb waiter and looked at his Elder. "I bet she can fit in there."

"How did we not see that?" Chevalier asked, dumbfounded.

Kyle chuckled. "You have to sit on the toilet to see the door. How often do we do that?"

"This entire time, she's been taking the dumb waiter down!" Mark growled.

Chevalier winced when Mark tore the chain off of the small box that carried supplies down the stairs and then heard it smash against the ground, five floors below.

Mark stood up, still livid. "I can't wait to tell her it's gone."

"Why don't we not?" Kyle asked, smiling.

A smile crossed Mark's face. "That's good…"

"We let her think she can get away… then when she tries, she'll find it bricked over."

Chevalier called for servants to brick over the dumb waiter's door and make it look exactly like the rest of the wall.

***

Emily drove past the heku at the gate to her mansion and parked in front. Megara was fast asleep in her car seat, so she picked her up gently and went inside to tuck her into bed.

Alec met them as soon as they stepped inside, and he followed Emily up to the nursery. When she came out, he was waiting for her in the hallway.

"I was worried about you," Alec told her.

"I just had to go do something," Emily said, and walked past him.

"We have a small problem."

"What?"

"That empty property behind the house… the Valle put a bid on it."

Emily gasped. "They did?"

"Yes"

"I didn't even know it was for sale."

Alec shrugged. "It came up for sale a few days ago, but I couldn't find you."

"Do you know their bid?"

"No, but I would imagine it's a lot."

Emily walked down the stairs, deep in thought. "If they buy that, they'll build a house, and I'll have another set of babysitters."

Alec nodded. "Yes, you will."

"Then I'll make a counter offer."

Alec followed Emily into the kitchen and sat down when she started making coffee. "You can't outbid the Valle though."

"That's true. Maybe they'll back off if I counter."

"They won't. It's so close to you, that they'd kill for it."

"Is it the Valle Faction that's put in an offer or just a random Valle?"

"The Council put in an offer."

"Damnit… well all I can do is counter it," Emily said, and then sat

down with the steaming cup.

"You need to enlist the Equites," Alec told her. "You don't have enough to prevent them from purchasing it."

"I have Exavior's money."

Alec winced slightly and then sighed, "Even Exavior didn't have enough to outbid the Valle."

"Yeah, the Equites and I aren't on very good terms right now," Emily said, deep in thought. "All I can do is put in an offer. I'll put all of Exavior's money as my first offer if I have to and let them know I'm not kidding."

"There is a chance if you put up a good enough cash offer, with the stipulation that you need the property within... say... two days. They may just sell it before the Valle can even counter," Alec suggested.

"That's a good idea."

"What are you going to do with that lot? It's close to six acres."

"Not sure really. I could put in livestock."

"We're not zoned for that here."

Emily lightly tapped her finger against the cup as she thought. "What is it zoned for?"

"Residential only," Alec said.

"Fine, then I'll build a house for Alexis and Garrett."

"He can't move out of Council City."

"Why not?"

"It's part of being a guard."

"Well, hell then... I'll just build a house and leave it abandoned. I don't really care, as long as the Valle aren't in my back yard."

"You really should tell the Council."

"No, I don't need them in my business any more than I need the Valle."

Alec nodded. "I would put in the offer today. I don't know how long ago the Valle put in theirs, so it could close soon."

"I'll go in right now," she said, and quickly finished her coffee.

"I'll watch the baby."

"Is Dain here?"

"Yes, but I wish you would trust me," Alec said. "I wouldn't hurt you or the baby."

She studied him and then nodded. "I know... I would just feel better if Dain is here. I don't think Chev has replaced the guards on the property yet."

Alec smiled. "Yes, he has."

"We'll talk about this later. I need to go put in an offer on the property."

Alec nodded, and Emily got into the Jeep after making sure Dain

was actually home. After getting the agent off of the property listing, she drove directly to her office.

"May I help you?" the reception asked.

"Yes, I need to speak to Judy."

"Do you have an appointment?"

"No"

"Have a seat. I'll tell her you're here."

Emily nodded and checked to make sure she had everything she needed. It was almost an hour later when a younger woman came in. Her polyester suit and awkward heels made her look unreliable, but Emily smiled cheerfully and shook her hand.

"I'm Judy, what can I do for you?" she asked.

"I want to put an offer on the 6-acre property you have for sale."

"Oh, come to my office, and we can discuss it. I was just about to notify one of the bidders that their offer had been accepted."

Emily followed Judy back to a small, cluttered office and then sat down.

Judy looked through a few stacks of papers before pulling out a file and sitting down. "Let's see. It's 5.86 acres zoned for residential."

"Right, but I need it immediately. I'll need to close within two days."

"That could be a problem."

"Why's that?"

"Well, that doesn't leave anyone else the option to bid higher."

Emily smiled. "My offer may be worth it."

"Oh?"

Emily slid a piece of paper across the desk with double the amount the property was listed for.

Judy gasped. "Are you serious?"

"Yes, my stipulations are that no other offers can be accepted, my purchase has to remain secret, and I have to sign in two days."

"I'm... well, I'm sure they won't mind."

"I'll wait for your call then," Emily said, and stood up.

"Actually, the property belongs to a bank," Judy explained. "I can probably get your answer right now."

Emily smiled and then sat down while Judy left the room. She pulled out her phone and began playing games. Judy finally returned and sat down with another stack of papers.

"So?" Emily asked, leaning forward slightly.

"The bank accepted your offer and your terms, as long as they get the money within three hours."

"I can do that. Just tell me where to wire it."

Emily got the bank information and then quickly drove toward

Council City, where Exavior's bank account information was sitting in a safe in Chevalier's bedroom.

She stopped just shy of the gate guards being able to see her and tried to think of how to get in there, get out, and get to the bank in the next 2 ½ hours. Figuring she didn't have time to come up with a good plan, she decided to wing it.

The gate guards waved her through, but she was certain they had also alerted Mark that she was back in the city.

Before she'd even reached the front doors of the palace, Mark, Silas, and Kyle were waiting for her. She stopped the Jeep and took a deep breath before climbing out.

"I'll pull that into the garage for you," one of the door guards told her as he rounded the Jeep.

"No, I'm not staying," she told him. He looked at Mark and then started to get into the Jeep anyway. One small flash of a burn, and he gasped and backed away. "I said no."

The door guard glanced at Kyle and then returned to his post.

Emily walked past the three heku and into the palace without saying another word. She quickly ran up the stairs, followed by the guards. When she walked into the bedroom, they tried to follow her, but she shut the door in their faces and then smiled and knelt down at the wall safe.

She started digging through the papers in the safe and turned only when she heard the door open.

Chevalier came in and shut the door. "Is there a problem?"

"No"

"What are you looking for?"

"My bank book from Exavior."

Chevalier sat down to watch her while she searched.

When she found what she was looking for, she locked the safe, stood up, and slipped the bank book into her back pocket. She headed for the door, but it wouldn't open.

Sighing, she turned to Chevalier. "I'm on a bit of a time crunch."

"To do what?" he asked softly.

"None of your business. Let me out."

"I can't… it's too dangerous."

"I'm not doing anything dangerous! Let me out before I lose this chance."

"No"

"Fine, then let me out before I lose my temper."

"It's too dangerous for you out there."

Emily crossed her arms and glared at him. "Just get out of here."

He nodded and then left, shutting the door behind him.

She quickly went into the bathroom and knelt down beside the door

to the dumb waiter. When she couldn't open it as usual, she tried to pry it with her fingers, with no luck.

After a few more minutes, she stood up, furious. Hoping to find a new way out the window, she opened it and looked out over the lawn. She instantly spotted one of the city guards standing post on the ground below her window.

Smiling, Emily had an idea, albeit an unpleasant one. She leaned out of the window and whispered, "Hey."

The city guard looked up as she climbed out the window and sat on the sill.

"Catch," she whispered, and then scooted off the window. She stifled a scream during the fall but grabbed a hold of the city guard when he caught her.

"Are you okay?" he gasped, and set her down.

Emily watched him for a moment and then smiled when he looked over at her.

"Oh, Lady Emily," he said, bowing. "Can I help you?"

"No, I was just telling you thanks for guarding my window," she said, smiling.

He bowed again. "You're welcome."

Emily spun and ran toward the front doors of the palace. She growled softly when she saw her Jeep wasn't there anymore and then she wiped the memory of the door guards after she ran by.

She checked her watch and had only 90 minutes before the deal ended. Rounding the corner into the garage, she spotted her Jeep and quickly crawled inside.

Emily hit the steering wheel when the Jeep wouldn't start and then glared at Chevalier and Kyle when they slowly walked up.

"Fix it!" she yelled, tapping her fingers against the steering wheel.

"Come out," Chevalier told her, and opened the door.

"Fix it!"

"No, come talk to me for a few minutes."

"I don't have time."

"What's so important that you don't have a few minutes?" Kyle asked.

"Personal stuff that's none of your business."

Kyle put his hand out. "Come on."

"No! I'm not a child, and I have business that I have to attend to."

"You're running," Chevalier said. "Plain and simple…"

"So help me… let me go, or you'll both regret it. I don't care if Kyle's the only one that can revive anyone."

"You won't ash us," Kyle said, and then smiled. "So you might as well come with us."

"Fine," Emily said, and turned both Chevalier and Kyle to ash. She sped out of the garage in Chevalier's Humvee and pulled out her phone.

"Encala Council," Elder Iuna said.

"It's Emily."

"Oh, good to hear from you!"

"Thanks... I need a favor."

"Name it," William said, sounding pleased.

"I need you to send your Chief Enforcer to the Equites as soon as possible."

"Is there a problem?"

"No, but I ashed Chev and Kyle, so they will need someone to revive them."

William chuckled. "Do we get a reason?"

"They stopped me from leaving the garage, and I have business to attend to."

"Are they restraining you again?" a strange voice asked.

"Yes... they've gone to new levels."

"Did they say why?"

"I went to the cave... ran into two Ancients... so they're all..."

"What?!" William yelled. "You were tracking Ancients when you told us you were going to check on Exavior?"

"No! I did go check on Exavior... but there were two Ancients there."

"Are you okay?"

"Yes, I'm fine. Now though, the Equites don't trust a thing I do and shackled me in their council chambers."

Chapter 16

Emily looked up at the bland ceiling and tried to find something interesting to think about. Since she'd turned Chevalier and Kyle to ash, then called in the Encala for help, they'd had her locked in the recliner during the day and in the bedroom at night. She bought the land behind her mansion and was anxious to do something with it, but she hadn't been allowed out of the Council's firm grasp since then.

She absentmindedly scratched under the shackle on her ankle before sighing and bringing her hands up to see if there were any nails to pick at. Boredom was the worst part of her day, and she hadn't discovered anything to do yet.

Kicked back completely, she didn't have to look at the Council or their prisoners, but all she could see was the dark brown ceiling. Finding a hang-nail, she pulled it off, bringing a tiny drop of blood to the surface.

"Emily," Zohn sighed. "How exactly are you drawing blood over there?"

She grinned but didn't look over at him. "I'm just that good."

"Will you not?"

Emily looked up and saw that the Chief Interrogator and the Chief of Staff had the prisoner restrained as he hissed and clawed to get to her.

"I can't help it. I'm bored."

"So you draw blood to spice things up?" Chevalier asked her.

"No, I saw a hangnail and removed it… the blood was a byproduct of that."

"Well, refrain from that in the future."

She sighed, "Then get me something to do!"

"Read"

"I don't want to read anymore."

"What would you like to do?"

"Talk on the phone."

"No"

"See!" she yelled, and laid the recliner back to look at the ceiling.

Kyle thought. "We said no laptop, but what if we give it a try?"

Emily looked over at him. "I'd go for my laptop."

"Fine," Chevalier said, and then called for Derrick to get her laptop.

She smiled and took it from him, then looked over at the Council. They were still watching her. "Go ahead…"

Zohn sighed and turned back to his prisoner.

Emily's fingers flew over the keyboard as she tried to connect to the wireless network she'd installed throughout the palace.

When she still couldn't find an access point, she looked over at Chevalier. "I can't do anything without the Internet."

"You aren't getting it."

"Why not?"

"You'd find trouble," Zohn told her.

Emily glared at him. "The laptop is useless without it."

Chevalier thought for a moment and then called Silas.

"Yes, Elder?" Silas asked after smiling at Emily.

"Can you arrange for Emily to have the Internet without being able to contact the Encala on the laptop?"

Her eyes narrowed, and she crossed her arms.

"Right away, Elder," Silas said. He avoided looking at Emily as he left the council chambers.

Within only a few minutes, Emily saw her laptop connect, and she immediately remoted into her office's computer and used it to send a text message directly to Andrew.

She sat back and watched the heku on trial beg for his life, until Kyle walked down and banished him for 750 years.

Derrick stepped in and glanced at Emily before approaching the Council. "The Encala Council is on the phone requesting an immediately audience."

Chevalier looked over at Emily. "Did you contact them?"

She smiled and nodded.

"Damnit," Zohn growled. "Patch them through."

"Why is she restrained?!" Andrew yelled.

"It's for her own good," Chevalier told him.

"Let her go."

"No, and tell your Council to stop interrupting our meetings," Quinn said.

Andrew suddenly sounded amused. "I am on the Council... and we will always respond to messages for help from Emily."

Emily gasped. "What?"

"Since when are you on the Encala's Council?" Chevalier asked.

"None of your business... now let her go."

Emily frowned. "Andrew?"

"Em, did they let you go?"

"You're on the Council?" She suddenly sounded concerned.

"I need to talk to her in private."

Zohn nodded. "Fine... we'll give her cell phone back to her. Call her in five minutes."

Andrew answered by hanging up.

Chevalier handed her the cell phone and knelt down. "What's wrong?"

She shook her head, obviously upset.

"We'll need to know what position he holds on the Council."

Emily opened the phone and put it to her ear when it rang, but she didn't speak. Chevalier moved back to his seat and sat down to watch her.

"Emily?" Andrew asked softly.

"Why?" she finally managed to whisper.

"It's a promotion... I was honored."

She swallowed hard. "What are you?"

"I'm the Chief Interrogator."

She gasped. "What? Why that?"

"I'll be good at it."

"No! Tell them no."

"I can't tell them no. I'm already sworn in."

After a few minutes of silence while Emily mulled over Andrew's promotion, he finally spoke again. "What's wrong... just tell me."

Emily swallowed hard. "You can't be on the Council."

"It won't change anything."

"Yes, it will!" she said, raising her voice. "It changes everything!"

"Calm down... nothing's going to..."

"Bullshit! Now I'll lose you too."

He thought about that for a moment. "What do you mean you'll lose me?"

"I lost Chev when he made Elder... I lost Kyle when he made Enforcer..."

"Em...," Chevalier said softly.

"You didn't lose us," Kyle told her, frowning.

"I won't be like that..." Andrew started.

"Yes, you will! Before you know it, you'll be trying to kidnap me or too busy to take a phone call. It starts with a simple promotion and turns into you leaving me," she said, fighting back the tears.

"I promise you'll always be my top priority."

"No, you won't! And why that? Why do you have to take that one? Do something less dangerous like... Court Reporter... or Records Keeper."

Jerry, the Equites' Records Keeper, looked over at the Elder. "Is my position not dangerous?"

Chevalier shrugged. "She doesn't understand your full position."

"I'm the Interrogator, Em," Andrew said. "I'll be a damned good one too."

"No! You're too nice to be in that position!" Emily yelled. "Tell William you'll be the Court Reporter."

The Equites' Court Reporter looked over and frowned. "I'm nice?"

"I'm starting to get offended," Jerry whispered.

"Tell him!" Emily screamed.

"I can't change positions on the Council," Andrew told her. "The old Interrogator made too many mistakes and was banished."

Emily gasped. "You banished him?"

"Yes... we had to..."

"Bring him back," Emily said, and stood up quickly. Being shackled to the wall was all that was keeping her from going to the Encala.

"We can't. This is how the heku work."

"Screw the heku!"

Zohn's eyebrows rose. "Interesting."

"Emily... he can't be on the Council anymore. He was showing great weakness," Andrew explained.

"Tell William to bring him back and reinstate you to the palace guards," Emily growled.

"No..." Andrew's words were cut off when Emily threw her phone at the nearby wall, and it broke into pieces.

"Em...," Chevalier said from beside her.

She looked up at him, shaking with rage. "Let me go."

"You can't run off to the Encala just because they replaced a member of their Council."

"I have to bring him to you... you all owe him... they brought you back, so I'll have Kyle revive him."

Kyle shook his head. "We can't do that."

"You owe him!"

"No... we owe the Council. He was replaced, as is tradition."

Emily sat down suddenly and laid back in the chair, then turned onto her side away from them.

Chevalier touched her shoulder softly, but she pushed his hand off and pulled the blanket over her.

He nodded and returned to his seat.

Zohn cleared his throat and spoke so Emily could hear, "Can you please tell us what position he holds on the Council?"

"Yes, I can," she mumbled.

There was a pause before Quinn chuckled. "Okay then, which one?"

"None," she said, but didn't turn to the Council. "As soon as I get out of here, I'm bringing back the old one, and he'll return as a guard."

"It doesn't work that way."

"Leave me alone," she whispered, and then shut her eyes to hide the tears that were forming.

"What did she mean by losing you and the Chief Enforcer?" the Chief of Staff asked Chevalier.

"I don't really want to get into that," Chevalier told him. "I'll talk to her later about it."

Kyle nodded. "I think I should too."

"Very well," Zohn said, and then called for the next appointment.

As the heku in the trial area petitioned to start a new Coven, Emily slowly drifted off to sleep.

"We're busy, what do you want?" Chevalier asked her. Emily looked over at him, Kyle, Sotomar, and Andrew as they sat at a large conference table. She grabbed onto the bars of the cage she was in and tried to open the door.

"I can't get out."

Andrew shrugged. "You're safer in there."

Emily reached down and began to pull at the shackle on her ankle. "I have to get out."

Salazar walked into the room, and the other heku ignored him as he went over to the cage and sat down. "Stop complaining."

"Chev!" Emily screamed, and pulled against the shackle. She looked up at the heku at the table, and none of them were even looking at her.

Salazar glanced at them and then shrugged. "Guess they're too busy to help you. So let's get on with it. You killed me... in repayment, it's time for your torture to resume."

"No," Emily whispered, and grabbed onto the shackle on her ankle.

"Em's having a bad dream," Chevalier said when the heku on trial was taken back to his cell.

Zohn looked over at her. "About what?"

"I'd have to touch her to see that."

"I wonder why she doesn't scream anymore."

"No idea," he said, and walked down to the overstuffed chair. He knelt beside the chair and gently touched her arm.

All of a sudden, Emily screamed and jerked away from him, diving over the edge of the chair. When she hit the ground, she began frantically tugging at the shackle on her ankle.

"Em... calm down," Chevalier said softly, and started unlocking the metal. "Stop fighting me."

Emily's fingers dug at the metal and kept getting in the way of Chevalier's key.

"Kyle...," he called out.

Kyle blurred behind Emily and gently took her wrists in his hands. Once Chevalier removed the shackle, she put her shaking hands over her face and gasped in quick breaths.

Chevalier lightly put his hand on her shoulder, but she cried out and scooted away from him and then returned her face to her hands. When she calmed enough to breathe slowly, she looked up and saw the Council had left, leaving her, Kyle, and Chevalier alone in the council chambers.

"I'm okay," she whispered, and stood up slowly.

"I'm sorry. We won't do that again," Chevalier told her. He reached out to take her hand, but she pulled away from him.

"Don't touch me... right now... I can't...," she mumbled, and then quickly walked out of the room.

Kyle looked over at Chevalier. "Do we go talk to her about what she said?"

He thought and then nodded. "Let's go."

The heku followed Emily up to the bedroom and then walked in after her. She sat down and put her hands out toward the roaring fire as Chevalier and Kyle each took a seat beside her.

"Want to talk about Andrew?" Kyle asked her.

She shook her head.

"We want to talk about what you said about us," Chevalier told her.

Again, she just shook her head.

"I don't like that you feel you've lost us because we joined the Council."

"It's true," she said softly, and then pulled a blanket over her legs.

"You haven't lost us," Kyle said, frowning.

Emily looked over at them. "When's the last time you took a day off... or we went on vacation... or even to a movie?"

"All you have to do is ask."

She shook her head.

"Talk to us," Chevalier said. "Please."

"Don't shackle me."

"We won't. That was a bad idea, I'm sorry."

"I need to go talk to the Encala," she whispered, still watching the fire.

"Why?"

"They have to release Andrew from the Council."

"They can't... he's sworn in."

She shook her head. "They will for me. I'll threaten them if they don't."

Chevalier touched her arm lightly. "Em... you should be happy for him. Any position on the Council is an honor."

"No, it's not. It's a death sentence."

"Death sentence?" Kyle asked.

"Yes... maybe not in the literal sense, but in other ways."

"Can you explain that?"

Emily looked over at Kyle. "We used to go horseback riding."

"Yes, we still can."

"We watched movies, played games, we joked, and hung around the castle."

"We can still do that."

"No, we can't," she whispered, and her lip quivered slightly. "Not since you joined the Council."

"I was already on the Council when we met," Chevalier said. "How have you lost me?"

"Becoming an Elder... leaving the island... they took you away from me. I can't..." She fought back the tears. "I can't take losing another heku I care about because of the bloody Councils."

"You haven't lost us, Em," Kyle said, and touched her leg softly.

"Before we moved here, I was never locked up, or restrained, or confined. I was allowed to walk the island and do what I wanted. We spent time on the yacht. We went on walks. We had fun."

"Things are more dangerous now," Chevalier reminded her. "Back on the island, the Valle and Encala didn't really know about you yet."

Emily stood up and headed for the door. "I'm going back to my house... away from the heku."

"Em, we need you to stay here."

"No," she said, and went into the nursery to get Megara.

Kyle silently ordered the Cavalry to return to posts around Emily's mansion and then looked over at Chevalier. "She's going to go to the Encala."

"I know. I guess we better warn them."

When Emily came back out with the toddler, Kyle turned to her. "We really need you to stay."

"I have business to attend to that I can't do from here."

"Daddy," Megara said, and then held her hands out for him.

"No, baby... we're leaving."

"No! Daddy go."

"She can stay here if she wants," Chevalier told her, and then took the toddler from Emily.

"Fine," Emily snapped, and then ran out of the room.

Kyle watched them for a minute and sighed, "You two have turned into a divorced couple."

"What?" Chevalier growled.

"Separate houses... fighting over the kids..."

He sighed, "You're right. How do I fix that though? I can't live at her house, and she won't stay here."

"I'm not sure."

                                    ***

"Emi?" Alec called from the back of the house.

"Yeah, it's me," she said, and set her keys on the table.

He walked up to her and frowned. "I've been worried about you. Did you get the land?"

"Yes... then the Equites decided to confine me."

"For what?!"

"They tried to stop me from leaving the palace, so I ashed Kyle and Chev... but then I felt bad and called the Encala to revive them."

Alec chuckled. "That's awesome."

"Yeah, they didn't think so."

"Where's Megs?"

"She prefers her dad, apparently."

Alec and Emily stood in silence for a few minutes before Alec spoke, "Should we go check out the new lot?"

"Sure, let's go see how bad it is."

They walked out the back door and across to the empty property. It was overgrown with weeds and littered with trash.

Emily sighed, "This place is disgusting."

Alec nodded and picked up the remains of a rat.

"Ew, put that down," she said, and wrinkled her nose.

He tossed the carcass out away from them. "We'll get it cleaned up, then what?"

"I have no idea... I may try to get it zoned for livestock."

"No house?"

"I changed my mind about that."

Alec nodded and then his eyes narrowed. "Someone's coming."

"Who?" Emily asked, and then looked over when eight men came into view.

Alec crouched. "Valle."

"Stand up," Emily whispered. "I got them."

He hesitated and then stood up straight and moved to her side. As they got closer, Emily recognized Sotomar, the Valle's Chief Interrogator, and six Imperial Guards.

"What do you want?" Emily asked, crossing her arms.

Sotomar looked around. "I had a feeling you bought this."

"Yeah, it's mine... so go away."

He looked over at Alec and his eyes narrowed. "You need to turn him over to us."

"Why would I do that?"

"He's a traitor and needs punished."

She glared at him. "You know me better than that."

Sotomar smiled. "I do... and I also know that your Cavalry was a few minutes late getting here, and they don't know you and Alec are out here."

"I can take care of you myself."

"And risk passing out and getting buried?"

"I won't pass out with only eight of you."

Alec smiled at Sotomar.

Sotomar glared at him. "You'd let her protect you?"

"Nope," Alec assured him. "However, I won't tell her what to do, and I won't stop her from doing what she thinks is right."

"How very mortal of you."

He just smiled at the Valle.

"Get off of my property, Sotomar," Emily said, irritated.

"Not until we agree what to do with Alec."

"Oh, we already agreed that you all leave him alone or turn to ash."

"He's ours to punish though. Heku tradition dicta…"

"Oh my God! I don't adhere to heku traditions, and I've about had it with the heku period."

Sotomar thought for a moment. "Why is that?"

"Here's the deal. I ash you… your Council tells Chev… the Equites Council figures out that I took land away from you… they get mad… I get restrained… it's all annoying. Why don't you save us both the heartache and just leave?"

"The Equites restrained you again?"

"Of course."

"Why?"

"Not that it's any of your business…, but I took off on personal business and ran into two Ancients."

"You did?!"

"Yes… I ashed them and brought them to the Equites… for that I was punished."

"They could have killed you!"

"They didn't…"

"Where were you?"

Emily glared at him. "Again… none of your business."

Sotomar stepped closer. "Where were you that you encountered two Ancients?"

"Get back!"

"Tell me!"

Alec sighed when the Valle turned to ash. He reached out and steadied Emily when she swayed slightly.

"Damnit… this is going to cause more problems than I'm ready to deal with."

"So, let's bury them. No one'll know."

Emily smiled. "I like how you think… but I always get caught."

"Call the Encala to revive them?"

"They'll tell Chev."

Alec nodded. "Then we face the music."

"We? You aren't going to be in trouble for this."

"They were after me."

"But I ashed them," she said, and started back for the house, followed by Alec.

"She's over here!" one of the Cavalry called out when Emily scaled the fence separating the properties.

Silas rounded the corner and blurred up to her. "What were you doing over there?"

"Nothing… just looking at my new land."

"You bought that?"

"Yes"

"Why?" he asked, looking over at the weeds and trash.

"Why not?"

"Go check it out," Silas said to two members of the Cavalry.

"Wait! No…," Emily said. "You might as well just call Kyle."

Silas looked at her with wide eyes. "There's ash over there?"

She shrugged.

"Who, Em?"

"Just Valle," she mumbled, and headed into the house.

Alec watched her and then turned to Silas. "Please, just call Kyle to talk to Emily. Don't tell him why."

"Why not?" Silas asked him. None of the Cavalry trusted Alec.

"Because it'll be easier on Emi if the Council doesn't find out."

Silas glanced at the weeds again. "Who was it?"

"Sotomar, their Chief Interrogator, and six Imperial Guards."

"Damnit!" Silas growled. "I have to tell the Council that!"

Alec thought before turning to Silas. "Bring Kyle here. Have him tell Emi that he'll not tell the Council if she'll move back into the palace."

Silas' eyes narrowed. "Why do you want her back in the palace?"

"She misses Chevalier… she needs him around."

"That's all?"

"That's enough. Believe it or not, I want only what's best for her."

Silas shrugged. "I'll try it, but it'll be up to the Chief Enforcer if he wants to follow through."

***

Emily followed Kyle into the palace and then started up the stairs when he smiled and walked toward the back entrance to the council chambers. His deal was the best way out of the Council finding out about her interaction with the Valle.

Her time away from Council City had put some of the horse care on the back burner, and she wanted to try to get some of that done today before she found out if she was to be confined to the recliner in the council chambers during the day again.

After putting on some chaps, riding gloves, and slipping on her cowboy hat, she grabbed a rope from beside the door and headed down the stairs. She was just tying it into a lasso when she saw Chevalier in the fourth floor foyer talking to Zohn. He was facing away from her, and a smile crossed her lips as she readied the lasso.

Aiming carefully, she let the lasso go and then gasped when Chevalier's hand shot up and caught it before he even turned around.

"How'd you do that?" Emily asked, re-coiling the rope.

Chevalier chuckled. "I'm just that good."

She smiled and shrugged. "Fine, be that way."

"Why are you back?"

"I thought I lived here."

He smiled. "You do… I'm just surprised is all."

"Yeah well… I have work to do," she said, and headed down the stairs. She wasn't at all surprised when she heard heku behind her all of a sudden, but it did surprise her when she turned and saw palace guards. "Where's the Cavalry?"

"They are heading out soon, ma'am," the closest replied.

"Okay, but stay out of my way."

"Yes, ma'am."

Emily glanced at him again and then headed into the stables. She planned on breaking in one of the colts now that he was over 2-years-old, and she didn't need over-anxious new guards interrupting her. It wasn't until she got into the stables, that she decided to check on each of the 120 horses.

She saw Chevalier's ornery Arabian stallion lying down in his stall with his head down also, and she wasn't sure if he was even alive. When his stall door opened, he slowly looked up at her and her heart sunk. His cataract eyes told her all she needed to know.

"How are you, old boy?" she asked him, then knelt down and ran her hand along his neck. He lightly sniffed at her hat as she examined his legs and found signs of severe arthritis in his front left fetlock.

After running a hose into the stall, Emily began dousing his leg with cold water and waited for the swelling to go down. When it didn't, she pulled a large tube of paste out of the storage room along with a pair of latex gloves. She applied the salve to his leg and then haltered him and gently got him to his feet again.

Once in the empty corral, Emily was able to slowly walk the stallion, so she could fully ascertain how bad off he was. He stumbled a

few times but followed her around the corral.

"What? No yelling at him?" Chevalier asked from beside the corral.

Emily wrapped her arms around the Arabian's neck and looked over at Chevalier. "He's officially retired."

"What's wrong?"

She buried her forehead against his velvety muzzle and pet the sides of his face. "He's old... very old, and it's time he gets to lounge around and eat."

"Is he going to be okay though?"

Emily nodded and started the slow walk again. "Yes, with some treatment, he should be okay."

"We could call Thukil and put him out to pasture."

She looked over and glared at him. "You're so ready to get rid of him?"

Chevalier sighed, "That's not what I meant... I just mean they have empty fields he can graze in. We only have this corral."

"He'll be okay," she whispered, and then kissed the stallion on the nose and looked into his eyes. "You're okay, aren't you, old boy?"

He sniffed at her hair and then turned to pick at a dandelion at his feet.

Chevalier watched her, amazed at how quickly she showed care and concern for an animal she'd had nothing but disdain from since she met him. "I missed you."

She nodded and then headed into the stable with the horse. "I missed you too. We'll just have to see how living here goes."

"Why did you move back?"

Emily put the horse in his stall and then sat down on a bale of hay. "I just want to give it another try."

"Well, I'm glad," he said, and sat down next to her. He studied her for a moment. "Why the chaps?"

"I was going to go up north of the leech pond and run my horse, but I got side tracked."

"They're kind of sexy."

She shook her head and looked around the stables. "Am I going to be stuck in the council chambers all day?"

"No"

"Why the change?"

Chevalier took her hand. "Because I don't want you moving away again."

"Then don't hold on that tight."

"I know."

Emily patted his knee lightly. "I have work to do."

"Like what?"

She stood up and headed down the stalls. "Kralen's mare is in heat. I want to breed her with Amin's stallion."

"Fun"

"Wanna help?" she asked as she opened the stall to the mare.

"Nope, I'll be in my office."

She nodded and led the mare out to the corral. Once the stallion joined her, she went back into the stables and started cleaning the tack room.

***

"Good morning," Chevalier said as he brushed the hair away from her face.

She nodded and looked up at the clock. "Is it really 5am?"

"Yes"

Sighing, she laid back down. "Let's go back to sleep."

He kissed her forehead. "You go back to sleep. I'm heading down."

She nodded and pulled the covers up to her shoulders and then watched him leave. She'd been back in the palace for four days, and so far, no one had done anything that might scare her off. She'd kept busy in the stables and was waiting for the Cavalry to get back so she could shift around the horses she was currently using.

Emily woke up again a few hours later and grabbed coffee on the way out the door. This morning she had city guards, and they fell in behind her as she walked down the stairs.

Derrick smiled when he saw her. "Lady Emily…"

"No," she said, cutting him off.

"But…"

"No." Emily kept walking and was soon in the stables. After telling the city guards to stay out of the stables, she took Chevalier's old horse and slowly walked him out into the corral for some fresh air. He nosed around the ground, trying to use his dying eye sight to pick at grass along the edges of the corral as Emily watched him carefully.

Just as she slipped the bridle back on the old horse to take him inside, she heard a rush of movement in the stables and then froze when horses ran from it at full speed. Someone had let them out of their stalls and spooked them.

The city guards watched with wide eyes as she ran past them and went to her stallion, the only horse left in the stables. She quickly threw a saddle on him and then filled the packs full of bridles. Emily kicked him hard after grabbing a lasso and calling for Devia to follow. She tore past the Council when they blurred to see what was going on.

"Em, stop!" Kyle yelled when she passed them. He growled and

blurred after her, pushing harder when Chevalier passed him. The entire Council fanned out in the city but only found eight of the loose horses. The rest had headed out of the gates.

Emily lassoed the first horse she came to and then Devia herded one back to her as she put a bridle on the first one. Once both were tied to a nearby tree, she quickly started out after another, now with the wolves at her horse's feet.

She saw an image blur ahead of her and figured the Council had come out into the trees to help. It wasn't until the Taser prongs embedded in her skin that she realized it wasn't the Equites around her. The horse reared and whinnied angrily. She wasn't able to stop as she fell back off the horse and felt her head slam against the hard ground. The pain from electricity stopped just as blackness took over.

***

"Lock her," Emily heard Valle Elder Ryan whisper.

"She's not fully awake yet," Sotomar replied. "Wait and I'll do it. Are we ready?"

"Yes," a strange voice said. "This is our only option."

"It's going to take weeks to get it correct."

"I know... but we trust the Valle with this."

"The deal stands. We do this, but we keep her," Sotomar whispered.

Emily tried to speak but only a soft moan escaped her lips.

"Do it before she wakes up and resists," the strange voice urged.

Chapter 17

"Ms. Russo?" he asked, looking down at the woman in the house.

Emily looked up, trying not to gasp as she saw that the men stood almost two feet taller than her and had broad shoulders that threatened to bulge out of the gray, long-sleeved shirts. "Ryan, was it?"

"Yes, ma'am."

"Please, call me Emily... and you're a little early, so why don't you wait in the barn, and I'll be out in a bit," she told him, and shut the door when he and his friend headed toward the rustic barn. Something bothered her about the color of his shirt, but it seemed such a picky thing to concentrate on, so she ignored the odd feeling and started to get ready.

Emily quickly ran a brush through her hair and pulled on her riding gloves before heading out. She glanced once around the house for Sam, the overseer, but he was still out plowing. Her attackers were all tall and muscular. She couldn't help but wonder if these two were also going to attack her. She took a deep breath and headed out to the barn. They needed this sale if they were going to buy feed.

"Sorry about that," she said, and skirted around the two men as she went to the stalls. "Can you ride a horse?"

"Yes, ma'am, I can," Ryan said, watching her closely. The man with him was looking casually around the barn.

"Great, then you and I will head out," Emily said, and started putting a saddle on a beautiful Arabian mare.

Emily led the horse out to him. "Will your friend be okay here in the barn for a while?"

Ryan smiled. "Yes, he'll be fine."

Emily swiftly hoisted herself, bareback, onto a painted mare. "Let's go then."

The heat was stifling. She hated this time of year when the heat from the ground beat upwards and added to the heat the horse put off, immediately soaking both her and the horse in sweat.

"You're not from here. I'm guessing Texas?" she asked him, trying to break the awkward silence.

Ryan nodded. "Yes, we're from Texas."

"What brings you up to Montana for cows then?"

"I come for the best. Might I ask you a personal question?"

Emily glanced back at him as they neared the cattle. "Depends on what the question is."

"Are you a donor?" he asked, and it seemed to her like he was nervous about the question.

Emily frowned slightly. It seemed like such a personal question. "Like an organ donor?"

"Never mind, these are exactly as specified. We'll take fifty of them."

"We can gather them. You said you only wanted one bull?" Emily asked, glancing back at him. As he looked over the cattle, she studied him to see if she could figure out why she had the urge to run. Some instinct deep within her told her to get away from him.

"Yes, you said he has papers?"

She nodded and turned back for the barn. "Yes, we'll have them ready tomorrow if you can get them."

"Will Saturday be okay?" he asked.

"Saturday's fine. My husband's gone for a few days but will be back by then."

They went the rest of the way in silence. She could feel him watching her, adding to the tension between them. She was relieved to see Sam standing beside Ryan's friend.

"Sam, what's wrong?" Emily asked when they approached him.

"You okay, Ms. Em?" he asked her, glaring at Ryan.

"I'm fine... Ryan is going to buy 50 head of cattle," she told him, and slid off of the mare.

Sam nodded. "I'll hep dem. You git inside outa da heat."

Emily nodded and glanced nervously at Ryan before handing the reins over to Sam. She turned and ran into the house and locked the door, then looked out the window as Sam spoke to the two men.

Once they left, she started on dinner. Keith wouldn't be back for two more days, so she planned on cleaning up and getting to bed early so she could help Sam feed the cows before she went in to work in the morning.

Sam seemed more quiet than usual during dinner. He never ate much, but this night, he just pushed his food around on the plate in silence.

After what seemed like an unnaturally long evening, she headed in to bed when Sam left. The night seemed extremely short when her alarm went off the next morning. Emily crawled out of bed, and within two hours, was walking into the tall office building in downtown Great Falls.

"H... hello... Emily," a young man said. He smiled broadly and stood up to greet her.

"Hello, Harold," she mumbled, and then tried to step around him, but he moved to block her.

"Have a nice night?"

She nodded. "Yes."

"So... umm..." Everything about the young man was awkward. Even though a few years older than her, he was socially uncomfortable around women, more so around Emily. "Do you... you know... want to

get a drink… after work?"

The morning ritual was getting old, and Emily sighed before speaking, "I'm married, Harold."

"Oh! I know… just… drinks, ya know?"

"No, thank you. I have cattle to get ready to sell."

"Okay, well, next time maybe." She hated how he looked at her face, and she knew he was checking for more bruises. Normally, she wore sun glasses when she had a black eye and then kept to her office, but Harold had sworn to protect her from Keith. Keith stood a good six inches taller than Harold and Harold's lanky build would be no match for Keith's muscular frame.

Emily nodded and finally made it past him. She shut her office door behind her, hoping to avoid more conversations with Harold and then turned on the numerous computers.

The day passed by slowly, and by the time it reached 5pm, Emily was anxious to get back to the ranch and help Sam gather the cattle that the men had purchased. She also knew that Keith would be back in the morning, and she wasn't looking forward to his return.

Sam was already out gathering cows when Emily got back to the ranch. She quickly saddled Patra and rode out to meet him. It was dark when they finished, and she was eager to get into a hot bath and get back to her book. She hardly had time to read anymore, with the full-time coding job and the ranch to run.

The hot water felt amazing, and she clipped her hair to the back of her head and then leaned back to read as the smell of bubbles surrounded her and washed away the stresses of the day.

"Hello." Sotomar's voice rang out through the small ranch house.

***

She cleared her throat before speaking. "Déjà vu, huh?"

Sotomar smiled over at her. "Why yes… it is oddly familiar."

"Did you really kill Keith?" She already knew the answer.

"Yes."

"I'm sorry he made you do that."

"I'm not. I've wanted to do that for months," he said matter-of-factly. "Warren called me back when he heard the shouting and smelled blood."

She saw Sotomar's jaw tighten and knew he was still mad.

"Your life would be so much simpler if you'd have kept going," Emily told him, pulling her seat back into the upright position.

"He was going to kill you."

She whispered, "I've never seen him that mad before."

"He didn't deserve to share this planet with you. I just wish it hadn't come down to..." He quit talking, his jaw flexing again in anger.

She reached out to touch his arm. "Thank you."

"You aren't mad?"

She shook her head and was silent, her mind deep in thought for the next hour. It was hard to imagine that Keith was dead.

"Who is Ulrich?"

Sotomar glanced at her before speaking. "Do you remember the story I told you about Elizabeth Winchester marrying a heku? The one that started all of this?"

"Yes"

"Ulrich is the one."

She sat up straighter. "And what's his claim to me?"

"How do you know about that?"

"I heard you talking to Sam."

He sighed, "He's been watching over his family. He thinks I may corrupt you."

"Corrupt me?" She didn't like the sound of that. "Where is your Coven anyway?"

"I can't say. It's safer not to speak of the location."

"Why is that? No one's in the car but us."

"It's just safer, take my word for it."

"End of subject, gotcha."

He grinned.

"Warren packed some sandwiches, are you hungry?" He reached behind the seat and pulled out a small cooler.

***

"I just don't know," Emily said, looking around the room.

Sotomar smiled. "I realize you don't love me... that's not my reasoning. The Valle Elders won't let you stay here unless we're bonded. It's not normal for a mortal to live in a coven."

"It just seems a lot like getting married."

"It's not. It's just a way to solidify you as a member of my coven."

"It still sounds like marriage."

"It's not..."

"Well then, what are you suggesting?"

"An immortal bonding... sealing us together, forever, as mates."

She frowned. "Mates?! See, this is a marriage."

Sotomar leaned his head back and laughed. "We'll know we aren't... but the Elders and the coven will think we are."

She sighed, "What exactly does it entail?"

"Well… normally… it's a small ceremony with just one other witness present."

She could tell he was leaving something out. "And?"

"Well to finalize it… there's an… well an exchange."

Her eyes narrowed. "An exchange of what?"

"The ceremony is for immortals."

"Don't you see one tiny problem with that?" Emily set her empty cocoa cup on the table.

"It can be done with a mortal too… it's just different for them."

"How? You're trying not to tell me something, and that's making me nervous."

"It's an exchange of…," he sighed, "blood."

Emily was horrified. "Ew! No way!"

"Well I knew you would feel that way, so I figured we could improvise and use the mortal replacement for blood… wine."

"For both of us?" She could feel the panic rise to her throat.

"I'm an immortal."

She spoke in a whisper, her hand on her throat. "You're going to bite me?"

"It won't hurt. If done right, you might actually enjoy it."

"I don't…." She couldn't even speak clearly.

Sotomar laughed. "Stop worrying about it… we'll do it tonight and then you won't have time to worry."

***

The Council was already convened and waiting their arrival. Emily looked up, wide eyed, as the twelve heku looked down at them. The chair to the right of Elder Defriez was empty. The Council erupted in an odd murmur when they caught the scent of Emily.

Emily shifted uneasily, and Sotomar glared at them as they turned back around.

Elder Valara stood. "Thank you for coming so quickly, Chief Enforcer." She was speaking to Sotomar but looking curiously at Emily.

Emily shifted nervously and grasped Sotomar's arm tighter.

"I see you brought your second in Command." She nodded to Warren.

She flashed a warm smile to Emily. "Good to see you again, child."

Emily looked up at her and fought to keep from running. She didn't realize how intimidating the council chambers were, with their bright lights pointed directly at whoever was addressing the Council and the way the Council looked so far down on them.

Valara sat and Defriez stood. "Let's get started. We have numerous

complaints from the Equites Elders. We'll read them now."

As Elder Defriez read the accusations, Emily could feel Sotomar tense.

> *Destroyed Equites coven Thukil*
> *Maliciously slaughtered innocent heku*
> *Sought out and killed the unarmed Lord of Thukil*
> *Freed two prisoners from the dungeons of the castle*
> *Tortured and killed top Thukil officers*
> *Kidnapped the granddaughter of the Lord of Thukil*
> *Viciously tortured a mortal man found within the city of Thukil*
> *Stole the city crest that was housed in the castle*

When he was done, he looked at Sotomar. "You had a busy day."

Sotomar glared up at him. "Lies, they are lies. Surely, you know that."

Defriez nodded and turned to Warren. "Let's address each one, shall we? Begin with destroying the city of Thukil."

Warren stepped forward. "We didn't harm the actual city, but we did kill anyone we came across, as ordered."

"Did you order such?" Defriez asked Sotomar.

"Yes, I did." He stood tall.

"Under what power do you call upon to order the killing of innocent heku?"

Sotomar looked straight into his eyes. "Under the power I was given to do all I could to retrieve what we were after."

Elder Valara grinned. "We did give him that power."

Defriez nodded. "That also answers the second accusation. Did you seek out and kill the unarmed lord, Lord Ulrich?"

Sotomar looked up at him. "He wasn't unarmed, just over matched."

"Easy enough," Defriez said, and then paused before continuing. "Did you free two prisoners from the dungeons?"

Warren answered. "We freed one prisoner, the one who led us to Emily, and I'm guessing she was the second prisoner we freed."

Defriez frowned. "Was she in the prison?"

Sotomar nodded. "Yes, hanging by her wrists from the rafters after having been beaten."

Emily blushed and looked at the floor.

"Is this correct, child?" She was too embarrassed and simply nodded to the floor.

"We will return to that. Did you torture high-ranking officials?"

Sotomar stifled a grin. "Yes, I did, when they wouldn't give me

straight answers."

"I see, and the granddaughter?" he asked.

Sotomar looked at Emily. "I don't think it was a kidnap as much as a rescue."

Defriez turned to Sotomar. "I don't understand how you can justify torturing a mortal man, though, Chief Enforcer."

Sotomar began to speak, but Emily interrupted him. "I think that was me."

***

"Emily, breathe," Warren whispered, and grinned. "Just walk to him."

Emily's eyes met Sotomar's. He was sitting at the other end of the room, watching her. She focused on him as the guard escorted her through the room, then she felt the eyes of thousands of gray robed heku on her and began to blush. Things again seemed to shift in her eyes. For one fleeting moment, the gray décor turned green but then returned, and she frowned slightly at the odd change.

At the foot of the stairs leading up to the platform with the Elders, the guard stopped and Emily looked up at Sotomar.

Elder Remi stood and smiled at Emily. She watched him as he spoke to those gathered in a language she didn't understand. The heku in the room all responded with an unfamiliar word. Defriez then stood and addressed them, and again, Emily wasn't able to understand what was being said.

Finally, Sotomar stood and held his hand out for Emily. She picked her dress up a bit and walked up the stairs to take his hand. He squeezed her hand tightly and smiled at her. She tried to avoid turning around to face the heku, but once he sat in his chair, he motioned for her to stand by his side.

It seemed like an eternity to Emily before Defriez excused the heku, and they began to file out of the room. Sotomar stood when the coronation hall was empty. He took Emily in his arms and held her tightly, but she pulled away from him and wrapped her arms around herself. She didn't want his arms around her and didn't want to make him think she was falling for him.

"Welcome home, Em," he said.

"We are so glad to have you here, Emily," Defriez said, smiling.

"At least someone is," she told him.

"What do you mean?" he asked.

She shook her head. "Nothing." Her mind ran through the different emotions from the crowd of heku, from angry, to happy, to disappointed.

Remi smiled slightly. "It's okay, child. They are just not used to a mortal in the palace."

Sotomar's eyes narrowed. "They better watch themselves."

"Why don't you show Emily to your new room? I'm sure she'd like to get settled. I will have some dinner brought up."

"Good idea."

Emily followed silently through the enormous palace. She watched the servants bow to Sotomar and eye her suspiciously. She kept glancing behind her as the hairs on the back of her neck stood up. Something bad was going to happen, she could feel it in the air.

The room was dark and cold. There were candles burning instead of lamps, which threw most of the room into shadows. She opened the first door to reveal a large bathroom.

"I'll have something put in that. They aren't used to needing bathrooms," Sotomar assured her.

She nodded and opened the next door and walked inside. She entered into a light blue nursery full of toys and stuffed pillows. The crib was cherry wood and matched the small wardrobe and changing table.

"I didn't tell them to put in a nursery, I swear. I told them you can't have children," he said.

* * *

"Finally, we meet again," the Ancient said when he was alone with Emily.

She stood still, not answering. She felt his dry, rough hands trail down her face and finally rest under her chin. "You look so much like my Elizabeth."

She listened carefully as he walked around her.

"You're shorter than your mother, more muscular though." She felt his hands move across the contours of her abdomen. Emily jumped slightly when she felt a light scratching on her thigh.

"I expect full obedience from you, child," he said, and she could feel his breath on her face. "You cannot turn enough of the Equites to ash to make it worth your pain if you try. Obedience will be enforced through punishment. Do you understand?"

Emily nodded.

"You turned me to ash once... as a child. You were two," he said, still walking around her slowly. "Quite painful, I assure you. Luckily, I wasn't alone, and the Equites were able to revive me."

Emily heard the door open and the Ancient speak. "Ahhh, Chevalier. I was waiting for you."

"I'm sorry to have kept you waiting," a deep voice replied.

"This is my daughter, Emily," the Ancient said.

"Let me look at her," Chevalier said.

Emily felt somehow drawn to his voice.

"She is beautiful," Chevalier hissed, and Emily felt his hands run from her waist down to her exposed thighs. "She's just a little thing though."

"Do not underestimate the Winchesters, Elder," the Ancient said, amused.

Emily fought the urge to pull away when she felt Chevalier run his nose along her chin to her neck and inhale deeply. "Mmmm, soon you will be mine, child."

"We will be expecting a female child soon," the Ancient said, pleased.

"I don't think that will be a problem," Chevalier replied, and then kissed her roughly. His hand wound around the back of her neck. Emily didn't fight, didn't try to get away, but she also didn't return the kiss.

"You'll have to wait until after the ceremony," the Ancient laughed.

"I'll have that ring off of her finger by midnight," Chevalier said, and his hands followed down the curve of her back.

Emily felt the blindfold loosening, and the sudden brightness made her squeeze her eyes shut. She opened them and let them adjust to the light. The Ancient was still in the room. His skin was pale and cracked with age.

"Behave, child, and this will go easier," the Ancient reminded her.

"Release my hands," she said softly.

Emily's feet left the ground as Chevalier put his hands under her arms, and lifted her up, so she was even with him.

"Look at those eyes," he said, grinning at her. His breath smelled like decaying flesh, and Emily's stomach turned.

"Yes, I always loved her mother's eyes," the Ancient said sadly.

Chevalier moved his face to her neck and ran his tongue along the pounding vein.

"Tonight, child," he said, and set her back down. "Can we release her hands?"

"Yes, yes, it's her eyes we have to worry about," the Ancient chuckled.

Chevalier moved behind her and released her hands and then wound his arms around her shoulders.

"It's time," the Ancient said. "I will see you in there." He left quickly, leaving Emily and Chevalier alone.

Chevalier began to kiss Emily's neck and shoulders as his hands ran lightly across her exposed skin. "Mmm you will love me, child. I promise you that."

***

Emily woke with a jump and heard an alarm sound from the city. She looked around the room, but she was alone. Sam came in from the other room.

"What's going on?" she asked him.

"I don't know," Sam said, then shut his eyes and listened closely.

"The Encala are attacking," Sam said.

Emily frowned. "The Encala? Here in the city?"

Sam nodded. "Yes, the troops are at a standoff outside of the city, and their Council is meeting with ours right now."

"I should go," Emily said.

Emily could hear the booming voices from outside of the council chambers. She used the back door so her entrance was behind the Valle Council. As she appeared at Sotomar's side, the entire room grew quiet, and she put her hand on his shoulder.

"Is this a threat?" William asked.

"She is not here to threaten you. Though, I find it hard to believe that you are here peacefully with an entire army," Defriez said angrily.

"What exactly are your demands?" Valle Elder Anthony asked them.

"We demand the return of the last remaining Equites council member, and the return of his mate," William said, and glared at Emily.

Emily frowned.

"What concern is it of yours that we hold Chevalier?" Anthony questioned.

"We have formed an alliance with the Equites and are helping them rebuild, as such, we demand the return of what was taken," William said to Anthony.

"We can peacefully discuss the return of Chevalier, but we don't recognize the bonding enforced by an ancient," Defriez said calmly.

"We don't have to peacefully discuss anything! With the Equites and Encala forces joined, we outnumber you, and will get what we want, one way or the other," Encala Elder Reese yelled.

"Don't talk about me like I'm not standing right here," Emily said finally, and all eyes turned to her.

"She's to be turned over to us and returned to her mate," William snapped.

"Again, we do not abide by any ritual performed by an ancient," Defriez said.

"Does she bear the mark of the Equites?" William asked, grinning.

"For now," Defriez told him.

"You have heard our demands. If they are not met in full, then we

attack at dawn," William said, and the Encala Council swept out of the council chambers.

"You always pick the worst times to make an entrance," Scott, the Valle's Chief Enforcer, said to Emily.

"Kiss my ass," she yelled.

"Stop it!" Defriez said. "This is not the time for you two to bicker."

"Yes, sir," Scott said, and looked straight forward.

"We have three hours to make a plan," Anthony said.

"I've summoned all covens within a three-hour travel time, but we will still be outnumbered," Sotomar said.

"Not with me here. I can take out a few thousand," Emily reminded them.

"We can't risk it. The last time, we weren't sure you would survive," Defriez reminded her.

Emily frowned.

"What do we lose by giving them Chevalier?" Anthony asked.

"We lose the ability to shut him up when he calls Emily," Sotomar said, irritated.

"Which causes pain, right?"

"Yes"

"Pain that I can handle. Hand him over," Emily said.

***

Emily started to sleep slightly as she waited for her masseuse. When he came in, he said nothing but pulled the sheet down off of her back and began working the knots in her neck with warm, scented oil.

"That's a unique smell, what is it?" Emily asked.

The masseuse laughed softly. "It's a blend I make, to help you relax."

"Mmm, it's working." Emily could feel her neck and back calming as he gently massaged the knots. The scent was soothing, and she felt herself relaxing more.

He moved onto her arms and massaged down to her fingers. "That's a lovely ring."

"Thanks," Emily said, her words slightly slurred.

"Why so tense all of a sudden?" He asked her.

Emily shrugged. She still felt relaxed and sluggish from the massage and all of the scents. She felt like hours had passed, even though she had only signed up for an hour-long massage. The room was quiet as the masseuse worked on her feet, and the scents were growing stronger.

"Turn over, dear," he said to her.

She held the sheet while she rolled over, and he immediately put a warm rag over her eyes.

All at once, she felt lips press against hers as hands slid lower down her chest and lightly brushed her breast. She pushed the face away from her and sat up, clutching the sheet close to her. She pulled the washcloth off of her eyes and stared at the masseuse while her eyes adjusted to the dark.

Emily's eyes narrowed. "Chevalier?"

Chevalier smiled. "You remember me."

"Oh, my God!" she screamed, and stood up. "What the hell?"

"Don't panic, I'm a trained masseuse," he said, and raised an eyebrow.

Emily put on the robe, keeping a close eye on Chevalier, and cinched it closed with the belt, "What the hell do you want?"

"Only to help you relax. You are quite tense. Seems the Valle aren't doing enough to keep you comfortable."

Emily glared at him. "Why can't you just leave me alone? I haven't attacked anyone in a long time. I'm tired of it."

"This isn't an attack. The Equites own this little place. I was called when you came in the door. It's nothing more than a business," he said, clearly amused.

Emily glanced at the massage oil and picked it up when she saw its crimson color. "Is this blood?"

"Some of it is. It's a special blend of oils like ochun and elegua." He took the bottle from her. "It's mine though. You'd need to make your own."

"You! You rubbed blood into my back? That's so… nasty!" Emily said, and tried to open the door, but it was locked. She turned around angrily. "Open it."

"It's customary to lock the door during a massage," Chevalier said, watching her.

Emily glared at him and watched him fall to his knees, clutching his chest and the familiar smell of burning filled the room. She frowned when he didn't turn to ash, and tried again. His screams filled the room, but he never fell.

"Can't do it, can you?" Chevalier asked, his voice strained as he stood up.

Emily began to panic. "What did you do?"

"Just a precaution, sadly temporary though," he said, and smiled. "Now come, finish your massage."

"Let me out of here," she glared.

He sat quietly and watched her. She studied him and fought the urge to trust him.

"Let me out," she said again.

"As a show of good faith, I will," Chevalier said, and unlocked the door.

Emily grabbed her purse and ran out of the building, still in the robe, and got into the Durango. She pulled quickly into traffic to head back to the city.

Emily glanced into her rear-view mirror and saw three identical red Lamborghini Reventon's right behind her. They spanned the three lanes of the Interstate and were quickly closing the distance. She pegged the Durango at 100 mph and kept a close eye on the approaching cars, then grabbed for her cell phone, but it wasn't in her purse anymore.

"Damnit," Emily yelled when one of the Reventon's quickly passed her on the median. She was now surrounded by the red cars. They were approaching the woods that eventually led to the west side of the palace, when the car in front of her began to slow, just as the sun set, and it started to get dark.

"Let's see you off-road those babies," Emily said, and popped the Durango into 4-wheel drive on the fly and then turned a hard right. She watched the Reventon's screech to a halt as she mowed down a barbed wire fence and sped across a rocky field.

The engine died at the tree line, and smoke began to pour from under the hood.

Emily glanced quickly behind her and then ran into the woods, cursing the bulky robe.

She realized she was running in a blind panic and stopped to lean against a tree to try and get her bearings. She couldn't see the sky through the dense trees but there was just enough light, she could see the ground. She found a patch of moss beside one of the trees and ran left, heading west toward the palace.

"Emmmily," she heard someone yell from behind her. She didn't turn around but kept running toward what she hoped would be the safety of the palace.

Emily suddenly saw a light ahead and realized it was a campfire. Soon, she could hear music playing. As she got closer, the music grew louder, and she heard the smashing of glass against a tree. She pushed harder and ran into the clearing. The music suddenly stopped, and the partying guards looked at her, confused.

Neils, one of her guards, came up from behind some of the others. "Emily?"

"Neils..." Emily panted. "Equites."

She felt a rush as the guards blurred to her.

"Where?" Neils asked, looking into the woods.

"Emmmmmily," someone yelled again from the dark woods.

Emily had barely even blinked when the clearing emptied out, and she heard the sounds of movement behind her. She turned and ran toward where the guards had gone. It wasn't far before she heard the sounds of fighting. She drew her pistol and ran forward, unsure how many Equites were after her.

The trees suddenly filled with fighting heku. Emily couldn't tell in the dark which were Equites and which were Valle.

Emily saw a Valle and ran toward him. He had three Equites attacking him, and she stood off to his side and concentrated. One of the Equites fell to the ground, screaming but didn't turn all the way into ash. He stood up slowly, and his eyes fixed on her.

Emily took a step back and raised her gun toward him.

"Go ahead, sweetheart, shoot me," Mark said, stepping toward her.

Emily pulled the trigger but the heku turned into a blur, and the gun was ripped from her hand. Mark smashed the butt of the gun against the side of her face, and she fell back against the mossy ground as blood poured from her cheek. She saw him disappear as someone slammed into him, then she slowly got to her feet and steadied herself against a tree as her head cleared.

A strong arm wrapped around her waist and lifted her from the ground as a hand pressed against her mouth.

"Shhhh, child, don't make this painful," Kralen whispered into her ear. "Come with me, and the Equites will leave some of your guards alive."

Emily bit his hand and her mouth filled with blood as he screamed but quickly began to heal. She head butted him hard and heard his nose shatter as she finally pulled loose from his grasp and took off running.

"Em, stop!" Neils yelled from behind her, and she turned slowly. She saw the familiar Valle guards step closer to her. They were covered in blood. Their clothes were torn, and some were supported by others as they fought against wounds that healed too slowly.

***

"Good morning, my love," Chevalier said, and kissed her softly.

Emily pulled away from him and sat on the edge of the bed.

"Come back and let me hold you," he said, and pulled her naked body against his. He'd banned her from wearing anything to bed since the hot tub, and replaced all of her dresses with sheer and lace ones that allowed him to see her body any time he wanted.

"Did you sleep well?" he asked, and began to kiss the back of her neck.

Emily didn't answer.

"You have to talk to me eventually," Chevalier said, and ran his fingers down the curve of her waist.

Emily got up from the bed and took the sheets with her, covering herself as she disappeared into the bathroom. She came out a few minutes later in a sheer black slip dress, with her arm covering her chest.

"I didn't give you those so you can hide yourself," Chevalier said, now sitting on the edge of the bed, fully dressed.

Emily walked over and sat in the bay window, pulling a blanket over herself.

He growled and pulled her out of the window by her arm and then gently pushed her against a wall. He smiled as he looked down at her body and the subtle hints of her curves he could see through the dress.

"You know... time's up," Chevalier told her. "Tonight I'm not taking no for an answer. You're my wife, and I'm going to treat you as such."

Emily gasped. "No."

"Yes, no more rejection from you," he said, and kissed her roughly. He pulled away and ran his eyes down her body again. "It's been too long, and tonight, it's time."

"Then you are no different than Jeff," Emily said, and fell to the floor when he backhanded her.

"I'm nothing like that lowlife."

"You're exactly like him," Emily said from the floor. She wiped the blood from her lip with the back of her hand. "And you're right... tonight is the night."

"It is?" Chevalier asked, surprised.

"Yes, the night I get out of here," she said, and wiped the trickle of blood from her nose.

Chevalier growled and appeared out in the hallway. The mansion was perfectly silent, and piles of ash lay across the floor. He swept into the bedroom and pulled Emily to her feet by her hair. He slapped her again and then dragged her out of the room by her neck.

"You'll pay for that," he hissed, and threw her into the interrogation room. She landed hard against the wooden table and turned to him, just as he backhanded her again. She felt the crunch when her cheekbone shattered as he hit her.

"When I lived in Rome, we called this the equuleus," Chevalier said as he forced her back into the rack. "The French call it Bac de Torture, that's one of my favorites. Course, Streckbank from the Germans was nice. It means 'stretching frame'."

Emily screamed when he turned the crank and stretched her, pulling at all of her joints.

"Now... how to revive my staff," he said, sitting down on a chair

beside her as her pain continued.

"I see that something also needs to happen between us for this to continue. How exactly am I going to prove to you that I am better for you than that Valle?" Chevalier asked, looking around at the various torture devices at his disposal.

***

Emily had never before felt such hunger or thirst. Her entire body ached from being restrained on the cold, dirt floor but the worst pain was in her dry throat and aching stomach. She'd lost track of how long she was there. Every few hours, a heku came in and gave her a shot of something that paralyzed her body but kept her mind alert. She could hear her heku guards talking to her through the day, but they fell silent at night, hoping she was asleep.

Her parched lips were cracked and bleeding, and she could taste the salty blood on her tongue. She could feel her resolve weakening and began to beg for death. She could no longer feel her legs. The back spasms caused them to fall numb after a few days. Her arms ached in the position, and she could feel her wrists swelling beneath the iron shackles.

"Can't you leave her alone?" Neils yelled when four heku came into the room.

Mark ignored him and sat beside Emily. "Congratulations, Winchester, you've made it past the first phase. You're almost there now."

He took her head in his hands and turned her to face him. Neils growled when he saw how easily the heku was able to lock Emily's gaze and had her fully under control.

"News from the home front, your beloved Sotomar came to rescue you and fell at the hands of my guards... funny how easily his head was removed from his body as his blood saturated my boots," Mark whispered.

"No! Emily, snap out of it!" Neils yelled. "Fight back, Em, come on."

"Four thousand and eighty four Valle died today, trying to get you. I wonder why they would do that. You're useless, nothing but a human. You cause more problems in that faction than you are worth, and now you've lost most of their army. The heku will figure it out, and will kill you. They hate you... the heku are bad, and they want nothing but to hurt you and cause you pain. Everything that's happening to you right now is done by a heku."

"Emily!" Neils roared.

"Now we release the rats and the mice, the ants and spiders, the

snakes and scorpions... feel them as they crawl across your body. Feel them as they nibble at your skin and tear at your flesh," Mark said, and grinned slightly. "They flood in, a never ending parade of them, all bent on coming to you and feeling your warmth against their wet noses and pointed claws."

Silas tore open the side of her jeans and removed them, leaving her in only a short halter top and panties, to maximize the amount of skin for their imaginary horde of scavengers to torment her.

Mark broke his gaze and glanced up. "No more medication is needed. She won't be able to focus enough to turn anyone to ash."

"Yes, sir," Silas replied, and left with the syringe.

"Enjoy, I'll be back for more," Mark said, and kissed Emily lightly before leaving.

"Emily, look at me," Neils growled.

Her inhuman screams slowly faded as her voice gave out but her panicked movements and painful whimpers continued for hours as the guards watched her helplessly.

On the morning of the ninth day, Emily was still screaming silently on the floor as imaginary rodents tore at her flesh. She pulled against the restraints, and her wrists and ankles were swollen and bloody.

"Your turn," Mark said, and walked in with a scalpel and clamps.

"Let her go or so help me...," Neils growled.

"Oh do behave, you'll be dead soon enough," he said, and cut Neils' right wrist until his blood trickled out. Mark then used a small clamp to hold open the wound, and soon, a slow stream of blood was dripping down his arms.

"Emily can you hear me?" Neils asked.

A slow hiss escaped her lips as she watched the blood drip to the floor. She could almost taste it and feel how it would wet her throat and stop the painful starvation.

"Want some of the blood now, human?" Kralen asked, grinning. "See... you can't take your eyes off of it. Don't worry, you'll get it soon enough."

Emily hissed softly and pulled her eyes away from her bloody companions to watch the heku in the room.

"Day ten, my dear, tomorrow we will turn the infamous Winchester," he told her, though she didn't seem to understand.

"It won't work! Stop now before you kill her," Neils growled.

"Oh this'll work. Master was very sure of that," he said, and grinned.

"Who is your Master?" Neils asked scathingly.

"In due time. He'll be here for the turning. I'm sure," Silas told Neils and then leaned over her. "This part won't be hard at all, not with

that back injury of yours."

"Stop this! You know it's wrong," Neils yelled.

Kralen took a short log from a servant and turned back to Emily. He quickly lifted her back from the floor and slipped the log beneath her. When he let her go, she screamed in agony as her back began to spasm again at the odd angle.

"See, easy enough, there's more though… 12 hours is all, and we'll be done with it. Then we turn you," he told her, and left the room.

When the spasms began to die down, Kralen returned with a sharp knife and proceeded to slice long, deep cuts into her arms, legs, and abdomen. He grabbed a small bag from his coat and sprinkled salt into the bloody wounds as her silent screams became more harrowing.

"Do you have no compassion? Why are you doing this?" Neils asked.

"Compassion for a Winchester? None," he said bluntly, and then left the room.

"No!" Neils screamed when thirteen heku entered, twelve in blue robes and one in black. "Don't do this."

The heku in black knelt down beside Emily and touched her cheek softly. "It will be over soon."

"Stop this!" Neils yelled.

"Mortal, do you know where you are?" one of the heku in blue asked.

"She does," the heku in black replied.

Neils gasped. "Chevalier!"

"Do you know what is about to happen?"

"She does."

"Do you do so willingly and without coercion?"

There was amusement in his voice. "She does."

"Proceed"

Hisses were heard from around the room as the heku in blue knelt down beside her and sunk their teeth into her soft flesh. She gasped at the pain and her back arched.

"Chevalier, stop it!" Neils growled. "There are other ways to get back at Sotomar."

As she was about to lose consciousness, she felt something placed against her mouth. At first, she struggled but when the blood wet her dry lips, she began to drink feverishly.

The twelve heku in the blue robes all pulled away from her and stood back along the circular walls. Chevalier stayed knelt by her as she drank heartily from his wrist. After a few minutes, he stood up, pulling himself forcefully away from her.

Chevalier took a stick and wrote runes in the dirt around Emily as

she began to convulse and her eyes rolled back in her head. The twelve in blue began to chant and sway slightly in place as the runes were etched into the blood-soaked mud.

"Stop!" Neils yelled. "Chevalier, stop it!"

He brought the stick above his head, and poised it over her chest, ready to plunge it into her heart, stopping it and bringing her into immortality.

***

Emily was shaking with fear as she looked up at Chevalier from inside her cage. He was sitting comfortably in a rocking chair, watching her as she suffered.

He finally sighed, "All I want is for you to try to have a baby for the Equites."

She curled up into a ball and began to rock.

"I know doctors said you can't, but you have to try, or you'll never get out of this cage."

All she managed was a soft gasp as he blurred to the cage and slammed his fists into the top of it.

"You are mine! When they buried you alive, it should have proven to you that they no longer want you around."

After only a few seconds of silence, he yelled, "Speak to me!"

Her entire body shook with fear, and her forearms hurt from a recent punishment.

"Fine, if you want to be insolent," Chevalier growled. He tore open the door and dragged her out by her arm. "You don't even deserve the courtesy of shackles anymore. Shackles help the prisoner to stay still during a lashing… you will have to do it by yourself."

Chevalier took her arm and slammed her against a wall when she didn't answer. "Remove your shirt and get into position."

With shaky hands, she began to slip off the worn, dirty t-shirt she wore. When it took too long, he ripped it off of her and again slammed her into the wall. "Hands up… you so much as flinch, and it will get a lot worse."

When the thick leather straps hit her back and cut the tender flesh, she gasped but held perfectly still. She'd done this before. One small move and he would bring out the whip with the leather straps and single chain, the one that tore her back to shreds.

She fought back a scream as he hit her again, and she could feel the blood slide down her legs.

"You should be honored that I'm willing to procreate with you," Chevalier hissed. "You should jump at the chance to carry a mighty

heku in your weak, pathetic little body."

Her hands tightened into fists as the lashing continued, and he grew more furious.

"Sotomar doesn't want you… the Valle don't want you, or they wouldn't have buried you," Chevalier said, finally lowering his arm. He began to walk around her as she stood her position. "I can't even figure out why the Valle have kept you around for all these years. You're ugly, even for a mortal, and you sit in filth in my home day after day and do nothing you're told."

When her legs finally gave out, and she slumped to the floor, Chevalier began to laugh.

Chapter 18

"Good morning," Sotomar said as Emily rolled over in bed. He was nervous to see if it had worked, and this exact moment would tell him.

Emily shrugged and stretched. "What time is it?"

"It's 9am. You slept late."

She nodded and then called out for pancakes. Sotomar was pleased. If she was a prisoner, she wouldn't be eating. She finally stood up and pulled on a robe before walking into the bathroom. When the shower started, Sotomar stepped out and met up with the Council.

"So?" Elder Ryan asked.

He smiled. "It worked. She's calm but doesn't seem very pleasant."

"We should tell the true Council of the Equites immediately."

"Let's not for now," Sotomar suggested. "Let's make sure this doesn't somehow backfire on us."

He nodded and then the Council returned to the council chambers. Sotomar took the plate of pancakes and walked back into the bedroom when he heard the shower turn off. Emily came out a short time later in a long black dress and then sat down to eat.

"You look lovely, my dear," Sotomar said, sitting down beside her.

She ignored his complement. "What are you doing today?"

"I will have trials. Did you have plans?"

"I was going to help Hillock put in those video conferencing units in SDR Coven."

"Oh, that's right. Take Winchester 1, will you? It'll be faster than driving."

Not sure why, her stomach lurched at the thought of flying. "I'd rather drive."

"Why?"

She shrugged. "I just would. We'll be back in a few days."

He nodded. "Very well... take guards though."

"Do I have a choice?"

"No"

"Then sure," she mumbled. Sotomar looked around the room once before heading to trials. Emily packed a quick bag and then started down for the garage.

"We aren't flying?" one of the Imperial Guards said as he fell in behind her.

"No, Hillock, I'd rather drive."

"You just want out of the palace longer."

She nodded. "Don't you?"

"No"

"Did you get the equipment gathered?" she asked as she crawled

into the seat of the black Tahoe.

"Sure did. Let's get going," Hillock said when he slid into the driver's seat. He turned and looked over at Emily. "Are you okay?"

"Yeah, why?" she asked, though that wasn't entirely true. She felt strange, as if things we covered by a façade, or she wasn't in touch with the things around her. It seemed that if she were to reach out and touch something, it might not be solid beneath her fingers.

"You're just quiet."

"I'm just running through what we need to do. I want to get this over with and get back."

He pulled out of the Valle's city and started along the interstate.

"We aren't going near the Equites, are we?" she asked, looking back at the guards with them.

"Nope, far from it."

"We can protect you from them, though," one of the Imperial Guards said.

Emily looked at him, unbelieving. "The five of you are going to protect me from the largest faction?"

"Well... not the entire faction."

"I just don't want to go near them. I'm tired of getting kidnapped."

Hillock smiled. "We'll be okay."

"The Equites might back off if you'd publicly swear your allegiance to the Valle," one of the Imperial Guards said after a few minutes of silence.

"I told you... that doesn't feel right to me."

"But why?"

"I don't know. Maybe because I'm mortal."

"You're more heku than mortal."

She shrugged and watched out the window. If they were going to keep bugging her about it, this would be a long trip. She hated when they brought it up. Nothing to her felt right about swearing her allegiance to the Valle.

Sotomar was the one pushing for that the most, and it irritated her at times. She hated how she remained bonded to him, even though there was no love between them, well, love from her to him. She often suspected that Sotomar was in love with her, but she'd never felt that way about him.

Late that night they arrived at SDR Coven, one of the largest and most technologically advanced in the Valle. They were greeted at the gates by six guards in gray capes, and they inspected each in the Tahoe before waving them into the compound.

"Cheery bunch," Emily said when they passed through the thick cement walls.

Hillock smiled. "They have every right to be cautious."

"Still, I'm on the Council for hell's sake... they could at least be nice," she grumbled.

He chuckled and pulled up to the large house, located in the center of the compound. Guards rushed out and opened the door for those from the main city.

"Are we ready?" Hillock asked the closest one.

"Yes, sir," the heku replied, and then showed them into the house.

"Lady Emily!" the Coven Lord said. "It's such an honor to have you here in my home."

She decided to dispense with any pleasantries. "Where will we be setting up the cameras?"

"In our main conference room. Let me show you," he said, and then gently took her arm. Emily had the fleeting image of someone grabbing the Coven Lord and tearing him apart for touching her, but the thought was unwarranted. Sotomar didn't care who touched her, as long as it was appropriate and gentle.

The conference room was massive, with a sizeable table in the center made of ancient oak. The chairs were all large enough to comfortably accommodate any heku, so when Emily sat down, she was instantly uncomfortable.

"We're going to check on the routers we put up," Hillock said. "Why don't you start setting up the camera and laptop?"

She nodded. "Fine."

Emily looked again around the conference room and then opened the laptop and started setting up its internal camera. She nodded when she saw the wireless kick on and then loaded up the program that they would use to contact the Valle Council.

The prompt came up for the IP address of the one to call, and she frowned slightly when a number popped into her head. Shrugging, she typed the IP into the box and then pressed connect.

"... *Connecting to Andrew Jones*" flashed onto the screen. She gasped and quickly disconnected the line, then checked to make sure no one knew. She wondered how it was she knew the IP address to contact the Encala's Chief Interrogator but knew how mad Sotomar would be if he found out.

Emily dug through the registry, erasing any evidence of the IP address before she put in the one for the Valle Council.

"... *Connecting Valle Council*" appeared, and she waited for them to answer.

"Oh, that was fast," Elder Ryan said. Emily watched as the three Valle Elders came into view. "How does it look?"

"Looks clear from here. How is it there?"

"Beautiful," Sotomar said, amused. Emily tensed and then adjusted the audio settings. "How was the trip?"

"Boring, actually," she said as her fingers flew over the keyboard. "Why don't you turn over to the cam with the full Council?"

Ryan nodded and then reached out and pushed a button. Emily looked up and this time saw a far-away view of the entire Council. "I don't like that one."

"Why not?" Valle Elder Randall asked.

"I can't make any of you out. You're too tiny."

"You're one to talk," he said, laughing.

She changed some settings on the laptop. "I wouldn't use that one unless you have to."

"How's it going?" Hillock asked, stepping in.

"Fine," Emily said. "I don't like the signal strength though. It's going to make them choppy to the Council."

"It does seem slow," Sotomar said.

Hillock spun suddenly toward the door. "Wait…"

Emily looked over. "What's wrong?"

He growled, "We're under attack."

"What?! Who?" she gasped, and stood up.

"Equites…"

"Get her out of there!" Sotomar yelled.

"No," Emily said, frowning. "I'm not running from the Equites."

"Hillock…," Ryan hissed.

She reached over and shut the laptop, cutting off the connection to the Valle Council.

"Let's go," Hillock said, taking her arm. "There's a safe passage out of the compound from in the castle."

"No," she told him, pulling her arm out of his grasp. "I'm going to have a chat with them."

"The Council said…"

She cut him off with a glare and then walked out of the castle. There was a siren going off, but the rest of the city was eerily quiet. She heard shouting as she neared the front of the compound and then saw heku gathered, ready to defend their city.

"We won't stand by and take it," a familiar voice yelled.

Emily pushed through to the front and came face-to-face with General Skinner from the Equites' Powan Coven.

"What's the meaning of this?" she asked, crossing her arms.

General Skinner gasped. "Commander Emily!"

"Yeah… I'm here… so I suggest you get your asses out of here before I turn all your puppies to ash."

His eyes narrowed. "Let her go."

She glared at him. "Let me go? No one's holding me here."

"But… are you okay?"

"Like you care! Leave this coven alone or face me."

"I… I don't understand," he said, and took a step back.

"What don't you understand? I'm not going to let the Equites bully us around just because you're bigger," she told him.

He frowned slightly and then called a retreat before turning back to her. "We'll protect you if you want to come with us."

Emily started to laugh. "Why would I leave with you?"

"We can take you back to Council City."

"Ohhh, I get it," Emily said sarcastically. "You don't wanna bother kidnapping me this time, so instead, you'll ask me to come nicely?"

"Wh… what?" Skinner asked, confused.

"Ashing your canines in three…"

Skinner backed up slowly, still watching her.

"Two…"

Suddenly, the entire area disappeared of Powans.

Emily smiled and turned to Hillock. "There…"

"Sotomar didn't want you to confront them. He wanted you to leave," Hillock reminded her.

"I don't run from a fight," she said, and started back for the city.

***

"She what?" Chevalier asked, frowning.

General Skinner nodded. "We offered to help her, and she just threatened us to leave."

"She could be protecting the Powans," Kyle said.

"At least now we know for certain the Valle have her," Zohn said, turning to Chevalier.

"Anything else?" Chevalier asked the Powan Coven Lord.

"No, sir. She looked to be in good health and well taken care of."

"Very well, you may go."

General Skinner disappeared.

Kyle turned to Chevalier. "We going then?"

"Yes, I want to find out from the Valle what the hell they are thinking," Chevalier said.

"Wait a few days," Zohn suggested. "Maybe Emily will return to the palace."

"Damnit, protecting the Powans may have gotten her punished."

"You can't tell?" Quinn asked.

"No, actually. For some reason, I'm not getting anything from her right now."

"That's weird. The bond is still there?"

"Yes, though it's weakening."

"Wait a few days… then we'll go talk to them."

Chevalier hissed, "It's been three weeks…"

"A few more days and maybe she will have returned to the palace," Quinn said.

***

"If it's hurt badly, the Council will kill us," one of the Valle palace guards said, grimacing.

Emily looked down at her thumb. "Honestly… I just tore a nail on the bowling ball."

"Still… there's blood."

"They can't blame you for that! I'm accident prone."

"Let me look," one of the Imperial Guards said, and then gently took her hand.

Emily looked over when she heard shouting. "Who's the Council fighting with?"

"The Equites are here," he said, and then flipped her hand over to study the other side.

"Would you stop?" Emily sighed. "It's a tiny cut."

When the shouting got louder, she headed toward the door guard posted outside of the council chambers.

"They're nasty today, Lady Emily," he told her. "Elder Sotomar requested that you not go in."

She crossed her arms and faced him. "He's not my Elder."

The door guard chuckled and watched her walk in.

"Behave!" she shouted.

Chevalier, Kyle, Mark, and Kralen turned suddenly toward her. They watched, confused, as she skirted around them and made her way up to the council stand, where she sat beside Sotomar. They were shocked to see her in all black with her hair hanging down against her back. Her features seemed darker and somehow malevolent.

"I suggest you keep a civil tongue, or I'll ash you," Emily said, glaring at the Equites.

"Em?" Chevalier asked, frowning. "Are you okay?"

"I'm none of your concern."

"But…"

"Leave her alone," Sotomar said. "We can carry on this conversation civilly now."

"Return her to us!" Kyle yelled.

Ryan smiled. "Why would we turn her over to you?"

"She's my wife," Chevalier growled.

Emily stood up and leaned forward. "Wife?! You tortured me into marrying you! I've divorced you already, so drop the wife shit and leave me alone."

"I've never tortured you."

"Oh... so my time in your Alaska mansion was what? A figment of my imagination?"

"My Alaska mansion?"

"I thought heku had perfect memory... how about the two years you kept me from the Valle and locked me in a cage... that torture ring a bell?" she asked angrily.

Sotomar sat back and smiled where Emily couldn't see him.

"That wasn't him," Kyle said to her. "Do... do you believe that?"

"Of course it was him!" she yelled.

"What did you do?" Chevalier growled at the Council.

"We aren't sure what you mean," Randall said calmly.

Emily met Chevalier's eye. "Try to remember when the Equites kidnapped me so my Ancient father could try to force me to marry you... I wiped out the entire Equites palace and half of the city... and now I'm tempted to do it again."

"That wasn't us," Kralen said, shocked. "That was the Encala..."

"Shut up!"

"But..."

"No more lies. Stop blaming the Encala too... it's pathetic. You're the largest faction, yet you can't even take responsibility for your own stupidity," Emily yelled, and then sat down.

Kyle studied her for a second before speaking. "What about your children?"

She shook her head and smiled slightly. "I can't have children. I thought that was well known."

"You have to believe us, Em," Chevalier said softly. "It's got to be in there somewhere... the truth..."

She glared at him. "Finish your business and get out of my city."

"We'll behave if we can talk to the Valle Council alone."

"No"

"I actually think we're done," Sotomar said.

"We'll be in touch," Mark said as Kyle forced Chevalier out of the room.

Once the Equites were back on the Interstate headed for Council City, Chevalier spoke, "What happened?"

"Brainwashed by the Valle again," Mark suggested.

"How much though?"

Kyle shrugged. "Leave it to the Valle to figure out how to embed

themselves into her psyche."

"It's disturbing to see how she glares at us like she does when the Valle visit," Kralen said as he watched out the window.

"So what now?" Kyle asked. "They've somehow placed Chevalier in a lot of really bad incidents in her life."

"We kidnap her and see if we can erase what they've done," Chevalier said.

"How hard can it be?" Mark asked. "They kidnap her all the time."

"We just need to keep Kyle away from any interaction with her," Chevalier said.

"What? Why?" Kyle asked.

"She's never hesitated ashing a Chief Enforcer before. I'd rather not have to call the Encala back yet again."

"Speaking of Encala," Mark said. "I wonder if they know."

"I don't know. They may not care as long as the Valle let her stay friends with them."

"Once we have her, what do we do?" Kralen asked.

"We find out how they did what they did and try to reverse it."

"If we can…"

"Let's just get back and see what we can find," Chevalier said. "If we can, we'll call in some of our spies from the Valle palace."

"She looks different though," Mark mentioned.

Chevalier just nodded and drove toward Council City.

***

"How frustrating!" Emily yelled as she paced across her bedroom after yet another screaming match with the Equites.

"It's okay," Sotomar told her. "Just calm down."

"I don't want to calm down! How dare he walk in here and act like he's never done anything wrong to me. They keep coming here to visit and just deny they've done anything!"

"The Equites are playing at something is all. Probably, another misguided attempt to kidnap you."

"Yeah, well they may not have to wait long…"

"What are you planning?" Sotomar asked, his body tensing.

"I'm going to go to their precious city and wipe them out."

"I know that sounds like a good idea to you… but… please, just wait this out."

"How can I? They won't leave me alone… they'll never leave me alone."

Sotomar felt the first pangs of guilt but bottled them up inside. "They will. I promise. Someday, this will all be over, and you'll be able

to comfortably live with the knowledge that no one will ever take you away from the Valle."

She shook her head. "It'll never happen. I'm not a real being to the factions. I'm a soulless lump that's passed around and used to serve the whim of the heku."

"That's not true."

"Yes, it is," she said, tearing up. "It's like when the Equites kidnapped me and used me to wipe out Valle and Encala Covens." When she couldn't fight the tears any longer, she ran into the bathroom and locked the door.

Sotomar watched her and silently hoped that soon she'd feel safe with the Valle. He wasn't sure how many centuries it would take for Chevalier's hold on her to fully release, but he figured within the next fifty years, she may be somewhat free from his grasp, and he hers.

Emily sat in the bathroom and had a good cry. She couldn't explain the hole she felt in her heart but wrongly assumed it was because of the visit by the Equites. She looked around the bathroom, trying to figure out again why nothing seemed real, why nothing seemed like it belonged.

When she stepped out into the bedroom, Sotomar was gone, and she was alone. Boredom set in quickly, so she set out to find something to do. The four Imperial Guards fell in behind her as she walked up the stairs to the roof.

Once there, she sat on a high turret and looked out over the Valle's city. The colors were drab and brown, and the first snow was only a few days away. The wind nipped at her skin as she studied the city and tried to figure out why none of it seemed real.

"Are you okay?" Hillock asked as he sat down beside her.

She nodded.

"I'm worried about you."

"Why's that?"

"You just seem quiet lately."

Sotomar had asked Hillock to try to see if their re-memory was wearing off. In the three months Emily had been with the Valle, she'd grown closer to Hillock than any other heku. Sotomar secretly wondered if it was because of how much Hillock resembled Chevalier.

She shrugged. "I'd think you all would appreciate that."

"Well… it has been nice." He watched her to see if his comment brought out any of her famous playfulness.

Emily turned back to the city as her feet dangled far above the ground.

"Are you still upset about the Equites?"

"They are so irritating!" she groaned. "I can't imagine the nerve of

Chevalier acting like he didn't know what I was talking about."

"I'm sure he hasn't forgotten about them," Hillock said as he studied her. "I would think he's just trying to frustrate you."

"Well it worked."

"Elder Sotomar told me that you are considering wiping out Council City."

"I could do it."

"Of that we have no doubt. We'd much rather you not though."

"I don't even think it would be hard."

He sighed and then looked out over the city. "It's just that when you did it before, when you wiped out the Equites City and 3400 of its heku, you almost died."

"A few months of sleep would be worth it to be done with them."

Hillock checked behind him to make sure they were out of sight of her guards and then tenderly took her hand and kissed it. "Promise me, you won't."

Emily moved closer to him and put her head against his shoulder. "I can't promise that."

He moved her chin with his hand, so she was looking at him. "Promise me."

"Hill, I can't…"

Her words were cut off with his lips, and she instinctively pressed closer to him. After a few seconds, he pulled away from her and then smiled and brushed a stray hair off of her face.

Emily checked behind them for her guards and then whispered, "It's not fair that I can't be with you."

"Sotomar would have me killed if he knew."

"I know… but I don't love him."

"I wish the Council knew that your bonding was a façade."

"Let's run away together," she suggested, and then curled up against his chest.

"They would find us." He wrapped his arms around her.

"They're going to find us anyway."

"True… but hopefully I can find a way for us to be together before then."

She sighed and shut her eyes to listen to his heart.

Without warning, Hillock pushed Emily away from him and then cleared his throat. "The Valle will take care of them without you risking your life."

She shrugged and then turned around when she heard footsteps. She wasn't at all surprised to see Sotomar coming up behind them.

"It's getting cold out here," he said, and handed Emily a jacket.

She slipped it on and then turned back around and watched the heku

in the city get ready for what was supposed to be a massive snow storm.

***

"You're off of your mission," Quinn said to the Valle Imperial Guard standing before them. "We want a full report on Emily."

He nodded. "None of us know what happened... but a few weeks after the Valle kidnapped her, she's completely changed. It looks like, in her mind, Sotomar has replaced Elder Chevalier... then Elder Chevalier has replaced Exavior, and Salazar, and any other heku that's wronged her."

"She has no idea any of the true past?"

"Not that I saw as her guard."

"Anything else?"

"She's change, Elder. Keep in mind I didn't know Lady Emily well, but from what I saw, she was pretty happy and spirited. She's now rather angry all the time. I would say maybe depressed. I know she wears only black and walks silently around the halls of the Valle palace with her four Imperial Guards behind her."

"No games? No teasing or joking?" Kyle asked.

"No, Chief Enforcer. I don't believe I've even seen her smile."

Quinn nodded. "It stands to reason that by changing everything that's happened over the last 30 or so years... they changed her personality. Our personalities are formed out of experiences and encounters. As far as we know, it's all changed."

"She gives no indication at all that things have changed?" Chevalier asked.

"None, sir," the heku replied.

"Return to your coven after giving Mark a full report," Zohn told him.

The heku bowed and then blurred out of the council chambers.

"Her personality change could be permanent," the Coven Liaison Officer said.

Chevalier nodded. "I know... I just hope we can undo what the Valle did, and it will return."

"First we have to figure out how," Zohn said.

"There was an incident... it was in 820 BC, and one of the Valle Old Ones reworked the entire history of an old mortal man, just to see if it could be done."

"What happened?"

"It drove him mad," Chevalier said, looking over at them. "He kept saying he didn't belong and that nothing was real. After that, the practice was banned."

"Until now, it seems."

"It took months to redo his memory. The Valle started by walking him through his earliest memories from childhood. When he said, say, that he went to tend the sheep, the Valle would change it to tending cows."

"Months?" Kyle asked.

"Yes... every bit of information had to be reworked. With Emily, they only had to do 50 years," Chevalier told him.

"Or 30," Quinn said. "Just from when you first met."

He nodded. "I'm positive that's what was done. I just find it hard to believe that Sotomar allowed it. He saw what it did to the man."

"He was there?"

"Yes... he actually did it. I do believe it was his idea and then it was his order that banned the Valle. As soon as we heard, we banned it from the Equites, and shortly thereafter, the Encala banned it also."

***

"God, I want you," Hillock said before kissing Emily passionately. She sat on his lap, facing him, and her hands were wound through his black hair.

The dark room, long abandoned, was safe from onlookers. Hillock would hear anyone approaching, and the medical supplies were an easy excuse to be in there. Everyone knew that Emily had fallen off of a ladder earlier, and it would be common for her to be in the infirmary with a guard.

She lightly kissed down his neck and began to unbutton his shirt. "No one's stopping you."

He lifted her face and then pressed his lips hard against hers as his hands trailed up her back softly. When she released the last button on his shirt, she slipped it off and ran her hands along his chiseled chest.

He whispered softly as he ran his fingers along her spine. "I told you... we can't."

"Why not?" She leaned forward and lightly ran her tongue along the vein in his neck and then bit softly.

He shivered and slipped her t-shirt over her head, and tossed it onto the medical bed they were sitting on. His strong hands pulled her close against him, and his mouth met hers again.

Emily's body ached to be closer to him, and she pressed hard against him as her hands felt along his broad shoulders. Not able to wait any longer, she quickly pulled away from him slightly and began to unfasten his belt.

Hillock took her hands in his and looked into her eyes. "We can't."

"Why not?"

"Heku can tell," he said, and then tried to kiss her again, but she pulled away from him.

"How?"

"They can smell the hormones… they would smell me on you."

"What if I don't care?"

"The Council would kill us both," Hillock explained. "Adultery is serious…, but adultery with an Elder's wife is worse."

"I'm tired of being alone," she whispered, and then leaned forward and put her forehead on his chest. "I've been alone for 30 years."

"I love you, Emily," Hillock said, and then wrapped his strong arms around her.

"Then give me this," she said, and kissed him softly.

He pulled away from her. "I won't risk them killing you."

"Maybe death is better."

Hillock grabbed her shirt and handed it to her. "Sotomar is asking where you are."

She sighed and then slipped it back on. "I hate him."

"I know… but you can't divorce an Elder."

"Has it ever been done?"

"No, death comes first," he explained.

"So, I get to be alone forever…"

"… I'll think of a way."

"I love you," she whispered, and then kissed him again before standing up. "Figure out how we can be together."

"I will."

She gasped and grabbed her essence ring when it fell off of her finger. With wide eyes, she looked up at him.

"No," he whispered, too afraid to speak.

"I… I'll hide it… he won't know," she said, barely making a noise.

"He'll know. Heku can feel the bond break."

"We're dead then."

Hillock looked up at the door and tried to figure out how to handle this without letting on that she wasn't bonded to Sotomar. "I wonder why he hasn't blurred in here and killed me yet."

She turned to the door. "What are the chances that he doesn't know?"

"He has to. The heku can feel the bond and can feel when it breaks."

"Run then. Let's get away."

"They'll find us," Hillock said as his body tensed.

"How did it break? We didn't…"

"Admitting you love me was a betrayal."

"Damnit"

"He's in the council chambers. I can hear them, and he acts like nothing's happened."

Emily frowned. "Then we're safe. I just hide my hand, and he won't notice."

"I don't think we have much of a choice."

***

"It's broken," Chevalier said, and then looked over at the Council.

"What is?" Zohn asked, unconcerned.

"The bond."

Kyle gasped. "Is she dead?"

"I don't know," Chevalier told him. "We better contact the Valle and see."

"Or not," Quinn said, turning to Chevalier. "If she's alive, then she's either agreed to join the Valle or has found someone else. Either way, there's nothing we can do, and it could worsen things if we push the issue."

"I have to know."

"We'll find out. I'll see if Jelith knows," the Court Reporter said before disappearing from the room.

"What if she did find someone else?"

"She thinks she's bonded to Sotomar," the Chief of Staff said. "Maybe she fell in love with him."

Chevalier disappeared from the room.

***

"Are you sure you're okay?" Sotomar asked Emily. She was sitting in a recliner in the bedroom with a blanket over her.

"Yes"

"You've seemed distant recently."

She shrugged. It was by luck alone that he hadn't seen the missing ring, and Emily still wondered how it was he didn't know the bond was broken. After five weeks, she considered herself safe from him finding out. The main problem was that the more she fell in love with Hillock, the more she hated her husband.

Sotomar squatted down by the chair and looked at her. "You'd tell me if something was wrong?"

"Yes"

"Then what's going on? It's been almost a month since I've even really seen you."

Getting up the nerve, she looked at him and tried to hide her hatred from him. "Do you feel our bond?"

"Of course I do."

"Always, or does it come and go?"

"I always feel it. It lets me know you're safe," he said, and then smiled and brushed her hair off of her shoulder.

She forced herself to smile. "I'm okay. Go down to the trials."

He studied her face and kissed her softly before leaving. Emily wrinkled her nose and wiped her mouth on her sleeve and then looked around the room. She was trying to figure out how Sotomar didn't know the bond was broken.

"Come in," she said when someone knocked, then smiled when Hillock came in.

He looked around the room and then walked over. "Elder Sotomar wants me to stay with you today."

"How convenient."

He grinned. "Yes, well. He's worried about you."

"He still doesn't know," she said, finally pulling her hands out of the blanket.

"He probably just hasn't noticed," he said as he sat down beside her and took her hand.

"I'm not so sure about that."

"What do you mean?"

Emily shrugged. "I just feel like something's not right. I keep getting these flashes… images… of places I don't recognize, things I've never done. When I look at him, I see something underlying his image."

Hillock frowned. "Maybe we should have the doctor look at you."

"No way! He'll think I'm crazy. I just feel like maybe Sotomar isn't what he seems."

Hillock watched her as she looked out the window. He wasn't sure how to report this new information to the Council without admitting that the bond was broken, which would put both of their lives at risk. He was afraid if she found the truth, he would lose her, and he wasn't sure his heart could take it.

"There's a lot of tension right now with the Council. Both the Encala and the Equites are causing problems. I would imagine those problems are masking the bond breaking."

She shook her head. "I just don't think so. I need to get to the bottom of it though."

"The images you see are probably from a traumatic experience. Maybe images from Chevalier's Alaskan mansion or even inside the Equites palace."

"I guess."

He smiled and then leaned over and kissed her. She instantly responded to his touch and leaned into him.

When he pulled back, she could see the longing in his eyes. "It's so hard to be away from you."

"We have to be together," she told him. "There's a huge hole in my heart that's only filled when I'm in your arms. It's painful, and I can't take it. I've been alone for too long."

Hillock started to feel guilty. As hard as he was falling for her, he knew that it was Chevalier her heart ached for, and not him. Without a word, he stood up and blurred out of the room. Being that near to her made it hard to fight back the deep desire he had. He put both of their lives at risk by allowing himself to love her.

Emily sighed when he left and then looked outside, trying to figure out how to stop the feeling that things weren't right. The empty fireplace caught her eye, and she turned toward it when it flashed into two fireplaces, both roaring with fire and then returned to the dark remains of the burnt out fire.

She focused on the fireplace, willing it to change again. When it did, the image was clearer and even the smells in the room changed. It seemed familiar, but she couldn't place it. The image disappeared suddenly, and with it left the warmth and contentment she felt when it was covering the dark room. As she looked around her bedroom, her heart again sunk, and the pain of loneliness returned.

"Enter," she said when someone knocked.

One of her Imperial Guards opened the door. "The Council is asking for you to come mediate a meeting with the Equites and the Encala."

She nodded and then stood up once he left. She pulled on a long-sleeved black sweater and pulled it down to cover her hands before wrapping her arms around herself and walking out.

The Council turned to her when she walked in but immediately returned to face forward when it was obvious that she wasn't in a pleasant mood. She sat down beside Sotomar and pulled her hand away when he tried to take it.

"Let them in," Elder Ryan called out after glancing at her quickly.

Encala Elder William and Andrew, their new Chief Interrogator, came in, followed by Zohn and Richard, the Equites Chief Interrogator. They stood before the Valle Council after scanning all of them carefully. They were all relieved to see that Emily really was alive, though it was obvious she was angry, and she had a menacing aura.

"Why have you come uninvited?" Sotomar asked them.

What the Valle didn't know, was that the Encala and Equites had spoken ahead of time so as not to say anything that would go against things the Valle had Emily believing.

William addressed him. "We came to ensure the Winchester is being taken care of."

Ryan looked at Emily. "Seems she's fine."

"When are you going to get it through your heads that my welfare is none of your business?" Emily snapped.

Richard studied her while Zohn spoke, "It's well known that the well-being of the last Winchester is the responsibility of all factions."

Emily frowned slightly. As Zohn spoke, Sotomar's image replaced his briefly.

"Are you okay?" Richard asked her.

She cleared her head and then glared at him. "Your only reason for driving all the way over here is to check on me?"

"No," William said. "We also want to know what the Valle are going to do about the Togon Coven."

Sotomar smiled. "Why would we do anything about them?"

"They're breaking heku law," Zohn told him. "We have no business being involved in mortal sports."

"They aren't hurting anyone," Ryan said. "They've agreed not to win the competition, so we see no reason why they can't compete."

"What gives you the right to break the laws of the heku?"

"Not breaking… bending…," Sotomar told them. "The rules specifically state that heku cannot influence mortal sports, not that we can't join them at all."

"Not the rules we were speaking of," William said.

Sotomar's eyes narrowed. "I'm aware of that."

Emily looked from Sotomar to William. "What do you mean?"

"We're done, dear," Sotomar said to her. "You may go."

"No, I want to know."

She sighed when four Imperial Guards entered through the back doors and escorted her out after she looked hard at Zohn. He was watching her carefully, and it felt familiar and she wondered why part of her was drawn to him.

Sotomar leaned forward. "What do the Encala care that we have Emily?"

It was obvious that Andrew was furious. "We care because it was done against heku law, and it interferes with her relationship with our faction."

"We didn't turn her against you though," Ryan said. "We just turned her against the Equites."

"She obvious doesn't remember our friendship!"

Ryan smiled. "We might have skipped that part…"

"We're not going to stand by and watch this!" Zohn yelled. "You know as well as we do what happened to the last person you did this to."

"I'm surprised Chevalier even heard about that," Sotomar said, unaffected by his anger. "I was more careful this time."

"It's too dangerous, and it's a personal violation that ranks up with the Ancients."

"We're done," Sotomar said, and motioned for the door guard to open them. "See them out."

"This is going to backfire on you," Zohn said to him. "We're not going to clean up the mess."

"Neither are we," William said.

"So you've joined?" Ryan asked.

"No, we've not aligned... however... when a common mission is found, we will cooperate long enough to see it through."

Zohn turned to Richard. "Shall we go?"

"Yes, I got what I needed."

"Which is what, exactly?" Sotomar asked the Equites Chief Interrogator.

Richard simply smiled and walked out with Zohn, followed by the Encala. Once in Equites 2 and headed back to Council City, they were free to talk.

"She has doubts," Andrew said, breaking the silence.

"I saw that," Richard replied. "I saw flickers of disbelief."

"So it's close to when the re-memory may break?" Zohn asked. He had been concentrating on Sotomar and hadn't seen what the Chief Interrogators picked up.

"If I had to guess... yes," Andrew told him.

"Then that's when she could lose her mind."

"Yes"

"What else?"

Richard smiled. "She hates Sotomar."

"And... she's hiding her hands," Andrew added.

"He may not know the bond is broken," William said. "So how is it then?"

"She may have found someone other than Sotomar," Richard suggested, "or... she may have just finally sworn her allegiance to the Valle."

"If Sotomar finds out how badly she hates him, he's not going to be happy."

"The hate isn't mutual," Richard said. "Sotomar is very much in love with her."

"It's common around her, though," Zohn reminded him.

"Still, it makes things more dangerous."

"So what do you suggest?" William asked. "The Encala are in on a rescue mission."

"We can handle the Valle alone," Zohn assured him. "We just don't want to end up getting turned to ash and risking her falling into another coma doing it."

"I want to be there," Andrew said.

"We know that. We can't attack though."

"So we wait?"

Richard lightly tapped his fingers against the armrest. "She's close to breaking out. The more things we can do to remind her of before the re-memory, the more she'll come out."

"You copying what Sotomar says about Winchester safety brought a glimmer of doubt. I could see it," Andrew said.

"How do we time our attack with her revelation that it's all a lie?" Zohn asked.

"More importantly, how do we handle the realization?" Andrew asked. "If she did find someone else... she'll realize that she cheated on your Elder."

"That's not her fault."

"Will he know that?"

Zohn started to say yes and then paused. "I would think so."

"Will she know that?"

"I don't know."

***

Emily was bored. She was certain the Equites and Encala would have come back, but they hadn't returned since their meeting two weeks ago. Sotomar was out of the palace on a mission and had taken Hillock with him. She wandered the palace alone, not sure what to do. The four guards following her seemed put-out to be on her guard duty and were even more irritated that she walked aimlessly around the palace.

"A book maybe?" one of them suggested.

"No," she told him.

"Movie?"

"No," she said, and then started up to the ninth floor of the palace to see what she could find.

"What's up here you need?" one of them asked.

"I don't know."

"Just go back to your room then."

"I don't want to. If you're so bored... go away."

"Elder's orders are we're to stay with you."

"Joy"

"We don't want to be here any more than you want us to be, princess," he hissed.

Emily sighed and decided to appease them and go find a book. "Fine… library then."

Her guards had cleared out the library before she arrived and then took up post outside of the door. There was only one way in and out of the massive expanse of books, so they were allowed to let her look by herself.

She thumbed through some of the books, finally coming across one of her favorite books, Anna Karenina. She picked the book up and inspected it as she ran her fingers along the crisp pages. Not sure why, she half expected to find the pages warped from water damage. She didn't feel like that serious of a book though, so she returned it to the shelf.

After almost an hour of searching for something to read, Emily passed yet another tall ladder and decided that she would actually climb this one to see what books were on the shelves almost two stories above her head.

Emily found that the higher she climbed, the less fiction she came across and the more she ran into hand-written books that seemed older than anything she'd seen before. One was bound in a thin leather, and the pages were scribbled in Latin with a hasty pen. The entire book smelled of rotten flesh and she quickly put it back on the shelf, no longer wanting to know what was in it. Up higher, she discovered a rolled parchment that contained nothing but runes.

After rolling up the parchment and returning it to the shelf, Emily saw something that seemed out of place. Off to her right was a hardback book that was in pristine condition and hundreds of years newer than anything else she'd seen up this high.

She reached over for it, but her fingers could only barely touch it. Hanging farther off the ladder, she was able to finally grab it but lost her balance and fell a few feet before her foot caught on the ladder rung, and she was able to grip the shelf tightly. Once her heart calmed from her close-call, she looked at the book.

There was nothing special about the book, *Generations by Camber Smith*. She started to put the book back but then saw a copy of the Equites Crest on the spine. Wondering why the Valle wanted an Equites book, she opened it and was shocked to see a picture of Ulrich. The first page she turned to was titled "Miles Winchester." Sitting down on the rung of the ladder, she began to flip through the pages of her history.

Emily smiled when she found a picture of her Mother with her stallion. She lightly ran her finger over the picture and then saw Sam standing behind her. She had to admit she missed him a bit, especially when she felt as alone as she had lately.

When the next page showed a black-and-white photo of Chevalier,

Emily frowned and began to read. She was completely absorbed in what she was reading, because it was in contrast to her memories of the events described. She distinctly remembered her first encounter with Sotomar, though the book depicted the incident correctly, they had it listed as Chevalier and not Sotomar that had whisked her away to Colorado.

By the time she finished the book and read about the three children, Allen, Alexis, and Dain, Emily began to wonder about the validity of the book as opposed to her memories, which seemed faded and distant suddenly.

Emily put the book back where she found it and quickly climbed down the ladder. She wasn't sure what to do about the feelings she had that things around her weren't real, or that things she felt were masking something deeper. Hillock was the only one she felt comfortable talking to, and he was out with Sotomar, who she despised and didn't trust. She briefly wondered if there was something Sotomar was covering up and then if Hillock was in on it also.

"Where to now?" one of her guards asked.

Emily didn't answer but walked down the stairs and toward the kitchen. She always enjoyed baking and thought it would give her a chance to think. Nothing cleared heku out of the kitchen faster than the smell of baking cookies. After loading up a cookie tray, Emily turned to put it in the oven but stopped when she'd turned to a cupboard instead. She could clearly remember the oven being there, but now it was just a cupboard.

She dropped the cookie sheet on the counter and then sat down on the floor and wrapped her arms around her knees. She couldn't figure out what was happening to her. Nothing seemed real. Nothing seemed solid or plausible. For almost thirty years she'd been with the Valle, yet only recently had she begun to feel like she didn't belong.

Trumpets sounded, letting the palace know that Sotomar was back. Emily stood up and decided to talk to Hillock about her suspicions and concerns. Heading up the stairs, she could hear the heku coming down the stairway.

"Emily," Sotomar said, smiling brightly. He put his hands out for her, but she walked past him and up to Hillock.

"I need to talk to you."

He glanced nervously at the Elder and then back to Emily. "Okay, what's up?"

"Alone"

Sotomar nodded when Hillock looked for approval, so he led Emily up the stairs to a private conference room. Once they sat down and Hillock confirmed no one was listening to them, Emily took his hands and looked into his eyes.

"You love me, right?"

"Of course I do."

"Then tell me the truth when I ask you…"

"What's going on, Emily?" Hillock asked when he noticed how nervous she'd become.

"Is something weird going on?"

"Like what?"

"Like… I don't even know. Something that would make me feel like things aren't like they should be. Something that alters my perception of events in my life?"

"What's causing this?"

"I don't know how to explain it, but it's getting worse."

"You need to see a doctor."

"No, I don't. I need you to tell me what's going on."

Hillock frowned slightly. "Nothing's going on."

She cocked her head to the side slightly and then got a strange look on her face. "You're lying to me."

"No, I'm not."

"Yes, you are. I… I can tell."

He sighed, "You can't tell if someone's lying, Emily."

She let go of his hands. "You're in on it."

"Nothing's going on to be in on. Maybe you're coming down with something."

"You're lying to me," she whispered, and then stood up. "I trusted you."

"Emily, listen to me. We just need to talk to the Council about this."

"No, we don't! Why would I go to them about this?"

Hillock surprised her by appearing at her back and restraining her from behind. "Let's go… it's what's best."

"No, take me in there, and I tell Sotomar everything."

He gasped and let go of her. "What?"

Thinking quickly, Emily spun and then kissed him passionately as her fingers wound through his hair and grabbed a handful.

He fought for only a moment before returning her kiss and spinning around to put her on the table. She wrapped her legs around him and pressed her body against his.

After a few minutes, Hillock pulled away from her and looked into her eyes. "This was all a ruse to get us alone?"

She smiled and started to unbutton his shirt as she nodded.

"You just can't be trusted, can you?" he asked, amused. "We can't though, the Council is waiting for me."

Faking a pout, Emily watched Hillock walk out, and she looked

around, not sure what to do from here. It was obvious that Hillock was in on whatever was going on. Without even trying, she could see the lie forming on his face, and it infuriated her. She felt the hole in her heart grow larger as she thought about his lies.

Emily had to find out what was wrong, what was causing her to feel like this. She felt on the brink of discovery but didn't know how to bring it all to the front, so she could fully see what was happening.

Not sure what else to do, she headed into the Valle's prison to seek out Larry and Cody. The Equites had them first, and she wondered if the two former V.E.S. leaders knew anything about her history.

"Lady Emily, you can't come down here," one of the prison guards told her.

"I won't be but a second."

"Go back up," he said, and took her arm.

Emily yanked her arm away from him. "Don't touch me."

"Then get out of the prison."

As he growled and took her arm again, her eyes focused in on the electrical control panel high above the guard's desk. She saw herself climbing onto the desk to reach it and then running off down the corridor following a strange Encala heku.

"Lady Emily?" the guard asked, suddenly concerned that she'd fallen silent.

"I need to go lay down," she whispered, and then headed back up the stairs. No one said anything to her, and she was able to go into her room and lie down on the bed undisturbed. The image was solid in her mind, following an Encala through the Valle's prison system, looking for Chevalier and Kyle.

"Emily?" Sotomar's soft voice penetrated the dark room.

"What?" she whispered.

"Are you okay?"

"I just don't feel well." That wasn't entirely a lie. Her stomach was tied into knots and trying to clear the fleeting images in her mind was giving her a headache.

"Shall I call a doctor?"

"No"

He sat down beside her on the bed, and the room fell silent for a few minutes.

"Talk to me, please."

"About what?" she asked, though she didn't look over at him.

"About why you are so quiet. Why do you ignore me and can't look me in the eye?"

"I don't know why."

"Have I done something to you?"

"No"

He sighed, "You know I care a great deal about you, right?"

She shrugged.

"If you need anything, just tell me. I would give you the world."

"I just want to be alone."

"Very well," he whispered, and then disappeared.

Following pure instincts, Emily got out of bed, walked over to the corner of the room and then sat down and pulled her legs up against her chest. She wrapped her arms around them and buried her face between her arms as she began to rock. This odd position gave her more comfort than she had felt in years, and she felt the stress of the images begin to fade as her mind calmed.

> *"Can you tell me how to get you to sleep in the bed? You've been sleeping on the floor for almost three years from the sounds of it."*

Emily frowned as she heard Chevalier's voice in her head. She calmed her breathing and put the hatred for him in the back of her mind to focus on his words. She remembered those words. They were spoken by Sotomar during her recovery from Chevalier's 2-year control of her.

> *"You're not going to be lashed here. Not for anything."*

Again, it was Chevalier's voice saying what Emily remembered Sotomar telling her. Why would her mind pick an enemy to say those caring words?

Emily's mind replayed when she first found out that Sotomar loved her. It was just after her bout with pneumonia shortly after they met. When her mind showed her the image though, it was Chevalier and not Sotomar that was speaking.

> *"Leave it, Love."*

> *"Don't look at me like that, you knew it all along."* His face was stern, but then he grinned.

It was Chevalier's face, not Sotomar's who grinned at her. She thought back and couldn't remember Sotomar ever smiling at her the way she remembered in that instance.

She could feel memories, emotions, and feelings all rushing forward, so she concentrated hard on them, trying to bring them to the surface. She suddenly realized that's what had been missing from her

life, true, raw emotions.

With an impact that caused her head to pound, it all came back to her, and she gasped and looked around the room. Her breath caught when she saw the gray of the Valle room and then she remembered her last eight months with them. How she lived in their palace as a Valle, as Sotomar's wife. Her heart sunk when she remembered her time with Hillock and how it broke the bond she'd assumed was from Sotomar.

With anger rising to the surface, she picked up her cell phone and quickly dialed.

"Equites Council," Kyle said. "Who is this?"

"Be here at 6am," Emily said, and then hung up before anyone from the Valle could hear more.

Kyle turned off the phone and looked over at Chevalier.

His heart jumped. "Do it."

"We're still under attack by the former Council," the Chief of Staff said.

"We can't leave her there. She obviously has some kind of plan," Kyle said.

"I'll go," Chevalier said, and then stood up.

"We can't separate the Elders during an attack that is attempting to banish the Council," Zohn reminded him.

"For once, I don't give a damn about this Council. I'm not leaving her with the Valle."

"I'll go too," Kyle said, "I'll take Cavalry Team 7."

"We can't have you both gone," Quinn said. "Kyle can stay."

"What if that's not enough?"

"It will be."

***

"Good morning," Sotomar said as Emily stretched in bed. "Do you feel better this morning?"

"Yes," she sighed and then rolled onto her side. "I just want more sleep."

He bent down and lightly kissed her forehead. "Sleep as late as you like, my dear."

Once Sotomar was out of the room, Emily scrambled out of bed and got dressed in all black. She had 30 minutes before she'd asked the Equites to arrive. Thirty minutes gave her plenty of time to make the Valle pay for the last eight months.

"Good mo…" the Imperial Guard's words were cut off when they fell to ash at Emily's feet. She quickly ran down the stairs toward the council chambers, and her bare feet barely made a sound.

"Where are your guards?" the door guard asked.

Emily glared at him and then stepped over his ashes to get to the door.

"Emily, we're busy," Elder Ryan said when she walked in.

She ignored him and moved closer, obviously mad.

"What's wrong, child?" the Chief Interrogator asked.

"I wanted you to watch," Emily hissed.

"Watch what?" Sotomar asked, frowning.

Emily's face showed her concentration, and a steady stream of blood began to drip down from her nose.

"What are you doing?!" Sotomar asked, standing slowly.

"Stop her!" the Chief of Defense roared as reports started coming in from the city that they were under attack.

"Emily, stop it this instant!"

She fell to her knees before turning her attention to the Valle Elders. As her eyes narrowed, they were hit with the excruciatingly painful burn in their chests. Their screams fell on empty hallways as the echoes of their pain rushed past piles and piles of ash.

Emily leaned forward when the last of the Valle Council fell to ash. Her head hurt beyond reason, and she could feel the fog covering her mind and clouding her thoughts.

**

"Valle from Equites 2," Kralen called over the radio again. "Elder, I'm still not getting an answer."

Chevalier nodded. "I'm not seeing any movement out there at all."

"Land it?"

"Put it down on the front lawn but be ready to pull out of here if it's a trap."

Kralen nodded and gently set the helicopter down on the lawn. When no one appeared, the heku jumped out onto the enemy grass and looked around the silent city.

"Damnit," Chevalier hissed and then rushed into the palace, noticing all of the piles of ash along the way.

Kralen was the first to catch her scent, and the Equites followed him to the council chambers. He rushed over to where Emily was lying on the cold, dirt floor, and turned her onto her back. It was oddly reminiscent of the last time she'd taken out the city and then slept for three months.

"Em?" Kralen asked softly.

Chevalier walked up to the council stand and ordered the Cavalry to gather the ashes before ,going back to Emily. He reached down and picked her up gently and then scanned the room.

"I'm sure an alarm went out. We have to get out of here," Chevalier whispered.

Kralen nodded and ordered Team 7 out of the building. It was amazingly easy and seemed surreal as they took off over the quiet city with Emily tucked carefully into a sleeping bag on the floor.

Chapter 19

Emily felt the headache as she swam out of the darkness and began to wake up. The room was dark, and she wasn't sure where she was. Turning the Valle to ash began to come back to her, and she quickly opened her eyes and sat up, only to see that she was in her bedroom in the Equites Palace.

She grabbed her cell phone and then checked the date. She'd been asleep for just over three weeks. Looking at the door, she wasn't sure who to call for. She wasn't sure how mad Chevalier was that the bond was broken, yet again, nor was she sure if he knew how.

After removing the I.V. from her arm, she pulled on a robe and then steadied herself against the bedpost until she felt strong enough to stand. She spun suddenly when she heard Chevalier outside of her door.

"I know you're awake," he said. "Can I please come in?"

Emily froze, not sure what to do. She'd cheated on him and didn't know if he knew or if he blamed her for it as badly as she blamed herself. She was shaking when she barely whispered for him to come in.

Chevalier came into the room and then shut the door behind him. He watched her for a moment before he smiled. "It's good to have you back."

She nodded and studied his face.

"I'm not mad."

Again, she only nodded and then fought back the tears.

He took one step toward her, his face calm and caring. "I just have one question."

"Okay," she whispered.

"Did you sleep with him?"

Emily shook her head as her eyes filled with tears.

"It wasn't your fault."

"I should have known."

"You couldn't have known. They re-worked every memory you had from the moment Jerry came to you for cattle."

She looked around the room as she wrapped her arms around herself.

"Who was it?" He took another step toward her, wanting badly to wrap his arms around her.

She debated not telling him but finally decided he had a right to know. "Hillock."

He smiled. "Sotomar didn't even know."

"I know."

"We have Sotomar in our prison still but had to let the rest of them go."

She nodded.

"Where's Hillock?"

Emily smiled crookedly. "How did you know I took him?"

"I just know you. Where is he?"

She didn't want to tell him. Emily was sure that Chevalier wanted to get his hands on the heku she had fallen in love with, but she felt he was hers to punish.

He saw the hesitation in her eyes. "I want to talk to him."

"I know."

"I can make him suffer more than banishment."

She teared up again and spoke in a hushed whisper. "I was so alone."

"I'm not blaming you. I realize that you believed you were alone for 30 years. It's natural to seek out a companion."

Emily glanced over at the black clothes she wore for her assault on the Valle palace.

Chevalier followed her gaze and then walked over and picked up her shirt. He felt around and dropped it into the chair before picking up the black pants. When he got to the bottom of the pants, he felt a lump and pulled a small bag of ashes out of a hidden pocket inside the lower leg.

"When I'm done with Hillock, I want to re-bond and then head out on the yacht for a bit," Chevalier told her as he headed toward the door.

"No," she whispered, and then shook her head when he looked at her.

"Why not?"

With shaky hands, Emily held out the essence ring. "I cheated on you."

"No, you didn't." He didn't move to take the ring. "That wasn't your fault."

She swallowed hard. "I thought I loved him."

"Em..."

"No. This time the bond was broken validly... I cheated on you, and you shouldn't take me back."

"I don't blame you."

"You should."

He studied her for a few minutes. "Why should I blame you? You were alone for 30 years and didn't even remember me as anything other than an enemy. Why would I blame you for finding someone to love?"

"Get mad," she whispered.

"No"

"Get mad!" she yelled, and suddenly fury showed in her eyes. "Yell... scream... choke me! I don't care what you do, but get mad at

me."

"I'm not mad."

She moved to him suddenly, and he took her hands when she tried to push him. "Get mad!"

"No"

"I cheated on you, damnit."

"No, you didn't."

"I loved him."

"I realize that."

Emily tried to get her hands away from Chevalier, but he held her wrists tightly. "It's not your fault."

"I wanted to sleep with him."

She saw a brief flicker of anger cross his face before he calmed. "Emily... stop..."

Not getting the anger she wanted, Emily sent a flash of burning at him and felt his hands tighten on her wrists as he gasped. Before she saw any movement, Mark and Silas appeared in the bedroom and took her from Chevalier, then restrained her against the far wall.

"Calm down," Mark said to her.

Chevalier pulled at his shirt a bit, trying to relieve lingering pain as he watched Emily closely. He finally regained his control and walked up to her while she watched him with tears streaming down her face.

"Let her go," he said softly.

Mark and Silas both let go of her but stayed close, in case she did it again.

Chevalier gently lifted her chin, so she was looking up at him. "What do you want, Em?"

Her voice cracked. "I want you to get mad. I want you to punish me for cheating on you."

"You didn't cheat on me."

"I did... I loved him."

"You can't cheat on someone you don't even remember."

"Get mad, damnit!"

"I am... just not at you."

Emily sunk down against the wall when all three of the heku left her room, and Mark shut the door after them.

"Are you okay, Elder?" Kralen asked from the hallway.

He nodded and smiled slightly. "She was trying to pick a fight."

"She'll be okay."

Chevalier nodded and then headed down the stairs with Hillock's ashes.

She sat back against the wall, deep in thought about her actions while with the Valle. The only thing she had to be ashamed of was her

time with Hillock. She was glad that she'd never caved to pressure and swore her allegiance to the Valle.

Chevalier dumped Hillock's ashes out of the small bag onto the floor of the trial area. Sotomar watched angrily and then glared down at the ashes before turning to Chevalier as he sat in his chair.

"Who is that?" Sotomar asked, irritated.

"That's your Hillock," Chevalier explained and then nodded to Kyle.

"Why is he here?"

"You'll see."

Kyle revived the Valle, and it shocked the Equites how much he looked like Chevalier, albeit a few inches shorter and not quite as muscular.

Hillock pulled on a blue robe and then turned to face the Equites Council, his eyes wide. "Oh my God."

"Yeah… better start praying, boy," Chevalier hissed.

Sotomar faced the Elders. "What right do you have holding me here?"

"What right did you have to alter Emily's memory?" Zohn asked him.

"We'll do what it takes to rightfully return her to our faction."

"You know how dangerous that was!"

"Emily's stronger than the weak-minded man I did that on before."

"Faking a bonding with her was a strong violation," Kyle growled.

"It wasn't a physical bonding," Sotomar told him. "She wouldn't have that."

Chevalier smiled. "We realize that or the bond would have broken earlier."

He frowned. "She didn't break the bond. You aren't listening. It was never physically consummated."

Hillock shifted nervously.

"The bond was broken while Emily was with you," Chevalier explained. "It was about four months ago."

"Then it was by betrayal."

"Care to explain it to him?" Chevalier asked, looking at Hillock.

Sotomar turned to his Imperial Guard. "Explain what?"

"No, sir, I don't," he whispered, and glanced at Chevalier.

"You took away Emily's memory of me," Chevalier said. "You fully expected her to be alone for 30 years and not seek out someone?"

Sotomar's eyes narrowed. "Explain yourself."

"It's common for mortals to want companionship and physical affection. What made you think that she would be happy without that for the 30 years you changed?"

"She was though…"

"She was happy?" Kyle asked. "She looked to us, on our visit, like she was very displeased with her life."

"She was fine!"

"She was miserable," Hillock said softly.

Sotomar glared at him. "Shut up."

"Emily and Hillock became an item behind your back," Quinn said, smiling. "So much so, the bond with Chevalier was broken four months ago."

"Is that true?!" Sotomar yelled at his guard.

Hillock nodded. "I love her."

"Did you sleep with her?"

"No, Elder."

"Did you kiss?"

Hillock simply nodded as he watched the floor.

"How dare you cheat with an Elder's wife!"

"Wife?" Hillock asked, his eyes suddenly furious. "Your bond was a sham to explain the ring! There was no love, and she hated you for making her do it."

"She did love me."

"No, she didn't. You treated her like a trophy wife! She hated every second with you."

"So you decided to risk your life for her?"

"For someone I care about, yes. You were too blind to see that you were ruining her. She was miserable!"

The Equites Council sat back, amused, and watched the Valle fight in the trial area.

"You will pay for your treason when we get back," Sotomar hissed.

Hillock smiled. "The Equites aren't going to let me go. So nothing's stopping me from telling you what an idiot you are to have altered her memories! It was low, disgusting, and entirely beneath you."

Sotomar's hands balled into fists. "You don't know what you're talking about…"

"I know her better than you do. The nights that I spent holding her while she told me how much she hated you and wanted to run away from the Valle that she so loathes."

"Lies!"

"They aren't lies. She felt trapped by the bond you forced on her and wasn't in the least bit upset when she told me she loved me, and it broke."

Chevalier shifted nervously as he watched them and started to get mad.

"She was my wife…," Sotomar hissed, and then took a step closer

to his guard.

"Well your wife begged me to make love to her…"

"What?!" Chevalier yelled, standing up.

Hillock's eyes grew wide and he turned to Chevalier. "We didn't though."

Sotomar was on Hillock instantly, and they blurred into a fight. Chevalier tried to jump into the fight, but Zohn and Kyle held him back. Four of the Equites Council jumped the desk and dove into the fray, finally pulling the two Valle apart.

"I won't allow you to kill him," Chevalier growled, trying again to get to Hillock.

"He's mine to punish," Sotomar said angrily.

"She's my wife."

"She was mine!"

"Stop it!" Quinn yelled, and his booming voice echoed off of the walls in the palace. "Take the Valle to cells."

Four prison guards came in and hauled the Valle away. Sotomar struggled against them, but Hillock walked out calmly.

"It wasn't her fault," Kyle said to Chevalier.

"I'm not blaming her!" he yelled. "I'm blaming the imbeciles who changed her memories."

"Then calm down, or she'll think you're mad at her."

Chevalier seemed to calm instantly and sat down. "She already does."

Zohn sat down beside him. "It stands to reason that she's blaming herself for this. You said you were going to take her away on the yacht for a week or so."

"She doesn't want to go."

"She wants punished," Quinn said. "Physical pain is sometimes used to erase emotional pain."

"Do you think Hillock was right about her request?" the Chief of Staff asked.

"I don't know," Chevalier told him. "Does it matter? A woman alone for 30 years has the right to find a suitable companion."

"He looks a lot like you," Zohn said. "I would imagine that's why she was drawn to him."

"Sotomar does too though," Kyle said.

"Yes, well… she doesn't like Sotomar. That may have been too ingrained to erase."

"I would imagine this goes deeper than we envision," Quinn said. "She takes personal violations so badly… yet she's broken a bond she held as a great treasure."

"That wasn't her fault," Chevalier said again.

"She's going to be hard to convince."

"Then stick with your plan to take her away," Kyle said. "Getting her away from everything around here is your best bet."

"We're still under constant attack though," Chevalier said. "I can't leave when we're on the verge of being replaced."

"Then what do you suggest?" Zohn asked.

"I suggest I wing it," Chevalier told him, and then walked out of the council chambers.

"Great," Kyle whispered, and turned back to a ledger. "Winging it works so well."

Chevalier stopped outside of his bedroom door and looked over at Kralen and Horace, who were standing outside of the Elder Guard's room. "She's in there?"

"Yes, Elder," Kralen said.

"It's dirty and cold in there," Chevalier said as he walked over and knocked.

"Actually, Mark saw this coming, and it's cleaned and stocked," Horace explained.

"Em, it's me. Can I come in?" he asked.

***

Emily headed down the back stairs, hoping to avoid being called into the council chambers. She was on a mission to break one horse and get her stallion out for a good run. First, she wanted to go check on Chevalier's aging stallion. She adjusted her chaps and ran quickly down the stairs, followed by four members of the Cavalry she'd never met.

First, she checked on Chevalier's retired stallion but found his stall empty. After checking the corral, she called for Mark and then let the colt she was going to break into the corral.

"Good to see you out," Mark said as he, Silas, and Kralen walked up.

She didn't turn toward them. "Where is he?"

"The Elder's horse?"

"Yes"

"Thukil took him."

"So Chev just sent him away?"

"Well... I guess," Mark said, trying to figure out how this could turn on him.

"What's up with the chaps?" Kralen asked as he leaned on the fence next to her.

"Gonna break in that colt and then take my horse out."

"But chaps?"

"I don't want to ruin my pants."

He shrugged and then smiled. "Just not seen you in them in a while."

"I haven't broken in a horse in a while."

"Why don't you let me do it?" Mark asked.

"Ever consider how breaking in a horse is a lot like my life?" she asked, still watching the colt in the corral.

"What do you mean?"

"I hold on," she said softly. "I hold on while he bucks and tries to knock me off. When he finally does… and he always does… I brush myself off and get back on."

Mark frowned as he watched her.

"I always hold on tighter when I crawl back on… but then he bucks harder until I fall off again."

Silas started to say something, but her soft voice cut him off, "What do I do?"

"Em…," Kralen said, and touched her shoulder.

"Nothing's ever changed. Yes, I had peace for a few years, but then it all went back to normal. The Encala are too spontaneous to be trusted. The Equites are bullies, and the Valle will go to any length to get me to join them."

Not sure what she was about to do, Mark called for Chevalier.

"What do I do?" she whispered as she studied the horse.

"Em?" Chevalier asked from behind her.

She turned and crossed her arms as she leaned back against the fence. "You tell me what to do."

"What do you mean?"

"Do I break him?"

Chevalier looked over at the horse but had a feeling something else was going on. "Tell me what's up."

"Breaking in the same horse for eternity seems like a waste of time."

When she turned back around and leaned her forearms on the fence, Mark filled the Elder in on what was said before he arrived.

"Let's ride," Chevalier said, and held out his hand.

Emily frowned slightly and turned to look at him. "Now?"

"Yes"

"You and I?"

"Yes," he said, smiling.

"How many Cavalry?"

"I don't need Cavalry," he said, and took a step closer to her. She hesitated and then put her gloved hand in his. The Cavalry disappeared when they walked into the stables and slipped saddles onto two of the

horses.

When Emily walked her horse out, Chevalier was already waiting for her. She mounted easily and then kicked him into a slow walk through the city.

"You never go riding anymore," she said, and then looked over when he slid sunglasses on.

"That's going to change."

"How so?"

"You and I will be getting more time together."

She nodded slightly when the gate guards bowed to them and then she headed into the trees east of the city.

"Do you want to talk about it?" he asked after a few minutes of silence.

She smiled at him. "I was just rambling."

"It sounded serious."

"Maybe"

"So the Equites are bullies?"

Her smile grew, and he couldn't help but grin when she spoke, "Yes... you are."

"I see."

"You're bigger, meaner, and you usually get your way because no one can fight you. Doesn't that sound like a bully?"

"If you put it into juvenile words..., then, yes."

"Maybe I wouldn't make a better Encala," she said as she stopped her horse at the derelict Durango and then tied him to the bumper before sitting on the rotted seat.

Chevalier dismounted and slid into what used to be the driver's seat. "Dare I ask?"

"I'm a bully too... so maybe I fit in better with the Equites."

"How are you a bully?"

She looked over at him. "You'd be amazed at what I do to get my way."

He smiled. "I already know."

She leaned back and put her feet on the leaf covered dash. "Then he bucks harder... and I fall off."

Chevalier reached out and took her hand. "But you always get back on."

"Forever seems like a long time to have a bruised ass," she said, suddenly turning serious.

"Tell me what you want."

"No, tell me what you want. You offer me the world... maybe it's time you get a say in it."

He chuckled and laced his fingers with hers. "I want you to be safe

and happy. I want the factions to back off of you and let you live a normal life."

She shook her head and smiled. "That's what you want for me. What do you want for you?"

He met her eyes and whispered, "You."

She brushed her lips lightly across his and then looked into his eyes. "You already have me."

"No, I don't."

"The ring?"

He nodded and smiled.

She pulled it out of her pocket and ran her finger lightly over the inlaid gems. "We must have our bond broken more than anyone in the history of heku."

"Probably," he said, and took it from her. "So let's give it another go."

"I cheated on you."

"No, you didn't."

"Then why did the ring come off?"

He shook his head. "Fine… so you kind of did. However, it wasn't your fault."

"Your logic drives me batty."

"It's foreign to you. I know."

She gasped and then hit him on the arm. "I'm not that bad."

"Marry me," he said, and then flashed a smile at her.

"Again"

"Again"

"Ceremonial room?"

"Nope"

She smiled. "Really?"

"Once is enough."

Chapter 20

"So?" Mark asked as Emily rode a Pinto mare around the corral.

"I'm not seeing what he's seeing."

"He said she's been limping."

"Do you see it?"

"Well... no."

She kicked the mare, and she moved from a slow walk into a trot. "I don't know. She seems fine now."

"I'll tell him to just ride her then."

"Let's take her out and run her," Emily said, moving the horse up to the gate.

"I have a meeting. Silas wants to go with you."

She nodded as he opened the gate, and she rode the mare out toward the stables. Silas was already waiting for her, and she was surprised to see that it was just him.

"No posse?"

He smiled. "Nope, you're stuck with just me."

She shrugged. "You'll be easy enough to ditch alone."

"Hey now...," he said sternly.

She smiled and then kicked the mare into a canter. When Silas and Emily met up on the grassy hills outside of the city, the canter turned into a gallop and they both flew across the grass.

Mark walked into the council chambers with Derrick, and both moved to stand before the Elders.

"She's out," Mark told them.

Chevalier nodded and looked over at Kyle. "Report?"

"They're still gathered around Banks Coven and have completely blocked off access," Kyle explained. "Powan scouted the area, and the Valle have over 4,000 heku."

Zohn hissed, "What caused this?"

"We haven't been able to contact Lord Banks. All forms of communication have been cut off. The Valle won't tell us what's going on."

"So we receive the head of the top officer for Banks, with no note, no explanation?" Quinn asked, frowning.

"Yes, Elder," Kyle said, obviously furious.

"I suggest we call in all level 4 covens and above," Zohn said, and looked down the row. "That gives us 3500."

Chevalier shook his head. "Or I go with just Mark and Emily."

Mark gasped. "Elder?"

He smiled. "It'd be good for her. She's still acting stand-offish, and she loves nothing more than to bully the Valle."

"No, it's too dangerous," Zohn said.

Quinn lightly tapped his fingers on the desk. "Let me think this out."

"She wouldn't necessarily ash all 4,000 of them," Chevalier said. "I say we just let Emily go and see what she comes up with. I bet she can stop this standoff faster than we can with brute force."

"I can't believe you're suggesting this," Kyle hissed.

Chevalier's smile widened. "It's a good idea."

"Four thousand are too dangerous though," Zohn said. He was still shocked that Chevalier even suggested it.

"I'm betting she wouldn't even have to turn them to ash."

"If it backfired, we'd be handing all three of you over to the Valle."

"Think about it," Chevalier said. "We take 3,500 in to wipe out 4,000. Yes, we'd win, but our losses would be substantial. However, if we waited long enough to gather 4,000, then we risk the life of every heku in Banks."

"How are you even suggesting this?" the Chief of Finance asked. "Any mention of Emily using her abilities, and you immediately veto it."

"We've just talked lately, and she really doesn't have a lot to do around here now that the Cavalry is learning to take care of their own horses."

"So we send her out on dangerous missions?"

"It won't be dangerous. The Valle are going to wet themselves and run when she shows up," he said, and then grinned.

"I thought she called us bullies though," Quinn reminded him.

"She did... then admitted she's a bit of a bully herself."

Quinn finally sighed, "I'll agree if the Cavalry goes too."

Chevalier nodded and then stood up. "Bring'em out, Mark. We leave in ten."

Mark nodded and disappeared while Chevalier went out to talk to Emily.

Silas and Emily rode up to the stables, and she eyed Chevalier carefully. "What'd I do now?"

"We need to go to Banks Coven," he told her as he took the reins on her horse.

"I don't want to visit Banks."

"Not a social call... they're under attack."

Her eyes narrowed. "You're letting me go?"

"You're letting her go?" Silas mirrored, surprised.

"Yup, let's go," Chevalier said.

Excited, Emily slipped off of her horse and followed after him. "Who's attacking?"

"The Valle," Chevalier told her as he walked up to the Cavalry.

"Head out in five."

Mark nodded, and the Cavalry began preparing for the run.

"Why are you letting me go?" Emily asked, leaning up against Chevalier's Humvee.

"Because it's time we stop keeping you out of things."

"I don't trust you."

He chuckled. "We hope that they see you and scatter."

"Why are they attacking?"

"We don't know. We haven't had contact from inside the coven."

Emily watched as Chevalier met with the Cavalry battalion leaders and then he turned to her. "Time to go."

She crawled into the Humvee but frowned when Chevalier reached in and picked her up.

"We're running it," he said, and checked to make sure everyone was ready.

"Running? To Banks?!"

"Yes"

She crossed her arms and glared at him as the heku took off running for the Banks Coven. It wasn't long before he set her down and met up with the Cavalry again. Emily followed him to find out what was going on.

"We're going to try this differently," Chevalier explained. "I want it known, first thing, that Emily is with us."

"Can I just ash them all?" Emily asked.

"No, there are 4,000 of them."

"Damn," Kralen growled. "What did Banks even do?"

"We don't know… let's go."

The heku matched Emily's pace as they walked up the dirt road leading to the Banks compound. The sounds of talking grew louder as they approached.

"Behind us!" a voice called out when the heku came into view.

Emily stepped forward when the Cavalry stopped, and then she crossed her arms and waited. "What the hell is this?"

There was a loud rumble, and the Valle parted to let Valle Elder Randall and their Chief of Defense through.

Randall looked over the Cavalry and then focused in on Emily. "Why are you here?"

"Because you're messing with my faction."

"Your faction?"

"Yes"

He grinned. "Mortals don't have a faction."

"Mortals don't follow instructions either," she said, and then smiled as she wiped a drop of blood from under her nose.

Randall spun and received word that 300 of the Valle had just fallen to ash.

"Stop it!" he roared. "Give us back Sotomar."

"Is that what this is over? Sotomar?"

"Mostly"

Emily's face showed her concentration. "There… now Sotomar's ash too."

"How dare you," he hissed. "You are breaking every…"

"You wanna talk about breaking heku laws?" she asked, taking a step closer. "Let's start with changing my memory."

"That was necessary."

"So is this," she said, and then swayed slightly when another 200 Valle fell to ash. Chevalier appeared by her side and steadied her.

"You let her fight for you now?" Randall asked him.

Chevalier shrugged. "We let her fight as we let any Equites fight."

"She's not an Equites!"

"I am too," Emily said, glaring at him. "Now take off and go tell Ryan that I was bullying you in the playground."

"I'm not afraid of a little girl," he said seethingly.

"Great! I'm not afraid of you either," Emily said, and then started forward. Chevalier took her arm, but she shrugged him off, and he returned to the Cavalry.

"What are you doing?!" Randall yelled as his troops split to let her through.

Emily smiled and walked up to the front gate, past the stunned Valle army.

"Flynn?" someone gasped from behind her. She turned and studied the Valle that was looking at her with wide eyes.

A smile slowly crossed her face. "Chuck Norris?"

He was obviously shocked. "I had no idea you were the fabled Winchester."

Emily took a step toward him, and Chevalier held his hand out to hold the Cavalry back.

"You're a Valle? When did you turn?" she asked, a frown forming.

"About six years ago. Oh my God. You haven't changed at all," he said, glancing nervously at his Elder.

"Why did you turn?"

"It was the perfect opportunity. There's no work in Cascade. The last real job I had was working with Keith on your dad's old place."

She looked back at Chevalier and then reached her hand out. "Come with me."

"I can't…"

"Yes, you can. You can stay with the Equites." She ignored the

low growl from Randall.

"Why don't you join the Valle and stay with me? We had fun times… remember cow-tipping on Old Miller's place?"

She laughed but then turned serious. "Come to the Equites."

"I can't, Emi," he said, but she cut him off.

"Yes, you can. I'll protect you from them."

"I should rephrase that… I won't. I'm a Valle and proud of it."

"Chuck…"

"I'm in a new coven, a new agricultural coven," he said to her. The entire clearing had grown quiet and listened to them. "Why don't you help me start it? You and your dad both had the most amazing ability to run a ranch. I've never seen animals react to anyone like yours do."

Emily walked up and took his hand. "Come on… to the Equites…"

He studied her and then shook his head. "No, Emi. But I'll wait for you with the Valle."

"Please…," she whispered. "I can offer you more than the Valle can."

"Em," Chevalier said from behind her. He put a hand on her shoulder, ready to tear the Valle apart if he made one wrong move. "He can't just leave the Valle and join the Equites."

Emily pulled away from him. "He's from Cascade though."

"I know."

"He helped me hide from Keith once…," she said, looking up at Chuck. "Do you remember that?"

He nodded. "Yes, but that might have been a mistake."

"What? Why?"

Chevalier took her hand and led her back to the Cavalry.

"Chuck Norris?" one of the Valle asked him, amused.

He chuckled. "It's Charles Morris… but Emi started calling me Chuck Norris in Elementary school, and by Junior High, everyone did."

"You won't let him join us?" Emily looked up at Mark and Chevalier when they reached the Cavalry.

"It's not that easy to switch sides," Chevalier told her.

"It doesn't look like he wants to either," Mark said softly.

She turned and started back for the Valle. "Chuck, I have an idea…"

Chevalier took her hand to stop her. "Em, he can't just become an Equites."

Randall was studying Emily's old acquaintance.

Emily looked over and saw him staring at Chuck. "Hey, dick for brains…"

Randall turned toward her, furious.

"Touch him for that, and I'll hide you like I did Frederick."

A smile crossed his lips. "Oh, he won't be harmed."

She pulled away from Chevalier and started back for the gate. The Valle moved again and formed a clear path, much to their Elder's dismay.

Once there, she hit the call button.

"We told you, we're not speaking to you," a harsh voice sounded.

"It's Emily," she said, and then smiled at the Valle next to her.

"Is it clear then?"

"No... is everyone inside okay?"

"Yes, ma'am."

Chevalier chuckled at the terror on the faces of the Valle. He marveled at how they didn't dare touch her and had let her walk up to talk to the Banks Coven as they split to the sides. Randall was fuming about their behavior, and Mark was watching him carefully in case he decided to attack Emily himself.

"Just hang tight while I see what I can do," Emily said before turning around and walking out to the Cavalry. She shrugged at Chevalier, smiled, and then turned back to Randall. "Okay, now let's talk about what this is all about."

Randall glared down at her and took a step forward. "Not only do the Equites hold our Elder, but they aren't the rightful Council..."

"Oh my God! Are you still harping on that?"

"But also... you should be turned over to the Valle to be punished for crimes against the heku."

"That all?"

"No, that's not all. You purchased land out from under the Valle..."

She cringed inwardly.

"... and Banks Coven's members assaulted two Valle in a donor bar."

"Em, I got this," Chevalier said from behind her.

"No, let me do this," she said without turning around. "First of all... Sotomar's crimes were akin to those by the Ancients..."

Randall growled, and his hands balled into fists.

"It's the Equites right to seek justice for such actions. They are the rightful Council, and you need to stay the hell out of it. It's my land, so deal with it... and lastly... I'm sure your Valle deserved what they got."

"I won't stand here and be spoken to in such a manner by the likes of you!" Randall yelled. "You have a hundred heku against our thousands... what are you going to do now?"

She moved closer to him and glared up at him. "What I'm going to do is take your precious little book of covens and go to each one. When I'm done, you won't find enough ashes to revive!"

Randall moved to backhand her, but Chevalier caught his hand mid-

air. "Do not hit her."

"I've had it with the Valle!" she screamed as Mark pulled her back to the Cavalry. "I have no attachment to you as a faction and have no qualms about wiping you out."

Silas and Horace each took an arm when she tried to get to Randall.

"Get her," Randall hissed.

"Touch my Cavalry and I swear... I'll scatter your ashes!" she yelled. The Valle shifted nervously and looked at one another. Their Elder had ordered an attack, but Emily was famous for scattering the ashes of heku that wronged her.

"I said to get her!" Randall screamed.

The first few to move even a step forward turned to ash as Emily glared at them. "I warned you..."

"That's enough," Kralen said when she swayed slightly. "We can get the rest of them."

Randall said something quietly and was immediately tackled by Chevalier. Emily watched the fast blur and then looked over at the Valle. "Leave them alone. If you try to help your Elder... you'll have to deal with me."

Silas and Horace held tighter, making sure Emily didn't try to join in the fight either.

Emily smiled when the fight stopped, and Chevalier had Randall pinned to the ground by his neck, with barely even a scratch on Chevalier. Randall was severely beaten and grabbing at Chevalier's hand, so he could breathe.

Silas and Horace let her go as she walked forward and squatted down beside Randall. "Get out of my sight."

Chevalier twisted his hand and snapped Randall's neck before standing up.

Emily shook her head at him. "Show off."

He grinned and walked back over by the Cavalry.

"Someone get your Elder and get out of here," Emily said to the gathered Valle. The Cavalry watched as Chuck stepped out of the Valle and studied Emily.

Randall was just getting to his feet when Emily turned to the Cavalry. "Now what?"

"We go see how Banks is," Chevalier said, stepping forward.

Emily shrugged, turned, and then smiled. "Damn, that was fast."

The Valle were gone, leaving no sign they'd even been there.

"We make a good team," Chevalier said. He took her hand, and they walked forward.

Silas hit the call button in front of the security gate.

"Lord Banks here," a rough voice said.

"It's clear. Let us in," Silas said to him. The security camera moved to see them and then a click was heard when the thick cement gate unlocked. Four heku immediately came out to take posts outside of the gate after bowing to Chevalier briefly.

Emily clung tightly to Chevalier's arm as they walked past the Banks Coven houses and toward the main house. The last time she'd been in there she was beaten and cut with a knife, and she was feeling tense walking toward the house again.

"They won't hurt you," Chevalier whispered when he noticed her slowing.

"Maybe I should wait out by the gate," Emily replied, and then let go of his arm and headed the other way.

Mark smiled and took her arm. "Come on."

She hesitated and sighed before following them into Banks Castle.

"Elder!" Lord Banks said, coming forward. "Thank you, sir."

"We need a conference room," Chevalier said bluntly. He hadn't forgotten how Banks had treated Emily either but had business to attend to.

"Lady Emily," Lord Banks said softly, and then bowed toward her. She tensed unconsciously and moved to grip Chevalier's arm again. He smiled and then started down a hallway. "We'll meet in here."

Chevalier gave brief orders to Silas and then stepped into the conference room with Emily and Mark. Lord Banks sat down next to the top officers in his coven, one of which Emily recognized as the heku that'd threatened to cut her baby from her.

She glanced at the door, but Chevalier slipped an arm around her and led her to a seat. Before she'd sat down, an ice cold Coke was sitting in a glass in front of her. She sat down but averted her eyes away from those from Banks.

Chevalier had told her a few years back that Equites Covens kept mortal food and drink around, just in case she showed up. It was important that the covens make a good impression on Chevalier, and keeping Emily happy was a big part of that.

"What caused this?" Chevalier asked as he sat down.

"Our refusal to follow the Council that banished you."

Chevalier's eyes narrowed. "Keep going."

Lord Banks shifted nervously. "They came to us last week, the 12 former Council that's left…"

"…12?"

"Yes, only 12 are left. When they found out that their Chief Enforcer left the dagger, he was killed immediately."

Emily looked over at Mark, and he smiled at her, then turned back to Lord Banks.

"They insisted that we lead an attack on Council City. Said it was our duty to follow the true Council. We refused…"

"Why doesn't the Council know this?"

Lord Banks sighed, "It's all complicated. We support you as a Council 100%, but we understand that we shouldn't."

"What?!" Emily yelled.

Chevalier put a hand out to stop her from standing. "We know it's all going against heku tradition, but you should have told us. Do they have any supporters?"

"Not as far as we know," Lord Banks said, avoiding looking at Emily. "The laws that came down from that Council were bad. No one really liked them, but we had to follow them. Now we're all confused. We aren't supposed to follow you, you know that."

Chevalier simply nodded.

"No one's going to follow the former Council. However, we all wish you would banish them to make this all official."

Chevalier looked over at Mark before speaking. "We may need to make that a priority. We've let it go because they backed off."

"They aren't going to stop, and they have the support of the Valle."

Emily looked over at Chevalier. "I can take care of the Valle… again…"

He smiled. "No, let us do this. It's our right to seek revenge on the former Council, and we can't let you have all the fun."

She shrugged and picked up the Coke.

Chevalier studied Lord Banks for a moment before speaking. "I want to see you and your top officers tomorrow morning."

Lord Banks swallowed hard and nodded. "Yes, Elder."

Chevalier stood and put his hand out. "Let's go."

Emily looked at the way Lord Banks had paled and then took Chevalier's hand and followed him out. "What'd you do to Banks?"

"He has some explaining to do is all," Chevalier said as he gently lifted her into a cradle.

"Is he in trouble?"

"Maybe"

"Are you going to kill him?" She buried her face in his shoulder when he began to blur toward Council City. The speed made her nervous, and it was easier not to look.

"Probably not," he said, though his voice was strained.

She clutched tighter to him when she saw the Cavalry falling behind. It was hard for heku to keep up with an Old One, but usually, Chevalier held back to stay with the group.

She felt him laugh. "I'm not going to drop you."

"I don't think you are," she whispered as Mark disappeared behind

them.

"Then why are you afraid all of a sudden?"

"I'm not."

"You forget... when we re-bonded, I can pick up your emotions again. You also tensed when I left the others."

"I'm not afraid."

He gently kissed the top of her head, but she could feel him laughing and couldn't help but tighten her grip.

Chevalier came to a sudden halt in the council chambers, and Emily gasped at the unexpected change in speed. She hit him on the arm when he put her down, then she turned and headed for the doors.

"Emily?" Zohn called out.

She sighed, still looking at how close the doors were. She briefly wondered if Derrick would stop her if she tried to run. He answered her silent question by appearing in the doorway and smiling at her.

Emily studied him before he motioned for the Council and whispered, "Turn around."

She bit her bottom lip. "I think I can take you."

He chuckled and returned to his post after shutting the door.

When she turned to the Council, she saw the Elders were facing way from her, deep in conversation, but the rest of the Council was watching her.

"Welcome back," Kyle said, smiling. "Have fun?"

She shrugged and then nodded slightly. She couldn't help but feel panic when standing before the Council. It irritated her, but she couldn't control the ingrained fear of the 13 Equites leaders.

"Calm down," Richard, the Chief Interrogator said softly. "I can see lies forming in your mind, but we haven't even asked anything."

"Feeling guilty?" Kyle chuckled.

Emily looked over at the soft recliner sitting in the back of the trial area and then turned toward Kyle and shook her head.

"We're not going to lock you up."

Richard smiled, trying to defuse her fear. "We just have a simple question."

"What?" she asked softly.

"We want to know what position Andrew holds on the Encala," he explained. "They aren't willing to tell us, for some reason. We suspect he's the Interrogator but would like confirmation."

Emily glanced back at the door.

"Em...," Kyle said, and then smiled at her when she turned. "No running off. We need to know."

Chevalier sensed her fear building and looked over at her. "What's going on?"

"We want to know what position Andrew holds," Richard told him.

Now she had the attention of the three Elders also.

"It's…"

"It's okay, Em," Chevalier said. "We won't tell them you told us. If we had any spies over there we'd already know."

"You don't have even one?"

"Not one inside the palace. That takes time, and as the Encala are so new…"

She knew what he meant. Chevalier had systematically wiped out the Encala, and they were still rebuilding. "Well…"

Richard leaned forward, and she eyed him nervously.

"He's not going to be on the Council when I go talk to William," she said. "So there's no reason to even say."

"They won't release him. Now, he's been on the Council long enough that he would need banished if he's removed," the Chief of Staff told her.

Emily gasped and took a step back as Kyle glared at him. "Why would you say that?"

The Chief of Staff looked nervously at the Elders. "It's…"

"We know it's the truth… but why would you even mention Andrew being banished?" Chevalier asked him glaringly.

"Is he going to be banished?" Emily managed to whisper.

"No," Kyle told her. "I'm sure Andrew is fine."

Emily spun and ran out of the room. Derrick didn't try to stop her. They all knew she was going to her office to web cam into the Encala Council.

Chevalier sighed and then turned to Zohn. "Has Sotomar been revived."

Zohn frowned. "What happened to Sotomar?"

"Emily turned him to ash from Banks."

Kyle whispered and then turned to them. "He's not been turned to ash."

"Guess he was too far away."

"We should record that," the Records Keeper mentioned. "I'd like to get a distance down on her abilities."

As soon as Emily got to her office, she shut the door behind her and locked it. Heku couldn't break the lock, and she needed the Equites to stay out of what she was about to do.

Her laptop came to life, and within only a few minutes, she'd entered the Encala Council's IP and was waiting for a response.

William appeared and smiled broadly. "Hello, Emily."

"Where's Andrew?" she asked, frowning.

William spun the camera over to where Andrew was sitting. "I'm

right here."

Her heart slowed a bit with proof he hadn't been banished. "Are you on the chopping block?"

His eyebrows rose. "I don't believe so."

William turned the camera back to the three Encala Elders.

"What's wrong?" William asked.

She crossed her arms. "Are you about to banish Andrew?"

"No"

It was obvious she didn't believe them. "Then I insist that you release him from the Council and put him back as head of the guard…"

"We can't do that," Elder Iuna said.

She studied him and her eyes narrowed. "Do it."

"Em…," she heard Andrew sigh.

"We can't release him," William explained. "He's a damned good Interrogator and…"

"Do it!" she yelled.

"What's wrong?"

Her eyes darted between them. "Release him without banishment, or I'll ash you."

"No, you won't," William said softly. "Tell me what's wrong."

"Did you just promote him because he's my friend?"

"No, he has an exceptionally keen ability to see if someone's lying," William said.

"He also has great interrogation techniques," Encala Elder Patrick said.

Emily gasped and William glared at him. "Enough."

"If you banish him…"

"He's not going to be banished."

She started to panic. "What can I do to get you to let him return to his guard post?"

"We need him."

"Em?" Andrew said from off camera. William turned it to face him. "Can I come talk to you?"

She shook her head. "Why does every heku I care about end up on the bloody Council? Why is that?! Next thing I know, Chuck'll be running the Valle."

"Who's Chuck?"

Emily spun suddenly and looked at the strange office. "Where am I?" she whispered.

"Emily, what's wrong?" William asked.

She turned and looked, wide eyed, at the screen on the laptop. "The Encala?"

William frowned and started to speak, but she quickly shut the

laptop before anyone could see she was talking to the Encala Council. She looked carefully around the office, trying to figure out where in the Valle Palace she was to be alone in an office full of computers.

When she left, she saw the four members of the Cavalry and backed up against the wall, glaring at them. "Green?!"

Kralen frowned. "What's going on?"

"Am I with the Equites?"

"Of course..."

"Damnit!" she screamed, turning them all to ash. She mumbled about being kidnapped again and headed down to the council chambers.

She was tired of being kidnapped from her home with the Valle and planned on making an example of the Equites by turning their city to ash. She wondered how long she'd been in the Equites care and if the Valle had already tried to get her back. She knew Sotomar would be furious that the Equites had again taken his wife.

"Good even..." Derrick started to say, but he instantly turned to ash. She stepped over him and through the door to the council chambers.

Zohn looked up from a roster. "Hello, Emily. Do you need something?"

She stormed forward and crossed her arms, glaring at the Council. "When will you stop?!"

"Stop what?" Chevalier asked, looking at her curiously.

"Stop kidnapping me! What the hell do you think I'm talking about? You keep taking me from my home, and I'm not letting you get away with it this time."

"Kidnapped?" Kyle asked, confused.

"Don't act stupid with me. You know I belong with the Valle. My home is there. My husband is there..."

"Wait!" Quinn said quickly, and she glared at him. "Who are you bonded to?"

"That's a stupid question," Emily snapped. "You know I'm bonded to Sotomar and have been for over 30 years."

"I see," he said, leaning back.

"Damnit," Chevalier hissed too low for her to hear.

"So this is what I'm going to do," Emily said. Kyle cocked his head slightly to the side when reports of ash came from around the palace. "I'm going to wipe out your beloved city... and make you watch."

Her eyes narrowed, and Chevalier roared and fell back in pain when the burning hit. Kyle was on her in an instant, and without thinking, sunk his teeth into her neck. When she relaxed beneath him, Quinn knelt down at her side and locked her gaze.

Chevalier caught his breath and then was caught in the tight hands of the Chief Interrogator and Chief Investigator when he lunged at

Emily. It took him a few minutes to regain his control, then they let him go, and he slowly walked down to where Quinn had Emily locked.

"Edwards," he whispered, and then knelt down beside Kyle. He inspected the bite carefully and saw that Kyle was no longer feeding but was keeping contact, in case she broke Quinn's gaze.

"What's wrong?" Dr. Edwards asked when he entered the council chambers and saw Emily pinned to the ground. Quinn had her hands trapped above her head, just in case she broke his gaze.

"Knock her ass out," Zohn snapped.

Dr. Edwards nodded and then readied a sedative. He injected it, and less than a minute later, Emily fell unconscious.

Kyle let go of her neck and looked up. "I didn't know what else to do…"

"I know," Chevalier said, and slapped him on the back. "You probably saved Council City."

"Ash reports?" Zohn called out. Palace guards reported that the four members of the Cavalry guarding Emily and the council chamber door guard, Derrick, were all turned to ash. Everyone in the city had felt the burn, but none had been turned completely to ash.

Chevalier gently picked Emily up, and she hung limply in his arms. "I thought once she remembered, that their façade would be gone."

"Apparently not," Quinn said.

"Start reviving," Zohn said to Kyle. Kyle glanced once more at Emily and then left the room.

"Now what?"

Chevalier watched her sleep. "We're enemies. It's going to be hard to keep her here."

"So we restrain her to the bed… again," the Chief of Finance suggested.

"In Chevalier's room? Bad idea," Quinn told him.

"Why?" Chevalier asked.

"You're the main enemy, remember? You hold everything Exavior did, everything Salazar did, the Encala… you are responsible for all of that. It may not behoove us to keep her in your room."

He sighed, "True."

"We've never successfully kept her restrained though," Quinn said. "Before we know it, she'll be back with the Valle."

"So put her in prison," the Records Keeper said. "She can't get out of a cell."

"She's tormented in prison," Zohn said. "They call for her blood…"

"We have the old oubliettes," Richard said. "So we put her in there."

Chevalier frowned. "How fast can we humanize one of them? She'll need a bed, table, chairs, warmth, a bathroom... we need to be able to pass food in to her."

Zohn called out orders into the air, including turning the adjacent oubliette into a mortal bathroom and then turned to Chevalier. "Now how do we keep her from turning Council City to ash?"

Mark came into the room. "I heard..."

"Suggestions?" Quinn asked.

"I suggest we make someone immune," Mark said. "She's proven that she won't ash a city if there's still one person alive that would have full control of her if she passes out."

Chevalier watched her face as she slept and then nodded. "Let's do it. She may test it though, so we have to actually make one of us immune."

"It should be you," Zohn said. "She already hates you."

He nodded and laid her down. "Get it over with."

Quinn knelt down beside Chevalier and then looked at him before sinking a fingernail deep into his arm. They watched as the blood drained out of him, and he turned pale and began to pant softly.

"When he's done... get her into the oubliette while we calm him," Zohn whispered to Mark.

Mark nodded and picked Emily up, then let one of her arms fall to her side for Chevalier's use. Silas and Kralen both appeared and put themselves between Chevalier and Emily.

Kralen took her arm and held it out when Chevalier's blood stopped draining. "You get her wrist only."

Chevalier stood up and tensed his body, ready to attack.

"Wrist," Silas hissed.

Chevalier immediately grabbed her hand and roughly sunk his teeth into her wrist. The council chambers fell silent while Dr. Edwards watched Emily for signs of hypovolemic shock.

It was only a few minutes later when the doctor spoke, "Enough..."

"Elder," Silas said, putting a hand on Chevalier's arm. He growled deeply but kept drinking.

"We got him," Zohn said, and then slammed into Chevalier, knocking him away from Emily's wrist. Quinn, Silas, and Kralen both tackled Chevalier when he knocked Zohn flying. When Chevalier looked up, Emily was already gone, and he angrily growled at the Council as they blocked him from the door.

"Elder...," Kyle said, walking into the room.

Chevalier blinked a few times and then bent over with his hands on his knees, trying to clear his head.

Quinn smiled. "Easy enough... now you're immune."

"Everyone's revived," Kyle said. "Mark has Emily in the oubliette. Everything's done except the bathroom, but it'll be ready in the next two hours and then they'll break a door between the two rooms."

Chevalier nodded and finally returned to his seat. "That's so dangerous."

"We had to," Zohn said, sitting down. He grasped his side as he recovered from a nasty bite from Chevalier.

"Sorry," he said, smiling slightly.

Zohn shrugged and leaned back in his chair.

"I want you watching her for a while," Quinn said to the doctor. "Make sure she has what she needs."

Dr. Edwards nodded and disappeared.

"Can we lock her and do what the Valle did?" Quinn asked.

Chevalier shrugged. "Do we dare mess with her mind again?"

"It's too risky," Kyle said. "Someday that's going to scramble her brain, and she'll lose her mind."

"Hasn't she already?" Zohn whispered.

***

Emily sighed and rolled over, then opened her eyes to look at the strange bed. The bed was soft and comfortable and the covers were warm, but there was an odd feeling in the room.

She sat up. The room was small and dark, with only a tiny window, high on the wall that was covered by thick bars. Besides the bed she was in, there was a table and chair, a desk, and a couch near a large TV. She noticed a small trap door along the floor beneath the tiny barred window.

Emily stood up and steadied herself against the headboard on the bed before walking over to turn on a lamp. With the added light, she could see a hole in the wall across from her bed, and she peered through it into a small bathroom with a toilet, tub, sink, and shower.

After making sure she was alone, she walked up to the wall with the tiny window, but it was too far above her head to see out.

"Hey!" she yelled. "Get me out of here!"

Dr. Edwards peered in at her. "Emily… who am I?"

She glared at him. "You're one of the Equites stooges. Let me out or I'll ash your city."

"You cannot," he said. "Chevalier is immune to you. Turn the city to ash, and you will pass out and be at his mercy."

She growled slightly and then crossed her arms.

"How are you feeling?" he asked, studying her.

"Pissed"

He smiled. "I would imagine. Your dinner will be here shortly."

Chapter 21

Mark came into the council chambers and walked up to Chevalier. "It's a no-go. She's not eating."

Chevalier pinched his nose between his thumb and finger. "Of course she's not eating."

"Has she said anything?" Zohn asked.

Mark smiled crookedly. "She's called us lots of way fun names."

"Other than that?"

"No, Elder. She's keeping pretty quiet, all things considered."

Chevalier shrugged. "I guess I could go talk to her."

"She's not going to talk to you," Kyle said. "Send Hillock."

"I hate to do that. He could say something to validate what she thinks is real."

"He might be able to get her to eat though. He's been cooperating."

"He loves her," Richard reminded them. The Chief Interrogator had spent a lot of time with Hillock and was shocked at his intense feelings for Emily.

"I'm thinking," Chevalier said, tapping his fingers lightly on the desk. "It's been four days and she's not eaten, and history proves that she'd starve to death before doing so."

The Council fell silent when they heard Emily scream from the oubliette. "Hey, old piece of shit! Face me like a man, why don't ya? Stop hiding behind your jockeys and come fight me!"

Chevalier chuckled. "Well at least we know she's alive."

"Want me to go talk to her?" Kyle asked.

"Nope, I'll go," he said, standing up. "Might as well let her think her name calling is getting her somewhere."

Zohn grinned and watched him leave.

Chevalier walked down to the oubliettes on the first floor. They hadn't been used in almost 1500 years, and most of the staff didn't even know they were there until they were instructed to modify them to hold Emily.

"Elder," Silas said, smiling crookedly.

Chevalier shook his head and then stood on the small stool that allowed them to see into the high window. "You called?"

Emily glared up at him. "Oh look… you actually came. Get in here so I can show you how much I appreciate you showing up."

He smiled. "I'm not going in there. What do you need?"

"I need you to stop being an asshole and let me go!"

"No, is there anything else?"

She crossed her arms. "Yeah."

"What?"

He ducked down just as her lunch tray slammed into the tiny window, sending food splattering across the hall.

Once clear, he peeked back into the window. "Feel better?"

"The Valle won't stand for this."

"The Valle will live. Now how do we get you to eat?"

"Oh, that's an easy deal."

"Name it."

"You die, and I'll eat."

"I'll make sure you're notified if I do," he said, hiding his amusement.

"Why don't you go blow your Council and leave me alone," she said, and sat down on the couch, facing away from him.

Chevalier stepped down and looked over as Silas stifled a laugh. "That went well."

"Yeah well... if she won't eat, we're going to have to put Hillock in there with her."

Silas grimaced. "Seriously?"

"Do you have any ideas?"

Silas thought for a moment and then shook his head. "Not really."

"Kralen, you're with me," Chevalier said as he headed down into the prison, followed by Kralen. The prison fell completely silent when he walked in, all too afraid of catching the Elder's attention and being punished. His callous ways of inventing new torture had them all terrified.

He walked over and looked into Hillock's cell. The Valle stood up to face them. "What now?"

Chevalier studied him before speaking. "Emily's not eating."

"Is she okay?" he asked, frowning.

"The Valle's planted memories surfaced again, and she thinks she's an Equites prisoner."

He sighed and sat down. "Great."

"Yeah... well, we think you can get her to eat."

"Does she remember me?"

"We actually haven't asked."

He shrugged. "I'll try."

"There's a stipulation," Chevalier said, irritated. "You aren't to validate anything she believes is real right now."

"Okay," he said, hesitantly.

"You get her to eat... that's all."

"Can I stay with her in the oubliette?"

"No," both Kralen and Chevalier said at once.

He nodded. "Fine... tell me what you've told her, and I'll stick with the story."

"We've told her the truth, about what the Valle planted," Kralen told him. "She doesn't believe any of it though. We aren't even sure seeing a Valle will help, but we want you back in uniform."

He nodded and took his old Imperial Guard uniform from one of the palace guards.

"Traitor!" Sotomar yelled, his voice echoing through the prison. "It's disgusting how you help them."

"She's not eating," Hillock called back. "You always said it's our responsibility as Valle to make sure Emily's taken care of."

"I can't wait to get you back to the Council," Sotomar growled.

Chevalier chuckled and followed as Kralen escorted Hillock out of the prison. They stood before the only door into the oubliette.

"I'll be watching you," Chevalier told him. "Don't fuck with me on this."

"I won't," Hillock said. He knew that even if he wanted to defy the Equites, the Old One wouldn't allow him to do it for long.

Kralen opened the ceiling entrance and saw Emily look up and move just before Hillock dropped down.

"Oh my God, Hill!" Emily yelled, and ran into his arms.

He wrapped his arms around her. "I've been worried about you."

She pulled away from him and looked up at the ceiling panel that was removed to access the oubliette. "Let's get out of here then."

He led her over to the soft couch and sat down beside her. "I need you to listen to me... okay?"

She looked over when Chevalier's face appeared at the window, and then she turned back to Hillock.

"The Valle... we... well... we altered your memories...," Hillock explained.

She pulled her hand away when he tried to take it. "Stop doing what that oaf of an Equites told you to do! What? Did he torture you?"

"He didn't torture me for this," Hillock said. "I'm telling you the truth... you are, and always have been, an Equites."

She glared at him. "Are you an Equites spy?"

"No! I'm trying to help you. You live here in the Equites palace. You have children, you h…"

"Stop it!"

"Listen to me, Em. The Valle screwed up your memories. It'll come back, and as soon as it does, they will let you out of here."

She leaned back against the wall and watched him. "Then who am I bonded to?"

"Chevalier"

She laughed sarcastically. "That buffoon? No way."

Hillock looked over at the untouched food on her table. "You need

to eat, Em."

"No, I don't. They'll have to let me go before I die."

Chevalier sighed and then ordered Hillock out of the oubliette.

"I have to go," Hillock said, and stood up.

Emily rushed to him and put her hand on his chest. "Don't leave me here alone."

His eyes narrowed, and he glanced at Chevalier briefly before looking down at Emily. "Eat, and I can stay."

Emily glared at Chevalier in the small window and then nodded. "Fine."

Chevalier was relieved when she sat at the table and started to eat while Hillock got instructions from Mark on how to behave. When she was done eating, Emily moved to the couch and started flipping through channels, trying to find something to do.

Hillock sat beside her, making sure not to touch her while Chevalier was watching. She smiled and then laid down with her head in Hillock's lap. He gasped and looked up at Chevalier, but he was no longer watching.

"How did they get you?" Emily asked after a few minutes.

"Same time they got you," Hillock explained. He lightly began to run his fingers through her hair.

"Anyone else?"

"Nope"

"Bastards, can't they leave me alone?"

"I'm guessing not." He jerked his hand away quickly when Kyle peered in and growled lightly.

Feeling comforted that she was no longer alone, she soon fell asleep. When Kyle disappeared from the window, Hillock lightly began to rub her back as he watched her sleep.

***

Chevalier looked up suddenly when he was called to the oubliette immediately. He set Megara down gently and then instantly appeared at the small window.

"You psychopathic piece of shit!" Emily screamed.

Chevalier looked in, and his eyes grew wide. Emily was sitting on Hillock's chest as he laid flat on the floor. She was screaming at the top of her lungs and accentuating each word with a vicious punch to his face and neck. His hands covered his face protectively, but he didn't return her attack.

"Do we stop her?" Mark asked, peeking into the room.

"How dare you come in here…" Emily continued to beat the heku.

"Well," Chevalier said, thinking. "If we do she may turn on us. Does she remember then?"

"I'm not really sure. She woke up, saw Hillock, and immediately attacked."

"Emily?" Chevalier called in through the barred window.

She stood up and swiftly kicked Hillock in the groin. "Never touch me!"

"Em..."

"What?" she asked, looking over at him. She cried out when Hillock lunged from the floor and slammed into her, knocking her to the floor.

Mark and Chevalier both ran for the oubliette's door on the second floor of the palace. Even though they moved as fast as they could, when they appeared in the oubliette, Hillock had already hit Emily once and was poised to do it again when Mark plowed into him.

Emily got onto her knees and rubbed off the blood that was coming from the corner of her mouth. Chevalier squatted down to her level. "Are you okay?"

She nodded and reached up to touch the bruise on her cheek. "Sonofabitch hit me."

"Well... not to defend him, but it's dangerous work to cause pain to a heku," he said, and then put a hand out to help her up. "It's instinctual to fight back."

Emily spun and saw Mark had Hillock restrained by the far wall with his hands behind his back. She ran up, planted her foot, and kicked him in the groin again, as hard as she could.

Chevalier chuckled and pulled her back when Mark hauled Hillock out of the room, kicking and screaming to get to her.

Emily pulled away from him, still fuming, and looked around the room. "What is this place?"

"It's an oubliette," Chevalier explained as he watched her. "We don't use them anymore."

"Except to restrain me now," she said, irritated.

"We didn't have a choice."

"This time... next time you'll stick me in here for no good reason."

"We won't..."

"... then I'll have to ash you all to get out..."

"Em"

"What?"

"Do you want out?"

She looked up. "Who the hell put the door on the ceiling?"

"We did. That's what an oubliette is."

"Fine"

He wrapped his arms around her, kissed the top of her head, and then blurred her up to the council chambers and put her down.

She looked over at the Council and then turned on her heels and headed for the door.

"Em?" Kyle said, amused.

Emily sighed and looked over her shoulder at him. "What?"

"Are you okay?"

"Peachy"

"Do you want Dr. Edwards to look at your eye?"

"No"

He smiled. "Heard you gave him quite the beating."

She couldn't help but grin and then left the council chambers. She immediately headed to the prison. It had been a while since she'd been down there, but she had business to attend to. Kralen backed off the other three guards and went down with her.

"Lady Emily," the first prison guard said, bowing. He then stood up. "You aren't authorized to be down here anymore."

She sighed and started to talk, but Kralen cut him off. "Stand down."

"Yes, Captain," he replied, and then moved back by his post.

"Where's Sotomar?" Emily asked.

"Row 17, cell 8."

She glanced back at Kralen and then walked down the rows of cells. Things were noisy in the prison. Neither Emily nor Kralen were a big threat, so the prisoners continued to visit and move around their cells. She thought it was funny that if Chevalier were to walk in, you could hear a pin drop in there.

Sotomar smiled when Emily walked up to his cell. "Good to see you."

She glared at him. "Get rid of that crap you put in my head."

"It's... I thought it was gone."

"Well it's not. So get rid of it."

He studied her for a moment. "What triggered it?"

"I don't know. I don't care. Just get rid of it!"

"I don't know how," Sotomar said before sitting down on his bed. Kralen was pretty sure he was telling the truth and not upset about it.

"You control me long enough to erase it, easy enough."

"He's not controlling you again," Kralen said.

Emily ignored him. "I don't care how long it takes."

"No," Sotomar said bluntly. "If it's still active, then there is a chance you will return to the Valle."

She simply screamed and then stormed off, meeting up with the other three members of the Cavalry that were posted outside the prison

doors. They could tell she was furious when she came out of the prison, and they fell quiet. As they headed out to the stables, Kralen filled the Council in on Emily's interaction with Sotomar.

"Stay out here," Emily said before disappearing into the stables. Kralen watched her and then sent two of the guards to the back door. Only a few minutes later, Emily came out and headed inside.

Kralen shrugged and followed her in.

"Wait here," she said when she opened the door to the prison. Kralen nodded and told the other three to stay and then headed down the stairs to the prison.

"You too," Emily said when she saw him.

"Why?"

"Because I asked nicely."

He studied her before speaking. "What are you up to?"

"Nothing… just stay, please."

"No"

"Listen… I know I promised you I wouldn't ash you or wipe your memory… but I will if you don't back off. This is at least a warning."

He growled softly. "No."

She walked past him and down into the prison as he returned to the other three members of the Cavalry, slightly confused.

"Did she wipe my memory?" Kralen asked them.

"Not sure, sir."

He looked around the hallway. "I don't remember coming down here."

"Do you remember the stables?"

"With Em?"

"Yes"

He sighed, "No, I don't."

"Sorry, Captain," the guard said.

Kralen's hands balled into fists, and he headed down into the prison. When he heard gunshots ring out through the palace, he quickly blurred to Sotomar's cell and grabbed the 9mm from Emily.

"Give it back!" she screamed at him.

Kralen looked in at the blood covered walls and noticed it was taking a bit for Sotomar to heal. "No."

"Now!"

"You wiped my memory!" he yelled at her. "You swore you wouldn't do that."

"Then back off when I tell you to."

"That wasn't part of the deal!"

She lunged for her gun, but he held it higher. "I have half a mind to throw you over my knee for this."

Emily glared at him. "I'm not a child."

"Then stop acting like one."

"You have no right to say that!" Emily screamed.

"You can't just come down here and shoot prisoners."

"I can too! He owes me."

"There's a process in punishing a prisoner! You know that."

Chevalier and Kyle rounded the corner to Sotomar's cell just as Emily jumped at Kralen and slapped him. Chevalier took Kralen by the arm when he went after Emily, and Kyle pulled her away from her guard.

"You promised me!" Kralen yelled.

"Yeah, well I lied!" Emily screamed back. "Seems common in your species. You should be used to it!"

"Calm down," Chevalier told them sternly.

Kralen jerked his arm away from the Elder and then blurred to just inches away from Emily with his finger pointed at her chest. "I've never lied to you. You had no right wiping my memory!"

"Enough," Chevalier growled.

"You would have stopped me!" Emily said, struggling to get away from Kyle.

"Em, stop," he said, and held tighter.

"You need stopped!" Kralen roared. "I'm not going to stand by and watch anyone hurt you…, but you seem to seek it out! It's like you want tortured!"

Emily kicked out at him, so Kyle blurred her up the stairs.

Kralen turned his livid eyes to Chevalier.

"Are you under control?" Chevalier asked him.

His face softened and he nodded. "Yeah, I guess."

"Take the day off. Go feed."

"I'm not…"

"That's an order."

Kralen nodded and walked slowly up the stairs. Chevalier turned to Sotomar, and he was just barely crawling to his feet.

"I don't believe I've ever had an entire clip emptied into me," he said, still out of breath.

"You're lucky I don't let her have at you."

"I'm not erasing the new memories… not if there's a chance it will bring her to the Valle."

"Won't matter to you. You're stuck here."

"It'd be worth it to know she's returned to her true family."

Chevalier shook his head and followed Emily's scent to their bedroom. Four new members of the Cavalry were standing outside of her door, and he could hear Emily screaming at Kyle from inside the room.

Chevalier sighed, "I'm not sure I want to go in there."

Horace grinned but didn't speak.

They all turned to the door when they heard Kyle starting to get mad. Chevalier instantly blurred into the room and stood between them just as Kyle started to yell.

"Don't push me on this!" he said, pointing at her.

"Calm down," Chevalier told him.

"He has no right treating me like a child!" Emily screamed.

Chevalier saw Kyle starting to lose control and ordered him to leave. When the door slammed behind him, Chevalier turned to Emily. "You're on a roll..."

"What does that mean?" she asked, glaring at him.

"Angering four heku in an hour."

She sighed, "I want to go talk to the Valle."

He sat down and patted the bed beside him. "About what?"

"About their feeble attempt at kidnapping me. About trying to stake some misguided claim on me." Emily sat down beside him and took his hand.

Chevalier thought for a moment. He knew she'd already made up her mind to go, and no one could stop her now. "Why don't you and I go?"

"Just us?"

"Yes, just us."

She smiled. "Really?"

"I don't want Megara that close to the Valle... so yes, really."

"When?"

Chevalier stood up. "Now."

Emily hurried and slipped on a jacket. "No Cavalry?"

"No, it'll just be us."

She turned to him and frowned. "What if they keep us?"

Chevalier smiled. "Then we'll call it a second honeymoon."

"How romantic," she said, and walked past him.

"Sir...," Horace said. "I really think..."

"Emily and I will handle this alone," Chevalier told him.

"But Sir..."

"It's not up for discussion."

"Yes, sir," Horace said, obviously irritated.

"Maybe you should take our Faction Liaison," Zohn said as they passed the fourth floor.

Emily smiled at him and took Chevalier's hand when he shook his head.

They took off in the Humvee, headed for the Valle's main city as the Cavalry watched. Mark stood out front, hoping they would change

their minds and allow some of them to go. Late the next evening they arrived and Chevalier parked just outside the city gates.

Emily watched the Valle guards move forward. "They look mad already."

"They're just being cautious." Chevalier stepped out of the Humvee, and when the guards saw who it was, they immediately called for Imperial Guards.

Emily joined Chevalier at the gates, and they waited for an escort to see the Council. When their escort came, she could feel Chevalier chuckle. The Council had sent over 30 Imperial Guards, who all seemed on high alert and rather angry to see the two of them.

"One toe out of line and we're to immediately destroy you both," the lead Imperial Guard said.

"Of course," Chevalier replied, sounding amused.

Emily clung to his arm as they walked toward the palace. Once inside, they waited at the door to the council chambers.

"Emi?" Emily smiled and turned around when she recognized Chuck's voice, her friend from Cascade.

"Hiya, Chuck."

"It's Charles, actually," he said, smugly.

"You're in the palace now?"

"Yup"

"Because you know me?"

He shrugged. "Not sure really."

She sighed, "Why the Valle, Chuck?"

"Em…," Chevalier whispered. It was rude to ask a heku why they made their faction choice.

"I was turned into the faction," Charles explained.

"By who?"

He smiled. "No one you know. You're looking good though, haven't changed a bit since high school."

"Yeah, that's kind of my thing."

"How about you? Why the Equites?"

Chevalier growled softly. Emily didn't know better than to ask rude questions, but this heku did.

She shrugged. "Luck of the draw, I guess."

"You can always change," Charles said, smiling.

She shook her head. "Become a Valle? No way."

Charles eyed Chevalier. "I heard about what happened to Keith."

"Yeah, so? He had it coming."

"He wasn't all bad."

"No, but the parts that were bad were exceptionally so."

"Why don't you hang back when Chevalier returns? We can catch

up."

Emily smiled. "Chuck... friend or no, you're a Valle now. They aren't exactly on my list of people to visit."

"You can trust me."

"Maybe"

Charles turned toward the door. "The Council is ready for you. They wonder if they can talk to Chevalier alone."

"Nope, they can't," she said, and took Chevalier's hand. He chuckled, and they walked into the council chambers together. The Council was furious that they had come without Sotomar, and his empty chair made everyone all the more tense.

Chevalier let go of Emily's hand, and she felt him tense beside her when they stood before the Valle Council.

"Why have you come?" Randall asked.

"To end this," Chevalier said. "Emily has a right to be left alone."

"She has no such right."

"I do too!" Emily said. "You all screwed with my mind, and I want it reversed."

Ryan smiled. "It's not gone?"

"No"

Chevalier cleared his throat. "She fell back into it for a few days. It's not safe, and we're worried about long-term effects."

"You have Sotomar. Have him remove it," Randall suggested.

"Yeah, like I didn't think to try that," Emily said, irritated.

"We have no reason to remove it. Especially if someday it brings Emily back into our care."

"Your care? You mean your prisoner."

"You were happy here."

"Bullshit!"

"Em...," Chevalier whispered. He turned back to the Council. "It's been almost 40 years. You have to see that Emily is, and always will be, an Equites."

"No, we don't see that. Forty years is nothing when you are an immortal, and you know that," Ryan said. "We do feel that someday the Equites will overstep, and we will be there with open arms."

Her eyes narrowed. "I'd go to the Encala before you."

"You are too much like a Valle to join the Encala."

"Don't insult me."

Ryan studied them for a moment. "I'm surprised you came without guards. You realize you aren't leaving here."

"Like I'm going to allow that to happen," Emily said as she crossed her arms.

"Chevalier won't allow you to turn our city to ash."

"Well maybe Chevalier won't have a choice."

"Guards… take them to a cell," the Valle's Chief of Staff said with a smile.

Chevalier sighed, "You know better than that."

Imperial Guards flooded into the council chambers and escorted Chevalier and Emily into the prison. Chevalier went calmly, knowing it was only temporary, but Emily put up a fight and was able to incapacitate one heku before being fully restrained by two others.

They were thrown into a cell, and when the door locked, Emily turned to Chevalier and a smile crossed her face when she saw he was on the verge of laughing.

"What's so funny?" she asked him.

"We're in the Valle prison," he answered, and then started to laugh. Emily joined him when the irony hit her.

They finally stopped laughing when a gruff voice sounded after someone banged on the cell door. "This isn't a playground you two. Keep it down."

Chevalier, still amused, looked around the stark cell. It had the same cement floor and heavy cement door as the last time they were in the Valle prison together, and again, there were no chairs for Emily to sit on.

Emily looked around the room. "Well… I guess it could be worse."

Chevalier sat down and patted his lap. "Kyle could be here, and you could be pregnant?"

She sat down and leaned against him. "Exactly. This could actually be fun."

"How so?"

"We get time together."

He chuckled. "We don't need to be in prison to get time together."

She gently ran her nails up his forearm. "My bet is two days."

"Until the Equites spring us?"

"Yes"

"I say two weeks."

"Why so long?"

"Well, the Valle will offer to exchange me for Sotomar…, but the Equites want you back… that's harder."

"So I ash them and we leave."

"They know I'll try to stop you."

She rolled her eyes. "Like you've ever been able to stop me from anything."

"True"

Chevalier moved Emily's hair aside and lightly kissed the nape of her neck. She shivered and spun in his lap to face him and pressed her

lips to his.

"Hey! You two knock it off!" someone yelled from outside the door.

Emily's eyes narrowed. "They can hear a kiss?"

Chevalier nodded, took her face in his hands, and kissed her again. She melted into him and wrapped her arms around his neck.

"Stop it!" the guard said again, and hit something up against the door.

Chevalier chuckled and looked to the cement door.

Emily sighed, "You never told me the entire palace could hear us kiss…, which means… anything else too."

"They don't care," he said, and brushed the hair away from her face.

"Still!"

"Honestly… it's something you'd have to try to hear. The Valle are just being a pain in the ass."

She looked toward the door. "Why are we even in a cell together?"

"They know I'm going to try to stop you from ashing their city. If we are separated, you'd do it out of sheer annoyance."

Emily smirked. "Well, that's true."

Chevalier kissed her again and then grinned when they got yelled at through the door.

"Just because you haven't gotten laid in the last century, doesn't mean you have to ruin our fun," Emily said toward the door.

Chevalier laughed. "Nice."

"Knock it off, or I separate you two," the Valle said through the door. "You're in custody for hell's sake."

Emily looked at Chevalier. "Yeah… Encala it is."

Chevalier sat back and took her hands. "Well beings how that's out of the question… now what do you want to do?"

She shrugged and again looked around the dull gray room. "I could pick off the Council, just for fun."

"Let's not… let the Equites step in."

"They're probably already on the way."

"Probably, this was very predictable."

Emily studied his eyes while he wondered what she was thinking. Finally, she broke the silence. "What was your name before you turned?"

"Why?"

"I just want to know… was it Equitis?"

"So do I finally get to find out why you pop off with Equitis once in a while when you're mad?"

"Maybe… was that your name?"

"Not until I turned, no."

"So what was it?"

"Why does that name make you mad?"

"The name doesn't."

"Okay, so why do you say it when you're mad at me?"

She thought for a moment before speaking. "I know you were the first non-Ancient on the Council."

"Okay"

"I also know that the Chief Enforcer started out punishing mortals."

"That was a long time ago," Chevalier said softly. He was trying to see where this line of conversation was going.

Emily watched him for a moment as she bit at her bottom lip.

"We've got nothing but time. You might as well tell me what this is all about."

"How many dads sought you out to marry their daughters?"

He sighed, "How do you even know about that?"

"How many?"

"I didn't count."

"More than ten?"

Chevalier debated lying but figured it wasn't worth it. "Yes."

"So you hated mortals."

"Em, that was a long time ago."

"Then you turned, and the Ancients were so proud of you for viewing mortals like they did... that they made you Chief Enforcer."

He nodded.

"Some are shocked you married me because I was mortal. That tells me your mortal hating was long-term."

"I don't hate mortals."

"You did."

"Yes"

"Until you met me?"

"You were different."

"Right, I'm only 49% mortal."

"I didn't know that at the time though."

"You sure?"

"Em..."

"No... Ancients can tell from my scent that I have Ancient blood. So you could tell too."

"No, I couldn't. Ancient's senses are a lot stronger than mine."

"But why else fall for a mortal when you hated us?"

Chevalier tried to pick his words carefully. "It's not natural for a heku to fall for a mortal. I didn't know why I had feelings for you. They were abnormal and uncharacteristic. However, I did fall for you."

"So you hated mortals until you met me?" she asked, trying to understand.

"Hate is a strong word."

"What word would you use?"

"Disdain"

"How can a Chief Enforcer protect mortals if you hate them?"

"I thought we just covered that I don't hate mortals."

"Not now maybe... but you did."

Chevalier took her hand. "I did hate mortals... I hated myself for being one, even before I knew what a heku was. I liked fighting, and war, and conflict. Then when I was forced to turn, I realized how much mortals complain and whine about everything. I admit to hating them and punishing them as Chief Enforcer."

She watched him, trying to understand.

"What I didn't agree with was how the Ancients treated them. I didn't think any creature of intelligence should be tormented and tortured just for fun. We banished the Ancients, the Chief Enforcer's role changed, and I accepted the change."

"But you still hated mortals at that point?"

"By then it was more disgust. They were not a civil species, and I hated how they complained and lied. When I met you, I still felt some loathing for mortals, I'll admit to that. You though... when I saw you sitting in the bath tub reading, I was hit with something I'd never felt before, and I wasn't sure how to react, so I put my feelings on the back burner and went about my job."

He studied her before continuing. "In Colorado, when I finally allowed myself to feel, I realized I was falling for you and didn't know why. You though, didn't complain or cower, you were strong and intelligent. I think you opened my eyes to what some mortals were like. When we found out you were mostly heku, I thought maybe in some way I sensed that. There's no way to be sure."

"You hated mortal women more than the men," Emily said.

"Yes, I did. The men at least fought for what they believed in. The men weren't as gossipy and didn't complain nearly as much as the women. No, I didn't marry. I couldn't see being tied down to someone who nagged and made my life a living hell."

"I've done that."

He smiled. "No, you haven't. I was focused on wars and keeping my village safe. I didn't have time to cater to the whims of an over-emotional wife."

"You married an over-emotional woman though."

"No, I didn't. I married the strongest woman I've ever met. I married someone who compliments my strengths and fills in for my weaknesses."

She frowned. "You don't have any weaknesses."

"In the realm of emotions I do," he explained. "I'm maybe not the most compassionate person…"

"You don't have a compassionate bone in your body."

"Exactly, so you make up for that."

"I just don't see how you fell for someone you thought was fully mortal."

"I don't either…, but I did."

"Do you swear to me that you didn't know I was part Ancient when we met?"

Thoughts ran quickly through his head, and he decided to voice them. "Had I walked into that house knowing you were half Ancient… I would have killed you instantly."

She gasped. "What? You told me you wouldn't have!"

"It was the code…, and I didn't know you."

She crossed her arms. "I wouldn't have let you kill me."

"So are we good?" he asked, watching her eyes.

Emily raised her eyebrows. "You think you could kill me?"

"Yes," he said quickly, and then grinned.

"I wouldn't even need to ash you to stop that."

Chevalier blurred forward and pinned her to the hard cement. "How exactly would you stop me?"

"I have my ways." She brought her knee up quickly toward his groin, but he dodged and straddled her hips.

"That all you got?"

She squirmed to get out of his firm grip. "No… I just don't want to hurt you, so it's not fair."

Chevalier reached down and lightly ran his lips along hers. They both looked over when the door flew open and four prison guards stormed in.

"Oh good, did you come to save me?" Emily asked, still pinned to the cement.

"No, you're to be separated," the closest guard said with disgust. "You're incarcerated! Act like it!"

Emily stood up when Chevalier let go of her, and she brushed herself off. "Fine… no more little Winchesters for now then."

Chevalier laughed as they took Emily out and put her in the cell across from his. He peered out of the tiny barred window and looked into her cell when the guards left. "Can you see out the window?"

Emily's hand appeared in hers. "This one?"

"Yes"

"Are you kidding? You'd have to be a giant to see out that thing."

"I can see out."

"Point proven."

"Just hang tight… the Equites will get us."

"I can't believe we were sequestered for making out in prison."

Chevalier laughed and returned to the hard cement floor. Emily looked around her room and then sat down on a cot in the corner. At least it was better than sitting on cement all day.

It was only a couple of hours later when Emily got bored enough to get into trouble. She pushed the cot over to the door and stood on it to look out the window. She quickly slipped her bra off under her shirt and then took aim. When Keith had been in a good mood, she often shot her bra at him and had become adept at hitting her mark. She hoped that hadn't gone away.

With one quick flick, her bra sailed through Chevalier's window, and she ducked down when she heard him laugh.

"Would you stay dressed?" he said, amused. The entire prison suddenly fell silent. Emily hadn't noticed how noisy the Valle prison was until everyone stopped talking, and she blushed when she realized why.

"Well you didn't have to announce that I'm undressing," she said, blushing deeper.

"You can't have your bra back."

She gasped. "What? No way… send it over."

"Nope"

"If you don't send it over, I'll send my panties over next."

"I'd keep those too."

She grinned and climbed down off of her bed when she heard guards approaching.

"The Council wants to see you two," one of them said as they opened their doors.

Chevalier carried her bra in his hand as they walked out of the prison.

"Give it back," she whispered, laughing.

"Nope"

Just after walking into the council chambers, Emily bumped Chevalier with her hip and then dodged when he tried to slap her butt.

"My God!" Ryan screamed. "We've never had such inappropriate conduct from a prisoner before."

Chevalier shrugged.

"Do you realize how serious this is?"

"Apparently not," Emily said, and then smiled.

"Return her brassiere," the Chief of Defense said.

"No, it's mine," Chevalier told him.

"You two are acting like children," Randall snapped. "Do we have to put Chevalier into interrogation to get you to take this seriously?"

Emily nodded. "I'm okay with that."

Chevalier looked at her with raised eyebrows. "You're okay if they torture me?"

"Sure"

"Now you're really not getting your bra back."

"Want the matching panties?" she asked as she undid the top button on her jeans.

"Stop!" Ryan roared. "Enough of this."

Emily looked up at him, suddenly serious. "Touch one hair on his head, and I'll obliterate your city and you know it."

"Do not threaten me."

She broke out laughing and looked at Chevalier. "I can't keep a straight face…"

"Return them to their separate cells," the Chief Interrogator said angrily.

"Aww man, well… remember me by my bra," Emily said, returning to laughter when she was escorted out.

Chevalier grinned at the Valle Council and was walked out by six Imperial Guards.

Chapter 22

"They'll come for us," Chevalier said through the tiny barred window on the door of his cell.

Emily shrugged. "It's not fun anymore."

"I know. I'm sure they're trying."

"I give the Equites two more days, and I'm getting us out."

"They have to have prepared for that. I'm thinking it wouldn't work somehow."

"How?"

"I don't know."

Emily disappeared from the window to her cell when she climbed down off of the hard cot. She was just pushing it to the far wall when the door opened.

"Emi, it's time to go," Charles said.

Emily turned to him. "Go where?"

"You'll see. Come on."

She crossed her arms. "No."

Charles hissed softly. "Don't give me any trouble… you've always been nothing but one big problem, and the Valle are done with you."

"Meaning?"

"Meaning… I worked with Keith. He told me what a bitch you are, how you stole from him, cheated on him, and how you spent all of the money he earned…"

"And you believed Keith?" she asked, irritated.

"Of course! He tried to get a handle on you but couldn't. Keith was a good guy, and you made his life a living hell… then you allowed your heku to kill him."

"I'm not going with you."

"Leave her alone," Chevalier growled from behind them. He watched from in his cell as Charles and another Valle advanced on Emily. She fought against them but was forcibly dragged from her cell.

Once in the hallway, the two Valle turned to ash, and Emily looked up at Chevalier fearfully. "I'll cut the power."

"No," Chevalier said hurriedly. "Listen to me… I don't know where they were taking you. You have to get out of here. Ash who you have to and run…"

"I'm not leaving you here."

"You have to! The Equites can get me back. They might be taking you to interrogation. Ash them and get the hell out of here."

Emily spun and ran down the hallway. Chevalier watched her go, and his heart sank. He felt the intense fear emanating from her and silently urged her to run.

"Stop!" someone shouted.

Chevalier tried to see down the hallway but couldn't.

"You're not turning off the current," another voice said. There was a loud scuffle followed by Emily's scream as it echoed through the palace.

Chevalier slammed up against the door, hoping to break it down, but it was reinforced against even an Old One. When her screams died down, he heard Valle guards talking about the sedative and when it might wear off.

"Hurt her and you'll have to deal with me," Chevalier called out.

"She's no longer any concern of the Valle," a voice said.

"What does that mean?"

"Mind your own business, prisoner."

Chevalier heard the guards talking. One of them finally agreed to pick Emily up, and she was carried out of the prison.

***

Chevalier hadn't heard from anyone in four days. The Valle didn't come, nor did he get the Council summons indicating the Equites were there to get him back. He knew wherever Emily was she was not only afraid but was in pain and seemed to suffer continuously.

He sat and made plans to exterminate the Valle, even going so far as to enlist the help of the Encala if he had to. While the Encala had backed off of Emily and had become a friend, the Valle continued to harass her, and he was tired of it.

At twilight on the 15th day, Chevalier heard someone coming, and he stood up and watched the cell door open.

Charles, Emily's childhood friend, entered. "The Council wants to see you."

"Where's Emily?" Chevalier asked, glaring at the young heku.

Charles didn't answer but moved aside so Chevalier could exit. He growled softly, balled his hands into fists, and then followed seven Imperial Guards out of the prison and into the council chambers.

He wasn't surprised to see Sotomar at his seat, and Kyle, Zohn, and Kralen standing in the trial area.

Chevalier moved quickly to the Council. "Where is she?!"

"Wait," Kyle said. "You said you were returning both of them."

"Emily is no longer ours to give. You may take your Elder and go," Valle Elder Randall said to them.

"I'm not asking again," Chevalier told them. "Where is she?"

Sotomar smiled. "She's been turned over to the true Equites Council to be tried for crimes against the Equites and the species."

"What?!" Chevalier roared. "They torture her!"

"Maybe it's what's needed in this case," Valle Elder Ryan said.

Kyle put a hand on Chevalier's arm. "Elder… we'll get her back."

"No, you are to be banished so the true Council can resume their positions," Sotomar said. "For now though, you may go."

"I'm not finished with you," Chevalier said to Sotomar. "She's in pain… and she's afraid…"

Sotomar's face showed a brief flicker of alarm before falling neutral. "I'm sure they are only doing what they need to."

Just after Equites 1 took off for Council City with Kralen at the helm, Chevalier turned to Zohn. "Do we know where she is?"

"No, we thought she was still with you."

"They took her on the fourth day, and she was screaming," he whispered. Kyle glanced over, not surprised at the malevolent look on Chevalier's face.

"We'll find her," Zohn said. "The former Council has been contacting covens all over the world looking for supporters. If we get the word out, one of the covens can follow them back and give us a location."

"She's in pain," Chevalier told him as he watched out the window. "Why do they always have to hurt her?"

"Because it's the only way they can get back at her. She's too strong to cave."

"I'm sure they know by now they can't kill her too," Kyle added. "I just wish she'd give in to their wishes until we can get her back. It'd save her a lot of pain."

Chevalier looked down at his hands. "I told her to ash the city and run…"

"Did she try?"

"No, she ignored me and tried to set me free."

"Damnit"

***

"Then we've hit an impasse," Kirt said. He believed himself to be one of the Equites Elders, although none of the Equites covens had agreed to follow them.

Emily nodded.

"We realize we can't banish you or kill you," their Chief Interrogator said. "However, once we reclaim our seats in the true palace, we will have to deal with you."

Emily stayed silent.

"For now, you will return to your cell. If you decide to help us and

follow heku tradition, then we will reconsider," Kirt told her. He motioned for the heku at the door to return her to her cell.

She jumped slightly when the heavy metal bars slammed shut behind her and then she looked around the small cement cell. There were no windows, no furniture, and nothing to keep her warm. She wrapped her arms around herself, cringing at the pain in her forearms from their interrogation, and sat against the cold cement wall.

Fear gripped her, and she couldn't bring herself to look any heku in the eye or speak. Without thinking about it, she curled up into a ball and began to rock on the hard, cold floor. She knew they were getting mad at her silence, but they had learned from the Valle, proven by her forearm pain, and she was sure they were going to go the way of Salazar.

She couldn't cry but continued to rock slowly as the sounds of the prison swarmed around her. Prisoners called for help for anyone that could hear them. They were tortured relentlessly and unjustly imprisoned by the Equites pseudo-Council.

***

"How many are here now?" Chevalier asked as he looked out over the mass of heku on the lawn.

Captain Darren from Thukil looked over the gathered army. "We're at just over 1800."

General Skinner came up with a stack of papers. "We've assigned groups, each led by a member of your Cavalry. The groups have been given an area of the globe. It's still going to be hard to find this other Council… so we're going to have to focus in on Emily's scent."

Chevalier nodded. "Break up into the teams then. I want to see it."

Kyle blurred up. "Still no word. The Valle and Encala have denied allowing Bahadir Coven to join them."

"Then they've joined the pseudo-Council."

"That's all we can figure. They haven't been wiped out. Our sources saw them in their coven. They just aren't answering calls from us."

"Send Mark's team immediately to Istanbul then," Chevalier told him. "We'll start looking there. If they have joined the pseudo-Council, then they would have to be close by. Either way, I want them killed."

Kyle nodded and disappeared to talk to Mark.

"Elder…," Silas said. Chevalier looked at him and then followed his gaze.

"What the hell is he doing here?" Chevalier whispered when he saw Andrew coming toward the castle, followed by four city guards.

"My guess is he wants to help."

"Well get rid of him."

Silas nodded and then walked up to Andrew. "We don't need your help."

"Yes, you do," Andrew said. "You don't know what kind of state Emily is going to be in, and she trusts me."

"She trusts us too."

"Not as much as she does me. I know how to take care of her if they've used Salazar's methods."

"We can handle it," Silas growled.

Chevalier sighed when he realized that Andrew was right. "Wait up…"

Andrew looked up at the Elder and crossed his arms. "Going to throw me out?"

"No, I'm going to put you in Silas' group."

"What?!" Silas hissed.

"He's right. Emily trusts him. I'm not sure if the pseudo-Council will turn her against the Encala, but they sure as hell will try to turn her against the rest of us."

"Get in line," Silas said to Andrew and then returned to his team. "We've been given Western Europe, specifically Holland, Belgium, France, and Switzerland."

"It's The Netherlands now, and that's a lot of area for this little group," Andrew said from the back row.

Silas' jaw tightened. "We're going to be splitting up and checking in with HQ each night. If you don't call, we'll assume you are in trouble, and you damned well better be because if we have to come find you, we'll be off Emily's track by then."

Andrew was ignoring Silas and watching Mark's team. They seemed ready to head out and anxious to check something out. He broke formation and walked over to Chevalier.

"I'm going with Mark," Andrew told him.

"No, you're not."

Andrew's eyes narrowed. "They're heading out first. He's the highest ranking of your elite. They think they know where she is."

"They aren't even going out after Emily," Chevalier told him. "Get back with Silas."

Andrew glared at Chevalier and then walked over and stood in the back row of Silas' group.

Mark watched the transport helicopter land and then ordered his team of 22 to get on board. They would be taken to the Equites hangar outside of New York City, and a jet would take them the rest of the way into Turkey.

The entire flight was silent, broken only when Gifford, a member of

the Cavalry from Thukil, finally spoke, "We haven't been told when we look for Emily."

Mark looked over at him. "Once we ascertain where Bahadir Coven is, we'll head out. We are going to cover Turkey, Bulgaria, Romania, and the Ukraine."

"Is it suspected that Bahadir may have her?" a heku from Powan asked.

"No, but they aren't responding to Council summons so something's up."

"Where are we landing?"

"Atakurk Airport in Istanbul. From there it's only an hour to Bahadir Coven."

"We running it then?" another heku asked.

Mark nodded and then looked outside when the pilot gave the ten minute warning until landing.

"What do we do if they're not in trouble?" Gifford asked Mark.

"If they've swapped sides or joined the pseudo-Council, then we kill them."

"How many?"

"There are 133 in Bahadir Coven. Lady Seden is the Coven Leader, and she's been holding a grudge against the Council since the early 1500s."

"About what?" one of the heku from Thukil asked.

"The Council didn't say. They strongly suspect that Bahadir has joined the Valle."

Once the jet landed, the heku readied themselves for the run and then immediately headed out for the small compound outside of Gebze, Turkey. The compound sat eerily quiet and dark in the thick trees surrounding it. The high cement walls weren't patrolled and there wasn't the soft humming of electricity.

"I don't hear a single heku," Mark whispered. "Gifford, get closer."

The heku nodded and stealthily moved forward until he was up against the cement. He turned to Mark and motioned that he heard nothing.

Mark frowned and then thought for a moment. "Team 3, you're with me. I want Teams 1 and 2 to follow us in two minutes after we get inside the walls."

When the heku acknowledged their orders, Mark moved in with seven heku following him. He stopped just inside the walls and looked down at the two sleeping heku at the gate.

Gifford knelt down and studied the closest. "He's not dead... he's... well... sleeping."

Mark's heart pounded in his chest. "Damnit... find Emily. She has

to be here."

Mark's heku spread out quickly through the compound and counted out the 120 heku they found unconscious throughout the compound. When they met at the center, Mark looked around the area.

"There are 13 missing," he whispered to himself.

"Maybe they were attacked and 13 got away," the heku from Powan said.

"I've never seen unconscious heku with no sign of trauma," another said.

Mark sighed, "This doesn't leave these walls. We were able to keep it pretty quiet, but this is what happens when you try to turn Emily."

"Turn her?" Gifford gasped.

"The 13 have to be in the ceremonial room where they tried to turn Emily. The rest of the coven will wake eventually."

"I didn't see a ceremonial room."

"It has to be in the main house then. Let's go," Mark said as he started for the largest house, offset a bit from the center of the coven.

The main house's door was already open from when the heku had gone through it on initial checks. Mark immediately caught the faint scent of Winchester blood, and he looked around the dark house. Gifford looked down at a female heku lying along the foot of the stairs. "This must be Lady Seden."

Mark finally returned his voice to normal volume. "Search everything in this house. She's either here or been here."

"I don't catch her scent," a heku from Banks Coven said.

"I do. It's very faint though."

Mark's team spread out through the house, and within ten minutes, had located the heavy door leading into the ceremonial room. Mark appeared shortly after he was called and looked around at the 13 unconscious heku in robes.

"Damnit, she was here," Mark said. By now, the rest of the heku could smell the faint trace of blood from Emily.

One of Mark's team blurred around the room and removed the hoods from each of the unconscious heku, revealing their identity.

"None look familiar, except him," the heku from Powan said, pointing to the one in black.

"Who is he?" Mark asked.

"He's the pseudo-Court Reporter."

Mark frowned. "Two of you go secure the gates. The rest of you stay here until I get back."

He passed two heku already guarding the front gates and continued on, well out of earshot of any heku that might be listening. Once his cell phone got signal, he dialed the Council.

"Zohn here."

"It's Mark. Is Chevalier around?"

"No, last I heard he's in Louisiana."

"Emily was here at Bahadir."

"Was?"

"The coven is asleep. There are 13 in the ceremonial room in robes."

There was silence while Zohn processed the information. "But she's not there?"

"No, she was though. Her scent is very faint."

"Do you recognize any of the 13?"

"One of them is a member of the pseudo-Council."

"Kill them all, but bring me that one. Send two heku back to Council City with him, and the rest of you find that Council."

"Yes, Elder," Mark said.

***

"He's awake?" Chevalier asked as his hands balled into fists.

"Yes," Zohn said. "Woke up this morning."

"Richard, you're with me," Chevalier said as he and the Chief Interrogator left for the palace's prison. Perkins, the pseudo-Council's Court Reporter, was already hanging from shackles when they arrived. His eyes grew wide when he saw the fury in Chevalier's features, and he immediately began to beg.

"Please... I'll talk...," Perkins said nervously.

Chevalier grabbed a Spanish flayer and turned to him. "Yes, you will."

"I meant without violence!"

Richard smiled. "He's way past being able to reason with you. Emily's been gone for three months, and we can't seem to find her. Not to mention, you morons tried to turn her against her will."

"It wasn't against her will! She asked us to... I swear... begged us to turn her," he said, seconds before screaming when the flayer slammed against his back and peeled the flesh away.

"She begged you to turn her?" Richard asked, studying his face.

He nodded vehemently.

Chevalier looked over at Richard. "Obviously a lie."

"No, actually... he's telling the truth, but there's something else."

"What?!" their prisoner screamed just as Chevalier removed a large chunk of flesh from Perkins' back with the Spanish flayer.

"Start talking," Chevalier hissed.

"N... no! She be... begged us. I swear."

"Wrong answer." Richard dug into a vat of salt and gingerly tossed it into the wounds on his back.

Chevalier stood back and studied him as his horrific screams filled the prison. When he'd healed enough to talk, Chevalier went over and put an iron poker into the fire.

"Please...," Perkins gasped.

"Emily wouldn't agree to be turned," Richard said to him. "So explain what you mean."

"It's the truth... she begged us to turn her."

"Why?"

"What?" Perkins asked, looking up with a wobbly head.

Chevalier reached down and tore his foot from his body. "He asked why. What possessed Emily to agree to be turned?"

Richard waited while Perkins healed enough to speak, but all he managed was a gurgled sob.

"Did you control her to agree?" Chevalier asked him.

"No," Perkins managed to whisper.

"I don't want to play the guessing game," Richard said, and headed for the fire.

"Wait! No!"

When the orange hot tip pressed against Perkins' lower back, he screamed and thrashed, trying to relieve the pain.

"Start talking or you get the tank," Chevalier said as he walked over to his newest torture device, a sealed tank of water.

Perkins looked over at it and gasped. "What is that?"

"My new toy... want to try it?"

"No," he squeaked.

"Why did Emily agree to be turned?" Richard asked calmly.

Perkins head lowered and he whispered, "Torture."

"You tortured her until she agreed to turn?"

He nodded slightly.

"What kind of torture?"

"I... I don't know... Lync did it all and wouldn't tell us."

"Who is Lync?"

"Chief Interrogator."

Richard studied him. "You don't know... but you saw the results..."

"Yes," Perkins whispered.

Chevalier walked forward. "I want to know what kind of torture you put her through, so she would agree to this."

"When... when she came into the ceremonial room... she had casts," he uttered.

"Where?"

"Lower arms," he said, and then started to cry tearlessly.

Richard shook his head and his lip curled. "You disgust me. Stop crying and act like a man for God's sake."

"I didn't do anything wrong."

"Sure you did! Part of the turning laws say no one can be tortured into it!"

"I didn't torture her! I asked if she'd been coerced, and she said no."

"But you knew she'd been tortured!" Chevalier yelled. "She had a cast on her arm."

"Both…" Perkins' words were cut off when Chevalier slammed his head into the rock wall and caved it in.

"They must not have heard that Emily can't be turned," Richard said as he sat on the rack to wait.

"Or they thought that by her agreeing to it, it would work."

Richard sighed, "It had to have taken a lot to get her in there."

"That damned forearm thing I'm guessing. The only ones that know about it won't say what the hell it is… Emily's been through it but won't tell me."

"Andrew knows," Richard reminded him.

Chevalier looked over at him. "He's on the Council… he was given the order to keep silent as a guard."

"Have we found out who removed Emily once the coven was unconscious?"

"No, no one's talking."

"What are you getting from her?"

Chevalier leaned back against the iron maiden. "Not much. There's lots of pain and always fear, but there are brief moments when it lessens."

"We'll find her."

"We have to," Chevalier said. "If the pseudo-Council can get Emily to follow them…"

"We'll find her first."

"No being, human or heku, can go through that much torture without eventually caving. To save herself, she'll have to agree and then we risk being re-banished and scattered."

"Now let's see if we can get him to tell us where the pseudo-Council is holed up," Richard said when Perkins began to stir.

***

Chevalier and Richard returned to the council chambers two days later. The rest of the Council was waiting for a report, and Mark was in the trial area.

"Did he talk?" Zohn asked when Chevalier sat down.

"They're in a tiny town outside of Prague called Holany," Chevalier said. "They have a temporary palace there and have been collecting unfactioned heku throughout Europe. They offer them re-admittance into the Equites faction if they join them."

Mark nodded. "So we head to Czech."

"There's something else," Chevalier said, and then turned to Kyle. "I don't think she's confined anymore."

"They let her go?"

"I don't know about that, but things have definitely changed. She's still afraid, but the pain is lessening, and I don't feel that she's panicked. Right now though, she's upset... more upset than I've ever felt her, and she's extremely desolate and alone."

"Then let's fly into Prague and find her."

Chevalier looked over at Mark. "Get all of the teams in Europe and have them meet us on the southeastern corner of Wenceslas Square tomorrow night."

Mark nodded and left to alert the troops.

"I don't like how alone she feels," Chevalier said softly. "If she's away from them, then why hasn't she contacted me? Why not seek out an Equites? We're all over that area."

"Maybe she's non-verbal again and afraid of being attacked," Richard suggested.

"I still think she would call us."

"Let's go to Prague and see," Kyle said, standing up.

Chevalier nodded and they both headed out to Equites 1.

***

"Elder," Silas said from the corner of the ancient square in downtown Prague. The heku were trying not to look conspicuous, but a group of U.S. Marines were watching them carefully.

Chevalier walked up. "Who's missing?"

"We're all here."

"Where's Andrew?"

"The Encala Council called him back for an emergency. I'm hoping he doesn't return."

Chevalier nodded. "Ceska Lipa Coven has agreed to let us meet there. Head out."

Silas nodded and whispered to the heku. It was only an hour later that they arrived at the Equites coven outside of Ceska Lipa. The Coven Lord immediately showed them into a grand hall where they could talk.

Chevalier stood up to address them. "Sources tell us that the pseudo-Council is shacked up in a makeshift palace in Holany, a tiny

town not far from here. They do have supporters, but we outnumber them."

"Sounds easy," Mark said. "Death or capture?"

"Kill all but the 11 members of the Council."

"And if we find Emily?"

Chevalier thought. "Don't make any sudden movements or loud noises. Just call for me. The coven here wants to assist, along with the Zahradky Coven, which we'll pass on our way. Holany is an old town, so keep quiet. We don't want to get the locals involved."

"Yes, Elder," Mark said before turning and giving orders to the heku. Once the Ceska Lipa Coven was filled in and readied, they all headed out to the compound outside of Holany.

The small village was quiet, and no street lights shown to guide the way. In the center of the town was an old church with a high steeple that housed a bell that alerted the citizens of a death. No one could be seen walking the streets that late at night, and even the quaint houses were shut up tight and silent.

Just off of the town was a lake, whose still surface perfectly reflected the clear night sky. Mark was the first to wade into the water and head to the large house sitting to the north of them. The heku were silent, barely causing waves as they swam toward their target.

The building was too new to have good security, but there were heku in groups of four patrolling the area around it. Chevalier moved up to Mark and, hidden by the reeds, whispered instructions.

"Take out the next four that come by. We then have 22 minutes until the next pass."

Mark nodded and then lunged at the four heku when they got near to the water's edge. Members of the Cavalry immediately quieted them and dragged them into the water before killing them and setting them afloat across the black surface.

Chevalier was out of the water first and blurring toward the double doors that led into the house. The 238 heku with him followed as quickly as they could, and soon, all were standing along the thick rock walls of the large house.

Silas and Kralen quickly dispatched the two door guards and then stood ready to fling the doors open for a surprise attack. Chevalier stood ready, his body tense and anxious for blood. The second the doors flew open, heku scattered and Chevalier walked in, followed by angry Equites.

"Don't kill the Council," he hissed, and the Equites spread out and began killing any heku they came to. He hoped Emily was in the house but far enough away from the bloodshed not to be affected.

Chevalier watched the fighting for a few minutes to ascertain they

were safe. There were more heku following the pseudo-Council than their informant let on, but they were still outnumbered and caught off guard.

"The council chamber's up on the second floor," Silas said, appearing beside the Elder. Chevalier nodded and headed up, followed by Silas and his team of 18.

Chevalier walked in and looked along the ten members of the pseudo-Council, all in the restraining grips of one of the Equites.

"You have no right!" Elder Neal screamed. "You were banished and are unfactioned!"

Chevalier ignored him and walked along them, looking into each of their faces carefully. The heku in the Chief of Defense's position seemed more nervous than the rest and watched Chevalier with wide eyes.

"Where's Emily?" he asked the uneasy heku.

He nervously glanced at the Council and then back to Chevalier. "She's not here."

"That's not what I asked."

"We don't know where she went."

Chevalier frowned and turned to Elder Kirt. "She got away?"

He snarled at the enemy Elder. "We let her go."

"You wouldn't let her go."

"We did. We had no more use for her, and she was causing too many problems."

"Elder," Mark said as he walked up behind them.

"Report," Chevalier said, still watching the Council.

"Everyone's dead but these in here. We found a cell in their prison that Emily was in at one time, but she hasn't been for a while."

"No other sign of her?"

"Just… just some evidence in their interrogation room."

Chevalier's eyes narrowed. "Who interrogated her?"

"I did," their Chief Interrogator said proudly.

"For what information?"

"For discipline and compliance. She had no information we needed."

"What did you do?" he asked, stepping angrily toward the smaller heku.

"I did whatever I had to, to get her to agree to our demands."

"Yes, to turn her against her will."

"She agreed."

Chevalier simply glared at him and moved down the row toward the Elders. "Where is she?"

Kirt smiled. "I told you. We let her go."

"You just let her go."

"Yes"

"Did you give her money?"

"No, we gave her nothing."

Chevalier nodded and then disappeared from the room. Mark heard him starting to go through the mansion on his own, so he moved toward the Council.

"Was she injured when you released her?" Mark asked the Elders.

Kirt shrugged. "She had some wounds, I guess."

"Some?"

"Well... casts on both arms, maybe a black eye and some bruises or cuts."

Mark growled softly and his hands turned into fists. "What did you do to her arms?"

"She's weak.   What we did shouldn't have caused that much damage."

"What did you do?!"

He smiled. "A little trick the Valle taught us... quite effective, I assure you."

Mark lunged for him but was held back by Kralen. "Don't hurt him yet. Elder's orders."

Mark hissed and turned to the Interrogator. "How long did you interrogate her?"

"Only around six hours," he said indignantly.

Silas thought for a moment and then gasped. "A day?"

"Of course... she's quite stubborn."

"You tortured her for six hours a day?!" Kralen roared.

Silas seemed more in control than Mark and Kralen, so he moved forward. "Do you know why she hasn't contacted the Equites at all?"

Kirt smiled. "Yes."

"Tell me."

"She's done with the species. I think we broke her of her unnatural attachment to the heku, and she wanted nothing more than to never see a heku again."

Silas' heart sank. "She said that?"

"She's not very talkative, but she did manage to say that."

"You're lucky she spoke at all."

"She didn't at first, but with enough torture, she finally spoke."

"How long ago did you kick her out?" Silas asked.

"It's been three weeks now, and we haven't heard from her since," Elder Neal said. "We don't expect her to ever speak to a heku again."

"Was that your plan then? Make her hate the heku and then when you take over, you don't have to deal with her?"

"Yes. She's a nuisance, and as we couldn't seem to turn her, and it's well known she can't die, then our only option was to rid her of her taste for the heku and send her packing."

"You kicked her out in a foreign country, covered in injures, with no money, no phone…"

"She deserved nothing."

Silas turned when Chevalier walked back in and stood beside him. "I heard it. He's not lying. She isn't here."

"Forget her… you'll be better off spending your eternity of banishment knowing that she hates your species," Neal said, smiling.

"Who, exactly, is going to banish me?" Chevalier asked him as he took a step closer.

"We will. We are the true Equites Council and have the backing of the Valle and many of your larger covens."

"Not Powan," a heku said from down in the trial area.

"Nor Thukil," another told them.

"Island Coven's not backing you… so the three largest are against you," one of Chevalier's coven said.

Chevalier smiled. "You had the backing of Bahadir, but Emily put them to sleep, and we killed them."

"Bahadir is small compared to others we have."

The Leader of Ceska Lipa Coven stepped forward. "I've spoken to every Coven Leader within 200 kilometers from here and none back you."

"You're running out of heku," Chevalier said. He nodded to Gifford, who immediately removed the head of the fake Chief of Defense.

"You have no right to kill us!" Neal yelled. "We are the true Equites Council."

Kralen stepped forward and faced the Chief Interrogator. "I want him."

"He tortured Emily," Chevalier said. "He's coming back with us. Kill the rest of them."

The struggle was brief, and when the Council was dead, all except for the Interrogator, the heku searched the house to make sure no other heku remained.

Chevalier turned to the Leader of Ceska Lipa. "When we leave… destroy this building and send out word to every coven that I want Emily found. She has to have left tracks… a tiny red-headed American lost in rural Czech."

"Yes, Elder," he replied, and then watched the American Equites head out.

Chapter 23

Zohn leaned forward and looked at the kneeling heku. "So you only brought back the one?"

"Yes," Chevalier said as he took his chair. "He's the one that tortured Emily for compliance, and I get the feeling he knows as much as the rest of the Council combined."

"I see… so where is she?" Zohn asked the kneeling heku.

"We let her go and haven't seen her since."

"Let her go or passed her off for another coven to hold?"

"Let her go."

Zohn sighed and sat back. "He's telling the truth."

"Tell me why Emily needed casts on her lower arms," Chevalier said to him.

He smiled. "That's a Valle secret that I'll take to my grave."

"So it's the forearm thing," Kyle said, mostly to himself. "They used it on her again."

"And we still don't even know what it is," the Chief Investigator said. "All we know is that it affects the forearms, and now we know it can require a cast to fix."

"Not a lot to go on."

"Let me take him into interrogation," Richard, the Chief Interrogator said. "Whatever it is, is bad. We've killed four heku that know what it is and no one would say."

Chevalier nodded. "Try it."

Four members of the Cavalry hauled the heku out, followed by Richard.

"So we search for her again?" Quinn asked. "That didn't go so well last time."

Chevalier lightly tapped his fingers on the table. "This time will be worse. I was pretty sure last time she stayed in the U.S., but she may not have the money to make it back here. We need to cover all of Europe and Asia too."

"It's dangerous for a single American to walk around Eastern Europe."

"We have to look."

"You sure she's alive?"

"Yes, she's alive, afraid, and lonely. She's not in pain and not confined, but that's all I'm getting."

"Why don't we wait until she contacts us?" the Chief of Defense said. "You didn't kick her out this time. She's proven she'll seek you out."

"I hate to leave it up to that. The Valle know she's out there, and I

suspect they will try to get to her first."

"Damn, you're right."

"Emily in the hands of the Valle is bad. If they can solidify what they planted, she may not remember the true past."

"Dad?" Alexis said from behind them. Chevalier turned and took Megara from her sister.

Megara laid her head on Chevalier's shoulder and hiccupped through a sob.

"What's wrong?" he asked, and then lightly kissed the top of her head.

"My tummy hurts," she said through sobs.

Alexis frowned. "She's been upset since you left, and she won't eat."

"Are you sick?" he asked her.

Megara shook her head and wrapped her arms around his neck.

He smiled. "So much like Em. You have to eat, Megs."

"I don't want to eat," she said, and looked over at Zohn when he shifted toward her.

"Maybe it's food she doesn't want," Zohn said.

"Did you try it?" Chevalier asked Alexis.

"No, Mom would shoot me."

"Well, have her try some. I'll take the heat," Chevalier said, and handed Megara over to Alexis.

"Daddy, no," Megara said, obviously upset.

"Go try to eat with Alexis, princess."

Alexis hurried out of the room through the back door, and the Council could hear Megara start screaming at her that she wanted her dad.

"Has she shown any ability to turn a heku to ash?" the Chief of Staff asked.

"None at all."

"Maybe she hasn't been threatened or afraid enough to."

"True, we'll just have to wait and see."

"Back to Emily," Zohn said. "Last time she contacted Allen."

"She hasn't this time. I already called him."

"Dain or Alexis?"

"Them either."

"It's odd that she hasn't attempted to contact anyone," Kyle whispered. "That's just not like her."

"Maybe she really has had enough of heku, and she's gone," the Coven Liaison Officer suggested.

"I want to say she wouldn't do that…," Chevalier started.

"It seems to me like the Valle have a lot to do with this," the Faction

Liaison Officer said. "More than just telling their Interrogator how to torture."

"You think they're in on it?"

"Why not? It puts Emily out there without Equites' protection."

"Ripe for the picking," Kyle added.

"We have to find her, or they'll use her to start wiping out Equites Covens," Zohn said.

"We can divide up again and go back out, but this time it's global," Chevalier said. "She mentioned when Mark found her that she'd made mistakes that she won't make again. It's going to be hard to find her."

"But this time we didn't do anything. She has no reason not to talk to us."

Chevalier shrugged. "Unless we don't know the entire truth."

Zohn stood up. "Well, I'm going to start by talking to the Valle. I agree. They have some stake in Emily's disappearance."

They watched Zohn leave and call for some of the Cavalry to meet him at Equites 2.

"Do we enlist the Encala?" Kyle asked. "They have a lot of covens throughout the Middle East and Asia."

"Not yet," Chevalier replied.

"Well…," Alexis said when she walked through the door.

The Council turned and saw Megara drinking scarlet liquid from a large glass.

Chevalier smiled. "Good, Megs?"

"No, it's icky," she said before taking another drink.

"Mommy said that?"

She nodded, finished the glass, and held it out for Alexis. "No more. It's icky."

"Yeah right." Alexis laughed and then carried Megara out of the room.

"I think we should focus on Europe," Kyle said.

"She's going to want to be close to home though… where she feels comfortable," Chevalier told him.

"Unless she thinks that's how we found her last time."

"This time seems different. This time we didn't kick her out." Chevalier stood up. "I'm going to call Allen again and see if he's heard from her."

When Chevalier left, Kyle turned to Quinn. "Let's have Powan, Banks, and Thukil start searching the U.S. We'll send the Cavalry into Europe and see what we can find there."

Chevalier returned after a few minutes and sat down. "He hasn't heard from her, but he's on the way to join the search. I'm searching too… I regret not helping more the last time."

"It's customary for Elders to let those below them search," the Chief of Staff said.

Chevalier glared at him, and he sat back in his chair.

Kyle showed Chevalier his rough sketch of search areas, and once it was approved, they both headed off, leaving Quinn and the Council as search contact.

The Chief of Staff looked over at Quinn. "Why do we search for her? We've never bothered finding missing mortals before."

"That missing mortal can obliterate every Equites in less than a year. There's no defense against her abilities, and besides... she's an Equites, and she needs help."

***

"So she follows more like Allen than the others," Zohn said when Megara left for class.

Chevalier nodded. "Yes."

"I'm amazed that she hasn't shown any Winchester abilities."

"I'm not sure she has them."

"Heading back out?" Quinn asked him.

Chevalier nodded. "Everything's fading... I can barely feel her anymore, and I want to find her before it disappears all together."

"Does it get stronger the closer you get to her?" the Chief of Defense asked.

"No, or I'd be able to find her."

Kyle tapped on the desk, irritated. "How can she still be gone? It's not like Emily not to contact her family, at least her children."

Zohn shrugged. "All I can come up with is that we don't have the entire story. They did something that's preventing her from contacting a single heku."

"What about that lead in Inveruno, Italy?" the Chief of Finance asked.

"Dead end," Chevalier told him. "That woman did have red hair, but she was years older."

"How can we not find her?! Next week, it'll be four months since she walked out of that house and went into hiding," Kyle growled.

"We'll find her," Quinn said. "She may not even be hiding. Seven billion people on this planet and we're looking for one tiny mortal."

"Well our spies say that the Valle thinks she's in Columbia," Zohn told them. "Thukil and Powan are there, and it's not a big country."

"I just hope when they run into the Valle, there isn't a war."

"I'm sure there would be some type of fight. I can't help but think the Valle know more about this than they're letting on."

***

"Why are we here? Mark would kill us," Silas said as he looked down the street to the dark face of St. Patrick's Cathedral.

Kralen glanced around. "She's afraid to go back to the U.S. Maybe she decided to try Ireland."

"Do you know how many Flynns are in Ireland? We can't track them all down to see if she sought out family."

"It's worth a try."

"Except that our teams are supposed to be in Edinburgh tonight."

Kralen smiled. "That's the beauty of it... our teams are in Edinburgh."

"We're supposed to be with them!"

"It's a hunch, Silas. Go with it," Kralen said as headed down the dark road.

"You and I are going to search 82,000 square kilometers of some pretty wild terrain?"

"Sure, why not?"

Silas just stared at him.

Kralen looked back at him. "Fine... according to Camber's book, the Flynns came from Bracknagh. It's only about 75 kilometers from here."

Silas started walking. "I've never heard of Bracknagh."

"No one has. It's not exactly a thriving metropolis."

"Well, at least if she's there she'll be easy to find," Silas said. "Lead on."

Kralen immediately blurred, heading west out of Dublin past dark houses and even darker fields. They both stopped a couple of hours later just before crossing the Figile River into the village.

Silas looked around. "You weren't kidding about small."

"There'll be a pub open," Kralen said as he pulled a picture of Emily out of his pocket.

"You carry a picture of Em?"

"Not normally, no."

"Fine, let's get this over with before Mark finds out."

Kralen kept to the shadows and headed deeper into the small village in search of a pub. It wasn't hard to find, and the noise from inside was loud and boisterous.

Silas shook his head and opened the door. No one seemed to notice the big strangers as they strolled over to the bar.

The bartender looked up at him and was obviously leery. "What can I get for you?"

Kralen smiled and held out Emily's picture. "We're looking for

her."

The bartender didn't even glance at the photograph. "Haven't seen her."

"You didn't look."

"Don't matter. I don't know her," he said in the deep Irish accent reserved for small town folks.

Silas put his hand on Kralen's arm. "Let's try someone else."

Kralen nodded and went over to a group playing darts. "Can I bother you gentlemen for a moment?"

"No gentlemen here," one of them said, and then turned and smiled at them. "What can we do for you?"

"We're looking for a woman…"

"… aren't we all?" he said, and was patted on the back by a laughing man behind him.

"Short, red hair, green eyes," Silas said.

"You're in Ireland, Lad. You just described half of the women in this county."

"Right," Silas said, and then took the picture from Kralen and handed it to him.

The man examined the picture and then handed it back. "You best leave her alone."

"You've seen her then?"

"Nope," he said, and turned back to the dart board.

Kralen studied him, and it was obvious he'd seen Emily and wanted nothing more to do with them.

Silas walked over to four men playing a poker game and laid the picture on the table. "Where can I find her?"

One man picked up the picture and then laid it back down. "Dunno."

"Have you seen her?"

"Dunno," he repeated.

Kralen took the picture and motioned Silas outside. Once out of earshot of the mortals, he turned to Silas. "I think they know her."

"I get that impression too."

"So let's do surveillance."

"She goes to a bar once a year. That could be a long surveillance."

"We could control one of them and ask," Kralen said.

Silas looked over as one patron stumbled out of the pub and headed down the street, singing a song about smiling Irish eyes.

Before Silas could disagree, Kralen blurred to the old man and had him instantly locked.

"The girl I showed you a picture of, have you seen her?" Kralen whispered to the man.

He replied in a soft whisper. "Aye."

"Where?"

"She comes to the pub every night."

"What's her name?"

"Elizabeth Flynn," he said in a monotone voice.

"Where does she live?"

"I don't know."

Kralen nodded and then broke the gaze. "You okay there?"

"Aye," the man mumbled. "I musta fallen asleep."

"Must have," Silas said, and they watched him stumble off.

"We better call in Mark," Kralen told him.

"Let's just wait it out until tomorrow and make sure before we call them all and admit that we aren't where we should be," Silas said.

Kralen grinned and backed into a shadow across from the old pub. They watched throughout the day as the small Irish community came to life and went about their lives. They hoped to catch sight of Emily but had no luck. It wasn't until nightfall that they moved to get a closer look at the pub's door.

They didn't have to wait long, and both watched in shock as Emily walked up to the bar and disappeared inside.

"Let's just go grab her," Kralen suggested.

"No, we need to get Mark here, now."

"You go. I'll keep an eye on her."

Silas nodded and stepped back to make the phone call.

"Mark here," he said, irritated.

"We found her," Silas whispered.

"I'll be in Edinburgh by morning. Where is she?"

Silas sighed, "We're not in Edinburgh... Kralen and I are outside of Dublin."

There was a soft growl. "Are you sure it's her?"

"Yes," Silas said, cringing inwardly at what he knew was a punishment coming from Mark when this was over. He gave Mark instructions on how to get to them and then walked over to Kralen, who was looking in the dirty window of the pub.

Emily was sitting across from a man in his late 60s. There was a crowd gathered around the small table, and it was obvious that bets were being made. The bartender dropped a shot glass in front of them and put a bottle of Green Spot between them.

Emily poured each a shot and then downed it at the same time as the man across from her.

"Great," Kralen whispered.

Silas and Kralen watched silently as Emily and the man across from her went on to drink 15 shots a piece. The old man was now leaning

crookedly on his seat, grasping the table as he watched Emily, and the cheers from the pub patrons grew louder.

"Hit me," Emily said steadily, and one of the patrons refilled their shot glasses.

"Do it Lass!" one of them yelled. Emily picked up the shot glass and quickly drank it, then watched the man across from her. With shaky hands, he picked up the shot and slowly brought it to his lips, spilling half of it on the way.

Suddenly, his eyes glassed over, and he toppled off the chair. The pub erupted in loud cheers and shouts, and money was quickly exchanged among them. Kralen focused in on Emily and the hollow look in her eyes. She poured herself another shot and downed it before standing up unsteadily and then she picked up her winnings and shoved them into her pocket.

One of the younger patrons stepped up toward her and took her arm. He was tall and solid, with dark-brown hair and a five o'clock shadow. "Let me drive you home, Elizabeth."

She jerked her arm away from him. "I don't need your help, Kelly."

"You going to walk home then?"

Emily didn't answer but stumbled toward the door. Kralen and Silas moved back into the shadows, so she wouldn't see him.

"Elizabeth," the bartender said, following her out. "You aren't driving are you?"

"I'm not driving," she said, irritated, and headed down the small street. She shocked the heku when she pulled a pack of cigarettes out of her pocket and lit up, inhaling deeply as she walked.

An old Ford Pickup was parked along a dark alley, and Kralen started to blur forward when she sat behind the wheel and started it up.

Silas stopped him. "We can't interfere. Wait until Mark gets here."

"She's too drunk to drive."

"You want her to turn you to ash? She's drunk and doesn't seem all that happy."

Emily finished her cigarette and then pulled onto the street, almost hitting a light pole on the way out. The heku blurred behind her, keeping to the shadows. She managed to make it to a ranch on the outskirts of town without hitting anything and stopped in front of a row of tiny, one-room cabins that served as bunk houses for the sheep ranch.

The heku watched as she fell out of her truck and then crawled into the closest cabin, locking the door behind her. They moved up to the only window to watch her inside.

Emily leaned against the wall to pull off her cowboy boots and then staggered and fell into the table but caught herself on a chair. She picked up a bottle off of the counter and took two pills with a glass of water

before falling into bed, still fully dressed, and instantly going to sleep.

Silas whispered, "There's so many things wrong with what we've just seen."

Kralen nodded, too mad to speak.

"Let's just keep an eye on her, and we'll fill Mark in. He'll get in touch with Chevalier, and they can figure out what to do."

The heku watched her sleep through the night without ever moving. It wasn't until the other field-hands started to stir that they were forced to move back into shadows.

An hour later, they heard Emily awake in the bunk house. They moved to an old, abandoned barn where they could see most of the farm. There were eight bunk houses total, and each housed a single field-hand. One central building seemed to be a shared shower and bathroom.

Emily walked out after a few minutes, wrapped only in a towel. It was obvious she was hung over and maybe even still a little tipsy.

"Damnit, Elizabeth. We're heading out in less than 20 minutes," an older man said from the largest house.

Emily flipped him off and headed for the showers.

"The men are showering in there," he called out.

"I won't look," she mumbled, and walked into the out-building. Seconds later, all seven men came barreling out of the building, wrapped in towels and in various stages of showering. One man was trying to keep the shampoo from running into his eyes, and yet another was holding a towel over himself that was too small to wrap around him.

"Do something!" one of them yelled to the older man at the house.

He sighed and walked up to the shower. "Elizabeth! You can't just go in there and shower with the men! We've told you that... you have to wait until they're done."

The men waited until Emily finally came out, freshly showered and still wrapped only in a towel. Kralen and Silas could both tell that she wasn't in a good mood.

"No more," the older man said to her. "It's not fair for you to traipse in there when they're showering!"

"Fuck off, Reilly," she grumbled, and headed for her bunk house.

"Bitch"

"Mick"

"Póg mo thóin." He turned when she shut her door. "Go finish showering, so we can get out of here."

The men hurried in to shower, and Kralen looked over at Silas. "Damn."

"Wonder what's up with that," Silas said.

The heku heard the man Emily called Reilly making dinner plans for the field-hands, so they knew they would be back by nightfall. They

decided to wait at the farm and search Emily's bunk house to see if they could find anything to help explain why she didn't seek out heku when she was released.

Emily came out later with her hair braided and an old black Stetson on her head. She was in her normal jeans and a long-sleeved t-shirt but had a red flannel shirt tied around her waist. The heku sighed when she produced a pack of cigarettes and lit up before walking over to where the field-hands were gathering.

She crawled into the back of a large truck with the others and then turned when Reilly pulled out a piece of paper. "Shawn, Michael, and Patrick will be checking the traps. I want Elizabeth and Aiden on castration, and I'll help Davin with docking."

"Why the fuck do I have to do castration again?" Emily said.

"Because that's what I said."

"Let me dock."

"No... besides... I'd think you would like cutting the balls off of something."

She just glared at him.

"You promised me I wouldn't have to work with her again," one of the men said.

"Bite me," Emily hissed at him.

"Stop being such a bitch!" he yelled.

They were still fighting when the truck took off across a muddy pasture toward a massive herd of sheep.

Kralen immediately headed for Emily's bunk house and found it unlocked. He and Silas stepped inside and shut the door behind them. The cabin was messy. Clothes were strewn around and there were empty whiskey bottles and ash trays full of ashes.

Silas covered his nose. "I hate the smell of tobacco."

Kralen nodded and picked up a bottle of pills from the counter and looked at it. "The bottle's not marked. Just some blue pills."

Silas looked over. "Take one for Dr. Edwards to see."

He nodded and slipped one into his pocket before kneeling down and opening the cabinet below them. "Damn."

Silas gasped when he saw the shelves of alcohol. "Wow."

"Drinking pretty heavily it seems."

"We'll see what Chevalier thinks."

Kralen nodded and then stood up and started looking through the drawers.

Silas grabbed a stack of mail and began going through it. He pulled one piece out and showed it to Kralen. "Cell phone bill."

"So she even has a cell phone but hasn't called us."

Silas tore it open and started to read. "She made four calls last

month."

"All month?"

"Yes, to the same number too."

"Call it."

Silas dialed the number, but no one answered. Just when he hung up, he heard Mark call to him from outside the cabin.

Kralen winced. "He's mad."

Silas nodded, and they both left and then blurred away as Mark led the way. Over forty heku were waiting in a grove of trees off of the ranch, and when Mark stopped and turned around, he was obviously livid.

"You were supposed to be in Edinburgh!" he shouted.

"Mark… I'm sorry, but I had a feeling she might seek out her dad's family here in Ireland," Kralen explained.

"So you felt free to break an order?!"

"We found her."

"I don't care! You do not break my orders!"

Silas tried to change the subject. "She's not well, Mark."

Mark frowned and looked over at him. "How so?"

"Drinking, smoking, taking some type of pills. She's moody, and it seems like the mortals here hate her."

Kralen nodded. "Not only drinking every night but driving after. She almost took out a light pole."

"That doesn't sound like Emily," Mark said, deep in thought. "Why would she smoke? And she hates pills."

"We don't really know. She has a cell phone bill but has only called one number."

"Where is she now?"

"Out working. They'll be back later today," Silas told him. "Is the Elder coming?"

"Not yet. He and Kyle are somewhere in Spain, and we can't get in touch with them," Mark explained. "Did she see you?"

Silas shook his head. "No."

"Okay, when she comes back, I'll let her see me, and I'll try to get her back here out of view of everyone else. I don't want to risk exposure."

Mark spent the day reprimanding Kralen and Silas for breaking orders, but they knew the real punishment was coming when the Council found out. Just before dusk, they saw the big farm truck return, and Mark ordered them all to stay in the trees while he headed toward the farm.

Emily lit a new cigarette and took a heavy drag before walking toward her bunk house. Her head was pounding, and she wanted nothing

more than a good, long drink. When she saw Mark, her heart skipped a beat, and she froze and looked to make sure it was him.

Mark stopped a ways off from her and motioned her forward silently.

She tapped out some ash and took another puff before slowly walking toward Mark as he backed up. Her mind reeled through what to say to him. By the time he disappeared into the trees, she'd made up her mind that she owed him nothing less than intense pain and suffering.

What Emily hadn't expected was how many heku were waiting for her. She stopped as soon as they emerged into a clearing full of heku, and her eyes narrowed as she scanned them.

"What do you want?" she asked as she dropped the cigarette butt and put it out with her cowboy boot.

"We've been looking for you," Mark said.

"Yeah, I bet you have."

"We don't know what happened, but it's safe to come back."

Mark cringed as she lit another cigarette and studied them before speaking. "How dare you tell me it's safe?! I expected more out of you."

Mark frowned. "Meaning?"

"Meaning I'm disappointed in all of you. I'm disgusted with you, and you have five seconds to leave my sight before I ash all of you and leave you here," she yelled.

"What did we do to deserve disappointment?" Kralen asked.

Emily smirked, and the anger shocked the heku. "You're all traitors... and you repulse me."

"Wait a minute...," Silas said, just before the heku turned to ash, except for Kralen.

Kralen gasped and looked around the clearing. "Why did you do that?"

"Because you've put all new meaning to the word proditor," she whispered harshly.

"We aren't traitors!"

"Leave me alone... last warning," Emily said. She concentrated on Kralen, and he fell to his knees as he was struck with intense burning pain throughout his body. When he fell unconscious, Emily backed up and returned to the farm.

When Kralen recovered, he carefully scooped up the ashes of his fallen heku and quickly blurred them to nearby Gael Coven on the outskirts of Dublin. From there, they contacted the Council and were told to wait until Kyle returned so they could revive the ash and figure out what to do.

Chapter 24

Kyle revived the last of the heku and then stood back while they recovered.

Chevalier walked over as soon as Mark stood. "Where is she?"

Mark looked over at Kralen. "Tell him everything you told me."

Kralen started with when he got the feeling Emily might return to her dad's family in Ireland. When he explained some of the behavior Emily had displayed, Chevalier was dumbstruck. It wasn't like Emily to do any of those things, and the self-destructive behavior was uncharacteristic for her.

"She called us traitors," Mark said to him.

"Did she say why?"

"We didn't have time to ask before she turned us to ash."

"What did she say to you?" Chevalier asked Kralen.

"She said we've put all new meaning to the word proditor and then she warned us to leave her alone."

"Kyle, you stay here then, if she's that trigger happy. I'll take Mark and go talk to Emily."

"I want to go too," Kralen told them.

Mark shrugged. "For some reason, she didn't turn him to ash. He can bring us back to Kyle."

Chevalier nodded. "Let's go."

They arrived in Bracknagh and headed to the pub. They were in the shadows when Emily walked into the pub and immediately disappeared in the crowd of rowdy drinkers. Four hours later she staggered out of the pub and headed for her old pick-up.

"Elizabeth, you can't drive home," one man said as he followed her.

"Go away."

"No, I'm not going to let you drink and drive."

"You're not my dad," Emily said as she climbed into the truck.

The man reached in and took the keys from her. "No."

"Damnit," she grumbled, and climbed unsteadily out of the truck. She tried to get the keys back, but he held them above her head.

"I'll take you home."

"Yeah I bet you will. Give me my keys!"

"No," he said, climbing into the truck. "Now get in."

Emily leaned back against the pub and lit a cigarette. She inhaled and then watched the man in her truck as she blew smoke into a light breeze.

"You can kill yourself tomorrow. Now get in," he told her. She finally let out a string of curses before climbing into the truck.

The heku took off after the truck and slid into the shadows around

Emily's bunk house. The man parked her truck and climbed into another one with a field-hand. Emily watched them leave and then went into the bunk house and locked the door behind her.

Chevalier, Mark, and Kralen watched secretly through her window as she dug out a bottle of Jack Daniels and poured it into a Styrofoam cup. She grabbed the bottle of pills, dumped some into her hand and then downed them with the whiskey.

Chevalier sighed and watched her strip down to a t-shirt and fall into bed, almost immediately falling asleep.

Mark whispered, "We need to intervene. I don't know what those pills do, but chances are she's not supposed to mix them with alcohol."

Kralen nodded. "I bet she's so far gone she won't even know if we take her."

Chevalier jimmied the window open and then slid easily inside. Emily didn't even stir as the heku watched her sleep. Chevalier studied her but saw nothing wrong, no injuries, and other than being thinner than usual she seemed in good health.

"Do we take her?" Kralen whispered.

Chevalier shook his head and then started going through her room. He picked up the pill bottle and slipped it into his pocket before opening the cabinet and finding the alcohol supply. Mark and Kralen watched him as he looked through the partially empty bottles and then shut the door and stood up.

He started looking through her mail and saw that all of it was addressed to Elizabeth Flynn. He put her phone bill into his pocket and opened up a drawer stuffed full of Euros. He figured she didn't have a lot of bills and had both her wages from the ranch and winnings from the bar all shoved into this unsecure location.

The drawer under the Euros was filled with various kinds of pain medication and boxes of gauze. He found four bottles of prescription pain meds and put them all into his pocket with the pills she took before bed. The rest were generic ibuprofen and acetaminophen tablets.

Buried underneath the pills was a small notebook that was tattered and worn. He opened it up and frowned as he read what appeared to be eulogies for him and each of the kids. His confusion deepened as he read through them and then put the notebook back where he'd found it.

All three turned to Emily when she whispered something incomprehensible and then rolled over and gripped her pillow tightly in her arms. Once she settled down, Chevalier went over and started to go through the few shirts she had hanging up in front of one of the windows. He thought it was odd that all of them were long sleeved, even though it was dead summer in Ireland.

Lastly, Chevalier opened up a box she had sitting on the windowsill

and pulled out five cartons of unfiltered cigarettes. He walked over and tossed them out of the window and then returned to sit down by Emily's side in bed.

"She thinks I'm dead," Chevalier told them.

"The ring though."

"We'll have to ask her about it," Chevalier said. "She either thinks the kids and I were killed or are going to be. She's written eulogies for us."

Mark shrugged. "Maybe it was her way of getting over you."

"What's our plan?" Kralen whispered.

"We hope she's sober and has an open mind when she wakes up," Chevalier said.

"Do you want to be alone with her?"

"No, because we don't know why she's not contacted us. I think we need to try not to scare her but show that we're not leaving without some answers."

When Emily started to wake, the heku moved back into the shadows of the tiny cabin, hoping not to startle her when she first saw them. She opened her eyes and looked up at the ceiling.

"I hate you for doing this to me," she whispered to the wooden rafters. After a few minutes, she leaned over and righted her Styrofoam cup before pulling a bottle of gin out from under her bed and pouring herself a glass.

Chevalier's sudden voice made her jerk and dump the gin onto her bedside table. "Isn't it a bit early to be drinking?"

She scrambled out of bed and pressed back against the wall when Chevalier, Mark, and Kralen stepped out into the cabin.

Chevalier studied her but couldn't place the look on her face. "I didn't mean to scare you."

Her eyes darted between them. "I warned you…"

"We're worried about you," Mark told her.

She nodded toward Chevalier. "And what's that shit?"

"Excuse me?" Chevalier asked.

"I thought it was against some stupid heku tradition to use a doppelganger," Emily said, looking directly at Mark. "First you turn traitor and then you break laws? Things just get better and better."

"I'm not a doppelganger, Em," Chevalier told her.

"Bullshit! I'm not stupid."

"Not stupid, no. Maybe misinformed."

Emily leaned over and pulled on her jeans and straightened the long-sleeve t-shirt she'd slept in. She studied them and then pulled a pack of cigarettes out of her pocket and lit up as she watched the heku.

"Why are you smoking?" Chevalier asked.

"So what's the deal?" Emily asked. "The Council needs my help? Maybe the Valle are picking on them, or the Encala have gotten too strong, and they are too weak to handle it themselves?"

"We aren't here to enlist your help," Mark said.

"Good, because if I so much as see any of the Equites Council, I'll wipe them out. Chief Enforcer included."

"Why are you so mad at the Council?"

"Here's what's going to happen," Emily said before taking another drag on the cigarette. "You're going to leave me the hell alone and go tell your Council, they can just forget me. I'm not helping them."

"Em... the Council doesn't need your help. I miss you," Chevalier said. "I'll do as you ask and leave you alone... if you'll just help me understand why you haven't contacted me. Why you've abandoned the kids and your friends."

She looked down at her feet and took another drag as she thought through her answer and fought back the tears.

"Talk to us, please," Kralen said. "You trust me... or you would have turned me to ash too."

"I didn't turn you to ash because I don't need the entire county filled with Equites."

"Why didn't you call me when they let you go?" Chevalier asked.

She laughed slightly. "Call you? You mean call the bloody Council? I'm not going to be a part of the sadistic banishment of innocent heku."

"I don't understand."

"Elizabeth!" someone yelled from outside. "You have five minutes, and we're leaving you."

Emily took another drag and then headed for the door. She opened it and turned to Mark and Kralen. "I can't believe how easily you turned and decided to back them."

"Emily, don't go," Chevalier said. "I'll pay you for the day's missed wages. Just stay here for a few minutes."

She glared at him and shut the door behind her. Soon, they heard the ranch truck take off for the fields.

"Who are we backing?" Kralen asked Mark.

He shrugged. "I wish I knew."

Chevalier sat down and looked around the cabin again. "We're missing something."

Kralen glanced at the messy cabin.

"Let's stay here then and talk to her when she gets back," Mark said. "Maybe we can keep her from going out to the pub and driving home drunk again. That's going to bite her in the ass one of these days."

Mark called the Council and checked in and then sat back with

Chevalier and Kralen to wait for Emily's return. The old truck pulled up late in the afternoon, and all three looked over at the door when Emily walked in.

"Why are you still here?" she asked as she dug through the cupboard full of alcohol.

"We want to know what's going on," Chevalier said. He inwardly winced when Emily poured herself a glass of whiskey and downed it in one shot.

She set the glass down and then sat in an old rocking chair that was off to the side of her bed. "What's going on is that the Council is shit. I'm not going to have anything to do with heku anymore, and you know why. Even if the current Council brought back the others, they can't make up for what they did."

Mark sighed, "That doesn't make any sense."

"And you two following the Council... I never thought I'd see the day," she told them as she lit a cigarette and took a long drag.

"We've always supported the Council. You already knew that," Kralen said.

"Bullshit! Your chicken ass way of saving your own skin is pathetic."

"Elizabeth, who are you talking to?" someone asked from outside the door. "We aren't supposed to have people in our cabins."

"Fuck off, George!" Emily yelled.

"God, you are such a bitch," he said, and they heard footsteps heading away from the cabin.

"What happened to you?" Chevalier asked as he studied her. The way she spoke, acted, and even moved wasn't like her at all. She seemed not to care about anything or anyone, even herself.

She ignored him and looked over at Mark as she poured herself another glass of whiskey. "So did you help the current Council do it? Or did you turn traitor later on?"

"I've always backed the current Council," Mark answered, getting mad. "You know I'm loyal to the Council. I've proven that."

"It's sick," she said, and then drank the glass at once.

Kralen sighed, "Em, that's probably a good three shots in each glass."

She stood suddenly and pushed Kralen, though he didn't move. "You have no right telling me what's right and wrong! You have no right coming in here and telling me that I should come support the current Council! I'm not a traitor, and I will always... always... support the former one."

"When did you decide to support the former Council?" Mark asked, frowning.

"Brainwashed again, maybe?" Kralen asked, too softly for Emily to hear.

Emily sat down hard when the whiskey began to make her unsteady. "I've always supported them. What kind of lame ass question is that?"

Chevalier suddenly had an idea. "Em, name the Council."

She stood up and walked past Kralen, purposely knocking her shoulder against him as she passed. She went over to the drawer filled with medications and opened it, then started shifting through what was left of the pill bottles.

"I took the narcotics out," Chevalier told her.

Emily turned toward him. "Give them back."

"No, you can't mix them with alcohol."

"For chrissake! Give me my fucking pills!"

"Name the Council," Chevalier said again.

"You name the fucking Council," she snapped.

When she grabbed the whiskey bottle to pour another drink, Mark gently took it out of her hand and stepped back.

Her shoulders sunk, and when she spoke, her voice sounded defeated and tired. "Why are you doing this to me? Haven't I been through enough?"

"I can't stand here and watch you kill yourself," Mark told her.

She looked up at him with red, teary eyes. "I wish I could kill myself. I don't want to be here."

Chevalier tried to take her hand, but she pulled away from him and sat down on the rocking chair.

"Talk to me," Mark said, sitting down on the bed. "Tell me what's going on."

"They took everything from me," she whispered. "I don't have anything more to give…, but they still felt compelled to send you to torment me. What do you want? What more could you possibly gain from coming here?"

Emily reached out to grab the box of cigarettes sitting on the table, so Kralen gently reached out and grabbed her arm. She gasped and jerked away when his hand hit her forearm, and then she cradled it close to her and turned away from them.

"What's wrong with your arm?" Chevalier asked, standing slowly.

"Give me my pills," she whispered.

"Pain or not, you can't mix those with alcohol."

"Why not? What's the worst that can happen?" she said as she looked out the small window. "I can't even die to forget."

"What are you trying so hard to forget?" Mark asked.

"You'd think after four months, the pain would lessen."

Chevalier sighed, "Just tell us what you are trying to forget. What's

causing this self-destructive behavior?""

"Why are you doing this to me?" she asked, and leaned over so her forehead was against her knees. She fought back tears for as long as she could but the hole in her heart grew larger, and she finally broke down.

Chevalier moved to her side and put a hand on her back. "Tell me."

"It hurts just to look at you. I miss him," she sobbed.

"Who do you miss?"

"God, I'm alone," she said through sobs.

"Em, name the Council."

She looked up at him with blood-shot eyes. "Why?"

"Name them."

"If I do, will you let me suffer in peace?"

"I'm starting to understand what's going on here," Chevalier said. "If you tell me, then I may be able to explain."

"Fine… there's Kirt, Neal…"

"Em, that Council is dead."

She shook her head. "No, they aren't. If I beg, will you just leave me alone?"

It was all starting to make sense to him. "The Council you know is still in power. I'm not dead… Kyle's at a nearby coven waiting for us…"

"I can't take this," she whispered.

"Did they tell you the kids were dead too?"

"I already know they are. Why are you telling me again? Do you just want to see me suffer?"

"The kids aren't dead, Em." Chevalier looked up at Kralen. "Get Allen here, now."

Kralen pulled out his cell phone while Emily watched.

"Have them bring in Dr. Edwards," Chevalier said to him.

Emily studied his face. "I don't understand."

"They lied to you," he explained. "We found them after we captured Perkins, and he told us where their palace was located. The pseudo-Council is dead… not even banished… dead."

"I can't believe that. All three factions joined just to lie to me?"

"What do you mean?"

"Ryan was there… and the Encala's Chief Investigator… I'm not stupid. I know that all three factions wouldn't agree to work together just to fuck with me."

Chevalier frowned. "They also told you that I am dead?"

Emily stood up and dug through the cabinet and poured a glass of vodka with shaking hands. Chevalier watched as she drank it quickly and then looked out the window with her hands wrapped around herself.

"They'll be here by morning," Kralen said when he got off the

phone.

"How many doppelgangers did you bring back?" Emily asked, still watching the sun set.

"They aren't doppelgangers."

Kralen frowned. "I'm finding it really hard not to be insulted that you think I allowed the Council to be banished and then followed a new one."

"You have to. Heku tradition... remember?"

"I didn't follow them the last time. Why would I now?"

"How should I know? To save your skin?"

"I'd die before I would turn traitor to the true Council!"

"Calm down," Mark said to him. Kralen's hands were tight fists, and he was losing his temper.

"I'm going to bed. It's been a long day," Emily whispered. She shocked them when she pulled off her long-sleeved t-shirt right in front of them. Mark and Kralen both spun instantly and faced away from her, but Chevalier watched as she changed into an old flannel nightgown. He couldn't help but notice that both forearms were tightly wrapped with gauze.

The others turned when she slipped into the small bed and rolled onto her side away from them.

"Em, what did they do to your arms?" Chevalier asked.

"Doesn't matter," she whispered. "It doesn't hurt nearly as much as my heart."

"Em?"

She looked over at him and didn't have time to react when he pressed his lips to hers and pulled her up against him. She pushed against his shoulders to get him to back off, but he didn't. Emily started to panic until she felt the familiarity of the kiss, and her heart skipped a beat in her chest.

Chevalier finally pulled away from her and then looked into her eyes. "You taste like alcohol."

She couldn't speak but continued to study him.

"The kids are fine... Quinn and Zohn are still Elders, and Kyle's out in hiding to revive us if you turn us to ash."

"The factions told me that all three want nothing to do with me."

"I don't know about the Valle..., but the Encala would disagree with that."

"Their Council was there too."

"We'll find out later what that was about."

"I can't trust you," she whispered, unable to speak louder. She wanted to believe that what she was told was a lie but couldn't bear to go through the pain of losing her family again.

"Who would you trust?"

Emily reached over and pulled her cell phone off of the desk. She looked at the heku in the cabin and then dialed the number she had committed to memory.

"Encala Council," William said, irritated. "How did you get this number?!"

She held the phone out to Chevalier. "Tell them who you are and then ask for Andrew."

He nodded. "It's Chevalier. I need to speak to Andrew."

Emily waited to see if the Encala sounded surprised to speak to him.

"Andrew here. Did you find her?"

She took the phone from Chevalier and whispered into the phone. "Don't let on that it's me."

Andrew cleared his throat. "What do you want, Chevalier?"

"Did the Encala send a representative to the Equites, one that came to tell me that the heku were done with me and wanted me to leave them alone forever?"

"What do you mean?"

"Just answer."

"No, we wouldn't do that!"

"What are they accusing us of doing now?" William asked.

"Who are the Equites Elders?" Emily whispered.

Andrew took a moment before speaking. "I'm sure Zohn and Quinn understand we didn't do that either."

"Not Neal and Kirt?"

"I don't know them, sorry."

Emily shut the phone when William came on the line.

"So?" Chevalier asked.

"I need a second."

He nodded and then walked over to the corner with Mark and Kralen. Emily curled up on her side away from them and tried to think through what she was being told. No noise came from the heku as her anger grew. She started to understand that she was told a lie by all three factions, and plans started to form in her head on how to deal with them.

After a few hours, she tried to get some sleep to clear her head but ended up staring at the back wall.

"Can't sleep?" Chevalier asked as he sat on the bed.

She shook her head.

"What can I do to make you believe it's really me?"

"You can leave me alone and let me sleep without an audience."

He stood up slowly. "We'll be back in the morning. Please don't go out to the fields tomorrow."

Kralen took up position outside of the tiny cabin where he could see

in the window without being seen himself. He watched as Emily sat up and looked around her cabin and then grabbed her cell phone and made a call.

"It's Liz," she whispered. It was obvious she knew there was someone watching her.

After a brief pause, she sighed, "Yes, can you deliver tonight?"

"Fine, 160mg Cor and some yellow-jackets."

Kralen frowned and moved closer so he was sure to hear everything. He watched as Emily hung up and then slipped on a pair of jeans before walking out of the cabin and waiting on the front step. Less than an hour later, an old Iveco van pulled up in front of her cabin. Emily went out to meet it and was soon heading back into her cabin with a small paper bag.

He moved over to the window again and watched as she took a couple of pills from each bottle and downed it with more vodka. Within 30 minutes, she was fast asleep, and he headed over to Gael Coven to give a report.

"Damnit, Kralen!" Chevalier growled. "You are supposed to be watching Em."

"She had a drug delivery," Kralen said quickly. He was still in trouble for not being in Edinburgh, but because he'd located Emily, things were slowly smoothing over, and he didn't need to get into trouble.

"What drug?" Dr. Edwards asked. He and Allen had just arrived from where they were looking for Emily in France.

"She called one Cor and one a yellow-jacket."

Dr. Edwards gasped. "Are you sure?"

"Yes"

"What are they?" Chevalier asked him.

Dr. Edwards looked over at him, still in shock. "A very powerful narcotic pain killer and an illegal barbiturate."

"So she's actually doing recreational drug use?!"

"I'm going to have to guess that she is. How long has she been taking them?"

Kralen shrugged. "I'm not sure, but she took them with vodka."

Dr. Edwards was visibly shaken. "Is she trying to kill herself?"

Chevalier sat down. "Between those, the chain smoking, and the drinking... I'm starting to think so."

"It's probably not consciously though," Silas said. "Lori mentioned once that mortals can have a subconscious desire to die."

Mark moved to look out the window. "Sounds to me like she thought her entire family was dead. I can see her taking that pretty hard, maybe hard enough to hit this self-destructive spiral."

"Why would she not fight back though?" Allen asked. "I mean...

she has to know Dad wasn't dead because of the ring. If he was simply banished, then she would have tried to free him."

"We'll have to ask her that," Chevalier said. "If I had to guess, she thought I was scattered or hidden away somewhere."

"Well now she knows it's not true. Why hit the drugs again?"

"She probably needs it to relax," Dr. Edwards said. "If she's been on them for the entire four months she's been away, she could be addicted."

"Let's kidnap her," Kralen said. "Take her back to Council City and get her off of it."

"And risk her turning the city to ash?" Allen asked.

"She's drugged out of her mind right now... and drunk to boot. By the time she wakes up, she'd be in Council City, and we could have all of the kids there to prove they aren't dead."

Chevalier watched Kralen as his idea sunk in. "That may not be a bad idea."

"At the very least, get her away from her dealer," Dr. Edwards told them. "It would take time to get another one in the U.S., and that could buy us some time."

"Let's do it then. Leave her cigarettes and alcohol here. She won't need them."

"We can't just cold-turkey her off of them. That's hard on the body."

"So we let her keep doing that? Drinking first thing in the morning, and chain smoking unfiltered cigarettes?"

"Yes, we do."

Chevalier growled and disappeared to go get Emily. Kyle and Mark followed him, and by the time they caught up with Chevalier, he already had Emily's things thrown into a bag and had her cradled in his arms. Within the hour, they were headed to the U.S. on the Equites jet with Emily safely tucked away in the back bedroom.

Zohn smiled when he saw Chevalier come in carrying Emily. "Oh great! You found her."

"Yeah well... clear out the palace," Mark told him. "She doesn't know she's back."

Zohn cringed and called for all non-essential personnel to leave the palace immediately.

"Is she okay?" Alexis asked as she ran up the stairs.

"She's fine... just... drunk and drugged," Chevalier told her. He walked into the bedroom and laid her down, then pulled the covers over her.

"You drugged her?"

"Nope, she drugged herself."

Alexis' eyes narrowed. "Mom took medication on her own?"

"What's that smell?" Quinn asked when he walked into the room. He covered his nose with his hand and looked around.

"Could be either the alcohol or the cigarettes," Kyle said.

Alexis gasped. "She's smoking too?"

"I'm guessing it's been a rough four months," Chevalier told her.

"Mommy!" Megara screamed, and then ran toward the bed. Alexis scooped her up.

"Mommy's sleeping," Alexis told her.

The 5-year-old looked over at her mom. "Is she sick?"

Alexis thought a moment before nodding and carrying the young girl from the room.

"Now what?" Chevalier asked Dr. Edwards. Lori came in with Silas.

"Is she filled in?" Dr. Edwards asked Silas.

"No, I just asked her to come."

"What's up?" Lori asked, and then wrinkled her nose. "Is someone smoking?"

Chevalier pulled the pill bottles from his pocket. "Em is… smoking, drinking, taking pills, reckless behavior…"

Lori frowned. "Do we know why?"

"She was told that the kids and I are dead."

She nodded. "I can work with that. She'll be okay."

"Unless she manages to kill herself first," Mark said. "I still don't like how many pills she took at once and mixed them with alcohol."

Lori turned to Chevalier. "Do you want her on suicide watch?"

"What does that entail?"

"Mostly confinement and observation. She'd never be left alone and would have no access to anything she can harm herself with."

"No… no confinement. Once she finds out that the kids and I are okay, she'll stop."

"Maybe"

"You doubt that?"

Lori shrugged. "It's not that easy to stop. What exactly is she taking?"

"Pentobarbital and OxyContin," Dr. Edwards said. "That's what she took last night, but there are pill bottles with morphine, Celecoxib, Demerol, and Ultram."

"Wow," Lori said, shocked. "Are there pills missing?"

"Yes"

"So is she in pain, or is she just taking them?"

"We aren't sure."

"Her arms are wrapped up," Chevalier said. He pulled the blanket

off of her right arm and lifted the sleeve, exposing the thick gauze around her forearms.

"When she wakes up, let me talk to her," Lori said. "Don't take anything away. Do we have her cigarettes?"

Mark nodded and pulled them out of her bag.

"Don't take away her alcohol either."

"We didn't bring that."

Silas smiled. "I'll get some."

When Silas left, Lori turned to the heku. "My recommendation is that she's not restrained or confined in any way. We let her take what she wants and do what she wants."

"She was drinking and driving though," Mark told her.

"Well... with that exception."

"We'll never get that smell out of the palace," Zohn complained.

"So let's take her to her home before she wakes up," Lori suggested. "That's even better. Neutral territory."

After a few more minutes of discussion, Chevalier picked Emily up and followed Mark down to the Humvee.

Chapter 25

Emily rolled over and nuzzled against the soft pillow. When she realized it wasn't the pillow she was used to in the cabin, her eyes flew open, and she jumped out of bed, stumbled, and fell to the floor with a loud thud.

Chevalier knocked on her bedroom door. "Are you okay?"

She looked at the door and then at her surroundings. Her mind was still foggy from the sleeping pills, but she couldn't remember coming back into the U.S.

"I'm okay," she mumbled, and then crawled to her feet. She saw a bottle of Cognac on the table beside her cigarettes, so she poured herself a shot and downed it before lighting up and again looking around her room. She was somewhat relieved that she was in her house and not in the palace, but she was irritated that she was brought back against her will.

"Em?" Chevalier said from outside the door.

"What?" she asked softly, though she knew he could hear her.

"We want to come in."

"Who is we?"

"Me and the kids."

Her heart began to pound in her chest. They were dead. All three Councils had gathered to tell her that for the good of the Equites, Chevalier had been banished and scattered, and his children had been killed. For three weeks, she'd laid in a foreign hotel room with nothing but bottles of whiskey to knock out the hole in her heart, living off of earnings from drinking competitions in local pubs.

She looked around for somewhere to put out her cigarette and finally opted to take one long drag before tossing it into the fire. She smoothed down the thin flannel nightgown and then opened the door.

Dain was the first to rush in and wrap her in a tight hug. He held back the grimace at the smell of cigarettes and held her. "I missed you."

Emily couldn't hold back. Seeing her kids again swept away any lingering control, and she silently cried against his chest.

"My turn," Allen said, pushing Dain aside. He wrapped his arms around her. "You scared me so badly when you didn't contact me."

"I thought you were dead," she whispered against his chest.

He smiled. "I know…"

"Girls turn," Alexis said from behind them. Emily pulled away from Allen and hugged Alexis tightly as Megara wrapped her arms around Emily's waist.

Chevalier smiled at the raw emotion Emily finally let show and had new hope that she would get over this setback too.

"Where did you go?" Megara asked. Emily smiled down at her beautiful green eyes and finally found her voice.

"I was in Ireland. I didn't know you were looking for me," she told the toddler.

Megara's brow furrowed. "They're making me drink blood."

Emily looked up at Chevalier.

"Wait a minute…," he said, trying not to laugh. "We aren't forcing anyone."

"Uh hu," she said, and then smiled and put her hands up for Chevalier to pick her up.

"Nope, not picking you up if you're going to try to get me in trouble."

"Oh," Megara said. She turned back to Emily. "Dain made me drink it."

"Hey! Brat," Dain growled.

Emily nodded and looked at Chevalier. "Guess I shouldn't be surprised."

"We weren't. What's surprising us is how much she tries to get us into trouble."

"Like what?"

He shrugged. "Anything… she told me Kralen hit her. She accused Zohn of taking her doll. Dain killed her once… no twice."

She sighed, "Enough… I get it."

"Out," Chevalier said as he watched Emily. She turned just as the kids left and shut the door behind them. Her hands were shaking, so she reached over and drank another shot of Cognac and lit a fresh cigarette.

"I wasn't hiding," she told him.

"I know. I realize you thought no one wanted to even find you."

Nodding, she sat down in front of the dead fireplace and took another puff.

"Cigarettes?" he asked, sitting down beside her.

"Helps me relax."

"And the pills?"

She looked over at him. "All three factions told me you were scattered."

"I know."

After flipping the spent cigarette into the fireplace, she stood up. "I need to go talk to the Encala Council."

"I figured, and I want to go with you."

She looked over at him. "You're not going to stop me?"

"No, you have a right to ask them why."

"What's the catch?"

He smiled. "Just no drinking and driving."

"I...," she started to lie, but then reconsidered. "Fine, you drive."

He frowned when she grabbed the bottle of Cognac and headed out the door. They were silent for a while as Chevalier drove west toward the Encala Council. Emily dozed on and off and finally agreed to stop and grab a hamburger on the way through a larger city.

After hours of silence, Chevalier decided to break the ice. "So who was there to tell you I was scattered?"

"The other Equites Council, Ryan, and the Encala's Chief Investigator."

"What did they say, specifically?"

"They told me that the Equites Council was re-banished and scattered, and to release any hold you had on the Equites, our children were killed."

"That's it?"

"Well... no. They pretty much said that the factions were done with me, and I wasn't to contact any of them again or I would be..."

"What?"

"Nothing," she said, and grabbed a cigarette from her purse. Chevalier glanced over and saw that she was shaking so badly it was hard to light her cigarette, but she finally managed and turned to look out the window.

"What happened to your arms?" He'd decided not to bring up the cigarettes quite yet.

"Interrogation"

"By who?"

"Lync... he's the Chief Interrogator..."

"We know who he is."

"Well then, you'll also know what a caring soul he has."

Chevalier looked over at her. "Tell me what method he used."

"No... I'm taking care of it."

"I saw the pain meds."

"Well, they work. I'll heal. I'm sure."

"Okay," he said, and then changed tactics. "Are you not sleeping well?"

"No"

"Do the pills help?"

"Yes"

"Do you always mix them with alcohol?"

She turned in her seat and looked at him. "I'm fine."

"I see that."

"Then drop it."

He nodded. "What exactly do you want to do with the Encala?"

"I don't know yet. I'll wing it."

"So you plan on ashing all of them or just the Investigator?"

"I'm not going to ash him... that's too easy."

"I don't think the others know," Chevalier said. "At the very least, William and Andrew were in the dark."

"I'll find out for sure."

"I won't interfere. I just didn't want you to go alone."

When she spoke, her voice cracked. "It was a long four months."

"I bet."

"I don't have anyone any more if you and the kids were to disappear."

"That's not going to happen."

"You don't know that. If it does, I'm alone."

"The pseudo-Council is dead... not banished, dead. I plan on dealing with the Valle, which I'm sure they are expecting. Once we know the Encala involvement, we can focus in on getting the Valle to back off."

"We?" she asked, not sure she heard right.

"Sure, we make a good team."

She smiled, something she hadn't done in a while. "Our team got our asses thrown into prison."

"That was my fault," he said, suddenly serious. "I didn't realize how deeply embedded the Valle was with the pseudo-Council."

"I don't blame you."

"I do. I knew better than to take you there without guards."

"I still don't blame you. I just want to know what they were going to accomplish by making me think you were dead."

"Or by turning you."

Emily looked over at him. "You know about that?"

"Yes"

She sat back in the chair. "I started to think it might work because I agreed to it."

"Through torture," Chevalier said, his hands tightening on the wheel.

"So you know all of it?"

"I'm not sure. I know you were tortured into consenting."

She nodded and looked out the window when Chevalier stopped outside of the Encala's front gates.

"Just drive past them."

"They'll set off the alarm."

"No, they won't."

Chevalier shrugged and sped past the guards, just as they fell to their knees in pain.

"You don't want to do this by the book?" Chevalier asked.

"No, I don't. I don't want them to know we're coming."

"Your call. I'm just here to make sure they don't attack you."

After knocking the door and palace guards they came to unconscious, Emily and Chevalier made their way to the council chamber's door.

He looked at her as she stared at the door and nervously wrung her hands.

"I'm here. It's okay," he said, and lightly touched her shoulder.

Emily nodded and then opened the door and stepped in.

"Emily!" William gasped, surprised.

She walked in, followed by Chevalier, and Andrew smiled. "So great to see they found you."

"Are you okay?" William asked when she walked up to stand before the Chief Investigator, ignoring the others on the Council.

"Why did you do it?" Emily asked him angrily.

"What's going on?" William turned to Chevalier.

"Let her do this," Chevalier said, moving to stand beside her.

The Council turned and saw the Chief Investigator shift nervously. "What do you mean?"

"You know damn well what I mean," Emily yelled. "Tell me why you did it!"

"Let's all calm down," Encala Elder Iuna said.

Emily's eyes narrowed, and the Chief Investigator screamed inhumanly and clutched at his chest. Chevalier crouched slightly at her side, ready for one of the Council to attack.

Andrew sighed, "Em… stop it, please."

Emily let him out of pain and asked again, "Tell me why you did it."

"Tell us what he did," William said.

"Tell me!" she screamed.

"No!" William said sternly. "You cannot lash out at someone on the Council, unless we know why."

"Tell us," Andrew encouraged her.

Emily's eyes bored into the Investigator as he got over the lingering burn.

"Chevalier, you cannot come in here and punish him," Encala Elder Patrick told him.

"I'm not punishing anyone… though I wouldn't mind getting my hands on him too," Chevalier said. "This is Emily's fight. I'm just here to make sure you don't get involved."

"We have to get involved," William told him. "She's torturing a member of our Council."

"I deserve an explanation," Emily said to him. "I deserve to know

why you joined the Valle and the now dead Equites Council in ostracizing me from the lives of every heku."

Iuna smiled. "Child, I'm sure you have things wrong."

"I have a right to know," she whispered to the Investigator. "Why did you back the Valle when they told me that my kids were dead, that Chevalier was scattered, and that no heku wanted anything to do with me? Why stoop to follow the Valle?"

William frowned at his Investigator. "Tell her it's not true."

"I did what I had to, to protect my faction," he said to her.

Andrew growled deeply. "You did those things?"

"Then you should be a Valle," Emily hissed.

The Investigator hurdled the desk but came face-to-face with Chevalier, who blocked Emily from the heku. "Don't touch her."

"She deserves to know!" the Investigator yelled. "This Council is too weak to tell her the truth. I'm not afraid of her, and she deserved what she got."

Emily moved around Chevalier and pushed the Investigator. "I'm not afraid of you either!"

Andrew and William both appeared beside their Investigator, and each took an arm.

"Did you have the backing of the Encala Council?" Emily asked him as Chevalier moved her away from him.

"Yes"

"No! He did not," William yelled. "How dare you go behind our backs and join the Valle!"

"I didn't join the Valle! I joined the joint factions in disposing of this thing…"

"Thing?" Emily screamed, and ran at him. Chevalier grabbed her before she could get to him.

"Yes, thing! You shouldn't even be here. If you would stay dead, we would have just killed you and been done with it. As it stands, when we couldn't turn you, we had no other choice."

"You had no right!"

"I have every right to protect the Encala!" the Investigator yelled as he pulled against William and Andrew.

"Well now your entire faction can pay for your stupidity," Emily whispered.

Chevalier looked down at her and then over to William quickly. Andrew frowned and let go of the Investigator. "Em…"

"No! I don't believe that you had no idea about this. You were my friends."

"We didn't know," Andrew said. "You have to believe us."

"I don't," she said to him, and then turned to leave. Andrew gently

took her arm, but she gasped and jerked away from him.

Andrew's eyes narrowed. "Did they do it again?"

"Do what?" Chevalier asked him.

Emily scanned the Encala and then nodded. "Of course."

Andrew spun toward the Investigator. "Did you torture her?"

The Investigator merely glared at his fellow Encala.

Andrew took Emily's hand and shoved her sleeves up, revealing the thick gauze. "How bad is it?"

She glanced at Chevalier and then whispered, "I'll heal."

"Why did they do it? What information could they possibly want?"

Emily swallowed hard. "It worked... I agreed to turn."

"What?!" William roared, and then turned to the Investigator. "Did you torture her until she agreed to turn?"

Chevalier gently took Emily's shoulder and moved her back when Andrew blurred into the Chief Investigator. She couldn't tell what was going on, and only Chevalier's firm grip kept her from joining in the fight.

"Let them do this, Em," Chevalier whispered. "He went behind the back of the Council and needs punished."

"I can punish him worse," she said.

"No, you can't. You can ash him... they can make him suffer."

Emily glanced at William and saw that he was carefully watching the fight. She started to understand by the anger on his face that the Encala didn't know what their Investigator was up to.

"Let's go," Emily said, taking Chevalier's arm. He nodded and followed her out. Just before he cleared the door, he looked back and saw Andrew break the neck of the Investigator and stand up.

The door guard stepped in front of them as they exited the Encala palace. "The Elders wish to see you."

"No, I've told them all I'm going to," Emily said.

"They're on their way out."

Emily pulled a pack of cigarettes from her pocket and lit up just as the three Encala Elders and Andrew came out toward the car.

"We didn't know," William told her, obviously angry.

She nodded and took a deep drag.

"Why are you smoking?" Andrew asked, confused.

Emily opened the car door. "I'm leaving."

"No, tell me what's going on," he said, and lightly touched her upper arm.

Without warning, Emily touched the burning end of her cigarette to his hand, and he quickly jerked it back. "Don't touch me."

Chevalier chuckled and crawled into the driver's seat of the Humvee.

"Em, talk to me," Andrew said. "What did they do to you?"

"It's not worth reliving. You're off the hook though, I believe you didn't know."

"How could you think we did that?"

She sighed and took another drag before answering in a whisper. "It's just been a long four months."

He looked over at Chevalier before leaning closer to whisper to Emily. "You need to tell them what they did to your arms. Their doctor might be able to help."

"I'm fine. I have pills."

"Pills and cigarettes? Is that how you're dealing? I can smell alcohol on you too."

"I don't need judged by you."

"I'm not judging. I'm worried."

"Don't be worried about me. Be worried about the Valle," she said as she crawled into the Humvee.

"Let me go with you to talk to them," Andrew said.

"No, it's my fight."

"Our fight," Chevalier said. "I'm going too."

She nodded and shut the door. The gate guards glared at her as they passed, still furious over being knocked unconscious earlier.

Chevalier pulled out onto the Interstate and then sat back for the long drive to Council City.

"Why won't you tell me about the forearm torture?" he asked after a few hours of driving in silence.

"Because you don't need new and inventive ways to torture someone."

He smiled. "But it's so much fun."

She looked over at him. "See? I won't be a part of that."

"I can do it back to those who did it to you though."

"Just stick them in your water tank and leave me out of it."

He thought for a moment. "How do you know about the water tank?"

"I can be very persuasive."

"So you bribed the guards?"

"Bribed... threatened... it's all a blur."

He chuckled. "I see."

"What?" Emily asked when Chevalier sighed slightly.

"I want to talk about the self-destructive behavior."

"I wasn't self-destructive."

"I beg to differ."

"I wasn't trying to kill myself. If I wanted to do that, I would put myself into one of your guillotines. I apparently can't die by poison,

might as well separate my head from my body."

He frowned. "It concerns me that you've thought that far about it."

"I didn't sign up for this long-life crap," she explained. "And I most certainly didn't sign up do it alone."

"So if I were to die, you would end up killing yourself?"

She looked out the window. "I'm surprised you didn't keep my pills."

"I wanted to."

"They help me sleep."

"I've noticed."

"Nothing else worked. I just sat up all night feeling alone."

"I'm sure Dr. Edwards can give you something safer."

"He wasn't there!"

"I'm not mad, okay?" Chevalier said. "I'm more worried about what happens if I do die someday."

"I don't want to talk about it."

"Why smoking?"

"Why not?"

"You hate the smell. It's just odd to see you with one."

"I don't know," she mumbled, and then pulled her knees up to her chest and wrapped her arms around them.

"Dr. Edwards thinks you might be addicted to all of it."

"I'm not."

"Do you remember when you came back from being gone for a year, and you finally relented and agreed to let me take care of you?"

"Yes"

"I want that back."

"No. I can take care of myself."

"I'm not so sure of that right now."

"Nothing I'm doing is out of control."

"Mixing alcohol and narcotics is out of control, Em." He sighed when she unbuckled and crawled into the very back of the Humvee where Kyle had tossed in some pillows and blankets.

***

Chevalier sat by the fire and watched Emily sleep. After getting into an argument with Mark and Silas over her smoking in the stables, she'd stormed up to her room and taken another handful of pills with the usual whiskey and was now sound asleep. It worried him how deeply she slept with the combination of drugs and alcohol, but he'd watched her toss and turn for nights on end, unable to sleep without it.

Her pills were running out. She'd been back in the palace for three

weeks and had only a few of the barbiturates left, though a lot of the pain pills. He noticed that she didn't take them often and only if she somehow bumped her forearms or someone touched her accidentally.

Lori was trying to slowly get back into Emily's life without acting too much like a psychiatrist. Silas helped, but now that she was mad at Silas and Mark, Chevalier wasn't sure she would warm up to Lori again. Dr. Edwards monitored her drug intake closely, but no one had yet to take anything from her or stop her from doing anything.

The Encala sent word that their former Chief Investigator had been thoroughly punished before being banished for 800 years. They sent apologies and gifts to Emily in hopes it didn't tarnish their relationship. The Valle knew they were next on her list, but they weren't sure how or when she would seek revenge for her four months away.

Because of a snowstorm, all three of Emily's dogs were in the bedroom, and the loud snoring of the Bulldog was starting to wear on even Chevalier's ancient patience.

Emily started to wake up after over 18 hours of hard sleep. Chevalier ordered some coffee to help her wake up and then shooed the dogs out of the room. Cavalry came and took them all out into the barn, and Emily opened her eyes just as the smell of coffee and hot muffins filled the room.

Chevalier moved over and sat down on the bed. "Good morning."

She opened her eyes and then sat up slowly. "Good morning."

He handed her a cup of steaming coffee, and she took a sip and looked over when a strong wind lashed against the side of the palace. "I was hoping this would clear up."

"It probably won't until Friday." Chevalier reached over and grabbed two rolls of ace bandage. "Dr. Edwards brought these over. He thought we could change your gauze out for these."

She shrugged. "The gauze helps."

"I know, and he thinks it's the pressure. So ace bandages will work better."

"Did he find out?" she asked, frowning.

"No, but it would help immensely if you would just tell us."

Emily reached out to take the ace bandages. "Fine, I'll try them."

Chevalier moved them out of her reach. "I'll put them on you. You can't do it right with one arm."

She smiled. "You won't see anything that will give it away."

His eyes narrowed when she put an arm out for him. Chevalier unwrapped her forearm and quickly studied the smooth skin underneath. She was right, and there was no sign at all that anything was wrong, nothing showing the pain she felt, and nothing to give any indication as to what the torture entailed.

When he was done, she pulled her sleeves down to cover the ace bandages and then leaned over and grabbed a pill bottle from the bedside table. After taking two, she sat back and watched Chevalier.

"What?" he asked, smiling.

"Shouldn't you be in trials or something?"

"I'll go in a bit." Chevalier reached into his pocket and pulled out a bottle, then handed it to Emily.

She took it and flipped it over to read. "What is this?"

"It's to help you stop smoking."

"I don't want to take pills."

He frowned. "You take them all the time now."

"More though?"

"You're back. It's time to stop."

"Maybe I don't want to stop. It helps me calm down."

"It's a disgusting habit that you're too strong to use as a crutch. Plus, it's stupid to stand outside in a snowstorm in sub-freezing weather just to smoke."

Emily stood up and threw the pack of cigarettes in the trash, shocking him. "I can stop without pills."

"It'll go easier if you take them," he said calmly. He actually hoped she would take them instead of subjecting the entire palace to her moody nicotine withdrawals, but he wasn't going to push the issue.

She flipped the bottle over in her hand a few times and then nodded. "I'll try them."

"You will?"

"Yes, now go to the trials. I have work to do."

Chevalier smiled at the Cavalry at her door and then headed to the council chambers. The rest of the Council was already seated when he sat down.

"I can't believe she's going to take them," Kyle said.

"I was surprised too, but it's still not going to be a fun few weeks."

"True," Zohn said, and then turned to Derrick. "Let the Valle in."

The Council watched as Elder Ryan and the Valle's Faction Liaison Officer came in with eight Imperial Guards.

"Your palace smells like cigarette smoke," Ryan said, wrinkling his nose.

"Is there some reason why you are here?" Quinn asked him.

"Yes, we have a lead on Emily's location and wanted to ensure that you understand that when we get her, she won't be back here."

Chevalier frowned slightly. "You know where she is?"

"Yes"

"Where?"

"We're not going to tell you that. We plan on keeping a close eye

on her and making sure the Equites don't interfere with her new life."

"You should also make sure she doesn't take up smoking," Kyle said, smiling.

Ryan's eyes flared. "She's here already?"

Chevalier nodded. "You're on her list too… so I suggest you watch it."

"We've done nothing to earn her wrath."

"So trying to turn her by torture was okay?" Zohn asked, irritated.

"We didn't try to turn her."

"But you gave the pseudo-Council the ammunition to force her to agree with it."

"We did no such thing!" Ryan yelled.

Chevalier leaned forward. "Then how did the pseudo-Council find out about this strange forearm torture that she's still suffering from? The Valle are the only ones I've known to use it."

Ryan's eyes narrowed. "I wasn't aware they knew of that method. I'm actually shocked they went to those extremes… I would imagine they tried lesser tactics first though, but she's stubborn."

"It would be a show of good faith if you tell us what that torture entails, so we can treat her injuries," Kyle told him.

He smiled. "I'm not going to do that. I'm sure she'll heal eventually."

"What was the threat if she contacted a heku?" Chevalier asked. "She won't tell us."

"I'm not obligated to tell you anything. I will inform the rest of the Valle Council that Emily is now here, and we will resume our stance on bringing her back to us," Ryan said, and then turned to leave.

Zohn sat back when the Valle came face-to-face with Mark and 15 members of the Cavalry.

"You're not done here," Mark said, blocking the door.

Quinn glared at Ryan when he turned around. "You tortured a mortal until she agreed to turn. That's breaking important heku laws, and you have to be held accountable for that."

"I didn't try to turn her!" Ryan yelled. "You have no right."

"Take them to prison," Kyle ordered.

***

"Has she said anything to you?" Chevalier asked Kralen, who was guarding her door.

"No, Elder. I don't even think she's left her room for four days."

Chevalier looked at the door. "She requested that I stay out."

Kralen nodded. "Us too, sir."

He thought for a moment. "We need to check on her though."

"Agreed"

"So you go in," Chevalier said, and smiled at Kralen.

Kralen grimaced. "Is that an order?"

"No, I'll go," he replied, and then broke the lock and walked in. He didn't see Emily anywhere in the room, so he walked over to the bathroom and heard her inside. "Em? Are you okay?"

"I'm alive," she mumbled.

Chevalier opened the door and saw her on the floor beside the toilet. She was pale and shaking, and shielded her eyes against the light from the bedroom. "Are you pregnant?"

"So help me, Chev…"

"Well, are you?"

"Who sealed my dumb waiter?"

"That was my decision." He studied her as she clutched her stomach and turned to the toilet. When she leaned back to the floor, he sat down. "Talk to me."

"I'm not pregnant."

"What's wrong then?"

"If you loved me, you'd give me just one cigarette."

"This'll work out. I swear."

Emily shook her head and looked over at him.

He smiled. "Don't even think about ashing me."

She finally crawled to her feet and started shakily out into the bedroom. Chevalier kept a hand close but didn't let her see it. It was obvious that she wasn't in the mood to be helped. She walked over to her bedside table and opened the small cupboard beneath it, revealing numerous bottles of alcohol.

"Em, where did you get those?" he asked, sighing.

"I have my ways."

"I thought we agreed you would cut out alcohol and cigarettes at the same time."

"No, you agreed… I nodded to appease you."

Just as she went to pour a shot of whiskey, Chevalier snatched the bottle from her and then stepped back when she turned furious eyes to him.

"Don't irritate me!"

"You need to get off of all of it."

"Give it back," Emily said, and took a step toward him.

"No… you've been drinking too much and chain smoking unfiltered cigarettes for four months. It's time to stop."

Emily simply screamed and tried to grab the bottle. He held it above his head and then braced himself for the oncoming assault. When

she started to pound on his chest, he silently called for Kralen and carefully tucked away his instinct to attack.

Kralen walked in and then his eyes grew wide when he saw Emily attempting to kill Chevalier. He quickly took her shoulders and backed her away from the Elder. She struggled against his hands, but he didn't relent and she grew even angrier when she couldn't get to Chevalier.

"Don't underestimate me," she snapped at him.

"I would never underestimate you," Chevalier told her. "However, you've made it four days without any nicotine or alcohol, so there's no use turning back now."

A malicious smile formed on Emily's lips. "I remember most of it…"

His eyes narrowed. "Most of what?"

"The incantation I'm not supposed to know."

"Don't do it," he said, getting angry.

Kralen called for backup and the room suddenly filled with members of the Council. Kyle hurried over and stood between Chevalier and Emily.

"I could do it to this entire palace," she said, staring at Chevalier.

He put his hands out and forced his voice to stay calm. "Think about it. You're mad now, but the ramifications are indescribable. You know, deep down, that we're trying to help you."

Her shoulders fell and the fragile way she held herself made his heart sink. She slowly sunk to the floor.

"I'm sorry," she whispered.

Chevalier ordered everyone out of the room and then pulled Emily into an embrace. "It'll be okay."

"I hurt," she said softly.

He lightly kissed the top of her head.

"I should call the Encala and apologize."

"You could always leave them afraid," he said, smiling.

"I shouldn't have threatened them, especially not Andrew."

"I don't like how Andrew looks at you."

Emily looked up at him. "How does he look at me?"

"He looks at you like I do."

"He's just a friend," she said, and leaned her head against his chest.

"Do you want to get away?"

"Where?"

"Palau… just you and me?"

She looked up curiously. "No kidding?"

"I'll do anything to help you get over this."

"What if we try to kill each other?"

"We won't."

"And Megs?"

He thought for a moment. "She's started Junior High level…"

Emily frowned. "She's only 5-years-old."

"I know, but she's above her age."

"Perfect"

"It'll be okay. Let's leave her too."

Emily looked over at her bedside table.

"No alcohol is going, and no pills unless Dr. Edwards thinks you need them."

"Is he going?"

"No"

She wrapped her arms around herself and nodded. "Yeah, let's go."

"I can be ready in 15 minutes."

Emily threw a few of her things into a bag, and when she looked around the room to see if anyone would notice a bottle of whiskey, she saw Silas in the corner, smiling at her.

"Don't even try it," he said, sounding amused.

***

"Sir, Miss Alexis wishes to address the Council," Derrick said from the doorway to the council chambers.

Quinn nodded. "Let her in."

Alexis seemed nervous as she walked forward to stand in front of the Elders.

"To what do we owe this honor?" Zohn asked, smiling.

"Well… I want to do this while Mom and Dad are out of the country," Alexis told them. She glanced back at the door and then turned to the Council.

"What's the problem?"

"No… no problem. I just… well… I realize that it's against heku laws… but I'm not a heku," she told them.

Zohn frowned slightly. "What law are we speaking of?"

Alexis sighed, "I want to adopt a baby."

"I see," Quinn said, sitting back on his chair.

The Records Keeper spoke up, "It's strictly forbidden for a heku to adopt a baby."

"I'm not heku," Alexis said again.

"Garrett is though."

"Well… yes."

"Plus, we have to assume you are immortal."

She nodded. "I realize that. Nevertheless, I want a baby, and I can't have one myself."

Zohn smiled comfortingly. "I realize that you have enough mortal blood to have the instinctual need to raise a child. However, the baby would have to be raised in Council City among the heku... it's too dangerous."

"I can protect it."

"It's not the blood-drinking that I'm speaking of."

"I know... and I can protect it."

"There are blood tests that are required to prove health of the parents," the Records Keeper said. "You probably can't pass them, and we know Garrett wouldn't."

"There's no proof that I can't pass a blood test."

Kyle leaned forward and put his elbows on the table. "Alex... it's too dangerous, and the laws are strictly adhered to."

"I'm not a heku."

"You're about as close as you can get though. Why do you not want Em and Chevalier to know?"

"Because I want to do this on my own. I'm tired of being the other Winchester, or an Elder's daughter. I want to be my own person with my own life."

"It's not that easy when you are such a rarity," Quinn told her.

"You've spoken to Garrett about this then?" Zohn asked.

"Not yet. He's too... well... by-the-book, and I know he would say no without even thinking about it. If I can get Council approval, he might consider it," she explained.

"A mortal child would need things we cannot give him," the Chief of Staff said. "Not only would you bring temptation to live in Council City, think of how the factions could use a child to lure you to them."

She glared at him. "I'm not dumb enough to let the Valle get a hold of my baby, and the Encala aren't stupid enough to try anything with me."

"You can't turn heku to ash massively like Emily can," Kyle said. "It'd be too dangerous. We'd have to put guards on it, and that's a lot of resources for a fully mortal child."

The Council could tell that Alexis was fighting back tears. "That's your final word? You won't even think about it?"

Quinn sighed, "We can't think about it. It's simply not done."

"Simply not done? You mean like moving a mortal into the palace? What about having a half-Ancient running around?" Alexis said, starting to panic. "There are a lot of things about my family that are breaking rules and stretching boundaries of what heku law says. I can't believe that you won't even consider it! I'm not heku, and I shouldn't be expected to live strictly by heku standards."

"Alexis," Kyle said sternly. "The Council said no."

She set her jaw and it reminded them of Emily. "Fine... then you're forcing me to go over your heads."

Alexis turned to leave but stopped when Quinn spoke, "No one is above us."

Alexis nodded and whispered, "My mom is."

Without turning again, she walked out, obviously upset.

Zohn waited a few minutes for her to leave and then had Derrick call for Garrett.

Garrett came in and bowed before the Council. "I was summoned."

"This meeting needs to remain confidential," Zohn said.

"Of course, Elder."

"Alexis has approached us, and when she left she was quite upset."

Garrett frowned. "What about?"

"She wants a baby."

"She wants you to turn a baby?!"

"No... she wants to adopt," Kyle told him. "We cannot allow that, and it greatly upset her that we said no."

"I didn't know she wanted one... I mean... she can't have one, so I thought that was the end of it."

"We need you to help us ensure that she doesn't go behind our backs and do it anyway. We assume that the blood-tests would show inaccurate readings for her and render her unable to adopt, but just in case, we need your help."

"The Council gave a solid no?" he asked, making sure.

"That is correct," Quinn said. "We cannot have mortal babies in Council City... or in any heku coven, for that matter."

Garrett nodded. "I will do what I can... but..."

"But?"

"She's a lot like her mom. If she gets something in her head..."

"We understand that."

"I'll try. I'll talk to her tonight."

"Just keep us out of it," Zohn said. "We don't need Alexis turning on the Council like her mom is prone to doing."

Garrett nodded, bowed and then left the council chambers.

***

"Let's just move here," Emily said when Chevalier brought a glass of juice to the chaise. She was sitting out in the hot Palau sun, reclined in a soft chaise and covered in sun screen.

He smiled. "You'd get bored."

"I think I could handle some boredom."

"For about a month, then you'd be begging to go back." Chevalier

slipped on sun glasses and sat down in the chaise next to her. They both quietly watched the crystal blue water lap against the white sands of the private island.

"It'd be worth a try."

"I'm sorry I was on the phone when you got up," he said, taking her hand. "How are the shakes and nausea?"

"Better"

"Dr. Edwards said you should be home free by next Friday."

"Dr. Edwards is a moron."

Chevalier smiled. "I'm sure he is…"

"It's gotten easier though… not that I wouldn't sell your left nut for a cigarette."

"Nice," Chevalier said, laughing.

"What was your meeting about?"

"The usual. The Valle now have paperwork proving that you need to be turned over to them for a trial."

"I didn't know heku had paperwork."

"Most don't… the Valle do apparently."

Emily sat up and crossed her legs, facing him. "What are you and I going to do about the Valle?"

"I'm not sure there's much we can do. We've been warring so long the world might come to an end if we stop."

"So we just let them keep finding new and inventive ways to kidnap me?"

"No, we just…"

"Double my guards? Lock me in the council chambers?"

Chevalier smiled. "No, we just do our best."

"That's boring. I want to do something pro-active."

"What, exactly, did you have in mind?"

"Why don't we wipe them out like you did the Encala a while back?"

"The Valle will be harder. There are twice as many of them."

"But this time I can help."

"If we start wiping out Valle covens, their Council is going to press harder to get you, and this time, they may choose death. At least for now, when they do have you, you aren't tortured or confined."

Emily sat back and looked out over the water. "It's amazing how things have changed since we first met."

"I know. It was simpler back then."

"Everything was. The castle scared the crap out of me. The thought of being surrounded by blood-thirsty immortals was terrifying. Now though, it's comfortable and I like it."

He smiled. "I sometimes wonder."

"I haven't been fed off of in a long time. Keith's a distant memory, although it seems he keeps coming into play."

"So tell me about Charles."

"Charles Morris," Emily said, and then a smile played across her lips. "He's two years older than I am, but his ranch was by ours, so we grew up together. I started calling him Chuck Norris before school even started. By the time I got into 5th grade, the entire school called him that. When I was 15, he started working for my dad under Keith's supervision."

"Keith told him some interesting things."

"Yeah, Keith always thought I was spending his money, sleeping around, stealing from him, that sort of thing."

"Sounds to me like he was accusing you of what he was doing."

"More than likely. After a few years of working with Keith, he started to act like him and became all around grouchy. By that time, Keith and I were married. One night, Keith and Chuck got drunk and started to play poker. Keith put a night with me up on the table, and Chuck won."

Chevalier frowned. "He's hit an all-time new low."

"Yes, well… when I found, out I refused. So Keith put me in the hospital for making him look bad. After that, Chuck kept trying for his one-night stand, and Keith let him, because no one goes back on a poker bet."

"Kept trying how?"

"Little things. He'd corner me in the barn and start kissing me. I can't count how many times I kneed him in the groin for being too handsy. After a couple of years, he quit trying, but by then, he hated me and would urge Keith into beatings. He'd tell Keith that he saw me in town with one of the Sani boys or coming out of a hotel with a stranger in a suit."

"Sounds more Encala than Valle," Chevalier said. He was surprised he was just hearing this after all of this time with Emily and briefly wondered why she was telling him.

"Last I heard from Chuck, he'd knocked up Bridget Kunzak and married her in a shotgun wedding… it was a real shotgun wedding too. Her dad stood behind the preacher with a 12 gauge."

"Was he still working for Keith when we met?"

"No, when Dad had his stroke and I inherited the ranch, I fired him. That was a fun night."

"I bet."

"When I got out of the hospital, Chuck had moved to Joplin, Missouri with Bridget, and within the year, he was in jail for beating her."

"Your past keeps rearing its ugly head," Chevalier said.

"That's the thing… it's the past. The past forms what we are and who we become. That's what's so frustrating about what the Valle did with the re-memory. It's bad enough to kidnap me and erase our relationship, but in doing so, they changed me."

"It's a dangerous road."

Emily looked over at him. "I can feel the memories surface once in a while, but when I realize I'm in the palace or in my house, I remember the truth. I'm afraid one of these days it's going to fully come back, and I won't ever remember."

"I am too."

"So fix it."

"It's too dangerous. We don't know what messing with your mind like that would do to you. You could wake up a complete amnesiac."

"Isn't that better than waking up a Valle?"

"We'll figure it out. I promise."

She nodded, and after a few minutes, spoke again, "I want to talk about Andrew."

Chevalier's body tensed slightly. "What about him?"

"He's my friend, and I trust him."

"I know."

"I want you to trust him also."

"My distrust goes far beyond his crush on you."

"He doesn't have a crush on me. You're so afraid I'm going to run off with some other heku that you think everyone's out to woo me."

He frowned. "Andrew looks at you like he's moments from carrying you off to bed."

"He's never even tried anything like that."

"Good to know. You just have bad luck with heku admirers, and you're closer to Andrew than any so far."

"Is it that or is it that he's an Encala?"

"That doesn't help."

"It would just be nice if you didn't scrutinize his every move when we're together."

"I just don't want him to hurt you like the others."

"You mean Exavior."

"You're so trusting. It scares me."

"He's earned his trust though."

"How is it you can tell him about the forearm torture, but you can't tell me?" Chevalier asked as he took her hand.

"Because he won't tell anyone, and he won't use it."

"I wouldn't be so sure of that."

"I am sure of that."

"So tell me what it is."

"No, it's nothing you need to do to a heku."

Chevalier thought for a moment. "You aren't upset with my water tank?"

"Not upset, no."

"Something else?"

"Scared to death may be more the term."

"Why's that?"

"Because I'm afraid if anything happens to you, someone will put me in it."

He involuntarily tightened his grip.

"Heku like to push my limits… but I can't take drowning."

"No one would put you in there."

She looked over at him. "You know they would."

"Then I'll get rid of it."

Emily sat back and shut her eyes for a moment before speaking again, "What did you do to Robin and Elliott?"

His voice sounded tense. "What do you mean?"

"They used to guard me but haven't since the run-in with Dion."

"I didn't do anything to them."

"Not even Robin?"

"No"

She smiled. "But you wanted to."

"Well, damn! He seriously broke the no-touching rule."

"So why aren't they guarding me anymore?"

"It was their request, actually."

She frowned. "Why?"

"Embarrassed, I would imagine. They asked to be assigned to the city only."

"I'll talk to them when we get back. That wasn't their faults."

"Elliott's not too bad. All he did was sing. Robin fears for his life."

"You won't touch him though, right?" Emily asked, looking over at him.

"No, though I wouldn't mind."

"It was Dion."

"The attraction had to be there first for it to surface."

"Beer goggles."

Chevalier grinned. "It wasn't beer goggles."

She shrugged and shut her eyes again to soak up the sun.

"I want to talk about your self-destructive behavior," Chevalier said.

"I don't have self-destructive behavior."

"Well no, not right now. I need to know that if I ever die or get banished, that you'll be okay."

"I won't let them banish you."

"Okay then, death."

She sighed, "I didn't sign up for this immortal crap. I never wanted to live forever, so I sure as hell am not going to do it without you."

"That's not very comforting."

"That's the way it is."

"But the kids…"

"The kids, Megara aside, don't need a mom anymore."

Chevalier took her hand. "They need you. No one else knows what it's like to be part-heku, except you."

"You're trying to get me to behave if you die, and I won't do it. Most heku had the option to stay alive forever. I didn't, and I wouldn't have chosen that."

"What's so bad about it? You get to see the changes in the human race. You get to see progression, make new friends, see new places…"

"Get one million colds, suffer from the flu, keep having babies, get in car wrecks, stub your toe for eternity. I don't want to keep watching tornadoes wipe out entire towns or hurricanes ruin the lives of anyone it crosses. I don't want to see World War III or find that my last relative is dead."

Chevalier sighed, "I'm sorry that you didn't get a choice. Killing yourself if I die isn't a good option though."

"I didn't necessarily try to kill myself."

"Probably not consciously, no."

Emily's voice dropped to a whisper. "It's the only way I could stop hurting."

"There has to be another way."

"No, end of discussion. If you and the kids disappear tomorrow, I'm going to somehow find a way to remove my head."

"Damnit, Emily. This isn't a joke."

"I'm not kidding."

He sighed, "That's what I'm afraid of."

"I'm not going to discuss this. If it happens, you obviously won't be around to stop it."

After a few minutes of silence, Chevalier looked at her again. "So were you going to tell me about buying land out from under the Valle?"

"I'm sorry about not telling you."

"What happened?"

"The land behind my house came for sale, and Alec found out that the Valle put in a bid. I didn't want a back-door babysitter, so I used Exavior's money, doubled the asked for price, and bought it with cash with the stipulation that no other bids could be taken."

He smiled. "That was pretty smart, actually."

"That's why I ashed you and Kyle. I had to get to the bank within three hours of the offer."

"An explanation would have been nice."

"I know, and I'm sorry."

"What are you going to do with the land?"

"I'm not sure actually. Alec is cleaning it up when he's available, and I'd like to get it zoned for livestock."

"You are putting a lot of trust in Alec."

"He's all of my dad I have left," Emily whispered.

"I know. I really do. I just get nervous when I think of you and he alone."

"I don't fully trust him, but I have to give him a shot and he's done nothing. When I took the land from the Valle, Sotomar showed up and threatened to punish him for leaving the Valle. It didn't seem like a show to me."

Chevalier nodded and took her hand. "Just be careful around him."

Chapter 26

"One more round," Emily said, and then she turned and watched a member of the Cavalry ride his mare around the corral.

"So?" he asked when he stopped in front of her.

"She's good to go. Let me know if the limp comes back."

He nodded and then rode off to catch up with his battalion. Emily turned and looked around the area with the stables before brushing off and heading back into the palace.

"Where are your guards?" the door guard asked as he bowed slightly and opened the door.

Emily turned and looked behind her. "Not sure actually."

The guard sighed softly.

"I didn't ditch them!" she said.

"I'll notify the General."

"Fine, but I didn't ditch them." Emily walked into the palace and headed up the stairs. She stopped on the fourth floor when she heard yelling from the council chambers.

Derrick blocked the door when she walked up. "Can I help you?"

"Who's yelling?"

"Wasim's Coven Lord."

"Why?"

Derrick smiled. "You'd have to take that up with the Council."

"Do they need me?"

"No"

She narrowed her eyes and then turned and walked up the stairs. She was only slightly surprised that Mark had replaced her guards already, and they were waiting at her bedroom door.

Silas watched her walk up. "Where are your guards?"

"I don't know. I didn't ditch them."

"Clipper said when you cleared his horse for return to the Cavalry, your guards were waiting by the stables."

"Well, I didn't see them."

"Welcome back, by the way," Silas said with a smile. He reached over and opened the door for her.

A smile played across her lips. "It was so nice."

"I bet."

"No phones… no kids… no guards…" Silas chuckled when Emily walked past him and into her room while she started to list everything in Council City.

Emily dropped her cowboy hat onto the table and pulled off her gloves as she looked at an envelope on the table by the fire. She walked over and looked at it. It was a simple white envelope with her name on

it. She opened it quickly and pulled out a note written on plain white paper. The note simply said, "If I were you, I would run."

She frowned and checked the envelope for something else, but it was empty. After re-reading the note a few times, she slipped it back into the envelope and buried it deep in her sock drawer, then walked over and opened the door.

Silas looked over at her as the other three members of the Cavalry moved back so she could step out. "Everything okay?"

"Did the cleaning crew come in here today?" she asked, trying to sound casual.

"Not today. Do I need to call them in?"

"No... was the bedroom door guarded?"

"No, what's wrong?"

She smiled. "Nothing, I was just curious."

Silas moved so he could see around her and into the room. "You sure?"

Emily pushed him back away from the door and shut it behind her, then turned and looked around the room. After checking the bathroom, closets, and even under the bed, she decided that whoever left the note had abandoned the room before her arrival.

She pulled the note out again and read it, then frowned and put it back into its hiding spot in her drawer.

"Mom?" Alexis said from behind her.

Emily jumped at the sudden voice and then smiled. "Hi, Alex."

"Sorry, I didn't mean to scare you."

"You didn't," Emily said, and then walked up to her daughter. She studied Alexis' face, and it wasn't hard to see she was on the verge of crying. "What's wrong?"

"Garrett...," she started, and then turned around when the tears began to flow.

Emily sighed, "Did you and Garrett get into a fight?"

Alexis nodded, unable to speak.

"Do you want me to shoot him?"

Alexis began to laugh through the tears. "It's tempting."

Emily smiled and pulled Alexis into a hug. "Tell me what happened."

Alexis finally spoke through sobs. "I told him I want a baby."

"And he said no?"

"He won't even talk about it."

Emily pulled Alexis over to the fireplace and they both sat down. "Have you brought it up before?"

"Not really, nothing more than telling him I can't have one."

"So you just shocked him, I would imagine."

"It's more than that…," Alexis said, and then looked down at her hands. "I asked the Council for permission to adopt."

Emily frowned. "Why is it any of their concern?"

"Garrett is heku."

"Right, and heku can't adopt. Well, you aren't a heku."

"I know. That's what I told them. They wouldn't even think about it though. I got a firm, solid, no. So then I asked Garrett if he would talk to them."

"Then they told him no too."

"No! He wouldn't even do it," Alexis said, breaking into a new round of tears.

Emily took her daughter's hand and watched her until she calmed down. "Maybe Garrett is too afraid the Council will get mad."

"No, he said he doesn't want to bother the Council with something as trivial as a baby."

"Ouch, okay…"

"So he's putting that bloody Council before me!"

"You're preaching to the choir," Emily said, and then looked around the room while she thought.

"Trivial… he said it's trivial."

"Heku have no sense of what's important," Emily told her. "Do you want me to talk to the Council?"

"No, I want Garrett to."

"He's not going to. I can promise that."

Alexis nodded. "Yes then… they wouldn't listen to me."

"They may not listen to me either, but I'll try. If the Council agrees, then you have to get Garrett to agree."

Alexis smiled. "Oh, he'll agree to it."

Emily laughed and then stood up. "I'll go see if they're done yelling at some angry Coven Lord."

Alexis nodded and grabbed for a tissue as Emily headed out. Derrick was watching Emily walk down the stairs and then smiled and opened the door when she walked up.

Emily nodded to him and then approached the Elders.

"What's up, Em?" Chevalier asked, a little leery.

She looked at the other two Elders. "I want to talk about what you told Alexis."

"We…," Zohn started, but Emily cut him off.

"She's not a heku and not bound by heku laws. If it were me, I wouldn't have even asked the Council."

"What's going on?" Chevalier asked.

"She may not be heku, but Garrett is," Kyle told her. "She cannot…"

"She's not going to live her life around heku rules when she's not a heku."

"Stop!" Chevalier yelled, and everyone looked at him. "Why am I not being told what's going on?"

Quinn turned his chair toward Chevalier. "Alexis came while you were away and asked for permission to adopt a baby."

"She did?!" he gasped.

Emily nodded. "Yes, and they told her no."

"It's against heku law to adopt for numerous reasons," Zohn told her. "Not only would it bring a mortal to live with the immortal, it would also risk exposing us."

"Not if it's done right," Emily said.

"There's also the blood test of the mother and father, to verify they aren't sick," the Records Keeper said.

Emily sighed, "There have to be ways around that. Just control them and tell them to approve you."

"No," Chevalier said sternly. "She cannot adopt."

"She's not a heku."

"She's close enough."

Emily studied them, and each member of the Council inwardly waited for the vicious onslaught that came when the Elders told her no. They were all surprised when she nodded.

"I have to help her," Emily said calmly.

"Em, it's important that you don't go off and do his alone," Kyle told her. "Think of how dangerous it is to have a mortal child living in Council City."

"I do know… I had three of them."

"No, you had three partial heku children."

She crossed her arms and studied him as her jaw tensed.

Kyle couldn't help but smile. "It's too dangerous. The laws for the heku were put in place to protect the mortal child."

"The laws were put in place for heku. Alexis isn't a heku."

"She exhibits more heku traits than mortal," Zohn said.

"Garrett would be the father, and he is heku," Quinn added.

"That's your final word?" Emily asked.

"Yes," Zohn replied. He decided to keep Chevalier out of the argument.

Emily shrugged and then turned back to the door. Before leaving, she mumbled under her breath, "Guess I'll just have to give her a half-heku baby."

Chevalier gasped and looked over at Kyle with wide eyes. Kyle was watching the door shut behind her. "She wouldn't…"

Richard, the Chief Interrogator sighed, "We know she would."

"She didn't scream at us," Quinn said, frowning slightly.

"I fully expected at least one of you to need revived," Kyle commented.

Emily walked up and found Garrett knocking on her bedroom door. "Come on, Alex. Just talk to me."

Emily stopped behind him and crossed her arms as she glared at his back. Silas cleared his throat and Garrett spun suddenly and faced them.

"How dare you put the Council before your wife," Emily said angrily.

"I didn't! I wouldn't do that…, but the Council isn't going to agree to this. There's no reason bugging them."

"Even if asking helps Alex?"

"How can being denied again help her?"

"You put the Council first… and now you're on my list," Emily said. She walked past him, purposely bumping her shoulder against his chest before disappearing into her room and slamming the door behind her.

Emily walked over and slumped down in a chair beside Alexis. "Figures… all men on the Council."

"They told you no, too?" Alexis asked.

"Pretty much."

"I've noticed that heku women don't even want kids."

Emily nodded. "It's hormonal, and they don't have those hormones."

"So I never get to be a mom."

"I wouldn't say that quite yet."

"What do you have in mind?" Alexis asked her.

"Well… I can pass a blood test. I'll just adopt."

"They won't adopt to a single woman, especially one so young."

Emily sat back in her chair. "That's true… bloody heku have me at 21-years-old. Course, I have a birth certificate to prove I'm in my 50s."

Alexis shook her head. "They wouldn't believe it."

"I hate being 20."

"Age wouldn't even matter as much as you're single as far as mortals are concerned," Alexis told her. Emily could see Alexis' heart drop as she fought back the tears again.

"I could find a husband," Emily said, smiling slightly.

Alexis looked up at her. "Do what?"

"I have money… a lot… I can just use Exavior's money to buy a mortal husband. We get married and adopt a baby."

"That's ludicrous."

"True… so then I'll have a baby for you."

"Dad'd never go for that."

"Your dad wouldn't have a choice," Emily said. "It's my body, and I can do what I want with it."

"Yeah, but Dad'd have to help."

"No, he wouldn't. We'll use artificial insemination and then Garrett can be the Dad."

"Out of the question," Chevalier said from behind them.

Emily jumped when he spoke and then she glared at him. "Don't sneak up and eavesdrop on us."

"I didn't sneak up," Chevalier said, sitting down beside them. "You're not going to have a baby for them."

"Why not?" Emily asked.

"Alexis, go."

Emily turned and watched Alexis leave their room, then she turned back to Chevalier. "I'm not talking to you about this. You don't understand."

"I do understand the mortal woman's need to reproduce, however…"

"No, you don't! Even mortal men don't understand that."

"Okay, maybe it's not first-hand, but I do understand there's a physiological need."

"There are two options. Either I adopt for her, or I have a baby for her."

"No"

"I have to help her, Chev."

"I'm your husband, and I don't want to watch you go through another pregnancy. What if the baby is full heku like Dain? He almost killed you."

"I don't care. I'll do whatever it takes to make Alex happy."

"She is happy! She'll get over the baby thing… we'll get her a dog maybe."

"Oh my God!" Emily screamed, and then stood up. "You are so ignorant!"

Chevalier frowned. "I think not. Now calm down."

"I will not calm down! You have no idea what you're talking about. This isn't like she wants a new bike. She wants to be a mother."

"Heku have long been appeased by raising animals."

Emily moved to him quickly, and he braced himself for a slap but she simply stood in front of him and whispered, "She's not a heku! Get that through your head. She doesn't have to live by heku rules, and if she wants a baby, then I'll get her one."

Chevalier took both of her hands, so she couldn't try to hit him. "She is my daughter, and she is a blood-drinker, therefore, bound by heku rules. She's married to a heku… and…"

"She had no more of a choice in this than I did. She wants a baby, not something that's going to bring down your species."

"It's too dangerous."

Emily jerked her hands away from Chevalier and walked out of the bedroom. He watched her go and wondered at how calmly she was acting. Normally, she would be screaming and hitting by now.

When she disappeared into the game room, Silas gave her location to Chevalier and received orders to watch her but leave her alone. Her temper was high, and it put her guards at risk of being turned to ash on a whim.

"Hey!" Silas yelled when he saw Emily spin the secret door and disappear into the bar.

Once standing, Emily focused on the game room and then turned to the shelves full of alcohol. She braced the door with a broken chair and walked over to clean out a shot glass.

Silas frowned and turned to the other three Cavalry with him. "Why are we in the game room?"

The one closest to him looked around. "We were guarding Lady Emily."

"I know… so where is she?"

"Probably in her room."

"She wiped our memories," Silas said, aggravated.

"Let's at least go check the room."

Silas nodded, and they all left the game room and started up for the fifth floor bedrooms. Once there, he listened at the bedroom door and then knocked. When no one answered, he opened the door and looked around the empty room.

"She ditched us," one of the Cavalry said, irritated.

Silas sighed and called for Mark.

A few minutes later, Mark walked into the room. "What's wrong?"

"Emily ditched us," Silas said.

One of the Cavalry turned to his General. "We were suddenly in the game room, and it was empty."

Mark nodded. "So she wiped your memory. My guess is that she's in the bar."

"Damnit!" Silas yelled, and blurred down to the game room, followed by the others. He walked over and tilted the mirror, but the door didn't spin.

Mark tried it and then pushed against the door, but it didn't move. "She has it blocked again."

"Emily!" Silas yelled. "Open this door, now!"

Mark called for Kralen and then turned to the door. "Let's all push and see if we can get in. Then we'll talk to the Elders about clearing out

that bar. I know they kept it for recreational use by the Council, but Emily's the only one using it."

The others nodded and braced against the door. When they pushed, the sound of shattering wood could be heard as they spun into the bar and stepped out. Emily looked down at them from her perch beside the high windows, and just as she locked eyes with Mark, she took a long drink from a bottle of bourbon.

"Damnit, Em," Mark sighed. "Why?"

She didn't answer but turned to face the boarded up windows that led down to the former Ancient's room.

Silas walked forward. "Why did you wipe my memory?!"

They all turned when the door spun again, and Kralen stepped in. "What's going... why are you drinking?!"

"Stop yelling at me," she whispered, but stayed facing the boards.

"I'm sorry... but why are you drinking?" he asked, calmer.

She shrugged and then dabbed at her eye with a tissue. When they realized she was crying, Mark ordered everyone out, except Kralen.

Kralen watched the others leave and then jumped up onto the ledge beside Emily. "Want to talk about it?"

She looked over at him. "Off the record?"

"Sure"

"I had an argument with the Council."

"Again"

"This is different... this time, they're messing with my family."

"Except that one of the Council is your family too."

"Yeah, one that doesn't really care about his daughter."

Kralen sighed, "Tell me what happened."

Emily looked over and took another drink before explaining. "Alexis wants a baby, so she asked the Council if she can adopt."

"And they said no, obviously."

"Right. What gives them the power to dictate what my daughter can and can't do? She's not a heku."

"She's pretty close though. There are rules among the heku that are more strictly adhered to than others... not adopting is one of the top."

"She's not a heku. So then I decided I would just have one for her, but Chev said no."

"I'm surprised you listened to him."

"Exactly, I've lost my mind," Emily said before taking another drink. "When did I start taking Chevalier's orders?"

"Maybe when you thought he was gone forever."

"She wants a baby. I can give her one."

"It's a pretty dangerous game. What if the baby is full heku? He could kill you."

"Chevalier said that too."

Kralen smiled. "It's true."

"Well, it's my body. If Alexis wants a baby, then I'll give her one."

"Most heku just adopt a dog."

"Heku women don't have the drive to be a mother like we do."

Kralen watched her and his eyes narrowed. "How much have you had to drink?"

"Enough that I'm not as mad right now."

"The Elder has her best interest at heart."

"Your Elder has the faction at heart. His kids have always been on a back burner behind the faction. So am I, for that matter."

"I wouldn't say that exactly."

"I would. Alexis never has really connected with Chev. They are polar opposites."

"I'm not going to argue with you on that," Kralen said. He shook his head when Emily offered him a drink.

"I know what it feels like to want a baby and not be able to have one. When I was told by the doctors that I couldn't have children, I thought my heart was going to shrivel up and die. I'm not going to make Alexis go through that all because her genes are screwed up."

"Adoption is too risky. I'll agree with the Council on that one. As for you having a baby for her, it seems logical. However, I do think that your husband should get a say in it."

"Why? It's my body."

"One that he cares a lot about. We were all scared to death when you had Dain, and you kept getting sicker and sicker."

She shrugged. "One out of four... chances are it'd be okay."

"Not good odds though."

"So what am I supposed to do?"

"My suggestion would be that you calm down and talk to the Elder again about having a baby for Alex. I wouldn't suggest you go behind the Council's back and adopt though."

She smiled. "That obvious I was going to do that?"

"Yes, it was."

Emily scooted down until she was lying in the window sill and then she set the bottle of bourbon beside her. "Now I just need a nap."

Kralen laughed slightly. "You aren't sleeping up here."

"Why not?"

"You'd fall off and break your neck." He picked her up and then jumped down and started for the revolving door. "I'll take you up to bed."

When they appeared in the game room, Mark and Silas were waiting. Kralen smiled at them and walked past when he noticed

Emily's eyes were shut.

Once Emily was in bed and sound asleep, they met up outside of her door and Mark turned to Kralen. "So what happened?"

"Same thing that we heard earlier. She wants to either adopt or have a baby for Alex," Kralen said.

"She drank over that?"

"It's important to her, and the rest of us kind of just blew off the idea."

"Let's go talk to the Elder," Silas suggested. "He needs to know she's been drinking."

"Been drinking?" Kralen asked. "She's downright drunk."

"Great," Mark sighed, and then led the way to the council chambers.

***

Chevalier watched her sleep. Since their fight over the baby almost three months ago, Emily had a hard time with confrontation and somehow managed to sneak alcohol into the palace unnoticed as a way of dealing with it. He used to think her running was the worst possible thing she could do but would take that over her continued self-destruction.

She seemed unnaturally compliant with the Council and hadn't told them no on anything. They were all on guard, waiting for her to revert to her defiant ways, but she seemed honestly trying to do as they asked and not cause any trouble. The alcohol was one way Chevalier suspected she was using to still feel somewhat in control when the Council began to interfere with her wishes.

Emily sat up and grabbed her head, then looked up when Chevalier shut the heavy blinds, throwing the room into darkness.

"There's some aspirin on the table beside you," he told her as he sat on the bed.

She grabbed it and took some with the hot coffee sitting beside it.

"Want to talk about it?" he asked.

"Not really."

"That's four times in the last month that you've gotten drunk."

"I'm sorry," she said, and then took another sip of coffee.

"I just want to make sure it's not getting out of control again."

"It's not."

"What caused it this time?"

"I don't want to talk about it, okay?"

He studied her. "If it's your guards, I can talk to them."

"It's not," she said, and then finally stood up and staggered into the bathroom for a shower.

Chevalier stepped out when he heard Mark outside of the door. Chevalier shut the door behind him. "What happened?"

Mark looked over at Horace. "Tell him."

Horace sighed, "It was my fault, and I apologize. She's been acting weird, and I caught her checking around a corner down on the first floor, and she had no guards."

Chevalier frowned. "Where were they?"

"She wiped our memory, Elder," one of the Cavalry explained.

"What was she looking for around the corner?"

Horace shrugged. "She wouldn't say. We've all gotten the impression that she's jumpy lately and maybe a tad paranoid, and I wanted to know what was going on."

"Did she say?"

"No, Elder, and when I kept pushing... she got mad."

"Damnit, that shouldn't cause her to drink though," Chevalier said.

"It doesn't take a lot," Mark said. "As for the paranoid behavior, we've all seen it."

"What the hell is she keeping from us now?"

"There's no telling."

"I'll talk to her..." Chevalier stopped talking when Emily opened the door.

"Heku convention?" she asked, stepping around him.

"Want to explain why you're paranoid lately?"

"Sounds to me like you are."

He smiled. "I'm watching you."

"Like that's anything new," she mumbled, and headed down the stairs for a swim. Horace and the other three heku followed her. She told them to stay out and then stripped and dove into the water in her bikini.

Hard laps would clear her head, so she immediately began pushing herself to swim from one end to the next. An hour later, she felt better, and the strain in her muscles faded to shaky arms and legs, so she leaned back and began to float. Something caught her eye, and she looked over and saw a bouquet of red roses sitting on a chaise by the pool. The telltale plain white envelope was sitting in front of it, and Emily cringed.

She'd found eight threatening notes now and was no closer to figuring out who was leaving them. She hadn't yet told any of the heku and didn't want to unless it got out of hand.

After crawling out and wrapping in a towel, she sat down and opened the envelope to read the note.

"I fear you aren't taking me seriously, so now I'll have to prove that I'm serious. Better say good-bye to something you care about."

Emily gasped and ran for the door, still clutching the note.

"Em?" Horace asked when she ran out wrapped in a towel. She cleared the front doors and took off for the palace, followed by confused guards. The door guards tried to find out what was wrong, but she ran past them and headed up to the fourth floor.

"Emily?" Derrick asked, confused as to why she was running through the palace wrapped in a towel.

She ignored him and ran into the council chambers, coming to a stop behind a heku on his knees in front of the Council.

"Is there a problem?" Chevalier asked, frowning. He hated when she showed any skin, and now she was running around in a towel.

Emily caught his eye and then calmed the panic that threatened to burst into insanity. "I'll let you know."

She turned without another word and ran out of the council chambers, then headed up to the school.

Megara and her teacher looked over at Emily when she came into the room. No one spoke and then Megara turned back to her studies when Emily walked out.

"Do we get to know what's wrong?" Kralen asked as he walked up. Horace had called for higher-ranking heku when it became obvious that something was wrong.

Emily gulped down air and then called for Dain.

"What's..." Dain looked down at his mom, and his eyebrows rose. "Some reason you're not dressed?"

"Go check on Alex," Emily said quickly, and then turned to Kralen and held her hand out. "Phone please."

Kralen handed over his cell phone and turned when Mark walked up and spoke, "What's going on?"

Emily quickly dialed Allen and waited what seemed like an eternity for him to answer.

"Good morning, Mom," Allen said.

"You're okay?" she asked.

"Sure, what's up?"

"Nothing weird going on?"

"No"

"Do me a favor. Stay on the island for a bit."

"I can't. I need to..."

"No! Do as I say!"

Allen sighed, "Fine, I'll stay on the island."

Emily hung up and then walked slower down the stairs, wondering what the note meant.

"What's in your hand?" Kralen asked her.

She looked down, having forgotten she was still clutching the threatening note. "Nothing important."

"So why are you running around half dressed?"

"I was swimming."

"I see that… and then you decided not to get dressed?"

Emily frowned as she went through things in her mind that the note could mean.

"Alex is fine," Dain said, blurring up to them. "What's wrong?"

She froze on the stairs and then mumbled before running down them. "The dogs…"

By the time they reached the stables, half of the Cavalry had been summoned, and Mark was trying to get Emily to stop long enough to tell them what was going on.

"Devia!" Emily called out from the stables. The Border collie ran up happily and licked at her hand. She called for Sebastian, the St. Bernard, and Quiesco, the Bulldog, as she checked on the horses.

Silas appeared with one of the soft pink robes from the pool room and handed it over to Emily. She dropped the towel and slipped into it as she checked the last row of horses.

"Sebastian! Quiesco!" she called out, and then looked up and down the long corridor.

"Last I heard, Sebastian is out with Gifford," Silas told her.

"Check on him."

Silas' lips moved, but Emily didn't hear anything until he faced her. "Sebastian's still with Gifford. So tell us what's going on."

"Where's Quiesco?"

"I haven't seen him today."

Her heart sunk. "Find him… please…"

Mark's eyes narrowed. "We're not putting out a manhunt for a dog until you tell us why."

Emily looked down at the note clutched in her hand and then shoved it deep into the pocket of her robe.

"Em?" Kyle asked, blurring up.

She turned pleading eyes to him. "I'm begging you. Help me find Quiesco."

"Did he run off?"

She swallowed dryly. "Maybe."

Kyle nodded to Mark, and she could tell they were having a conversation, but she couldn't tell what. She headed back into the stables to check the stalls again. Quiesco had a habit of finding new and inventive places to nap, so she checked some of the harder to see places as the panic set in.

"Em?" Kyle said from behind her.

She cried out slightly and spun. "Don't sneak up on me!"

"I didn't... we'll find him. He probably followed one of the Cavalry out."

She nodded but watched him.

"Want to tell me what's up?"

"No"

Kyle stood silently and watched as she fought back the tears and then wiped a stray one that escaped from her eye. "Please, tell me what's going on."

Chevalier appeared with them and studied her. "What's up?"

They both saw it in her eyes, indecision. She couldn't explain why she had an internal debate in the brief seconds it took her to decide. Her first instinct was to handle it herself, not to involve the heku, but another part of her craved help and wanted to stop always having to deal with things alone.

She swallowed hard. "I'm in over my head."

"With what?" Kyle asked.

"I'm getting threatening letters..."

"From who?" Chevalier hissed.

"I don't know. I'm sorry I kept it from you, but I think they have Quiesco."

Emily poured out the details to Chevalier and Kyle, all the while her inner voice was screaming at her to stop and to take care of it by herself. Her months alone though proved to her how much she needed Chevalier, and she now felt that she didn't want to deal with this by herself.

"I'm afraid he's dead," she said finally.

"We'll figure it out and get him back," Chevalier said, and then smiled and pulled her into a hug. He couldn't explain how much it meant to him that she enlisted his help.

She nodded and looked over at Kyle.

"Just stay dressed in the palace while we investigate," he said, smiling at her. He was still in shock that she told them what was happening.

"I was covered."

He smiled. "You have half of the palace staff scared to death that the Elder's coming after them."

"I was covered!"

"Barely"

Emily looked over Kyle's shoulder when Mark came up behind them. "Nothing yet. He's probably just asleep in some corner somewhere. He's too lazy to run off."

"You can smell him in the palace though, right?"

"No, his smell is all over the building anyway."

She turned and looked down the stalls again, hoping he'd waddle out from a good nap.

"Let's go get you changed," Mark said, moving aside to let Emily pass. She let go of Chevalier and followed her guards into the palace.

Once she changed and got ready to go back down to the stables, Emily grabbed her phone and saw the little green LED flashing. She thumbed through her phone to the waiting text message.

> *Your dog is mine now. Time to run off, princess, or you could be next.*

Emily's heart dropped when she realized that whoever was sending those messages had Quiesco. She couldn't run, not with someone out there threatening her. Up until now, the threats had been hollow and more of an annoyance. She knew she had to tell Chevalier the new information before they killed her dog.

She decided to start by letting him know she wasn't going to take it. Quickly typing in a reply to the text message, she re-read it and then finally pressed send.

> *Treading on dangerous water there, Hoss. Suggest you return my dog and back the hell off.*

The Cavalry fell in behind her when she walked down the stairs, and she noticed they all seemed on high alert.

Derrick smiled when she walked up. "Do you need to talk to the Council?"

"Just Chev," she told him, but couldn't help wringing her hands.

Derrick opened the door and stepped aside.

Emily walked in and immediately headed up the stairs.

"You okay?" Chevalier asked, turning his chair when she walked up behind him.

"He has Quiesco," Emily said, and handed him her phone. She glanced over at Kyle while Chevalier read the brief messages.

"Is that another threat?" Kyle asked.

She nodded and looked down at Chevalier. "So?"

His eyes narrowed. "Can I have your phone for an hour?"

"Yeah, I'm just going out to the stables.

"Don't take your eyes off of her," Chevalier said to her guards.

"Yes, Elder," the closest one said.

Emily hurried out of the council chambers when Chevalier began to explain the newest messages to the Equites Chief Investigator. Things seemed better when she got into the stables. She disappeared into the

tack room and came out with a long brown tube, then called for Gifford, the member of the Cavalry from Thukil.

"What is that?" Horace asked when she started to fill it with warm water.

She smiled. "Artificial vagina."

"Sorry I asked."

Gifford walked around the corner and saw her with the tube. "I'll get the mare and let you know as soon as she urinates in the corral."

Emily nodded and began to rub something into the tube.

"What exactly are you doing to your stallion?" one of the Cavalry asked when Emily slipped a bridle on him.

***

"It's disgusting," Richard hissed. The heku in the trial area was knelt down and had his eyes on the ground ahead of him.

Zohn glared at him. "I vote death."

Chevalier smiled. "Death's too easy…"

"You're saying not to kill him?" It was shocking. Chevalier normally chose to kill the heku.

He shrugged. "I think his time might be best served starving."

"Please…," the heku whispered.

"Why would we show you the lenience that you did not exhibit?" Quinn asked him.

"It was an accident."

"The rape or the murder?" Richard asked.

He shook his head. "It wasn't like that."

"You didn't even drain her. You broke her neck," Chevalier said. "That's not an accident."

"I don't believe there's more serious of an offense," Kyle told him. "To prey on the weaker species is pathetic."

"My vote is 800 years," Chevalier suggested.

"No! I can't… I can't do it," the heku pleaded.

"Why not?"

"I can't be hungry. I can't spend that long suffering!"

Zohn's eyes narrowed. "I concur, 800 years."

"No!" he screamed, and then tried to run. Kyle took his time walking down to the trial area while Derrick held the heku as he struggled.

His screams pierced the palace moments before he fell to ash at Kyle's feet. Kyle swept him into a small leather bag and tucked it away in his cloak.

"It's humiliating to have an Equites do that," Quinn said, still angry.

Chevalier nodded. "He'll learn his lesson."

"What's next?" Zohn asked the Records Keeper.

He glanced at a roster. "The Encala have representatives here."

"Did Emily call them in again?"

"No, Elder."

"Fine… see them in."

Derrick opened the door and allowed William, Andrew, and four of the Encala's palace guards to enter. They moved to stand before the Council.

"We should pre-empt this," Chevalier told them. "Emily's fine."

William smiled. "We have business besides Em, but thanks for the update."

"Very well, what?"

"We've come to seek the return of Jacobs."

"No"

"It's been long enough."

Andrew looked over at Chevalier. "What did he do to deserve being in your prison?"

Chevalier shrugged. "He's an Encala… that's enough."

"That's not enough! We have somewhat of an alliance, and we demand…"

"No, we don't," Kyle interrupted.

Andrew's eyes narrowed. "We've not fought for years."

"Just because Emily considers you friends, doesn't mean we do."

"Is that a threat?"

"No"

"What will it take to get Jacobs' return?" William asked. It was obvious he wasn't in the mood to watch Chevalier and Andrew bicker over Emily again.

Zohn spoke before Chevalier could. "We must put him on trial first, but we're still gathering information."

"What's he even accused of?"

"He was caught in the walls of Shepler Coven."

"Doing?"

"Reconnaissance, I do believe. He had a camera, notebook, and a backpack full of devices to help him perfectly map out that coven."

Andrew glanced at William and then turned to Zohn. "We weren't aware of anyone staking out Shepler."

"It doesn't matter. He was."

"Return him!" William yelled.

Zohn called out to Derrick. "Derrick, please have Emily come immediately."

"I don't need a peacekeeper," William said, irritated.

"We'll resume when she comes in."

Andrew crossed his arms and silently waited for Emily to arrive. It was a few minutes later when Derrick came into the trial area.

"She said she can't at the moment," Derrick said, smiling slightly.

"Did she say why?"

"Something about artificial insemination…" Derrick had barely finished his words when Chevalier and Kyle looked at each other and then disappeared from the room.

Following Mark's suggestion on Emily's location, both arrived in the corral in seconds and then screeched to a halt when they saw Emily and Gifford tag teaming Emily's stallion to gather semen.

Emily looked over when they first appeared. "What?"

Chevalier smiled, sort of embarrassed. "Just… you know… seeing what you're doing."

She glanced over at Gifford as he steadied the false mare. "We're collecting semen. Want to help?"

"Not really."

Kyle chuckled and walked up. "Why are you doing that?"

"Thukil has a racing mare they acquired. We're going to breed these two and see if we can produce faster horses."

Emily pulled the artificial vagina out from under the stallion and stepped back when Gifford got the stallion off of the false mare. She then walked over to Chevalier and looked up at him.

"Why do you look guilty?" she asked him.

He grimaced at the tube and took a step back. "I don't know what you're talking about. We just wondered what you were doing that you couldn't answer a summons."

"Jacking off a horse. Want to go tell the Council that?"

He smiled. "I think I'll just keep that to myself."

Gifford came out and took the tube from Emily and headed into the stables. She walked over and washed her hands.

"So you can come now?" Kyle asked her.

She turned and put her hands on her hips. "Why?"

"The Encala are having attitude issues."

"Who is it?"

"William and Andrew."

Chevalier couldn't help but grow angry when she smiled. "Andrew's here?"

"Well…," Kyle started, but stopped and followed Emily when she headed for the palace doors. Chevalier looked over at the false mare and then followed them inside.

Emily ran up and hugged Andrew when she walked into the trial area, then stepped back and smiled up at him. "What's up? You haven't

been here in ages."

"The Equites have an Encala that we want back," he told her, and then looked up the Equites Council.

"Do I know him?"

"Doubt it," William said. "He's accused of spying on an Equites coven."

She sighed, "You heku and your spies. Can't just leave each other alone, can you?"

He grinned. "What fun would that be?"

"Well, do it anyway."

Andrew's eyes narrowed. "How bad is it?"

Emily glanced up at the Equites Council and then lowered her voice to Andrew, "I'm okay."

"We need a conference room for a moment," Andrew said to Chevalier.

He looked at Emily, and when she shrugged and then hesitantly nodded, he ordered Derrick to show them to a conference room.

Quinn smiled and punched in a number on the speakerphone, and the conference room came onto audio.

"Hey!" William hissed. "That's a private conversation."

"Nothing's private in my palace," Zohn said, amused.

"And it's one-way, so no use trying to warn them," Quinn said.

The Council listened as Andrew and Emily sat down.

"How bad is it?" Andrew asked her again.

"I told you. I'm okay."

"Not what I asked."

"How do you even know?"

"You have on long-sleeves and it's 80 degrees outside."

Emily sighed and slipped the gloves off of her hand. "I'm handling it."

Andrew took her hands and flipped them over and then pushed her long sleeves up to her elbows, exposing the soft side of her forearms. He studied her arms before speaking. "The marks are gone though."

She nodded. "Yes, it was months ago."

"But you still have pain?"

"Some"

"What are you taking for it?"

"Depends on the day I…"

He looked into her eyes. "What?"

"Are you interrogating me?" she snapped, and then tried to pull her hands out of his, but he held tightly.

"No, but I want to know what you're taking for the pain."

"Why?"

"I'm concerned. I can smell medication on your blood."

"Then plug your nose."

"Tell me, please."

She sighed, "This morning was bad, so it's Vicodin."

"Did the Equites force you to take it?"

"No, in fact, I don't think they know I'm on it."

He nodded. "They know. It's pretty strong."

She finally managed to pull her hands away from him and slipped her sleeves down. "It's getting better."

"Did the Valle do it?" he asked, getting angry.

"No, it was the other Council."

"They're dead?"

"That's what I'm told," she said, and then whispered. "You're not using that in your interrogations are you?"

"No, I swore I wouldn't."

"I hate that you're an Interrogator."

"Why? It's fun."

She glared at him. "Torturing poor heku for no good reason isn't fun!"

"I didn't say I tortured them for no good reason. You're trying to make my job into something worse than it is. I get information. That's it."

"It happened though."

"What did?"

"You made the Council and then stopped coming around."

"You are the one that took off for four months. I don't really want to come and visit the Equites Council socially." It irritated her that he was finding this amusing.

"Still... I hate the Councils."

"I know, but I'll be around now that you're back. I was hoping we could start our videoconferencing again."

She smiled. "You just want to check up on me."

He studied her for a moment before speaking. "You're hiding something from me."

"I am not! Stop using your little Interrogator thing on me."

"I'm not using anything on you. It just seems to me like you're not telling me something."

"Can't you turn off that Interrogator crap around me? This is why Interrogators are my least favorite Council members," she whispered harshly.

He grinned. "You just lie too much and hate being caught."

Emily stood up. "We're done here."

"No, we're not. What are you hiding from me?"

"Nothing"

"Is it something the Equites did?"

She just watched him.

"Valle then?"

They had a small stand-off when no one spoke and then Andrew smiled and stood up. "I guess we're done here."

"I guess so," Emily said, and then headed back to the council chambers. Before they arrived, Quinn turned off the speakerphone and the Council waited. They could tell by how Emily walked in that she was irritated, but Andrew seemed amused at the last conversation.

"Everything okay?" Chevalier asked her.

"Fine," she said, and sat down beside him. She watched as William said something quietly to Andrew, who then turned to glare at the Council.

"I think we're done here," Zohn said. "We will put Jacobs on trial within the month and let you know its outcome."

"Call me tonight," Andrew said to Emily before leaving with the other Encala.

"Call me tonight," Emily mimicked.

Chevalier chuckled. "Problems?"

"Yeah, he's an Interrogator now… so he's on my list."

"List?" Richard asked.

She stood up and looked at him. "Yeah, you're on it too."

He just smiled.

"Em, you have a helicopter landing from Thukil?" Kyle asked.

"Oh! I have sperm for them," she said, and then ran out of the room.

Zohn and Quinn looked over at Chevalier.

"She's working with Thukil to breed a faster horse."

"She does the strangest things," Zohn said, laughing.

"How do I get off of this list?" Richard asked them.

Chevalier shrugged. "Tomorrow the list will change."

***

Emily headed up the stairs after a long day with three of Thukil's Generals. They wanted to see her racing stallion in action and then ended up doing patrols with the Council City Cavalry until late into the night. Exhausted, she went into the room as her guards took up their post outside of the door.

She immediately saw the manila envelope sitting on the table beside her dinner. The handwriting was familiar, and her heart constricted in her chest when she realized that her stalker had again gotten into the

bedroom.

With shaky hands, she opened the envelope and pulled out Quiesco's collar along with a dozen photographs of Emily sleeping in the bed. She gasped. The stalker was now watching her sleep.

Emily studied a photograph and then walked over to the bed, trying to determine if the room had a camera in it. From the distance and angle, she followed the point-of-view to a wall she had with a painting of each of the kids. She carefully removed each picture and looked along the frame and backing. It was on the back of Dain's picture that she found the tiny camera.

"Redecorating?" Chevalier asked from behind her.

She showed him the camera. "I'm under surveillance."

He hissed and took the pictures off of the table.

Emily looked over when the Chief Investigator came in and immediately began going through the pictures.

"What did you find on her phone?" Chevalier asked him.

The Investigator handed Emily her phone and then addressed his Elder. "The phone is one of those pay by the minute numbers. No way to trace it."

"Search this room. I want to know if there are more cameras."

"Yes, Elder," he said, and Emily watched as a team of heku entered and began tearing the room apart.

"Let's go to my office," Chevalier said, taking Emily's hand.

She nodded and followed him down, then sat in a chair across from his desk.

He leaned against his desk in front of her. "Do you want to talk about Andrew?"

"Not really."

"Did you call him?"

"No, I got busy with Thukil."

He nodded and then grinned and pinned her to the wall. When his lips met hers, the camera was forgotten.

Chapter 27

Emily smiled. "We'll only be gone for a few hours."

Chevalier's eyes narrowed as he looked over Emily and Alexis. "I don't like it. If you're so hell bent against guards, then I'll go."

"We don't want you to go either," Alexis said, and then took a step back when he looked at her.

Emily moved between them. "We're just going to talk, nothing more, but we can't do it with grumpy old men watching."

"Grumpy old men?"

"That'd be you."

He smiled and shook his head. "I got that. Fine... but check in every hour, or I'll send the Cavalry out."

"How sad it is, that that's not just an expression," Alexis said as she followed Emily out to the Rubicon.

Once settled in, they set off for the city and Emily drove while Alexis watched out the window.

"Oh, set the alarm on my phone for every hour," Emily told her daughter. "We don't need Mark showing up in the middle of this."

Alexis nodded and then began fiddling with Emily's phone. "Just talk though, right?"

"Yes, we need to know what's involved."

"I can't believe we're doing this."

"There's no commitment, just talk."

"I was shocked that you told Dad. I figured you'd tell him we were shopping or something."

Emily couldn't help but grin. "I've done that before. They're on to it."

"Not with me! I obey the Council," Alexis reminded her.

"You didn't used to."

"Well... no... but that got you shot, remember? Why exactly is Dad letting us do this when the Council said no to adoption?"

"He said it won't hurt just to go ask questions. Between you and me, I think he's hoping they talk you out of it."

Alexis nodded and looked out the window.

"Here we are," Emily said. They both looked up at the sheer face of the twelve story business complex. After finding a parking spot, Emily and Alexis headed inside to the fourth floor, where a small office with 'Melissa Quick, Adoption Attorney' was written on the door.

Alexis took a deep breath and walked inside, followed by Emily.

"Good morning. Can I help you?" a young woman asked from the reception desk.

"Yes, I have an appointment. I'm Emily Winchester," she said.

The woman looked over Emily and Alexis and then smiled.

"Have a seat. Ms. Quick will be right out."

Emily nodded and both of them sat down, obviously a bit nervous about the meeting. They were starting to get irritated when, 45 minutes later, an older woman came out of the office.

"Emily?" she asked, putting her hand out.

Emily shook her hand. "Yes."

"Come into my office."

Alexis swallowed hard and followed her mom into the cluttered office of the adoption attorney.

"Have a seat, please," Melissa said, and then sat down behind a large oak desk.

Emily sat down and took a deep breath. "We're just here to see about adopting a baby."

Four hours later, Emily and Alexis crawled back into the Jeep, and Alexis frowned at a single white rose sitting on the dashboard. "Oh no! Dad came anyway."

Emily reached out and took the card, and put it into her purse. "No he didn't. That's not from your dad."

"Who is it from?"

"You can keep a secret?" Emily asked, looking over at her daughter.

Alexis nodded. "Of course."

"It's someone threatening me."

"Do what?!"

Emily shrugged. "He leaves these envelopes and notes with flowers usually, and they contain threats."

"What kind of threats?"

"Pretty harmless… except he took Quiesco."

"So that's where the dog went. Let me guess though, you haven't told Dad."

"He knows."

"You told him?!"

"Yes"

Alexis sat back and thought for a moment. "You've changed."

"How so?"

"Six months ago you wouldn't have told Dad and would have just handled it on your own."

"Maybe I'm tired of doing it all on my own. It doesn't seem to be stopping, and I'm tired."

"It's good you told Dad."

"Well, don't tell Garrett. I don't want anyone else to know."

"Why not?"

"I just don't. The Council is enough."

"But they followed us today. That's scary."

"No, creepy maybe, but not scary. Just remember, keep that from Garrett."

Alexis began sifting through the mountain of paperwork the attorney had given them.

"Can we get Chinese food?" Emily asked as she pulled out of the parking lot.

"Sure, I'll call Dad and let him know."

It was a few minutes later before Alexis was connected to Chevalier. "Dad, we're going out for dinner and then we'll be back."

"Where?" he asked, sounding short and a bit irritated.

"I don't know. What's wrong?"

"Nothing, just be careful."

"Always," she said, and then smiled and hung up. "Must have had a bad day."

"Why's that?" Emily asked.

"He's grouchy."

"As opposed to…"

"Okay, so he's grouchier."

"I'll talk to him when we get back," Emily said. She pulled into the Chinese restaurant across from the heku's donor bar and cut the engine.

Alexis looked back at the bar. "Can't we pick another Chinese place?"

"This one has the best egg rolls though."

"I guess it's okay."

Emily glanced at the bar after getting out of the Jeep. "I'm sure we'll be okay."

"I know we will. I just hate that bar."

"Why?"

"Garrett goes there sometimes."

Emily shrugged. "A heku's got to eat."

"I don't know why he won't just feed off of me," Alexis snapped, and then headed into the Chinese Restaurant.

Emily was shocked and finally followed her inside, and they sat down in the booth across from her. "Does Garrett feed from you?"

"Sometimes," Alexis said, as she thumbed through the menu.

Emily's eyes grew wide. "You let him?"

"Of course! He wouldn't do it if I said no."

"But…"

Alexis put the menu down. "Mom, I don't mind… in fact… I kind of think it's a good way to relax after a stressful day. It's kind of, well, erotic too."

Emily wrinkled her nose. "No, it's not."

"You should really give it a go when no one's attacking you."

"No thanks," Emily said, and then turned to the waitress. "Lemon Chicken please, with an extra egg roll."

The waitress turned to Alexis, and she handed her the menus. "Same for me."

Once the waitress left, Emily leaned forward. "I can't believe you let him do that."

Alexis shrugged. "Why not? It's soothing."

"It's disgusting!"

"Not with someone you love."

"Still…"

"It's not disgusting."

Emily took Alexis' hands and flipped them over to examine the soft side of her wrists. "Does it hurt?"

"No, and he doesn't use my wrists."

She put her daughter's hands down and shook her head. "I'm not sure I like that."

"Why not? It's my choice. I love him, and I like it."

Emily frowned and took a drink of ice water as she thought about it.

Alexis finally broke the silence. "What did you think about our meeting?"

Emily looked up at her. "If it's what you want, then I'll do it."

"I don't know though. It's not the same as having one."

"Alex…"

"You don't have to tell me. I just don't know if it's worth it."

"That'll be your call. You heard her. It's not that easy to get a newborn."

"With the right money though, she said we can pre-arrange one."

"There's that. I have enough money that you can go that route."

"I'd rather Garrett and I pay for it."

"Does he have that kind of money?" Emily asked, somewhat impressed.

Alexis shook her head. "No. He's not old enough to have that kind of stockpile."

"I thought he wasn't going to go along with this anyway."

"True"

They both watched the waitress deliver their food, and Emily began to eat while Alexis just moved the food around on her plate.

"You're not going to eat?" Emily asked.

"I will… I hate it though. If I didn't get really tired after a few days of no mortal food, I wouldn't do it."

"I know, but you do… so eat up."

Alexis took a tentative bite and then grimaced as the slippery food

slid down her throat.

Emily grinned and took another bite.

After a few minutes, Alexis frowned. "So what's the note say today?"

"Oh, forgot about that," Emily said as she dug in her purse. She pulled out the plain white envelope with her name on it and dug out the paper. "It says… *Tired of the half-breeds and trying for a full mortal this time? Seems you've had enough brats, but who am I to judge?*"

Alexis's frown deepened. "So this person knows where we went."

"They seem to know everything I do."

"Meaning?"

"Meaning they watch me sleep, know when I'm working with the horses, or swimming…"

"Mom, this is bad!"

"Between your dad and me, we'll figure it out."

"Is that all you ladies want?" the waitress asked.

Emily nodded and then paid the bill. They gathered their purses and headed back out to the Jeep. Halfway there, they heard a soft hiss from behind them. Emily and Alexis looked at each other before turning slowly to see the source.

Four heku were standing behind them, all crouched slightly and smelling at the air.

Emily shook her head. "Seriously?"

Alexis fought the urge to meet their crouch, but instead, she sighed, "You cannot be that stupid."

The closest heku smiled and watched the vein in Emily's neck. "Two girls out unprotected… they smell so sweet."

Emily crossed her arms. "Don't be stupid. You're not feeding from us."

"You think, sweetheart?" he asked, and his tense body moved closer.

"Do you know who we are?" Alexis asked, irritated.

The heku furthest from them nodded. "Yes… you're too beautiful women left out here with no one to help you."

"Two beautiful Winchesters," Alexis corrected. "You missed that part."

Emily just nodded but watched the closest one carefully.

"Winchesters?" he asked, and stood up slowly. "What's that?"

"Where have you been?" Alexis asked.

"Away… we were unjustly imprisoned for the last 400… erm, 40 years."

"Ahh, that explains it. Well let me give you the crash course," Emily said. "The crash course is… try to feed from me, and I'll turn you

to ash."

He grinned, seemingly unafraid. "You don't know what you're talking about, so don't worry your pretty head about that."

Emily turned to Alexis just as the four heku dropped to their knees in agony. "What should we do with them?"

Alexis shrugged and watched their faces. "Well... we could take them for the Cavalry to play with. Garrett said the Cavalry Leaders were concerned about the lack of real-world training lately."

"Really?" Emily asked, and then glanced at the four heku.

"This'd be perfect... course... then Dad'll know that we were attacked while out."

"We weren't attacked, just threatened," Emily said. She let the heku out of their pain and cleared her throat. "So now that you know I don't need a Chief Enforcer, you can either get in the Jeep over there... or turn to ash."

"We... we can't...," one of them gasped. "We're unfactioned."

"Oh right, and we are supposed to kill unfactioned."

"No! Wait...," he said. "Please, they'll kill us."

"I'll kill you," Alexis said. Emily looked over with wide eyes and was amazed at the sudden evil that shrouded her daughter's beautiful features.

"Alex," Emily whispered.

"So there's the deal. Get in the car, or I'll tear you apart myself."

Emily turned and saw the four heku crawl into the Jeep, and she walked over and got into the driver's side.

When Alexis sat down, her face had returned to the sweet beauty that Emily was used to. Alexis saw her mom looking strangely at her. "What?"

"You were mad."

"Yeah, so?"

"I... I haven't... I guess seen you that way."

"I have very good control of it."

"Where are we going?" one of the heku asked from the back seat. He had regained enough strength to sit up.

Emily put the Jeep into drive and left the parking lot. "We're going to see how my husband is doing."

"How do you even know about us?" he asked, frowning.

Alexis smiled at him. "What do you make of me?"

His eyes narrowed. "You have an odd scent... a mixture..."

"Interesting"

"Who are you?" he asked, starting to panic.

"Us? Nobody important."

"Oh man, she has an essence ring!" one of them yelled when they

looked up at Emily.

Alexis smiled. "Okay, so maybe we are somebody important."

He tensed when Emily pulled into the private drive leading to Council City. "What?! We can't... they'll kill us!"

Emily shrugged. "I doubt it. I'll ask them not to."

"You may wish they would though," Alexis told them.

"Is this a joke?! How do you even know about this city?"

"We live here," Emily said as she slowed down for the gate guards.

One of them walked over to the Jeep and looked inside. "What did you find?"

Emily rolled down the window. "Four unfactioned."

The back door flew open, and the four heku blurred from the back of the Jeep. Before Emily even knew the Cavalry was close, four heku blew past them on horses, following the running unfactioned.

"Who was that?" Emily asked as they disappeared around the bend in the road.

"Silas, Garrett, Tiamen, and Luke," Alexis said.

"I hate that... I'm half heku. Why can't I see that?"

"Mom..."

Emily turned to see what Alexis was watching and saw Mark standing in front of the Jeep with his arms crossed, looking unhappy.

She sighed, "What? I didn't do anything wrong."

"I'll meet you in the garage," he snapped, and then disappeared.

"How can he be mad?" Emily asked Alexis.

"I don't know..., but he is."

"But I didn't do anything!"

"Just take the Jeep in and let's see."

Emily nodded and put the Jeep in gear after checking over her shoulder again. Once in the garage, she hid the adoption papers in the glove box and stepped out to face Mark and Kralen, who were waiting by the door.

"You can't get mad at me. I didn't do anything," she said, leaning back against the Jeep.

Alexis stood beside her. "Dad knew we were out."

"That's not the problem," Kralen said. "The Council wants to see you."

Emily looked up at the ceiling.

"Mom, let's just go see what they want," Alexis whispered.

"Not you, Alex. They just want to talk to Emily," Kralen told her.

Emily finally looked over at them. "Chev said that?"

"Elder Chevalier's not here right now," Mark said, irritated.

"So the rest of the Council wants me?"

"Yes"

"Then send Kyle here."

"Kyle's out with the Elder."

She started to panic. "I didn't do anything wrong though."

"Alex?" Garrett said from behind them.

Alexis turned and took his hand, and they left together as Emily watched Mark and Kralen. They both moved aside so she could walk into the palace, but she stayed by the Jeep.

Derrick appeared after a few minutes. "The Council said you aren't in trouble. They just want to ask you a question."

Emily hesitated and then sighed and started forward. "Fine."

"Did you want to bring the rose?" Kralen asked.

Emily glanced at the single white rose on her dashboard before reaching in and grabbing it. She then deposited the rose into the first trash bin she came to.

Derrick smiled at them and opened the door to the council chambers when they arrived.

Emily walked forward and looked up at Zohn. "I'm here."

He looked down at her, and even though she wasn't supposed to be in trouble, he seemed mad. "The Cavalry has advised us of your four passengers."

"Okay"

"Do you know who they are?"

"No"

"Did you go into the city after them?"

Her eyes narrowed. "Why would I go into the city after four heku that I don't know?"

"Did you?"

"No"

Quinn put his hand out to stop Zohn's questioning and then forced himself to calm down. "Where did you find them?"

"At the Chinese Restaurant," Emily said, and then glanced at the door before turning back. "When's Chev going to be back?"

"Soon... and you had no idea who they are?"

"None"

"Very well, you may go."

"So who are they?"

Richard studied her and then spoke, "They used to be Equites palace guards before they began a mutiny against the Council 416 years ago."

She frowned. "Okay, then they were banished."

"Yes. They revived two weeks ago, and we've been trying to find them since."

"You seem to lose a lot of prisoners."

"Not a lot, no. They weren't kept in the Ancient's room. They

were too low profile. Then they disappeared."

"Oh, well… there you go," she said, smiling.

"It's disturbing that they found you," Quinn said.

"To say the least," Zohn agreed.

"Not my fault," Emily reminded them.

"Still, they could easily have killed you."

"I'm not that easy to kill."

"Yes, you are… and…" Zohn looked up when Chevalier and Kyle walked into the trial area.

"What's up?" Chevalier asked as he walked up to Emily.

"Emily brought the four Ahabe followers back from the city," Richard told her.

He lightly kissed the top of her head. "Appreciate you grabbing them for us."

She frowned and looked up at him. "You aren't mad?"

Kyle chuckled and took his spot on the council stand.

"No, why would I be?" Chevalier asked.

"I didn't go out looking for them."

"I know."

She watched him walk up and sit down casually in his seat.

Zohn frowned and looked at Chevalier. "How can you not be upset?"

"That Em found our banished?"

"Yes… while out alone…"

"She can handle them herself."

"But…"

"No, she can take care of herself," Chevalier said again, and then turned to Emily. "Did you find out what you wanted?"

She nodded, still not sure what was going on.

"Did you need anything?"

"No… I guess not." Emily watched him for a few seconds and then quickly left the trial area.

***

Emily rolled over and clutched tightly to her pillow. She was so comfortable, that she didn't want to fully wake up, but a slight sound startled her, and she sat up suddenly and looked around the tiny oubliette. The past four days came flooding back to her, and she laid down and stared up at the door on the ceiling.

"Chev?" she called out, and waited for him to arrive. She ran over what had happened during the previous four days and mostly remembered turning almost all of the Cavalry to ash before being tackled

by Silas. He immediately began to feed, and she relaxed and finally fell asleep with the help of Dr. Edwards.

Chevalier's face appeared in the small window. "You called for me?"

She sighed and looked over at him. "How mad's the Cavalry?"

His face disappeared from the tiny window and almost instantly appeared above her as he dropped down into the oubliette. "Not really mad. They know you don't mean it."

"Still... I think I made them suffer a bit first," she told him.

He chuckled. "Yes, you did. They aren't mad though."

"I can't keep doing this."

"Do you want to call in Mitch?" he asked, and then sat down beside her and took her hand.

"Not really. This wasn't hypnosis... this was good, old fashioned, heku mind control."

"We are..."

Emily leaned up on her elbow. "There's no we. I want you to do it."

"What if it makes things worse?"

"I can't keep this up. One of these times I will ash the city."

He nodded. "I know. This one wasn't as bad though. You seemed to have doubts from the start."

"I did?"

"Yes, when you spoke about Sotomar... you paused, and it was almost as if you doubted what you were saying."

She sighed, "I guess."

"Let's just wait. I don't want to end up scrambling your mind to fix this."

Chevalier held out his hand and Emily took it and stood up. He kissed her softly and then blurred her up to the bedroom.

"Someone's been calling your cell phone," he said as he opened the thick blinds covering the windows. "We didn't answer it, figured it would be Andrew."

"Maybe," she said, and thumbed through her messages. One made her heart threaten to stop,

> *I love to hear you cursing out the Equites and defending the Valle. Soon, you'll do that all of the time. It'll be like at the top of Joe's... remember, Emi?*

"You okay?" Chevalier asked as he watched her.

"It's Chuck."

"The threats?"

Emily nodded. "He knows about the re-memory surfacing again."

"It's a lot easier now that we know who it is."

"But he has to have someone in the palace. I have an idea on how to find out who."

"Is it dangerous?"

"No"

He smiled. "Let me know what you find."

She nodded and watched Chevalier leave and then flipped open her laptop. Once she connected, she opened up her e-mail and replied to an ongoing message from Charles.

> *I'll never swear allegiance to the Valle. You know me better than that. I don't give in. Now stop the childish threatening shit and leave me alone! I haven't involved the entire faction, but if you don't knock it off, then I will have to. ~Emily*

After re-reading the message a few times, she sent it and then deleted all of the e-mails she'd gotten so far. Now she sat down to consider Chevalier's blasé attitude about her encountering four dangerous heku. It wasn't her fault, and she did handle it on her own, but she fully expected him to yell and threaten to lock her up.

Finally shrugging, she decided her time would be best spent figuring out how Charles was able to get the notes into the palace and how he knew everything about her day. The place to start would be with the floor guards. No one got to the fifth floor without the stair guards seeing them.

The four Cavalry fell in behind her when she went to the fifth floor foyer. She saw the two strange guards and walked over to them, trying to look casual, though her four guards found it odd and watched her carefully.

"How's it going?" Emily asked, smiling at the closest stair guard.

He looked over at the highest member of the Cavalry with Emily.

"They aren't authorized to speak to you," he explained.

"Oh, well I'm on the Council, and I'm authorizing it," she told them.

The member of the Cavalry shrugged and finally nodded. "Fine… you can talk."

"It's going fine, Lady Emily," the stair guard said nervously.

"Can I ask something?"

"Yes, M'Lady."

"Have you seen anyone come to the fifth floor lately that is maybe new?"

"No, M'Lady."

"No one? Maybe a new cleaning person, or a new guard?"

"No, M'Lady."

The closest member of the Cavalry looked over at her. "It takes a lot to get onto the fifth floor. The Council is very particular about who is allowed."

"Even a trusted guard or servant then," Emily said. "But maybe new to the palace?"

"No, M'Lady."

"What's going on?" Mark asked as she ascended the stairs.

Emily sighed. She should have known Mark would be called. "Nothing, just visiting with the stair guards."

"About?"

"Stuff"

"No, about access to the fifth floor."

"Is this about why you've been jumpy lately?" one of the Cavalry asked her.

"I'm not jumpy."

Mark studied her and then turned to the stair guards. "Go back to your duties."

They both bowed and returned to looking down toward the fourth floor.

Emily thought quickly. "I'm probably jumpy because I keep slipping back into Valle mode. I'm sorry about the ashing thing."

Mark couldn't help but smile. "We're just going to keep a closer eye on you. One sign of... what you call Valle mode, and we'll take care of it."

"You mean bite me."

"Yes, bite you."

"Why don't you carry sedatives or something? I hate to get bitten."

Mark grinned. "Our way is always accessible."

"And gross," Emily told him before heading back up to the bedrooms. She grabbed her laptop and decided to set up a small surveillance of her own. With a few more supplies, she walked out of her room and into the Elder Guard's room that was right across from hers.

"You aren't moving again, are you?" Horace asked from behind her.

She glanced up. "When did you get called?"

"I didn't... it's my shift."

"No, I'm not moving in here. I want to try something."

He watched her set up the laptop and then secure a webcam to the top of it, facing her bedroom door.

"This looks like you're putting surveillance on your bedroom."

She smiled and adjusted the camera. "I'm not. Why would I do that?"

Once she hid the camera behind a stack of pillows and set it up to record continuously, she stood up, looked around the room, and walked out, leaving both doors open.

Horace walked over to look at the laptop, but she had already blacked out the screen. After deciding nothing was illegal about recording your own bedroom, he walked out to see where they were going, easily catching up with Emily and her guards in the foyer.

***

"Send a team then," Kyle suggested as he looked along the row of Council.

Zohn shrugged. "It's none of our concern if the Valle are having internal problems."

"They aren't responding to our requests though," Quinn told him. "We have to know why. If they're being quiet because they're too busy planning an Equites war, then we have to know."

"It's not uncommon for the Valle to ignore us though."

"True, but I got the impression from the last meeting that something was happening," Richard said. His innate ability to know when someone was lying to him solidified his place as Equites Chief Interrogator.

Chevalier sat back in his chair. "At first, I thought it was because they had the four Ahabe followers and didn't want to give them back. Now though, I wonder what's up."

The Faction Liaison Officer turned to the Elders. "I could go and see what I can find out."

Zohn shook his head. "I don't think we should send anyone. Our sources say that it's an internal Valle issue that's creating the delay in responding to our request."

"If our sources are wrong, then the Valle could be stockpiling an army."

"We have nothing else?" Chevalier asked. "All they say is that it's internal?"

Quinn shrugged. "The messages we get from inside are always cryptic."

"Then let's pull out one of our spies and get answers."

"We want to break a hundred years of infiltration just to find out that the Valle Council is having a spat?"

Chevalier sighed, "No, I guess not. I would assume if the Valle were planning an attack, that our spies would let us know."

"They have in the past."

"Double the gate guards, just in case," Kyle said. Mark nodded and disappeared from the trial area to carry out the orders.

"Should we get the Ahabe followers out of the way?" the Court Reporter asked.

Quinn nodded. "Let's do. They are causing problems in the prison, and still trying to stage a mutiny, even after 400 years."

"It's not often that banishment doesn't cure a heku's appetite for criminal activity."

"Bring them in," Chevalier said to Derrick. It was almost 20 minutes later when eight prison guards wrestled the four heku into the trial area.

"What took so long?" Zohn asked them.

"They keep fighting us," one of the prison guards said as he forced one of the prisoners to his knees.

"Stay then. I don't feel like tackling them every time they make a break for it," Kyle said.

The prison guards nodded and stood behind the four on their knees.

The Court Reporter stood and addressed the Council. "Ryder, Crow, Gessop, and Lance were banished 416 years ago for attempting to mutiny the Council at the time. They were sentenced to 400 years banishment. When they revived a few weeks ago, they were immediately sought out to destroy as unfactioned. Lady Emily encountered them and brought them to us, where they ran from the Cavalry. The Cavalry caught up easily and imprisoned them, to be killed. Once in prison awaiting execution, they tried to rally the prison guards and all prisoners to mutiny against us again."

When the Court Reporter sat down, the Records Keeper passed around thick file folders full of information on the four heku. Each member of the Council began looking through the files while the council chambers remained completely silent.

After almost four hours of reading, they finished, and Zohn looked down at them. "How is it that after 400 years of suffering, you still want to banish us?

"Because we want the Equites to be the strongest faction," the Leader of the four snapped.

"We are," Zohn told him.

"No, you aren't! The Equites are big. That doesn't mean they are the strongest."

"We're the strongest and the largest."

"You have a mortal living here!"

Chevalier smiled. "I love how we're weak because of Emily, yet the factions fight to get her."

"They don't fight because she makes you strong," the heku said,

irritated. "They fight to get her, to get to you."

"Yet she burned you…"

"Someone did. I suspect the Chief Enforcer was there."

"Did you see me?" Kyle asked.

"No, you were hiding."

Chevalier sat back, smiling.

"Emily aside, we're still the strongest faction, and trying to stage a mutiny is a serious offense," Zohn said.

"I vote to kill them," Chevalier said calmly. "Apparently banishment didn't work."

"You can't kill us!" one of them yelled. "We're the Equites' only chance to come back to power."

"This from someone who was arrested by a mortal," Kyle chuckled.

"We were not! You were there. Don't try to deny it."

Quinn studied them. "Were all of you involved in trying to incite a riot in the prison and enlist the prison guards to let you stage a mutiny?"

The four looked at each other, but none spoke.

One of the prison guards kneed the leader in the back and then spoke, "They all four were working on it, Elder."

"Very well, then I vote death also," Quinn said.

Zohn nodded. "Death."

Kyle was just standing up when the four sprung to their feet and began a fight with the eight prison guards. Kyle sat back down, smiling, and watched the prison guards tear the mutinous heku to pieces. Once done, the prison guards moved up to stand before the Elders, all looking elated and excited to go tell the other guards about the small fight.

"You can't go in there…," Derrick said quickly.

"No, it's okay," Emily said as she walked into the council chambers. Her eyes grew wide at the carnage in the trial area, and she backed up suddenly to get farther away from part of a skull that sat on the blood-stained ground ahead of her.

"Em…," Chevalier said, instantly beside her.

She swallowed hard, cringing at a hand that was mangled and tossed off to the side. "What happened?"

He took her hand and led her through the mass of body parts to the Council's seats, where she sat down and looked at the blood covered guards. They shifted nervously and tried to pick pieces of heku from their clothing in a feeble attempt at cleaning up.

"Feel better?" she asked them, somewhat still in shock.

"Yes, Lady Emily," one of them said with a grin.

"Who was it?"

"The four hek…" He stopped suddenly when Chevalier glared at him.

"Which four heku?" Emily asked, looking up at Chevalier.

He sighed, "The four recently un-banished."

"The ones I brought you?!"

Chevalier nodded.

She looked around at the body parts again. "I think I told them I wouldn't let you kill them."

"I didn't know that," he said softly.

"Maybe I'm wrong… but… does it have to be so bloody?"

One of the prison guards stifled a grin and turned away to look at the butchery behind him.

"No, it doesn't," Zohn said. "However, they tried to run."

Chevalier took Emily's arm when she turned a slight shade of green. "Are you okay?"

"It's just… making me sick to my stomach," she whispered, staring at a nose on the floor in front of them.

"Are you pregnant?" Zohn asked suddenly.

She turned and frowned at him. "No."

He smiled. "Not an invalid question."

"I'm not always pregnant."

"Coulda fooled us," Kyle said jokingly.

She started to make a snide remark but thought speaking may actually make her throw up. When she began to pale, Chevalier chuckled and pulled her up to standing. "Let's go before you vomit."

"It's… so…," she whispered and then followed him out.

Quinn grinned and called for the trial area to be cleaned up and then released the Council for the day.

Zohn and Quinn started up for their rooms and decided to stop and see if Emily was feeling better. Chevalier was knelt beside the bed, while Emily sat on the bed and talked to him.

Zohn knocked, and both of them walked in when Chevalier told them to.

"Are you feeling better?" Quinn asked, smiling down at Emily. She was still slightly pale but was no longer a sickening green.

"Yes, that was disgusting."

"Derrick did ask that you not come in," Zohn reminded her.

Before Emily could start to argue with Zohn, Chevalier nodded toward the table by the fire. "You seem to have a note."

Emily looked over and then quickly got up and grabbed it.

"Anyone we know?" Zohn asked, frowning.

"Just another threat," she said, and shoved the note into her pocket.

"Not going to read it?"

"Nope"

Chevalier stood up. "Let's all go out riding."

"All of us?" Quinn asked, shocked.

Emily smiled. "He's afraid to go riding with me. The last time, I ditched him and got chased by all three factions before being taken down by Thukil."

Quinn chuckled. "I'm not afraid though."

"I haven't been on a horse in years," Zohn said. "I'll go."

"As will I," Quinn said, and then followed the group down into the stables.

"Is there a problem, Elders?" Silas asked when all three walked into the stables with Emily.

"No, we're going riding though… apparently," Zohn said, and then turned to Emily as she gathered the bridles.

"How many Cavalry do you want to go?"

Zohn turned to Emily. "Em?"

She thought for a moment. "How many usually accompany the Elders out on a field day?"

Silas chuckled. "I don't think the Elders have ever taken a field day."

"I don't think we need Cavalry," Emily said as she handed Quinn the reins to a horse.

Kyle came in and laughed. "They're with you, Em. You're walking trouble."

"I am not!" she said, and then tossed a bridle to him. "Wanna go?"

"Sure," he said before disappearing in to get his horse. Twenty minutes later, they were all saddled and ready to head out.

Emily looked over when she heard horses riding closer and saw Mark ride up with most of the Cavalry.

"We don't need that many guards," Emily told him.

He smiled. "You're walking trouble. Of course you do."

"Oh my God! I am not."

"We're here to guard the Elders and Chief Enforcer, not you," Mark said, amused. "You have to fend for yourself."

She smiled and kicked her horse into a slow walk. "True, they are kind of wimpy."

Chapter 28

Emily finally had a moment to herself. She wasn't sure, but she was suspicious that, for some reason, the Cavalry was told not to leave her alone anymore. She hadn't had one second to herself, and she wanted to check out the video feed from the laptop from when she got the last note the week before. Since that note, she hadn't heard from Charles.

Once locked in her office, she put her coffee down on her desk and fired up the computer. There were gigs and gigs of video files. The webcam had run continuously on her door for the past week. In just a few minutes, she pulled up the video footage of the day she received the last note, starting with when she left the bedroom for the morning.

She sat back with her coffee as the video played in fast-forward. It wasn't until hours later that she saw a lone figure knock on the bedroom door and then kneel down. She slowed the video and watched as the lock to their bedroom was picked, and someone walked in. He quickly put a note on the table, and just as he turned to leave, Emily caught a clear picture of his face. She didn't know him but had seen the heku in the palace before.

Once she was sure of who she was looking for, she left her office, Cavalry in tow, and went down to the first floor of the palace. Without a word, she began walking up and down the halls, stopping at each servant and studying them before moving on.

She'd always seen this particular heku on the main floor, so once she looked through all of the servants, she started over again, knowing that shift changes were scattered for security, and there was always a new heku to find. The Cavalry kept quiet, never asking what she was doing, but she knew her actions had to have gotten back to the Council.

After rounding the corner and heading toward the kitchen again, Emily saw him. He glanced up nervously from a corner he was mopping and then turned back to his cleaning. Emily took a deep breath, not sure what she was going to do exactly, and walked up to him.

"Excuse me," she said, stopping behind him.

He looked up nervously at the Cavalry.

"Don't look at them. I'm the one talking to you."

He finally nodded and went back to mopping.

Emily sighed, "Stop cleaning. I need to talk to you in private."

"Why?" Horace asked from behind her. She turned at the strange voice and wondered when Horace had been called in.

"Because I need to talk to him alone."

He smiled. "Why?"

"I just do," she told him, and then turned to the servant. "You and I need to have a chat."

The servant glanced nervously at Emily and slowly nodded.

"Start talking then," Horace said, crossing his arms.

"Not here," Emily said. "We'll meet in the conference room."

Horace finally nodded. "Sure, go ahead."

Emily started for the nearest conference room but had to stop and wait for the heku servant, who seemed to be hesitating and not in any hurry to be alone with her.

"Walk faster," Horace snapped at him.

The servant jerked slightly and then caught up with them. When Emily walked into the conference room, Horace stepped in also and shut the door.

"No, out," Emily said to him as the servant nervously sat down.

"No, why?" Horace asked.

"Because I'm on the Council, and I said so."

He smiled. "That doesn't work with me."

"Chevalier knows I'm doing this, so I'm on my own."

His eyes narrowed. "I'll be right outside the door." It was more directed toward the heku servant than to Emily. Horace eyed them both and then stepped out and shut the door.

Emily looked at the servant and then sat across from him. "What's your name?"

"Farmer," he whispered, looking down at the desk.

"Your name is Farmer?"

"Yes"

"Why?"

"Ma'am?" He looked up at her, confused.

"Never mind... why are you delivering notes from a Valle to me?"

"I'm not."

"Yes, you are," she said, starting to get angry. "Don't lie to me! Are you a Valle spy?"

He gulped. "No."

"Then why are you delivering notes from a Valle? Threatening notes, I might add."

"I'm not... only the one... it came to the farmhouse for you, and I just delivered it," he said as his eyes darted around the room.

"That's a lie. You picked the lock and delivered a threatening note from a Valle. Either fess up what's going on, or I call for Horace."

"No! Listen... I can't tell you, or they'll kill me."

Emily glared at him. "Tell me, or I'll kill you too."

"I can't..."

"I'm tired of this. Charles and I have a long history of distrust and not a lot of love between us. I'm tired of getting threatened, and I want my dog back," she told him.

He swallowed hard again and his hands began to shake. "I…"

"Let's start like this. You're a Valle spy."

He nodded slightly.

"You've been here for how long?"

"Seventy three years," he whispered.

"So Charles asked you to deliver the notes to me…"

"No, not Charles."

"Who then?"

"The Council… asked…"

Emily nodded. "Sotomar is in on it?"

He nodded.

"What are they hoping to accomplish?"

He sighed, knowing either way he went, he was a dead heku. "I'm to make sure you come out to the Durango next Friday night at midnight to retrieve your dog and to confront Charles."

After thinking it over, she nodded. "Fine. Next Friday night I'll meet up with Charles at the Durango."

"And what about me?" he asked timidly.

Emily smiled. "Horace?"

The heku Commander opened the door and stepped in. "Yes?"

"He's a Valle spy… do whatever you want with him," Emily said, smiling.

"What?! I helped you!" Farmer said suddenly, his eyes fearful.

"Valle spy?" Horace asked angrily, and took a step forward.

"No! She's… she's lying… she just wants to get me into trouble."

"Spy," Emily said again and then walked out of the room. She was a little afraid the heku might tear the spy apart, and she didn't want to see that kind of bloodshed again.

Horace grabbed the servant by the collar on his shirt and roughly pulled him up to the council chambers.

Derrick saw them coming and took the prisoner from the Commander. "What's this about?"

"Lady Emily said he's a Valle spy," Horace told him.

"I'm not!" the heku screamed.

Derrick shrugged and opened the door. He forcibly pushed the heku to his knees before the curious Council.

"What's up, Derrick?" Kyle asked him.

Derrick moved aside and let Horace answer. "Lady Emily was in the conference room with this heku, and now she claims he's a Valle spy."

Chevalier frowned. "Why were you alone in a conference room with her?"

"She… she came to where I was cleaning… and ordered me into a conference room. I'm not a spy! I've been a loyal servant for 73 years."

"Interesting," Richard said, scowling down at him. "He's lying."

"So you are a spy," Chevalier said to him.

"No!"

Richard nodded. "He is."

"How did Emily know?" Kyle asked him.

"She doesn't know anything. I'm not a spy!"

"Ask Emily to come here," Zohn said.

"Belay that," Chevalier countered. He then turned to Zohn. "Let's just figure it out on our own."

He nodded.

"Service records on Farmer," Kyle said.

The Records Keeper disappeared and then returned with a file. "Came to us from the Oahu Coven 73 years ago. Started out as second floor cleaning crew. No commendations, no disciplinary actions, clean record. He was moved to the first floor cleaning crew 17 years ago."

Chevalier thought for a moment. "So he started here before Emily came to the palace. At least he wasn't sent here specifically to spy on her."

"I'm not a spy," Farmer said again, his voice barely a whisper.

"You're lying, so shut up," Richard snapped at him.

***

Emily rolled over and turned off her phone alarm. She looked around the room quickly but saw that Chevalier wasn't there. He knew she was supposed to meet the Valle tonight, so she got up and got dressed to wait for him. It wasn't but ten minutes later when he came in with Kyle and 20 members of the Cavalry.

"Ready?" he asked, looking her over.

She nodded. "I'm still surprised you're letting me do this."

"Of course I am," he said, smiling. "What we're going to do is follow behind you a ways. Don't worry about us. Do what you want, and we'll take over when we feel it's necessary."

"Sounds easy enough," she said, and started down for the stables. Her horse was already waiting for her, and soon, she was riding toward the derelict Durango. A few yards from the clearing, she slipped off the stallion and tied him to a tree. She looked behind her toward the dark forest but saw no indication that the Equites were there.

When she stepped out into the clearing, she saw Charles turn suddenly toward her. There were 18 other Valle in the clearing, and all faced her.

She fought back any fear she felt and crossed her arms, reminding herself that he was the same Chuck Norris that she'd known since

infancy. "Why did you call me out here?"

He glared at her and took a step forward. "You know why. Don't be dim, Emi."

"Well, it's not going to work. I just came to get Quiesco and then I'm heading back."

He grinned. "No, you aren't. You're coming back to the Valle with us."

"Says who?"

"I say so. You're a menace to the heku, and you have to be dealt with."

Her face softened. "Why, Chuck? We were friends until Keith came along. I remember skinny-dipping in the irrigation ditch with you and your brothers."

"That was a long time ago, when I wasn't aware of how much of a bitch you are," he said, glaring at her.

"How can you believe Keith?"

"He was a great man and loved you more than you deserved. I can't believe what he put up with just to stay with you."

She nodded and then looked around. "Where's my dog?"

One of the Valle appeared holding the squirming Bulldog in his arms. "He's going to die unless you agree to come with us."

It all happened fast. Emily turned the heku with the dog to ash and was immediately tackled by another Valle. The entire area suddenly swarmed with heku in green as someone slammed into the Valle on top of her and threw him farther into the trees.

She got to her knees and pulled the Bulldog closer to her as heku blurred around her in a fight. She was ready to turn any left-over Valle to ash. One heku broke out of the pack and started for her angrily. Her eyes grew wide, and she stood up and took a step away from him.

Mark appeared behind the Valle and removed his head, spraying Emily with warm heku blood. Mark turned and disappeared after another Valle as Emily looked down at the headless heku at her feet.

When the fighting stopped, there were piles of dead Valle lying around her and still more piles of ash that she didn't create. Kyle smiled at her just as the last Valle turned to ash at his feet.

"Are you okay?" Chevalier asked, walking up to her. He gently brushed the hair away from her face and followed her gaze to the heku in front of her.

"Where's Chuck?" she asked, looking around at the Equites. None of the Equites were missing, and she was thankful the Valle hadn't killed one of the Cavalry.

"He's ash," Kyle said, showing her a small leather bag.

"Gather up the ashes and uniforms," Chevalier said, taking her hand

gently. She looked once more at the lifeless heku and started back to her stallion with him.

They stopped on the fourth floor, and Chevalier turned to Emily. "Do you want to be in on this trial?"

"Chuck's trial?"

"Yes"

"Not really."

He smiled. "Silas will come wait with you then, okay?"

She nodded and went up the stairs to wait.

Kyle and Chevalier headed into the trial area where the ten piles of ash were laid out beside the scattered clothing. Kyle went to work immediately, and Chevalier took his seat to wait. The fifth heku revived was Charles, Emily's friend from Cascade, Montana.

Charles was obviously furious as he turned to face the Council and glared at Chevalier.

Chevalier nodded. "Interesting to see you among them. I still have a bone to pick with you over Emily's attempted escape from the Valle prison."

"I wasn't going to let her go!" Charles snapped. "She needs controlled, and it will take the Valle to do it."

"So why did the Valle turn her over to the Equites pseudo-Council?"

"We mistakenly thought they could teach her obedience. We had no idea they were just going to let her go once we convinced her you were scattered."

"So you were in on that too?" Zohn asked him.

He smiled. "Proudly."

When all ten of the Valle were revived and had recovered from the burning pain, the Court Reporter stood. "You ten are now charged with crimes against a member of the Equites Council. How do you plead?"

Charles snarled. "Not guilty! She's not a member of the Council. She's a mortal pest who has managed to weasel her way into your lives."

The Court Reporter ignored most of what Charles had said, "Do all of you plead Not guilty?"

The rest of the Valle nodded.

"Very well, your trial will begin soon…"

Chevalier held his hand up. "We can try them now."

The Court Reporter nodded. "Then your trial is to begin now. The Valle will be advised as soon as the sentence is carried out. What are the charges?"

"We should ask Emily here to get her account of what happened," Zohn suggested.

"I'll tell you. I'm not afraid or ashamed of what I've done," Charles

said.

"Then by all means…"

"Shortly after Emi's return from Europe, I began sending threatening notes to her via one of your servants…"

"We know this part already," Chevalier said.

"She told you?" Charles asked, frowning.

"Go on."

"We ended up kidnapping her dog and holding him for ransom. Our plans were to drug her and then return her to the Valle."

"The Council was in on this then?"

"Not all of them. Sotomar was our main contact."

Zohn frowned. "I'm not sure if you're being a tattle-tale, or if you're showing bravery."

"Why deny it?" Charles asked. "Emi will tell you all of this is true, unless she decides to show her true colors and lie again."

"Just keep talking," Chevalier snapped.

Charles smiled. "When she arrived at the clearing, we shared a few heated words and then I headed for her to sedate her. Next thing I know, I'm being revived here."

The Court Reporter wrote for a few minutes and then turned to the Elders. "That leaves charges as harassment of a member of the Council, assault, theft, spying, trespassing, and attempted kidnapping."

"Quite the list," Chevalier said to Charles.

"Might as well add breaking and entering," he said, smiling.

"Are you not taking this seriously?"

"No, I'm not. I'm pretty sure Emi will come rescue me."

"So am I, so we're going to hold this trial and hand out the punishments now," Chevalier said. He then smiled when Charles' smile faded.

"But…"

"… Guilty."

"Wait!" Charles said, irritated. "That's not a trial."

Zohn chuckled. "A trial is simply a determination of a person's guilt or innocence by due process of the law. I do believe your admission of the findings is a clear guilty plea. I vote guilty."

The Council each, in turn, voted guilty, while Charles kept arguing that the trial was a farce.

The Court Reporter ignored his complaining and stood up. "The ten of you are hereby found guilty on all charges. The Elders will decide on a punishment that is to be carried out immediately."

"Wait!" Charles said frantically. "I want to talk to Emi first."

"No," Chevalier told him. "I'm not going to play that game. You've been a thorn in her side since you befriended Keith, and I'm

ready to be done with you."

"She'll be mad over this."

"No, she won't. I'll explain it to her. I vote death."

"Death?!" Charles yelled.

"Yes, death. I won't risk banishing you and having Em dig you up."

"Still…"

"How old are you?" Kyle asked the young heku.

"I was turned seven years ago."

"Damn, bad choices in one so young."

"I don't have bad choices! I was assigned by my Council…"

"Bad choices," Kyle said again.

Zohn tapped his fingers lightly. "I vote for banishment and burial in Powan."

Quinn looked at him. "That's not a bad idea."

"That way we can banish him, and Emily won't be able to dig him up. I hesitate to kill one so young."

Chevalier studied Charles.

"What?" Charles asked him, still angry.

"I think it's odd that you were friends with Emily from childhood, yet when Keith stepped into the picture, you turned on her."

"What can I say? He opened my eyes."

"So you went with the guy who had the nerve to bet a night with his wife in a poker game."

Charles' eyes narrowed. "I can't believe she told you that."

Kyle looked over at Chevalier. "That sonofabitch gave Emily away to this idiot in a poker game?"

Chevalier nodded. "Then when she refused, he put her in the hospital."

"She got bucked off of a horse…," Charles started, but then stopped suddenly and fell silent.

"Then you really are stupid. My vote stands at death, young or not," Chevalier said. "Where is your wife?"

Charles sighed, "She left me."

"I bet you cheated on her."

"Just once! I was drunk… it was an accident. Then she found us on the kitchen counter…"

Kyle couldn't help but chuckle.

"It's not funny!" Charles said, glaring at him.

"Oh, it is though. What did the Valle see in you to turn you?"

"I'm a really good mechanic," he said, and it seemed to the others like he might be fighting back tears. "Please, I'm sorry okay? If I can just apologize to Emily and then I swear to leave her alone."

"I agree with not allowing you to wait for Emily," Zohn said. "My vote stands at banishment in Powan."

Quinn nodded. "Banishment in Powan it is then."

"You're lucky," Chevalier said to him. "But when you are revived... you better watch out for me."

Charles gulped and then took a step back when Kyle stood. "How long?"

Quinn studied Charles and then shrugged. "Give them 400 years."

"No!" Charles yelled. "I can't do that, please."

Chevalier addressed him. "It's not often we banish one so young. Your thirst is much more prevalent, and it's an added punishment to have you suffer. However, we don't feel it's in the best interest of this Council to let you live."

"Then kill me."

"No. When you are un-banished, you may want to re-think your choices though."

Charles fought against the strong arms of the Cavalry when they were summoned. When such a large group was to be banished, it often took guards to help restrain them while Kyle did his job. Kyle went from heku to heku, leaving Charles for last because the panic he exhibited was getting stronger, and he wanted the young heku to suffer.

Once Kyle stood in front of the now cowering Charles, he smiled. "Your turn. You are hereby sentenced to 400 years of banishment. When you are un-banished, it will be up to the Valle if they want you back."

"Please..." was all Charles managed before falling to ash. Kyle walked slowly up to sit down to recover from so many banishments. As a servant was brought in to begin bagging the ashes, the back door opened and Megara came in.

Chevalier turned his chair and pulled her onto his lap and kissed her forehead softly.

She wrapped her arms around him and looked down at the scattered ash before Chevalier turned.

"Did Mommy do that?" Megara asked as she leaned back in Chevalier's arms.

"No, Kyle did that."

"Was it a bad heku?"

"Yes"

She frowned slightly and looked up at him. "Why can't I do that?"

"We don't know. Maybe you can," Chevalier said after ordering her something to drink.

"How can I find out?"

"I don't know that either."

She sighed and then looked over when Alexis came in. "Did you call her?"

Chevalier grinned and nodded. "Yes, you need to go with Alex. I have trials to finish."

Megara crossed her arms and glared at him. "No."

"You can't tell me no," he said, and handed her over to Alexis. "She has breakfast waiting."

Alexis nodded and then took Megara from the room.

"Let's finish up here so I can get back to Em," Chevalier told them.

***

Silas stepped out of the bedroom when Chevalier and Kyle came in and shut the door behind them.

"Did they hurt you?" Chevalier asked, trying to sound calm.

"No," she managed to say, though she seemed upset.

After a few minutes, she looked up and saw Kyle was in the room also. He smiled. "They were going to sedate you. I bet you're the most drugged mortal in history."

"Lovely," she said. "Where's Chuck?"

"We've sentenced him already," Chevalier told her.

She frowned. "Just Chuck or all of the Valle?"

"All ten of them."

"Sentenced... as in..."

He sighed, "Banished."

Emily frowned. "I hate that! No one should ever be banished."

"It's an effective... okay so mostly effective means of punishment though. It's that or death."

"It's awful. To suffer for hundreds of years."

"They at least recover from that," Kyle told her as he sat on the edge of the bed. "If we kill them, it's over."

"They do fully recover from a long banishment?"

"Of course."

"I still don't like it. Chuck's a good guy, he just... I don't know... lost this way."

Chevalier gently lifted Emily's chin, so she was looking into his eyes. "Charles was a Valle, and a puppet used to get to you. He had nothing but hatred, and that's dangerous."

"I don't know if I believe that."

"I know, which scares me. We've taken care of Charles and the Valle. Now though, I want to thank you for telling us you were getting threatened."

"Maybe I'm tired of getting beaten to a pulp. Course... if I tell you

every time, you may need to quit your job to have time."

Chevalier lightly kissed her and then peered into her eyes. "I always want to know if something's wrong."

"I know."

"You kept it for a while though, let it go on too long."

"I'm sorry."

"Why?"

She sighed, "The Council just got reinstated… they didn't need me to come tell them I was getting picked on."

"So you were protecting the Council?"

"No"

"You were. It's part of your charm."

"My charm?"

"Yes, it's endearing."

"You aren't mad?"

"Furious," he whispered and then pressed his lips to hers.

***

"The Valle have representatives here," Derrick said to Council.

Zohn sighed, "Probably mad that we banished Charles and his posse last week."

"Let them in," Chevalier told him.

Several seconds later, Valle Elder Ryan came in, followed by the Valle's Faction Liaison Officer and four Imperial Guards. The entire Equites Council watched them enter.

"Why are you here?" Quinn asked, a little shortly.

Ryan thought briefly before speaking. "We've come to inform you that Sotomar has been replaced."

Chevalier was stunned. "He has?"

"Yes, his undying infatuation with Emily made him a liability, and he's been banished."

"You banished him because of Emily?" Quinn asked, still not sure he heard right.

Ryan smiled. "No… not because of Emily. We wanted to make that very clear. He was in no way banished because of her. He was banished because he continually risked the Valle faction by trying to get to her."

The Valle's Faction Liaison Officer stepped forward. "We came peacefully to let you know because we are afraid of how the news will affect Lady Emily."

Kyle nodded. "She'll try to get him."

"We were afraid of that. He's been banished and then sent to a remote location for safety. We can't risk him being revived and

resuming his unnatural drive to obtain the last Winchester."

"You're okay with this?" Zohn asked Ryan.

Ryan sighed, "Sotomar was not only my friend but was my mentor in a way. I cannot, however, deny the fact that he continually threatened the Valle's way of life over his obsession."

"So Charles and his goons…"

"Was Sotomar working behind the backs of the rest of the Council."

"And telling Emily that I was banished and scattered?" Chevalier asked, knowing full well it was Ryan who represented the Valle.

"That was done by me under Council agreement. We thought it might end Sotomar's preoccupation with Emily, but it only made it worse."

"I'm still in shock," Quinn said.

"I know it was sudden, but it was necessary," Ryan explained. "We as a Council began to see a decline in Sotomar's ability to handle every-day business without involving Emily in it. He never once let a day pass without throwing out another idea on how to capture her and then how to keep her when we have her. The re-memory was impulsive, and we regret it."

"It still haunts her," Chevalier said, irritated.

"We're sorry. It shouldn't have happened. We've given Sotomar 800 years to calm down, but then he will most surely resume his quest."

Kyle nodded. "We all knew he was obsessed with her."

"You don't know the half of it," Ryan said, and then turned to Chevalier. "We leave it up to you. We can inform Emily if you feel that is what is needed to lessen the blow."

"No, I will need to," Chevalier said, already deep in thought.

"I apologize, but we saw no other way."

"Does this mean she'll get a break then?" Kyle asked, not believing them.

"Yes"

"So after almost 40 years, you're going to leave her alone?"

"Yes"

"Then you won't be surprised when we don't believe you."

Ryan smiled. "Not at all."

"Our main goal now is to try to regroup as a faction," the Valle's Faction Liaison Officer said. "We've all been so focused on obtaining Emily that things have been lax, and it's time we get back on track."

"Is he in prison waiting banishment or has it already been done?" Chevalier asked, still sounding unsure.

"He has already been put in the ground, far away from anywhere Emily would think to look," Ryan assured him.

Chevalier nodded. "We'll let Em know. Was there anything else?"

"We just ask that you as a faction leave us alone long enough to deal with his loss. He had the covens convinced that our main goal was obtaining Emily, and a lot of them were very angry that we replaced him. It's going to take time to rebuild and get back on track."

"We won't agree to back off… we are still at war," Zohn told him. "However, if you leave Emily alone, then we have no imminent reason to attack."

Ryan nodded. "Then we'll be off."

Once the Valle were escorted out, Quinn turned to Richard. "Impressions?"

"He was telling the truth," Richard said. "I saw nothing he said as a lie."

Zohn nodded. "Sotomar did seem to be behind all of the captures."

Chevalier sighed and looked up at the ceiling. "I don't know how to tell her."

"Should we tell her as a Council?"

"No, it's my responsibility to tell her and then handle the consequences."

Kyle smiled slightly. "She hates banishment, period."

"How can she be upset, with all that Sotomar has done to her?" the Chief of Staff asked.

Chevalier looked over at him. "Once you become a friend of Emily's, it's next to impossible to become an enemy. I don't know if she's going to be upset or not over his replacement, but she will be upset over a banishment."

"I can go with you," Kyle suggested.

"No, let me do this alone," he said before standing up. The Council watched him walk out.

Chevalier met Mark outside by the stables and asked that the training Cavalry bring Emily in from the trees. Mark saw the grim look in his eyes and immediately called the entire Cavalry back in and had them scatter through the city to watch over things.

Emily rode up and smiled. "Going to go riding?"

"No, Em, I need to talk to you," he said. He took the reins after she slipped off her horse and then turned and handed them to a member of the Cavalry.

"What's wrong?" she asked, slipping off her gloves.

"Not here, let's go upstairs."

She sighed, "This sounds bad."

He gently took her arm. "Let's go."

The two walked up in silence and Emily glanced back and saw that she didn't have any Cavalry guards behind her, which was unusual and highly frowned upon. Once they got to the fifth floor, they walked into

their room, and Chevalier shut the door behind them.

"Have a seat," he said, and then sat down in a chair by the fire.

Emily did the same. "What's wrong?"

"I need you to hear me out, okay?"

"You're scaring me."

"The Valle came to inform us that there's been a change in the Council."

"Change?"

"Sotomar has been replaced."

Emily frowned and looked into Chevalier's eyes. "He what?"

"The Valle realized his dangerous obsession with you was keeping him from fulfilling his duties as an Elder. He's been replaced."

She was finding it hard to speak. "He's buried..."

"Yes, for 800 years."

"But..."

"This is where you need to listen to me. This isn't like when all of the Council was banished. You can't get him and bring him back."

Emily stood up slowly as she grasped her neck. "It's not too late... the Encala will revive him."

Chevalier took her hand. "In preparation for that, Sotomar has been moved to an undisclosed location."

She didn't answer, but her eyes darted around the bedroom, desperately searching for something to help.

"Em, the Valle were right. Sotomar couldn't see anything other than owning you, and it put their faction at risk continually. He was a liability, and the only way to stop him was 800 years of banishment."

"Larsen," she whispered, and looked over at the window.

"Yes, he'll be like Larsen. They did it to protect the Valle."

"No, to protect me," she choked out as tears filled her eyes.

"No, it wasn't done to protect you. The rest of the Council doesn't care enough about you to banish an Elder for you. They were focused on the good of the Valle. His obsession wasn't your fault."

She spun suddenly and looked out the window. "He's going to suffer for 800 years."

"He's a liability."

"He doesn't deserve that kind of punishment."

"He does. He was warned repeatedly by the Valle to leave you alone. He couldn't do it. Everything the Valle have done in the last 35 years has been Sotomar's doing. He brought back Salazar and Exavior. He changed your memories. He enlisted Charles."

She shook her head and the tears began to spill down her cheeks. "I can't let him suffer.

"You can't do anything about it. I don't even know where Sotomar

was buried."

"Please… stop this," she said, turning pained eyes to him.

He gently took her hand. "This is the only way you can have peace. The Valle are in ruins because of following Sotomar's direction. It wasn't an easy decision for them to make, but it was a good one."

She clutched at the front of her shirt. "I'll have the Encala get him back."

"They aren't going to help you on this."

"They will! They brought you back."

"Em, that was different. We all know that Sotomar had a fixation with you that clouded his judgment and encased his every movement."

She slowly sunk to her knees. "For 800 years, he'll be in the ground, suffering and thinking about me."

"My guess is he'll spend that time realizing that he was wrong."

Emily suddenly dug in her pocket and pulled out her phone. She hit speed dial and waited.

"Em, they can't help you," Chevalier said softly. His face showed the concern over how desperately she was going to fight to save Sotomar from years of torment.

"Em! How are you?" Andrew asked, happy to hear her.

"Help him," Emily whispered, unable to speak. Her heart was constricting in her chest as she thought of the short year she had to save Sotomar.

"Help who? What's wrong?" Andrew asked frantically.

"Sotomar"

"What's wrong with him?"

"B… banished."

"Sotomar's been banished?!"

"Help him…"

"Em, I'm coming over. Stay with the Equites until I get there."

"Please," she whispered and then shut her phone and looked at Chevalier.

"Please wait for him," Chevalier said. He hated that an Encala was coming because of Emily's desperation, but he also knew she trusted him and he might be able to help convince her to leave it all alone.

"Kyle!" Emily called out. He arrived within seconds and shut the door behind him. Emily turned to him. "Do something."

"I can't do anything. Even if I wanted to, I don't know where he is. It's the best move the Valle could have done though. He was ruining them."

"Please." Emily wiped at the tears falling from her eyes and pleaded with him.

Kyle gently took her hands and pulled her into a hug. "Try to

understand that it's for the best. It's going to leave you alone to do what you want without always getting kidnapped. We can work through the re-memory without worrying about the Valle getting you. The Valle can..."

Emily pulled away from him. "Stop saying it's all good! He's going to suffer for 800 years... lying in the cold ground thinking about me, hating me..."

"He's not Larsen," Kyle said, seeing where she was coming from. "Sotomar's smarter than Larsen. He's going to spend that time trying to figure out how to get back into the Valle."

"No, he won't! He's going to be obsessing about me for hundreds of years."

"Calm down," he said, gently gripping her shoulders. "This is long overdue."

Emily pulled away from him and headed for the door.

"Em...," Chevalier said, and followed her out. Mark had already replaced her guards, and they headed down the stairs after her.

Chevalier appeared in front of her when she tried to get into the game room. "There's no alcohol in there anymore."

"Leave me alone," she snapped, and tried to push him out of the way.

"No"

Suddenly, she leaned her head against his chest and burst into tears, sobbing incomprehensibly as Chevalier's arms wrapped around her and held her tightly. He gently stroked her hair as she sobbed about the loss of a friend.

After a few minutes, she collapsed into his arms, and he cradled her tenderly and walked back up the stairs. The entire incident was reminiscent of Allen's death and how she cried in Keith's arms.

When he laid her down, she gripped tightly to his shirt, and he crawled into bed beside her and held her in her sleep. Her dreams were confusing and disturbed, never forming cognitive images or scenes. Once in a while she woke long enough to cry again and fall asleep in his arms.

When Andrew arrived, he waited patiently in the council chambers for her to wake up. She began to stir early the next morning and woke up, looking at Chevalier with red, swollen eyes.

He gently brushed the hair away from her face. "Are you feeling any better?"

"I have to ask the Encala."

"I know. Andrew is down in the council chambers."

She nodded and sat up, still dressed from the day before. Without even bothering to change, she took Chevalier's hand and walked down to

the council chambers with him.

Chevalier stayed with her when they walked into the council chambers. Andrew started forward to give her his usual hug but saw the pain in her face and froze in his tracks. "What's going on?"

She sniffed slightly and then wrapped her arms around herself before speaking. "Sotomar has been banished."

"Yes, after you told me, we confirmed it."

"I want the Encala to bring him back."

"You have him here?!"

"No, we have to find him first."

"He isn't being kept in the Valle Palace."

"We can find him."

He sighed, "Em... it makes sense for the Valle to replace him. I know he's your friend, but he was a dangerous friend, one that should probably have been an enemy."

She started to tear up again and scanned the Equites Council, looking for help. "No one will help me?"

Andrew glanced at Chevalier and then took Emily's hand. "We are helping you by leaving him where he is."

"What?" she asked, looking up at him with a frown.

"He wouldn't leave you alone. When the Encala backed off, he continued to push even harder. He was dangerous to you, and I'm more comforted knowing he's gone for a while."

She pulled her hand away from him roughly. "He's my friend!"

"I know that."

"Then help me."

Andrew sighed, "No. I'm sorry, and I speak for the Encala faction and its Council. We aren't going to help you revive Sotomar."

"Do it!" she screamed.

"Em... this isn't Chevalier," Andrew whispered.

Emily's shoulders fell and she watched him. "What?"

"What do you mean?" Chevalier asked the Encala.

"Sotomar, the black haired heku, an Old One, an Elder... if they can banish Sotomar, then they can banish you," Andrew explained.

Suddenly, it started to make sense to him, and Chevalier sighed as he looked down at her. "Is that it, Em?"

She unconsciously wrapped her arms tightly around herself and took a step back. "No."

"Sotomar isn't Chevalier," Andrew said softly. "His banishment doesn't mean that Chevalier's is coming."

Emily looked over at Chevalier, and he was shocked at the amount of fear. "What if I can't get to you next time?"

"Why does there need to be a next time?" Chevalier asked. "I've

been alive for a long time, and that's the first I'd been banished."

"They can turn on you in an instant," Emily whispered. "Sotomar didn't have time to fight back."

"He messed up."

"Everyone messes up!"

He softly took her arm. "Em, I'm not going to be banished."

Emily went to address the Council but found them all gone. Emily, Kyle, Chevalier, and Andrew were all that was left in the council chambers.

"Chevalier's not going to be banished," Andrew told her. "Sotomar will resurface in 800 years and will more than likely seek you out. When that time comes, I'm sure the Equites will be ready."

"All that time thinking about me," she said, and a shiver ran up her spine.

"You're free, Em," Kyle said, smiling. "No more Valle attacks."

"I'll never be free."

"The Encala aren't out to get you. The Valle have backed off... all you have now are unfactioned and rogues," Kyle said reassuringly.

She shook her head. "No, as long as someone I care about can be thrown into the ground. I won't be free."

Chevalier wrapped his arms around her and kissed the top of her head lightly. "You're protecting me again."

She nodded. "What if I can't get to you next time?"

He bent down and whispered into her ear. "There won't be a next time."

"You don't know that."

"I do know that. We have new measures in place to prevent what happened. I'm not going to run to the frontlines of war anymore either. It's time I step back and consider the impact on you if I were to die."

She looked at him, not quite sure she believed him. "You're going to evacuate with the Council?"

"Yes"

"Both of you?" Emily looked over at Kyle.

He frowned slightly. "I can't do that... we evacuate the Elders, mainly."

"We'll work on that, Em," Chevalier told her. "I just realized that we should evacuate Kyle too, as he's your second best bet to seek help if something separates us."

Andrew smiled. "Then there's me. If you ever need help, you can always come to me."

She nodded and then sighed, "Still... Sotomar's suffering."

"His suffering will protect the Valle. I'm pretty sure in 800 years, he's going to see that," Chevalier explained.

Emily began to tear up again. "He's going to be hungry and tormented."

Chevalier lifted her chin slightly so she was looking at him. "It's for the good of the Valle. His infatuation was destroying them. Their numbers were down, and there was no drive to rebuild. They had to take drastic action."

She swallowed hard. "Can I... maybe in a few years... ask that they reconsider?"

He smiled. "I'm sure it wouldn't hurt if you do just that."

Andrew chuckled. "It won't be the first appeal of a sentence."

"It isn't?" Emily looked over at him.

"Nope. Friends and loved ones of banished often appeal for new sentences. I don't believe it's ever helped, but there's a first for everything."

She sighed and nodded. "I guess if there's hope..."

"You're free now. I bet they even back off your bloody guards."

Emily looked up at Chevalier, and he grinned. "Not a chance. There are still unfactioned to think about."

She smiled. "I don't mind guards, I guess."

"You don't?" Kyle asked, a little surprised.

"I've kind of gotten used to them. I can always get away from them if I want to."

"I hate that."

Chevalier smiled. "Or she can just make up shopping stories, so I give her permission to go alone."

Emily couldn't help but smile slightly. "I didn't do that this last time. I told you the truth."

"This time... but Garrett thought you were shopping."

"Oh, right."

"I'm sure he figured it out. You hate to shop," Chevalier told her and then kissed her lightly. "Garrett and Alexis are working things out. The lawyer gave her some doubts about getting a baby, and Garrett has been given some time away from the Cavalry to try to help her cope."

She sighed, "Even if she decides that for now she doesn't want a baby, the desire will come back."

"Yes, it will. So Lori's helping them," Chevalier said. "You're off the hook. No Valle attacks. No Encala rescues. The Ferus are gone, and your daughter is grown up and can lean on her husband more. We've been working with Megara, and I honestly don't think she inherited any Winchester abilities."

"Well now what am I going to do?" Emily asked, a small twinkle returning to her eyes.

"I'm almost afraid to find out."